Sing As We Go

and

Wish Me Luck

Born in Gainsborough, Lincolnshire, Margaret Dickinson moved to the coast at the age of seven and so began her love for the sea and the Lincolnshire landscape.

Her ambition to be a writer began early and she had her first novel published at the age of twenty-five. This was followed by twenty further titles including *Plough the Furrow*, *Sow the Seed* and *Reap the Harvest*, which make up her Lincolnshire Fleethaven trilogy. Many of her novels are set in the heart of her home county, but in *Tangled Threads* and *Twisted Strands* the stories included not only Lincolnshire but also the framework knitting and lace industries of Nottingham. The Workhouse Museum at Southwell in Nottinghamshire inspired *Without Sin*, and the beautiful countryside of Derbyshire and the fascinating town of Macclesfield in Cheshire formed the backdrop for the story of *Pauper's Gold*. For *Sing As We Go* and *Wish Me Luck*, Margaret returns once more to her native Lincolnshire – known in the Second World War as Bomber County.

www.margaret-dickinson.co.uk

Also by Margaret Dickinson

Plough the Furrow

Sow the Seed

Reap the Harvest

The Miller's Daughter

Chaff upon the Wind

The Fisher Lass

The Tulip Girl

The River Folk

Tangled Threads

Twisted Strands

Red Sky in the Morning

Without Sin

Pauper's Gold

Margaret Dickinson

Sing As We Go

and

Wish Me Luck

PAN BOOKS

Sing As We Go first published 2008 by Pan Books
Wish Me Luck first published 2007 by Pan Books

This omnibus first published 2009 by Pan Books
an imprint of Pan Macmillan, a division of Macmillan Publishers Limited
Pan Macmillan, 20 New Wharf Road, London N1 9RR
Basingstoke and Oxford
Associated companies throughout the world
www.panmacmillan.com

ISBN 978-0-330-51754-6

1 3 5 7 9 8 6 4 2

A CIP catalogue record for this book is available from
the British Library.

Typeset by SetSystems Ltd, Saffron Walden, Essex
Printed in the UK by CPI Mackays, Chatham ME5 8TD

Sing As We Go

For my grandson, Zachary John

'*When I saw thee, I gave my heart away.*'
Longfellow

Acknowledgements

My grateful thanks to the staff of Lincoln Central Library and of Skegness Library for helping so much with all my research, and to Brian and Jean Gabbitass for the photo of Brian's father, James, who served with ENSA during the Second World War.

As always, my love and thanks to Robena and Fred Hill, David and Una Dickinson and Pauline Griggs for reading and commenting on the script, and to all my family and friends for their constant support and encouragement in so many ways.

Thank you to Darley Anderson and everyone at the Agency, and to Imogen Taylor, Trisha Jackson, Liz Cowen and all at Pan Macmillan, for always being there.

One

LINCOLNSHIRE 1939

Kathy pulled on her wellington boots and tied a headscarf over her blonde hair and under her chin with a quick, angry movement. She pulled open the back door of the farmhouse and, walking through it, slammed it behind her so that it shuddered on its hinges, the wood creaking in protest. Immediately, she regretted her action. Her mother deserved an extra few minutes in bed if anyone did. Especially after last night.

Pale fingers of a frosty dawn crept across the yard as she marched, hands thrust into her pockets, across the cobbles towards the cowshed. The cows had already been fetched from the field and her father's only greeting was, 'You're late.'

'You call half past six on a winter's morning "late"?' Kathy snapped, her blue eyes bright with resentment.

She banged the lower half of the byre door, making the cows move restlessly. Ben, their collie, ran to her, tail wagging, tongue lolling. She bent and gave him a friendly pat. She wouldn't vent her ill temper on him.

'Ya'd be able to get up in a morning if ya went to bed the same time as decent folk.'

'I was home before midnight. And you'd no right to

lock me out so that Mam had to come down and let me in.'

'I lock up every night at ten. If you're later than that, then I want to know. And I want to know why, an' all.'

'I went to the St Valentine's dance in the village hall. You know that. I did – ' her tone took on a sarcastic note – 'ask permission.'

'Aye, ya asked your mam because ya knew ya could wheedle your way around her. And don't use that tone of voice with me, my girl, else—'

'Else what?' Her eyes sparked rebellion and her small, neat chin jutted with determination. Two pink spots that had nothing to do with the cold morning burned in her cheeks. 'You'll take your belt to me? I'm a bit old at nineteen.'

Her father, shoulders permanently hunched, carried a bucket full of fresh, warm milk to the end of the cowshed. Pausing as he passed her, he thrust his gaunt, lined face close to hers. 'You're not of age until you're one and twenty, and until then ya'll do as I say or else . . .'

She faced him squarely, but her voice was quiet as she said, 'What, Dad? Just tell me what the "or else" is?'

'Ya can pack ya bags and go,' he growled. 'I'll not have a chit of a girl back-answering me in me own house.'

'Very well, then,' Kathy nodded calmly. 'I'll go. I'll go this very day – if that's what you want.'

For a moment Jim Burton stared at his daughter. Then he gave a sarcastic, humourless laugh. 'Oh aye. And where would ya go, eh?'

'Lincoln,' Kathy said promptly.

'And what d'ya plan to do there, eh? Ain't no cows in Lincoln. And that's all you're good for, girl.'

Kathy nodded slowly. 'Yes – yes, I have to admit you're right there. But that's down to you, isn't it? Making me leave school the minute I was old enough. Setting me to work on the farm for no pay—'

'Pay? What d'ya need paying for? Ya've everything you need.'

'Need, maybe. Want – no.'

'Who's been putting fancy ideas in your head, girl?' He eyed her keenly, his dark eyes narrowing. 'Is it your mother?'

Now Kathy laughed aloud. 'Mam? Put ideas like that into my head? Don't make me laugh. As if she'd dare, for a start.'

Jim grunted. He was thoughtful for a moment, dismissing his idea as nonsense. The girl was right. His wife wouldn't dare make any such suggestion. 'Then it's that chit of a Robinson girl. Flighty piece, she is.'

Kathy hid a smile. Amy Robinson was the only real friend she had. And Jim wasn't done yet. 'No better than she should be, that girl.' He'd seen Amy only the day before with a boy in the copse between his land and the Robinsons' farm. 'Up to no good they were, I'll be bound.' And after evening milking he'd marched across the fields to warn his neighbour that his daughter was going the right way to 'get 'ersen into trouble, if you ask me'.

For once, the mild Ted Robinson had been stung to retort, 'Well, no one's asking you, Jim Burton, and I'll thank you to keep your opinions to ya'sen. I trust my daughter. She'll come to no harm. What's a kiss and a cuddle in the woods, eh? We've all been young once, haven't we?' Ted had paused then and eyed his irate neighbour. 'Mind you, I have me doubts if you was ever young, Jim. Born old, I reckon you were.'

'Oh, so that's what you think, is it? Just because I've worked hard all me life and done me duty. Where'd me family's farm have been by now, eh, if I hadn't worked from the minute I was old enough?'

Ted's anger had died as swiftly as it had come. 'Aye, I know, Jim, I know. You've not had it easy with your dad dying when he was fifty and you having to take on the farm so young. And then losing your poor mam only a few years later in that dreadful flu epidemic of 'eighteen, but—' Ted Robinson had put his hand on the other man's shoulder. 'Look, Jim, I don't want to fall out with you. We've known each other a long time, but if you'll take my advice, you'll ease up a bit on that lass of yourn. If you don't allow the youngsters to have a bit of fun now and again, then they'll take it anyway, whether you like it or not.'

Jim had shaken off Ted's friendly gesture. 'And I'll thank *you* not to interfere with the way I bring *my* daughter up. She'll do as she's told else she'll feel the back o' me hand. And sharpish.' With that he had tramped back across the fields, his anger still simmering and bursting into rage when he found that Kathy had already gone out to a village dance.

'What d'you let her go for?' he'd thundered at his wife. 'Did I say she could go? Did I?'

'Well, no, Jim, but I th-thought it wouldn't matter. Just this once. They always have a d-dance in the village hall the Friday night after Valentine's Day . . .' Edith Burton had stammered, her faded eyes fearful, her thin face creased into lines of perpetual anxiety. Although still only in her late thirties, the harsh life she was forced to lead had taken its toll. Her shoulders were rounded in a permanent state of submission and her hair was prematurely grey. Kathy was the only brightness in Edith's cold and cheerless life. As a naïve nineteen-year-old girl, the youngest of five daughters of a hardworking farm labourer, marriage to Jim Burton, who'd inherited Thorpe Farm at the age of twenty, had seemed too good to be true. It was – as poor Edith had soon found out. She'd long ago realized she did not love her husband and she doubted now that he'd ever really loved her. She wondered if he'd ever known the real meaning of the word 'love'. All he'd wanted, after the death of his mother, was a housekeeper and someone to give him an heir. He'd picked Edith, thirteen years his junior, thinking that she would be sufficiently strong for farm work and healthy enough to bear him a son. But after the birth of their daughter, Edith had been told she should have no more children. Jim Burton's interest in her had ceased totally. Since that time, he'd treated her no better than he would a servant and while they still slept in the same room, in the same double bed for the sake of convention, all intimacy between them had ceased years ago.

'Valentine's! Sentimental rubbish! Don't you let her out again without my permission, d'you hear?'

'Yes, Jim,' Edith had said meekly.

Now, as Jim argued with his daughter in the cowshed, all his frustration and resentment surfaced again. Deep down, he envied his neighbour. Why couldn't he have found himself a wife like Ted's? Betty Robinson was, in Jim Burton's eyes, the perfect farmer's wife. She was a superb cook and a helpmate about the farm, while his own wife hardly lifted a finger to help him with the outside work. And it wasn't as if she was even a good housewife. Edith was a poor cook. Some of the meals she had placed before him in the early days of their marriage had been scarcely edible. And she barely kept the house clean. Edith was not a bit like his dear, house-proud mother. Sarah Burton must be turning in her grave. Oh, he'd made a bad mistake in marrying Edith. He'd not realized she'd been spoiled and cosseted by her parents and older siblings. She'd never been taught how to keep house or to cook. And that wasn't her only fault. She'd failed to give him a son like Betty Robinson had given her man. He remembered the surprise the whole village had felt at Maurice's birth. No one had even known that Ted's new wife had been expecting, until, all of a sudden, there was Betty proudly wheeling the little chap around the village in a huge black perambulator. It wasn't until five years later that Amy Robinson had been born, only two months after Jim's own daughter. And then, when the doctor told him the devastating news that it would be dangerous for Edith to have more children, the resentment had begun. Not bearing him a son had been Edith's greatest failing in her husband's eyes.

Jim's envy of the Robinsons made him critical. While part of him wanted to ally his daughter to that family by her marriage to Maurice, another devious and embittered part of him half hoped that one day Ted's perfect life would be shattered. And now he knew how that might happen.

'That lass – ' he jabbed his forefinger towards Kathy as he spoke of her friend again now – 'would do well to knuckle down and help her father on his farm, instead of acting like a whore with all and sundry. He's too soft with her, but then, of course – ' Kathy held her breath, knowing exactly what was coming next – 'Ted Robinson's got a son to help him.' Jim turned away with a swift, angry movement, slopping milk over the edge of the bucket.

Kathy's gaze followed her father for a moment, feeling a mixture of emotions. Just now and again she could find it in her heart to feel sorry for him. His disappointment in being blessed – or in his eyes cursed – with only one child, and a daughter to boot, was understandable, she supposed. It was a frustration he'd never tried to conceal, and Kathy had been aware of it for as long as she could remember. It never occurred to her father that Thorpe Farm, which had been in his family for four generations, could pass to a woman.

But Kathy's feelings of compassion lasted only a moment and her own resentment surfaced again. Adopting the same sarcastic tone he'd used, she said with deceptive mildness, 'I thought you liked the Robinson family. You're always trying to marry me off to Morry to give you a grandson.'

'Ya could do a lot worse,' Jim growled.

Yes, Kathy thought, I could. Morry Robinson was a nice lad but he had no ambition, no dreams to fulfil. He was perfectly content to work on his family's farm for the rest of his life. He didn't care if he never saw the world outside the farm gate. He even avoided trips to the local market town if he could. And as for visiting a city or – heaven forbid – London, well, he'd likely die of fright at the mere thought. Kathy smiled at the thought of Morry. She liked him. Of course she did. You couldn't help but like Morry. Everyone did. He was plump and cuddly like a teddy bear, with big, soft brown eyes, reddish brown hair and a round face liberally covered with freckles. She'd danced with him last night, feeling his hand hot on her waist and returning his shy, lopsided smile with kindness. He was the sort of chap you couldn't *dis*like, couldn't be cruel to, but as for marriage, well now, that was something very different. She could see her life mapped out so clearly if she were to marry Morry. Years and years of working on a farm from dawn to dusk. Oh, she liked the Robinson family – loved them, really. Amy was her best friend – had been since school. Ted Robinson was a darling of a man and his plump and homely wife, Betty, always had a smile of welcome for anyone who called. A cup of tea and a sample of her latest batch of baking were always readily on offer. There were constant laughter and playful teasing in Betty's kitchen and her energy was boundless. Just watching her made Kathy feel tired. The whole Robinson family, even Amy, was contented with their lot.

But it was not the sort of life Kathy wanted for the next fifty or sixty years. Not what she dreamed of. And her father had got it wrong. It was not Amy who was the flighty one, it was her. It was Kathy who yearned for the bright lights, for excitement and to see a bit of the world. But now, for once, she wisely held her tongue. She said no more and went to the end of the byre to milk the cow in the end stall.

'Now then, Buttercup,' she greeted the animal cheerfully. 'Let's hope you're in a good mood this morning.' She patted the cow's rump and then bent to her task.

'Have you been putting ideas into her head? I wouldn't put it past you,' Jim growled as he sat down at the supper table, while his wife hovered at his side ready to place the plate of cold ham and pickles in front of him.

Edith cast a frightened glance at her daughter and

then looked back at her husband. 'I – I don't know what you mean, Jim.'

'"I don't know what you mean, Jim,"' he mimicked in a high-pitched, whining tone.

Kathy sat down on the far side of the table and picked up her knife and fork as she said calmly, 'Dad threatened to turn me out, so I told him I'm going anyway.'

Edith's eyes widened in terror and she dropped the plate she was holding. It fell to the floor and broke into four pieces.

Jim rose slowly to his feet and raised his hand as if to strike her. 'Now look what you've done, you stupid, stupid woman.'

Kathy was on her feet at once and launched herself between them. 'Don't you dare lay a finger on her,' she blazed. 'It's only because of her that I've stayed this long.'

Father and daughter glared at each other, but then, for once, Jim's gaze was the first to fall away. Maybe he'd seen something – a new strength of resolve – in his daughter's eyes. Perhaps he realized that if he pushed her just that little bit too far, she would carry out her threat. She would leave.

What Jim did not realize – could never have believed it – was that Kathy had already made up her mind. Maybe not today, or tomorrow, but one day very soon, she really would go.

Two

'You coming to church this morning?'

Amy Robinson's merry face peered over the bottom half of the cowshed door. She leaned on the top of it and rested her chin on her arms to watch her friend finishing off the morning milking with Cowslip in the nearest stall. Amy's dark brown eyes danced with mischief. The light dusting of freckles across her nose only accentuated her natural prettiness, but her light brown hair was as wild as ever. No matter what Amy did to try to tame her locks into a smooth, sleek style, the unruly curls escaped. Kathy glanced up, smiling. 'Of course. Would I *ever* miss singing with the choir?'

Amy threw back her head and laughed aloud. 'Choir? You call that a choir? Old Mrs Pennyfeather warbling off key. Mr Jenkins growling at the back and three cheeky little brats trying to look angelic but actually dreaming up their next prank to play on poor old Miss Tong.'

Miss Tong was the organist who was also the unofficial choirmaster – or 'mistress', Kathy supposed – until someone more proficient should apply for the post. But no one seemed to want the job and St Cuthbert's motley choir struggled on to lead an ever-diminishing congregation at the Sunday services.

'My darling girl – ' Amy teased and adopted a lilting tone – 'you'd have to go to Wales to hear a proper choir, look you, isn't it?' She mimicked the accent perfectly, for her maternal grandmother had been Welsh and Amy had spent a week's holiday every summer on her granny's farm in the heart of the Welsh countryside. Even now her face sobered and took on a dreamy, faraway look as if she were reliving those happy days.

Pulling her friend back to the present, Kathy asked quietly, 'And how do you think the choir would manage without me?'

The question sounded arrogant and for a moment Amy blinked. It was so unlike her dearest friend to show even the faintest trace of conceit.

'Oh, 'ark at 'er!' she mocked. 'God's gift to St Cuthbert's choir, a' you?'

Pink embarrassment tinged Kathy's cheeks. 'I'm sorry,' she said swiftly. 'I – I didn't mean it to sound the way it came out . . .'

Amy laughed. 'I know you didn't, you daft 'aporth.' She pulled a comical face and gave an exaggerated sigh. 'It pains me to admit it, but you have got the best voice of anyone, apart perhaps from little Charlie Oates. You wouldn't think a little tyke like him could sing like an angel. Mind you, his voice'll break. Yours won't. You've got it for life. You're a lucky devil, you know. Dad says my singing sounds like a frog croaking – and an injured one at that!'

For a moment, Kathy's mouth was a hard line. 'Lucky, am I? Well, I'll tell you something, Amy. I'd swap places with you any day of the week, voice or no voice.'

Amy's face sobered at once. 'Aw, ducky, is your dad giving you a hard time about the other night?'

Kathy bit down hard on her lower lip to still its

sudden trembling. She didn't normally give way to self-pitying tears, but the concern in her friend's tone touched her. 'It's not only that. It's – it's – Oh, *everything*! The way he treats me. I'm nothing more to him than a servant. An unpaid one, an' all. I've a good mind to up sticks and go!"

'But – but if you go away – ne'er mind the choir – what would your poor mam do without you?'

Kathy sighed. 'I know. I've only stayed this long because of her. Because he'll take it out on her if I do leave.'

'Does – does he – hit her?'

Kathy bit her lip. 'He did once. She dared to answer him back about something. I don't know what. I was only ten and I wasn't actually in the room when it happened. I – I heard it though. Through the bedroom wall. She had a black eye for weeks.'

'Has he ever hit you?'

Kathy laughed wryly. 'Oh yes. With his belt. The last time was two years ago.' Kathy smiled at the memory, but it was a bitter smile. 'He hadn't realized how strong I'd grown with working on the farm. And I snatched the belt from his hand and told him that if he ever tried it again, I'd go. I meant it. And he knew I did.'

'But *can* you leave home? You're not twenty-one for another two years.'

'Well, he'd have a job to carry me back physically, wouldn't he? And first,' she added pointedly, 'he'd have to find me.'

No more was said, but Amy went home without the usual cheery smile on her face. 'What's up with you?' her brother, Morry, greeted her. 'Lost a shilling and found a farthing?'

Tears started in Amy's eyes.

At once, Morry put his arm about her. 'Hey, Sis, what's the matter?'

'Oh, Morry, it's Kathy,' Amy blurted out as the tears now trickled down her cheeks. 'She – she's talking about leaving home.'

Morry's round, gentle face was grim. 'Well, I can't say I blame her. Living with that ol' devil. But where would she go?'

Amy shook her head. 'She didn't say. I – I expect she doesn't trust me. And – to be honest – I can't blame her. You know what a blabbermouth I am. And if she does go, she doesn't want *him* to be able to find her.'

'Mm.' For a moment, Morry was thoughtful. 'I'll have a word with her. See if there's anything I – we can do.'

Amy scrubbed away her tears and glanced up at her brother. 'You could ask her to marry you.'

Morry didn't answer. He just smiled quietly.

'Maurice, lad. Nice to see you. Come away in. I'll get the missis to mek a cuppa. Or would you prefer a beer? And a piece of 'er currant cake.' Jim Burton's laugh was humourless, with more than a hint of cruelty in it. 'Or mebbe you'd prefer to give that last one a miss, lad. My missis's baking's not a patch on your mam's.'

Morry gave a weak smile, not sure how to respond. Jim's attitude towards his wife always made the young man feel uncomfortable. 'No thanks, Mr Burton. I – er – just wondered if Kathy was about, that's all. I – er – thought we could walk to church together.'

He felt the older man's eyes searching his face keenly. 'Ah, yes, well now . . .' Jim Burton's mouth was stretched into an unaccustomed smile. 'She's getting ready. I'll call her down.'

'No need, Mr Burton. I'll just wait. She'll not be long. She's never late for church.' He stood awkwardly in the middle of the yard, twirling his cap through nervous, slightly sweaty hands.

'Well, at least come into the kitchen, lad. It's cold to be standing out here.'

Reluctantly, Morry followed the man into the farmhouse kitchen. He'd much preferred to have waited out in the yard, however cold it was.

'Maurice is here, Edith. Mek the lad a cuppa.'

The thin, worried little woman hurried forward. She smiled at Morry, but the young man could see that though her smile for him was genuine, it did not touch her sad eyes. The thought sprang immediately to his mind: what would this nice little woman do if her daughter – her only child – left home? Maybe that was the way to touch Kathy's heart if . . .

'Hello, Maurice,' Edith Burton was saying. 'Come in. Sit down while I—'

But at that moment there were footsteps on the stairs and Kathy burst into the kitchen. 'I'll have to go, Mam, I'm late—' She stopped short. 'Oh, hello, Morry. What are you doing here?'

'He's come to walk you to church,' Jim Burton cut in and there was a warning note in his voice that said: Now, you be nice to this lad. He's the one I want as my son-in-law.

Kathy managed to quell the involuntary shudder that ran through her. She didn't want Morry to sense her revulsion. He was a lovely lad, but – not for her. She loved him dearly, but only as she would have loved a brother. She could never – would never – see him as a husband. As a lover! But, smiling brightly, she crossed the red tiled floor and linked her arm through his. 'Come on then, Morry. Best foot forward. You know the choir can't start without me. Bye, Mam . . .'

When they were a good distance down the lane from the farm, walking briskly both to keep warm and to arrive at the church on time – already the church bell was tolling through the frosty morning air – Morry could contain himself no longer.

'Amy says you're leaving.'

Kathy sucked her tongue against her front teeth to make a tutting sound of exasperation. But it was a good-natured expression. She rolled her eyes heavenwards as she said, 'Oh, that sister of yours! Can't keep a secret for love nor money, can she?'

'She was upset, Kathy. She was in tears.'

At once, Kathy was contrite. 'I'm sorry. I didn't mean to upset her. It's just – it's just – oh, Morry, I've got to go. I can't stand it any more.'

The young man was silent, his dark eyes full of sorrow. 'We don't want you to go, Kathy. *I* don't want you to go.' He stopped suddenly and stepped in front of her, bringing her to an abrupt halt. He caught hold of her arms. 'Kathy – please – don't go. Stay. Stay and – and marry me.'

Kathy's mouth dropped open in a silent gasp. She stared at him with wide blue eyes. When, after a few seconds, she found her voice, the words came out all wrong.

'What's he said to you? What's he promised you?'

For a brief moment, puzzlement clouded Morry's eyes, to be replaced, as understanding dawned, by hurt.

'Oh, Kathy – how can you think that of me? Don't you know how much I love you? Don't you know I've always loved you? For as long as I can remember.'

Now there were tears in Kathy's eyes as she reached up and cupped his round face between her hands. 'I'm sorry. I wouldn't hurt you for the world. You're a lovely, lovely man and I love you dearly – as a friend. But – but – Morry, I'm not in love with you. Not in that way. Not to *marry* you. I – I'm sorry, but I never could be.'

His kind face was creased with disappointment, but, strangely, there was no surprise, no shock or disbelief in his expression. Instead he sighed heavily and nodded, 'I – I thought as much, if I'm honest.'

'And we're always honest with each other, Morry, aren't we?' Kathy said softly. 'We're still friends, aren't we?'

Morry managed a weak, but genuine, smile. 'Oh, yes, Kathy, I'll always be your friend, no matter what.' Catching hold of her hands and gripping them tightly, he held them close to his broad chest. 'Whatever happens, Kathy, whatever you do, always remember that I'm your friend.'

Kathy's voice was husky as she whispered, 'I will, Morry. I will.'

It was not the 'I will' that Morry longed to hear her say, but it would have to do.

With a sudden, old-fashioned gesture of courtesy that was way out of character, Morry raised her cold, chapped fingers to his lips and kissed them. 'Good. And now we'd best start running. The bell's stopped.'

*

'So – did he ask you then?'

'Ask me what?' Kathy kept her voice calm but avoided meeting her father's eyes as she ladled potatoes onto his plate.

'To wed him, of course?'

The spoon trembled a little in her hand as she felt her mother's timorous glance. Kathy pulled in a deep breath and let it out slowly as she carried on serving both her mother and herself with vegetables.

'Well?' Jim Burton snapped. 'Are you going to answer me, girl?'

'He did ask me, yes.'

'And?'

'I – I refused.'

'You – did – what?'

A sudden calm settled over Kathy. Whatever her father might say – or do – no matter however much he ranted and raved, she knew her answer had been the right one. 'I refused him,' she repeated, but bit her lip as, out the corner of her eye, she saw her mother tremble and the colour drain from her face.

'You refused him? Have you gone mad, girl?' Jim Burton rose slowly to his feet, his dinner forgotten.

Without warning, he raised his right arm and struck her on the left side of her face. Kathy dropped the dish she was holding. It smashed to the floor, spilling hot potatoes across the tiles. She stumbled and almost fell, but managed to regain her balance by clutching the edge of the table.

'Jim—' Edith pleaded, but he waved his hand in dismissal and the cowed woman shrank back into her chair and shrivelled into terrified silence.

'Now you listen to me, girl—' Jim wagged his forefinger into Kathy's face. 'You get yourself over to the Robinson place this minute and you go down on your knees if necessary and you beg him to forgive you and you ask him to take you back.'

Kathy stared into her father's eyes, seeing him – really seeing him – for the first time. Not any longer as her father, the man who, though strict and dominating, must be honoured and obeyed, but as the man he really was: cruel and self-centred, without an ounce of love or compassion in his embittered soul. Though the side of her face was stinging, she gritted her teeth and determined not to put her hand up to it. She wouldn't give him the satisfaction of seeing that he had hurt her. But the physical hurt was nothing compared to the ache in her heart.

'You hear me. You'll do as I say.' It was a demand, not a request, and in that moment, Kathy's heart hardened irrevocably as he added, 'You'll go to the Robinsons' this very minute.'

Briefly, she glanced down at her mother. 'I'm sorry, Mam,' Kathy said softly. 'So sorry . . .'

For a long moment, mother and daughter gazed at each other and then the girl saw the brief flicker of a smile on the older woman's mouth. Edith gave an almost imperceptible little nod that told her daughter all she needed to know.

'And so you should be,' Jim growled. He sat down and picked up his knife and fork, confident that the matter was at an end, that now he would be obeyed.

Kathy moved round the table and knelt beside her mother's chair. Edith clasped her hand and leant forward to kiss the girl's forehead. 'God bless you,' she whispered so low that Kathy only just caught the words that released her, words that sprang the trap wide open.

She was free. Free to go, free to leave – and with her mother's blessing.

'You – you'll be all right?' Kathy whispered.

They both knew she wouldn't be – not really – but Edith patted her hand, managed to raise a smile and say, louder now, 'Off you go, love. You go to the Robinsons'.'

For a moment, Kathy leant her face against her mother's bony shoulder and whispered, 'I love you, Mam.'

'I know, my darling, I know,' the poor woman whispered back, 'but off you go. It's – it's for the best.'

With a final squeeze of her hand, Kathy rose and moved towards the door into the hall and the stairs. She glanced back just once. Her father was eating as if nothing had happened, his whole attention on the food in front of him, but her mother's gaze followed her.

Then Kathy turned and ran lightly upstairs to pack her battered suitcase.

Three

'Hello, lass.' Ted Robinson greeted her with a wave and began to cross the yard towards her. He was a big man, tall with strong, broad shoulders and a weather-beaten face that crinkled with laughter lines. 'Going on your holidays?'

Kathy set the heavy suitcase down, straightened up and smiled at him as he neared her. 'I've a favour to ask.'

'Owt, lass, you know that.'

'Could Morry take me to the station, please?'

The Robinsons had a dilapidated old truck that carried anything from pigs bound for market to the huge Christmas tree that Ted brought home every year.

'Of course he can. But – but where are you going?'

Suddenly, the euphoria at her sudden freedom that had carried her this far faltered. 'I – I don't really know.'

'Don't know?' For a moment Ted was puzzled. He moved closer, his gaze intent upon her face. 'What's been happening, lass? You've got a right old shiner coming up there.' He frowned, already half guessing what had been going on in the Burtons' unhappy household. He sighed and then said softly, 'You leaving home?'

Kathy bit her lip and nodded. Then she blurted out, 'Morry asked me to marry him and – and I said no.

I'm sorry, Mr Robinson, truly I am. He'll make someone a wonderful husband, but – but . . .'

'But not you, eh, lass?'

She nodded.

The big man sighed. 'I'm sorry too. Me an' the missis would've loved you as a daughter-in-law, but if you don't love the lad . . .' He searched her face for a glimmer of hope that she might – just might – change her mind. Not seeing it, he murmured, 'Aye, well, marriage is tough enough at times when you are in love, ne'er mind when you're not.' He glanced at her again, an unspoken question in his eyes.

She nodded slowly. 'I know. I've seen the consequences at first hand. I don't intend to make the same mistake. Not that I think Morry would be like that – like – like *him*, but . . .'

Ted put his huge, work-callused hand on her shoulder and gave it a gentle, understanding squeeze. 'Come along in,' he said firmly, in a tone that brooked no argument. 'And we'll see what's to do.' He picked up her suitcase and walked towards the back door of the sprawling farmhouse, leaving Kathy to follow in his wake.

'Mother,' he shouted to his wife as he opened the back door. 'We've got another for dinner. Set a place at the table, love.'

Betty Robinson bustled forward tutting with disapproval as she saw the red mark on the side of Kathy's face and the swelling already beginning around her eye. 'Now, what's that old devil been doing? You're welcome to stay here as long as you want, cariad.' Though Betty had been away from the valleys for many years, there was still a trace of the Celtic lilt in her voice. 'Amy – Amy, come here.'

It wasn't Amy who came into the kitchen, but Morry, his smile of welcome fading when he saw the telltale mark on Kathy's face. For a moment, his benign, kindly face creased into anger. 'Dad – we should go over there. We can't let him get away with this.'

Before Ted Robinson could answer, Amy bounced into the room. 'Kathy . . .' she began and then halted, staring open-mouthed at her friend. 'Wha. . .?'

'You might well ask,' Morry said grimly. 'Been hitting her, that's what he's been doing.'

'Now, now, let's sit down and we'll all have a bit of dinner together,' Ted said. 'You haven't eaten, lass, have you?'

Kathy shook her head. 'No—' She smiled faintly. 'It ended up on the kitchen floor.'

There was an awkward silence. No one knew quite what to say for a moment. Then Betty, ever motherly and sensible, said, 'Amy, come and help me dish up. We'll talk about it over dinner and decide what's to be done.'

They ate in silence for several moments, even though not one of them had much appetite. Each was busy with their own thoughts, working out in their own minds what to suggest. Ted and Betty Robinson were ready to offer the girl a home. Amy was planning much the same, eager to have her very best friend as a sister, and Morry was determined to repeat his proposal. But Kathy had made her mind up and when she laid her knife and fork side by side on the plate, she cleared her throat and forestalled all their schemes by saying, 'I've made up my mind. I'm leaving.'

The other four stared at her and then all seemed to speak at once.

'Oh now, cariad, don't be hasty . . .'

'You can't leave, Kathy. What'll I do without you?' Amy's eyes filled with ready tears.

'I meant what I said, Kathy . . .'

'You stay here, lass. Stay with us for a bit. That'll make the old bugger come to his senses.'

'It's very kind of you and I love you all for it, but I have to go. I – I've been thinking about it for some time anyway. The – the only thing that has kept me here this long is – is Mam.' Her voice broke then and she covered her face with her hands. The Robinsons glanced at each other uncomfortably, lost for words now.

Kathy pulled in a deep, steadying breath and raised her face, even managing to force a tremulous smile. 'But now Mam's sort of – sort of given me her blessing. But it – it doesn't make it any easier. I can't bear to think what might happen to her left alone with him.'

Betty touched Kathy's arm with her plump, comforting hand. 'She'll want what's best for you, cariad.' For a moment, her fond glance rested on her own son and daughter. 'Mothers always do. She'll cope and – if not – then she's always welcome to come here. We'd look after her.'

'You're very kind,' Kathy murmured and her eyes filled with tears. 'I – I don't deserve it.' She glanced apologetically at Morry.

'We know all about Morry's proposal,' Betty said cheerfully. 'And we're sorry it's not to be. But there it is. I wouldn't want you saying "yes" to him just because you want to get away from home. I wouldn't want you using him . . .'

'Mother, please.' Morry's face reddened as he protested.

'You know me, Morry. I always speak my mind. And Kathy should know that by now.'

'I wouldn't ever do that, Mrs Robinson. Not to anyone, and certainly not to Morry.'

Betty nodded, her chins wobbling as she patted Kathy's hand again. 'I know, I know. Morry will find the right girl one day. We all wish it could be you, but like I say, if it's not to be, then it's not to be.'

Now it was Morry who, still red-faced, cast a look of apology towards Kathy.

Ted, tired of all the romantic nonsense, changed the subject to one of practicalities. 'Where do you plan to go, lass?'

'Lincoln.'

They all stared at her for a moment and then, almost as if given a cue, they all laughed and relaxed.

'Lincoln. Why, that's nowt. Only a stone's throw away, lass. Ya not really leaving us at all. I thought you meant you were off to Lunnan or somewhere. Oh, that's all right then.'

Amy clapped her hands. 'I'll be able to come and stay with you and we can go out on the town . . .'

'Now, now, steady on, Amy. You hold your horses a bit,' Betty said. She turned to Kathy. 'Have you got somewhere to go to in Lincoln?'

Kathy shook her head. 'No. But I've got a little money saved up. Though how I've done it I don't know myself, since Dad never paid me a proper wage.' The unfairness of her life was a bitter taste in her mouth and, despite her anxiety over her mother, hardened her resolve.

She was doing the right thing. She was sure she was.

Betty glanced at her husband and voiced her thoughts

aloud. 'D'you think your sister would put her up for a bit? Just till she finds her feet?'

Ted blinked. 'Jemima? Ah, well now, I don't know about that. Not the sort of place you'd want a young lass staying.'

'Oh, I don't know,' Betty was smiling mischievously. 'Might do your Jemima the world of good to have a bright young thing like Kathy about the place. Might liven her up a bit.'

Amy was giggling uncontrollably and even Morry was smiling. Only Ted looked unsure as he glanced at Kathy. He cleared his throat. 'My sister is a spinster and lives alone in a little terraced house with just her cat for company. She does work, though. In one of the big stores in Lincoln. She – er – never married. She – er . . .'

'Such a shame,' Betty murmured as husband and wife exchanged a glance and Betty gave a tiny shake of her head. Ted fell silent, but Kathy had the distinct feeling that there was more to Aunt Jemima's story than either of them were telling.

'You can't send her there,' Amy spluttered. 'She'll have to be in bed by half past nine every night and she won't be allowed any "followers". How's Kathy ever to meet anyone? Make friends?'

'Well, like I say, it's only till she finds her feet,' Betty answered. 'Till she gets a job and can afford a place of her own. Then she can find a nice little bed-sit somewhere.'

Amy clapped her hands again. 'And I can go and stay. What fun we'll have, Kathy.'

'Now, take your things upstairs. Amy'll show you the spare room,' Betty said, rising from the table.

'You stay here the night and Morry can drive you into Lincoln in the morning. I'll come with you and talk to Jemima. All right?'

Kathy nodded. 'You're – you're very kind.'

'Think nothing of it, cariad. That's what friends are for.'

Ted stood up too and, as Kathy rose to follow Amy, she heard him say softly to his wife. 'I've a mind to slip across to Jim's and see how things are.'

'Leave it for tonight, Jim,' Betty whispered back. 'You might make things worse. Let's get her safely out the way and then you can go and see how poor Edith is.'

Kathy picked up her suitcase. The overheard conversation had eased her conscience and lightened her concern. The Robinsons would keep an eye on her mother, and now that she was to move in with a relative of theirs, Kathy would be able to hear if things were all right. The knowledge comforted her and assuaged her guilt – if only a little.

Kathy lay awake half the night, going over and over in her mind the events that had led up to the drastic action she'd taken. She lay in the Robinsons' spare bed, tense and anxious, expecting at any moment to hear a loud banging on their back door. She couldn't imagine that her father would let her go easily. For one thing, he would have to pay someone to do the work on the farm she did for nothing. And that was the last thing he would do. At any moment she expected him to arrive at the Robinsons' to drag her back, by her hair if necessary.

Then another thought struck her. Perhaps he hadn't

realized she'd gone. She'd crept quietly out of the house while he was asleep in the battered armchair near the range.

Only Kathy's mother had seen her go, had held her close for a few brief moments and then given her a gentle push towards the door. 'Go now. Quickly – before he wakes up,' Edith had whispered urgently.

But nothing disturbed the stillness of the frosty night; the only sound was Ted Robinson's noisy snoring in the next room. If her father did know, it was obvious now that he wasn't going to chase after her. No doubt he thought she would come back of her own accord like a whipped dog, contrite and begging forgiveness.

'Fat chance,' Kathy murmured aloud in the darkness. She turned over and, at last, fell asleep.

Four

'Good heavens! Whatever brings you to my door this early on a Monday morning? Is something wrong, Betty? Is it Edward?'

Kathy hid her smile at hearing the use of Ted Robinson's full and formal Christian name.

'No, no, Jemima cariad. We're fine. But we're early because we wanted to catch you before you went to work.'

'Come in, do. You're welcome any time of the day, Betty. It's good to see you.' As the tall, thin woman ushered them into the tiny terraced house, she was still firing questions. 'How *is* Edward? And Amy? Is my goddaughter behaving herself? Hello, Maurice, my dear boy, how nice to see you.' She proffered her gaunt cheek for Morry's dutiful kiss.

Then she turned her sharp grey eyes on Kathy. 'And who is this?'

'Kathy. Kathy Burton.'

Strangely, the grey eyes showed no surprise, not even when they glanced down briefly and took in the suitcase. 'Jim Burton's girl?'

When Betty nodded, Jemima's only reply was a swift nod and a soft, 'Ah.'

It seemed the woman understood without another word of explanation, for she led the way from the back door through the scullery and into the living kitchen.

Remains of her half-eaten breakfast lay on the table set against the wall, but she made no effort to return to it, saying instead, 'Would you like a cup of tea?'

'We mustn't keep you, Jemima. You'll be wanting to get to work.'

Jemima glanced at the clock on the mantelpiece above the range that took up the centre of one wall. 'I've never been late in all the twenty years I've worked there,' she said. 'I don't think they're going to dismiss me for being a few minutes late this morning. Besides, Mr Kendall is a very understanding young man.' She paused, sniffed, and seemed lost for a brief moment in her own thoughts. 'Poor young feller has to be,' she murmured. Then she shook herself and was brisk and businesslike once more. 'Sit down, sit down all of you. Maurice, my dear, fetch another chair from the front room. And then you can tell me what this is about – though I think I can guess.'

When they were all seated, Jemima sat down too, crossing her ankles neatly and folding her hands in her lap. She was dressed ready for work in a smart, navy blue two-piece costume that accentuated her slim figure. Her hair, once a bright auburn but now showing signs of grey here and there, was swept back from her face into a plaited coil at the nape of her neck, the plain style emphasizing the thinness of her face. Kathy guessed the woman must be in her late forties – like her brother and sister-in-law – but she looked older. There were tiny lines around her eyes and her mouth, but when she turned her clear, green eyes on Kathy and smiled, the severity left her face and Kathy could glimpse the pretty girl this woman must once have been.

'Now, my dear,' Jemima's tone was surprisingly kind. 'Leaving home, are you?'

Kathy could not prevent a little gasp of surprise and she glanced at Betty, who nodded encouragingly. 'Tell Aunt Jemima – I mean, Miss Robinson—'

Jemima waved her hand and said, 'Oh, "Aunt Jemima" will do fine. I'm sure we can make room for an adopted niece.' Her smile widened and her eyes actually twinkled for a brief moment. 'I'm sure the names the girls at work call me are far less polite.'

Kathy cleared her throat, suddenly nervous. Miss Robinson – Aunt Jemima – seemed kindly enough. There had been no note of disapproval in her tone, yet there was none of approval either. It had been a statement of fact that gave Kathy no real encouragement.

'Yes, I – er – um – I want to come and live in the city. Find a job. Stand on my own feet.'

Jemima's disconcerting gaze eyed her steadily. 'Why?'

Kathy swallowed and gnawed at her lower lip. Then the words came in a rush, as if she could contain herself no longer. 'Because – because I can't stand it at home any more. My father treats me like a servant. I get my keep, as he calls it, but no wage . . .' Now she met Jemima's gaze steadily. 'I want to stand on my own two feet. I want to see a bit of life.'

'I see,' Jemima said quietly. Slowly, the older woman turned her head towards her sister-in-law as she said softly, 'It could be me thirty years ago, Betty, couldn't it?'

Betty nodded. 'Yes, but things are worse for Kathy, Jemima. Your dad was strict, yes, but he was never cruel.' She nodded towards Kathy. 'See that black eye she's getting? He did that to her. Now your dad never hit you. Not that I know of, anyway.'

Jemima closed her eyes for a moment, as if lost in the past. When she opened them she sighed and murmured, 'Only the once, Betty, only the once, but maybe he had good reason, eh?'

Betty stared at her sister-in-law, but said nothing. Kathy looked at Morry, but he was studiously avoiding her glance. She guessed he knew what the two women were talking about, but no one was going to reveal a long-held family secret to her. Not even Morry.

Briskly now, Jemima turned back to Kathy. 'I know your father of old, my dear. Being neighbours, Edward and I, and your father, were all young together. I always thought him a cold fish even then and pitied any woman who was foolish enough to marry him. He came a-courting me once, but I sent him packing, I can tell you.' Her eyes sparkled suddenly with mischief but then, almost as suddenly as it had appeared, the twinkle was gone. 'But your poor mother.' Jemima sighed. 'I expect she was taken in by the thought of a young man owning his own farm.' She gave a quick nod. 'And, yes, it could have been a good life for any girl. Look at Betty here – I don't think she'd change her life with the Queen of England . . .'

Betty nodded and smiled her agreement.

'And your father can be very charming,' Jemima went on. 'When he wants to be!'

Kathy was on the point of arguing. She had never seen any 'charm' in her father, but then she stopped as she remembered how Jim always greeted Morry when he came to the farm. Oh yes, Jim Burton's attitude could be very different when he wanted something from someone.

'But I expect your poor mother rues the day she met Jim Burton,' Jemima added grimly.

For a moment – a very brief moment – Kathy almost felt moved to defend her father. Jemima's bluntness was almost rude. But the words she might have spoken died on her lips. What Jemima Robinson was saying was absolutely true. Harsh though her words were, there was no denying the truth in them.

'So, you want somewhere to stay in Lincoln, I take it?'

'Only temporary, Jemima, just till she finds a job and can afford a place of her own. A little bed-sit or – or something,' Betty finished lamely. She knew nothing of city life and couldn't imagine anything worse than being cooped up in a tiny room in a little house in a row of houses with street after street just the same. Give her the wide open spaces of the countryside any day. Sandy Furze Farm and the tiny village of Abbeytoft were all Betty needed or wanted. But, though she couldn't understand it herself, she could see that the lure of the busy streets and the bright lights were perhaps what the lonely Kathy Burton needed. She just hoped her Amy wouldn't want to follow her friend.

'You're very welcome to stay – for a short while,' Jemima said bluntly. 'But you'll have to try to fit in with me and my funny little ways. Taffy – that's my cat – and I like our routine.'

'Of course,' Kathy said at once. 'Just tell me what you want me to do and . . .'

'Oh, I will, make no mistake about that.' Jemima's gaze scrutinized the girl once more. 'And I might be able to help you find a job. There's a vacancy at the department store where I work. I'll talk to Miss Curtis – the head of the department – and to Mr Kendall.'

'Oh, thank you. That's – that's very kind of you.'

'Kindness has nothing to do with it,' Jemima said,

standing up as if giving a signal that it was time for Betty and Morry to leave and for her to go to work. 'The sooner you have a job and can earn your own living, the sooner Taffy and I will have our house back to ourselves.'

Kathy wasn't sure but she thought she saw – just briefly – the fleeting sparkle of mischief in Jemima's eyes.

Her first encounter with the other occupant of the terraced house was more frightening than meeting Aunt Jemima.

Taffy was a long-haired ginger tom, who padded silently about the house on huge white-tipped paws and glared balefully at the newcomer invading his territory. Their first confrontation happened in the scullery.

Aunt Jemima, having shown her to the tiny spare bedroom and given her a key for the back door, had left for work. Betty and Morry had gone and now Kathy was alone in the house and wondering what she should do. After being used to working from dawn to dusk – and sometimes beyond – she didn't know how to handle the hours that stretched emptily before her.

Perhaps I should go into the city myself and see if I can find work, she mused. But she didn't want to offend Aunt Jemima, who had promised to enquire about the vacancy at the large department store where she worked. So Kathy looked around the neat house to see if there was anything that needed doing. Then she spotted the breakfast things still left on the table. She carried the used crockery into the scullery to wash it. Standing at the deep white sink, she heard a snuffling and turned towards the round basket in the corner. The cat was stretching and yawning, showing sharp, white teeth and even sharper claws.

'Hello, boy. You must be Taffy. My, you're a beauty, aren't you?' Kathy squatted and held out her hand towards the cat, but he arched his back, his fur bristling, and spat at her. As his paw flicked out towards her, Kathy quickly pulled back her hand, narrowly missing receiving a deep scratch. 'That's not a very nice welcome, I must say. Mind you, I am a stranger in your home, so you've every right.'

His green eyes sparked anger and he hissed at her again.

'I'm not going to hurt you,' she carried on, talking in a soft soothing tone, but she made no attempt to touch the animal again. 'I've just come to stay here for a while.' She stood up and turned back to the sink, half expecting that at any moment she might feel those vicious claws raking the back of her leg.

After a moment, she risked a glance over her shoulder. The cat's bright green gaze was weighing her up, it seemed. Kathy tried again. 'I wonder how you get in and out while your mistress is out all day.' She looked around. At the bottom of the back door there was a hole cut in the woodwork and covering it was a metal-hinged flap that swung backwards and forwards. 'Oh, how clever,' she murmured.

Then she saw that the cat's bowls – one for milk and one for food – were filled. 'Seems you don't need my help,' she said as she dried the last plate and stowed it away in the cupboard.

She turned and went back into the kitchen and sat down in an easy chair near the range. Beside the chair and set in the alcove near the range was a shelf of books. Kathy leaned forward and perused the titles, smiling as she saw one of her favourite books there. *Pride and Prejudice*. In her last year at school the class had begun to read it, but she'd been forced by her father to leave school as soon as she was old enough. She'd never had the chance to finish the story. There were few books around at Thorpe Farm. Her father considered them a waste of time.

'Filling your head with such nonsense,' had been his view if he ever caught her reading. 'You'd be better doing something useful.' And by the time she climbed the stairs at night to her bedroom – the only place where she had any privacy – she was usually so dog-tired that her eyelids drooped before she'd read even half a page.

But now she'd time to spare. Carefully, she pulled the book from the shelf and opened it, her heart beating with a sudden excitement. She could read to her heart's content. There was no one to stop her. From this moment on, she could do exactly what she pleased with her life.

As she turned to the first page, the door into the scullery was pushed wider open and Taffy walked into the room. Kathy glanced up, watching him. He stood a moment, his green eyes staring at her. Then, with the easy grace of a big cat in the wild, he padded towards her, his gaze still holding hers. He sat down before her, still looking up at her, still assessing her. She could no longer read his expression; he was no longer spitting but neither did friendliness shine in his green eyes.

'Ah,' Kathy said aloud. 'Am I sitting in your mistress's chair? Is that it?' She smiled. Did she imagine it or did the green eyes soften just a little? Without warning, the cat lifted his front paw, balanced himself for a moment on his hind legs and then launched himself towards her, landing on her lap and sending the book slithering to the floor. His face close to hers for a moment, her stared at her again. Kathy, pressing herself back into the chair, stared back. Then Taffy broke the gaze and turned three times in a tight circle, kneading her lap with his white-tipped paws. Kathy held her breath, waiting. At last he lay down with the curve of his spine towards her and began to wash his foreleg. To her amazement, Kathy heard the deep-throated rumble of a contented purr. Tentatively she touched the cat's head and was rewarded by him pressing against her stroking fingers and purring even louder.

Carefully Kathy reached down to retrieve her book and they settled down together. The cat yawned, stretched his front paw, then curled his head round and closed his eyes. Strangely comforted by the warm little body on her lap, Kathy turned back to her book.

It wasn't until she heard the rattle of the back door opening that Kathy realized just how the morning had flown by. Lost in the wonderful story of Mr and Mrs Bennett and their five daughters, she had not once moved from the chair. And Taffy still slumbered on her lap.

Jemima stepped into the room and stopped, staring in surprise.

'Well, I never,' she exclaimed. 'Now that's something I never expected to see. Taffy's usually most unfriendly with visitors.' Jemima seemed impressed to see her pet sitting on Kathy's knee.

'He wasn't at first. He spat at me and tried to scratch

me, but I just ignored him and then he came and jumped up on to my knee of his own accord.'

Jemima laughed. 'That's the best way to treat him. One thing Taffy can't bear is to be ignored.'

Kathy set her book down and put her hands beneath the cat's hefty body to lift him off her knee. He woke with a start and leapt down, walking angrily towards the door, his ears flattened. The two women watched him as he stalked out and they heard the rattle of the flap in the back door.

Kathy got up quickly. 'I'm sorry,' she said again. 'I'd've done some housework for you, but I didn't like to presume . . .'

'No need,' Jemima said crisply. 'I don't expect you to do that – at least not on your first day. Obviously, I shall expect you to keep your room clean . . .'

'Of course,' Kathy said swiftly. 'And I'll help elsewhere – that is, if you want me to.'

'We'll see,' Jemima smiled.

'I could have got you some lunch ready if I'd known you came home.' Kathy was still apologetic.

'I don't normally, but I have some news for you. Mr Kendall, the manager, is willing to see you at three o'clock this afternoon. The vacant post is in the millinery department. Do you know anything about hats?'

Kathy laughed wryly. 'Not really. The only hat I possess is the one I always wear for church. And that's an old one of my mother's. Nineteen-twenties style!'

Jemima grimaced. 'Oh well, as long as you're a willing learner.' She glanced at the skirt and blouse that Kathy was wearing. Bluntly she said, 'Have you anything better to wear than that?'

Biting her lip, Kathy shook her head.

'Mm.' For a moment, Jemima was thoughtful.

'You're a little bit plumper than me . . .' She chuckled suddenly, her thin face lighting up. For a brief moment it made her look so much younger. 'But in all the right places, I must say. I have a costume that might just fit you.' She glanced at her wristwatch. 'You make us some sandwiches, Kathy, and I'll run upstairs and sort one or two things out. You can try them all on when I've gone back to work.'

While Kathy went into the scullery and found bread, butter, a joint of cooked ham and some cheese, Jemima ran lightly up the narrow staircase to her bedroom. As she prepared the snack, Kathy heard wardrobe doors opening and closing in the room above. Just as she placed a plate of the sandwiches on the table in the kitchen, she heard Jemima's steps on the stairs.

'I've laid out three suits for you and two blouses.' She glanced down at Kathy's feet. 'Your shoes will have to do, but there's polish under the sink in the scullery. Ah,' she said, seeing the sandwiches. 'This looks nice. Why is it,' she added, sitting down, 'that food always tastes so much nicer when someone else has prepared it? Even a few sandwiches.'

'I'd offer to cook for you,' Kathy said, sitting down too. 'But I've never had much chance to learn. Father always wanted me to work outside. Poor Mam had to . . .' Suddenly her throat was tight and she felt the prickle of tears behind her eyelids. But she pulled in a deep breath and steadied her voice. 'Had to manage in the kitchen all by herself.'

Pretending not to notice, Jemima said, 'Your poor mother wasn't cut out to be a farmer's wife. It's a hard life. A good life, mind you, but a hard one nevertheless.'

'Do you know,' Kathy said, surprised to hear herself

saying it and almost ashamed to admit it, 'I know very little about my parents' life. They hardly ever talk about the past and if they do, well, it's only my father grumbling how unfair life has been to him. The – the fact that he's never had a son. He – he's very jealous of your brother for having Morry to carry on the family farm.'

There was a long pause before Jemima asked, 'Is there anything between you and Maurice?'

'No . . . I mean – my father would like there to be and I – er – Morry would too, but . . .' Kathy felt her cheeks redden with embarrassment. Perhaps she had now offended Aunt Jemima by not being able to love her nephew, but the older woman's only answer was her soft, understanding, 'Ah.'

Five

Mr Kendall, the manager of the large department store on the High Street, was much younger than Kathy had expected. As she was ushered into his office by his secretary, Kathy almost gasped aloud in surprise. He looked to be in his late twenties. Young to hold such a position of authority, she thought.

Jemima had explained a little as they'd eaten their lunch. 'The Hammond family owns the store. Old Mr Hammond rarely comes in these days. He suffers cruelly with arthritis, so I understand. Mr James Hammond, his son and heir, comes in most days, but it's Mr Kendall we see about the store the most. He's – er – very actively involved,' she added, sounding amused about something, though Kathy could not understand what.

Now, as she stood before him, he rose, smiled at her and indicated a chair set in front of his desk for her to sit down. She noticed that he was very smartly dressed in a dark, pinstriped suit, gleaming white shirt and neat, sober tie. His short, black hair was sleek and shone in the pale winter sunlight from the window behind him. Though his face was in shadow, she could see the outline of a straight nose and a strong jawline. She couldn't, at this moment, see the colour of his eyes or the shape of his mouth . . .

'Please sit down, Miss Burton.' His voice was deep, but friendly.

Kathy perched nervously on the edge of the chair, gripping her handbag in front of her.

He looked at her for a moment and now she could see that his eyes were a gentle brown. 'Don't be nervous,' he said softly. 'I'm not such an ogre.'

Kathy smiled and relaxed a little. It wasn't really him she was nervous about. It was just that this interview was so important to her. She badly wanted – needed – this job. And having to borrow clothes from a woman more than twice her age wasn't exactly boosting her confidence!

'Now,' he rested his arms on the desk and leaned towards her. 'I understand from Miss Robinson that you would very much like to work for us, but that you have no experience at all.'

There was nothing else she could do except be absolutely frank. 'No, I'm sorry. I haven't. The only work I know is on a farm. My – my father's farm. But – but I so want to do something else.'

'I see,' he said slowly. 'And I presume you cannot furnish us with references?'

Kathy shook her head and her heart began to sink, but hope surged again as he continued, 'Well, in some ways your inexperience might be an advantage. We can train you from the start to our ways. You won't come with any preconceived ideas. Ideas that we might not like.' His smile broadened. 'And because of Miss Robinson's recommendation, I'm willing to give you a month's trial and see how we go.'

Kathy felt the colour rush into her face. 'Oh, thank you. Thank you very much. I won't let you down.'

'No,' Tony Kendall said softly. 'No, I don't think you will.' He stared at her for a long time, taking in the long, blonde hair swept back from her face over her ears and falling in a shining cascade of curls to her shoulders. Her clear complexion was tanned from her time spent working out of doors in all weathers but her blue eyes were direct and honest. She was not the sort of girl they usually employed, and he'd only agreed to interview her as a favour to Miss Robinson, who'd worked for the store for more than twenty years. Jemima Robinson was a revered member of staff who had worked her way up over the years to be head of the ladies' department. More recently, she'd been promoted to the position of supervisor of the whole of the first floor and was responsible for several departments, including mantles, outfitting – and hats! Under her keen eye were the heads of each department who, in turn, had several assistants and juniors below them. Miss Robinson was known to be strict with those under her, but fair. For her alone, Tony Kendall had been willing to give this girl a trial. But now that he saw Kathy Burton for himself, well, reason didn't come into it!

'I'll hand you over to my secretary. She'll fill out all the necessary paperwork and take you down to introduce you to the other girls in millinery.' He rose and moved around the desk, opened the door and called to the woman sitting before a typewriter in the outer office. 'Miss Foster, would you step in for a moment, please?'

'Certainly, Mr Kendall . . .'

'This is Miss Curtis.' Half an hour later, Miss Foster was introducing her to the head of the millinery department and to the other girl who worked there, Stella Matthews.

Miss Curtis was in her early thirties, Kathy surmised, slim with a … in the very latest … But her grey eyes … Kathy up and down … of her mouth. 'It's u… someone without con… She gave a small sniff o… and for the girl standi… he's the boss.'

'Miss Burton is here … Foster, an older, more ki… no experience, but Mr Ke… an advantage. You can train her to … ays, Miss Curtis.'

Muriel Curtis's eyes widened and she turned towards the secretary. 'No experience? None at all?' She tutted with disapproval and murmured, 'Whatever is he thinking of?' As her glance flickered back towards Kathy, there was a shrewd, knowing look in her eyes. 'Ah,' she said softly. 'Another of his fancy pieces, is she?'

'Really, Miss Curtis,' Emily Foster hissed angrily and, taking hold of the woman's arm, she pulled Muriel a short distance away. But Kathy's sharp ears still heard the rest of their conversation. 'That is a most inappropriate remark. And, for your information, he had not seen the girl before today.'

Muriel's smile was humourless. 'Oh really!' Kathy felt the woman's resentful gaze rest on her again. Grudgingly, she added, 'But with a pretty face like hers, one look would be enough.'

'Jealousy will get you nowhere, Muriel.' Emily's tone had softened and Kathy could detect a note of pity in it. Though her voice dropped even lower, she still heard enough of their conversation to understand. 'Forget worth it . . . not the first . . .

ered reply was even softer. 'It wasn't was *her*.'

ied to glance away, to make out she could r what was being said, but her gaze was held he sight of Muriel's sudden and obvious distress. or a brief moment, the young woman's face crumpled and she seemed about to burst into tears. But then, with a supreme effort, Muriel pulled in a deep breath, straightened her back and lifted her head. 'You're quite right, Miss Foster,' she said raising her voice deliberately. Obviously, she now intended Kathy to hear. 'Any girl who gets involved with him had better watch out.'

Emily Foster patted Muriel's arm and then turned back to Kathy. 'I'll leave you with Miss Curtis. Perhaps she can begin your instruction today, if she has time. We shall expect you here by eight forty-five in the morning to start work. Good afternoon.' She nodded and began to walk away.

'G-good afternoon, Miss Foster, and – thank you,' Kathy said, her nervousness making her stammer and blush like a gawky schoolgirl.

As the woman walked away, Muriel Curtis said frostily, 'I really haven't time to show you around today. Just mind you're here on time in the morning.' Her tone implied she thought it a waste of her time anyway with a young girl of absolutely no experience.

Kathy forced a polite smile. 'I will, Miss Curtis. Thank you.'

She turned and left the millinery department, walked down the wide staircase, passed through the ground floor and out into the street, straight into the blustery cold wind. Kathy shivered. Jemima's costume might be very smart, but it didn't keep her warm. For a moment, she thought longingly of the heavy raincoat and boots she wore about the farm. But the moment was brief and banished with a laugh as she revelled, yet again, in her newfound freedom.

Briskly, she walked from the city centre to the terraced house that would be her home for the next few weeks.

The following morning passed in a mesmerizing whirl, so that by lunchtime Kathy felt as if her head was spinning.

'We stagger the lunchtime period,' Muriel told her. All morning, her sharp voice had issued orders, explained the work expected crisply and watched Kathy's every move with her disapproving grey eyes. If Kathy had not seen for herself the woman's brief lapse, she would have believed that Muriel Curtis had a heart of stone. But the picture in her mind's eye of the crumpled face, close to tears, prevented the younger girl from disliking the woman on sight. 'Are you listening to me, Miss Burton?' Muriel's voice penetrated Kathy's wandering thoughts.

Kathy jumped. 'Oh – I – I'm sorry, Miss Curtis.'

'As I was saying—' Muriel's voice was frosty. 'We stagger the lunchtime period so that there are always two in the department. As there are only three of us, we can only take three-quarters of an hour each.' She looked at her watch and then glanced around her. 'It's only eleven forty-five, but we're quiet at the moment, so if you'd like to take your lunch now, I'll hold the fort while Miss Matthews shows you where the staff restroom is. And then later, when it goes quiet about four o'clock, she can take you on a tour of the store. It's important you know your way around and to be able to direct customers too.'

'Thank you, Miss Curtis,' Kathy said with unaccustomed meekness.

Away from the head of department's eagle eye, Stella chattered incessantly. 'I'm so glad you've come . . .' She was small, with mousy straight hair and hazel eyes. But her round face was continually wreathed in smiles – even when Miss Curtis found reason to reprimand her, which seemed often. 'There's only been the two of us for four weeks now. The other girl left and though Miss Curtis isn't a bad old stick really, it's been so hard not to have someone of my own age to gossip with.' She giggled – a delicious, infectious sound. 'Not that we're supposed to, of course, but you know how it is.'

Kathy smiled and nodded, but she didn't know. She'd never had anyone to chatter to, only Amy. And she'd only been able to do that once or twice a week. Her father had seen to that!

'How old are you? I'm seventeen. Just. I've been here ever since I left school . . .' The young girl prattled on, scarcely giving Kathy chance to reply. But she didn't mind. Stella was sociable and Kathy soaked up her friendliness like a flower devoid of rain. 'This is the restroom where we eat our lunch. Have you brought anything to eat?'

'Yes, some sandwiches.'

'I expect Miss Robinson told you we all bring our own food, did she?'

Kathy nodded. She wasn't quite sure how much Jemima wanted her connection to Kathy to be known among the rest of the staff. It seemed, however, that the store grapevine had already been busy.

'You're lucky to have been recommended by Miss Robinson, you know. I don't think Mr Kendall would dare *not* take you on.'

Kathy didn't know whether to feel grateful or mortified that she had got the job more because of Jemima Robinson's say-so than because of her own merit. She sighed. This was a whole new world. Things were very different from what she had been used to. But it was the sort of world she had craved and she'd better get used to it.

One thing she knew for sure, there was no turning back. She couldn't bear to think how her father would crow if she failed. Oh no, no matter whatever happened there was no going back.

The afternoon flew by and, before Kathy realized it, it was four o'clock.

'Now, Miss Matthews may take you on a tour of the store . . .' Muriel Curtis began, but at that moment a deep voice spoke behind her.

'That won't be necessary, Miss Curtis, thank you.'

They turned to see Tony Kendall striding towards them. He glanced briefly at Muriel but then turned towards Kathy with a beaming smile that crinkled his eyes and showed perfectly white, even teeth. 'And how is she shaping up, Miss Curtis?' As he spoke, his glance ran up and down Kathy as if implying: She shapes up very well in my eyes.

There was the slightest of pauses before Muriel replied stiffly, 'Reasonably well, Mr Kendall, considering . . .'

'Good, good,' he said, rubbing his hands together. 'I thought I'd come and show you around the store myself.' At last he turned towards the head of the millinery department. 'If you have no objection, of course, Miss Curtis.' The words were courteous, but even to Kathy's naïve ears his statement left the woman with no alternative but to say through tight lips, 'Of course not, Mr Kendall.'

He smiled again as he put out his arm as if to usher Kathy forward. The girl bit her lip and glanced anxiously at Miss Curtis, an unspoken question in her eyes. She didn't want to upset this woman. She would have to work with her – *under* her. Miss Curtis had it in her power to make life very uncomfortable for the younger girls in her charge. Even Stella looked down in the mouth. Obviously she'd looked forward to showing Kathy around the store.

'Come along, Miss Burton,' Tony Kendall ordered, and Kathy was relieved to see Miss Curtis give her a slight nod.

For the next half an hour Kathy followed the manager around the large store, through ladies' apparel, haberdashery, footwear, men's and boys' wear and then up the elegant staircase to carpets, household furnishings, linens and fabrics . . . The store seemed to sell anything and everything. On and on it went, until Kathy's head ached trying to remember where each department was situated.

'And now,' he beamed down at her as they arrived back at his office on the top floor, 'we'll end the day with a cup of tea in my office. I like to make all the newcomers feel welcome and that they can turn to me with any problem at any time. Please, come in.'

He opened the door into the outer office where Miss Foster was still typing, her nimble fingers flying over the keys.

'Would you get us tea, Miss Foster, please?' he asked.

The woman stopped her work at once and glanced up. For a moment, she stared at Kathy and then glanced at her boss. 'Of course, Mr Kendall,' she murmured and rose to her feet, frowning slightly.

Tony Kendall had moved towards his own office and opened the door, holding it for Kathy to enter.

With a strange feeling of trepidation that she could not understand, Kathy stepped ahead of him into his room.

'Did you enjoy being shown round by "sir"?' Stella's greeting when Kathy returned to the millinery department was distinctly cold. Gone was the easy chatter there had been before Mr Kendall had arrived on the scene.

Carefully, Kathy said, 'It was all right. But I'd much sooner you'd've shown me round. My head's aching with trying to remember where everywhere is. I'd've felt more comfortable with you. I could've asked you when I wasn't sure, but – but I daren't refuse to go with him. I'm sorry.'

Stella stared at her for a moment and then the merry smile was back on her face. She touched Kathy's arm. 'No – no, of course you couldn't. It's just that I was really looking forward to showing you round.'

Kathy nodded. 'Me too.'

Stella leaned closer. 'Miss Curtis isn't too pleased, either. She gets all huffy when he interferes with the running of her department. She's been here longer than him *and* she's older. Not much, of course. Mind you, when he first came here I think she fancied her chances with him. There were rumours . . .' Stella was chattering happily again, her brief moment of umbrage completely forgotten. She nudged Kathy and winked. 'Know what I mean?'

Kathy smiled, but said nothing.

The girl seemed about to confide more but instead she muttered suddenly, 'Look out! The dragon's here.'

Kathy glanced over her shoulder to see Jemima walking towards them, pausing every few moments as her glance ran over a display. Her sharp eyes missed nothing, from the tidiness of the counter to a thin film of dust on a shelf.

From nowhere, it seemed to Kathy, Miss Curtis appeared silently and fell into step beside her superior. A short distance from the girls, the two women stopped and turned to face each other. 'Has Miss Burton had a tour of the store yet?'

'Oh yes.' Miss Curtis's mouth tightened. 'She certainly has.' As Jemima's eyebrows rose in a question, Muriel added sarcastically, 'Mr Kendall showed her around himself.'

'Did he indeed?' There was no mistaking the disapproval in Jemima's tone and she added softly, 'Mm. Well, we'll have to see about that, won't we, Muriel?'

The other woman shrugged. 'But what can we do? You know what he's like.'

'I do,' Jemima sniffed. 'But this particular girl is staying with me for a while. Just until she gets on her feet. Maybe I can . . .' Now her voice dropped so low that even Kathy's acute hearing could not catch the rest of the conversation.

*

'So,' Jemima began as they walked home together after the store had closed. 'Do you think you'll like working with us?'

'Oh yes, yes I do. But – but there's a lot to learn.'

Jemima chuckled. 'I suppose there is. I've worked there so long, I suppose I don't see how it must be for someone just starting. Especially someone who's lived out in the sticks.'

Kathy smiled to herself. Jemima certainly didn't mince her words.

'I just hope I will suit. Miss Curtis seems a bit fearsome.'

'Oh, we all are,' Jemima said cheerfully. 'We don't tolerate slackness or slovenliness or idleness in any way, shape or form.'

Kathy was silent.

'But,' the older woman went on, her tone softening just a little, 'the main thing to remember is that the customer always – *always* – comes first and foremost. I know there's the saying "the customer's always right". Well, of course they're not, but you have to act as if they are. In short, my dear – it sounds a funny thing to say – but you have to let the customer walk all over you and still come up smiling.'

'Well, I should be good at that then,' Kathy remarked dryly. 'I've had plenty of practice at doing what I'm told.'

'Mm,' Jemima said as they arrived at the passageway between her home and the next-door house. They walked down it in single file. As they came to the door at the end of the passage leading into Jemima's back yard, she put her hand on the latch and turned to glance back at Kathy. 'Maybe so, but you've kicked over the traces now, haven't you? Well and truly.'

Without waiting for any reply, Jemima opened the door and, in a soft and tender tone, began to call, 'Taffy, where are you? Come to Mummy, Taffy.'

Six

With her first week's wages, Kathy bought herself a smart suit to wear for work. At least, she paid for part of it. Staff were allowed to have an account and, although she was only very newly appointed and still on trial, because she was Miss Robinson's' protégée, the rules had been relaxed.

'I'll need your help, Stella,' she said. 'You'll have to tell me what's suitable.'

As the doors closed on the Saturday evening, both girls approached Miss Curtis to ask if Kathy might be allowed to try on the two or three suits that Stella had picked out for her during quiet moments in the department.

Kathy felt Muriel's scrutiny. The woman's face was expressionless and Kathy couldn't guess what her superior was thinking. She would have been amazed – and dismayed – to know that the overriding emotion that Muriel was feeling at that moment was one of jealousy.

Kathy was quite unaware of her own natural beauty. With her lightly tanned, smooth complexion and well-proportioned features she was more than just 'pretty'. Perhaps the only thing that spoiled the classic beauty was the rather square, firm chin. Her blonde hair had now been styled into the fashion of the day – swept back from her face in pincurls and falling in a shining cascade of waves and curls to her shoulders. With the addition of a smart new suit and a few lessons in the art of applying subtle make-up, Kathy would be more than eye-catching. She would outshine all the other women and girls on the whole of the first floor. Muriel struggled with her feelings, quashing the natural instinct of the envy that one woman feels towards another, younger, prettier girl, and tried to decide whether the girl's looks would be an asset to the department or otherwise. Would her customers, striving for beauty themselves, be encouraged or disheartened by the loveliness of the sales assistant?

It was a question Muriel could not answer, and only time would tell.

Now, she plastered a smile on her face and tried to make her tone friendly. 'Of course. And though you wouldn't ordinarily be allowed staff discount yet, I'll see what I can do for you. Ask Miss Jenkins if you can look at the items in the stockroom. We had a big sale in January because of stock reduction and obviously there are always some items that don't sell even then. Not that I'm suggesting you should take anything you don't like,' Muriel added hastily, 'but it might be worth a look.'

'Thank you, Miss Curtis,' Kathy murmured, touched by the woman's sudden understanding and kindness.

Muriel was looking down at Kathy's feet.

'Er . . .' she began hesitantly, but Kathy, making it easier for her, said quickly, 'Yes, and I'll be needing some new shoes too, though I don't know if I can afford them this week. I must pay my way at Aunt . . . at Miss Robinson's.'

'Of course,' Muriel said swiftly. 'I'll have a word with my colleague in footwear. I'm sure something can be arranged.'

'I'm sure if you asked Mr Kendall, he'd let you have a pair on tick for a week,' Stella put in. Her face was innocent, but Kathy was sure she caught a wicked gleam in the young girl's eyes.

The smile disappeared from Muriel's face as she said tartly now, 'You'd better be quick trying on those suits. The store will be locked up in thirty minutes. Unless, of course, you want to spend the night here.' And with that last sarcastic barb, she turned away.

Kathy stared after her. 'Why did she say that?'

Stella was giggling. 'I think she was insinuating that you might want to get locked in on purpose. Mr Kendall is the only one who can get back into the store once it's been locked up for the night and the night-watchman's on duty.'

Kathy blinked. 'But why—?'

'I expect she thinks you're after him.'

Colour suffused Kathy's face. 'After him? Mr Kendall? Oh, surely she doesn't think that. She can't!'

'Why ever not? You're pretty and Mr Kendall likes a pretty face.'

Kathy was horrified. This job was going to be difficult enough to learn without her superior thinking she was setting her cap at the store's manager. 'But I'm not, I mean, I . . .' Then she groaned and closed her eyes. 'How can she even think such a thing?'

'Jealousy's a funny thing,' Stella said. Though she was younger than Kathy, Stella had a streetwise knowledge that the country girl had yet to acquire. 'And he's not helped. He's never even noticed me. He didn't take *me* round the store when I started here, so you'd better watch it, because I think – even if you're not interested in him – that he's got his eye on you.'

'Oh, crumbs!' Kathy muttered and her blush deepened.

Stella laughed. 'Don't look so woebegone. Just keep out of his way and do your best to butter up Miss Curtis. Now, come on, we'd better get these suits tried on else we really will get locked in.'

'Very nice, dear. Very suitable. You've got good taste. It must come naturally because I'm sure you've never had the chance to buy any smart clothes for yourself before.' Jemima, as ever, was blunt, and at her mention of the girl's former life Kathy wondered what on earth her father would say if he could see her now, dressed in the tailored black suit with a crisp, white blouse beneath it. And he would be outraged at the elegant court shoes in place of her muddy wellingtons. But Amy . . .

Jemima interrupted her wandering thoughts. 'But it will certainly be an asset if you choose to continue working at the store.'

Kathy smiled weakly. Did she really have any choice? Certainly not at the moment. She was honest enough to acknowledge that she had only been given a trial because of Jemima Robinson. Without her support and recommendation, there would have been no job. But she felt impelled to say, 'Stella picked the suits out as being right to wear for work, Miss Robinson, not me. I – I'm sorry.'

Jemima smiled. 'No matter. I like your truthfulness.

That goes a long way with me, my girl. I don't like being lied to. Now, we should think about supper . . .'

Over the meal, Kathy tried to broach the subject of Mr Kendall. 'He seems nice,' she began tentatively, but was shocked by Jemima's swift glance and the pursing of her lips. 'Oh, he is,' the older woman remarked dryly. 'Very nice.' Then she murmured, 'Too nice, sometimes.'

Kathy's sharp hearing had heard her words. 'What do you mean? "Too nice"? How can anyone be "too nice"?'

'He should remember his position. It doesn't do for a store manager to be too familiar with his staff. Especially with the young women. It puts ideas into their silly heads. It doesn't do at all.' She sighed. 'But I suppose he's only young himself. He's certainly very young to be in such a high position, but then I understand his mother . . .' For some strange reason Kathy was sure that Jemima's voice hardened as she mentioned Mr Kendall's mother. 'Pulled a few strings. She's well connected.'

'Oh? Is Mr Kendall from a wealthy family then?'

Jemima gave a wry laugh. 'Not really, his mother . . .' Jemima stopped abruptly. 'Dear me! What am I thinking of? Gossiping about my employers like this. I *never* do that. You're a witch, young Kathy, to loosen my tongue so. Dear me. This will never do,' she tutted primly.

Kathy was disappointed. She'd hoped to learn quite a lot about the people she was to work with, but Jemima was pursing her lips as if to stop any further indiscretions escaping them. She tried one last time. 'I just wondered if there was anything between him and Miss Curtis. She—'

'Whatever gave you that idea? Oh, I see . . .' Jemima added, answering her own question before giving Kathy time to say a word. 'Stella.'

'No,' Kathy burst out, anxious that she should not get the young girl into trouble. 'No, it wasn't Stella. It was – well, I saw Miss Foster and Miss Curtis talking and – and she seemed, well – upset.'

Jemima eyed her. 'Kathy, my dear, let me give you a word of advice and you'd do well to heed it. You young girls should learn to keep your eyes and ears open, but your mouths very firmly closed. Whatever you hear in the course of your work either about other members of staff or about customers, you should keep to yourself. It doesn't do to gossip, it really doesn't.'

With that Jemima stood up and began to clear the table, crashing the plates together with swift angry movements.

Kathy bowed her head, dismayed that she had angered the woman who was being so kind to her. She said no more, silently vowing never to raise such a topic of conversation with Jemima again. But in truth the older woman's very reticence had awoken a curiosity in Kathy.

There was some mystery about the handsome Mr Kendall and Miss Curtis, and Kathy was determined to find out what it was.

Seven

Almost three weeks after Kathy's arrival in Lincoln, Amy came to stay for the weekend, arriving on Friday evening when Kathy and Jemima got home from work. Taffy, ears flattened, fled the kitchen with a loud rattle of his cat-flap and retired to the washhouse at the bottom of the yard in a huff. All of a sudden there were too many people invading his domain!

'What fun we'll have!' Amy trilled, hugging her friend.

'That's as may be,' Jemima put in tartly. 'You may be on holiday, but Kathy has a job of work to do. And I don't want her appearing in the department bleary-eyed and looking like something the cat's dragged in.' She paused and looked about her. 'And talking of cats, where's Taffy?'

The two girls glanced at each other and stifled their laughter.

'I – I think he went out,' Kathy said, keeping her face straight with a supreme effort and vowing at the same time to make a big fuss of the animal the moment Amy left.

'Too many people about for his liking,' Jemima murmured, and the two girls were left in no doubt that she shared her pet's opinion.

'We'll go to the pictures tomorrow night,' Amy said. 'I'll have a look what's on when I go into town in the morning while you're at work.'

'It'll be in the *Echo*,' Jemima remarked. She reached down at the side of her chair and held out the local evening paper.

'What time do you finish work, Kathy?' Amy asked, scanning the pages for the advertisement or a review of the city's weekend entertainment.

'Seven on a Friday and Saturday.'

Amy pulled a face but forbore to make any comment in front of her aunt.

'Ah, here we are.' There was a slight pause, then she smiled. 'We're all right. The performance at the Regal is continuous from two o'clock until eleven, so we can just go in when you're ready and see the programme round.'

'What's on?'

'*The Texans* with Randolph Scott and *Trouble in Panama*.'

'That first one sounds like a cowboy picture,' Jemima murmured.

'Oh, I say!' Amy squeaked with delight. 'Tyrone Power's at the Central. He's dishy! Oh, do let's go and see him, Kathy. Please?'

Kathy smiled at her friend's girlish excitement. 'Whatever you want. I've only ever been to the pictures once before, so I really don't mind what I see. What film is it?'

'*Marie Antoinette* with Norma Shearer. It says it's a "spectacular drama of a scandal that rocked the world".'

'She gets her head chopped off in the end, doesn't she? Very cheerful, I must say.'

'But Kathy – Tyrone Power!'

'All right, all right,' Kathy laughed and held out her

hands in submission. 'We'll go. Is it a continuous performance like the other one?'

'Er – not sure, but I expect they'll all be the same, won't they?'

'Well, we'll give it a try.'

'And if we go tomorrow night, we can have a lie in on Sunday morning . . .'

'Oh no, you can't,' her aunt said. 'You'll be up to come to morning service in the cathedral with me.'

Amy's jaw dropped. 'The cathedral? You go to church at the *cathedral*?'

'Of course. Why ever not?' Jemima said.

Amy turned wide eyes on Kathy. 'Have you been?'

She nodded. 'Yes. Last week.'

'I go every week,' Jemima put in primly. 'If not to the cathedral, then to St Mary's. Anyone who stays with me is expected to accompany me. And tomorrow it's the cathedral.'

'And did they hear you sing?' Amy asked.

'Well . . .' Kathy hesitated, the colour rising in her face. 'I just sang along with the rest of the congregation.'

'You mean they didn't ask you to be in the choir?' Now Amy was teasing, but Jemima took her words seriously.

'Oh, you can't get into the cathedral choir as easily as that . . .'

Amy laughed. 'I know, Aunt Jemima. I was teasing Kathy. But she's got an amazing voice. Haven't you heard her?'

'Well, she was standing next to me and I heard her singing – of course I did – but it was nothing special.'

They were talking about Kathy as if she was not sitting there getting more embarrassed by the minute.

'Then she was obviously singing softly deliberately. You should hear her when she really lets rip.'

The corner of Jemima's mouth twitched with barely suppressed amusement. 'Then, my dear, this week,' she said, her eyes twinkling mischievously at Kathy, 'you'd better let it rip.'

As soon as they were alone in the bedroom, Kathy asked, 'Have you heard anything about my mother? Do you know if – if she's all right?'

'Dad went to Thorpe Farm the day you left and saw them both.'

Kathy pulled in a deep breath and held it, fearing what Amy might say next. But her friend was smiling. 'Your mam's fine. Dad said that your dad was furious when he realized what you'd done. He ranted and raved and carried on alarming, but all your mam did was smile and nod. As far as she's concerned, Kathy, you've done the right thing. There was no mistake about that. My dad said.'

Little by little, Kathy let out her breath, but her anxiety was not yet gone completely. 'And since? Has your dad been over since then?'

Amy nodded. 'Oh yes. He goes every other day or so. I heard him telling Mam that he's going to keep an eye on your mam. And your dad too, if it comes to that. He knows what he's like all right and he can't forgive him for the way he's treated your mam and you but, like he says, they've been neighbours all their lives and he'll not see him stuck. He'll let Morry go and help out if he sees your dad struggling with the work.'

Now Kathy let out the last of her breath in relief. She hugged Amy. 'Tell him "thanks", won't you? And ask him to give my love to my mam and tell her I'm fine.'

'Course I will.'

'I've never seen you clock-watching before,' Stella said at ten minutes to seven when she had seen Kathy glancing at the clock on the wall for the umpteenth time. 'Got a date, have you?'

Kathy laughed. 'Not really. My friend's come to stay for the weekend and we're going to the pictures tonight. She's meeting me outside when the store closes.'

Stella sighed. 'Lucky you! My dad's very strict. He won't let me go to the pictures on my own. Says it isn't "seemly".'

'Don't you have any friends to go with?'

The girl shrugged. 'How can I make friends with anyone if I don't go out? The only people I ever meet are at work.'

'Well, come with us tonight.'

Stella stared at her for a moment. 'Do you mean it?'

'Of course I mean it.'

'But – but you're going with your friend . . .'

'Amy won't mind.'

For a brief second the young girl's eyes lit up with pleasure at the anticipation of the unexpected treat. Then the joy in her face died. 'I can't. I'd have to ask my dad first.'

'Yes, I see,' Kathy said sympathetically. She knew, if anyone did, about a strict home life.

'Perhaps we could go another time. Just you and

me – when you've had a chance to ask your dad first, eh?'

Stella nodded and smiled again. 'Ooh yes, that'd be lovely. Thanks, Kathy, I'd really like that.'

As all the staff trooped out of the store, Mr Kendall was waiting by the main exit.

'Good night, ladies. Miss Robinson, good night. Ah, Miss Burton . . .' He put out his hand to draw her to one side. 'Could you spare me a moment?'

Kathy bit her lip. Amy would be waiting outside in the cold for her, but she smiled and stepped to one side. She saw Jemima glance back and raise her eyebrows but then she turned and walked on and out through the door.

'Good *night*, Mr Kendall,' Miss Curtis said pointedly a moment later as she passed by.

'Miss Curtis,' Mr Kendall murmured without looking at her, but he waited until Kathy's superior had got through the door and out into the street. Kathy watched her go and saw her glance back as the door closed behind her. The look on the other woman's face shocked the girl. It was hatred.

She was so shocked that it took her a few moments to gather her wits and to concentrate on what Mr Kendall was saying to her.

'I just wanted to tell you, Miss Burton, how very pleased I am with your progress. Better than I could possibly have hoped, and rather than keep you wondering for a further two weeks, I'd like you to know that I'm happy to confirm you appointment as permanent.'

'Oh!' Kathy blushed. 'Thank you very much, Mr Kendall.'

'Good night, Mr Kendall.' Another member of staff

passed by and the store manager smiled briefly and nodded 'good night'.

'And now that you're a permanent member of the staff here,' he went on. 'I was wondering if you would have dinner with me one evening.'

Kathy's eyes widened. 'Dinner? With – with you?'

He smiled and tiny lines around his dark brown eyes crinkled and then he adopted a hangdog look. 'You don't want to?'

'Oh yes, I mean, I don't know if I should. I mean – is it – well – allowed?' she stammered, completely at a loss to know what to say.

Of course she'd love to go out with this handsome, debonair man, but for some reason she could not explain, she had the uncomfortable feeling that Jemima Robinson would not approve.

Now he threw back his head and laughed aloud, and the last few stragglers leaving the store glanced at him in surprise. To her discomfort, Kathy saw two of the women from the ground floor, their heads close together, whispering to each other as they went out.

'That's one advantage of being the boss,' Tony Kendall said. 'There are only the store owners who might object and I don't think either of them will.' When she still said nothing, he added, 'So – would you like to go out with me?'

Suddenly there was something endearing about the little-boy hesitancy in his tone, as if he really feared she might refuse. Now Kathy felt shy too. It was the first time, the very first time that any man – apart from Morry, and he didn't count – had asked her out.

'I'd love to,' she said softly. 'If you're sure it would be all right.'

'Of course I'm sure, but perhaps – ' he touched her arm – 'it would be better to keep this our secret, eh?'

'Yes – er – yes, all right.'

'Then how about next Saturday night?'

'Yes, thank you,' she stammered. 'That – that would be lovely.'

'I'll book a table and let you know where to meet me. I'd offer to pick you up in my car, but you're still lodging with Miss Robinson, aren't you?'

Kathy nodded.

'Then I think it best we meet in town. All right?'

Again, she nodded and then found herself being ushered from the store, her head in a whirl.

As she stepped out on to the wet pavement, Amy hurried forward out of the shadows. 'There you are! I thought you'd got lost. Or had to stay behind in detention. Been a naughty girl, have you?' She linked her arm through Kathy's, not noticing how quiet her friend seemed. 'Come on, we'll have to hurry if we don't want to miss some of the programme. And I want to see every second of the gorgeous Tyrone . . .'

Kathy walked along the dark street. Her thoughts in a dream world, she scarcely heard Amy's ceaseless chatter.

Mr Kendall – Tony – had asked her to go out with him.

Eight

'So, did you enjoy the cinema last night?' Jemima enquired as they trudged up Steep Hill towards the cathedral the following morning.

'It was great,' Amy enthused, 'but Kathy seemed lost in a little world of her own.' She laughed. 'I think she must have fallen in love with Tyrone. Mind you,' she sighed ecstatically, 'can't say I blame her.'

Kathy smiled but said nothing. The truth was that the handsome and dashing Tyrone Power had reminded her very much of Tony Kendall. He had the same dark hair and eyes, the same handsome face and that smile! Oh, his heartbreaking smile was just the same . . .

'Dear me, I'll have to stop for a moment.' Jemima interrupted Kathy's daydreams and brought her back down to earth. 'I'm sure this hill gets steeper every week.'

All three of them paused for Jemima to catch her breath and Kathy looked about her. On either side of the steep, uneven road, quaint old buildings huddled together: dusty second-hand bookshops, crowded antique shops and artists' galleries. There were little tea-rooms too, enticing the weary walker struggling up the hill to step inside the old-world interior and seek refreshment. There was even a grocer and a greengrocer to serve the people living nearby. What a blessing, Kathy mused, not to have to go up and down the hill every time you ran out of sugar! Even though the establishments were all closed, Kathy peeked into every window until Jemima said, 'Do come along, Kathy. We shall be late.'

At the top of the hill they came to a square with the cathedral to the right and the castle to the left. Kathy cast a longing glance towards the round tower of the castle.

'Another time, Kathy,' Jemima said, reading her thoughts.

As they stepped through the huge doors and into the cathedral, Kathy caught her breath. Although it was the second time she had attended a service, she was struck afresh by the magnificence. She walked to her place in the congregation in a trance, drinking in the sight of the huge pillars supporting the vast ceiling. In front of her she saw the intricately carved dark wood of the choir.

'It's so beautiful,' she breathed and even Amy, seeing it all for the first time, was bereft of words, quite lost in wonder.

As the opening hymn began, Kathy let her pure, clear voice soar into the vastness.

For a few moments, caught up in the joy of singing, she even forgot about Tony Kendall.

As they emerged into the pale March sunlight after the service, Jemima said, 'Well, Amy, you were right about one thing. Kathy certainly has a beautiful voice.'

'She ought to be on the stage.'

'Oh now, I don't think that would be very suitable. Dear me, no, but I think there is a choral society in the city that she might be able to join. Would you like that, Kathy?' There was a pause before she prompted, 'Kathy?'

'I'm sorry. I was miles away. What did you say?'

'See?' Amy said. 'I told you. She's in a dream world. It must be love.'

Kathy felt Jemima's shrewd eyes upon her. 'Dear me, I do hope not,' she murmured, and Kathy felt a shudder of fear. What would Miss Robinson say if she knew that in only six days' time she, Kathy, would be having dinner with the manager of the department store?

'I said,' Jemima repeated, 'that I believe there's a choral society you might be able to join if you enjoy singing. I believe Mr Spencer next door is a member. I could ask him, if you like.'

Kathy thought quickly. If she joined some reputable society, maybe Jemima wouldn't question where she was going at nights. And if Tony Kendall were to ask her out again . . .

'Thank you, that would be lovely. I hadn't realized until today how much I missed singing.'

'Miss Burton, this is the third time today that I've had to reprimand you. Your mind really isn't on your work. Remember you are still on a month's trial. You must try harder or I shall be forced to recommend to Mr Kendall that you are not suitable for the position here.'

Kathy opened her mouth to retort that she'd already been told her appointment had been made permanent, but then she bit her tongue and instead said contritely, 'I'm so sorry, Miss Curtis.'

For the rest of the day Kathy tried hard to banish all thoughts of the handsome young manager. She didn't want to risk losing this job, for several reasons. But top of her list was now one that she was sure would not have pleased either Miss Curtis – or Miss Robinson.

The week seemed to drag, but at last Saturday arrived. As the store closed, Kathy was eager to get home to wash and to brush her hair, then hurry back to the hotel restaurant on the High Street to meet Tony. But Jemima walked her usual, steady pace and Kathy was forced to match her step.

'And with whom are you going to the cinema tonight?' asked Miss Robinson. Her grammar and her diction were always perfect. No trace of the Lincolnshire dialect that must once have been strong in her speech – like her brother's still was – remained. Kathy wondered fleetingly if she had ever taken elocution lessons.

'With – with a friend.'

'A friend? And who might that be? I didn't know you had any friends in the city.'

Kathy ran her tongue around dry lips. This was getting to be like home. Questions, questions, questions! But she answered Jemima politely. She needed to stay here just a little while longer, although she vowed silently to start looking for a place of her own the very next week. As soon as she could afford it, she'd be out of here, she promised herself.

'Stella.'

'Stella Matthews?'

Kathy nodded, regretting the deliberate lie immediately. She was normally a truthful girl. Chin high, she would stand up straight and tell the truth whatever that might be and however it might rebound on her. But this was different. She just couldn't take the risk. Miss Robinson had the power not only to make her homeless but also to get her dismissed instantly from her employment. Mr Kendall might say he had made her position permanent, but he was not the only one with the power to dismiss her and – even if he overrode such a decision – life could, and would, be made very uncomfortable for her by those with whom she worked. Miss Curtis, for one.

No, for once in her life, Kathy could not be truthful. But lying did not sit well with her. And now she would have to involve Stella in covering up for her too. She wondered if she could rely on the younger girl. Kathy swallowed and then opened her mouth to retract her statement and tell the truth. But the words remained frozen on her lips. Just this one time, she thought. I'll see how it goes. If this is just a one off, then it won't matter. But if he should ask me again, then . . . At this moment she didn't know exactly what she would do if Mr Kendall should ask her to go out with him again. Her heart lurched with excitement at the mere thought.

He was waiting outside the restaurant as they had arranged.

'You look lovely,' he smiled, tactfully making no remark that she was still wearing the suit that she wore every day for work.

As they entered the restaurant, Kathy felt awkward and out of place among all the diners dressed in evening clothes, the men in black suits and the women in silks and satins. Heads turned as they were ushered to their table by the head waiter and Kathy blushed in embarrassment.

When they were handed a menu each, Kathy was appalled to find that it was all written in French.

Tony leaned across the small table. 'Would you like me to order for you?'

'Yes, please,' she breathed thankfully.

'Is there anything you don't like?'

Kathy giggled nervously and shook her head. She'd never been asked such a question in the whole of her life. Choice had never been an option at home. She'd always had to eat whatever was put in front of her.

When the waiter had taken their order and moved away, she blurted out, 'I had to tell Miss Robinson a lie. I said I was going to the cinema with Stella.'

Tony leaned his elbows on the table and steepled his fingers. He smiled at her. 'Well, don't worry about a little white lie. Besides, is Miss Robinson your jailer? Do you have to tell her everywhere you go?'

'She – she's been very good to me. Taking me in and getting me the job . . .'

'You got the job on your own account. I admit I interviewed you initially on her recommendation, but once I saw you – ' his smile broadened – 'I couldn't resist you.' He reached across the table and took her hand. 'Now, tell me about yourself. I want to know all about you.'

'There's nothing much to tell. I'm just a country mouse come to town and it – it's all very strange in the city.'

'Are you enjoying your job?'

'Oh yes,' she said at once. 'I still make mistakes and Miss Curtis is very strict . . .'

Tony released her hand suddenly and sat back in his chair.

Thinking she had made a serious mistake in criticizing her senior, she said hurriedly. 'She's very good at her job, isn't she? I wish I could be like her one day. She's very smart and beautifully – oh, what's the word – groomed. That's it.'

When he still said nothing, she fell silent. She was babbling, but instead of covering her nervousness it only made her feel more foolish. She should have had the strength – and the sense – to refuse his invitation. She was out of her depth in such surroundings, ignorant of even the simplest rules of etiquette.

Tony cleared his throat and said stiffly, 'Miss Curtis is an excellent employee. She has been with us since leaving school.' His tone was expressionless and he was using words that he might have done in a letter of reference. There was no warmth, no . . .

He leant forward again and smiled, 'But let's not talk about work. I want to talk about you.'

The starter arrived and Kathy waited until she saw which knife, fork or spoon he picked up before she started to eat. And then she suddenly found she wasn't hungry. Butterflies in her stomach made eating impossible, and though she managed a few mouthfuls, her plate was removed with half the food left on it. She felt embarrassed. What would her father have said if he had seen such waste?

The main course arrived and Kathy's heart sank as she saw what seemed to her like a mountain of food placed before her.

'Are you looking for a place of your own?' Tony asked.

'Well, yes, but only looking. I really need to save

some money first . . .' She stopped, unsure whether she should be saying such things to him. She really would have to curb her tongue. She was far too outspoken for her own good sometimes.

'I might be able to help you there. I know one or two people who might have a bed-sitting room, or even a flat. It'd be tiny though, but at least you'd be able to come and go as you pleased and not be subjected to the third degree every time you wanted to go out. Leave it with me. I'll ask around and—'

The head waiter approached the table. 'Excuse me, Mr Kendall.'

So, Kathy thought at once, Tony was well known. The thought crossed her mind – I wonder how many other young women he's brought here? But the waiter was continuing, 'There is a telephone message for you, sir. Would you like to follow me?'

Tony sighed, threw his napkin on to the table and, without a word, rose and followed the man.

Kathy wasn't sure what she should do and besides, she was still having difficulty forcing the food down her throat. So, thankful for the respite, she laid her knife and fork down and waited until he came back.

After a few moments, Tony hurried towards her, a worried frown on his face. He did not sit down again but stood by the table. 'Kathy – I'm dreadfully sorry but I've had bad news. My mother has been taken ill. I'll have to go home at once.'

Kathy half-rose from her chair. 'I'm so sorry. Is there anything I can do?'

His answer was swift. 'No – no, but I must go. Look, you stay and finish your meal. I'll pay as I leave. Can you get home all right?'

'Of course, but I—'

He held out his hand, palm outwards as if to prevent her from making any more offers of help. Again he said, 'I'm really sorry. This is not how I wanted it to be.'

Kathy sank back down into her chair as she saw him approach the head waiter, speak to him briefly and slip something into his hand. The man looked across at her and nodded. As Tony hurried from the restaurant, the waiter approached her table.

'Mr Kendall has asked me to look after you, madam. I'm sorry your evening has been spoilt, but please enjoy the rest of your meal and let me know if there is anything else I can do for you.' He bowed obsequiously.

'Thank you,' Kathy murmured and picked up her knife and fork, pretending to eat. As he moved away, his sharp glance roaming round the rest of the room to check that no one needed him, Kathy glanced down at the food on her plate. She had scarcely touched it, but now, curiously, she found she was ravenously hungry. She tucked into the food as if she hadn't eaten for a week!

When she'd eaten pudding and the waiter had poured her a cup of coffee, she sat back and let her glance roam around the huge room. Elegant ladies and gentleman sat at the other tables. Her envious gaze lingered on the luxurious fabric of the ladies' gowns, their sparkling jewellery and their beautifully coiffured hairstyles. Kathy felt suddenly very much the little country mouse in her dark suit and sensible shoes.

She became aware that a woman at one of the tables on the far side of the room was staring at her and

Kathy dropped her gaze in embarrassment. Nervously, she raised her coffee cup to her lips to finish the drink and leave.

A shadow fell across the table and Kathy looked up to see the woman who had been watching her standing above her. Without being invited, she sat down in the chair opposite. At once the head waiter was at her side.

'Madam—?' he began, but she waved him away.

'I just need a word with my – friend here.'

'Very good, madam.' He bowed his head and then moved away.

Now it was Kathy who was staring. She didn't know her from Adam – or rather, Eve. She bit her lip. Oh dear, was it some customer that she should remember? Had she served her and—?

'My dear, please forgive this intrusion. Perhaps you won't thank me when you hear what I have to say, but I mean it with the very best of intentions.'

Kathy didn't know what to say, so she remained silent.

The woman leaned her elbows on the table and clasped her hands together. 'Tony Kendall. Have you known him long?'

Kathy shook her head saying with careful deliberation, 'No, not long.' Then she could not stop herself asking, 'Why?' She would liked to have added, 'What business is it of yours?' But she still couldn't place the woman, couldn't think if she should recognize her. But for once she held her tongue and let the woman continue.

'You look a nice girl, but – forgive me – rather an innocent one.'

Kathy felt the woman's glance take in her plain

serviceable suit, her home-styled hair, and her face, devoid of any cosmetic enhancement. In stark contrast, the woman sitting opposite her was beautifully made-up, her black hair smooth and shining like a raven's wing. She wore a blue and silver dinner gown and diamonds clustered at her throat. On the fourth finger of her left hand was the biggest sapphire ring that Kathy had ever seen. Not that she had seen many, she thought wryly. But the stranger's beauty and poise left Kathy feeling frumpish and plain.

'What do you know about Tony Kendall?'

Kathy stared at her. She couldn't believe this was happening. All sorts of ridiculous thoughts flitted through Kathy's mind, but nothing made any sense. She glanced across at the table where the woman had been sitting. A man sat alone there now, watching them with an amused smile. Was he the woman's fiancé?

Kathy took a deep breath. Be hanged if she was going to sit here and take this, even if it cost her her new job. A job she really was beginning to enjoy. Her natural feistiness reasserted itself and fleetingly she wondered how she'd become the meek, subservient being she'd been during the last few weeks. Of course, she'd been trying to please Aunt Jemima, trying to hold down a new job and adjust to the strange environment. She'd been trying to please everyone else. Well, it was high time she pleased herself. High time she stopped feeling guilty for keeping her meeting with Tony a secret, as if it were something to be ashamed of. Because it wasn't. She was attracted to Tony Kendall – yes, she had to admit it, she found him irresistible. Contrary to what she knew would be Jemima's advice, indeed everyone's advice at the department store – even against her own better instincts – she'd agreed to come out with him.

And now here was a complete stranger asking questions she'd no right to ask. Kathy had been in danger of cowering before the stranger, subsiding under the woman's scrutiny.

Suddenly, the old Kathy – the Kathy who'd walked out of her home, had come to the big city, determined to start a new life and to stand on her own two feet – was back. She quelled the sudden tremor of apprehension, and now, instead of shrinking, she met the woman's gaze squarely. Slowly she let out the breath she'd been holding and said quietly, keeping her tone respectful, 'What gives you the right to ask me?'

For a moment the woman blinked and then smiled. 'Nothing, my dear, except that I don't want to see a nice young girl taken in by him and hurt like so many others before you.'

Kathy gasped. 'So many others . . . ?' she began.

The woman's wry smile had a tinge of sadness too. 'I'm afraid so. And I should know, because I was one of them.'

Kathy glanced swiftly at the man across the room. He was still watching them.

'But I've been lucky,' the woman went on. 'I've met a wonderful man – a lovely man – who adores me and whom I love very much. But I have to tell you, my dear, that three years ago Tony Kendall broke my heart – and I wasn't the only one. I saw you come in with him and – forgive me – I've been watching you.' She smiled sadly, knowingly. 'The moment I saw the head waiter approach your table, I knew.'

'Knew?' Kathy snapped. 'Knew what?'

'That it was the same old routine.'

'Routine?' Kathy repeated stupidly. 'What d'you mean?'

The woman sighed. 'I think he must have some arrangement with the head waiter. He must give him some sort of signal that he wants to escape. It's his way of ending an affair—'

'Affair? This isn't an affair,' Kathy said impulsively. 'It's only the first time he's asked me out. How can he want to end it now? So soon?'

The stranger's smile was sympathetic. 'My dear, you have a lot to learn about men, I can see. And about Tony Kendall's sort in particular.'

'His – *sort*?'

'He's a philanderer. A heartbreaker. He'll pick you up and drop you just as quickly if he decides you don't – ' she paused and added pointedly – 'suit.'

'You're wrong,' Kathy was stung to retort. 'I know you're wrong. His mother was taken ill. He had to go . . .' Her voice trailed away as the woman's knowing expression didn't change. She sighed as she rose and, looking down at Kathy with what seemed like genuine concern, said softly, 'Like I say – the same old routine.'

Nine

Kathy walked home through the cold, dark streets, her head in a whirl, though not now with the euphoria of falling in love.

But it's too late, she thought. I like him – I really do – and he likes me. I know he does. She's just jealous. That's what it is. She lost him and she can't bear to see him with someone else. And as for all that rubbish about there being countless others – well, Kathy just didn't believe it. And the nonsense about the 'routine' to rid himself of an unwanted girlfriend? She didn't believe that either.

But a niggling thought burrowed its way into her mind. For some unaccountable reason, Miss Curtis's distressed face was before her and the whispered words with Emily Foster were replayed in her mind.

Kathy reached the tiled passageway leading between the two terraced houses and then the gate into the back yard. Before entering the house she visited the privy across the yard. As she came out, she saw Taffy sitting in the centre of the yard, his green eyes catching the pale moonlight and shining through the darkness.

'Hello, boy.' Glad to have a distraction, Kathy bent and stroked the cat's fine head. She knew he slept in the washhouse, where another hole cut in the door allowed him entry and exit whenever he wanted. How wonderful, she thought to have such freedom, and her heart quailed at the questioning she was about to face.

She braced herself mentally as she let herself into the house to find Jemima sitting in her chair by the range, a book in her lap, the wireless on the small table at one side of her playing softly.

Jemima looked up and smiled. 'Hello. Enjoy your evening?'

Evenly, Kathy replied, 'Yes, thank you.' She waited, expecting more questions, but Jemima's eyes went back to her book.

Kathy glanced at the clock and was surprised to see that it was half past ten. Now she understood Jemima's lack of questions. If she'd indeed gone to the cinema with Stella, this was about the time she would have arrived home.

Jemima believed her. She'd no reason to doubt Kathy's word, but instead of being relieved, she felt even guiltier for having lied to the woman who'd been so kind to her.

'Can I get you anything, Aunt Jemima?' she asked, trying to make amends, even though the woman was ignorant of the need for it.

'No, thank you, my dear,' Jemima murmured without raising her head.

'Then – then I'll say goodnight.' As she reached the door leading to the foot of the stairs, Jemima said, 'Oh – I almost forgot. I spoke to my neighbour, Mr Spencer.'

Kathy blinked and racked her brain. Then she remembered. 'Oh, yes. The man who belongs to the choral society.'

'That's right. He said if you sing as prettily as you look, they'd be glad to welcome you to their group.

You're to go along to their meeting on Thursday evening in the school on Monks Road, just beyond the Arboretum.'

'Yes, yes, I know it.' Kathy's was thinking quickly. 'Do they meet every week?'

'No, once a fortnight.'

Kathy smiled and nodded. She hoped that Tony Kendall would ask her out again and if he did, maybe she could suggest a Thursday evening.

Now all she said was, 'Thank you, Aunt Jemima. I'll certainly go along.'

As she climbed the stairs, Kathy hummed softly to herself. Not only would she be able to sing again – something she really enjoyed – but she would also have a cover story when she wanted to meet Tony in secret.

Now all she had to do, she realized, was to get Stella to back up her story about their supposed visit to the cinema together.

'You're a dark horse and no mistake,' Stella teased, her hazel eyes alight with pleasure at the intrigue. 'Hasn't taken you long to find yourself a beau.' She eyed Kathy speculatively. 'Or was it someone you knew before? Is he the reason you came to the city?'

Kathy shook her head. 'No – no. I – I've only met him since I've been here.'

Stella giggled. 'You're a fast worker and no mistake. Is it someone I might know?' She gripped Kathy's arm. 'I bet it's that spotty-faced lad in hardware.'

'No, no. It's no one you know.' More lies. Kathy sighed. But they were necessary ones.

She didn't see Tony Kendall at all until the Wednesday, and by this time she was feeling hurt and humiliated and almost ready to believe what the woman in the restaurant had said about him. He'd not bothered to give her one word of explanation for his hurried departure from the restaurant, leaving her feeling foolish. She so desperately wanted to ask him about the woman who'd spoken to her. Who was she? And were the things she'd said about him true?

Yet how could she ask him such personal questions on the strength of one date? And only half a one at that. Common sense told her to bide her time and wait until he made the first move.

But what had common sense ever had to do with falling in love?

For three days she worried. She tried hard to concentrate on her job and not incur Miss Curtis's wrath. She was very afraid that, at any moment, the well-dressed woman from the restaurant would walk into the department. Whatever would she say to her if she did?

And then there was Aunt Jemima. Every evening she was on tenterhooks in case the woman asked her about the film she'd supposedly seen. But at least Stella had agreed to cover for her. The young girl, who had little social life herself, had been only too pleased to help.

'Tell you what, though,' she'd said. 'We really should go to the pictures now and again. Then it won't be a real lie, will it?'

Kathy had smiled. 'You're on.'

'What about Saturday?'

'Well . . .' Kathy had hesitated.

'Oh, I get it. Lover boy might ask you out again.' Kathy's heart had melted at the sight of Stella's obvious disappointment.

'No, we'll go. Really,' she'd said impulsively, even though she was regretting it immediately. But the pleasure on the young girl's face was her reward. Like Kathy's own home life had been, Stella still lived under the strict rule of her parents and only the assurance that she was out with a girlfriend from work would make them relent and allow her to visit the cinema.

On the Wednesday afternoon, just as they were laying the covers over the counters and the displays, Miss Foster came into the millinery department. 'Excuse me, Miss Curtis. Mr Kendall has asked to see you in his office.'

Kathy glanced up and then looked away quickly, feeling the colour suffuse her face as she saw Miss Curtis follow the manager's secretary. The minutes passed and the time for closing came and went.

'We can't leave till she comes back and says we can go. I hope she's not going to be long. I'll miss my bus.' Stella groaned. 'Oh, I do hope *that's* not all starting up again.'

'What? What do you mean?'

'Her – and him.'

'I don't understand.'

'Miss Curtis and him. Mr Kendall. They used to go out together. I told you before, didn't I?'

Kathy felt as if the breath had been knocked from her body. 'Used to – go – out together?'

'Oh, yes,' Stella said airily, not realizing how her gossip was a devastating blow to her new-found friend.

Kathy swallowed uncomfortably. Perhaps what the woman in the restaurant had said had been the truth. Perhaps, after all, it was not just jealousy that had made her approach Kathy. Perhaps her concern had been genuine. Kathy opened her mouth to probe further, but at that moment Stella's face brightened and Kathy glanced over her shoulder to see Miss Curtis returning. As she walked towards them she glanced around her, checking the counters and the displays. 'Is everything done?'

'Yes, Miss Curtis,' Stella said.

'Then you may go, Miss Matthews, but as for you, Miss Burton . . . Mr Kendall wishes to see you.'

Kathy's heart skipped a beat, but she managed to say calmly, 'Thank you, Miss Curtis. Goodnight.'

'I shan't be leaving until you come back.' The woman's face was expressionless as Kathy turned away and made her way to the manager's office. As she entered the outer office, Miss Foster was covering her black typewriter.

'Go straight in, dear. He's waiting for you.'

Kathy tapped lightly on the door leading into the inner office and went in.

At once Tony rose from behind his desk. 'Ah Miss Burton, do come in.'

As soon as the door was closed behind her, he whispered, 'Has she gone?'

'Who?'

'Miss Foster?'

'I think she's just about to leave. She's tidying her desk.'

He came round the desk and took her hands in his. 'Kathy, I'm so, so sorry about the other night.'

'It's all right,' she said breathlessly, gazing up into his dark brown eyes and feeling as if her legs were going to give way beneath her. 'How – how is your mother?'

He gave a wry smile. 'She's all right. She's an invalid and this sort of thing often happens, I'm sorry to say.

And I'm sorry that I haven't had a chance to explain before today. I've been racking my brains to think of an excuse to send for you.' His smile broadened. 'And then I remembered, I hadn't officially confirmed your appointment. So now I have. I had to send for Miss Curtis to go through the procedure correctly. She says you're proving satisfactory, though she says you seem a little dreamy at times.' He chuckled. 'I couldn't very well tell her that that was probably my fault.' He squeezed her hands and added softly, 'At least, I hope you were thinking of me.'

Guilelessly, Kathy nodded. 'I was.'

They stood gazing at each other before she said, 'I'll have to go. She's waiting for me to get back before she leaves.'

'Oh, damn!' he muttered. 'I thought we might snatch a few moments alone. Look, what about Saturday night? Will you meet me again? We'll go to the cinema. My mother won't be able to get hold of me there.'

'Well, yes, but if she's ill and needs you . . .'

'My father will be at home this week. He works shifts and last week he was working nights. Mother was on her own, but she won't be this weekend. So, what do you say? Please say yes,' he added with that sudden boyish charm that bowled her over.

Forgetting the warning words of the stranger and without a thought of the promise she'd made to Stella, Kathy heard herself saying, 'Yes, of course I will.'

Kathy steeled her heart against the hurt look on Stella's face. 'We'll go next Wednesday instead,' she promised, trying to lessen the disappointment.

Stella shook her head. 'I can't. My dad won't let me go out in the week. Saturday's the only night he might have let me. Says I need my sleep to be fit for work. No gallivanting in the week, as he calls it.' She gave a wry smile. 'Still there's always another week. Unless, of course, lover boy's going to take you out every Saturday night.'

'Well—' Kathy hesitated. She'd been about to promise rashly that she would refuse one week and the two girls would go together, but her romance with Tony was so new and vulnerable. She didn't know how serious he was and she didn't want to give him the impression she wasn't interested in him. Far from it!

Lamely she said, 'If he doesn't ask me every week, we'll certainly go out together.'

'And I suppose I'm still expected to keep all this a secret and cover for you?'

'Do – do you mind?' Kathy pleaded.

Stella regarded her for a moment and then she smiled. 'Only if you promise me one thing. If I ever get a boyfriend, you'll do the same for me.'

Now Kathy could say willingly, 'Of course.'

On Thursday evening, Kathy went to the meeting of the choral society as Jemima had arranged for her. Mr Spencer, who was also the conductor, welcomed her warmly, but she was dismayed to see that most of the members were more Jemima's generation. There was no one of her own age at all.

'We could do with some younger blood,' Mr Spencer confided. 'Now, my dear, if you'd just like to sit there while we get started. We have a break for a cup of tea about half past eight and I'll give you a trial then.' Mr Spencer was short and bald, with tufts of springy hair growing just above his ears. He was very bow-legged and walked with a rolling gait, but his pale blue eyes twinkled merrily from behind the thick lenses of his spectacles. 'It doesn't do to take a family member's recommendation on trust, I'm afraid,' he went on apologetically. 'We once had a young man come. His mother had told me he'd the most marvellous baritone voice. But, oh dear me, the poor lad couldn't sing a note in tune. Not a single note. So you do see, my dear, don't you, why I must try you out?'

'Of course, Mr Spencer,' Kathy murmured. Briefly, she wondered if finding himself among the geriatric membership the young man had sung off key on purpose. For a moment, she was very tempted to follow his example, whether it had been deliberate or not. But as she sat and listened to the choir, she became entranced. Until now, she'd only been able to sing hymns in church and songs from her school days. Now, a whole new repertoire could open up for her. Giving herself up utterly to the soaring music and the beautiful voices, she even forgot about Tony Kendall.

When the group broke up to help themselves to a cup of tea and a biscuit at the far end of the school hall, Mr Spencer approached her. 'Now, my dear, if you'd like to come to the piano . . . ?' He led the way and sat down at the instrument. 'What would you like to sing for me?'

'Er – I only know hymns, Mr Spencer. How about "The day Thou gavest . . ."? It's one of my favourites.'

'Of course, my dear. Now let me see . . .' He picked up a hymn book that contained not only the words but the music too, propped it up on the music stand above the keyboard and began to play.

Kathy's pure, clear voice filled the hall and the tea-drinkers stopped their chatter and began to move down the hall towards the piano. Now it was they who sat and listened. As the hymn came to an end and the music died away, behind Kathy there was a spontaneous round of applause and she blushed.

'Wherever did you find her, Ron?'

Mr Spencer was smiling up at Kathy. 'Can't take the credit, I'm afraid. It was Miss Robinson who recommended her.'

There was a chorus of, 'You will join us, dear, won't you?'

'I'd love to,' Kathy said. At that moment, she could think of nothing she'd like better than to be able to sing to her heart's content every other week. And there were still the church services on Sunday mornings too.

When she arrived home, Jemima wanted to hear all about it and Kathy's enthusiasm was genuine.

'I'm pleased,' Jemima said. 'I'd wondered if you'd find them a little old for you. Still, it's the singing you're going for and you'll still be able to have your nights out with Stella, won't you?'

At once, the shiver of guilt that ran through her spoiled Kathy's delight in the evening.

Tony had asked Kathy to meet him after work on the Saturday evening. She waited in the shelter of the Stonebow's arches, just across the street from the department store, and watched all the staff leave one by one. At last, when everyone else had gone, she saw him come out of the door, locking it carefully behind him. Then, as he crossed the road towards her, she stepped out into the light.

'*There* you are,' Tony said and took her arm. 'Are you all right? You look a little tired. Are they working you too hard?'

Kathy smiled up at him. If she was tired, it was because her nights were disturbed by thoughts of him. 'I'm fine,' she assured him. 'Where are we going?'

'I thought we'd go for a drive in the country instead of going to the cinema.'

'In the dark?'

'We'll call at a nice little pub where no one will know us.'

'Can you be sure of that? There was a woman in the restaurant last week who knew you. She came and spoke to me after you left.'

'Was there?' he said casually. 'Well, an awful lot of people know me. It's the job, you know. Ah, here we are. This is my car.'

At the kerbside stood a dark green open-top car.

'This is very smart,' Kathy said and was rewarded by the beam of delight that spread across his face.

'It's an Alvis Roadster,' he said proudly as he opened the door for her. 'Hop in.'

Kathy wasn't quite sure how to 'hop in' and ended up scrambling into the vehicle in a most undignified and unladylike manner. She giggled as she imagined what Aunt Jemima would say if she could have seen her.

Tony went round the other side and vaulted neatly over the low door and slid down into the seat.

'Now why didn't I think of doing that?' Kathy said and they both laughed.

'Are you going to be warm enough? March is a little early to have the hood down, but I never put it up unless it's raining.'

'I'll be fine,' Kathy assured him, tucking her scarf around her neck. 'I'm used to outdoor life, remember.'

As he drove out of the city, the wind blew in her hair and she felt exhilarated by the speed and the freedom.

'Now I know how Mr Toad felt,' she shouted to him above the noise of the engine.

'Who?'

'Oh, never mind,' she laughed.

The country pub was cosy and informal and they both relaxed. Though there were no other women in the pub, no one seemed to give her a disapproving glance and, even if they had, she wouldn't have cared. For the first time in Tony's company, Kathy felt she could be herself. This was more her kind of scene. She felt more at home in a country pub than in the formal surroundings of a fancy city restaurant. For the first time she could forget that he was the boss and she just a lowly employee. Here, she could feel she was his equal. Tony too seemed more at ease. He laughed and joked and teased her gently.

'You know, you really are a very pretty girl. So fresh and unspoilt.'

'Unsophisticated and ignorant, you mean,' she laughed. 'A real country mouse lost in the big city.'

'No, I don't mean that,' he said gently and his dark brown eyes looked deeply into hers. 'But you do seem more at home here than in the city, I must say.'

Kathy shrugged. 'Well, I've lived all my life in the country. This pub is very like the one we've got in Abbeytoft.'

'And who used to take you to this pub? Have I got a rival for your affections?'

Kathy laughed as she felt herself blush. 'No, it was

only Morry.' Then she felt guilty at dismissing him as 'only Morry'. Swiftly she said, 'Morry is my best friend's brother. He – he's a good friend to me too. And he's Miss Robinson's nephew.'

'Ah! Do I detect a bit of matchmaking?'

'They can try,' she answered pertly. 'But it won't work.' She forbore to tell him that it never would have done in a million years. That would have sounded very cruel to Morry.

He moved closer to her along the bench seat, picked up her left hand and touched her fourth finger. A shiver of delight coursed through her. 'So,' he murmured, his voice low and deep, 'You're not "spoken for"?'

Kathy's heart felt as if it were turning somersaults in her chest. 'No,' she whispered. 'I'm not spoken for.'

'Good,' he said with an air of authority. Then he raised her hand to his lips and kissed it, while his brown eyes caressed her.

On the way back towards the city, he pulled to a halt down a country lane and stopped the engine. Then he turned and took her in his arms, kissing her gently on the mouth.

'But now, my darling girl, you can consider yourself "spoken for".'

Ten

'Amy's coming for Easter,' Jemima informed her during the first week in April, as she opened a letter at the breakfast table. 'I can't imagine why the interest in visiting her maiden aunt all of a sudden,' she said airily, but her eyes were twinkling with merriment.

Kathy stared at her for a moment and then forced a smile. She had to appear delighted that her best friend was visiting, but in truth her heart was sinking at the thought that she wouldn't be able to meet Tony if he should ask her.

'Do you mind?' she asked, hoping that Jemima would express irritation at yet another intrusion on her quiet, well-ordered life.

'Of course not,' Jemima replied spiritedly. 'She's my god-daughter as well as my niece.' For a moment her eyes took on a faraway, dreamy expression. 'You know, that was one of the nicest things anyone's ever done for me. Asking me to be godmother to their precious daughter. Especially . . .' Her voice faded away and she shook herself and came back to the present with a jolt. Briskly, she added, 'It's nice to see the child, even if it is you she's coming to see.'

'I'm sure—' Kathy began.

'Now, now, no little white lies to make me feel better. I can't abide being lied to, whatever the reason.' There was a pause before she went on. 'I thought I might treat the three of us to a day at the seaside on Monday. There's an excursion with the local bus company to Saltershaven. Would you like that?'

'The seaside?' Kathy's eyes shone. 'Oh, I would. I've never been.'

Jemima stared at her. 'You mean to tell me you've never seen the sea?'

Kathy bit her lip as she shook her head. It did sound ridiculous that a girl of nineteen had never seen the sea.

Jemima shook her head slowly. 'Your father—' she began but then stopped and altered whatever it was she'd been going to say. 'Then we'd better rectify that omission, my dear.' She rose from the table. 'But for now, we'd better get ready for work, else we'll both be late and that would never do.'

Kathy rose to clear away the breakfast things feeling yet another stab of guilt at the deceit she was practising on this good, kind woman.

Maybe I should tell her the truth, she pondered, but although the romance with Tony was progressing, he'd left her in no doubt that he wanted it kept secret. As the days passed she had the niggling doubt that his reasons were more than just the impropriety of the manager going out with a lowly junior assistant. And to add to her worries, he'd made no mention of plans for the coming weekend.

Very well then, Kathy tossed her head as she marched into work, I'll make other arrangements.

'Stella,' she said when there was a break in the morning routine. 'My friend Amy's coming to stay this weekend. And I know she loves the pictures. Would you like to come with us on Saturday night?'

'Why?' Stella asked bluntly. 'Lover boy not coming up to scratch? Not asked you out this week, then?'

Kathy sighed, but forced a smile to her face. 'No,' she said carefully. 'It's time I kept my promise to you and I'd like you to meet Amy. You'll like her. She's bubbly and fun.'

Stella's prickliness dissolved and she said, 'I'd love to. I'll ask my dad tonight.'

'Blimey!' Stella greeted Kathy the following morning. 'Talk about the third degree. My dad wanted to know where I was going, who with and what time I'd be home. Then he said what picture were we going to and was it "suitable" . . .' She rolled her eyes. 'And *then* he said "Are there any boys going, because I don't want you consorting" – consorting if you please, that's what he actually said – "with boys?" ' She spread her hands helplessly. 'How am I ever going to get married if I'm not allowed to "consort" with boys? I ask you!'

Kathy laughed wryly. 'Tell me about it. Why do you think I left home?'

'Was that why? Because your dad wouldn't let you go out?'

'Partly,' Kathy said, realizing she'd said too much. It had been Morry's proposal and her father's anger at her refusal that had precipitated Kathy's flight, but she didn't want to confide that much to Stella. The chatterbox might let something slip in front of Amy and Kathy had no wish to hurt her friend's feelings and certainly not dear old Morry's. Sometimes she regretted that she couldn't feel for him what everyone wanted her to. Life would have been so much simpler. But now that she'd met Tony Kendall, she knew she'd been right.

'Anyway, can you come with us?'

'After all that – yes, I can.'

Kathy squeezed Stella's arm. 'Great! We'll have a lovely time.'

Kathy and Amy waited outside the cinema for half an hour.

'Isn't Stella coming? I thought she'd've left work with you,' Amy said, hopping from one foot to the other. 'Oh, do let's go inside. I'm freezing!'

'I don't know what can have happened to her. Miss Foster came for her about ten minutes before closing time. Said there was a message for her in the office and I haven't seen her since. I do hope nothing's wrong, but, you're right, we'd better go inside. She knows where we are.'

The two girls sat in the back row of the cinema among the courting couples feeling as if they were playing gooseberry. 'But we'll be able to see if Stella comes in late,' Amy suggested as they chose their seats.

Later, as they walked home through the dark streets, Amy said, 'I wonder what happened to your friend from work?'

Kathy gave a very unladylike snort of wry laughter. 'Her father. I'd bet my last penny that somehow he stopped her coming at the very last minute. I wouldn't put it past him to drive into the city on his tractor and carry her off home.'

'Poor thing.' Amy tucked her arm through Kathy's. 'She'll end up doing what you've done. Leaving home.'

'Maybe,' Kathy said, abstractedly.

They walked another few yards.

'What's up, Kathy? There's something on your mind. I can tell. Is it Aunt Jemima? Getting on your nerves, is she? 'Cos I can't say I blame you if she is. She's a dear, but I don't think I could live with her for long. Her pernickety ways would drive me potty.'

'No, no,' Kathy said at once. 'She's been very kind to me and I like living there, but . . .' Her voice trailed away.

'But?' Amy prompted.

Kathy took a deep breath. She hated not confiding in Amy – her best friend in all the world. She felt a stab of guilt that already Tony had become more important to her than Amy and, even worse, more important than being totally honest at all times. It was something she'd prided herself on always being. She might have many faults, but being untruthful was not one of them. Until now. Until Tony. She didn't enjoy deceiving Aunt Jemima and, even more, she hated not telling Amy. But she just daren't confide in her. If you told just one person – and particularly Amy – then a secret was no longer a secret. Although Amy was lovable in every way, she'd never been able to keep a confidence. The only thing that assuaged Kathy's guilt was that she knew Amy herself would cheerfully acknowledge her own failing and had been heard to remark many times, 'If it's a secret, then please don't tell me.'

'But I think I'm intruding on her peace and quiet. I – I ought to look for a place of my own as soon as I can afford it.'

Amy chuckled. 'Well, we could do just what we liked then, when I come to stay. Stay out all night, if we wanted to. We wouldn't have to trot home like obedient children as soon as the pictures finished. I bet she's watching the clock this very minute and calculating just how long it takes for us to walk home from town. Ooh, wouldn't I love to be an hour late home. Just once.'

Kathy laughed. 'But we won't be, will we?'

Amy gave an exaggerated sigh. 'No, we won't. Because she'd tell my dad and he wouldn't let me come any more.' There was a slight pause before, with a note of surprise in her tone, Amy added, 'But to be truthful, I wouldn't want to worry the old dear.'

Kathy said nothing. There was nothing she could say, but a fresh wave of guilt swept through her at the deception she was practising.

As the three of them boarded the bus on the Easter Monday morning, even Jemima seemed excited. The day was warm and sunny and she wore a flowery dress, broad-brimmed white hat and carried a parasol. It took over two hours to reach the seaside resort of Saltershaven on the east coast and everyone was thankful to climb down.

'Come along, let's complete your education,' Amy teased, linking her arm through Kathy's. 'It's high time a girl of your age saw the sea.'

From the clock tower set near the sea front, they walked until they could see the sea and the beach.

Kathy gasped. 'Oh my! Isn't it big! I had no idea.' She stood and gazed at the expanse of water before her, fascinated by the gentle waves rolling languidly on to the shore. Already bare-footed children were playing on the warm sand, building sandcastles and digging a moat around them, then running to the sea's edge to fill buckets to pour into it.

'I should have brought my bucket and spade.' Kathy laughed. 'I've a whole childhood to catch up on.' There was a distinct note of sadness in her tone. She felt a sense of loss for all the fun she'd missed. A time she would never be able to recapture, at least not until she'd children of her own. Her heart gave a little leap as she thought about Tony. Perhaps one day . . .

'Come along, girls,' Jemima interrupted her. 'I don't know about you, but I need a cup of tea. I think there's a little café at the pier entrance.'

They walked along the sea front until they came to the pier. 'Do let's go on it, Aunt Jemima. Look – it goes right out into the sea. Let's go and stand right at the end of it.'

'When we've had a cup of tea,' Jemima said firmly, but there was a smile on her face.

The day was a huge success. The girls had a donkey ride, giggling as they bounced up and down and ignoring the jibes of the group of children who stood watching the grown-ups acting like children. They weren't to know that, for one of the girls, it was her first taste of seaside fun. They rode on the big dipper, squealing with terrified delight and clutching each other. Aunt Jemima watched from the ground, smiling gently and congratulating herself on having suggested the day trip. As the time approached for them to board the bus again, they walked back to the pick-up point along the sea front eating ice cream and admiring the well-kept gardens and the smooth bowling greens on the foreshore.

All three were tired, but contented. Though she loved Amy dearly and was becoming very fond of Jemima, Kathy's only disappointment was that Tony had not been there to share the day.

If Kathy had placed her bet, she would have won.

'My dad stopped me coming,' Stella greeted her mournfully on the Tuesday morning. 'At the very last minute. He actually rang up Mr Kendall on Saturday afternoon and told him – told him, mind you – to send me straight home after work. And I was so looking forward to it. I even came to work in my Sunday best coat and all. I cried all night, but that man's got a heart of stone. Even my mam couldn't persuade him. Mind you, I don't think she tried very hard. She's almost as bad as him.'

Kathy bit back the remark, I thought as much. Instead, she adopted a sympathetic expression. 'I'm so sorry. We wondered where you'd got to. We waited outside for you for about half an hour.'

'Was the picture good?' Stella asked eagerly. 'Oh, I do wish I'd been strong enough to defy him, but – ' she sighed heavily – 'until I can get a place of my own in the city I daren't cross him.'

'Miss Matthews . . . Miss Burton . . .' They both jumped as they heard Muriel's sharp tone. 'Were you thinking of doing any work today?'

'Of course, Miss Curtis. Sorry, Miss Curtis,' Stella said meekly, and hurried away to greet a customer who had just entered the department. Kathy said nothing but tilted the hat she was arranging on a display to a slightly jauntier angle. As she did so, she glanced thoughtfully after Stella. I wonder . . .

Kathy thought about her idea for several days. Could she and Stella find a flat somewhere near the city centre to share? But as the days passed, the idea became less appealing. Although she liked the girl well enough, she doubted she could live with her. Stella was a moody girl. One moment she was friendly, laughing and chattering and sharing confidences. The next she'd taken offence at some simple remark or action and had retreated into sulky silence. While this might be because of her home life under the harsh regime of her strict father, Kathy felt she daren't take the risk. She very much doubted that Stella, once she knew who 'lover boy' really was, would be able to keep it secret. And, if they lived together, Stella was bound to find out.

Besides, Kathy told herself, things were settling down into a very nice routine in the little terraced house. Jemima had made no hints that she wanted her lodger to move out and Kathy's outings with Tony were covered by Stella's willingness to enter into the intrigue and by Kathy's membership of the choral society.

Throughout the summer, Kathy lived in a little world of her own. While Jemima read the newspapers avidly and listened more and more to the news on her little battery-operated wireless, Kathy was blithely ignorant of the gloom that was pervading the country. Her only thoughts were of the next meeting with Tony, whenever that might be. She ignored the times he arranged an outing and then cancelled it at the last minute, always giving the same excuse. 'My mother's not well . . .'

The first time they planned to go to the pictures on a Thursday evening, Kathy waited for over an hour outside the cinema, earning herself one or two very strange looks from passers-by. She blushed to realize what they must be thinking. Deciding at last that Tony was not coming, Kathy walked towards home, tears of disappointment stinging her throat. Was he tiring of her? Was this his way of ending it?

As she neared the end of the street where she lived, Kathy realized that it was far too early to go home yet. Aunt Jemima believed her to be at the choral society meeting, so that's exactly where she'd go. Instead of turning into the street, Kathy walked on to the school just beyond the Arboretum. She let herself into the main door and tiptoed into the hall, taking her place at the end of the second row, near the other two sopranos. Mrs Sims smiled at her and shared her songbook. After a few moments, miraculously Kathy had forgotten all about Tony as her voice soared to the rafters and the members of the choir smiled at each other, delighted that their little songbird had come after all.

'I'm so sorry I was late,' Kathy apologized swiftly to Ron Spencer as they broke for tea and biscuits halfway through their allotted three-hour meeting.

'We missed you, my dear,' was all the kindly man said. But he asked no probing questions. It wasn't in his nature and for that, Kathy was grateful. But she mentally crossed her fingers, hoping that neither Ron nor his wife Mabel would mention to Jemima that Kathy had arrived late that evening.

The following morning, Tony whispered a hurried apology as he passed through the millinery department, adding, 'Saturday? Are you all right for Saturday?'

Kathy's heart leapt. He still wanted her. 'Of course,' she breathed, her anguish of the previous night swept away.

'Meet me at the restaurant we went to that first evening. Remember?'

She nodded, glancing around to make sure that neither Miss Curtis nor Stella was watching.

'Till Saturday, darling,' he murmured as he moved away. 'Eight thirty.'

For the rest of the day, Kathy hummed happily to herself.

'You're in a good mood,' Stella muttered. 'Got a date with lover boy, have we?'

'Might have,' Kathy said airily.

The younger girl glared at her balefully. 'I really think you might let me in on the big secret. Specially as I'm covering for you. Don't you trust me?'

'Of course I do,' Kathy said a little too swiftly and Stella eyed her suspiciously. 'Look, you've been a brick – a real pal – and . . . and I will tell you. Very soon. Just – just give me a few more weeks. Please, Stella.'

'All right,' the girl agreed reluctantly. 'But I don't know what all the mystery is about. Are you ashamed of him, or something?'

'No, no, of course I'm not,' Kathy declared hotly. 'It's just – just that . . . well, to tell you the truth, I'm not sure of him. I mean – if he really likes me. If – if he's serious.'

'Oh.' Stella was thoughtful for a moment. In her ignorance, she was struggling to understand how it must feel to fall in love. The only experience she had was from the books she'd read or the films she'd seen on the very rare occasions she'd been allowed to go to the cinema. 'You mean, you sort of feel . . . that if you tell anyone it might – well – it might ruin it.'

'Something like that,' Kathy agreed carefully. More lies, she thought sadly. She'd heard it said that if you told one lie you ended up telling a lot more to cover the first one. She was finding out that the saying was true.

Stella was nodding now and smiling, pleased with her philosophy. 'I do understand. But you can tell me, you know. I wouldn't say a word. Not to anyone.'

Kathy doubted it, but she smiled in return, promising, 'You'll be the first to know.'

Placated, Stella was in a better mood for the rest of the day.

Kathy was at the restaurant on the Saturday evening by eight fifteen, hovering uncertainly on the pavement outside. Tony was never early, and rather than run the gauntlet of disapproving glances, she took a deep breath and pushed open the door of the restaurant. Menu in hand, the head waiter approached her. He smiled obsequiously and gave a little bow. 'Good evening, madam? Have you booked?'

'I – er – no. I mean, I'm not sure. I – I'm meeting someone.'

'I see, madam.' He raised his eyebrows in a question. 'Perhaps your dinner partner has placed a reservation with us?'

'Er – yes. Perhaps he has. It's – it's Mr Kendall.'

'Ah yes, madam. Of course. I should have remembered you. I do apologize.' He bowed again and ushered her towards a secluded table at the far side of the restaurant. He held out the chair for her to be seated. As she took her place, Kathy had the feeling that he'd remembered her very well, but that he was far too discreet to mention it. Perhaps he feared that Mr

Kendall might well, by now, have transferred his affections elsewhere and that, for a man in his position, the head waiter would have been committing an unforgivable *faux pas*.

'Would madam care to order a drink?' he asked, shaking out the white napkin and laying it across her lap.

'No – no, thank you. I'll wait.'

'Very good, madam.' He bowed again and moved away, his sharp eyes raking the room, checking that everything in his domain was in order.

Holding her breath, Kathy now risked a glance around. She was so afraid there might be someone there who knew her. And even worse, the woman who'd been there before and had said such awful things about Tony. Slowly, Kathy let out her breath. There was no one she recognized, but then, that didn't mean that there was no one there who knew her. Customers had an unfortunate habit of recognizing shop staff, whereas Kathy found it difficult to remember each and every woman who came in to the millinery department.

The minutes ticked by. Eight thirty came and went and the hand on the clock on the wall crept towards nine o'clock.

'Are you sure I can't get you something, madam?' The head waiter was at her elbow once more.

'No, really, I . . .' She glanced up and breathed a sigh of relief to see Tony threading his way between the tables towards her.

'Darling, I'm so sorry . . .' He slid into the seat opposite her and took the menu the head waiter was holding out to him. 'Thank you, Gregson. Have you ordered, darling?'

'No. I was waiting for you.'

Swiftly, without deferring to her, Tony ordered for them both, but Kathy was quite happy for him to do so. She was just so thankful that he was here.

Eleven

They'd almost finished their meal and had been chatting amiably before the telephone call that Kathy had been half expecting all evening came. Gregson approached their table with an apologetic look on his face.

'There's a telephone call for you, sir.'

For a brief moment, Tony looked genuinely angry. Then he sighed, shrugged his shoulders and rose. 'I won't be a moment, darling.'

As he hurried away, Gregson leaned forward and refilled Kathy's glass.

'Thank you,' she murmured as he moved away, wondering for the second time if there'd been a prearranged signal between them.

Kathy kept her eyes downcast and twirled the slender-stemmed wineglass between nervous fingers. She felt as if everyone in the restaurant knew what was going on but her. It was a foolish notion, of course, but it was how she felt.

'I'm sorry,' he said as soon as he sat down again. 'It's mother. She's alone in the house and she's frightened.'

'Frightened?' Kathy snapped, her patience beginning to wear thin. 'What of?'

'Of being alone.'

'I see,' she said shortly. 'Then you'd better go.'

'No, no. We'll finish first. She'll be all right for a little while. I've tried to reassure her and promised I won't be late.'

They finished the pudding in complete silence and when their coffee had been served, Tony reached across the table and took her hand. 'Darling, you're so understanding about all this. No one else has ever – I mean – no one else would be so good. My mother is a sick woman and it's very hard for her and for my father too. I – I feel I have to help as much as I can.'

Kathy was suddenly overwhelmed with guilt. Not this time, on account of her deceit, but because she was criticizing a loyal and loving son. She was reminded too that she'd walked away from her own mother's difficult life and had selfishly followed her own desires. Shame swept through her and made her squeeze his hand and say huskily, 'It's all right. She can't help being ill.'

Tony raised her hand to his lips and kissed it. 'Sweetheart, you're so kind and generous. I do love you. There's so much I want to say to you – was going to say to you tonight – but now . . .'

It was all she needed to hear. He'd said those three little words that meant so much to any girl and especially to her. She would never doubt him again, she vowed silently. She'd be kind and understanding and forgiving whenever their evenings were interrupted or their arrangements cancelled.

'Never mind,' she heard herself saying. 'You go and I'll find my own way home. It's such a nice evening, I don't mind the walk.'

'If you're sure, darling . . . ?' And he was gone.

*

The summer rolled on. Towards the end of August, Amy came again.

'Dad says I've worked so hard with the harvest, I deserve a bit of fun.'

Kathy said nothing, but she wondered just how her father was coping at such a busy time of year without her. She hoped he hadn't forced her mother to take her place. As if reading her friend's thoughts, Amy said, 'And before you ask, your mam's fine and Morry's been helping your dad with his harvest. Just in case he had it in mind to get your poor mam driving the tractor or lugging bales. Now,' she went on briskly, 'What's on at the pictures this weekend?'

Half way through the programme the Pathé News came on and by the time it had finished, the cinema-goers had little heart to sit and watch the next film.

'Let's go, Kathy,' Amy whispered. 'I can't sit here any longer after what we've just seen.'

As they walked home, arm in arm, clutching each other for comfort, Amy whispered, 'I'm scared. All that talk of emergency powers and the sight of those students building great walls of sandbags outside that London hospital. It – it can only mean one thing, can't it? There's going to be a war, isn't there?'

'It was the sound of those sirens that got me. I know they weren't for real this time but . . .' Kathy shuddered as she added, 'I'd no idea things had got so bad. I – I haven't been taking much notice of the news lately.' She bit her lip, longing to confide in her dearest friend, but she still daren't say a word.

'Neither have I,' Amy answered in an unusually subdued voice. 'We've been so busy just lately, I don't think even Dad realizes just how serious things are now. But don't let's say anything to Aunt Jemima. We don't want to worry the old dear.'

Kathy agreed, but when they arrived home, Jemima was listening to the nine o'clock news on the wireless, leaning towards it, not wanting to miss a word. The book she had been reading had fallen, discarded, to the floor.

'Hello, Auntie,' Amy began breezily.

'Shush! I'm listening.'

The two girls exchanged a glance and shrugged.

'Oh well,' Kathy murmured. 'She'll hear soon enough at work on Monday. They'll be talking of nothing else. And come to think of it, she's been devouring the newspapers for weeks. Maybe she's far more aware of what's going on than we are.'

The news bulletin ended and Jemima switched off the wireless. She sat motionless, staring pensively at nothing in particular.

'I'll make the cocoa,' Amy said gently and went into the scullery, while Kathy sat down in the chair on the opposite side of the range. She didn't know what to say, so she said nothing but waited until Jemima should speak.

At last Jemima gave a huge sigh and then said flatly, 'So – it's all going to start again, is it? You'd really think, wouldn't you, that we'd all have learned our lesson the last time? Enough to know not to let it all happen again. The war to end all wars, they called it. Huh!'

The last sound was uttered with an ironic despair.

Though Kathy had no memory of the Great War and little knowledge, she knew it was only twenty-one years since it had ended. Her own parents – and Amy's too – had lived through it and the woman sitting opposite her now must have been about Kathy's age at the start of it. Kathy watched her now and saw the raw suffering in Jemima's eyes. There was a hurt, a wound in them that would never heal. She wanted to ask what had happened back then but she couldn't. But later, when they were on their own, she would quiz Amy. She might know what had happened to her aunt all those years ago.

Amy came in with three mugs of cocoa. 'There now, this will make us all feel better.' She handed them round and then sat down on a chair near the table. 'Perhaps it won't happen,' she said, trying to be cheerful.

Jemima sipped her cocoa but said nothing. She was older and a lot wiser than the two young girls and she was very much afraid that it would.

As they came out of the cathedral the following morning, Jemima stopped to speak to an acquaintance. Kathy took the opportunity to whisper to Amy, 'Your aunt seems very upset by all this talk of war. I mean, more than normal. I know we're all worried, but it's really seemed to affect her badly. And usually she's so – she's so . . .'

'Strong? Resilient?' Amy suggested with a fond smile.

'Exactly. So why?'

Amy glanced back at her aunt, who was still deep in serious conversation, a worried frown creasing her forehead. The girl bit her lip and, for a moment, there was a look of uncertainty in her eyes. She seemed to be struggling to find the right words – or to decide if she should even say them.

Then she gave a little sigh and shrugged. 'I think she – she lost someone in the last war. Dad's always very protective of her and Mum, well, I've heard her say "poor Jemima" more than once. And yet, to me, she's anything but "poor". She's smart. She has a good job, a nice home and she lives in the city. She can do anything she likes. She's not "poor" in any way. I rather envy her. But – I think – there was . . . something . . .' Her voice trailed away and she avoided meeting Kathy's direct, enquiring gaze.

'I bet your mum thinks Aunt Jemima's lonely. Family means everything to your mum. Perhaps she feels sorry for Aunt Jemima because she has no husband or family,' Kathy suggested, trying to prise more out of the usually loquacious Amy. There was a pause as they walked slowly to the top of Steep Hill and then stopped, waiting for Jemima to catch them up. Kathy glanced at Amy, but the girl had her lips pressed firmly together as if to stop them saying any more.

'Well,' Kathy said quietly, 'if you're right and she did lose someone she loved in the war, then that's why she's so upset to think there might be another one. It's going to bring the nightmare all back.'

Still Amy said nothing as they turned to watch Jemima come towards them. She walked straight-backed, her head held high.

'She's still a good-looking woman, you know,' Kathy said. 'She must have been a stunner in her younger days.'

'She was,' Amy said. 'There's a photo of her on the sideboard in our front room. You must have seen it.'

Kathy turned to gape at her friend. '*That's* Jemima? But – but she was beautiful.'

'I know.'

And they both turned to stare at the older woman again.

'Well, well, well,' Kathy murmured.

'Now you two, I've decided we're going out for lunch today. My treat. I need cheering up a little.'

The two girls stepped on either side of her and linked their arms through hers.

'That's what I call a good idea. Where are you taking us?'

'There's a nice little café just down here. It's sometimes open for Sunday lunch in the summer.'

'I need to speak to you,' Tony whispered to Kathy as he passed through the department just after opening the following morning, ostensibly on his rounds to check that all was in order throughout the store. 'My office. After work.'

'I can't . . .' she began, but he'd moved on, smiling and nodding to other members of staff.

Kathy bit her lip anxiously. She and Jemima always walked home together unless Kathy had planned to stay in town. But Jemima didn't like surprises being sprung upon her. She planned their meals meticulously, shopping only for what they needed. She didn't like having her routine altered at short notice.

'What's up?' Stella asked. 'Has the war started?'

Kathy smiled weakly. If Jemima were to find out about her and Tony, there would certainly be a war of words if nothing worse.

The talk at work this last week had been of little

else but the uncertainty about the war. Everyone was worried.

'Is it lover boy? Has he packed you in?'

'No – it's just that – look, I've got to meet him tonight urgently . . .'

Stella's eyes widened. 'You're not in trouble, are you?'

Kathy gasped. 'Good Heavens, no! He's – he's sent word that he wants to speak to me. That's all.'

Stella's eyes narrowed as she searched Kathy's embarrassed face. The girl was thinking, calculating. She glanced round the department. 'I didn't see anyone bring you a message and we've had no customers in yet. The only person I've seen speak to you this morning is . . . Oh my God! It's *him*, isn't it?'

Kathy tried hard to stop the colour flooding into her face, but failed. She grasped Stella's arm. 'Stella – please. Don't say anything. Please don't tell anyone.'

'Oh, don't you worry, I won't. But you're an idiot. A fool.'

'What – what do you mean?'

'He'll break your heart. That's what I mean. Just like he's broken a whole string of 'em before you. Miss Curtis for one and God only knows how many more. But I know there's been a few because when it was all going off with our dear Muriel I overheard snippets. Oh, he's a real lady-killer and no mistake. I wouldn't touch him if he was the last man on earth. And that's a fact.'

Kathy's heart felt like lead in her chest. 'I don't believe you,' she said, but her protest was feeble. And she knew it.

Twelve

'You go on ahead,' Kathy said as closing time approached. 'I've just got something to finish off. I won't be long.'

'Very well then,' Jemima murmured. Her mind on other things, she didn't think to ask questions and Kathy heaved a sigh of relief. She'd worried all day as to how she could snatch just a few moments with Tony after work and then it had been so easy. All she had to do was to pretend she had to stay behind to finish something. That excuse wouldn't work more than once or twice, she realized. But tonight, Jemima seemed distracted. All day the talk among customers as well as the staff had been of the impending war. The merry lunch Jemima and the two girls had enjoyed the previous day had faded already. Once again, Jemima seemed lost in her own thoughts and memories.

When the store had emptied, Kathy made her way to the manager's office. He was hovering in the outer office, waiting for her. At once, he took her hands in his, drew her into his office and closed the door.

'Darling, we can't talk long. I have to get home, but can you meet me on Thursday night?'

'Thursday? Yes, yes, of course I can, but, Tony, I have to ask you . . .'

'Good. I'll pick you up near the main gate of the Arboretum at about seven?' He pulled her to him and kissed her hard on the mouth. 'I must go, but we'll have time to chat on Thursday.' He smiled. 'All the time in the world, my darling. Whatever it is you want to ask me will just have to wait until then.' Before she could say another word, he'd hustled her out of his office and down the stairs. Without realizing quite how it had happened, she found herself outside on the street with the door firmly closed behind her. She stood a moment, looking back, but Tony had disappeared.

Oh well, she thought, shrugging her shoulders. I'll find out on Thursday.

She was only ten minutes later arriving home than normal and to her relief Jemima asked no questions. Kathy hugged her secret to herself. Luckily, this Thursday was her night for the choral society meeting. It would be easy for her to meet Tony instead, without Jemima suspecting a thing.

All she had to do was to be sure she wasn't any later home than usual.

The next three days passed by so slowly. Stella ignored her. Gone in an instant was all the friendliness. At last, Kathy couldn't stand the uncomfortable silence from the girl whom she had thought was her friend any longer.

As they left the store on Wednesday night, she caught hold of Stella's arm. 'Look, Stella . . .'

'I'll miss my bus,' the girl said shortly. 'Then my dad'll want to know what I've been up to. I don't want to be in trouble. You're going to be in enough for both of us as it is. When everyone finds out.'

'But you promised—'

Stella whirled around to face her. 'And I keep my promises,' she said and added pointedly, 'even if others don't.' Kathy felt guilt sweep through her afresh as Stella went on. 'But how long do you think you can keep it secret, eh?'

'We've managed it up to now. Why should anyone find out?'

Stella sighed and shook her head. 'I guessed, didn't I? Oh, I know everyone sees me as a naïve kid. A plain girl who's never had a boyfriend – nor likely too the way my dad keeps me locked up – but even I'm not daft enough to think you can get away with something like this. He's poison, that man. Keep away from him, Kathy, if you've any sense left in that pretty head of yours. I can see why he likes you but he'll not stay with you, you mark my words.' Then she twisted herself free of Kathy's grasp and hurried away towards her bus stop.

Kathy watched her go, suddenly feeling very lonely.

On the Thursday evening, Kathy dressed with extra care. Over the last few weeks she had been able to buy herself a pretty dress and a pair of dainty shoes. She knew she should be saving to be able to afford her own bed-sit or flat, but she couldn't always go out with Tony in the suit she wore every day for work. And the few clothes she had brought from home, well, they were fit only for the ragbag.

'You look nice,' Jemima smiled, looking up from her book as Kathy headed for the back door. Curled on his mistress's lap, Taffy raised his ginger head and regarded her with his green gaze. Kathy hesitated, then crossed the room to stroke the cat's head. If she missed anything from home, apart from her mother of course, it was the animals.

And the Robinsons. She missed the Robinson family. All of them. But the one person she pushed from her mind and determined not to think about was her father.

'I'll be home the usual time,' she called back as she closed the back door behind her. Outside in the back yard, she breathed a sigh of relief and hurried along the passage and out into the street, hoping that Ron Spencer wouldn't emerge from his house and walk along with her to the choral society meeting. She held her breath until she was safely at the top of the street and well beyond his house. Then she walked briskly across the road to the city's park.

Tony's car was nowhere to be seen when she arrived at the main gate. She had waited a few moments when she saw a member of the choral society cycling along the road towards her. Quickly she ran into the park and waited behind a tree until he had passed by.

Still there was no sign of Tony's car and she began to wonder if he was about to stand her up again when she heard the familiar roar of the car's engine. With a squeal of tyres, he pulled up in front of her, leapt out and ran around the car to open the passenger's door for her.

'Sorry, I'm a little late, darling. Mother had one of her turns and I couldn't get away until Father came home. What a pretty dress you're wearing. Blue's certainly your colour. It matches your eyes.' He smiled down at her as he carefully tucked her dress into the car and closed the door. His compliment gave her a warm glow and made her feel special.

'I'm sorry to hear about your mother. Shouldn't you go home? I quite understand if . . .'

'Maybe I'd better not be too long . . .' He turned the car around and drove back across the High Street, then turned up the hill, twisting and turning among streets Kathy didn't know.

'So, where are we going?'

'You'll see,' he said mysteriously. 'It's a surprise.'

Within minutes he was drawing to a halt outside a large house on the corner of Mill Road.

Kathy gasped and her eyes widened. 'Are you taking me to meet your parents? Oh, you might have warned me. I . . .'

'No, no, darling, it's something much better than that. I've found a little flat for you.'

'For me, but . . .'

'She's a very nice old lady. She's been widowed for about five years and after her family had left home and her husband died, she found the house too big for just her. But – she didn't want to leave the home she'd had all her married life, so she turned the upstairs into a nice little flat.'

Kathy looked around her with renewed interest. It was a nice area and the house was certainly big enough to have been converted into two flats.

'I – I don't think I would be able to afford it,' she said quietly. 'It's very kind of you, but . . .'

He patted her hand. 'Now you're not to worry about that. I want you to be independent of Miss Robinson. It's little better than living at home, as far as I can see.'

Kathy almost laughed aloud. If only he knew! But she said nothing as he went on, 'Whenever we're out, you're always clock-watching. And it must be difficult for you working with her too. I can understand that. So – if you have your own place, you'll be able to come and go as you please. Mrs Sutton won't be keeping tabs on you, I promise.'

'Do – do you know her?'

'I've known her years.' He paused. 'She's – er – a good customer of ours. So – shall we go and have a look? It's a lovely flat. I'm sure you're going to be happy here.'

The flat was just as he'd said – lovely. It was self-contained, with a sitting room, bedroom and tiny kitchen that had obviously been converted from a small bedroom. It even had its own bathroom, complete with water closet. A luxury that Kathy had never known. Even Miss Robinson's lavatory was across the back yard. And Mrs Sutton was a dear. She greeted Tony like an old friend, kissing him on the cheek.

'I shan't come up with you. It's my legs, dear. I can't climb the stairs like I used to. You show your young lady round, Mr Kendall, while I make a nice cup of tea. Then we can have a nice chat and see if we'll suit each other.' She smiled at Kathy.

'So do you like it?' Tony asked, when they had seen all the rooms. 'It's not much further to walk to work than you do now, but just in the opposite direction. What do you think?'

'What rent does she want?'

'I told you not to worry about that. I'll help you with the first few months and I'll see about giving you a raise at work so that you'll be able to afford it yourself. What do you say?' He put his head on one side and smiled at her, the lines around his eyes crinkling. Her heart melted. She knew now that she was helplessly in love with him. He was so kind and thoughtful, She really couldn't believe that he was the philanderer that Stella made out. Maybe he just hadn't found the right girl – until now. She loved him and she was sure he loved her. He'd told her so often. Tony Kendall made her feel special, made her feel really loved . . .

'Yes, all right,' she agreed. 'But as soon as I can afford it for myself—'

He laughed and patted her hand. 'Yes, yes, Miss Independent. So, we'll go down and tell Mrs Sutton yes. The old dear will be setting out tea and scones on paper doilies. Come along, we won't keep her waiting any longer.'

As she walked home, Kathy felt she was walking on air. She skipped down the dark passage, in through the gate and then the back door leading into the scullery. She took a deep breath before she opened the door into the kitchen.

Jemima was sitting where Kathy had left her, in her chair near the range.

'Sorry I'm a little late. The practice went on a little longer than normal . . .' Kathy stopped. Jemima was looking at her with a strange expression on her face.

'Did it indeed?' Her voice was hard and cold, and her sharp eyes held Kathy's gaze. Taffy jumped down from her knee and, ears flattened, headed for the door. He miaowed to be let through to the scullery and Kathy opened it. He scuttled through and they both heard the rattle as he pushed his way out of his own little door.

'Close the door, Kathy, and come and sit down.'

'Shall I – make the cocoa?'

'Not just now.' Jemima nodded towards the chair opposite her. 'Sit down.'

For a moment there was silence in the room. At last

Jemima asked quietly. 'Where have you been tonight, Kathy? And I want the truth.'

Kathy thought quickly. Somehow, Jemima knew that she had not attended choir practice.

'I – I've been out with a – a friend.'

'You haven't been to the choral society meeting?'

Kathy bit her lip and shook her head. Then she looked up defiantly and met the older woman's gaze calmly. After all, she was not answerable to Miss Robinson. As long as she respected the woman's home, which she did, and came in at a reasonable hour, which she did also, what right had Jemima to question her?

But it seemed as if Jemima felt she had every right to question her. 'And this – er – friend. Would it be a male friend, by any chance?'

Kathy's chin rose higher. 'And what if it is?'

Jemima sighed. 'Kathy, I'm not trying to play the heavy father here. You've had enough of that, I know. But – but it's who this friend is that I'm concerned about.'

'It's no one you know.'

'No more lies, Kathy, if you please,' Jemima snapped, her patience at an end. She closed her eyes for a moment and sighed heavily. 'You disappoint me, Kathy. I thought you were an honest girl. Betty vouched for you. Amy thinks the world of you, and Maurice – well – as for poor Maurice, I expect you've quite broken his gentle heart.'

There was a stillness, as if the whole room was holding its breath.

'I've had two visitors tonight, Kathy. One – Mr Spencer – has only just left a few minutes ago. He came round as soon as he got home to enquire if you were all right, as you hadn't been to the meeting.' She paused and then went on. 'The other was a little earlier. Miss Curtis called to see me and what she had to tell me has disturbed me greatly.'

'Is she not satisfied with my work? Is that it? Does she want me to leave?'

'No, no, not at all. As it happens she's very pleased with your work. She says you're doing very well, particularly bearing in mind that you've had no previous experience.'

Kathy frowned. 'Then – what?'

'She happened to be walking down High Street earlier this evening when she saw Mr Kendall's car. A car, I might add, that she is very familiar with.' Jemima paused to let her words sink in.

So, Kathy thought, the secret was out and Miss Curtis had wasted no time in telling tales to the woman who was not only her landlady but also had the power to have her dismissed immediately and without a reference.

'Is there a company rule against a friendship between employees?' Kathy asked stiffly.

'No,' Jemima said carefully, 'although it is unwise between two people of such differing ranks, shall we say. It can lead to resentment among the other staff if they were to perceive any favouritism.'

'But we – he – has certainly not shown any favouritism towards me at all. He hardly ever comes into the department, let alone . . .'

'I know. I realize that. If he had, I might well have smelt a rat before now.'

'A rat!' Kathy's anger flared. 'Is that how you view – our – our friendship?'

Jemima pursed her mouth and nodded, but there was a hint of sadness in her eyes. 'My dear, you might not believe me, but I really do have your best interests at heart.'

Kathy's expression was sceptical and Jemima, catching sight of it, closed her eyes and shook her head in a gesture of helplessness.

After a long pause, Jemima opened her eyes and looked directly at Kathy. 'There are a few things you should know about Mr Kendall, my dear—' she began, but Kathy jumped to her feet.

'I don't want to hear them and anyway, I'm moving out. I won't be a trouble to you any more. Tony's found me a flat and—'

'Ah, the flat. The famous flat. He's setting you up in the flat, is he? This is worse than I thought.'

'No, he's not setting me up in it, as you put it. You make me sound like a – a mistress!'

'And aren't you?' Jemima asked bluntly.

Kathy felt an embarrassed flush flood into her face. 'No, I am not,' she answered heatedly. 'How dare you imply any such thing?'

'Well, that's one good thing, I suppose,' Jemima murmured, unperturbed by the girl's outburst. 'But once he gets you into that flat where he can visit you any time he likes—' She paused and then added, 'It's the flat on Mill Road, I suppose?'

Kathy's mouth dropped open as she stared at Jemima. Her voice was husky as she faltered, 'What – what do you mean? *The* flat on Mill Road?'

'Kathy – please – sit down. At least listen to what I've got to tell you.'

Slowly, Kathy sank back into the chair. She sat forward, tense and fearful, her hands so tightly clasped together in her lap that her knuckles were white. Against her will, she waited to hear what Jemima had to say.

Thirteen

'Tony Kendall is a very nice young man, I won't deny that—'

'Then why—?' Kathy began, but Jemima held up her hand to silence her.

'He comes from a good background – ' she hesitated briefly before adding, 'but it's his family that's the problem.' She paused. 'He's related to the Hammond family.'

Kathy gasped. 'The – the owners of the store?'

Jemima nodded. 'It isn't talked about because the obvious would be said.'

'What d'you mean? The obvious?'

'That he's very young to be in such an important position. It could be seen as nepotism.' She smiled wryly. 'James Hammond is his mother's cousin and many would say Tony's only the manager because of his relationship to the Hammond family.'

'So his mother was a Hammond?

Jemima nodded. 'It was *her* mother, to be precise, who was the Hammond. She was sister to the old man, as we call him, Mr Anthony Hammond.'

'Tony did say we should keep our – our meetings secret,' Kathy said slowly. 'I expect he thinks Mr James wouldn't approve.'

'Actually, Mr James is a very nice man, down to earth and not in any way snobbish. No, I'm afraid the problem is Tony's own mother.'

'His mother? Has she got something to do with the store?'

'Oh no. But Tony – whom she always calls Anthony, by the way – is her only son. Her only child and she – is a very possessive woman.' Jemima met Kathy's puzzled gaze. 'You haven't met her yet, I take it?'

Kathy shook her head. Suddenly she was feeling very cold inside. This wasn't at all what she had expected Jemima to say and for some inexplicable reason she feared what was coming next.

'How many times have you been out with Tony?'

'Well – several times over the weeks.'

'And how many times has he left suddenly, not turned up at all or cancelled at the last minute?'

Kathy's mouth dropped open as she stared, horrified, at Jemima. 'How – how did you know?'

'Because it's happened before. It's what always happens to his girlfriends.'

Remembering what Stella had told her, Kathy whispered, 'Miss Curtis? It happened to her?'

'You know about Muriel?'

'Yes – someone told me.'

'Stella, I expect,' Jemima murmured.

'Oh, please, I don't want to get her into trouble . . .'

'It's all right. Actually, I'm pleased she has. Perhaps it will help you to believe what I'm telling you now.'

For a moment, Kathy covered her face with her hands and gave a little sob. Then with a supreme effort, she raised her head and said quietly, 'I do believe you. I know you wouldn't lie to me. And – and I'm sorry that I ever lied to you. I hated doing it. I really am a very truthful person – usually. But somehow, I knew you'd try to stop me seeing him if you found out.'

'I most certainly would have done,' Jemima said briskly. 'Make no mistake about that.'

There was silence between them for a moment until Kathy said, 'But his mother's – well – some sort of invalid, isn't she? I mean, if she needed him when his father was working, I didn't mind.'

'Personally, I think she's a hypochondriac who uses her so-called ill-health to manipulate both her husband and her son.' Jemima's expression softened as she added, 'George – Tony's dad – is, by all accounts, a lovely fellow. He's too good, if you know what I mean.' Not having met Tony's parents, Kathy didn't really know. Though she was starting to understand a little more. And she didn't like what she was hearing. 'Beatrice Kendall is a selfish, devious woman who will stop at nothing to keep her son living at home with her.'

'What happened to Muriel – Miss Curtis?'

Jemima shook her head, as if she was still unable to believe herself what she was about to confide in Kathy. 'Poor Muriel. I think she was very fond of Tony and we all thought he was fond of her too. We were pleased for them. Oh, we'd heard rumours about other girlfriends he'd had, but we thought this time it was the real thing – for both of them.' She sighed. 'But then he took her home to meet his parents. Beatrice was very unpleasant towards Muriel. But worse than that, she made it her business to find out about the girl's family. Years ago, there was a scandal about Muriel's father embezzling money from the firm he worked for. Not Muriel's fault, of course. She was only a child at the time. It was nothing to do with her. But Beatrice latched on to it. She tried to persuade Tony that Muriel was not right for him. That his involvement with her would damage his career and his reputation.'

'And he believed her and ended the – the friendship?'

'No – no, credit due to him, he didn't. It was Muriel who ended it.'

'*Muriel*? Why?'

Jemima held her gaze for a moment. 'You do realize that I am trusting you not to say a word about all this to anyone. Not *anyone*, Kathy. I only know about it because poor Muriel was so distressed at work – well, let's just say she confided in me. I shouldn't really be telling you. I never betray confidences.' Despite the gravity of their conversation she allowed herself a small smile. 'Just like you never lie. We both seem to be breaking our own rules, don't we?'

Kathy smiled guiltily.

'Anyway,' Jemima went on. 'It seems that Beatrice sent for Muriel to go to their house – *without* Tony being present. She told her that Tony was too loyal to end the relationship himself, but that if she, Muriel, had any true feelings for him, she would end it to save his career and his good name.' Jemima sighed. 'I suppose Muriel felt she had no choice. There would never have been any kind of friendliness with her in-laws, Beatrice would've made sure of that. And Tony would have been in the middle of what would probably have become a battleground.' She was silent for a few moments, allowing Kathy time to digest it all.

'So Muriel loved him enough to sacrifice her own happiness.'

'That's how Beatrice made her see it, yes.' Jemima sniffed. 'But in my opinion she would have been better to have fought for her man.' Then she sighed. 'Muriel is an excellent head of department, but I'm afraid she lacked the courage to stand up to the woman.'

'And you think I do too?'

For a moment Jemima regarded her solemnly, then slowly, she smiled. 'No,' she said quietly. 'No, I think you're made of sterner stuff. But I can still see you losing in the end. Beatrice is a formidable woman and her methods are clever. No one dares to call her bluff. Certainly, poor George and Tony dare not. She might, indeed, be genuinely ill.' She sighed. 'I expect nothing I say can dissuade you, but at least I wanted you to know exactly what you are getting yourself into.'

Kathy nodded.

'And as for moving into this flat, well, there's no need for that. If you want to stay here, you can.'

'Even if I go on seeing him?'

Jemima nodded and now her smile was pensive. 'Oh Kathy, you might not think it to look at me now, but once upon a time I was young and in love and – I have to admit – very, very foolish.'

'And – you think I am?'

Again Jemima regarded her solemnly, searching the pretty face before her, seeing the determined set of Kathy's chin, the spark of defiance in her eyes. 'I think,' she said slowly, 'that you could be letting yourself in for a lot of heartache. Falling in love should be a happy time, the most joyous time . . .' For a moment Jemima's eyes were alight with joy at her own memories but then they were suddenly clouded with sorrow. Kathy, who had been on the point of asking what had happened to Jemima in her youth, now dared not ask the question. If even thinking about it in her own mind brought back such a sad and haunted look, then asking Jemima to talk about it would be cruel. Though Kathy longed to know. Perhaps she could ask Amy, though she doubted her friend knew any more than she did. It seemed to be a closely guarded family secret.

Instead, she said, 'Thank you for telling me and, yes, I would like to stay here. I can't really afford the flat and I don't want to be – well – I don't want Tony to be paying for it. That wouldn't be right. But – ' she paused and her tone took on a determined edge – 'I do intend to go on seeing him.'

Jemima sighed but said, 'Very well. As long as you understand you will be the subject of some unpleasant gossip and possibly even ridicule for a while. Until they find someone else to tear to shreds,' she added tartly. 'You'll have all sorts of people telling you tales about all the girlfriends he's had and how he's left a trail of broken hearts behind him.'

'I've already had a couple. The first time he took me out, he left halfway through the meal – just like you said – because a message came that his mother had been taken ill. After he'd gone, a woman from another table came and spoke to me. Evidently, she was one of his former girlfriends. At the time, I thought she was just being spiteful. Now I see that perhaps she was genuinely trying to warn me.'

'It'd be a lot easier if he was really a cad,' Jemima sighed. 'But he isn't. He's a nice young man, just weak where his mother is concerned. And whether that can be classed as a fault, even I'm not sure. And usually,' she smiled mischievously, 'I have no problem in making my mind up about folks and saying so too, if I think fit.'

'I've noticed,' Kathy teased and the two women exchanged a glance. In it there was a new understanding, even a fondness for each other that had grown over the weeks that Kathy had been there and had been even more strengthened by tonight's conversation.

'So,' Kathy went on. 'You and Taffy don't want your house to yourselves again then?'

Jemima laughed out loud. 'I like having you around, but I have to admit it's mainly because of Taffy that I'm asking you to stay. If he has taken to you – and he certainly has – then you must be all right.'

The two women laughed together and, getting up, Kathy said, 'I'll make the cocoa and call him in to give him an extra saucer of milk to say thank you.'

Fourteen

The first few days back at work were difficult. The gossip had spread, and Kathy tried to ignore the glances, the whispered conversations that halted as soon as she came near. Hardest to bear was Stella's attitude. One moment she was friendly enough, the next cold and distant.

But it was Miss Curtis who caused Kathy the most discomfort. It must have been her who had told work colleagues. She didn't think Stella would have broken her word and yet now she couldn't be sure. Once or twice she saw her whispering to the young assistant from lingerie, their conversation ceasing as soon as Kathy drew near. She knew that Jemima would say nothing to anyone. So – that left Muriel. Kathy longed to talk to her superior about it, but she couldn't. That would be betraying Jemima's confidence and, now that they had arrived at a mutual understanding and respect, she had no intention of doing so.

As if he too realized that 'the word was out', Tony started coming to the millinery department and speaking to her, making no attempt now to hide the fact that they were walking out together.

'Actually,' he whispered. 'I'm glad it's out. I don't like all this cloak-and-dagger stuff. It's exciting at first, but then it gets a bit wearing.'

Kathy smiled weakly, biting back the retort: Well, you should know about that!

'Have you made up your mind about the flat?'

'Yes, I have. I'm staying where I am for the moment. Now there's no need for secrecy, I'm happy with Miss Robinson. She's been very kind to me.'

Tony looked disappointed. 'Well, if you're sure. It won't be so easy to be together, though, will it? She'll still be keeping her beady eye on you.'

'We can go out to the pictures, to restaurants, for drives in the country.'

'Yes, but I want to be alone with you. I want to – well, you know . . .'

Though a faint blush rose in her cheeks, Kathy faced him squarely. 'I'm not that sort of girl, Tony. Maybe your past girlfriends – and oh yes, I do know there have been a few – have let you have your way with them, but not this one.' With that she had flounced away, leaving him staring after her in confusion.

That night when he took her out to dinner, Tony said, 'You misunderstood me earlier today. I can guess what the gossip is about me, but I want you to believe me that it's not true. Yes, I've had a few girlfriends – ' he sighed – 'but there was only ever one other before you that I was serious about. And she – she was the one who finished our friendship. Not me.'

Before Kathy thought to stop herself, she blurted out, 'Muriel Curtis?'

Tony's eyes widened. 'How d'you know?'

Kathy could have bitten her tongue off. 'I – I guessed,' she lied. 'I saw she was very upset when you'd been into the department one day and I – I overheard a conversation I shouldn't have done.'

'I see.' He was quiet for a moment, though he

seemed to accept her explanation and Kathy inwardly breathed a sigh of relief.

After a few moments, when she had gathered her wits, she asked carefully, 'You had the flat then?'

'Yes, but not for the reasons that I'm sure you and everyone else is thinking.' There was a bitter edge to his tone. Then he sighed. 'I – I have problems at home. Because of my mother's ill-health. I'm sorry, Kathy.' He spread his hands helplessly and looked at her with such a 'little boy lost' look that quite melted her heart. 'I took the flat in the first place because I intended to live there myself. Move out from home, but – well – it became impossible. I was still spending more time at home than I was in the flat. Anyway, I kept it on just so there was somewhere for us to go, just – just to talk and be together.'

Kathy couldn't quite believe what he was implying – that there had never been anything more than a kiss and a cuddle with his previous girlfriends. And what about Muriel Curtis? Surely that had led to 'something more'? But it was none of her business. It was what happened from now on that mattered to Kathy. Whatever had happened in the past was just that. In the past.

'You see,' he went on, as if it explained everything – and in a way, it did. 'You see, I can't take anyone home. Mother doesn't like it.'

On the Saturday evening Kathy was hurrying to leave work on time. Tony was calling for her at eight o'clock. Now there was no need for secrecy, he came openly to the little terraced house and was welcomed by Jemima. Though Taffy made it very clear that he did not welcome yet another stranger. Whenever Tony appeared, the cat stalked out of the room, his ears flattened and his tail thrashing angrily.

'Miss Matthews, you may go,' Muriel said as the last customer left the department and the sheets were placed over the displays. 'But, Miss Burton, could you spare me a moment? I'd like a word.'

Kathy's heart began to beat rapidly and she cast a glance at Stella. But the younger girl studiously avoided meeting her gaze.

'Of course, Miss Curtis,' Kathy replied evenly, though she was dreading what the woman had to say to her. Had Miss Curtis engineered her dismissal to try to separate her from Tony? As other staff called their 'good nights', Muriel drew Kathy to one side.

'I don't want you to think I'm interfering and I want you to know that this is said out of a genuine concern for you . . .'

Kathy was not sure she believed her, but she said nothing.

'You – you must know that Mr Kendall and I were once—' Muriel's lip trembled and Kathy felt sorry for her. But, not trusting herself to speak and afraid that she would say things she shouldn't, Kathy just nodded. 'He – he asked me to marry him.' Kathy stared at her. She hadn't known that. Maybe no one else knew that much. 'But – but his mother intervened. She – she didn't like me. I don't think she would like any girl – that her son got close to.' Muriel ran her tongue round her dry lips. 'He – he took me home to meet her, but she hated me. And no, that's not too strong a word for it. It was hatred – pure and simple. Of course, we could have gone away and got married. But I couldn't do that to him. I couldn't let him be estranged from his family. I couldn't let him carry the guilt of making his mother ill, maybe even of causing her death. How could anyone live with that? I couldn't and I wouldn't want him to either.'

Still, Kathy said nothing.

'You haven't met her yet?' Muriel asked.

Kathy shook her head.

'If and when you do, just be aware that she will hate you on sight and do everything she can to break your relationship up.'

'Well, I can't speak for Tony, but I know one thing. There's nothing she can do to make me end it. Nothing.'

Tears trembled in Muriel's eyes as she smiled sadly and said softly, 'Are you sure about that, Kathy?'

Kathy nodded. 'Oh yes, I'm very sure.'

'Then, I wish you well, my dear. Truly I do. The only thing I have ever wanted was to see him happy. And if you can do it, then I wish you all the luck in the world. Make him happy, Kathy. That's all I ask.'

It was a strange conversation to have taken place between a former girlfriend and the current one. Now she had very mixed feelings about Muriel. On the one hand, Kathy admired her for her selfless love for Tony, on the other she rather despised her for not being strong enough to fight for her man. She told no one about their talk. She didn't even confide in Jemima and certainly not in Stella. She was unsure now just how much she could trust Stella. She had the uncomfortable feeling that the gossip that had spread like wildfire through the store had come not from Muriel but from the younger girl. With her new understanding, she couldn't believe that Muriel would be the instigator of tales that would include her own broken romance.

No, in future, Kathy would be careful just how much she confided in Stella Matthews.

The gossip ran on for another few days, but then something happened that drove all thoughts of Tony Kendall and his latest girlfriend from everybody's mind.

On the morning of Sunday, 3 September, Kathy woke with a strange feeling of foreboding. She lay a moment in her bed as if to hold on to the warmth and the security. She had the strangest feeling that once she got out of bed, nothing would ever be quite the same again. There was a soft knock at the door and Jemima appeared carrying a cup of tea.

'I couldn't sleep. The Prime Minister's going to speak at about quarter past eleven on the wireless, so I'm not going to morning service. Maybe I'll go along to St Mary's later.' She placed the tea on the bedside table and moved across the room to open the curtains. She stood a moment, looking above the rooftops to the blue sky. She gave a soft sigh and murmured, 'It's far too nice a day to be declaring war.'

Kathy sat up. 'Is – is that what he's going to do?'

'I'm very much afraid so.' There was another pause before Jemima shook herself, turned away from the window and said briskly, 'Now, my dear, drink your tea and get dressed. Breakfast will be all ready by the time you come down.'

'I should've—' Kathy began, but Jemima smiled and held up her hand.

'It's quite all right. I couldn't sleep. I've been up ages.'

*

They sat down, one either side of the wireless set, at eleven o'clock. It seemed an age before they heard the sound of the Prime Minister's voice and listened to his solemn words. At the end of his statement, they waited in silence until the notes of the national anthem died away.

'So,' Jemima murmured, stroking Taffy absently, 'it's all going to happen again.'

In a small voice, Kathy asked, 'What exactly is going to happen?'

'I really don't know, my dear. Of course they'll use the regular army first, but no doubt they'll expect volunteers and, after a while, they'll bring in conscription.'

'What – what's conscription?' Kathy felt very ignorant. She'd never heard her father, or anyone else in their small village, speak about the last war. She knew very little about it.

'Call-up. They set an age range and then all young men between those ages have to go for a medical. If they're passed fit for service, then – they have to go.'

'Will – will Tony have to go?' Swiftly, conscious of sounding selfish, Kathy added, 'And Morry?'

'They may be able to apply for deferment for Maurice because he works on a farm. But as for Tony – how old is he?'

'Twenty-six, I think.'

'Then he may not have to go yet, but eventually . . .' Her voice trailed away and Kathy shuddered.

At the store the next morning, there was a buzz of excitement running among all the staff. Stella, red-faced and breathless, came running into the department at five minutes past nine. Muriel opened her mouth to reprimand the girl, but before she could speak, Stella burst out.

'They're going to close the store for an hour and we've all got to go to the manager's office at ten o'clock. Mr James is coming in to speak to us all. I'm to go round all the store, Mr Kendall said, and tell everyone,' Stella went on importantly. Then, without even asking for permission from her superior, she marched off to carry out her mission.

Muriel turned slowly to look at Kathy, her expression bleak. 'I wonder how this will affect us all?'

Kathy's hands were trembling, but she tried to speak calmly and hopefully. 'Perhaps – perhaps it won't last very long. When this man, Hitler, realizes that there are people prepared to stand up to him, then – then . . .'

'Germany's a very strong nation, very – committed. My father fought in the last one. He was wounded. He's got medals, you know.' Muriel's voice took on a bitter note, 'But no one remembers the good people do, they only remember their mistakes.'

Kathy said nothing, but she knew Muriel was referring to the scandal surrounding her father that Tony's mother had used against her.

At last Muriel whispered what was really on her mind. 'He might go. Tony might have to go.'

Kathy stared at her, miserably. 'I know,' she whispered, her voice breaking. No longer could she hide her worst fear.

Muriel was the first to speak again. 'Come, we'd better do as we've been told. We'd better tell all the customers in the department that the store will be closed for an hour between ten and eleven.'

*

At ten minutes past ten all the staff made their way to the manager's office. Miss Robinson stood beside Tony, and the supervisors from each department squeezed into his office. The rest of the staff crowded into Miss Foster's office. Kathy was careful to stand at the back along with Muriel and Stella. She and Muriel were quiet and subdued, but Stella's eyes were shining with an excitement that seemed to rub off on the younger members of staff.

'I shall volunteer,' a young boy from the warehouse declared.

'You're not old enough. You're only fifteen.'

The spotty-faced youth flushed, but he still vowed, 'Well, as soon as I am then.'

'Sh,' someone hissed. 'Mr Hammond's coming.'

Kathy looked round to see the tall silver-haired man, smartly dressed in a dark suit and blue tie, weaving his way through the crowded office. He paused now and again to nod and smile at the members of his staff.

'He's a nice man, isn't he?' Stella whispered. 'Always has a word for us. Not stuck up and hoity-toity like some owners'd be.'

Now it was Kathy who, afraid that Mr Hammond might overhear, said, 'Sh.'

He stood in the doorway of Tony's office so that all the staff could hear him. 'This is an anxious day for all of us,' he said, his voice soft and deep and full of concern. 'But we must all pull together and do what we can to face whatever is coming. I want you to know that whatever problems this war brings, you can always come to either Mr Kendall or to me and we'll do our very best to help you. The Hammonds like to feel that the members of their staff are one big family and, in troubled times, that's what families do. Help each other. And for those of you who volunteer – ' the grin on the face of the young boy from the warehouse seemed to reach his ears – 'or are called up, then as long as Hammonds is still here, your job will be waiting for you when you come back.'

Though the kindly man used the word 'when' and not 'if', the thought was in everyone's mind. How many of those who went to fight would ever come back?

But Mr Hammond remained positive. He smiled and nodded at the staff in the outer office and then turned to speak to Tony and the heads of department. Knowing they were dismissed, the rest of the staff drifted back to their departments ready for the store to reopen, but Kathy lingered at the end of the corridor, hoping for a brief word with Tony. But it was Jemima who emerged from the office first, white-faced and stiff-backed. She walked towards Kathy, but didn't seem to see her. She just walked straight ahead as if lost in a trance. Kathy stepped forward, 'Aunt Jemima – I mean, Miss Robinson,' she added swiftly, forgetting in the tension of the moment how she always addressed her when at work. But Jemima didn't notice, didn't even realize she was being spoken to. She was walking in a trance. Kathy touched her arm and Jemima jumped, startled out of her reverie.

'Are you all right?' Kathy asked.

'I—' Jemima hesitated. Her eyes were dark, anguished pools. 'No, I'm not.' For a moment she sagged against Kathy and the younger girl supported her weight. Then she felt and heard Jemima let out a long, deep sigh.

'Let me take you to the staff restroom and make you a cup of tea. You've had a shock.'

With a supreme effort, Jemima straightened up. 'Thank you. I think I need one. Pity we're not allowed a little medicinal brandy. I could certainly do with—'

Suddenly, Mr Hammond was at the other side of her, taking her arm and helping Kathy to support her. 'I think that's an excellent idea. We'll go back to Mr Kendall's office.' He smiled at Kathy above Jemima's head. 'But don't tell the rest of the staff.'

Together, one either side of her, they helped Jemima back into Tony's office.

'Miss Foster, would you be so kind as to get us some tea? Miss Robinson is feeling a little – well, like the rest of us – shocked.'

'Of course. At once, Mr James.' And the fussy little spinster hurried off to do his bidding.

Inside the office, Tony placed a chair for Jemima and Mr Hammond and Kathy helped her into it.

'Tony, my boy, I hope you still keep a bottle of medicinal brandy in the bottom drawer like I always did.'

'Of course,' Tony smiled as he reached for it, but his concerned glance was on Jemima.

Miss Foster returned with the tea and James Hammond poured a generous measure of brandy into it. 'We're all in a turmoil, not quite knowing what it's all going to mean for us.' Standing by her chair, he looked down at her with a serious expression. 'But we do, don't we, Miss Robinson?' he added gently. 'We know exactly what we're all in for.'

Jemima looked up at him sadly as she murmured, 'I'm afraid we do, Mr James. I'm very much afraid we do.'

Fifteen

As soon as they arrived home that evening, Jemima said, 'Go and light the fire in the front room while I get the tea ready.'

'The – the front room?' Kathy gaped at her. 'But – but you – we – never sit in there.'

'Well, we will tonight. Go and light the fire and then make yourself pretty.' Jemima had fully recovered from her brief moment of doubt and uncertainly. Now she was her old self once more, full of determination and fortitude. Her eyes were full of mischief as she added, 'Not that you're not already, but you know what I mean. Tony's coming round later, isn't he?'

'Yes, but—'

'I'll explain when Tony gets here, but first let's have our tea,' was all Jemima would say, but Kathy was thankful that she seemed almost back to her old self. And yet there was something strange about her, something resolute and determined. She's up to something, Kathy thought, as she laid sticks and paper and pieces of coal in the grate. Although it was only early September and not exactly cold, she understood Jemima's desire for a comforting fire this evening of all evenings.

Once the fire was well alight, Kathy ran upstairs to change into her dress and brush her hair. As they sat down at the table together in the kitchen, Jemima picked up the heavy teapot and poured out two cups of tea, passing one to Kathy.

'Help yourself to sugar,' she murmured. 'And make the most of it. I expect it will be on ration soon enough.'

'Ration?' Kathy stared at her. 'What do you mean?'

Jemima set the teapot down carefully. 'Towards the end of the last war, certain foods were put on ration. I expect they'll do it even sooner this time. Of course,' she went on, musing aloud, 'they'll be all right out on the farm, but in the city we'll all have to start queuing for whatever we can get.' A little smile twitched the corner of her mouth. 'You might want to go home.'

'Never,' Kathy declared as she buttered a piece of bread, spreading it thickly. 'I'd sooner starve.'

'Bravely said, my dear,' Jemima said, sipping her tea and looking as if she was relishing every drop. As perhaps she was. 'But not so easy to do.'

'This war changes everything,' Jemima said as, a little later, the three of them sat in her front parlour before the blazing fire. Kathy and Tony sat side by side on the battered sofa, Jemima in the armchair to one side of the hearthrug. The room was cosy, the fire casting a warm, flickering light around the room, illuminating briefly Jemima's heavy old-fashioned furniture. 'I'm guessing that there won't be conscription for a while. They'll depend on the regular army and volunteers. And I expect there will be plenty of them – just like last time.' For a moment she was pensive. Kathy could only guess at her painful memories and her fears for the immediate future too.

Jemima pulled herself out of her brief reverie. 'But if

it goes on for some time, then they will bring it in. I'm sure of it.' Her glance now rested on Tony. 'And if they do, you'll undoubtedly be called up.'

He nodded, not in the least surprised, though Kathy could not help a startled gasp. She hadn't thought it would happen so soon.

She clutched at Tony's hand and held onto it tightly, as if by her willpower she would physically stop him from going to war.

'You must make the most of the time you have together,' Jemima went on. 'And you can meet here. This room can be your haven from the world.' She looked hard at Tony. 'But I'm going to be very blunt. I'm trusting you not to bring shame upon Kathy.'

The young man blushed, seeming for a moment nothing like the competent manager of the big city store, but a rather boyish and shy young man. 'Of course I won't. I – I do care about Kathy. Truly, Miss Robinson, despite what you might think because of my – well – because of my past.'

Jemima waved her hand dismissively. 'I'm not one of the gossips. I do know a little more than you might think and I am aware that it is not all your fault. However, that said, I am *not* in agreement with this flat you have in town. If you set Kathy up there, it would be announcing to the world that she's your mistress—'

'But I'm not,' Kathy declared hotly.

'I know that,' Jemima answered patiently. 'But I'm afraid the gossips wouldn't believe it. They would have a field day and – to be honest – who could blame them? But it'll be very different if you meet here, under my roof.'

Tony and Kathy exchanged an amused glance, realizing that no one would dare to question their conduct if it had Miss Robinson's blessing.

'That's very kind of you and, yes, I do see what you mean about the flat—' Tony pulled a wry face. 'But it was all I could think of. You see – ' now he turned to Kathy as if this concerned her more than Jemima, yet he spoke freely in front of the older woman, wanting her to understand too – 'you see, I can't – I daren't—'

Kathy touched his hand in a tender gesture. 'I know,' she said sympathetically. 'It must be so difficult for you with your mother being an invalid.'

Tony squeezed her hand and murmured, 'You're sweet to be so understanding. Not – not everyone is.'

Though Jemima said nothing, Kathy heard her give a disbelieving sniff.

Now Kathy too began to scour the daily papers for news of the progress of the war. Poland had been overcome, but the expected onslaught on Britain did not happen. Instead, every home was bombarded with public information leaflets and lists of regulations.

'But it's better than bombs,' Kathy remarked, trying to sort out which list of dos and don'ts applied to them.

'They'll come soon enough,' Jemima replied tartly, sifting through the leaflets. 'Identity cards. We've got to carry identity cards and gasmasks at all times. Even children.'

'Did you know that a lot of children from Leeds have been evacuated to the Lincoln area already? They arrived with luggage labels attached to their coats. Poor little mites.'

Jemima frowned. 'Yes, I had heard. I'd like to help, but with us both out all day, it's hardly suitable for us to have a young child, is it? I expect Betty will be the first in the queue to take a little one though.' Her face softened. 'A real mother is Betty,' she whispered. 'Bless her.'

Kathy stared at her. It was the first time she'd seen Jemima sentimental, but the next moment the older woman had shaken herself out of her daydreaming and was briskly asking Kathy to hold the tape while she measured the windows for blackout curtains.

'Mr Hammond has instructed that all the staff can have their curtains made up for free and they can buy the material at cost price. The workroom's going to be busy, but he's certainly setting a good example. I think he's already looking for more staff for the dressmaking department.'

'Mm,' Kathy murmured, holding the end of the tape measure. 'I wish I'd leant to sew. It's going to be useful.'

'I have to admit, it's not one of my skills,' Jemima said, stepping down from the stool and writing figures on a piece of paper. She straightened up. 'Your turn to climb up. But we're lucky, you know,' she went on as Kathy reached up to the top of the curtain rail. 'At least we can get any sewing work done at the store.'

'Stella was saying that the fabric department has been so busy the last few days, some of the shelves are empty. Mind you, we've been quiet. I expect buying a new hat is the last thing on people's minds at the moment.'

'They'll drift back. Things will settle down into a routine soon enough and folks will start to act normally again.'

'You think so?' Kathy was doubtful. 'I don't think things will ever feel "normal" again.'

Now Jemima did not answer.

'Will you have to go?' It was the question Kathy was asking continually.

'Not yet,' Tony tried to reassure her. He smiled and pulled a wry face. 'And if my mother has anything to do with it, I shan't be going at all.'

'Why? What can she do?'

'Nothing. At least, I don't think so, but she's quite determined that her precious boy won't have to go and fight.'

Kathy smiled and linked her arm through his as they walked down High Street towards their favourite hotel restaurant, where Tony had booked a table. Whatever the tales were about his mother, if she could pull strings to keep Tony safely out of the war, then she had Kathy's whole-hearted approval.

Surprisingly, the place was full.

'It's a good job I booked or we wouldn't have got in, by the look of it. Ah, good evening, Gregson,' he added as the head waiter hurried forward to hold out Kathy's chair for her and then to hand them each a menu. 'You seem busy tonight.'

'We certainly are, sir.' He leaned forward as if imparting a confidence. 'I think everyone's determined to make the most of the time they have together.'

Kathy glanced round. Many of the diners were young couples like themselves, who at any moment might be caught up in the conflict and parted for goodness knew how long. Perhaps forever. Kathy shuddered and sent up a silent prayer that Tony's mother would start pulling strings right now!

They were halfway through their main course when Gregson approached the table, an expression of apology on his face.

'There's a telephone call for you, sir.'

Tony sighed, but got up at once. 'Sorry, darling. I won't be a minute . . .'

Kathy, now knowing what to expect, carried on with her meal. She had finished eating by the time Tony returned to the table, her arms folded, determination on her face.

He didn't sit down, but hovered near her. 'I'm sorry, darling, but—'

'Tony, sit down and finish your dinner. At least this course,' she added, softening just a little.

'I really can't—' he began.

'Yes, you can,' Kathy said firmly. 'Five minutes isn't going to make any difference.'

'It might. Mother thinks she's having a heart attack and Father's at work. I have to go, Kathy, really I do.'

Kathy rose. 'Then I'm coming with you.'

Tony stared at her, consternation on his face. 'Oh – well now – I don't think—'

'I'm coming.' And for once, Kathy would not take 'no' for an answer.

They reached the house where Tony lived with his parents in less than fifteen minutes.

'Please, Kathy, stay in the car. It's – it's not the right moment for you to meet her. It – it'll upset her even more.'

'Why?' Kathy asked, feigning innocence.

'She might be really bad. I might have to call the

doctor – or – or even an ambulance. Please, Kathy – please stay in the car at least until I see how bad she is.'

Kathy sighed. If the woman really was ill, she didn't want to be guilty of making her worse. And Tony had his 'little boy look' on his face. 'All right then, but if there's anything I can do to help . . .'

'Yes, yes, of course,' Tony said quickly and hurried away into the house.

He was gone a long time. So long in fact that it began to get dark. And still Kathy waited, but now she was growing impatient. Surely Tony hadn't forgotten that she was sitting out here?

A car drew up in front of Tony's. A well-built man with broad shoulders, a bald head and glasses eased his way out from behind the driving seat and reached into the back seat for his medical bag. Kathy watched as he went up the garden path of the Kendalls' home and rang the bell. Almost immediately, the door opened and she saw Tony usher him into the house. As he was about to close the door again, Tony glanced down the path and saw her. For a brief moment he hesitated, seeming unsure, but then, leaving the door half-open, he loped down the path and came to the passenger's window.

'Darling, I'm so sorry. You're still here. I thought you might have gone by now. Let me call you a taxi. Mother's in a dreadful state. I've had to call the doctor . . .'

'I saw,' Kathy replied shortly, trying to keep the impatience out of her tone, but failing. She bit her lip, feeling suddenly guilty at being so selfish. 'I'm so sorry your mother is ill. Is there anything I can do?'

Tony shook his head. The worried look never left

his face and Kathy could see that he was anxious to get back into the house. 'Let me call you a taxi,' he said again.

'It's all right,' Kathy said, climbing out of the car. 'I'll walk home. It's a nice evening.'

'But it's right the other side of the city. It's almost dark and now we've got these blackout regulations, I don't like you walking all that way on your own.'

'It's a clear night. I'll see enough by the moonlight. We're used to black nights in the country. It won't bother me.'

He smiled wryly as he closed the car door. 'A beautiful romantic evening and I can't even walk my girl home. I truly am sorry, darling.'

She touched his face gently. 'Don't worry,' she said softly and kissed his cheek. 'Go back to your mother. I do hope she'll be better soon.'

'I know what's caused it,' Tony blurted out.

You being out with your girlfriend, Kathy thought, but aloud she said, 'Oh?'

'The young man next door's been called up. His mother's in a dreadful state. She came round to see Mother. I do wish she hadn't. She should know how delicate Mother is.'

Kathy almost snapped: And what about the poor woman whose son has gone to war? Are none of you sparing a thought for her? Automatically, Kathy's glance went to the next-door house. It was all in darkness. In mourning already, it seemed, though she knew it was really because the occupants were following blackout regulations.

She pulled in a deep breath and once again tried to see it from Mrs Kendall's view. Although she didn't know the woman – yet – she could imagine a gentle, delicate, doll-like creature for whom life in general and this dreadful war in particular was just too much for her to bear.

She pictured her as an ageing Dora out of *David Copperfield*, a sweet-natured woman on whom all her family doted. With this picture in her mind, Kathy could find it in her heart to forgive the woman who appeared so selfish. Perhaps it wasn't all her fault. Perhaps . . .

'I must go in,' Tony said, kissing Kathy's cheek swiftly and squeezing her hand. 'Do take care, darling.'

The haunted look on his face was genuine. He was torn between the two women in his life. Anxious not to add to his worries, Kathy smiled and reassured him. 'I'll be fine.'

With that they parted, she to walk through the dark streets of the blacked-out city, he to rush indoors to care for his mother. For a moment she lingered, watching until the door closed behind him. Then she sighed and turned away. As she did so, she cannoned into a man walking up the street.

'Oh, I'm so sorry, I didn't see you,' she cried.

The man reached out and caught hold of her steadying her. 'That's all right, miss. No harm done.'

Peering at him through the poor light, she could see that he was dressed in workman's clothes and heavy boots, but his voice was deep and gentle. He nodded to her as he released his hold on her and stepped back. Touching his cap he moved away, but to her surprise, instead of walking on further up the street, he turned into the gate of the Kendalls' house.

Kathy couldn't move. Her curiosity held her there as she saw him go in at the side gate leading round to the back of the house. The gate closed behind him and his shadowy figure in the moonlight was lost to her. For a few moments longer, Kathy stood staring at the house before turning away and walking slowly down the street, her thoughts in a whirl.

Could the man she had bumped into have been Tony's father?

Sixteen

'You're home early,' Jemima greeted her as she stepped into the comparatively bright light of the kitchen. 'Oh, don't tell me! His mother's been taken ill. Again!'

Kathy sighed as she slumped into the easy chair opposite Jemima.

'Got it in one!' she murmured, still half lost in thought. After a moment she asked, 'Aunt Jemima, do you know Tony's parents?'

'No, not really. I know a bit *about* them. And I do remember seeing his mother in the store years ago when she was a young woman and I was a junior. And I do believe – ' she pondered a moment – 'Tony's father has been in the store a few times. But his mother never comes in any more. Not now. She rarely goes out anywhere – so I believe.'

'What's his father like?'

Jemima wrinkled her forehead. 'An older version of Tony. Dark hair – going grey now.' She snorted in an unladylike manner that was so out of character for Miss Jemima Robinson that Kathy almost laughed aloud. 'But you can't wonder at it with that wife of his,' Jemima went on. 'But he strikes me as being a nice sort of chap. Quiet. Ordinary, just like you and me, really. Not at all the sort of chap you'd have thought Beatrice Charlesworth would have married. Oh dear me no. Far too ordinary for her.'

'She must have fallen in love with him.'

'Maybe.' Jemima sounded doubtful.

'Are you trying to say she married beneath her?'

Jemima frowned. 'It's all a bit of a mystery really. Mr Anthony Hammond took over the store from the people who started it. He continued to build it up and obviously he's become quite well to do. Deservedly so, for he's a hard worker and a clever businessman. He's Beatrice Kendall's uncle – her mother's brother. The Charlesworths were actually quite ordinary, but rumour had it that Beatrice was spoiled rotten by her doting uncle. Mr Anthony only had one son – Mr James. No daughter, you see. And he lavished attention and gifts on his niece instead. I believe he even paid for her to go to a private girls' school.'

How ironic, Kathy thought. My father longed for a son and Mr Anthony Hammond craved a daughter. Aloud, she said, 'So how come she didn't marry someone – well – more top drawer?'

'*That's* the mystery.'

'Then she must have loved George Kendall.' Kathy, so in love herself, was adamant. But Jemima merely smiled and conceded softly, 'Perhaps. She wouldn't be the first to fall for someone totally unsuitable.'

Kathy said nothing, but she was left wondering if Jemima still felt that her romance with Tony Kendall was doomed for one reason – or another.

'I think I might have bumped into his father.' Swiftly she explained how she had come to be outside the Kendalls' house and she described the man she had seen.

'That certainly sounds like him. He'd've been coming home from his shift. He works at an engineering firm. Poor George.' Jemima sighed and murmured again, 'Poor, poor George.'

The following day, Kathy heard nothing from Tony all morning. At her lunch break, she headed for his office without waiting for his summons. She knocked, then entered the outer office.

'Good morning, Miss Foster. Is Mr Kendall in today?'

'Oh – er – yes, good morning, Miss Burton. Yes, yes. I believe he is. Er – please would you sit down a moment while I—'

Kathy smiled. She had been about to go straight into Tony's office. Why shouldn't she? Everyone knew they were practically engaged now. But she was amused by his secretary's guardianship and she didn't want to offend the kindly little woman. So she sat down meekly and folded her hands in her lap to wait.

Miss Foster returned. 'He's engaged on the telephone at the moment. If you wouldn't mind waiting a moment, then you may go in.'

'Thank you, Miss Foster.'

Miss Foster returned to her desk and continued to tot up a long line of figures. It was so quiet in the outer office, the only noise the plopping of the gas fire, that they both heard the 'ting' of the telephone receiver being replaced in the inner room.

Miss Foster quickly scribbled a figure and then looked up. 'You may go in now, Miss Burton.'

'How is she? How is your mother?' Kathy asked as soon as she'd entered his office and closed the door behind her.

Tony stood up and came around the desk to take

her in his arms. 'Not too bad. She's resting. Dad's stayed off work today to look after her and I'm taking tomorrow off. Darling, I'm so sorry our date was spoilt and, the way things are at the moment, I don't know when I'll be able to see you again.'

Kathy swallowed her disappointment and smiled bravely. 'That's all right. I understand. I just hope she'll soon feel better.'

'You're very sweet. Not many girls would be as understanding as you are.'

'It's not your fault.' She put the palms of her hands flat on his chest and smiled up into his face. 'But just promise me one thing.'

'I will if I can. You know that.'

'When she's well again, you'll take me home to meet both your parents.'

A look of horror flitted across Tony's face. 'Oh, I don't know about that. She – she doesn't like visitors.'

Kathy put her head on one side and regarded him steadily. 'What you mean is – ' she spoke softly, but now there was a note of firmness in her tone – 'that she won't want to meet *me*. Your girlfriend.'

Tony closed his eyes and groaned. 'You've heard the gossip about Muriel and me, I suppose? You shouldn't believe everything you hear.'

Determined not to tell any more outright lies, instead Kathy said carefully, 'Then tell me what happened with Muriel.'

'I hate talking about this. It – it doesn't seem right.'

'I promise I won't say anything to her. I wouldn't be so cruel. I – I think she still has feelings for you.'

His mouth hardened. 'I doubt it. And I certainly don't feel anything for her now. She ended our – our friendship suddenly and without any explanation. All she would say was that "it would be for the best". I didn't understand it. I still don't.'

So, Kathy thought, with a pang of sympathy for the other girl, Muriel had acted so very nobly that Tony was still unaware that his own mother had been instrumental in bringing about the end of the affair. Muriel had loved him so much that she had spared his feelings. She had even protected his mother, who certainly didn't deserve such thoughtfulness. Yet, Kathy supposed, Muriel had realized that in telling the whole truth she would hurt Tony too.

'Tony – please be honest with me. It's important. If Muriel were to explain everything and – and wanted you back, would you—?'

He didn't even let her finish. 'No,' he cried vehemently. 'No. It's you I love, Kathy. Really I do and – I don't suppose you'll believe me – ' he gave a wry, lopsided grin that melted her heart – 'but I've never felt this way about anyone before. Not the way I feel about you.'

'I bet you say that to all the girls.' Kathy laughed flippantly.

But Tony's face was utterly serious. 'No, I swear I haven't ever said that before. Not to anyone.'

'Not even to Muriel?' Now Kathy's question was serious. She needed to know.

He looked directly into her eyes and she knew he was speaking the truth when he said soberly, 'Not even to Muriel.'

Kathy gave a huge sigh that came from deep within her being. She believed him and vowed she would never again mention his relationship with Muriel, though she spared a sympathetic thought for the other girl and hoped that she too might one day find the kind of happiness that Kathy herself now felt.

But there was still one problem – apart from the obvious one of the war – that overshadowed their happiness. Tony's mother.

'He doesn't want to take me home to meet his mother.'

'Are you surprised?' Jemima retorted tartly. 'He's afraid the same thing will happen again.'

'He doesn't seem to know the full story about what happened between his mother and Muriel,' Kathy said and related what Tony had told her.

Jemima pulled a sceptical expression. 'You surprise me. But then, if I think about it, Muriel was so besotted with him that I expect she sacrificed her own feelings for the sake of his. How very noble!'

'You don't sound as if you admire her for that.'

'I don't. She should have stood up to his mother. Fought for him.' She glanced at Kathy over the top of the steel-rimmed spectacles she wore for reading or knitting and sewing. Her busy hands were already knitting socks for the troops. She had joined the local branch of the WVS and, two or three evenings a week, she was disappearing to meetings involved with war work. 'I don't expect you'll give in to that dreadful woman quite so easily, will you?'

Kathy grinned. 'You bet your life I won't.'

'Good.'

'Only thing is – I can't get him to take me home to meet his parents.'

'Then go and see them yourself. Nothing to stop you.'

Kathy gasped. 'You mean – on my own? Without him being there? Without him even *knowing*?'

Jemima pondered for a moment. 'No . . .' she said slowly. 'No, I wouldn't do that. But what I *would* do is to tell him that if he is serious about you, then you would like to meet his parents and that if he doesn't take you, you will go on your own.'

Kathy stared at her. 'You're absolutely right. That's exactly what I'll do.' Then she laughed ruefully. 'Only thing is, I'm a bit stuck if he turns the tables on me and demands to meet *my* parents too.'

Jemima smiled. 'Ah, well now, that's another story.'

'Are we having a Morrison shelter in the front room or an Anderson shelter in the back yard?'

'Neither,' Jemima answered promptly. 'There's a big cupboard under the stairs. You can get into it from the front room. I'm going to clear that out and make it so we can both get in it. It'll be as safe as any shelter. More so, probably.'

'Right you are. Can I help?'

'I tell you what you can do. Pack up my mother's best tea service out of the china cabinet into boxes and we'll push them to the narrow end of the cupboard.' She was thoughtful for a moment, then murmured. 'I'm sure there's other things I ought to put in there for safety, but I can't think what at the moment.'

Kathy smiled. Jemima had so much on her mind now, she often seemed to go off into a little world of her own. The girl rather suspected she was reliving the events of the last war and that her memories were far from pleasant. But she dared not ask. Jemima Robinson was not the kind of person one asked personal questions. Instead, Kathy said brightly, 'Where can I get some suitable boxes?'

'Mm? Oh yes. Boxes. Er – ' Jemima wrinkled her forehead – 'you could try the shop on Monks Road. They might have something.'

A little later Kathy returned triumphantly with two sturdy boxes and something wrapped up in newspaper. 'Guess what I've got? Four sausages and two lovely pieces of fish.'

'Well done,' Jemima smiled. 'We'd better make the most of them. I'm sure there are going to be shortages very soon. I hear they're cutting the bus services already because of a shortage of fuel, and men to drive them, if it comes to that.'

'They'll have to take on women bus drivers then, won't they?' Kathy laughed jokingly, but Jemima's answer was quite serious. 'Yes, they will.'

'Kathy, please don't do that,' Tony begged.

'Then take me to meet them yourself.'

Already it was almost the end of October. It had snowed during the day, but they were cosy, sitting close together on the old sofa in Jemima's front room, the only light coming from the flickering fire.

Tony ran his hand distractedly through his hair. 'I can't. I really can't.'

'Why?'

'Because – because – ' he took a deep breath – 'Mother won't like you. Oh, that sounds awful,' he added swiftly, gripping her hand tightly in apology. 'It's not you personally she won't like. She doesn't like anyone I take home. Anyone who I might marry and leave home for.'

'She wants to keep you at home, tied to her apron strings forever, does she?'

He smiled ruefully. 'I suppose that's about the size of it, but put like that, so bluntly – it – it makes me sound very weak.'

Kathy did not contradict him outright. Instead she said slowly, 'I can see that it's very difficult for you. If she's ill and depends on both you and your father, it would be rather brutal of you just to leave. I do see that.' She bit her lip, longing to ask if his mother really was as ill as she made out. Instead, she toned down the bluntness a little by asking, 'How ill is she?'

Tony shrugged. 'Who's to say? When she has one of her attacks, she certainly seems genuinely poorly. And the doctor's never once hinted that she's not really ill. Mind you, he gets paid for every visit and her stays in the private nursing home – marvellous though it is – cost us quite a lot.'

'When you say "us", I take it you mean that you contribute?'

He nodded. 'Dad works very hard. Does a lot of overtime whenever he can get it, but even then he couldn't afford the fees on his wage.'

He returned her steady gaze. 'You're wondering if she's putting it on just to make me stay at home. To keep me tied to her.'

'No,' Kathy said carefully. 'I didn't say that. I wouldn't accuse her of that. At least,' she added, trying to lighten their conversation a little, 'not yet.'

But Tony could not see anything funny in his situation. He was caught between his ailing mother and the girl he loved. 'Kathy, I know this must sound like a trite line, but I swear it isn't. I've truly never felt this way about any other girl. And oh yes, I know there've been a few, but I've never – ever – asked anyone else to marry me.' He squeezed her hands. 'Marry me, Kathy. Please – say you'll be my wife.'

Tears sprang to her eyes. Tough as she could be, Kathy was always moved by a romantic gesture. There had been so few of them in her life and certainly from no one that she cared deeply about. Even in that moment – the happiest moment in her life – she spared a fleeting thought for poor Morry. How happy she would have made him if she had been able to have given him the answer she was about to give Tony. And how much simpler life would have been. She would have pleased everyone. Her father, her mother – especially her poor, dear mother – and even the Robinsons would have been delighted. But she didn't love Morry, not in the way she loved Tony.

She put her arms around his neck and gently kissed his lips, murmuring. 'Yes, oh yes, please.'

He held her close and they kissed long and hard.

'Let's go and tell Aunt Jemima,' Kathy said at last. 'Oh, I can't wait to tell the whole world.'

'Hey, hey, wait a minute. Slow down,' he protested, but he was laughing as he said it. 'Let's not say anything. Not until I've bought you a ring and we can announce it officially.'

Kathy was disappointed. 'But surely we can tell Aunt Jemima?'

'I'd rather you didn't. I – I must tell my parents first.'

Kathy felt her heart sink. Still, he was afraid of his mother's reaction.

'I see,' she said flatly.

'Darling,' he caught hold of her hand. 'Don't look like that. Just a day or two. That's all I ask. Please?'

She forced a smile and nodded. 'All right. A week. I'll give you a week.' She tapped him playfully on the end of his nose. 'But no longer. That gives you plenty of time to pick out an engagement ring for me and also to tell your mother and father. Then next Sunday afternoon, we'll go to see them.'

Tony pulled in a deep breath and now it was his turn to force a smile. 'All right,' he agreed and Kathy tried hard to ignore the reluctance in his tone.

Seventeen

Beatrice Kendall was nothing like Kathy had imagined. True, she lay languidly on a couch in front of a roaring fire in the front room of the semi-detached house. The room was cluttered with heavy mahogany furniture and ornaments on every available flat surface. But there, any resemblance to Kathy's romantic picture of a pretty, but delicate, woman ended.

Tony's mother was sharp-featured and beady-eyed. Her face was pale and thin, her grey hair straight and cut in a twenties-style bob.

'And who might this be?' was her greeting as Tony ushered Kathy, rather nervously she thought, into the room. The woman spoke with an upper-class accent that Kathy was sure was put on.

'This is Kathy, Mother.'

'Kathy who?'

'Kathy Burton. She – she's a friend of Miss Robinson.'

'Miss Robinson? You mean Miss Robinson at the store?'

'That's right.'

The woman's thin lips curled with obvious disapproval. 'And why have you brought her here, pray?'

'I – she wanted to meet you.'

'To meet me? Whatever for?'

Kathy stepped forward, plastered a smile on her face and held out her hand.

'Tony and I have been going out together now for over seven months so I thought it was high time I met you. And Mr Kendall too, of course.'

There was a brief, fleeting glimpse of fury in Beatrice's eyes and a tightening – if that were possible – of her thin lips. But only Kathy saw all this, for the next moment, Beatrice covered her face with her bony, wrinkled hands and let out a pathetic cry. 'Oh, Anthony, how could you?'

'Please don't upset yourself, Mother. Kathy and I are just friends. We—'

'We're getting engaged,' Kathy interrupted.

Now the woman let out a high-pitched wail and let her head fall back against the pillows. Tony hurried forward, almost pushing Kathy aside in his haste.

'You'd better go,' he muttered to Kathy as he bent over his mother. 'She's having one of her turns.'

'I'm going nowhere,' Kathy said firmly. 'Are you calling the doctor?'

'No, no,' Beatrice protested weakly. 'There's no need. I just need rest and quiet. You've given me such a shock, Anthony. How could you do it?' Her face crumpled and she dissolved into tears, dabbing at her cheeks with her lace handkerchief. 'How could you become engaged without even telling me?'

Kathy noticed the word 'me' rather than 'us' and she was even more shocked and hurt when Tony cast an accusing look at her and said harshly, 'I really think you'd better go, Kathy.'

Her only answer was to sit down in the armchair near the fire. 'I said, "I'm going nowhere," and I meant it.'

'Please, Kathy . . .'

'Anthony, my pills . . . They're on my bedside table. I forgot to bring them down with me this morning.'

'I'll get them,' he said at once and hurried out of the room.

The second the door closed and they were alone, Beatrice sat up and said in a strong, clear voice, 'I don't know what you think you're playing at. My Anthony will never marry the likes of you.'

'Really?' Kathy replied keeping her voice pleasant. 'And how do you know what "the likes of me" is exactly, since you haven't taken the trouble to find out anything about me? I could be anyone.'

'Exactly!' Her glance scanned Kathy from head to toe and her lips curled again. 'Just look at you. Cheap shoes and handbag and a cotton dress. Home-made, I shouldn't wonder.'

'The dress was bought at the store,' Kathy replied calmly.

'A "sale" item, I've no doubt.'

Now the woman had hit the nail on the head, so Kathy remained silent, while Beatrice gave a smirk of satisfaction.

'You're a nobody,' she hissed as they both heard footsteps on the stairs. 'And the best thing you can do for Tony is to disappear out of his life. He'll never marry you. I'll make sure of that . . .'

As the door opened, she lay back against the pillows again and closed her eyes and gave a weak gasp.

'Here we are, Mother.' He was carrying a small brown bottle and a glass of water. He hurried across the room and knelt on the floor beside her chair, holding out the glass. She opened her eyes and raised herself a little, wincing as she did so. She took the water with a trembling hand and held out her other hand for him to shake a pill out of the bottle into her palm.

'Thank you, darling,' she murmured and lay back again, adding bravely, 'I'll be all right now. It was just such a shock. Such a terrible shock. You know I can't do with visitors and for her to tell me such news . . .'

'I'm sorry, Mother—'

What more penitent noises he might have made were cut short by the sound of the back door of the house banging.

'That'll be Dad,' Tony said and got to his feet. 'I'll go and tell him what's happened. Kathy – ' his voice was firmer now – 'you'd better come with me. We'll leave Mother to rest.'

As Kathy rose reluctantly, Tony took hold of her elbow and propelled her towards the door. She glanced over her shoulder and smiled brightly. 'I'll see you again, Mrs Kendall.'

Again, there was a fleeting vicious look in Beatrice's cold eyes. 'I don't think so,' she murmured so that only Kathy might hear.

In the kitchen, Kathy came face to face with the man she had encountered briefly in the street. He was sitting at the table, reading his newspaper. He had not changed from his working clothes and lines of weariness were etched deeply into his face.

He looked up as Tony and Kathy entered. He nodded briefly at his son but his glance rested on Kathy. He smiled at her and some of the tiredness disappeared from his face. His eyes were dark, like his son's, and kindly.

'Hello, love. You're the lass I saw out in the street a while back, aren't you?'

Kathy nodded.

'Never forget a pretty face,' George Kendall chuckled. 'I'd shek yar 'and, love. But ah'm a bit mucky.'

Kathy stared at him in amazement. He spoke with a broad Lincolnshire dialect. She warmed to him at once. Stepping forward, she held out her hand and her smile was wide and genuine as she said, 'I'm used to good honest muck, Mr Kendall. Born and bred on a farm. Please, don't get up,' she added swiftly as he made to rise. 'You look as if you've had a hard day.'

'Aye well, I have to tek the overtime when I can, lass. Needs must.'

'Can I make you a cup of tea or a meal even?'

'Aw no, lass, I couldn't possibly impose on you like that. You'm a guest . . .'

Kathy laughed. 'I'm hoping to become family . . .'

'Kathy, please . . .' Tony began warningly, but she ignored him. Somehow she knew instinctively that she would not get the same reaction from Mr Kendall that she had had from his wife. She was right. A beam spread across his face. 'Well, I nivver.' He glanced at his son. 'Ya've got yasen a good 'un here, lad.'

Tony smiled thinly, still uncomfortable.

Kathy glanced around the neat kitchen. Whoever kept it so clean and tidy, she wondered. Perhaps they had a daily help.

'What can I do? Tell me what you'd planned for your evening meal and I'll get it ready.'

'Ah well, I haven't got much in, lass. Haven't had time to stand in the queues. I'm not hungry when I get in from work. The Mrs eats like a bird and I thought Tony'd be out again. If I'd known he was bringing you home, though, I'd have got something nice in.'

'Then I'll just see what I can rustle up for us,' Kathy said and began opening cupboard doors.

A little later, she set the three plates of food – an omelette with potatoes and vegetables – on the table and called Tony and his father to sit down, saying, 'I'll just take a tray into Mrs Kendall.'

Tony leapt up and almost snatched the tray from her hands. 'I'll take it.'

She stared at him for a moment and then capitulated prettily. 'All right. I hope she likes it.'

Tony disappeared and as she sat down, George Kendall said, 'Thanks for this, lass. It's a rare treat for me to sit down to a meal someone else has made.'

Kathy picked up her knife and fork and smiled at him archly. 'Well, it could become a regular habit if you'll allow me to visit often.'

The man sighed and wrinkled his forehead. 'Truth be told, I'd like nowt better, but the missis . . .'

'Ah. Yes. Of course,' Kathy said gently, but then added briskly, 'Come on, eat up before it goes cold.'

They ate in companionable silence, but Tony did not return to the table and the meal Kathy had prepared with such love and care went cold upon the plate.

'It doesn't surprise me,' Jemima said tartly when Kathy told her about Beatrice Kendall's hostile attitude. 'Not one bit. I did warn you.'

'What's supposed to be the matter with her?'

An amused smile played on Jemima's lips. 'You're quick on the uptake, Kathy. No one knows. She's an invalid. That's all we know. Heart, probably. But how much of it is real and how much is put on, your guess is as good as mine.'

Kathy giggled. 'You mean she enjoys ill-health.'

'Exactly.' Jemima laughed but then her expression sobered. 'But it's George and Tony I feel sorry for. They're in such a difficult position.'

'Why? Why don't they just call her bluff?'

Jemima smiled at her. She was becoming very fond of this rather outspoken but straightforward young woman. She had quite forgiven her for the deception over her blossoming friendship with the store's young manager. Jemima was honest enough to admit that, in Kathy's position, she would have done just the same. 'Think about it for a moment, my dear. How can they? If she really *is* ill, such an action might precipitate a heart attack and how would they feel then, eh?'

Kathy was thoughtful for a moment. 'Yes,' she said slowly. 'I do see.' Then she added vehemently, 'How – how horrible of her to behave like that.'

'Oh yes,' Jemima said calmly. 'She's horrible all right. I'd even go as far as to say evil. The silly, spiteful woman is not only ruining her own life but George's and her son's too. And how – how any mother can – can do that to her own son, I don't know.'

To Kathy's surprise she heard a quaver in Jemima's voice and the older woman turned her head away quickly and struggled to find her handkerchief. Shocked and at a loss to know what to do or say, Kathy sat silently, but Jemima had recovered in a second and turned back with a bright smile on her face. 'Tread carefully, Kathy, where Beatrice Kendall is concerned. That's the only advice I can give you. I can't tell you not to fall for her son. It's too late for that, I know. But I'll tell you now, I just don't know how much Tony is prepared to stand up to his mother. Not even, my dear, for you.'

'You shouldn't have done it, Kathy. You could have made her really ill.'

Kathy stared at him. Was he really so naïve?

They were standing in Jemima's front room. He had arrived a few moments earlier and, as he stepped in through the back door, both women had seen the agitation on his face.

'Good evening, Tony,' Jemima had said calmly, rising from her chair. 'You two go through to the front. I'll make some tea.'

And now they were standing facing each other, Tony with an angry frown on his face, Kathy with shock and disbelief.

She sighed and put her hand on his arm. 'Tony, listen to me. She's not as ill as she's making out. When you went out of the room, she—'

'How can you say such a thing?' Tony said harshly, his voice rising in anger. 'How *dare* you?'

'I dare because I love you and I can't bear to see you taken in like this—'

'Taken in? What on earth do you mean, Kathy? And what gives you the right to say such things about my mother. For heaven's sake, you've only just met her. You don't know her at all. You don't know the years of suffering she's borne. How could you?'

'When you went out of the room, Tony, she was perfectly all right. She sat up and told me that you would never marry the likes of me. She'd see to that, she said.'

Tony stared at her. 'I don't believe you. You're making it up. You—'

'I don't tell lies,' Kathy shouted, incensed that he refused to hear a word said against his mother. Was he so blind that he couldn't see through her devious ways?

The door swung open and Jemima came into the room carrying a tray with three cups of tea on it.

'Now, you two, just stop this arguing. Sit down and drink your tea and talk about the situation calmly.' She set the tray down on a low table and sat down. 'Come along,' she added briskly as the two younger ones remained where they were, glaring at each other. Woodenly, they moved to sit in chairs either side of the fireplace.

'Now,' Jemima began as she handed them each a cup of tea. 'As I've told you before, you're very welcome to meet here if you don't want Kathy to come to your home, Tony.'

'But I could do so much to help with the housework and the cooking. His poor father looks worn out. He'll be the one having the heart attack, if they don't watch out. Not her.'

'She's no right to say that Mother is malingering. No right at all. She's only just met her. How can she possibly know?'

Now they were not talking directly to each other but were using Jemima as a go-between.

'I could tell. When he went out the room, she sat up and spoke normally. The moment she heard him coming, she flopped back on the pillows and acted all weak and faint. And he – ' she jabbed her forefinger towards Tony – 'won't believe me.'

'That's how her illness is. She can be fine one day. She even does a bit of cooking if she feels up to it . . .'

Kathy snorted and muttered. 'I bet that's not often.'

Tony glared at her resentfully, but went on, 'Of course the housework, cleaning and that, is too much for her, but she gets a meal ready for us now and again.'

'Really?' Kathy murmured, sceptically.

Jemima sipped her tea thoughtfully. 'So, Tony, are you really saying that you don't want Kathy to come to your house any more?'

'Not if she's going to treat my mother like that, no.'

'And how – exactly – did she treat her? I mean, I realize she's said things since that you don't agree with, but surely she didn't say them to your mother.' She swivelled to look at Kathy. 'Did you?'

'Of course not,' Kathy denied hotly.

'I don't know what was said when I was out of the room fetching Mother's pills.'

'I've told you – ' now Kathy was speaking directly to Tony again – 'she said she'd make sure you never married me.'

'Do you want to know what I think?' Jemima set her empty cup and saucer back on the tray. 'Well, I'm going to tell you whether you want me to or not,' she added. 'I think that Kathy should continue to visit your home, that she should help with the cooking and perhaps a little cleaning too. Make herself useful. She should treat your mother with respect and make no reference whatsoever – ' here her tone became even firmer – 'to your mother's – er – condition. She should accept it just as you and your father do.'

'You sound as if you don't believe it either,' Tony said.

Jemima shrugged. 'How can I possibly tell? I haven't

seen your mother for years. Nor am I likely to, except perhaps,' she added impishly, 'at your wedding.'

'I don't think that will be happening for a while yet,' Tony began, while Kathy looked crestfallen at his words.

'You're likely to get called up before long,' Jemima reminded him gently. 'Wouldn't you want to get married before you go?'

'I don't expect to be going. Mother says she'll be able to organize a deferment.'

'Really?' Jemima said dryly. 'The only way I could see that happening is if you got yourself a job on Kathy's father's farm.'

'And *that* won't happen,' Kathy murmured. 'Not in a million years.'

'Mother will ask her cousin to apply for a deferment for me. I'm needed at the store.'

'If the store remains open, your job could be done by a woman,' Jemima remarked.

'A woman? A woman as manager?' Tony laughed.

But Jemima's face remained stonily straight. 'And why not, pray? Women did extraordinary jobs in the last war, so why not in this one? Kathy's age group might well be called up too, but I won't be. And for your information, young man, I could do your job standing on my head.' She got up and picked up the tray.

'Miss Robinson – I'm sorry. I didn't mean to offend you.'

'You haven't. I can't blame you for thinking all women and weak and ineffectual, now can I?'

It was an oblique reference to his mother and they were all aware of it, but it had been said in such a way that Tony could not accuse her of it. Instead, he rose with a sigh and opened the door for her. As she passed by him, she paused and said, 'Now the two of you talk this through – sensibly. You have a problem and you must both deal with it.'

He closed the door behind her, leant against it for a moment and looked across at Kathy. Then he moved towards her and opened his arms wide. With a little sob, she rose and flew across the space between them.

'I'm sorry. I'm so sorry. I didn't mean to be horrid about your mother. But I couldn't bear it if she came between us.'

'I know, I know,' Tony whispered and stroked her hair. 'And we won't let her. I promise. But – but you have to believe me, Kathy. She really is ill. I know she is.'

Against his shoulder, she screwed up her face and bit down hard upon her lower lip. And there and then she made her decision. She would put on the greatest act of her life. She would pretend to believe him. She would pander to the woman just like Tony and his father did. Perhaps the way forward was not by confrontation, but by little acts of kindness that would slowly break down the barriers. It was worth a try. Anything was worth a try if she wanted to keep Tony's love.

And about that, there was no question.

Kathy lifted her head and kissed him gently. His arms tightened around her and he returned her kiss with passion.

For just a little while all thoughts of Beatrice Kendall were driven from both their minds.

Eighteen

Without any warning, Amy arrived to stay the weekend at the beginning of December.

'I've brought you some butter and a few eggs and a chicken. Dad only killed it this morning so it's quite fresh.'

Jemima pounced on them as if they were gold dust. 'How thoughtful of you. Kathy had to queue last week, just to get a couple of ounces of butter.'

'Now, I don't want to put you out, Aunt Jemima,' Amy went on. 'I can sleep with Kathy.' The two girls hugged each other as Jemima answered, 'You won't put me out, my dear. I'm delighted to see you. How's that brother of yours?'

'Oh, Morry's fine. You know Morry.'

'Yes,' Jemima murmured and suddenly her tone was wistful. 'Yes, I know Maurice. He's not going to do anything silly, is he? Like volunteering?'

'Don't think so,' Amy grinned. 'But I am.'

'What d'you mean?' Kathy and Jemima spoke together.

'I'm going to join the Wrens. That's why I'm here. I'm going to find the nearest recruiting office. There is one in Lincoln, isn't there?'

'I haven't the faintest idea, but we can find out, I've no doubt.' Jemima regarded her seriously. 'But Amy, are you sure about this? I mean, wouldn't you be better helping your father on the farm?'

Amy laughed. 'Dad doesn't need me. He's got Morry and he can apply for a deferment for him. Besides, all the old boys in the village are coming forward to help out. What about you, Kathy? Are you going to join up? You'd look cracking in uniform.'

'I might if – if Tony's called up. But I don't want to before he has to leave.'

'But I thought you told me that his mother will get him out of it?'

Before Kathy could reply, Jemima put in, 'She can try, but I doubt she'll manage it. Being a manager in a store selling fripperies is hardly likely to be viewed as valuable war work.'

Kathy leant forward to say in a loud whisper that was intended for Jemima to hear, 'He made the unforgivable mistake of saying that a woman couldn't do his job.'

The two girls giggled and looked at Jemima, who wriggled her shoulders and declared, 'Well, like I told him, I could do his job standing on my head.'

The smile faded from Amy's face as she murmured, 'You might very well have to. Oh, not standing on your head, Auntie, but if this war goes on, you might very well have to step into his shoes.'

At this and all that her remark implied, the three women fell silent.

Despite the cloud hanging over everyone and the restrictions of the blackout, the two girls enjoyed a merry weekend together. Kathy was given Saturday off and they treated themselves to afternoon tea in Boots' café and then to the cinema.

'Aren't you seeing Tony?' Amy asked. 'I don't want to play gooseberry.'

Kathy shook her head. 'No. We thought it best for him to stay at home this weekend.' She had told Amy all about her visit to the Kendalls' house and the quarrel she'd had with Tony afterwards. It felt good to have a friend she could confide in. She hadn't realized just how much she was missing Amy and their girlie chats. Impulsively, she reached out across the table and clutched Amy's hand. 'Oh, I do miss you so much. How is everyone at home? Your mum and dad and – and Morry?'

'They're fine.' She squeezed Kathy's hand as she added, 'And Morry's fine. Don't you worry about him. He's friendly with a girl in the village. Eve Jackson. Do you remember her?'

'A pretty blonde girl.'

'That's the one.'

'I'm so glad,' Kathy heaved a sigh of relief. Somehow, she still felt responsible for Morry's happiness – or rather for having made him unhappy by her refusal to marry him. If he was seeing someone else, then . . . But at Amy's next words her hopes were dashed. 'Of course, it's not serious. Not on Morry's part. There's only one girl for him.'

Kathy groaned. 'Don't, Amy. You make me feel awful.'

Amy laughed. 'Well, don't, you silly goose. No one's blaming you. Not even Morry. We all know – and Morry too if he's honest – that it's no good marrying him if you don't love him.'

There was silence between them until Kathy asked hesitantly, 'Have you – have you heard how my mam is?'

'She's all right,' Amy said gently. 'Mum's been across to see her and Dad keeps in touch with your father. I won't say she's "fine" but she is all right. He's not hitting her, if that's what's worrying you. Mum asked her straight out and told her to come to our house if that happened.'

'Thanks.' Kathy's gratitude was heartfelt. 'And please thank your mum and dad for me. They're the best. They really are. You're so lucky, you and Morry.'

'I know,' Amy said simply. They were silent for a few moments before Amy said with a briskness that was very like Aunt Jemima's. 'Now, let's go and find out where the nearest recruiting office is.'

The days leading up to Christmas were the busiest Kathy had known since she had come to work at Hammonds.

'You wouldn't think they'd be wanting to buy hats, would you?' she remarked to Stella as the two scuttled about the department, with scarcely a minute's breather between serving customers.

'Defiance, that's what it is,' the younger girl said with an astute flash of insight. 'We're showing that Hitler feller he can't get us down. Oh, Kathy, just look at this hat! Isn't it the prettiest you've ever seen?' She sighed. 'I do wish I could afford it.'

'Put it on your Christmas list.'

'Huh!' Stella's mouth tightened in disgust. 'And what good d'you think that'd be? Do you know what I'm getting for Christmas?'

Kathy stared at her and shook her head.

'War Bonds. That's what my father's present to me is.'

Kathy found it hard to hide a wry smile. It was just the sort of thing her own father would have done. But she was saved from having to answer the girl, as three more customers arrived in the store at once.

'What are you doing for Christmas, Kathy?' Jemima asked a week before the day. 'We're lucky this year. With Christmas Day falling on a Monday, we'll get three days off work. I shall go to Sandy Furze Farm as usual and Betty has invited you too. If you want to go, that is.'

Kathy was torn. Once, she'd have liked nothing better than to spend Christmas enveloped in the warmth of the Robinson family. For years she'd lived out the cheerless austerity at home, longing to escape across the fields to her friend's house. Some years she'd managed a visit on Boxing Day and the stark contrast between the homes had left her feeling even more dissatisfied with her own. But now there was Tony.

'I'll let you know tomorrow night. I'll try to find out what Tony's plans are.'

Jemima looked sceptical but she said nothing. Privately, she hoped that for once the young man just might have the courage to stand up to his mother. She sighed. He was soon going to have to summon up another kind of bravery. She hoped he would be up to it.

During her lunch break the next day, Kathy went to the manager's office.

'Go straight in, Miss Burton.' Miss Foster smiled at her fondly.

Kathy entered and closed the door behind her,

leaning on it a moment to watch Tony working over a sheaf of papers. When he looked up, a smile lit up his face. He jumped up at once and came round the desk, his hands outstretched. They snatched a brief kiss, before Kathy launched into the reason for her visit to his office.

'I'm sorry if you're busy—'

'No, no, it's all right. It's just all this form filling one has to do these days. There's so many new regulations now, my head aches with it all.' But he was laughing as he said it.

'Am I going to be able to see you over Christmas?' she asked. 'Because, if not, I've been invited to go with Miss Robinson to her family.'

Tony ran his hand across his forehead, agonizing over the decision. 'I want nothing more than to spend Christmas with you, darling, especially if Miss Robinson's away and we'd have the house to ourselves.' He pretended to leer at her. But Kathy couldn't smile in return. She'd already guessed what was coming next. 'Darling, you know I'm likely to be called up soon. It – it might be the last Christmas I get to spend with Mother . . . and Father,' he added hurriedly.

Now Kathy smiled, surprised to find his decision didn't hurt as much as she'd thought it would. She wound her arms around him, not caring for once if anyone came in. 'It's all right. Really, but there's just one thing.'

'What?' Tony was anxious.

'You're spending New Year's Eve with me.'

His worried expression cleared. He kissed the tip of her nose. 'Darling, I do love you so.'

*

'I do hope you're not breaking any food rationing regulations, Edward,' Jemima said primly, as they all sat around the laden table watching Ted Robinson carve the goose. 'We've all received our ration cards, you know.' But there was a mischievous twinkle in her eyes, which was mirrored in her brother's glance.

'Aye well, didn't Betty tell you? This is going to cost you two coupons a slice.'

'Now, don't you listen to him, cariad,' Betty said, bustling in with dishes of steaming vegetables. 'Rationing doesn't start in earnest until January.'

'Maybe not – officially, but there are already shortages in the city,' Jemima said seriously now.

'Then you let us know what you need and we'll send it,' Betty said firmly. 'Living on a farm, we'll be luckier than most.'

'That's kind of you, dear,' Jemima murmured. 'But then, you've always been good to me, Betty, haven't you?'

The two women exchanged a look across the table and smiled at each other.

'More potatoes, Kathy?' Morry, sitting beside her, passed the dish.

'I thought you had an evacuee staying with you?' she asked as she helped herself.

'We did,' Morry answered. 'A comical little chap from London. A typical cockney. Half the folk round here couldn't understand him.'

'I could,' Amy declared. 'He's a little sweetheart, Kathy. He'll be back in January, but he went home for Christmas.' She glanced across at her father and smiled. 'Dad paid for his fare home.'

'Now, now, Amy lass, don't go giving all my secrets away.'

'You know me, Dad. I always say if you've anything to hide, don't tell me.'

'Is it safe for him to go back?' Kathy asked.

'I think they're hoping that there won't be any bombing over Christmas.'

'Like in the last lot, you mean, when the soldiers on both sides got out of their trenches and played football?'

Everyone laughed, but beneath his breath so that only Kathy could hear, Morry said, 'I wouldn't trust Hitler to do anything like that. I hope the little chap's going to be all right.'

'Eat up, everyone,' Betty said cheerfully as she sat down. 'There's plenty more.'

'Aye, we'd better make the most of it. Goodness knows what we might all be eating by next year.'

'Oh, it'll not last as long as that, Ted,' Betty said, ever the optimist. 'We'll all be back to normal before you know it. Now, let's forget all about the war and enjoy our meal. And don't forget, we've got a little surprise for Kathy after our dinner.'

'A surprise? For – for me? What is it?' Kathy looked across at Amy, who shrugged her shoulders and said, 'I don't know. They haven't told me.'

'Of course we haven't,' Morry laughed. 'Else it certainly wouldn't stay a surprise for more than two minutes, would it?'

Everyone, including Amy, laughed, but Kathy could wheedle nothing more out of anyone.

'Wait and see, cariad,' was all Betty would say.

While the women cleared away and washed up the mountain of pots after a superb Christmas dinner,

Morry disappeared. From the kitchen, they heard the engine of the old farm truck start up.

'Where's he going?' Amy asked.

'Wait and see,' Betty said again, her plump arms deep in the sink.

'It must be a big present for Kathy if he's got to fetch it in the truck.' Amy tried to prise something out of her mother, but Betty was tight-lipped.

Half an hour later, they heard the vehicle returning.

'Go and open the door for him, Kathy,' Betty said.

'I'll go,' Amy said, throwing down the tea towel and heading for the door, but Betty stopped her.

'No, Amy – let Kathy go,' her mother said, quite sharply for the easy-going Betty.

Kathy shrugged and went to the back door. Opening it, she saw her mother climbing out of the passenger seat.

'Mam, Oh, Mam.' Tears coursed down her face as she threw her arms wide and ran towards Edith.

'My darling girl,' Edith whispered, holding her close. 'I haven't long. Your father's asleep by the range. He doesn't know I've come and Maurice has promised to take me back in half an hour. Let's hope he doesn't wake up before then.'

Betty appeared near the back door. 'Come in, come in.'

'I didn't ought to,' Edith said, as arm in arm she and Kathy moved towards the house. 'I've had to come out in my wellingtons. When I go back, I'm going to make out I've been feeding the hens.'

She hugged Kathy's arm to her side and smiled up at her, almost enjoying the intrigue and, hopefully, getting the better of her husband for once.

'Oh, Mam,' Kathy whispered, her tears of joy

turning to sadness. How awful it was that her mother was like a prisoner in her own home, that she daren't even come out to see her daughter for a brief half hour.

'Come away in, cariad,' Betty insisted. 'Don't you think I'm used to wellingtons tramping in and out all day?'

'Well, just into the kitchen then.'

They were left alone together, just the two of them, sitting in Betty's warm kitchen over a cup of tea. They talked non-stop, Edith wanting to know everything that had happened to her daughter since she'd left home. She'd heard snippets from the Robinsons, but it meant so much more to hear it from Kathy herself.

Edith held her daughter's hands tightly. 'Are you happy, my darling? Truly happy?'

'I'm happy with Tony, Mam. You'd love him, I know you would. But – but it's his mother . . .' She went on, the words spilling out about Beatrice Kendall's possessiveness.

When, at last, Kathy fell silent, Edith smiled gently. 'I can understand it. A mother's love is something very special. Some say, the strongest love there is. But sometimes, it can become "smother" love and that can be dangerous. But I feel for her. She must be desperately anxious about him being called up.'

'Along with thousands of other mothers. Why can't she just let him live his own life? You did with me.'

Fresh tears welled in Edith's eyes. 'It wasn't easy, darling. In fact it was the hardest thing I've ever had to do in my life.'

'Then – then why did you let me go?'

'Because it was the best for you,' she said simply, and her unselfish love for her daughter was summed up in those few words.

There was a soft knock and Morry poked his head around the kitchen door. 'I hate to do this, but you've been here nearly an hour, Mrs Burton, and . . .'

'Oh my Lor',' Edith cried, jumping up at once, her eyes wide with fear. 'If he's woken up . . .'

Morry moved into the room and put his arm around her shoulders. 'I'll park in the lane and we'll walk up to the farm and then sneak into the henhouse . . .'

'No, no, I'd best go on my own. If he sees you there, he'll start asking questions. I'll be all right.' She hugged Kathy swiftly. 'Whatever happens, it was worth it just to see you, darling.'

'Oh, Mam,' Kathy said shakily and hugged her hard in return.

Later, Kathy kissed Morry on the cheek. 'That was the very best Christmas present you could have given me. Thank you.'

Morry didn't answer but the look in his eyes said it all. I'd do anything for you, Kathy. Anything at all.

Nineteen

'Mr Kendall, whatever are you doing here?'

The man stood awkwardly in the centre of the millinery department, twirling his cloth cap through his agitated fingers and looking decidedly uncomfortable. Kathy hurried towards him. 'Is something wrong?'

''Fraid so, lass. Can you tell me where I can find our Tony?'

'Of course. I'll take you straight to his office.' She put her hand on his arm and was about to lead him through the maze of departments and corridors when she saw Muriel coming towards them.

'Ah,' she murmured. 'I'd better ask permission to leave the floor. Miss Curtis, Mr Kendall needs to see his son on a matter of urgency. May I take him up?'

Muriel nodded towards Mr Kendall, who smiled thinly. 'Of course, but come straight back. Stella is on her lunch break and we're quite busy this morning.'

As they hurried up the stairs, Kathy asked, 'What's wrong? Is it Mrs Kendall?'

'Sort of, lass. She's had a nasty shock and fainted clean away. Good job I was at home. I've been on nights and I was in me bed. I heard this thump and went downstairs and there she was on the floor with a letter in her hand.'

'A letter? A letter had caused her to pass out?'

He nodded grimly. 'It's Tony's call-up papers, lass. He's got to go.'

As they reached the top of the stairs, Kathy stopped and turned to face him. 'But – but I thought your wife said she could arrange a deferment for him?'

Sadly, George shook his head. 'She'd like to think she could, love. But the truth is there'll be nothing she can do. Nothing anyone can do. He's not in the sort of job that could get deferment. Now she's clinging to the hope that he'll fail his medical.' He leaned closer and lowered his voice. 'She even asked our doc if he'd write a certificate saying Tony has a weak heart.'

Kathy gasped and her eyes widened. 'He can't do that, surely?'

'Of course he can't. Something like that could end his career.'

'Then – then Tony'll really have to go?'

''Fraid so, lass. Now, where's his office?'

'I don't care what he says, I'm going to their house.'

'I wouldn't,' Jemima warned. 'It's snowing like mad out there. There's a couple of inches fallen already and a lot more on the way by the look of the sky this afternoon. With the blackout too . . .' Seeing the determined look on the girl's face, Jemima stopped, sighed and shrugged.

'I've not even seen him. If his father hadn't come looking for him, I wouldn't even have known.' She was feeling hurt that Tony hadn't sought her out at once to tell her that his call-up papers had come.

'He left the store to go home to his mother,' Jemima said.

'Now why doesn't that surprise me?' Kathy said, unable for once to keep the bitterness from her tone.

For once, Jemima gave up. 'Be careful, dear. Wrap up warmly. It's bitterly cold. I'm just thankful it's Sunday tomorrow.' She stroked the cat on her knee. 'Taffy and I intend to stay snug and warm by the fire.'

Kathy trudged through the darkness, pulling her coat tightly around her and squinting against the driving snow that stung her cheeks and caught her breath. But her anger and resentment drove her on. She was ready to do battle, but when she arrived at the Kendalls' home Kathy found Beatrice Kendall in a state of collapse. She could see at once that this time the woman's distress was genuine. Beatrice lay back on the sofa, looking thin and white. Tony sat on a footstool beside her, chafing her hand as if trying to bring some warmth, some life almost, back into her.

He glanced up, a mixture of pleasure and apprehension on his face, as his father ushered Kathy into the stuffy, cluttered room.

'Look who's here,' George said cheerfully. 'Come to see if she can lend a hand. Isn't that kind of her?' Before giving anyone time to make a comment, George went on. 'Tell you the truth, lass, I'm glad to see you. I could really do with a hand in the kitchen. I've to go to work. I'm late for me shift already with all this to-do and I haven't had time to cook Tony a meal or try to tempt Beatty with a little something. Mind you, I've done the shopping, so there's everything you need. I could only get sausages at the butchers. The shortages are starting already, I reckon. There'll be enough for you, an' all. I shan't have time to stay to eat.'

'Can I make you some sandwiches to take with you?'

'Oh no, lass,' he smiled. 'Me pack-up's all done. I just haven't time to eat now. Still,' he laughed and patted his rotund stomach. 'Won't hurt me to miss a meal for once, will it? Now, I'll show you where everything is and if you could make a milky rice pudding for the Mrs, she might manage a bit of that.'

'I couldn't eat a thing,' came Beatrice's quavering voice from the couch. 'Whatever are we going to do? I can't bear it. This is going to kill me.'

'Now, Mother, don't take on so. Please. I'll be all right and I'll come home just as often as I can.'

'But I'll never see you,' the woman wailed. 'You'll want to be with – with *her*, won't you? She'll take you away from me.'

'Kathy can come here, then I can be with both of you.'

Beatrice raised her head from her pillow and pointed a trembling finger at Kathy. 'I won't have her here. I won't have her in my house. Get her out!' Her voice rose hysterically. '*Get her out!*'

'Now, now, Beatty. You know I've got to go, and this lass here has kindly offered to cook Tony's meal for him. You don't mind her doing that, surely?' Before his wife could answer, he took Kathy's arm. 'Tek no notice, lass,' he whispered as they left the room. 'She's overwrought with the news. She'll calm down in a bit. Let's leave Tony with her. It's him she wants with her when she has a bad turn.'

Don't I know it! Kathy thought, but she said nothing.

George left for work and Kathy busied herself in the unfamiliar kitchen. First, she made up a rice pudding, as it would take the longest to cook. She peeled potatoes and set them to steam and then found a frying pan for the sausages. 'Bangers and mash,' she murmured, and smiled, thinking that it was hardly what she would have wished for as a meal she was preparing for her future husband.

When everything was ready, she tapped on the door of the sitting room and entered carrying a tray set with a snowy white tray cloth and a bowl of the rice pudding with a dollop of jam in the centre.

'Mr Kendall thought you might be able to eat a little rice pudding. I hope you like it.'

Beatrice raised her head and glared up at her.

'Isn't that kind of Kathy, Mother? Now let me help you sit up.'

As Kathy leant forward to place the tray on Beatrice's lap, the woman suddenly lashed out, hitting the tray upwards. The rice pudding splashed down the front of Kathy's blouse and skirt, and the bowl and tray clattered to the floor.

'What on earth did you do that for?' For once, Tony was angry. 'Kathy was only trying to help.'

'Get – her – out – of – my – house,' Beatrice gasped. Then she clutched dramatically at her chest and moaned. 'Tony – my pills. Fetch my pills.'

As Tony hurried out of the room once more, Kathy stood looking down at Beatrice. 'You know, if you carry on like this, you will lose him. Sooner or later, he's going to see right through you and then – he'll go.'

Through gritted teeth, Beatrice spat, 'Get out.'

'Oh, I'm going – for now. But I'll be back. You won't get me to give up like poor Muriel Curtis did.' As they heard Tony returning, Kathy leant forward. Putting her face close to Beatrice's, she said, 'You won't get rid of me quite so easily. I promise you.'

'We'll see about that, won't we?' Beatrice hissed and

then flopped back against the pillows as Tony entered the room.

As he passed close to her, he faltered and looked into Kathy's face. 'I'm so sorry. I don't know what came over her. It must have been an accident. I'm sure she didn't mean to do it.'

Swiftly, Kathy made her decision. She smiled sweetly. 'Of course not, darling. I'll go and clean myself up and then I'll see to this.' She indicated the smashed bowl on the floor and the splashes of rice pudding on the carpet.

'Oh, I'll see to it . . .' Tony began, but Kathy interrupted firmly, 'No, your dinner's waiting for you in the kitchen. As soon as you've given your mother her pills, you go and get it. I'll keep an eye on her and fetch you if she needs you.'

'Well . . .' He was torn between the two of them, and to tell the truth he was very hungry. He hadn't eaten since breakfast.

Kathy went back to the kitchen and cleaned the front of her blouse and skirt as best she could, then, finding a dustpan and brush and a cloth to mop the carpet, she returned to the front room.

'Off you go,' she said gently to Tony.

'You'll fetch me if she needs me.'

'Of course I will.'

With that he left the room, but as the door closed behind him, Kathy moved towards the sofa and bent over Beatrice.

'Round one to me, I think,' she said softly.

Twenty

'I'm to join the RAF. I'm to report on Monday, the nineteenth of February.'

Kathy could see both excitement and apprehension in his eyes. She wound her arms around his neck and laid her cheek against his shoulder, as she whispered, 'You will be careful, won't you?'

His arms tightened around her. 'Of course I will,' he said gently. He smoothed the hair back and kissed her forehead. 'Do you really think I'd endanger our future together?'

She raised her head and looked up at him. 'You really think we have a future together?'

'Of course.' It was obvious he was shocked that she could doubt it. 'Oh darling, I know Mother's difficult and I'm so sorry for what happened the other day.'

Kathy smiled weakly but said nothing.

'I had a long talk with Dad last night. He – he told me a lot of things about the past that I hadn't either known or realized. It – well – I suppose it explains a lot of things.' He paused. Still Kathy said nothing. She'd never been one to pry into the secrets of others. If Tony wanted to confide in her then he would. If not, then it was really none of her business what had happened in his family's past. All that concerned her was – their future. Hers and Tony's.

'His advice to me was that I should take this opportunity to cut loose the apron strings, as he put it.' Tony smiled. 'And the very best piece of advice he gave me was to say that I should marry you and be quick about it before some other eligible chap snaps you up behind my back.'

Kathy gasped and stared up at him in surprise. Then she threw back her head and laughed aloud. 'Well, that's the best I've heard yet. That a young man is "under orders" from his father to get married.'

Tony laughed with her, though slightly sheepishly. 'So, what do you say? Will you marry me? Right away? Before I go? I mean, there's only just over three weeks.'

Kathy hugged him tightly. 'Oh yes, yes, *yes*!'

'Can you arrange everything for the Saturday before I go?'

'Just try and stop me.'

'We might need a special licence. I'll sort that out. Will you want to get married at home? In your local church?'

Kathy bit her lip and tears sprang to her eyes. Wordlessly, she shook her head. Her girlish dream had been to float down the aisle of the little village church on her father's arm to the sound of her friends in the choir singing for her. But it was not going to happen. Apart from anything else, her father would more than likely stay away from her wedding. But if that happened, she knew the very person she would ask to give her away. Ted Robinson. She didn't know quite how Morry would take the news, but Amy and her parents would be thrilled for her. And Amy of course would be her bridesmaid. That had never been in doubt.

But there was one cloud blighting her happiness. Would her mother be able to attend the ceremony?

Would she be brave enough to go against her husband and attend?

'I'll have to go home and tell them, but, no, we'll be married here, in Lincoln. It'll be easier, since we're both living here. And – and – well – things could be difficult back home.'

'Whatever you think best, darling. And now – ' he tapped her nose playfully – 'you'd better go and talk to Miss Robinson and see if she can sort out a wedding dress for you.'

'Oh, but I don't know if I can afford . . .'

'Now, now, it can all be put on account and you can pay a bit off each week. And I should be able to send you some of my pay as a married serviceman.'

It sounded very strange to hear Tony refer to himself as a 'serviceman' but even more so as 'married'.

'Come on,' he said, grabbing her hand. 'Let's go into the kitchen and tell Miss Robinson.'

A few moments later, passers-by might have heard a squeal of delight from the kitchen of the little terraced house as Jemima threw her hands in the air and then hugged both Kathy and Tony. She was not given to such displays of emotion, so it made the moment all the more special for the three of them. Only Taffy, ears flattened, rushed for the back door, his tail thrashing wildly in disgust at the commotion.

'You're doing the right thing, my dears. I know you are. You are so right to grab your happiness in these uncertain times. Never mind what anyone else says, just don't listen to them. You must do what is right for you.' She glanced at them, first one and then the other. 'And I can see by your faces that it is right for both of you.' She laid her hand on Tony's shoulder and added,

'And forgive me for saying so, young man, but this will be the making of you.'

Far from taking offence, Tony laughed. 'D'you know, that's just what my dad said.'

Jemima nodded and said softly, 'Well, he would. Your dad's a sensible chap – most of the time.' Then she shook herself and added, 'And now we'd better think about your wedding finery. We haven't much time. Despite the shortages, I think we can find you a gown in the wedding department and there should be a dress to fit Amy. Oh . . .' She clapped her hand over her mouth and her eyes brimmed with laughter. 'I'm rather taking things for granted, aren't I?'

'Don't worry,' Kathy reassured her. 'Who else would I have other than my very best friend as my bridesmaid?'

'Well, let's just hope she's not gone before then.'

'I hope so, but first – I'll have to go home.'

Jemima's face sobered. 'Yes, my dear, you will. After all, you're under twenty-one. I think you'll need your father's consent.'

Kathy's lips parted in a startled gasp and her eyes widened in horror as she stared at Jemima. 'Oh no!'

Kathy was trembling as she pushed open the gate into the farmyard of her childhood home the following Saturday afternoon. Jemima had given her the day off, and though Muriel had raised her eyebrows, she had said nothing, not daring to argue with her superior.

Kathy had brought a small overnight suitcase, but she wasn't sure of a welcome. But if necessary, she knew she could stay with the Robinsons. Despite her having hurt Morry, the Robinsons were big-hearted enough to welcome her any time. And her unexpected arrival would cause them no trouble. Betty always kept the spare room bed made up and aired.

Sounds of early evening milking came from the cowshed and Kathy breathed a sigh of relief. Perhaps she could find her mother first and put off the moment she would have to face her father for a little longer. She pushed open the back door and tiptoed through the washhouse and into the kitchen. She saw her mother standing at the kitchen sink washing up.

'Hello, Mam.'

Despite the softness of Kathy's voice, Edith jumped and turned with frightened eyes towards the door. Seeing her daughter, she gave a cry of delight and rushed across the space between them to throw soapy hands around her. Laughing, Kathy hugged her in return.

Edith drew back and, after the first joyful reaction, her eyes were suddenly anxious. 'Is something wrong? Have you come back home?' There was both hope and apprehension in her tone. While she would have loved to have her daughter back home, she knew that would not be the best for Kathy.

'No, Mam, I've come to tell you something and – and to ask your permission.'

Edith pulled in a sharp breath. 'Oh no! You – you're going to join up, aren't you? Oh, Kathy, are you sure?'

'No, Mam, I'm not volunteering. I – I'm getting married.'

'Married!'

If she had told her mother that she was flying to the moon, Edith could not have been more shocked.

'But – but who?' Then suddenly, her face cleared and her joy was complete. 'Oh it's Maurice, isn't it? Oh, do say it's Maurice!'

Kathy shook her head. 'No, I'm sorry. It isn't Morry. It's – it's Tony Kendall. I told you about him at Christmas. Remember? He's the manager of the store where I work. He's the great-nephew of the owner.'

'But you haven't known him long.'

'I love him, Mam, and he loves me. And he's been called up.'

'Ah.' Her mother sighed deeply and let her hands fall away. 'So you want to get married before he goes.'

'Yes.'

'And when do you plan to—?'

'Three weeks today, so there's not much time, and because I'm under twenty-one, I need your consent.'

'Your father's consent, you mean, and he'll never give it.'

'Wouldn't yours do, Mam? Surely it doesn't have to be both parents, does it?'

'I don't know.' Edith rubbed her hands nervously down the front of her apron. 'I don't think I dare . . .' She stopped and was suddenly very still for a long moment. Then she raised her head and met Kathy's eyes. With more firmness in her tone than Kathy had ever heard, Edith said, 'Yes, yes, I'll do it. If you're sure it's what you want, then I'll give my consent, whatever your father says.'

'Oh Mam . . .' Tears flooded down Kathy's face as she enveloped her mother in a bear-hug.

At last Edith patted her back. 'There, there, love. Now you'd better go and tell your father.'

'Mam, are you really sure? I don't want him to take it out on you later.'

Edith gave a wan smile. 'Oh, I don't mind. All I care about is your happiness. It's too late for me now. But you – you've got all your life in front of you.'

'Why don't you leave him, Mam?'

Edith shrugged. 'Where would I go?' she asked simply.

'To me. To us,' Kathy said impulsively. 'When we're settled in a home of our own, you can come and live with us.'

Edith smiled gently. 'We'll see, love, we'll see,' was all she would say.

'I suppose you're pregnant, a' ya?'

Shocked, Kathy stared at her father, her heart pounding in her chest. She felt a guilty flush creep up her face. The previous night, while Jemima had been at one of her WVS meetings, Tony had made love to Kathy in the big lumpy bed she occupied in the spare room. It had been her first time and she had been nervous at first. But Tony had been so gentle, so loving, that she had given herself to him willingly and, finally, with joyful abandon. Amid all the uncertainty everyone now faced, their few hours together had been an oasis of bliss. But now, facing her father, she felt the flush creep up her face. Hoping he would see it as indignation, she declared hotly, 'Of course I'm not!' Mentally she crossed her fingers, hoping that what she said was the truth.

'Then why the hurry? And who is this chap anyway?'

Kathy explained, but her reasons were lost on her

father. 'Now if it was Maurice you were marrying, well, that'd be different.'

'So you won't give your consent?'

'No.'

Kathy shrugged. 'Very well then.'

Her father glanced at her suspiciously. Suddenly, there was a gleam in his eyes. 'And don't think your mother can give her consent instead. It has to be me.' Kathy stared at him as he smiled with satisfaction. 'Aye, I thought so. Wheedled your way round her, have you? Got her to promise to give her consent 'cos you knew I wouldn't.'

Kathy wasn't sure of the law, but she would find out. For the moment, she turned away without another word and went back into the house.

Standing in the middle of the kitchen, she told her mother tearfully. 'He says you can't do it. I didn't tell him, Mam,' she added hastily, 'but he guessed.'

'He would,' Edith muttered bitterly. 'To be honest I'm not sure either, but there must be a way round it.' She laughed softly. It was the first time that Kathy could remember her mother laughing in years. 'If the worst comes to the worst, you'll have to run away to Gretna Green. But then, I suppose his parents would be upset if you did that.'

'His father would, but his mother . . .' Kathy hesitated. 'She's even more against our marriage than Dad is – if that's possible!'

'Doesn't she like you?'

'No, but then she has never liked any girl Tony has taken home. She's an invalid and she plays on it to keep him tied to her apron strings. Well, that's what it seems like, anyway,' Kathy added hastily, anxious not give her mother a false impression. She sighed. 'She has her husband and her son wrapped around her little finger, but to be honest, no one knows for sure just how ill she is. Not even they do.'

'Yes, I remember.' Edith sighed. 'It sounds as if you're taking on a lot, Kathy love. Are you sure?'

'Yes, Mum. Whatever the problems, I love Tony and I want to marry him.'

'I tell you what, go and talk to Mr Nightingale. He'll know.'

Kathy's face cleared. 'Of course.' She giggled. 'Only trouble is I might get roped in to sing with the choir tomorrow morning.'

Her mother smiled. 'Well, that'd be nice, wouldn't it?'

'Yes. Yes, actually it would be very nice.'

Kathy sang her heart out at morning service in the little village church where she had worshipped since childhood. Afterwards, as she walked home arm in arm with Amy, she felt more at peace than she could ever remember.

'That was a lovely sermon old Mr Nightingale gave. Evidently he was a padre in the last war, so he knows what's ahead.' Amy sighed. 'D'you know, Kathy, part of me's terrified about joining up and yet – I can't help it – I'm excited too.'

'I don't blame you. I would feel just the same.'

'Why don't you join up?'

'If I wasn't getting married, I would, but I want to be there for Tony whenever he can get leave. I shall volunteer to do some sort of war work in Lincoln instead.'

'Are you coming for dinner with us? Mam and Dad'd love to see you and there's always plenty – even with the rationing!'

'No, if you don't mind, I'll go home. I want to see as much of Mam as I can while I'm here.' She sighed. 'If I marry Tony, I doubt I'll be welcome at home any more.'

Amy squeezed her arm. 'Well, you're always welcome at our place, you know that.'

Kathy felt a lump in her throat. It was good to have such loyal friends.

They parted at the fork in the lane where one path led to Amy's home, the other way to Thorpe Farm.

As she pushed open the gate she looked up in surprise to see her father standing in the middle of the yard. It was obvious he was waiting for her. Without any kind of greeting, he said, 'I'll give my consent on one condition.'

Kathy drew in a deep breath of surprise. She said nothing, just stared at him, waiting for him to go on, knowing that she probably wasn't going to like what he had to say.

'I'll make a new will leaving everything to Maurice Robinson. If you marry this chap, you won't get a penny.'

Kathy tried hard to hide her delight, but failed. 'You mean it, you really mean it? You'll give your consent?'

He stared at her for a moment before saying harshly, 'Does this farm mean nothing to you? It's been in my family for years. Don't you care?'

Kathy shrugged. 'You've never made me feel as if I'd a right to care. Because I'm not a boy, you never once gave me any reason to think you'd pass it on to me. All you could ever think about was marrying me off to Morry and him having the farm. Well, as far as I'm concerned, he can have it and good luck to him.'

With that she marched into the house and slammed the back door behind her, leaving her father staring after her with a puzzled expression on his face.

Twenty-One

With her father's written consent secured, Kathy returned to Lincoln on the Sunday evening.

'You do surprise me,' Jemima said when Kathy told her the news. 'He's a vindictive old beggar, isn't he? Fancy any father cutting his only child out of his will like that. Mind you – ' her bright eyes twinkled mischievously – 'it's all the better for Maurice.'

Kathy laughed and hugged Jemima impulsively. 'And it couldn't happen to a nicer bloke. I mean it, I'm more than happy that it would be Morry to benefit.'

Jemima smiled sadly. 'I'm sure he'd rather have you than all the farms in Lincolnshire, though.'

Kathy sighed. 'I am sorry, truly I am. But I can't pretend to be in love with him. I've seen at first hand what a loveless marriage is like. I don't want that for myself – or for Morry. And a one-sided marriage would probably be even worse in a way.'

'I expect you're right, dear,' Jemima said briskly. 'Now, we'd better get this wedding planned. Who's going to give you away?'

'I'd like to ask your brother, but is it fair? I mean – because of Morry?'

'Don't worry about that. Ted will be tickled pink. You can phone him from work tomorrow.' The Robinsons had been the first in the village, apart from the vicar and the local doctor, of course, to have a telephone installed.

'I can't wait to see Tony in the morning and tell him the good news.'

'Let's just hope . . .' Jemima began and then stopped.

'What?'

'Oh nothing, dear, nothing. Now, let's get to bed. We've got an exciting three weeks ahead of us.'

Later the following morning, during her dinner break, Kathy rushed upstairs to Tony's office. As she knocked and opened the door he sprang up from behind his desk and came towards her. He swept her off her feet and swung her round. 'I've organized the licence and James has agreed to be my best man.'

'Mr Hammond has? Oh how wonderful.'

'He is my mother's cousin.'

'I bet that's pleased her, hasn't it?'

The smile faded from Tony's face. 'Darling, nothing – but nothing – will please my mother. She's refusing to come to the wedding.'

'That makes both our parents. Mam would come but I don't know if she'll dare and as for Dad . . .' She took a deep breath and told him all that had happened over the weekend ending, 'You – you don't mind about the farm? I mean, I'm not bringing anything to the marriage.'

Tony hugged her to him and kissed her firmly on the mouth, murmuring, 'You silly goose. You're all I want. Besides, what would I do with a farm? I hardly know which end of a cow the milk comes out of.'

Kathy giggled. 'It comes out in the middle. Well, sort of.'

'There you are then? What do I know?'

'Miss Curtis, could I have a word with you, please?' It was the moment Kathy had been dreading all day, yet it was something she had decided that she must do herself. She should be the one to tell Muriel.

'Of course . . .' Muriel glanced at her watch. 'We close in five minutes. We'll talk then.' She smiled at Kathy's worried face. 'I do hope you're not going to leave us to join up. You've proved yourself to be an excellent sales assistant. I wouldn't want to lose you.'

Kathy smiled thinly but said nothing.

When all the other staff had left the floor, Muriel said, 'Now, what is it?'

Kathy took a deep breath. 'I wanted to tell you myself, I didn't want you to hear it from anyone else. Tony and I are getting married on the seventeenth. You probably know he's been called up and – and we want to be married before he goes.'

For a moment Muriel stared at her, then tears welled in her eyes.

'I'm so sorry. I know it must hurt you.' Kathy was crying too.

Muriel shook her head. 'I'm being silly. It would never have worked for us. I know that. I – I just want him to be happy. That's all I've ever wanted. So, I wish you joy. Really I do, Kathy. But – please – make him happy. That's all I ask. Make him happy.'

Impulsively, Kathy hugged her. 'You're such a good,

generous person. You will come to the wedding, won't you?'

'No – don't be offended, but no, I won't come.' She smiled tremulously through her tears. 'That would be asking a bit much, don't you think?'

Kathy nodded. 'Yes, I suppose so.'

'But I wish you well – both of you. Truly I do. Now,' Muriel went on, gently easing herself from Kathy's arms. 'Have you got everything you need for the big day? If we can help you, we will.'

'Aunt Jemima – I mean, Miss Robinson – told me to wait for her here and she'd help me look out a wedding dress. She'll have spoken to the head of the department by now.'

Muriel brushed away the last of her tears and smiled bravely. 'May I help? I used to work in that department until they made me head of millinery. There are rumours that eventually we'll have clothes coupons too, so make the most of it and get everything you need. We can put it on account for you.'

Tactfully, Kathy didn't remark: That's what Tony said. Instead she said tentatively, 'If – if you're sure, then, yes, that would be lovely. I'd value your opinion.'

The three women spent the next two hours happily. Even Muriel buried her own thoughts and threw herself into helping Kathy choose her wedding finery, never tiring of carrying gown after gown for Kathy to try on.

'It's such a pity you haven't time to have one made, but the workroom is so busy just now. Now, try this one, Kathy. It's last year's model, but it really is pretty.'

Carefully she helped Kathy ease the gown over her head, while Jemima stood, her head on one side, appraising each one.

The silk gown had a fitted bodice, buttoning down the back, long sleeves and a full skirt and train with scalloped-edge pleats. A long veil, reaching to the ground, completed the ensemble.

'That's the one,' Jemima nodded, firmly. 'You look a picture, dear.'

By the time the three women left the store, Kathy had not only a wedding dress and veil, but shoes and silky white underwear too.

'I've had a letter from Auntie Betty. Uncle Ted's said he'd be delighted to give me away and they're all coming to the wedding. Even – even Morry.'

'I should hope so too,' Jemima answered with asperity. 'I should think a lot less of him if he stayed away out of pique.'

Kathy smiled. She guessed that wasn't strictly true, but she understood what Jemima meant. Her smile widened as she added, 'And guess what? They're bringing my mother.'

'My dear, I am so pleased for you.'

'I can hardly believe it. She's really dared to stand up to my father.' Kathy's eyes clouded. 'I – I just hope he won't take it out on her afterwards.'

'Don't you worry your pretty head about that. Ted and Betty will keep an eye on her. You just enjoy your big day. It's what she would want.'

'I know, and it'll mean the world to me to have her there. I just wish . . .' Kathy began and then stopped.

'That your father would come too,' Jemima said softly, but Kathy shook her head.

'No, actually, it was Tony's mother I was thinking about. I wish she would change her mind and come to the wedding. I know it would make Tony's day if she did.'

'His father will come though, won't he?'

Kathy grimaced and shrugged. 'I don't know. I expect she'll try to stop him. And she'll probably succeed.'

'Oh well,' Jemima said kindly, but without much real hope. 'Maybe George will manage to persuade her to come.'

'I do hope so,' Kathy said fervently.

Jemima glanced at her, but said nothing. It wouldn't do to say so, the older woman was thinking, but it might be a lot better if Beatrice Kendall did stay away from the wedding.

The following Sunday morning, Kathy walked across the city carrying two shopping bags containing everything she needed to cook a Sunday roast lunch for the Kendalls. She'd had to queue for all the things she needed and now, with the rumours that meat was going on ration at the beginning of March, that too was getting scarce. But she'd managed to get a piece of mutton.

She knew that George wasn't finishing his night shift until eight o'clock or even later, and she knew the poor man would be weary. The last thing he needed was to have to come home and start cooking. As she trudged up the slope of the hill on which their house stood, she saw him ahead of her, pushing his bicycle through the gate.

'Mr Kendall,' she called.

As he looked up and saw her, his face break into a

welcoming smile. Well, Kathy thought, there was no mistaking that he, at least, approved of her.

'Hello, lass, what are you doing here?' He chuckled. 'I'd've thought you'd be busy sorting out your trousseau.'

Kathy laughed. 'It's all sorted, Mr Kendall. Such as it is.'

'You'll look a smasher whatever you wear, love,' he said gallantly.

'Now I can see who your son takes after. Flattery will get you everywhere. At least, a Sunday dinner,' she teased.

'A Sunday dinner?' He eyed the bags she was carrying. 'You don't mean you've come all this way just to cook us a dinner, lass, do you?'

'I certainly have. I thought you could do with a little help, seeing as you're on nights. And Tony tells me the extent of his culinary skills is boiling an egg.'

George laughed. 'That's about the size of it, lass. Well, this is a nice surprise. You must have known it's my birthday. Did you?'

Kathy's eyes widened. 'No. Is it?'

'Actually, it was yesterday, but no one remembered 'cept me.'

Kathy was shocked. 'Not even Tony?'

George shrugged. 'He's a lot on his mind. Not only the wedding, of course, but his mother's taken the news very badly, lass, I'm sorry to say. She had a nasty turn yesterday. Tony was called home from work. Did you know?'

'I guessed as much when he sent a message that he couldn't see me last night. That's partly why I've come today. I thought – I thought if your wife realized I'm not trying to take him away from her, that I – I'd like to be thought of as one of the family, then . . .' Her voice trailed away.

'You're already one of the family as far as I'm concerned.' He sighed. 'But I don't mind telling you, love, you've got a battle on your hands before Beatty will see it that way.'

'But while Tony's away, I thought – well – I thought I could be company for her. For both of you. I could help out – if you'd let me.'

'Oh, I'd let you, lass, no doubt about that. And you'd be a daughter to me. Always wanted a daughter, I did,' he murmured dreamily.

I wish you'd tell my dad that, Kathy thought.

He shook himself out of his reverie. 'Let's get inside and you can get cracking. My word, I'm looking forward to this. Tony'll be that pleased to see you.'

Will he? Kathy wondered, but she did not voice her doubts.

Tony was surprised to see her there and a little on edge. 'Look, it's good of you to come, but do you mind staying in the kitchen? That way Mother won't know you're here.'

'You mean if she knows I've cooked the dinner, she won't eat it?'

Tony shrugged. 'Probably not. We'll not tell her.'

'I'll do whatever you want me to do, darling. Besides, I'll need to be in the kitchen most of the time anyway. We'll eat in here, if you like.'

'We usually do,' George said as he washed his hands at the deep sink in the scullery. 'Now, lass, is there anything I can do?'

'No, you go upstairs and have a rest. Tony will call you when dinner's ready. You go back to your mother,

Tony, but if you don't want her to realize I'm here you'd better keep popping out to see when it's all ready.'

'Right you are and – thanks.'

'It's okay,' she said, deliberately keeping her tone light. But it wasn't really okay. It was anything but. It was a ridiculous situation and she couldn't see how it was ever going to be resolved.

Twenty-Two

As they were finishing dinner, the little bell that Beatrice kept close at hand tinkled and Tony went rushing through to see what she wanted. He came back carrying the tray with an empty plate on it. As he set it down on the table, he laughed. 'Mother says your cooking's improving, Dad.'

George chuckled and winked at Kathy. 'You've done it now, lass. You'll have to come again.'

'Any time. I've enjoyed doing it for you.'

'It was a real treat, I don't mind telling you. And now I insist you let me and Tony do the washing up.'

'No, no. Tony, you go back and sit with your mother. And you – ' she wagged her finger at her future father-in-law – 'should go back upstairs and sleep.'

'I will when I've helped you. You wash, I'll dry,' he said, picking up a tea towel. 'And I won't take "no" for an answer.'

Kathy laughed and capitulated. As they worked together, Kathy asked tentatively, 'How long has Mrs Kendall been an invalid?'

George sighed. 'It's a long story, love. I don't know if you'd be interested.'

'Of course I'm interested. And not just about Tony either.' She had grown very fond of George Kendall. He was such a kind, gentle man, but she couldn't for the life of her see how he had become entangled with someone like Beatrice, let alone married her!

He sighed, and his round, pleasant face fell into lines of weariness and disappointment as he chose his words carefully. 'It seems such a long time ago now,' he murmured. He forced a smile as he began, 'Once upon a time . . .'

Kathy smiled too, knowing that he was trying to lighten a story that perhaps had little happiness or joy in the telling.

'I belonged – ' now he sighed heavily again – 'to a reasonably wealthy family. My grandfather – my father's father, that is – was a farmer at Wellingore. We lived in a very nice house on the edge of the hill there overlooking all his lands. They were good days. I had an idyllic childhood. Although we never lost our broad dialect . . .' His smile widened and Kathy knew he was not apologizing. He was proud of his birthright.

'Quite right too,' she said stoutly. There were traces of it in her own speech, a trait she had no intention of trying to eradicate.

'I think you could say we were classed as "country gentlemen". My father held shooting parties on his land and mixed with the businessmen and dignitaries of the city.'

His eyes clouded with painful memories. 'And then came the depression. A lot of people went bankrupt. My father among them. He had to sell up, and on the day of the sale, when strangers where tramping through the house, poking and prodding into personal belongings, he took his twelve-bore shotgun and went into a little copse at the end of the meadow. It was where he and I had spent our happiest times. When I was little, he'd play hide and seek or cowboys and

Indians. My dad could be great fun. But that all ended in the little copse.'

'You mean – he – he—'

George nodded and said flatly, 'He shot himself. My mother never got over the shock. She died only six months later. And Beatty, of course, well, she's never got over the shame.'

'Poor man,' Kathy murmured. 'I know how hard it was then. I was only ten or so, but I've heard my father and Ted Robinson talk about those times.' She was pensive for a moment, realizing, perhaps for the first time, just how hard her father had worked to save his own family's farm. But surely, she reasoned, even if he'd been through some hard times, there was no reason why he'd become so embittered.

There was a long silence before Kathy asked tentatively, 'So – when you married Beatrice your folks were – ' she smiled – 'well breeched?'

George gave a wry laugh. 'You could say that. It was through her uncle I met her. Have you seen the old boy yet?'

'Only once. His son brought him through the store in a wheelchair.'

'Aye well, he'll be getting on a bit now. He must be nearly ninety.'

'He still looked bright as a button,' Kathy laughed. 'I overheard him finding fault with a display. "See to it, boy," he said. He called Mr James "boy".' She was giggling now at the memory.

Despite the gravity of their conversation, even George chuckled. 'Aye, he was always the success of that family, old Anthony.'

'I presume Tony's named after him?'

'Oh yes,' George smiled wryly. 'Beatty always had

her eye on the main chance, though where she got her social-climbing ideas from, goodness knows. Her parents were lovely folk. Oh dear – ' he grimaced comically – 'that sounds terribly disloyal to my wife, doesn't it?'

Kathy whispered, 'There's only you and me here and you can trust me.'

His dark eyes, so like Tony's, looked deeply into her. His voice was a little unsteady as he said, 'Aye, I know that, lass. I know that.' He paused and then went on with his story. 'Her uncle – the old boy – used to come shooting on our land. James too, when he was old enough. And because Anthony had no daughter of his own – James was his only child – he used to make a big fuss of Beatty. Perhaps that's how she got a taste for the luxurious life. Her own father, John Charlesworth, was just a good, honest working man but he wasn't a high flyer like his brother-in-law. It was always said Anthony had the Midas touch. He started as a market trader on Lincoln market, would you believe? And look at him now. Must be worth thousands. I wouldn't be surprised if he's not a millionaire.'

'And you fell in love with Beatrice?'

George sighed again. 'I suppose I must have done.' It seemed he was having difficulty in believing it himself. So much had happened since then to kill any love he'd had for the resentful, bitter woman that he could hardly remember the golden days of their youth. 'Oh, that sounds awful,' he groaned. 'But you wouldn't recognize the girl she was then in the woman you see now.'

'But what's made her like she is? Is it just because of what happened in your family?'

'I suppose so. Unless it's because I'm so – so boring and – and ordinary. I think she despises me.'

'She's no right to do that,' Kathy declared hotly. 'You're a lovely man.'

He smiled sadly. 'You're a dear girl to say so.'

'It's true. She should've supported you when your family hit such a terrible time. Not – not turned against you and blamed you.'

'She thought she was marrying into a well-to-do family. Folks with land and property and a prosperous future. She didn't know it was all going to disappear. Nor did any of us. I have to say her uncle's been good to us. Still is. He, and James too, have given Tony a marvellous opportunity. But even then Beatrice is still resentful, seeing it as a right rather than a privilege. I sometimes wonder, though, if he's really up to the job. If he's just there because of who his relatives are.'

Kathy tried to be objective. 'I don't think so. Everyone thinks very well of Tony, at least—' she hesitated.

'What? Tell me, lass.' He smiled wryly. 'Since we're being honest with each other.'

Kathy lifted her shoulders in a helpless gesture. 'It was just that he was known as rather a "ladies' man". He had a reputation for having several girlfriends and – and, well – not treating them very well.'

George nodded. 'I guessed as much.'

'You – you knew about the flat?'

'I guessed. When he didn't come home some nights, I guessed he must be staying somewhere. For some time I though it was at a friend's house or at a girlfriend's. But when he never brought any of them home, I guessed he must have a little place of his own somewhere.'

'But he brought Muriel Curtis home, didn't he?'

'Yes. She was the first.' He was quiet for a moment before murmuring, 'In fact, the only serious one before you. Poor Muriel. She was a nice lass. I never really knew what happened and to be honest, I don't think Tony did either. He was quite cut up when she broke off their engagement without giving any real explanation.' He held Kathy's gaze steadily. 'I always thought Beatty had something to do with it, but I don't know what.'

Kathy couldn't prevent the colour rising in her face.

'But you know, don't you?' he added softly.

She couldn't lie to him. Slowly, she nodded. 'Yes, I do know, but I was told in confidence and I can't betray that person's trust.' Already she'd tested Jemima's belief in her, and she would never again lie to the woman who had befriended her or break her confidence. 'The only thing I will tell you is that, yes, you're right. Your wife did interfere.'

'Aye, well, lass, you're not breaking your promise to anyone by telling me that. I guessed as much and I'm sorry.'

George put his hand on her shoulder and gave it a gentle squeeze. His voice was husky as he added, 'Just mind you don't let her break you two up, eh?'

'No,' Kathy said firmly. 'I won't.'

'You're lucky with the weather, my dear. It's cold but fine – at the moment. Let's hope it holds,' Jemima said, as she entered Kathy's bedroom on the morning of the wedding carrying a tray of cereal, toast and a small pot of tea.

'Now, sit up,' she commanded. She set the tray across Kathy's knees and then moved across the room to open the curtains.

'Oh, Aunt Jemima, you shouldn't have!'

'Every bride should have breakfast in bed on her wedding day and since your mother isn't here to do it, I'm the next best thing.'

'You're very good to me,' Kathy said huskily, her eyes filling with tears.

'Now, now, none of that. This is a happy day, the happiest day of your life.'

Kathy smiled but said nothing. Though she didn't voice it, her tears were not for herself but for this woman who had shown her such brisk kindness. A woman whose own past was something of a mystery, but who, Kathy believed, had once known love herself. And yet, though something must have gone terribly wrong, Jemima, instead of wallowing in bitterness, had done everything she could to encourage Kathy's romance with Tony. 'Aunt Jemima,' Kathy said hesitantly.

'Yes, my dear. What is it?'

'Just – thank you. Thank you for everything.'

Jemima waved her hand and said, 'Oh, phooey, girl. I've enjoyed every minute of it. And here comes Taffy to wish you well today.'

The cat jumped on to the end of the bed, kneaded the eiderdown with his huge paws, turned round three times and then lay down, curling himself into a neat circle.

Kathy laughed. 'Are you sure, or does he just want a comfy bed to sleep on?'

Jemima's eyes twinkled. 'Probably the latter. Shall I take him away?'

'No, no, I like having him here. He'll be company while I get ready.'

'All right, but just don't let him get his claws in your wedding gown.'

Kathy finished the bowl of cereal and nibbled at the toast. She drank half the cup of tea and then lay back against the pillows and glanced through the open curtains.

Fluffy white clouds scudded across the sky, but the pale winter sun was shining and today she was going to marry the man she adored.

What more could a girl ask for?

She was almost ready when there was a flurry of activity downstairs and the sound of voices all talking at once. Footsteps sounded on the stairs and the bedroom door was flung open.

'There you are,' Amy began and then stopped, her mouth open in a gasp. 'Oh Kathy, you look beautiful.'

'I was just beginning to get a bit worried. You'll have to be quick getting ready.'

Amy waved her hand in the air nonchalantly. 'Don't worry. I'm all ready apart from putting my dress on. Are you okay? Need any help?'

'It's just my veil, but I was waiting deliberately. I – I was hoping Mam might help me put it on. I think she'd like that. She – she has come, hasn't she?'

'Well – er – yes. She's on her way,' Amy said, as she stepped into her dress and Kathy helped her with the tiny buttons.

'What do you mean "on her way"? Didn't she come with you?'

'No. There wasn't room for both of them in our car, not with the four of us.'

'Both of them?' Kathy was startled. 'You – you don't mean . . . ?'

Amy nodded. 'I do. Your father's come and he's insisting on giving you away. Says he doesn't want the neighbours gossiping about him for refusing to give his daughter away.'

'I see,' Kathy said grimly. 'It's not because he wants to do it either for me or for himself, but because of what others might say.'

'I – suppose so. I'm sorry, Kathy.'

'It's not your fault.'

There were soft footsteps on the stairs and the two girls said no more as Edith came into the room, her arms outstretched to envelop her daughter and tears of happiness in her eyes.

'Oh Mam, I'm so glad you're here.'

'Amy's told you? About your dad?'

Kathy forced a smile. 'Yes. Isn't it great?'

'Ted understands. He says he's pleased 'cos it's only right and proper.'

Kathy nodded. If truth be told, she would rather have had the kindly Ted Robinson leading her up the aisle than her own father. But that secret thought remained unspoken.

Edith drew back and looked at her daughter. 'Darling girl, you look beautiful.'

Jemima's voice drifted up the stairs. 'Edith, Amy – time you were going to the church.'

There was a flurry of activity downstairs and then the house was suddenly quiet. Taking a deep breath as she prepared to face her father, Kathy went carefully down the narrow stairs and into the kitchen.

Her father was standing with his back to the range. They stared at each other for several moments, before Kathy felt obliged to say, 'Thanks for coming, Dad.'

He frowned and muttered. 'I hope you're not going to expect me to pay for any of this. Hiring a car, for heaven's sake. A lot of fuss. And it won't last. You mark my words, it won't last. A man in his position marrying someone like you. Huh!'

'Mr Hammond has lent us his chauffeur for the day. It's not costing us anything.'

'Who's Mr Hammond when he's at home?'

'The owner of the store where I work and where Tony is the manager. Tony's related to him.'

For a moment, Jim Burton's eyes gleamed. 'Wealthy, is he? Is the lad in line to take over some day then? Maybe you've got a bit more sense that I gave you credit for.'

'Mr Hammond senior is Tony's mother's uncle and I think he will always see that Tony has a good job. But no, he's not in line to take over as you put it. Mr Hammond has a son of his own.'

Jim sniffed. 'Huh! I thought as much. I thought you hadn't the sense you were born with.'

There was the sound of the car drawing up outside. Relieved, Kathy said, 'Time to go, Dad.'

They paused in the porch and Amy, smiling from ear to ear, slipped in behind them as the organ music struck up and they began the slow procession up the aisle. The congregation was pathetically small, but Kathy felt a flood of happiness sweep through her. The only people who really mattered to her were all here. Even Morry. Though she knew she could never love him as he deserved to be loved, in the way that he wanted, she was extremely fond of him and the only cloud on her day was the thought that she was hurting him. As she drew level with the end of the pew where he was sitting, she risked a glance at his face.

Morry's eyes were full of tears but he was smiling and he gave a little nod of encouragement. He leant forward and whispered, 'You look wonderful, Kathy. Be happy.'

Those words from Morry meant more to her than anything anyone else could say to her on her wedding day.

A few more steps and she was standing beside Tony. She looked up at him to find him smiling down at her. He looked so handsome in his dark suit that her heart turned over with love for him. She glanced beyond him and saw that James Hammond was standing beside him as his best man. A movement in the pew just behind them caught her eye. Kathy's eyes widened as she saw Tony's father sitting there, and beside him, dressed in black from head to toe, was Beatrice Kendall.

Twenty-Three

Kathy smiled tremulously at Tony, who reached out and squeezed her hand. 'This is it, darling? You ready?'

'Oh, yes,' she breathed, as the vicar moved closer and opened his prayer book. He smiled benignly at the young couple, silently praying that their hopes and dreams would be fulfilled and that their future would not be torn asunder by this dreadful war. He was conducting so many marriages these days, hastily arranged, before the imminent departure of the groom into the armed forces. This, he knew, was another such one.

'Dearly beloved . . .' he began, and Kathy, delirious with happiness, tried to concentrate on what he was saying and on being sure she made the right responses in the right place.

The service went on, and then it came to that moment that all brides and grooms joke about and tease each other. 'Therefore if any man can show any just cause, why they may not lawfully be joined together . . .'

The vicar got no further. From the front pew came a gasp, a moan and then a thud. Everyone turned to see that Beatrice had slumped sideways onto the pew and had only been prevent from rolling on to the floor by George grabbing her. He knelt in front of her.

'Beatty – Beatty!' he hissed in a fierce whisper, but the woman only moaned and put her hand to her chest.

Her eyes closed, her face white, she whispered, 'Oh the pain, the pain. George – my pills.'

Tony turned away from Kathy and knelt beside his father, cradling his mother in his arms, while George scrabbled in her handbag for the box of pills.

A murmuring ran around the small congregation and necks craned to see what was happening. Kathy stood watching the scene. Her heart pounded. Her hands trembled until her bouquet shook and all the happiness slowly drained out of her. But no one was taking any notice of Kathy. All their attention was focused on Beatrice Kendall.

'Dad, we should call an ambulance,' Tony whispered worriedly. 'This is a bad one.'

'Let's see if her pills work first. Just hang on a moment, son.'

'Dad, I'll never forgive myself if . . .'

'Hold on, son, just hold on a minute.'

'Can I help?' the vicar enquired. 'A glass of water, perhaps?'

Tony glanced up, 'Yes, yes, please.'

The vicar laid down his book and hurried away towards the vestry. He returned in a moment with a glass of water, but by now Beatrice was limp in Tony's arms, her eyes closed, her mouth gagging open.

'Dad, she's unconscious. We must call an ambulance.'

George stood up, pausing only a brief moment to look down at his wife before he turned to James Hammond, who was standing close by looking on anxiously. 'James, would you find the nearest telephone box and ring for an ambulance, please?'

James hurried down the aisle and the murmuring amongst the guests grew louder.

'What's up with her?' Jim muttered in Kathy's ear.

Kathy ran her tongue around her dry lips. 'She – she has a bad heart.'

She heard her father's familiar sniff of disapproval. 'Huh! Very convenient, if you ask me.'

For once, Kathy was in full agreement with her father.

There was no way they could continue the service with the groom's mother apparently unconscious in the front pew and waiting for the arrival of an emergency vehicle.

Kathy felt the vicar's light touch on her shoulder. He cleared his throat, obviously embarrassed at what he had to say. 'My dear, I am sorry, but I have another wedding service in an hour. There are so many to fit in these days . . .' His voice trailed away apologetically.

Kathy tried to smile. 'If we could just wait for the ambulance, maybe . . .'

At that moment there was the sound of a clanging bell and a noisy motor drew up outside the church. Two ambulance men hurried in, carrying a stretcher between them.

'Here – down here.' Morry had stepped into the aisle and was pointing towards the front pew. He was directing them towards the sick woman, but his anxious glance was upon Kathy. There was no mistaking that his whole concern was really for her.

Kathy stood motionless, watching while the ambulance men gently lifted a limp and unresponsive Beatrice on to the stretcher. They picked it up and carried her down the aisle and out of the church.

George walked close behind and Tony, without even so much as a glance at his bride, followed him. Halfway down the aisle, George stopped and glanced back.

Kathy saw the surprise on his face as he realized his son was just behind him. He said something, though Kathy could not hear his words, but she saw him gesture towards her. And then she saw Tony shake his head. Anger crossed George's face and he pointed at Kathy and spoke again and this time his voice was raised high enough for Kathy to hear, loud enough for everyone in the church to hear. 'You go back to that lass and carry on.'

Tony hesitated and then turned and hurried back towards her. 'Kathy – darling,' he caught hold of her hands and gripped them tightly. 'I have to go with her. It looks bad. If anything happened, I . . . You do understand, don't you? Wait for me, darling, please. I will come back . . .'

Without even waiting for her answer, he turned and almost ran back down the aisle. He did not even look back at her. Not once.

'Well, this is a find how-do-ya-do, I must say,' Jim Burton growled. 'What happens now, might I ask?'

Kathy had not moved. She was motionless, still staring down the aisle, her eyes fixed on the point where Tony had disappeared from her sight. The truth came at her like a tidal wave, flooding through her, engulfing her, swamping her. It would always be like this. Even though Tony would have to go away, would have to serve his country, and it looked as if even his mother could not prevent that, Kathy could see that there was no future for her within his family. While George might welcome her, he was as helpless against Beatrice as his son.

Dimly, she was aware that two people were moving towards her, coming to stand one on either side of her.

Jemima took her arm and Morry put his arm around her waist.

'Come, my dear, let's go to the vestry and see what the vicar has to say.'

For a moment Kathy gave no sign that she had even heard, but then, slowly, she shook her head.

'No,' she whispered. 'It's no use. There's no future for us. How blind I've been.' With stiff, jerky movements, she began to walk down the aisle.

'Hey, what's going on?' Jim's voice blared, echoing round the church, but Kathy walked on, tears blinding her. Morry hurried after her and caught hold of her arm. 'Kathy . . .'

She pressed her lips together and shook her head, unable now even to speak.

As she emerged from the church door, Morry still at her side, the photographer with his box camera on a tripod called, 'Ah, the happy couple, hold it there. Let's get a nice picture of you.'

Kathy continued to walk towards him.

'I say, wait a minute—'

She paused beside him, stared at him for a moment and then flung her bouquet at him. 'There's been no wedding. Nor will there be. You'd better go home.'

'But – but – Mr Hammond—'

Kathy stalked towards the car that had brought her to the church.

'You'd better go into the church. They'll explain,' she heard Morry tell him as she climbed into the car. Then he hurried after her and climbed in beside her.

'Morry, please. I want to be on my own.'

'You probably do, but for once, Kathy, I'm taking no notice of you. I'm not leaving you on your own.'

'Oh Morry, I've been such a fool.' Tears were close now. She fought valiantly to stem the flow, but failed. Morry mopped her face with a clean, white handkerchief. 'No, you haven't. It's a difficult situation,' he said, with gentle reason. 'Jemima's told me what Mrs Kendall's like, but really, you can't blame Tony. If it was my mother, I'd be just the same. I know I would.'

Kathy tried to smile, but it was only a wry twist of her mouth. 'You're very understanding – and forgiving. I don't think I can be that generous. Not – not today.'

'I know. It's dreadful for you. It's your bad luck that the vicar is so hard pressed that he can't just give us an hour or two to see what happens. Perhaps, when they've got her settled in hospital, Tony will come back and the vicar can perform the ceremony later. I know your special day is in tatters and none of us can say whether Mrs Kendall's illness is real or – or induced at just the right moment to halt the ceremony.'

'It's that all right,' Kathy said bitterly. 'I know it is.'

'But can you really, in your heart of hearts, Kathy, blame Tony? Can you really expect any man with any decency to turn his back on his mother, to ignore her cries for help? You see, he can't be sure, can he? He can never be sure. If she's really ill – if she were to die even, he'd have to live with that for the rest of his life. He'd never be able to forgive himself. Or – you.'

'It'll always be like this, won't it?'

'Maybe not. Perhaps when he's been away from home in the forces – and that's nobody's fault – things might change. If she can't deal with that either, then that's not Tony's fault or yours. But maybe when the break with him has been forced upon her, there's just a chance that things might be different.'

Kathy lifted her tear-streaked face and looked into Morry's round, open and honest face. 'Oh Morry – ' she bent her head against his shoulder and wept bitterly – 'Oh Morry, why couldn't I have loved you?'

Morry whispered huskily, 'I only wish you could, Kathy.

The house was deathly still as Morry opened the back door with the key that Jemima had slipped to him. Kathy got stiffly out of the car and walked down the passageway towards the back gate, ignoring the curious glances of the neighbours. Time enough for the gossip to spread, she thought.

As they stepped inside, Kathy turned to him. 'Thank you for your kindness, Morry. I'll never be able to thank you enough, but now I'm going upstairs. I need to be alone.'

Understanding as ever, Morry nodded. 'Of course you do. I'll stop anyone coming up.'

'Thank you. Just one more thing, could you undo the buttons down the back of my dress.'

She turned away from him, her back towards him.

'Oh Kathy, I . . .'

'Please, Morry, just do it.'

She felt his fingers trembling as he struggled with the tiny buttons.

'That's fine,' she said, pulling away when she felt that he had undone enough for her to slip out of the garment. 'Thanks.' Without a backward glance, she headed for the stairs and the sanctuary of her bedroom.

A little later she heard voices downstairs and knew that the others had returned from the church. Then she heard her father's raised voice.

'Get out of my way, Maurice. I've a right to see my own daughter.'

There were sounds of a scuffle and then of heavy footsteps on the stairs. Kathy closed her eyes briefly and groaned. This was what she had dreaded most.

'Jim, please, leave her alone . . .' Edith's voice drifted up the stairs.

'Shut up, woman, and leave this to me.'

The door opened and he was in the room, slamming it behind him with such force that it bounced open again. But Jim was too intent upon shaking his fist at his daughter to notice.

'You want horsewhipping, girl. Bringing such shame on me like this. Well, I'll give you one last chance. You come home now with us and you settle down and wed Maurice and we'll say no more about it. Though there's plenty I could say. Plenty.'

And you will, Kathy thought bitterly. I shall have all this dragged up and thrown at me for the rest of my life – or rather for the rest of yours. She shook her head. Her voice was husky, but there was a note of resolution in her tone. 'No, Dad, I will not marry Morry. I wouldn't do that to him.'

'Huh!' Jim was scathing. 'So I was right. You are expecting that whippersnapper's bastard, are you? Well, Maurice will still marry you. He's besotted with you. God only knows why, but he is. I'll pay him, if I have to.'

Wearily, Kathy said, 'Dad, for the last time, I'm not pregnant.'

'So what's the problem?'

'I don't love Morry.'

'What's that got to do with anything? I've never loved your mother.'

Slowly Kathy raised her head to look at him. 'No,' she said quietly. 'And that's the tragedy of both your lives.'

They stared at each other until quick, light footsteps sounded on the stairs and the bedroom door was flung wide.

'Jim Burton,' Jemima said coldly, 'Leave my house this instant. We've heard every word of your conversation. *Every* word. Kathy stays with me. You're a stupid man, Jim. You don't realize what a fine girl you've got.'

'Fine? Fine, you say, when she's brought all this shame on me.'

'Shame? What shame?'

Jim's lips curled. 'Well, you wouldn't know anything about that, Jemima Robinson, would you? You're nowt but a dried-up old spinster 'cos none of us village lads were good enough for you, were we? Turned your nose up at us, didn't ya? Thought you could do better for yarsen in the city, but it dun't look to have got you far.'

'Get out!' Jemima, her eyes sparking with fiery anger, spat at him. 'Get out of my house.'

'I'm going.' He turned towards Kathy one last time and pointed his finger at her. 'But if I do, don't you ever, ever come knocking on my door again. From this day forward, you're no daughter of mine.'

It wasn't his threat, it wasn't the fact that she might never see him – or her mother – again, that was Kathy's undoing. It was his use of the words from the marriage ceremony that tore at her heart and caused her face to crumple and the tears to flow again.

'Aye, you can cry, girl. But you've brought all this on yourself. You've only yourself to blame.'

With that, he turned and stamped out of the room and down the stairs. The last words she heard were, 'Come along, Edith, we're going home, and if you ever have anything to do with that girl again, I'll throw you out an' all.'

The back door slammed and there was a stunned silence throughout the whole house.

Twenty-Four

'Well, I never did hear the like.' Kathy heard Betty's voice drift up the stairs. They were still all sitting down there in Jemima's front room, drinking tea and talking over the shattering events of the day. Kathy stayed alone in her room. She couldn't face the kindly faces of the Robinsons and their sympathy. Only Jemima's brisk attitude was bearable at the moment.

She was best left alone and they all seemed to sense this.

'What's going to happen, d'you think? Will they get married, quiet like, another day?' Ted's booming voice asked.

'I really don't know,' Jemima said in a matter-of-fact way. 'It's up to them. They're best left to sort it out between themselves.'

'I doubt very much whether that young man will ever be able to do that.' Ted sighed. 'It's a real shame. He seems like a nice young feller. A bit weak, mebbe, where his mother's concerned, but who are we to judge?'

'Precisely,' Jemima said. 'More tea, Betty?'

'No thank you, Jemima cariad. We'd best be on our way. We want to be home before dark. Before the blackout. Oh dear me, and to think that poor Tony will be gone on Monday. I don't think there's going to be much time for them to sort anything out, do you?'

'Sadly, no, I don't. His mother will do her best to keep him at her bedside until Monday morning. Still, don't you worry about Kathy. I'll look after her.'

'Shall we say goodbye to her?'

'Best not. I'll tell her later. And I'm sure she knows she has your support.'

'Give her our love and tell her there's always a home for her with us – whatever happens.' This last was from Ted, and Kathy's tears flowed afresh at the kindness in his tone.

Why, oh why, couldn't she have fallen in love with Morry? Life would have been so simple then. But she knew she could never marry him. He was a dear, dear friend but – for her – nothing more.

She could hear Amy's tearful voice. 'Tell her I'll write, because I don't know when I might have to – to go.'

'I will, dear. Now, chin up, you'll soon be a Wren. Wrens don't cry.'

'This one does.' Amy tried to laugh through her tears.

There was much hugging and kissing and calls of 'goodbyes' before Kathy heard them all clattering down the passage and out into the street. Car doors banged, the engine started and they were gone.

Kathy heard Jemima moving about below, heard the clatter of pots and cutlery, and knew she should go down and help. But she couldn't move. She remained sitting motionless on the edge of the bed, still in her wedding dress with the buttons undone down the back, her fingers knotted so tightly together that the knuckles were white.

Footsteps on the stairs and Jemima came in bearing

a cup of hot, strong tea. 'Now, my dear, dry your tears and drink this. Then we must think what to do.'

She sat down on a spindly-legged bedroom chair facing Kathy. 'Come along, drink it up.'

Kathy obeyed meekly and suddenly found she was very thirsty.

'Would you like me to trot along and see the vicar? Just to ask if there's a chance he can fit the ceremony in some time tomorrow?'

Kathy shook her head. 'It's no use unless we hear from Tony.'

'I take your point.' She was silent a moment before adding, 'Perhaps we'll hear something from him this evening.'

Kathy raised her head and looked directly into Jemima's honest eyes. 'Do – do you think her attack was genuine?'

'No – I don't. It was too contrived. Oh, I don't say she couldn't have suffered some sort of attack during the service with the stress of it all, but to happen just at that very moment, just when he was asking the congregation that all important question. It was straight out of *Jane Eyre*, now wasn't it? So melodramatic as to be unbelievable.'

'I know,' Kathy agreed sadly. 'But we can't prove it. No one can. And Mr Kendall and Tony just – just daren't take the risk of calling her bluff.'

'Well, if the worst comes to the worst, we'll just have to arrange a very quiet ceremony when Tony gets his first leave.'

Kathy set her cup down carefully on the bedside table. 'But the same thing will happen. It'll go on happening. She said – she told me that she'd see to it that he never married me. I didn't believe she could do it, but she has. She's managed it.'

'You might find that this enforced separation – Tony having to go into the armed forces – will be the making of him. I've never said a word against him. He's a nice young man but, between you and me, maybe that's his main fault. He's *too* nice. He's not strong enough to stand up to his mother, but now he's going to be forced to make the break. It's being done for him and it might turn out to be a blessing in disguise. You might well find that when he comes home on leave he'll be a very different person.'

'I – I don't really want him to be any different. I love him as he is . . .' She smiled sadly as she added wryly, 'Despite his mother.'

'Well, in that case, my dear, you'll never be free of her and you can take it from me that she'll never stop trying to prevent your marriage. And, even if you succeed in that, she'll never stop interfering in your lives. If Tony survives the war—'

Kathy covered her face with her hands and cried out, 'Oh no, don't say that, Aunt Jemima. Please, don't even think it.'

'It's a possibility that has to be faced, my dear,' she said quietly, and added in a whisper, 'And I should know.'

Guiltily, Kathy raised her face. Here she was selfishly taking all the generous support Jemima had to give when the poor woman had spent a lifetime of loneliness. Somehow, she had lost the love of her life. Kathy was sure of it.

'I'm being very selfish and self-centred, Aunt Jemima. I'm sorry.'

'Oh, phooey.' Jemima flapped her hand. 'We've just got to think what's best to be done now.'

There was nothing to be done. Tony didn't come to Jemima's house that evening or the next morning. After breakfast, of which Kathy ate hardly anything and even Jemima ate only a little cereal instead of her usual bowlful followed by toast and marmalade, they washed up the pots together and then sat in the kitchen, waiting. As the clock crawled to half past eleven, Jemima jumped up from her chair.

'I can't abide all this sitting about. Shall we walk up to the hospital and make enquiries? At least we might find out if there's any chance he . . .'

Kathy shook her head. 'He'll come when he can. It – it must have been more serious than we thought. I feel so guilty now for having thought badly of her.'

'Huh!' Jemima was not yet ready to be so understanding. 'Either that or she's keeping up a very good act. She should have been on the stage, that one.' She paused and paced up and down the small space for a moment. As if she could not bear to sit, she muttered, 'Then I'll walk along to the church and see if . . .'

'It's no good,' Kathy said, sounding far more reasonable than she was actually feeling inside.

'Come on, girl, don't give up. Not now. At least if we could get you married today . . .'

Again, Kathy shook her head. 'That's not how I want it to be. Not all rushed and – and underhand as if – as if . . .'

'As if you've *got* to get married?'

Kathy lowered her gaze and said nothing. Jemima

sank into her chair and leant her head back, closing her eyes. 'Yes,' she said flatly, 'you're right. I'm pushing you too hard. It's just – it's just . . . Oh, I'd so like to have seen you married before he has to go away. It'd give you both something to hang on to. It's not going to be easy for either of you. He's going to have to face God only knows what and it's going to be hard for you, trying to carry on as normal when nothing's ever going to be "normal" again. Oh why, why, can't those in power see the futility, the stupid, stupid waste of it all?'

The clock ticked steadily on as the two women fell silent again and waited once more.

He came just after five o'clock, looking white and dishevelled. He was still wearing his wedding suit; dark shadows ringed his eyes and anxiety clouded their brightness.

'They're keeping her in for observation.'

'Where is she?'

'At the moment, she's in the County but we're trying to get her moved to the Bromhead Nursing Home.'

Jemima sniffed. 'I should leave her where she is. It's a good hospital.'

'Well, yes, I know, but she likes her own room. She likes her privacy.' He turned to Kathy and took her hands. 'Darling, I am so sorry about what happened. I couldn't help it. You do believe that, don't you?'

Before Kathy could answer, Jemima said, 'Well, now you're here, I – er – have to go out. I must see Mabel Spencer. WVS business, you know. We've – um – a lot to discuss.'

They both knew she was deliberately leaving them alone together. Within minutes she had donned her hat and coat. 'Just feed Taffy for me at six o'clock. You know how he likes his routine.' And then she was gone.

'Let's go into the front room. Jemima insisted on lighting a fire in there – in case you came.'

'In *case* I came? Darling, surely you knew I would come as soon as I could?'

'Well, yes, of course I did,' Kathy said, trying to sound as if she meant it. 'But I didn't know when that would be, did I? And – and you have to catch the early train tomorrow morning, don't you?'

'Yes, I do. And there's nothing I can do about that. I could be on a charge if I'm late reporting.'

They sat, huddled together, on the sofa. 'We should be on our honeymoon now. You should have been Mrs Kendall for a whole twenty-eight hours. Darling, I am so, so sorry.'

'I know,' Kathy said simply. She twisted in his arms to look up at him. 'But – but we could still have our honeymoon. At least, a bit of it. We—' She blushed as she said shyly, 'We could go upstairs. Aunt Jemima won't be back for ages . . .'

Their lovemaking was bitter sweet, each of them knowing deep in their hearts that this night together might be all they ever had, and afterwards they lay in each other's arms. While Tony slept, Kathy wept silently against his shoulder.

Only when Taffy's meowing outside the bedroom door reminded her that she had forgotten to feed him did they rouse, dress and go downstairs.

'I don't suppose she'd mind if you stayed. I – I think she'd understand.'

Tony shook his head sadly. 'I have to go back to the hospital before visiting ends. And then – then I have to pack.'

'Of course,' Kathy said huskily. She was about to offer to help him but she bit back the words, realizing that his father, too, deserved a little time with his son before . . . She closed her eyes and dared not think about what was to happen in the morning.

Just before he left, Tony handed her a long, thin box. 'I was going to give you this on our wedding night. I still want you to have it.'

Kathy opened the box and gasped when she saw the single string of pearls nestling against the dark blue velvet lining. 'Oh darling, it's beautiful. Thank you.'

As she kissed him, he murmured, 'Wear them always for me, Kathy. And remember, whatever happens I really do love you.'

Twenty-Five

'How did it all go then?'

Stella was excited the next morning. She had so wanted to attend the wedding, but with Kathy, Miss Robinson, Tony and even Mr James Hammond all off for the day, the store had been severely understaffed.

'It didn't,' Kathy said shortly. Out of the corner of her eye, she saw Muriel Curtis moving closer.

Stella gasped. 'What do you mean "it didn't"? Do – do you mean he jilted you? Left you standing at the altar?'

'Not exactly.'

'What then?'

Kathy raised her eyes and glanced around. There were no customers yet, so she moved towards Muriel with Stella following in her wake. 'I might as well tell you together. The wedding didn't happen,' she said bluntly.

Kathy watched Muriel's face closely, half expecting to see relief, perhaps even triumph, on the other woman's face. But to Muriel's credit, there was neither. Instead, she frowned and asked in a concerned tone, 'Why? What happened? Oh . . .' She sighed heavily and closed her eyes briefly, saying flatly, 'Don't tell me. His mother was taken ill.'

'How . . . ?' Kathy began and then stopped. She'd been about to say: How did you know? But of course she realized exactly how Muriel knew. Instead, she said flatly, 'Yes. During the service. Just at the moment when the vicar asks the congregation about "just cause" and all that.'

'Huh! I call that perfect timing,' Muriel said sarcastically. 'I'm so sorry, Kathy, truly I am. I – just want to see him happy. You know that. And if you were the one to do it, then I wished you well.' She gave a wry smile. 'I tried as hard as I knew how to hate you when you first started going out with Tony. But I couldn't. And I'd have liked nothing better – now – than to see the two of you happy together.'

'You're very generous,' Kathy said huskily. 'But it doesn't look as if it's going to happen now. He – he left this morning on the early train. And goodness knows when he'll get leave.'

'He should get a few days when he's completed his basic training and been posted,' Stella said. 'My cousin did. Mind you, that was the Army. Mr Kendall's joined the RAF, hasn't he?'

Kathy nodded, not trusting herself to speak for the huge lump that felt as if it was growing in her throat.

'Work, that's the best thing for you,' Muriel said, almost adopting Jemima's brisk manner. 'And here's the first customer of the day. Forward, Miss Burton, if you please,' she added with a smile. As Kathy moved towards the lady entering the department, Muriel whispered to Stella, 'As we don't work on commission here, Stella, perhaps you'd let Kathy take most of the customers today. Keep her busy.'

'Of course, Miss Curtis. Poor thing. What a dreadful thing to happen.'

'Yes,' Muriel murmured. 'Isn't it?'

*

With the help of her colleagues' thoughtful actions, Kathy was kept busy all day and the time passed quickly. About mid-morning, Jemima walked through the department. It was not unusual, so Kathy thought nothing of it. It was also quite normal for the supervisor to stop and speak to the head of department, so seeing Jemima and Muriel with their heads together in conversation caused Kathy no discomfort. Though, perhaps, if she had thought for a moment, she might have guessed that this morning their exchange was not wholly about stock and displays.

'I expect she's told you,' Jemima began, and Muriel nodded.

'I'm so sorry.'

'That's generous of you, in the circumstances.'

'What happened to me was nothing to do with Kathy and I'm sorry to see nothing has changed. That woman . . .'

'Precisely, but sadly there's nothing any of us can do. If I had thought for a moment that interference from me would have helped, I'd have been up at their house in a trice. But I knew such an action would only make matters worse.' Jemima pulled a wry grimace. 'If they could get much worse. He's gone this morning, you know.'

'Yes.' Now Muriel's voice was husky. She still loved him and, even though now she was seeing him with someone else, she was trying to move on with her own life. And there would always be a place in her heart for her lost love. A part of her that would be devastated if he should be hurt or – God forbid – killed. 'I'm trying to keep her busy. Trying to keep her mind off things.'

'Good. Thank you, Muriel.' Jemima moved on, and

without even a glance towards Kathy, who was serving a customer, she left the department.

Evenings were going to be the most difficult. The long hours that stretched into an even longer night. Hours of darkness when Kathy lay staring into nothingness, wondering what might have been and what, if anything, could be done. Once more, Jemima attempted to come to the rescue.

Kathy arrived home before her that first evening and was feeding Taffy, still apologetic that she had neglected him the previous night, though, as he arched his back under her gentle stroke, she believed herself forgiven. He wound himself around her legs as she prepared his dinner and miaowed and purred in ecstatic anticipation.

As she placed his dish on the floor, she heard Jemima's quick tripping steps down the passageway.

'I've just been talking to Ron Spencer,' Jemima began, almost before she'd stepped inside and closed the door. 'He wants to know if you're going to the choral society on Thursday evening. Evidently they're trying to get a special concert together for the war effort. In fact, he'll probably ask you if you can spare any more time. I told him I'd ask you.'

Kathy hid her smile. She wondered just which of them it really had been who had suggested trying to fill Kathy's empty evenings. Touched by their kindness, Kathy said at once, 'Yes, of course I'd be glad to help. I'd been thinking of offering to help you at the WVS too, but I do want to go and see Mr Kendall. Just – just to see if I can help him at all. He'll miss Tony's help with – with . . .'

'He certainly will and I'm sure he'll welcome you with open arms. But what *she* will do is another matter.'

Kathy climbed the hill to the Kendalls' house the very next evening, but no one answered her knock. She tried to squint through the blackout curtains to see if anyone was in, but the whole house appeared empty.

Perhaps Mrs Kendall was still in hospital and George was visiting her or was still at work on the evening shift. Kathy turned away and retraced her steps. As she turned into the side street, she saw Ron wheeling his bicycle up the slope towards her.

'Hello, love. I'm just on my way to the school now. Are you going to join us?' His eyes showed his concern for her, but he made no mention of her disastrous wedding day. For that, she was grateful.

Kathy took a deep breath and forced a smile. 'Why? Is there a practice tonight? It's only Tuesday.'

'Not exactly. A few of us are meeting to discuss how we can help the war effort. Some chap in London has set up an entertainments' unit of civilian artistes who are willing to travel anywhere to entertain not only troops but factory workers, shipyards, hospitals – in fact, any group of workers involved in the war. Some of us in the society would like to get involved.'

'I see. But – but you said travelling. I mean – I have a job, and – and I want to be here whenever Tony comes home on leave.'

Ron patted her shoulder understandingly. He had heard all about Saturday's fiasco and his heart went out to this girl. 'Of course you do, my dear. But – tell you what – come along with me now and at least hear what's involved. We're none of us too sure ourselves yet, but we've got some bod coming from London to talk to us tonight. We might all know a bit more by the end of the evening about exactly what they're looking for a group like us to do. A lot of our members have day jobs, but they'd be able to travel reasonable distances in the evenings and at weekends. Besides, some employers can be surprisingly helpful if they know it's for the war effort.'

Kathy shrugged. 'Well, I've nothing else to do. Why not?'

'That's the ticket.'

The evening was a merry one. The 'bod' from London was something of an entertainer himself, and his talk to the company was littered with jokes and anecdotes that had the members of the normally rather staid choral society rocking with laughter. There was also a young man there, a stalwart of the Lincoln Operatic & Dramatic Society, Martin Montgomery. He was tall and broad with fair hair. His chin was firm and square and he had the cheekiest grin and the most mischievous blue eyes that Kathy had ever seen.

He doubled as a stage manager for the local society, he told them, but his real love was being on stage. He then proceeded to demonstrate with monologues and a comedy routine that had the audience in stitches. Between them, the two visitors gave the choral society much to think about.

As they walked home together through the blackout, Ron Spencer pushing his bicycle so that he could walk alongside her, they were both still chuckling.

'I was rather impressed with his idea of forming a

concert party that was more than just singing,' Ron remarked.

'Yes. The man from London – what was his name again?'

'Sid Warren, I think. Yes, that's it, because it made me think of rabbits.' Ron chuckled. 'I wonder if he includes producing a rabbit out of a top hat in his act.'

'He said the show should include a comedian, a juggler and a speciality act. What's that, exactly?'

'It's an act that's a bit out of the ordinary. Like a hypnotist. That sort of thing. And, of course, there should be pretty dancing girls. Are you any good at dancing, Kathy, because you're certainly pretty enough?'

Kathy laughed. 'I've got two left feet. No, I'll stick to singing, if you don't mind.'

'Fair enough. The dancing world's loss is the singing world's gain. But I'll keep in touch, Kathy. I still think you might be able to help, even if you can't travel far. Goodnight, love,' he said as they reached the passageway leading to his back gate.

''Night, Mr Spencer.'

'So, how did it go?' Jemima asked as soon as Kathy was in the house.

'It didn't,' she said, referring to her attempt to visit Mr and Mrs Kendall, but then she went on to tell Jemima about the choral society's meeting. 'They're disbanding the usual meetings and putting all their efforts into entertaining war workers and such.'

'That sounds wonderful. D'you know, I've never even heard you sing, dear. Solo, that is, only beside me in church. I really should have come along to one of the society's concerts. How remiss of me.'

Kathy laughed. 'You wouldn't have heard me among

all the rest there either. Mind you, I did do a bit of a solo one evening.'

'Well, if you decide to join their entertainment party I'll certainly come and hear you if you're performing locally. Be sure to tell me.'

'I will,' Kathy promised, but now her mind was drifting back to Tony, wondering where he was and what he was doing. And if he was thinking of her.

The days dragged on. Ten dates later, a letter arrived from Tony, reassuring Kathy of his love and promising her that they would be married during his leave.

Basic training's going well, he wrote, *and I'm thrilled because I've been selected to train as a fighter pilot. I'll likely be posted down south though, as that's where all the fighter action is likely to be . . .*

His letter was like one from an excited schoolboy who has been sent away to boarding school for the first time and finds, to his astonishment, that he loves it. To Kathy's surprise, Tony didn't even mention his mother. She couldn't help wondering what his letters home were like.

The next Sunday, she went again to the Kendalls' house and this time George opened the back door to her knock.

'Hello, lass. You're a sight for sore eyes and no mistake. Come away in.'

'How's Mrs Kendall?' Kathy asked as she stepped over the threshold. 'Is she home from the hospital?'

'Oh yes. They only kept her in three days. Just until after Tony had gone.'

So, Kathy thought, the woman had been in when she had called the previous week.

George's face fell into lines of sadness. 'I told them what had happened, like, and how he had been called up and was leaving early on the Monday morning. They said they'd keep her and see how she coped with him leaving.'

'And did she?'

'What?'

'Cope?'

George shrugged. 'Case of having to, love, isn't it? But she's very down. Tony's very good, though. He writes to her every other day or so.' He pulled a wry expression. 'Mind you, I'm not sure if it helps or not. She gets so upset when a letter comes, yet I know she'd fret if he didn't write at all.'

Kathy swallowed her resentment. Tony had only written to her once in the two weeks since he'd been gone. But instead she smiled brightly at George Kendall and asked, 'Is there anything I can do to help you?'

He gazed at her for a moment and then shook his head as if he couldn't believe what he was hearing. 'You are a remarkable lass, you know. Not many'd come here and offer to help after what happened last week. I just wish . . .' His voice broke and he stopped, as if unable to go on.

Kathy touched his arm. 'I know,' she said gently. 'I know you wish the marriage had taken place.' She took a deep breath and smiled tremulously. 'But it can't be helped now. Maybe when Tony gets leave, well, we'll have to see.'

'Just do it, lass. Next time, don't tell anyone except p'raps Miss Robinson. Just slip away, the two of you, and do it.'

Kathy smiled sadly. 'Yes, I think you're right.' Then she took a deep breath and said, with new determination, 'Now, what can I do?'

For the next two hours, Kathy helped George cook a meal. Then she cleaned the kitchen, ending up by washing the red tiled floor. Just as she was finishing, she glanced up to see a pair of feet standing just in front of her. Feet encased in women's shoes. Kathy held her breath as, slowly, her gaze travelled up and up, stopping eventually when she met the hostile eyes of Beatrice Kendall.

'And what, may I ask, are *you* doing here?'

Kathy scrambled to her feet and dropped the floorcloth into the bucket of soapy hot water. 'Helping out.' She smiled brightly. 'I thought Mr Kendall could do with a hand now Tony's not here to help.'

Beatrice put her hand to her chest and staggered to one side, slumping against the table. 'Oh, you cruel, heartless girl,' she gasped. 'How could you say such a thing to me?'

Kathy spread her hands helplessly. 'What have I said wrong? I'm only stating the obvious.'

Tears trickled down Beatrice's face. 'But to remind me so callously.'

Kathy said quietly, 'I wouldn't have thought you needed reminding. I certainly don't. Look, Mrs Kendall, why can't we be friends? I'd like to help you. Help your husband care for you . . .'

'Friends?' the woman shrieked. 'Friends, you say, when you're trying to steal my son away from me. My only child, who's everything in the world to me. If I lose him, I don't want to live any more.'

'But don't you see – can't you see – you'd be gaining

a daughter? I don't want to take him away from you. I'd never dream of doing any such thing.'

'You already have. I've hardly seen him these last few weeks. These precious last few weeks. What if he never comes back? What if he gets killed . . . ?' Her voice rose hysterically.

Kathy felt the colour drain from her face. 'Don't say that! Don't even think it!'

George came hurrying into the room. 'Oh, Beatty, what are you doing in here?' Beatrice leant against her husband. 'Send her away, George. I don't want her here. She reminds me . . .'

'Come along, dear, let's get you settled back on the couch and then we'll talk about it.'

While George half carried his wife back to the front room, Kathy emptied the bucket of dirty water down the drain in the back yard and replaced it in the wash-house. Returning to the kitchen, she washed her hands at the now sparkling white sink and took down her coat from the peg. She stood, listening a moment and then, when there was no sound of George returning, she let herself quietly out of the back door.

The formation of the concert party was going well, and by the end of March Ron Spencer had rounded up enough people to make up a variety show.

'I'm just short of a soprano,' Mr Spencer said, sitting down in Jemima's kitchen and picking up the cup of tea she had offered him. He looked across at Kathy. 'Won't you reconsider, Kathy? You're perfect.'

'But you're going to be travelling all round the country, aren't you?'

'Well, I have to admit, that's the idea now. We've found enough folk who are free for one reason or another. One or two are even prepared to leave their jobs. They're trying to make their way into the entertainment world and they see this as an ideal opportunity to get themselves known. And we've got official backing from ENSA and we're even going to be paid for our efforts. There's no stopping us now. We can go anywhere we're wanted.'

'I could see if Mr James would keep your job open for you, dear,' Jemima put in. 'He's anxious to do whatever he can to help with the war effort and, to tell you the truth, we don't need so many staff nowadays. Sales are dropping alarmingly.' There was silence between the three of them. They all knew that many of the items that the store sold could be classed as luxury items. 'It's a case of "make do and mend" now. Mr James is seriously looking at what else they can stock. Things that people really need and want.'

'Yes, I'm afraid a lot of things are going to change.' Ron glanced again at Kathy. 'So, what d'you say?'

Kathy ran her tongue around dry lips. 'I – I'll think about it,' she murmured, avoiding his gaze. She would have loved nothing better than to have said 'yes' there and then. But there was another worry niggling at her mind now. A worry that gripped her afresh each morning as she leant over the bowl in her bedroom and retched.

Twenty-Six

'You're pregnant, aren't you?' Jemima said bluntly as, for the fourth morning in a row, Kathy pushed aside the untouched bowl of cereal.

Kathy hung her head, unable to meet Jemima's eyes. Miserably, she whispered, 'I think I must be.' She'd managed to hide the morning sickness for a month. At first she'd believed it was just because she was so devastated by her ruined wedding day. Then, as the days went on and there was only one letter from Tony, her misery had deepened. But now, she had to admit, the sickness was happening far too regularly to be just that. The truth had to be faced. How gleeful her father would be, she thought bitterly, that what he had accused her of was now a fact.

Jemima sighed heavily and lowered herself into the chair on the opposite side of the table. It was Sunday morning, so there was no need to rush. 'So, what are you going to do about it?'

Kathy's head snapped up. 'I'm not going to get rid of it, if that's what you're thinking.'

Jemima shook her head sadly. 'Kathy, how can you even think that I could suggest such a thing?'

Kathy hung her head again. 'I'm sorry,' she muttered. 'I – I'm not thinking straight.'

'I know, I know,' Jemima whispered. There was a

pause before she added, 'So, what are we going to do about it?'

'We?' Kathy's voice was high-pitched. 'Don't you mean me? What am I going to do about it? This is my problem. I don't want to bring shame on you. I'll – I'll think of something.' Her voice trailed away, because she had no idea at this moment what that 'something' might be.

There was a long silence in the room before Jemima said softly. 'Kathy, my dear, I'm going to tell you something now that will probably shock you. I'm sure most people – including you – view me as a dried-up old spinster who has never known a man, who has never – ' her lower lip trembled for an instant – 'has never known love and passion. But you'd be wrong. Quite wrong. You see, during the last war – rather like you – I wanted to get away from the farm. I wanted to do my bit, so I joined up to be a nurse. A VAD nurse. I even went to France.' Now her eyes took on a dreamy expression, but there was sadness there too. 'I saw some terrible sights, Kathy. Sights no young girl should ever see, and death and suffering that no young man should ever know. That's why I was so upset when this war started. You see, the very people who should know better have let it all happen again.'

She paused and was pensive for a few moments. 'I met someone out there, Kathy. An officer. And we fell in love.'

Kathy was silent. She didn't want to break the spell. Besides, she didn't really know what to say.

'Of course, such – such liaisons were frowned upon. He could have been in serious trouble and so could I, but we didn't care. We were in love and we lived for the moment. We had to, because we didn't know if we had a future. Either of us.'

Now Kathy could guess what had happened. At least, part of it. 'Was he – was he killed?'

Jemima nodded. Her voice was flat and emotionless as she went on. 'I came home. I – had to. I was pregnant.'

Kathy gasped. She had not expected this. 'But – I mean – what . . . ?' She fell silent. Now she really was lost for words.

Jemima looked up with a half smile. 'Can't you guess?'

Kathy stared at her. Conflicting thoughts were whirling around her head. What was she supposed to guess? That the baby had died? That it had been adopted? What? Slowly she shook her head.

'I had a baby boy,' Jemima whispered, as if trying to give her a clue.

Kathy was still puzzled.

'When I came home my father was so angry I thought for a moment he was actually going to kill me.'

Suddenly, Kathy remembered the exchange of glances, the strange conversation between Jemima and her sister-in-law, Betty Robinson. She had thought it odd at the time but had never dreamed it could have such significance.

Jemima paused only briefly and then continued. 'Ted never went to the war. His work was on the land, and just about the time I came home he and Betty were about to get married. They took my baby and brought him up as their own.'

Kathy's mouth dropped open. 'Morry?' she breathed. 'Morry is your son?'

Jemima's smile flickered briefly as she said, 'Yes, he is. And I don't regret his birth for one minute. Not one minute, Kathy. He's all I have left of Charlie.' Then her smile faded, to be replaced by a haunted look of anticipated anguish. 'But now? Who knows? Maybe I'm going to lose him too.'

Kathy moved forward and took her hands. 'Oh no. Morry won't have to go. He's a farmer. He won't *have* to go.' She paused and, as if the doubt had pervaded her own mind, added, 'Will he?'

Jemima sighed. 'Who knows? Who can guess what regulations they'll bring in? But, of course, he may – feel it's his duty to go. He may volunteer.'

'Does – does Morry know? I mean – that he's your—?'

'Oh yes. And Amy too.'

'*Amy* knew?' Kathy burst out before she could stop herself. Chatterbox Amy, who couldn't keep a secret for love nor money, had never breathed a word, never even hinted at such a family skeleton.

Jemima smiled fondly. 'Yes, even Amy has kept my secret. And I'm asking you to do the same now. There was no point in hiding such a thing – at least not from the members of my family. And we all agreed that Maurice should always be told the truth, though I'm not sure about the neighbours.' She cast a comical look at Kathy. 'I'm sure the gossip was that Ted and Betty had had a shotgun wedding.' She laughed wryly. 'I don't expect your father would have been so keen to marry you off to Maurice if he'd known he was my bastard son.'

Kathy flinched. 'Don't call Morry that. It sounds awful.'

'It's what he is, but thanks to Ted and Betty he's

never had to suffer because of it. But remember, Kathy, I have trusted my secret with you. Not a word to a soul.'

Kathy shook her head and said huskily, 'Of course not.'

'And so you see now why I say, "What are *we* going to do about it?"'

Now Kathy raised her head slowly, tears in her eyes. She had fully expected to be thrown out of the house, to be cast out in disgrace with no home, no family and nowhere to go. She had, like all the girls at work she was sure, viewed Jemima Robinson as a strait-laced spinster who had perhaps never known romance, let alone borne a child. The news came as a shock to Kathy, yet now she understood why Jemima was not turning her back on her and why she was offering, so generously, to stand by her and help her.

But there was one difference between their plights. A huge difference. Jemima's lover had been killed before he even knew about the child. There was nothing he could have done even if he had wanted to. But the father of Kathy's child was still alive.

As if reading her thoughts, Jemima said, 'Can we get in touch with Tony? Perhaps he can get compassionate leave and you can be married.'

'No!' The word came out like the crack of a whiplash. Then more quietly, Kathy said, 'I – I don't want him to know.'

'Don't want him to know?' Jemima repeated. 'Why ever not?'

'Because I don't want anyone saying he married me because he *had* to.'

'But – but, that's not the case.' Jemima was mystified. 'You were going to be married.' She gave a snort of disgust as she remembered Beatrice's antics. 'You almost were.'

'I know,' Kathy said flatly, 'but it's different now.'

'Why is it different? Tony loves you. He'll probably be thrilled about the baby anyway.'

'He – he's only written to me once.'

'Oh, phooey! The poor man's probably exhausted. Basic training must be pretty tough.'

Kathy met Jemima's open gaze. 'But he's written every other day to his mother.'

Jemima raised her eyebrows. 'How do you know?'

'Because his dad told me.'

'I see,' Jemima said thoughtfully, then added, 'Well, I expect he's trying to keep her happy.'

'Mm.' Kathy was not convinced.

There was a silence. 'Let's get ready and go to St Mary's. Aren't you singing there today with the choral society before they disband?'

Kathy sighed. 'Yes. And I'm supposed to be singing a solo. But I don't know if I'll manage it.'

Jemima forced a smile. She'd looked forward to hearing the girl sing, but the occasion would be spoilt by the dark cloud hanging over their heads.

'Courage, my dear. Now's the time to show your mettle. Put a brave face on. Hold your head up high. Now, you go and get ready while I clear away.'

Kathy began to protest, but Jemima waved her away. 'I'll do it.'

Upstairs, Kathy sat on her bed and stared vacantly into space. She had to face the awful truth. She was pregnant. And she couldn't help but think how gleeful her father would be that he'd been proved right.

She heard the back door open and close and Jemima's footsteps trot along the passage. She glanced at her alarm clock, wondering if she had lost track of time and Jemima was already setting off to church. But no, she had only been sitting there for ten minutes or so.

With a sigh, Kathy got up. Perhaps Jemima was going to see Ron Spencer, was going to tell him the news, tell him that there was no way that Kathy could become a member of his concert party now.

She felt a little cross that Jemima might be spreading the news so quickly, but then she sighed. He would have to know sooner or later, though, and at least Jemima was saving her, Kathy, the embarrassment of having to tell him herself.

When she went downstairs a little later, Jemima was waiting for her. 'Come along, we'll have to hurry.'

There was no chance for conversation as they walked quickly along side by side. This morning they were attending the church where Kathy and Tony should have been married. When they reached the church porch, Ron was waiting for them. 'I was getting a bit anxious. I thought you weren't coming.'

Kathy smiled weakly. Why should he think that? she wondered. Surely Jemima had told him they would be attending service when she'd spoken to him earlier?

Ron fussed around her, leading her to her place in the choir and ensuring that she had everything she needed for her solo.

'Don't be nervous,' he said patting her hand. 'You'll be fine.'

Reading far more into his words than just encouragement for her performance, tears sprang to her eyes.

The service went well and when Kathy stood up to sing, she closed her eyes and blanked her mind of everything except the words and the music. Her clear voice echoed through the church and, emotional as she was feeling, she put such feeling into the words of the hymn that there was scarcely a dry eye in the congregation when she had finished.

As the worshippers filed out, Kathy found herself being shaken by the hand or patted on the back. People she hardly knew smiled and congratulated her.

'Does everyone know?'

'Of course they don't,' Jemima retorted. 'They're praising you for your singing, my dear. Nothing else. I hardly think,' she added dryly, 'that many here would consider your – er – news as something for congratulation.'

'But did you . . .?' she began, but at that moment, Ron Spencer came towards them, rubbing his hands with glee. 'Beautiful, my dear girl, just beautiful. Now, have you made up your mind about joining the concert party? I do hope it's going to be a yes.'

Kathy stared at him. She'd been wrong. He knew nothing about her condition. She bit her lip and shook her head. 'I'm so sorry, Mr Spencer, but it – it has to be no.'

His face fell. 'Well, I'm disappointed. Very disappointed. Perhaps you'll change your mind once your young man's been home and you've got him hooked, eh?' He laughed at his own joke.

Kathy flinched. Even if Tony came home and they were married, she could imagine some of the gossip when word got out that she was expecting his child.

'Couldn't escape a second time, could he?'

'Made sure she got him this time, eh?'

And so on.

There and then on the steps of the church where six

weeks ago she should have been married, Kathy made her decision.

She would not marry Tony at all. By the time he came home on leave, she would be gone. She would disappear and no one would know where she had gone. Only perhaps one person. She would confide in Jemima.

When they turned into the street, Kathy saw the Robinsons' car parked outside the front of Jemima's house.

'Oh no!' she breathed and stopped. 'Did you know they were coming today? I can't face them. Please . . .'

Jemima took hold of her arm with a firm grip. 'Kathy, my dear, listen to me. I rang them from the telephone box at the end of the street.'

Kathy wrenched herself free and turned to face Jemima. 'You did what?'

'I telephoned Betty,' Jemima repeated calmly, quite unapologetic. 'You should go home.'

'Home?' Kathy's laugh had a note of hysteria. 'Are you mad?'

'Well, if not to your parents, then to Betty and Ted's. They'll look after you.'

'No.' Kathy shook her head. She was adamant. 'No. I will go away, but not back to Abbeytoft. Never back there.'

'At least come in and talk about it. Please.'

'You – you've told them?'

'I had to. We need their help.'

'No, I don't. I'll—'

'Stop being so melodramatic, Kathy. You're not the first and you're certainly not going to be the last.' Again she took hold of Kathy's arm, and this time there was no wriggling free.

Kathy's heart plummeted even further as she stepped into the kitchen and saw that there was only one member of the Robinson family there.

'Hello, Morry,' she said flatly, avoiding his eyes.

'Kathy.'

'Go into the front room,' Jemima said briskly, peeling off her gloves and removing her hat, 'while I make some tea.'

Woodenly, Kathy led the way through and sat stiffly on a chair beside the empty grate, while Morry sat awkwardly on the sofa. The same sofa where she had spent so many happy hours with Tony . . .

She averted her gaze.

'Does he know? Have you told him?'

'No, and I'm not going to. He's been gone six weeks and I've only had one letter, right at the beginning, yet he's written to his mother every other day. Just shows where his thoughts are, doesn't it?' she added bitterly. She pulled in a deep breath. 'I've made up my mind. I'm not going to marry him. I'm not even going to tell him. It's over.'

'Everyone wants you to come home with me,' Morry blurted out. 'We'll take care of you.'

'Oh, Morry, don't be kind to me. I don't deserve it.'

'I could never be unkind to you, Kathy.' His hand tightened on hers. 'You know how I feel about you.'

'Stop it! You'll make me cry.' But already it was too late. Tears were coursing down her face.

Morry knelt beside her chair. 'I'd do anything for you, Kathy. Marry me and I'll take care of you and your baby. I swear I'd treat it as my own. You'd never hear a word of reproach from me. I promise you.'

For a moment she closed her eyes and rested her head against his shoulder. How very easy it would be to give in. To take this wonderful man's offer. To let him care for her for the rest of their lives. And she knew he would. She would be safe and secure and, yes, loved by a good man . . .

'I can't,' she whispered. 'I can't do that to you.'

'I don't expect you to love me.' Morry was still not ready to give up. 'Well, not in the way I love you. But we're friends, aren't we? Maybe in time . . .'

Kathy raised her head and shook it slowly. 'You deserve so much more, Morry.'

'What if I don't want any more, Kathy? What if all I really want is you?'

'Morry, don't,' she moaned. 'You make me feel so – so ashamed.'

'You've nothing to be ashamed about, Kathy. You – you loved him and you thought you were going to be married. Don't blame yourself.'

'I should have known,' she said flatly. 'I should have known that somehow his mother would stop it. She told she would. She told me she'd never let him marry me. And now it looks as if she's got her wish.'

'Come home with me. We'll look after you anyway, even if – even if you really don't want to marry me.'

She closed her eyes, trying to hold back the tears, trying to remain firm in her resolve. 'I can't. It's – it's too near home. You know what my father's like. He – he'd make my life a misery. And probably yours and all your family's too.'

Morry gave a wry laugh. 'Do you really think Jim Burton's ranting bothers my dad? Or any of us for that matter?'

'It wouldn't be fair,' Kathy was adamant, her mind made up. 'I'm going away, Morry. Right away.'

'Where, Kathy? How will you manage?'

'I – I don't know yet. But I've got to handle this on my own. As my father would say, I've made my bed so now I've got to lie on it.'

Morry knew he was beaten, but even yet, he couldn't quite let go. 'You'll write to me, Kathy? Just to let me – us – know that you're all right? At least do that. Please?'

'All right. Just so long as you promise not to try to find me.'

He sighed, defeated at last. 'All right. I promise.'

She didn't know if she believed him, but it was all she could do.

They begged, they pleaded, they reasoned, but Kathy was adamant. She was going away. Somewhere where no one knew her. She would find some sort of work until she couldn't work any more and then she would go into a mother and baby home until the child was born.

'And then?' Jemima asked bluntly. 'What then?'

'I – I don't know.'

'You mean you'll give it up for adoption?'

Kathy's head snapped up. 'No. Never. I'll never do that.'

'But how will you manage? Society doesn't look kindly on unmarried mothers.'

Kathy flinched at Jemima's bluntness, but she was only speaking the truth, painful though it was to hear it.

'I – I don't know. But I'll manage somehow.'

There was a long silence before Morry rose. 'I must be getting back.' He stood looking down at Kathy for a long moment. Then he put his hand on her shoulder and squeezed it gently. 'I know you don't want me to come looking for you, but promise me one thing, please, Kathy.'

She looked up at him.

'Promise me that if ever you need a friend you will come to me.'

Slowly, Kathy nodded.

Twenty-Seven

Kathy stood on the sea front looking out across the cold grey water.

She had been living in Saltershaven for five months now. The day after Morry's visit she had packed her suitcase, accepted the money that Jemima pressed upon her and gone to Lincoln bus station. She hadn't even looked where the bus was heading, and after a journey that had seemed to last for ever but was in fact only about two and a half hours, she had found herself in the seaside town. As she'd stepped down from the bus, she'd allowed herself a wry smile. How different she felt this time. The day she'd spent here the previous Easter with Amy and Aunt Jemima had been filled with happiness. The only cloud in her sky then had been because Tony had not been there too. And now – only a year later – she was running away from them all.

For the first two nights, Kathy was obliged to spend some of the precious money Jemima had given her at a bed and breakfast. But when the local newspaper came out on the Wednesday, she found lodgings among the advertisements. '*Furnished rooms. Season or longer. Full board if required.*' There was a box number to answer. She went into the paper's office and left a short note. The next day she was contacted and went to view the rooms.

'How long will you be here?'

'I'm not sure, but it will be for at least four months. Perhaps a little longer.'

'Mm . . .' The woman owner of the house divided into bed-sitting rooms seemed doubtful as she looked Kathy up and down. Slyly, Kathy said, 'I can pay you a month's rent in advance instead of the week you're asking for, if you like.'

That clinched it, as the woman held out her greedy hand. 'No pets, no children and no followers,' she said tartly.

Kathy did not answer.

From the same newspaper, Kathy listed two or three jobs from the 'Wanted' column and the following day tramped the streets looking for work. She found it as a waitress in one of the seafront cafés for the season.

'You'll probably only be needed until September, if we get any kind of a season at all with the wretched war on,' Mr Bates, the proprietor – a doleful man in his fifties – informed her.

'That's fine. That's all I want anyway.'

'And the work'll be quite hard. You'll be on your feet all day.' He too looked her up and down, just like the landlady had done. But he seemed to like what he saw, for he smiled and said, 'But you look strong.'

Now Kathy could raise a smile. 'Oh, I am. I worked on my father's farm,' she told him, but did not add about her months working in the fancy department store in the city.

The weeks and months had passed quickly and already it was September. And today, the young girl who was the kitchen maid in the café had said, 'By heck, Kathy, I reckon you're putting on weight but I don't know how you're managing it with all this rationing. Poor Mr Bates is doing 'is nut 'cos he can't get the stuff he wants.'

Kathy had been able to conceal her condition with the loose overall she wore when working. But now the growing bulge could no longer be hidden.

She sighed as she watched the waves rolling in towards the shore and breaking on the smooth sand. It was a lovely beach and she longed to walk on it, but ugly rolls of barbed wire barred the way and danger signs forbade entry.

Hands deep in the pockets of her coat, Kathy walked along the seafront as far as she could. She was trying to come to a decision. Jemima's final words to her had been, 'Wherever you're going, my dear, you must see a doctor, and don't forget to sort out your ration books.'

Kathy had handed her ration book to her landlady, who provided her meals, but she had not been able to bring herself to visit a doctor. However, she'd found out that there was a home for unmarried mothers and their babies on the outskirts of the town. And today she must visit it and seek admittance. She was putting off the moment for as long as possible, but by lunch-time she forced herself to walk along the road leading southwards out of the town towards the square house that sat in its own grounds.

She walked through the gateway, noticing that, though there were posts and hinges, the gates had been removed. For the war effort, she supposed. She crunched up the gravel driveway and pulled on the bell rope. After what seemed an age, in which she almost lost her nerve and ran back down the drive, footsteps approached and the door was pulled open.

A young girl, obviously far advanced in pregnancy,

stood there. Kathy and the girl exchanged a solemn glance of mutual sympathy and understanding before the girl smiled and invited Kathy inside.

'I . . .' Kathy faltered, not knowing how to begin, but the girl filled the moment of awkwardness by saying, 'My name's Lizzie Marsh. We call each other by our Christian names but the staff here call us by our surnames.' She grimaced and laughed wryly. 'It's supposed to make us feel even more degraded than we do already.' She put her arm through Kathy's. 'Don't look so terrified. It's not so bad. If you behave yourself and do exactly as they tell you, you'll be fine.' She laughed again and this time there was a brief hint of a mischievous sparkle in her eyes. 'I don't, so I'm always in trouble.'

Kathy warmed at once to the girl. 'I'm – I'm Kathy Burton.' So nearly had she become Mrs Kathy Kendall. Another few minutes and she would not be having to seek sanctuary in such a place.

'I'll take you to see Matron.' Lizzie leaned closer and whispered. 'That's what we all have to call her – "Matron". But I won't tell you what we call her behind her back. You'll hear soon enough.'

The girl led the way and knocked on a door on the left-hand side of the wide hallway. In a moment, Kathy found herself standing in front of a broad desk behind which was sitting a large, sour-faced woman in a navy blue dress with a white cap perched on top of her short, straight grey hair. The bright light from the window behind the woman shone in Kathy's eyes.

'Thank you, Marsh,' the matron snapped and Lizzie turned to leave. Unseen by the matron she gave Kathy a broad wink.

Once the girl had gone the matron appraised Kathy from head to toe, but she did not invite her to sit down.

'How far gone are you?'

'Nearly seven months.'

'Have you seen a doctor?'

'No.'

'Is this your first pregnancy?'

Kathy felt the colour creep up her face. Embarrassment, shame – a tumult of emotions – swept through her. But she tilted her chin a little higher and met the woman's cold stare. Deliberately deciding to take Lizzie's advice – at least for the moment – she said, with feigned humility, 'Yes, Matron.'

The woman pulled a notepad towards her and picked up her pen. 'I'd better take some details. Name . . .'

The questions went on, endlessly it seemed to Kathy, until her feet were aching.

'I shall need a referral from a doctor. Are you registered with anyone locally?'

Kathy shook her head.

'I'll see that you are put on Dr Williamson's list. It was he who started this place and he attends the confinements of all our inmates.'

Kathy flinched at the word. It sounded like the workhouse and she was suddenly very much afraid that it would be little better.

The matron laid down her pen at last, rested her elbows on the desk and steepled her fingers. 'This place is run on charity. Women of standing in the community raise funds and support our efforts. And the girls are expected to contribute by working. We employ no staff other than myself and two more part-time qualified nurses who come in when required. All other work – cooking, cleaning and laundry – is done by the inmates.'

That dreadful word again, Kathy thought, and now it sounds even more like a workhouse.

'I understand, Matron.'

'We also keep chickens, pigs and a small herd of cows. We grow our own vegetables. Even more so, since the war started.' She glanced down at her notes. 'I see you were brought up on a farm, so no doubt you would be most suited to the outside work.'

Kathy felt hysterical laughter bubbling up inside her. She had left home to escape a life of drudgery and now, just because she had made the mistake of falling in love with Tony Kendall, she was back at the start. It was like a game of snakes and ladders and she had just slid down a very long snake.

She quelled her laughter and composed her face, saying meekly, 'Yes, Matron.'

'Now, if you'll sign these papers of consent, then I'll be able to admit you.'

In a blur of misery and shame, Kathy scribbled her name at the foot of several typewritten sheets of paper, which the matron laid before her. Then she returned to her lodgings to pack her few belongings and collect her ration book. Carrying her suitcase, she gave in her notice at the café and trudged back to the isolated house that was to be her home for the next few months.

Kathy couldn't remember ever feeling so lonely in the whole of her life.

The days passed with monotonous routine. The work was hard, though no worse than Kathy had been used to on her father's farm. But the months of comparatively soft living in the city made feeding pigs, milking cows and cleaning out the chicken huts seem doubly hard. Kathy was lucky. She was physically strong, and after a week or so slipped back into the routine as if she had never left it. She even helped some of the girls who found it exhausting, though this earned her a reprimand from the matron.

'They're here to work,' Miss Delamere reminded her.

'To be punished, you mean,' Kathy muttered.

'What did you say?'

'Yes, Matron,' Kathy said, staring boldly into the woman's steely eyes.

'Get on with your work,' she snapped, turned and marched away. Behind her back, Kathy pulled a face and one of the other girls laughed. The matron glanced back, glared at Kathy for a moment and then walked on. But Kathy knew she had made an enemy.

Despite the harsh routine and the unhappy circumstances that brought them together, friendships grew among the girls. There were one or two spats, as was inevitable amongst a group of lonely, frightened young woman forced to live day and night in each other's company. But the others quickly resolved any arguments. From feeling desolate when she entered the house, Kathy soon felt among friends. Only the matron and nurses held themselves aloof and disapproving. Even Dr Williamson seemed to be a benign benefactor. He was middle-aged, round-faced and balding, and smiled over his steel-rimmed spectacles at Kathy when she entered his consulting room.

When he had finished his examination of her he

pronounced her fit and healthy. 'You'll have a fine baby, my dear, that some lucky couple will be delighted to adopt.'

Kathy stared at him. 'Adopt? What – what do you mean?'

The doctor smiled at her. 'Well, you are not in a position to keep the baby, are you, my dear?'

Kathy gasped. 'Not – not keep my baby?'

'Oh no. That's out of the question. We cannot allow it. You came in here of your own free will, didn't you? Nobody forced you to, now did they?'

'Well, no, but I didn't realize—'

'So, you thought you could come in here . . .' Suddenly, the blue eyes behind the spectacles were no longer friendly. They were sharp and greedy. 'Be cared for and cosseted. And then what did you expect? After the birth? That you'd be found a home and supported? I think not, my dear. I don't know your background or your circumstances, but obviously you don't have a family prepared to forgive you and support you, else you wouldn't be here.'

Kathy leapt to her feet. 'Then I won't stay here. I had no idea that I'd be expected to allow my baby to be adopted.'

The once benign face suddenly creased into an angry frown. 'You signed the papers when you came in.'

Kathy gasped and stared at him in horror. 'I – I thought they were just something to do with my admittance here. I was never told that it was anything to do with – adoption.'

Dr Williamson shrugged. 'You were told—'

'I was not told anything of the sort,' Kathy shouted.

'Don't raise your voice to me, young lady.' All

pretence at benevolence was gone. 'You've signed the papers. Your child will be adopted. Look,' he said, his tone softening. 'Sit down and let me explain.'

Slowly, Kathy sank back down into her chair. Not so much because she wished to sit, but because she felt as if her trembling legs would no longer keep her standing upright.

'Look, my dear . . .' The cajoling tone was back, but now Kathy knew it was insincere. 'If your baby is taken by a couple who are unable to have children of their own and are desperate to adopt, isn't it going to have a much better life than with you? All its life it will bear the stigma of being a bastard.' Kathy flinched and Dr Williamson nodded sagely. 'Yes, you may well wince, but that, my dear girl, is exactly what your child will suffer the whole of its life. It will have that dreadful name called after it in the playground, in the street. It will never be able to hold its head up. It will be an outcast from society. It will never get a decent job, or marry well. The stigma will follow it all its days,' he ended pompously.

Kathy closed her eyes and groaned inwardly. Had she been wrong to run away from those who would have helped her? Jemima and all the Robinson family? And Morry? Especially Morry? She even wondered if she should have given Tony another chance. Perhaps she should have waited until he'd come home on leave instead of rushing away in pique.

But no. If nothing else, she was an honest girl. She could no more force Tony into marriage than she could accept Morry's proposal. And yet . . . Now she was being forced to give up her baby. She'd never even thought of such a thing. Yet now she had to face it.

Calmer now, she stood up. 'I'll think about it.'

The doctor was all smiles again, though now Kathy saw them as sinister. She gave him a brief nod and marched out of the room. She would talk to Lizzie and the other girls. Surely, she thought, there are others here who don't want to give up their babies?

'Of course we don't *want* to,' Lizzie said as three of the girls huddled together in the dormitory after lights out. 'But what other choice do we have?'

'How can we work and look after our babies?' Pamela put in. She was near her time and every day her eyes became sadder and more haunted with the thought of what she must do. 'I would if I could, believe me. I don't want to give my baby away.' Tears filled her eyes and Lizzie put her arm about her. 'But your baby will go to a good home.'

'You make it sound like a litter of puppies that goes to "a good home",' Kathy snapped.

Lizzie shrugged philosophically.

'Why can't we get a place together? Three or four of us and help each other.' Kathy was clutching at preposterous ideas. 'We could get work and one of us could look after the babies.'

'I thought of that, but it's been done,' Pamela sighed, wiping her eyes.

'And?'

'It didn't work. The locals accused the girls of keeping a brothel.'

Kathy stared at her, open-mouthed, to think that people could be so cruel. 'You'd think in nineteen forty and in the middle of a war, folks would be a bit more understanding, wouldn't you?'

'You would,' Lizzie said quietly. 'But they're not. We're still "fallen women" in most folk's eyes.'

'So – is everyone here giving their babies up for adoption?'

No one spoke. No one denied it.

'Lizzie?'

'It's the best for the child,' Lizzie said, though her voice trembled.

'But what about your baby's father. Won't he . . . ?'

Lizzie pursed her lips, trying to hold back the tears. She shook her head. 'No. He didn't want to know. He – he even said he didn't know if the baby was his.' Now her tears fell. 'How could he say such a thing to me? He was my first boyfriend and he knew that.'

'I was an absolute fool,' Pamela murmured. 'My baby's father was married, but I was so head over heels in love with him . . .' She needed to say no more. Each one of them knew what it was to fall in love, to be so sure that their lover felt the same. That nothing would ever come between them . . . Oh they'd heard it all before but they believed it would be so different for them. But it wasn't. And now they found themselves here, brought together by a common bond, their only fault having loved too much.

'And – and I take it your parents . . . ?' Kathy began, but she got no further. There was wry laughter.

'You must be joking,' Pamela said. 'My parents arranged for me to come here. I can only go home again when it's all over and then only so long as it's without the baby.'

'But it's their grandchild. How can they . . . ?'

'Oh they can. Very easily, it seems,' Pamela said.

'My parents just turned me out,' Lizzie said dolefully. 'I'd nowhere else to go except a place like this. A friend of mine whose sister had a baby out of wedlock told me about Willow House.'

Two other girls told their similar, sorry, tales and then all eyes turned to Kathy.

'I was almost married,' she said bitterly. 'Five minutes more and I would have been.' And she went on to tell them the details of that chaotic day.

'That's awful, but couldn't you have waited till he came on leave again? It doesn't sound as if he's deserted you. Just – just circumstances,' Lizzie said logically.

'I know,' Kathy sighed. 'Maybe I've been a bit hasty. I see that now. But I still don't think there's much hope. He's a mother's boy and that's never going to change.'

'Does he know? About the baby?'

'No,' Kathy said firmly. 'And he's not going to. Not from me and no one knows where I am. I – wanted to handle it myself, but – but I didn't realize it involved giving up my baby.' She turned to Lizzie and said softly, 'And I'm not going to. Once I've had it, I'm out of here and taking my baby with me. At least I do have a place to go back to. Someone I lived with in – in the city. She'll stand by me. I know she will.'

The girls all glanced at each other. 'You're lucky then,' Pamela said. 'Good luck to you.'

They crept back to their beds and Kathy lay staring into the darkness and planning how she could escape from this place that was like a prison.

Twenty-Eight

Pamela gave birth to a baby girl. She refused to look at it or hold it and the child was handed over to eager parents at a week old. The next day, Pamela said her goodbyes and returned home. Several other girls gave birth and stayed for about six weeks, caring for their child, feeding it, dressing it and bathing it.

When the day came that they too had to part with their babies, they were heartbroken.

'I'll never see her again,' a young girl called Rachel sobbed on Kathy's shoulder. 'I'll never see her smile or nurse her when she's teething. I won't be there when she starts to walk. And it won't be me she learns to call "Mummy".'

Kathy held her close and stroked her hair, but she could think of nothing to say to comfort the girl. There was nothing she could say.

And then it was Lizzie's turn.

'Stay with me,' she begged Kathy. 'Don't leave me. I'm so frightened.'

'There's nothing to be frightened of,' Kathy tried to reassure her as the girl writhed on her bed in agony.

But there was plenty for Lizzie to be afraid of. She endured three days in labour to be delivered in the end of a stillborn child. A week later, distraught and weakened, Lizzie succumbed to an infection and followed her child to the pauper's grave in the nearest churchyard.

On the morning of the funeral, Kathy sat by the window looking down the road towards the church. She had begged and pleaded to be allowed to attend her friend's funeral but Matron was adamant in her refusal. 'You cannot appear in public in your condition,' she was told harshly, making her feel even more ashamed.

Now Kathy had no one left to whisper with. No new girls had come into the home since she had arrived, and with all those that had gone recently, there were only a handful left. She tried to make friends with one or two but they were withdrawn and uncommunicative, lost in their own private world of sadness and shame.

Once more, Kathy felt completely alone.

Kathy felt the first pangs of labour one cold, blustery November morning. She was put in the labour room and left.

'I'll be back soon. You've a long way to go yet.'

There was no one to sit with her, no one to comfort her. When the pains grew stronger and closer together and Kathy cried out, the nurse put her head round the door and said, 'You can stop making all that noise. It'll get worse yet.' And she disappeared.

Kathy sobbed and cried out again, but no one came. There was no one who cared. Anger flooded through her, and the next time the pain came in a huge, crescendo, she bit hard down and refused to cry out. Over the next twenty minutes she made no sound, and her silence brought the nurse in faster than had her cries.

The birth was long and exhausting. As the pain

became unbearable and Kathy could no longer quell her cries, she was aware that Matron had entered the room.

With experienced, but ungentle, hands the two women positioned her to give birth and then barked orders at her. 'Push down hard. Now pant – now push . . .' until with one valiant effort that took the last ounce of her strength, Kathy felt a strange emptying feeling and heard a baby's cry.

'Oh – oh. What is it?'

No one answered. She tried to raise herself up to see, but weariness overwhelmed her and she fell back. She was aware of movement in the room and the cries of her child grew fainter.

'Please . . .' she begged, but then she remembered no more.

When she came round, she was back in her own bed in the ward. She felt battered and bruised. She tried to sit up, but pain seared through her and she gave a cry.

One of the young girls, Peggy, who had come in the week before, came to her bedside.

'Can I get you anything? Would you like a drink of water?'

'Please,' Kathy croaked through parched lips.

Peggy raised her up and held a glass to her parched lips. Kathy drank gratefully.

As she lay back again, she asked, 'My baby? Where's my baby?'

The girl shrugged. 'They've taken him away.'

'A boy? It was a boy?'

'Yes.'

'Where've they taken him?'

The girl shrugged. 'He'll have gone to his new parents, I suppose.'

'What? Already? They can't do that. I haven't even seen him. I haven't given my permission. I haven't even – even held him.' Tears coursed down her face. 'They should have let me hold him. I should have him with me for a few weeks. Why – why have they taken him?'

Peggy leant closer. 'I heard Matron talking to one of the nurses, telling her not to let you have him. "She's trouble, that one," she said. "Doctor said she wants to keep him, but he's got an ideal couple waiting. Keep her sedated for two days. When she comes round, he'll be gone. And she won't be able to find out where." That's what she said.'

'Have I been asleep for two days?'

Peggy nodded. 'They kept rousing you and giving you more pills or they stuck a needle in you.'

'But how can they do that? I thought the rules were that mothers nursed the babies for five or six weeks.' Kathy passed her hand over her clammy forehead. She was still feeling dizzy and sick. It must be all the sedatives they'd given her.

'What rules?' Peggy laughed wryly. 'They make their own rules here, believe me. Matron – and the doctor. They can do whatever they like because they own this place between them. Didn't you know? They're brother and sister.'

No, she hadn't known. And now she was beginning to doubt the integrity of this place. But she was too weak to do anything about it. Too exhausted even to get out of bed. Her strength had drained from her and even her spirit was defeated and broken.

Kathy turned her face to the wall and wept bitter, scalding tears.

*

When Kathy was strong enough, she dressed and walked down to the matron's office.

She faced the woman across the desk. 'I didn't know that those papers you had me sign when I came in here were adoption papers. You never told me what they were.'

The matron smiled. 'Now, sit down, my dear. You've been through a very difficult birth and you're not feeling strong yet. We can let you stay another week but then you'll have to leave.'

'But my baby,' Kathy felt tears of weakness flow down her face. 'What have you done with my baby?'

'He's gone to a loving couple. He will have a wonderful home, my dear. Everything that you could never give him. Isn't that the very best thing for him?'

'Where's he gone? Who's taken him?'

'I can't possibly tell you that. It wouldn't do.'

'But what are they like, these people? Surely you can tell me something?'

'It's our rules that neither side know the names or anything about each other. Secrecy is best for all concerned. All we can do is assure you that the adoptive parents are respectable people and suitable to bring up your child as if he was their own. Now, dry your tears and concentrate on getting yourself fit and well. Then you can leave and get on with your life. But if you'll take my advice, you won't be so foolish enough to find yourself in here again.'

Kathy rose and left the room without another word. As she reached for the door handle, she caught sight of three wooden filing cabinets, each with four drawers, placed against the wall just inside the door of the matron's office. On each drawer there were letters A–B, C–D and so on through the alphabet. Kathy didn't pause in her movement towards the door and out of the room, but as she left, her heart was beating a little faster.

In those drawers were the details of the people who had taken her baby. She was sure of it.

Kathy told no one of her plan. If only Lizzie were still here, or even Pamela, she might have confided in one of them, but she didn't feel as if she knew the girls that were left well enough to trust them. They all seemed downtrodden, with no spirit left in them. She waited impatiently for another two nights, until she felt stronger. Luckily, she was now in a room on her own, so when she thought the household would be asleep, she crept out of her room and down the stairs, stopping in alarm every time a tread creaked. It sounded so loud in the silence of the night.

She reached the door to the matron's office and tried the door handle. To her relief, it wasn't locked. Quietly, she slipped into the darkened room. She didn't want to turn on a light, so she opened the curtains to let the bright moonlight shine in. Then she went to the cabinets. They were locked. She bit her lip and looked about her. Then she tiptoed to the desk and quietly opened the middle drawer. A bunch of various-sized keys lay there. She lifted it up, wincing as the keys jangled together. She paused and listened, holding her breath, but there was no sound of anyone coming to investigate.

She tried various keys in the topmost drawer, A–B. She was beginning to lose hope and her heart was beating faster, fearing that at any moment she would be discovered. But then, she argued, what more could they do to her? They had already robbed her of her baby. She worked on, trying every key in the bunch. The last key but one fitted and turned the lock. She pulled open the drawer, wincing as it squeaked loudly.

The files were in alphabetical order and she pulled out the one marked B. She turned to the back of the file, knowing 'Burton' would be one of the last. And there were the notes in the matron's own handwriting made on the day Kathy had first visited the place. If only she had turned tail and run then. She scanned through the pages until she came to the place where she had signed. Reading now, for the first time, she saw that she had indeed signed a paragraph that gave permission for her baby to be adopted. Kathy groaned and then read on. As she did so, her pulse quickened with excitement. The names of the couple who had adopted her baby boy were Mr and Mrs Henry Wainwright and the address was right here, in Saltershaven.

Carefully, Kathy replaced the file, closed the drawer and locked it, returned the keys to the drawer in the desk and then closed the curtains. She tiptoed from the room and quietly shut the door of the matron's room. She had no need to write down the name and address. It was seared in her mind.

She gained her room without discovery and, once back in bed, began to breathe more easily. She couldn't believe that she had not been caught, that it had been so easy. If the matron had locked the office, or taken the keys to the filing cabinet with her at night, there would have been nothing she could have done. She wondered if other mothers ever did what she'd done or if they, unlike her, were relieved to part with their child.

'But not this mother,' Kathy whispered into the

night. 'Not this one. I'll find my baby and I'll snatch him back if I have to.'

By the end of two weeks since the birth of her child, though she wasn't really fully recovered, Matron deemed her fit enough to leave Willow House.

Kathy had the feeling that the woman wanted to be rid of her, so she packed her suitcase and left without a backward glance, glad to be free of the place. She walked back to where she had rented a bed-sitting room, on the top floor of a row of three-storey, terraced town houses.

'Oh, it's you. Been away, 'ave ya?' The woman who owned the house and lived on the ground floor greeted her.

'Yes, but I'm back now. Any chance of a room again?'

'Yes, as a matter of fact your old room's just come vacant again. Young feller who worked at the bank moved out. Bin called up, 'ee 'as.'

'May I take it then? Straight away?'

'What, now?' Mrs Benson looked her up and down.

'Yes, I – I've just arrived back and I've nowhere else to stay.'

'You look a bit peaky. You look thinner. Not sickening for summat, a' ya? Don't want no illness in the place.'

'No – no, I'm fine.'

Mrs Benson pulled open the door with a sniff. 'Ya'd better come in then. Same terms as afore. No children, no pets an' no followers.'

'That's fine,' Kathy said. She still had some thinking to do about how she could find her child and what she would do when she did. Obviously, where they would live together would be something else she would have to think about. And what they would live on was another worry. Her money was fast running out and she was too proud to ask Jemima for more.

She settled quickly back into her old room and in some ways it was as if she'd never been away from it. Sleep didn't come easily as she lay awake staring into the darkness and laying her plans.

The following morning, Kathy asked Mrs Benson if she knew the road where the Wainwrights lived, but she didn't mention their name.

'Oh aye, it's near the golf course on the way to the Point. Right on the seafront. Them's posh houses up there. Why a' ya asking? Hoping to get a job there, a' ya?'

Kathy stared at her, her mind working quickly. That hadn't occurred to her.

'I – er – saw an advert for a housekeeper,' she lied. 'I thought I might go and have a look.'

'If I'd known you were planning on leaving so soon, I wouldn't have let you have ya room back.' She sniffed. 'Messing me about. Them's usually live-in jobs.'

'I'm not messing you about, Mrs Benson. I'll be here at least the month I've paid you for.'

'Aye, well, mind you are. All this coming and going and changing ya mind. I can't be doin' with it.'

Kathy had walked at least a mile along the road Mrs Benson had indicated she should take. She stopped to rest on a low wall in front of one of the houses. Perhaps she'd been foolish to try to walk so far, so soon. But she was anxious to see where her baby son was.

A delivery boy, with a huge basket on the front of his bicycle, came riding past, whistling loudly.

'Excuse me . . . ?' Kathy put out her hand to attract his attention.

'Yes, miss,' he grinned as he applied his brakes and the bicycle slithered to a halt. 'Can I 'elp ya?'

Kathy explained and the boy said, 'A bit further along, you'll see the golf course, turn left up the road leading towards the sea just before it. Then at the end of the road turn right and that's the road you want. Looking for anyone in particular?'

'The Wainwrights.'

'Oh aye, that's the big house right at the end. Big white one.'

Thanking him, Kathy walked on again wrapping her coat tightly around her as the cool breeze whipped in off the beach. At last she stood before the huge wrought-iron gates, peering through them at the elegant house at the end of the steep driveway. It was a magnificent house, painted white with gleaming windows overlooking the sandhills and the beach, right to the sea.

As Kathy stood there uncertainly, she saw a woman emerge from a side door, turn and pull a perambulator into view. Kathy's heart skipped a beat. Her son was in that pram. Her little boy. The woman, whom Kathy presumed to be Mrs Wainwright, pushed the pram down the drive towards the gate. She was smiling and talking all the while to the child in the pram. Kathy shrank back and began to walk away. Her heart was thumping in her chest. She had to see the baby, but she knew she must seem like a passer-by, merely making a polite enquiry. She mustn't appear too interested. She mustn't alarm the woman. She strolled along as if out taking a walk, but in truth was waiting for Mrs Wainwright to catch up with her. As she heard the wheels of the pram behind her, Kathy stepped off the pavement and stopped, turning to look back as if to let the woman and her baby pass by. She smiled and nodded casually, but Kathy was actually taking in every detail of her appearance. She was a little older than Kathy would have imagined, but dressed in a smart, well-cut navy blue coat. Her smooth complexion was expertly made up and her black hair peeped out from beneath a small hat that matched her coat.

'Hello,' Kathy said in a friendly manner. The woman's smile widened and she stopped.

'May – may I see your baby?'

'Of course. I'm so proud of him. He's beautiful and so good. He's only two weeks old and this is his first time out. You have to be so careful with November weather, don't you?'

Mrs Wainwright leaned forward and pushed back the hood and Kathy looked down on her son for the first time. He was asleep, but she could see his smooth skin, the silky black hair and his round little face. Tears welled in her eyes as she searched the tiny face for any hint of likeness to herself or to Tony.

'He's lovely. Perfectly lovely,' she said, trying to keep her voice steady.

'Oh, he is. We're so lucky.'

Kathy straightened up and turned to face the woman. 'You look very well. Should you be out walking so soon after the birth?'

The woman smiled a little sadly. 'We've adopted him. My husband and I couldn't have children of our own. We've had our names down with various adoption societies for ages and then last week, out of the blue, we got word from Willow House that there was a baby suitable for us. And he is, Oh, he is. He could be our very own. We shall spoil him, I know, but he will have everything that we can give him. And Oh, how he will be loved.' She shook her head in wonderment, as if she still could not believe their luck. 'We feel very blessed.' She looked straight at Kathy with clear, earnest blue eyes. 'To have been given such a gift and entrusted with his care. He will want for nothing.'

'I – I can – can see that,' Kathy whispered. 'May I ask what – what his name is?'

'James,' the woman said. 'After my husband's father. And I shall insist on him always being called James, not Jim or Jimmy.'

Kathy nodded unable to speak. How ironic, she thought, that Tony's child should be given a family name. She wondered what Beatrice Kendall would say if she knew that she had a grandson named James. And what, indeed, would James Hammond think if he knew?

Mrs Wainwright was speaking again and moving on. 'I must go. I'm just going to the end of the road and then back home again. It's far enough for his first outing.'

As they walked along, Mrs Wainwright chattered. 'Do you live nearby?'

'No – I – er – I've only just arrived. I've found lodgings and tomorrow I'll look for work.' Her answers came automatically, she was hardly thinking clearly. Her thoughts were in turmoil. She couldn't do it. Her plans lay in tatters. She couldn't snatch her baby away from this happy, loving woman who would give little James everything. What could she, an unmarried girl, with no proper home, no job, scarcely any money left, give him in comparison? She faced the awful, heart-wrenching truth. The answer was 'nothing'. She could give her son nothing, except love. But love alone could not feed him, clothe him and keep him warm.

They reached the end of the road and Mrs Wainwright turned the pram around. 'There, my little precious, time to go home.'

The baby whimpered and she leant forward, pulling down the coverlet. 'Are you hungry, my little one? Soon be home.'

Kathy felt a tingling in her breasts as if, hearing her baby's cry, her body responded naturally. Kathy tore her gaze away from the baby to meet the woman's eyes.

'I must go,' Mrs Wainwright said pleasantly. 'I think he wants feeding. Goodbye. It's nice to have met you. I hope you find a job.'

Kathy nodded, unable to speak as Mrs Wainwright walked away, every step taking Kathy's son further and further away from her. She stood watching them walk the length of the road, saw the gate open and them disappear through it. Not until then did Kathy turn away and begin her long, lonely walk home.

She didn't cry. She couldn't. She felt as if there was a leaden weight in her chest, a sadness too deep even for tears.

Twenty-Nine

It was the wrong time of the year to seek work back at the café, but Kathy was lucky. She found work at one of the local cinemas, the Grand, which had a stage that could be used for live theatre. There were two different programmes of films during the week, each one lasting three days. Sometimes on Sunday evenings there was a live show, usually with a wartime theme. Artistes from units of the forces stationed in the district put together a programme of music and orchestras, and bands from the Royal Marines played.

During the day Kathy worked in the box office, at night she was an usherette.

'I'm so glad I took you on,' Larry Johnson, the cinema's manager told her. 'You're so willing to do anything we ask you.' He was young, fresh-faced and eager and Kathy wondered why he had not been called up. It wasn't long before he was confiding, 'I wanted to join the RAF, but I have a weak heart, so – ' he spread his hands, almost apologetically – 'I thought I'd try to do something to keep everyone's spirits up.'

Kathy smiled sympathetically, 'I'm sure you're doing a wonderful job and I'm only too glad to help out.'

She wanted to fill every waking moment. Nights were the worst, when she lay lonely and sleepless, aching to hold the warm little body in her arms. Then she would turn and sob into her pillow until exhaustion overtook her. She grew thinner and paler, but still she pushed herself on, no longer caring what became of her.

Any time she had free during the day she took the long walk out of the town towards the south, just on the offchance of meeting Mrs Wainwright wheeling James out in his perambulator. In the evenings, the darkness of the cinema hid her tears.

Five girls, smartly dressed in WRNS uniform, came up the steps and into the cinema a little after the start of the evening's programme. Mrs Riley, the elderly, grey-haired lady who manned the box office in the evening, gave them their tickets and directed them to the door leading into the stalls. 'The film's only just started, you've not missed much.'

Kathy forced a smile on to her face as the girls entered the auditorium, stumbling and giggling in the darkness.

'Sh,' someone from a nearby seat hissed. 'Can't you be quiet?'

'Sorry we're late,' Kathy heard a familiar voice say. 'We've only just got off duty.'

The complaining voice was mollified. 'Oh, Wrens, are you? Well, we'll let you off then. There are seats here.' The man stood up, inviting them to sit beside him.

'Sorry, I think my friends want to be nearer the front,' the girl said cheerfully and turned to follow the wavering light of Kathy's torch leading them down the aisle.

As she stood, pointing the beam of her torch

towards the empty row of seats about half way down the aisle, she felt someone touch her arm and the voice she knew say softly, 'Kathy!' Then boisterous arms were flung around her and she was hugged tightly. 'Oh, darling Kathy, it is you.'

A chorus of 'sh' came out of the darkness.

'Amy – sit down,' Kathy whispered. 'I'll see you later.'

'You won't disappear? You promise?'

'I promise, but please – sit down now, or else you'll get me the sack.'

Amy squeezed her hand but sat down without another word, while Kathy walked back to her seat near the door, ready for any more latecomers.

Kathy sat in the darkness staring at the brightly lit screen, yet she saw and heard nothing. Her mind was in a turmoil. She was tempted to break her promise, plead sickness to the cinema manager and leave before the interval, when she knew Amy would seek her out. But something held her in her seat. Was it an overwhelming desire to see her dearest friend again? To feel, just for an hour or so, that someone cared for her? She longed to know how the Robinson family were. All of them, Ted and Betty, Morry and, of course, Aunt Jemima. And she wanted to hear any news that Amy might have of her mother. She wondered if Edith knew that she had a grandchild. Would the Robinsons have told her parents that she had been – as her father rightly predicted – pregnant? She didn't think they would betray her secret, yet Betty might have succumbed to an overwhelming desire to tell Edith. Part of Kathy hoped she had done so.

The first film ended and the Pathé News came on.

As the house lights went up, Amy was out of her seat and running up the aisle towards her before anyone else had moved.

'Kathy, Oh Kathy, I'm so glad I've found you. Why didn't you write, you naughty girl? We've been so worried – all of us. Can we go somewhere to talk?'

'Not until after the last film,' Kathy said. 'I'm still on duty.'

'Of course. All right.'

'You coming to the bar across the road, Amy?'

'Yes – yes, you go on. Port and lemon for me, please. I'll be there in a mo. I've just met an old friend.'

'We gathered,' the other girl smiled and another quipped, 'That's her way of getting out of paying for the drinks.' She winked at Kathy. 'I bet she doesn't know you from Adam – or rather Eve – does she?'

'Oh, yes,' Kathy said huskily. 'She – she's my best friend.'

Another hug and Amy followed her friends, saying again, 'Don't you dare disappear again. I'll see you afterwards in the bar. Okay? And the drinks will be on me.'

Kathy looked forward to, and yet at the same time dreaded, the end of the show.

When all the cinema-goers had finally gone, Kathy took a deep breath and made her way across the road.

'Here she is.' Amy jumped up at once and beckoned her to the corner where the five girls were seated. She made the introductions. 'This is Dorothy, Millie, Janet and Vicky.'

'What are you doing here?'

'We're just up the road at a holiday camp that's been turned into a training camp for the Navy,' Amy explained. 'It's my first posting. But none of us know how long we're here for.' She hugged Kathy again enthusiastically. 'Oh, it's so good to see you. Tell me everything.'

'Well . . .' she hesitated, not wanting to talk freely in front of the others.

'Look,' Dorothy said, perceptive to Kathy's hesitation. 'You two go off on your own. We're fine here. We'll give you a shout when we're ready to leave. The Liberty Bus leaves in fifty minutes and we mustn't miss it.'

'The Liberty Bus?' Kathy smiled as they rose and, carrying their drinks, moved to a table in a quiet corner where, above the hubbub, their conversation would not be heard. 'Whatever's that?'

'It's the bus that brings us from camp into town,' Amy giggled. 'Brings us to liberty, I suppose.'

There was a pause before Kathy asked haltingly, 'How – how's everyone? Your mum and dad and – and Morry?'

'They're all fine, but we've all been so worried about you. Tell me everything, Kathy. How've you been and – ' she lowered her voice – 'what about the baby?'

Suddenly it all came pouring out, like the floodgates opening. She told Amy everything that had happened to her since she had left Lincoln, ending with, 'He – he's been adopted by a nice woman, I have to admit. She looks smart and lives in a big house on the outskirts of the town. And there's no doubt she – she loves him.'

'You – you know who she is? I thought they didn't let you know anything about the adoptive parents, just in case . . .' Amy faltered and stopped.

'Just in case I tried to snatch him back or made a nuisance of myself, you mean?'

'Well – yes.'

Kathy sighed, and explained how she had found out the Wainwrights' address.

'You rogue,' Amy said with admiration. 'I wouldn't have dared.'

'I think that's what the matron depends on. Why she's not more careful to secure her records. She doesn't think anyone would dare to go into her office. Mind you, I'm surprised no one has.'

'Perhaps they have. They're not going to tell anyone, are they? Any more than you've done.'

'No,' Kathy smiled. 'I suppose not.'

'So, what are you going to do? Try to get him back somehow?'

Kathy was silent for a long moment while she searched her heart and her mind. Her heart told her to run to the house this very minute, bang on their door and demand her child. But her head told her that the Wainwrights could give her son everything that she could not. And, most important of all, Kathy had seen for herself the love that Mrs Wainwright had for the baby boy. He would be cared for and cosseted and loved. He would have a legitimate name, not some vile insult called after him in the playground. Her head won. Slowly she said, 'No, I can't. I can't do that to him. He deserves better than I can give him. And besides, it's too late. That woman loves him, really loves him. How can I do that to her now?'

'But he's your child. You're his mother. He should be with you,' Amy persisted.

Kathy closed her eyes and groaned. 'I know, I know. But he'd carry the stigma of illegitimacy all his life.

This way he has a good home with people who love him and can give him everything.'

Softly Amy said, 'But you love him, don't you?'

'Of course I do,' Kathy cried out so loudly that one or two nearby glanced round at her. She turned her face away to hide her tears. 'Of course I do,' she whispered again. 'And that's why I know it's the right thing that he should stay where he is. Oh, it wasn't done in the right way. Those people at the home – there should be a law against what they're doing – but in the end, what choice do I really have?'

'You could come home and marry Morry,' Amy said simply.

Kathy went with them to the bus. Amy hugged her as they parted. 'If you change your mind, you know where we still live and Morry won't ever change his.'

Amy's words did nothing to ease Kathy's conscience over Morry, yet she knew she was right not to give in. A one-sided marriage was no marriage at all. And she was too fond of Morry to do that to him, even if, at the moment, he might think otherwise.

'Won't you at least come home for Christmas? I've been really lucky; I've got a seventy-two. We could go together.'

'I—' For a moment Kathy was very tempted. She yearned to be enveloped in the loving Robinson family. 'I can't,' she said at last and her tone was full of regret. 'I have to work.'

Amy pulled a face, hugged her swiftly one last time and climbed aboard the bus. She was still waving from the back seat as it drew away.

Kathy walked back to her lodgings feeling a turmoil

of emotion. Seeing Amy had been wonderful and yet it left her with a strange feeling of unrest.

'I must move on,' she murmured aloud as she walked home through the blacked-out streets, with only a thin pencil line of a torchlight to guide her. 'Go somewhere else. Now Amy has found me, I'll have the whole Robinson clan down on me.' And yet she couldn't drag herself away from the place where her son lived. Though she couldn't see him, couldn't hold him, she did feel close to him. She could stand outside the gate and look up at the windows and imagine him in his cot or lying on a rug in front of the fire, while Mrs Wainwright knelt beside him, playing with him, caressing him with adoring eyes.

But the days passed and no one came. She saw Amy briefly now and again, until on one meeting in the pub in late March after Kathy had finished her duty, Amy said, 'I've been posted down south. I've a week's leave before I go, so I'm going home. Do – do you still want me to keep quiet about where you are?'

Kathy raised her eyebrows, surprised that her loquacious friend had kept her secret thus far. But then she remembered. Despite giving the opposite impression, Amy was really very good at keeping secrets. Kathy nodded. 'I don't expect you to lie for me if anyone asks you straight out, but unless they do, yes, I'd prefer that no one knows.'

'Okay,' Amy nodded. 'I don't suppose they'll think to ask me anyway. But . . .' she bit her lip and looked awkwardly at Kathy.

'What? What is it?'

'Well, there is some news. Not good, I'm afraid.'

'Is it – is it my mam?'

'No, no, not that. They're fine, at least – ' Amy pulled a face – 'as fine as they'll ever be.'

Kathy smiled weakly. But she could see from Amy's worried expression that the news had something to do with her.

'Tell me.'

'Aunt Jemima told us. She only heard quite recently and Mum's written to tell me. But, of course, she didn't realize that I often see you.' Amy took a deep breath and took hold of both Kathy's hands, gripping them tightly. 'You know that Tony went to train to be a fighter pilot?'

Kathy nodded, her heart beating painfully. She almost knew what was coming before Amy said the words. 'It seems he was involved in the Battle of Britain. You know, all that fighting that went on in the south and over the Channel last autumn?'

'I – I've heard about it, though at the time . . .' Kathy's voice faded away and she shuddered as she remembered being shut up behind the grim walls of Willow House, cut off in shame from the world outside and everything that was happening. She began to tremble. She couldn't speak, could hardly breathe.

'He – he was shot down and – he was posted missing, presumed killed.'

The room seemed to spin. Kathy clutched at the table, her hands pulling free of Amy's grasp as she felt herself falling sideways. She knew no more until she opened her eyes to see Amy's face bending over her, chafing her hand.

'She's coming round,' a strange voice said. 'Don't let her get up too quickly though. There, steadily does it.'

'Can we help?' said a man's voice and Kathy found herself lifted bodily from the floor by two sailors and placed gently on the chair where she'd been sitting.

'Can I get you anything?' one asked.

'Thank you, she'll be fine now. I – I just had to give her some bad news.'

The fresh-faced young man grimaced. 'Tell me about it. Well, if you're sure you're all right . . .'

'We're fine, but thanks for your help.'

'Don't mention it.' He laid his hand gently on Kathy's shoulder. 'Hope you'll be all right, miss.'

Kathy murmured her thanks. Her head was still woolly as the landlord of the pub arrived at the table. 'Here, miss, drink this brandy. It'll help. On the house, love,' he said to Amy as she offered to pay.

Kathy sipped the liquid and colour came back into her cheeks.

'Are you going to be all right?' Amy said anxiously. 'Because I daren't miss the bus.'

'I'll be fine in a minute. It was – it was just the shock.'

They sat a few moments longer in silence, neither knowing what to say now, until Amy was obliged to say, 'I'll have to go.'

'Yes, yes. I know. I'll be all right. Honestly.'

Amy kissed her. 'This is "au revoir" for the moment then. Take care of yourself, and I'm so sorry I had to break such news to you, but – but I thought you should know.'

'Of course,' Kathy said flatly.

All hope was gone now. Any dreams she might have had that one day she would meet Tony again were blown away by those few words. 'Missing, presumed killed.'

But even amid her own sorrow, Kathy spared a thought for Beatrice Kendall.

It was the first time she'd felt any sympathy for the woman. Now that she had given birth to her own son, and lost him, she understood the devastation Tony's mother would be feeling.

Thirty

After she knew Amy had gone, Kathy felt even more bereft than ever. And to be left with such heartbreaking news, too, was almost too much to bear. The days now passed in a blur. Kathy was hardly aware of what she was doing. She did her job but she couldn't even force the cheery smile she always plastered on her face. Before she knew it, it was spring and Saltershaven was flooded with personnel from the RAF training centre that had been set up in the town.

One Sunday evening towards the end of April, when there was a live show on the stage of the cinema instead of a film, several airmen came to the cinema, laughing and joking and flirting with any girl in sight.

Kathy looked at them with bitterness. Why should they be alive when Tony was dead? Immediately she felt guilty.

'Cheer up, love, it'll never happen,' said one cheery young man. He looked no more than a boy, Kathy thought. He looked as if he shouldn't be out of short trousers yet, never mind flying off to face the enemy.

Now, for the first time since Amy had told her the awful news, Kathy's smile was genuine as she said huskily, 'Not with you brave boys defending us, it won't. Good luck to you.'

The young man's face sobered for a moment and then he nodded and said, 'Thanks, but tonight, we've got a night off. We're looking forward to this. Have you seen the show before?'

Kathy shook her head. 'No. It's the first time this particular concert party's been here.'

'I hear they're from Lincoln?'

'Really?' Kathy glanced down at the programme she held in her hand. So lost had she been in her own private grief that she hadn't really taken in the name of the concert party appearing tonight. But now she saw the name on the programme she gave a gasp of delight. 'The Lindum Lovelies' bring you *Sing As We Go*, a musical extravaganza of laughter and song,' she murmured aloud. 'Of course! I should have known.'

The lights began to dim as she showed the young man into his seat. Then, taking her own seat at the back, Kathy looked eagerly towards the stage, wondering if there would be anyone among the artistes whom she might recognize. And there was. The very first person to come on to the stage as compère for the evening was none other than Ron Spencer.

He stepped up to the microphone and spread his arms wide. 'Ladies and gentlemen, welcome one and all . . .'

Kathy smiled in the darkness and sat back to enjoy the show, pushing aside, just for a couple of hours, the sadness in her heart. But it was not quite what she had expected. Knowing Ron, she had anticipated a programme of choral works, but instead it was more like a music-hall revue. Then she remembered the plans that they'd had just before she'd left so hurriedly. This is exactly what they'd planned. She smiled in the darkness, thrilled that it had all come about just as they'd hoped.

The young comedian, with a pencil-line moustache

and a garish suit, shamelessly impersonated the great Max Miller, while the girl vocalist sang a medley of favourite songs of the thirties from 'Roll out the Barrel' to 'Smoke Gets in Your Eyes'. But throughout her performance, Kathy couldn't help wincing. The girl, Melody Miles, though pretty and vivacious and attracting whistles and catcalls from the young men in the audience, could hardly sing in tune. The three dancers, with long shapely legs, were a definite hit with the audience and were seen in various guises in the comedy sketches, as too was Melody. And in two of the sketches, Kathy spotted Martin Montgomery. What a good actor he was, she thought in admiration. They all were, and Melody was a much better actress than she was a vocalist. Her comic timing was perfect and the audience's laughter threatened to damage the roof far more than any bomb!

The finale brought a medley of sentimental ballads and the whole show ended with a rousing rendition of 'Land of Hope and Glory' followed by the National Anthem, led, Kathy was thankful to see, by the male vocalist, who could sing in tune!

As the curtain fell, Kathy stood up. As soon as the audience had filed out, she went backstage. There was a lot of chatter and laughter coming from the dressing rooms.

'Do you know where Mr Spencer is?' she asked a woman carrying an armful of dresses.

'Star dressing room, love. Just 'cos he formed the party, he reckons he's top billing. If you ask me that should go to the female vocalist – if we had a proper one, that is. Melody's a lovely girl, but she can't sing for toffee.' She leant forward. 'But don't tell 'er I said so. Mind you, she's a good little actress. I'll give her that. Funny, too. What's the word? Coquettish. That's it. And sparkle! That girl sparkles more than all the sequins on these dresses.'

Kathy smiled weakly. She said nothing, but she couldn't help agreeing with the woman she presumed was the wardrobe mistress. The cameo parts the girl had played in the sketches had been brilliant, but like the woman said she couldn't sing for toffee.

Kathy knocked on the door and heard Ron's familiar voice. 'Come in.'

He was sitting at the dressing table, removing his stage make-up. When he saw in the mirror who was standing behind him in the doorway, he sprang to his feet and turned with his arms outstretched all in one movement. 'Kathy! My dear girl. How wonderful to see you? Whatever are you doing here?'

'I work here. In this cinema.'

'Oh, are you the resident singer?'

'No – no, I'm an usherette and—'

'An usherette! My dear girl, with your talent. An usherette! Oh dear me, we can't have that! Here, sit down.' He moved some clothes from a chair and dusted it. 'We must talk about this.'

His tone brooked no argument and, smiling self-consciously, Kathy did as he bade her.

'It was a lovely show, Mr Spencer.'

Ron chuckled. 'Oh, it's Ron now, to one and all. No standing on ceremony these days, love.'

'So – it all worked then? All the plans you were making when I – I left.'

Ron regarded her solemnly for a moment. He seemed about to question her, but then he changed his mind, smiled and nodded. 'Yes, and we're all having a great time.' His smile faded briefly as he added, 'Of course, we see some dreadful sights, when we go to hospitals especially. And it's heartbreaking seeing all the bomb damage in the cities. And then, of course, when we go to the docks when the army lads are going abroad, that's hard, Kathy, that's really hard.'

'You go all round the country then?'

Ron nodded. 'We were in Coventry in February.' He sighed and shook his head. 'My, that's a dreadful sight, Kathy. And London's had it very bad, haven't they? And even poor old Lincoln got a bit of a pasting last month.'

'Yes, we had a couple of raids here too. What about our street? Is it okay?'

'So far, love. Mabel writes regularly. I always let her know where we're going to be. She keeps me up to date with all the news.'

'I presume you're here because of all the forces personnel in the area?'

'That's right. We have a list of all the theatres near to army camps, airfields and training centres. Lincolnshire's becoming known for its airfields and, of course, there's the naval training centre up the road and so – here we are.' He spread his hands as if that explained everything. And in a way, it did. 'Of course,' he went on, 'we have to travel a lot and it means staying away from home, sometimes for weeks at a time, but Mabel's all for it. She says she's lucky I haven't got to go into the forces and she's busy with her war work in the WVS. She and Miss Robinson do a lot of work together.'

Suddenly, Kathy was overwhelmed by a wave of homesickness. Not for the farm and her parents, but for the tiny terraced house in Lincoln, Aunt Jemima and her cat.

'How – how is Miss Robinson?'

Ron eyed her keenly. 'Missing you,' he said as bluntly as Jemima herself would have answered. He leaned forward and patted her hand. 'We were all sorry about what happened on your wedding day, but we've all missed you, Kathy. Don't hide yourself away here forever, will you? Unless, of course, there's someone here . . . ?'

Kathy took a deep breath. Oh yes, there was someone here all right, and for a brief moment she was very tempted to tell Ron everything. What a relief it would be to spill it all out. Yet, still something held her back. Instead, she shook her head, not trusting herself to speak the lie aloud.

'Then would you consider joining us?' He smiled ruefully. 'I expect you heard poor little Melody tonight. She's a great little actress, but she's not a singer. Now you . . .' Again he spread his hands and then went on. 'They're a good crowd, very friendly and most of them are a similar age to you. You'd fit in very well. Kathy, dear girl . . .' He grasped her hands and held them tightly. 'Please say you'll think about it.'

Kathy smiled and said impulsively, 'I don't need time to think. The answer's yes. I'd love to join you all.'

Now he put his arms around her and held her close. 'I'm so pleased. We're in the area until next Saturday night. Can you leave with us first thing on Sunday morning? I'll see the cinema manager if you have any problems leaving your job.'

'I'll talk to him. I'm sure he'll be all right about it.'

'That's wonderful. Wonderful! I can't wait to tell the others. They'll be thrilled. We've really missed having a decent female vocalist with us.'

'But what about Melody? Won't she be hurt?'

Ron laughed. 'Heavens, no! The poor girl will be relieved. She's been begging me to find someone to take her place. Oh, she'll not leave us. Like I say, she's brilliant in the sketches and she helps Martin write some of them too. No, no, you don't need to worry about Melody. She's very talented in all sorts of ways, but sadly not in singing.'

For the first time since her disastrous wedding day, Kathy walked home feeling she had some hope for the future.

The cinema manager was most understanding and released her from her job at once. He made up her pay packet until the end of the week and even gave her another week's wages on top.

'Just in case you need a few things,' Larry said kindly. 'But I do feel a little put out.'

'I know – and I'm sorry if I'm letting you down . . .' she began, but he interrupted.

'No, it's not that. I just wish I'd known you could sing. I'd've had you on that stage myself before you could say "Jack Flash", especially when we had one or two acts we'd booked for our Sunday shows let us down. We were booked to have an RAF band last night, you know, but there was some sort of flap on and they cancelled. This concert party was the only replacement I could get at short notice, but I wasn't sure if we were doing the right thing having a variety show on a Sunday,' Larry added worriedly. 'Some people might think it a bit out of place.'

'I think people are relaxing their attitude a bit these days,' Kathy tried to reassure him. 'I wouldn't worry.'

'I'm sure you're right. It's a difficult time for all of us, but "The show must go on" is a very good adage to cling to just now. There are a lot of people with cause for tears but they put a smile on their face and carry on, and if concert parties like the one you're about to join can help folks to do that, then good luck to you.'

Kathy nodded. She could not speak for the tears that welled in her throat, but she took the kindly man's words to heart. Though her own heart felt as if it was breaking, she would put on a brave smile and sing to bring a little joy into the lives of others. Maybe it would help ease her own heartache, even if only for a little while.

Kathy's landlady was not so understanding. 'I need a week's notice. That's what you agreed to, so if you're leaving on Sunday, you'll 'ave to pay me for next week, an' all.'

'That's all right,' Kathy said, silently blessing the manager's generosity.

'Oh, flush are we?' the woman said sarcastically. 'I've a good mind to demand another week.'

'Well, you won't get it. Here, this is what I owe you and that's all you're getting.'

Kathy pushed the money into the greedy woman's hand and headed for the stairs, thankful she'd some packing to do. With a bit of luck, she'd never be back here again.

But once in her room, as she closed the door behind her and leant against it for a moment, she realized that of course she would come back. Perhaps not to this dingy room, if she could avoid it, but she would come back to the town. Oh yes, she'd be back, if only to try to catch a fleeting glimpse of her son.

Thirty-One

On the Saturday afternoon Kathy walked along the road running parallel to the beach to the white house at the end. As she neared the entrance she could see that the wrought-iron gates had disappeared, taken, no doubt, for the war effort. Hungrily she gazed at the house, wondering which of the windows was her son's nursery. She ached to see him. He'd be five months old by now. Was he trying to sit up yet? Was he smiling and laughing? Oh, how she wished she could hear his baby laughter.

She saw a face at one of the upstairs windows and saw that the woman was standing there with a child in her arms. Her heart skipped a beat and she held her breath, gazing up at the window, squinting to see the child more clearly. Mrs Wainwright stared down at her for a few moments and then moved away. Kathy waited but she did not come back to the window. With a sigh, Kathy was about to turn away when she saw the front door open and Mrs Wainwright hurried down the steps and came towards her.

Kathy made to turn away, but the woman called out, 'Wait!'

Kathy bit her lip and her heart beat a little faster. She didn't want to cause any trouble. She just wanted to . . .

'Hello again,' Mrs Wainwright greeted her pleasantly. 'I thought it was you. In fact I think I've see you once or twice.'

'Yes, yes, I just walk along to the end here and – and back again. It – it makes a pleasant walk along here. With the sea just over the sandhills. In fact, I think I'll go back along the beach.'

Mrs Wainwright smiled and nodded. 'If you go down that little path there through the bushes, you'll come to the beach.'

'Thanks,' Kathy smiled. 'Nice to see you again. I – I'm leaving tomorrow. I've joined a concert party touring round to entertain troops and war workers.'

'How wonderful. I would've liked to have done something like that, but now I have the baby . . .' She smiled, not in the least unhappy that she could no longer do any such thing.

'Of course. How – how is he?'

'He's fine. Growing fast. Would you like to see him?'

'I – I'd love to, if you don't mind.'

'Of course I don't. I'm such a doting mother, I must be boring all my friends with my constant baby chatter. Come along in. Perhaps you'd like a cup of tea before you walk back into town.'

'Thank you. That would be nice,' Kathy said mechanically, but her heart was skipping madly. She was going to see her son.

She followed the woman into the house, through the vast high hall and into a room on the right-hand side.

Mrs Wainwright opened the door quietly, 'Here he is, my little darling,' she said as she approached the sofa where the child was lying, surrounded by cushions.

Mrs Wainwright laughed. 'I have to put these here when I leave him for a few moments. He can nearly roll over now and I'm so frightened he might fall off the settee.' She picked him up and rocked him for a moment, looking down into the little face with such love that Kathy felt a lump in her throat. The child reached out and touched the woman's face with his tiny fingers. And then he smiled and Kathy's heart melted.

'I'll just make some tea,' Mrs Wainwright said. 'Would you like to hold him while I fetch it?'

Kathy sat down on the sofa and held out her arms. Trembling a little, she took the warm little body into her arms and looked down at him with eyes that were blurred with tears. 'He's beautiful,' she said huskily. Then she whispered, 'Hello, James. Hello, my darling boy.'

The tea forgotten, Mrs Wainwright sat down in the armchair. 'You're – you're his real mother, aren't you?' she said.

Kathy looked up and met her steady gaze. She couldn't read the expression in the woman's eyes, but she was relieved to see there was no fear or panic.

She looked down again at the little boy in her arms as, trying to keep her voice calm and level, she said, 'I believe I am his natural mother, yes. But you are the one he is going to know as his mother. And please, don't think I'm going to cause trouble for you, because I'm not. I – we're not supposed to know who the adoptive parents are, but I found out.'

'I see. Yes, we were assured that you would not be given our name and certainly not our address.' Still Mrs Wainwright spoke calmly.

'But you see, I signed the papers when I went into Willow House thinking they were just admission papers. I never dreamed I was signing away all rights to my baby even then. And after he was born – I had a difficult time – they took him away. They never even showed him to me, never let me hold him. I didn't even know it was a boy until one of the other girls told me.'

Now Mrs Wainwright gasped. 'That's dreadful. We were told that his mother had been given every chance to keep him herself but that she was adamant that she wanted him adopted.'

'That's certainly not the case,' Kathy said, 'More than anything I wanted him. But since then I've realized that you can give him a far better life than ever I can now.' She took a deep breath. 'James's father and I were to be married. Five minutes more and we would have been.'

'Five minutes?' Mrs Wainwright's smooth brow puckered. 'Whatever do you mean?'

'Tony's mother was taken ill during the service, just before – just before we were to make our vows.' She smiled with wry sadness. 'You know the part in the service where they vicar asks the congregation whether they know of any just cause . . . ?' Wordlessly, Mrs Wainwright nodded. 'That's when Mrs Kendall – very conveniently – had a heart attack.'

There was a pause before Mrs Wainwright asked hesitantly, 'Do you – do you mean his mother was against the marriage?'

'Yes,' Kathy said bitterly. 'She told me to my face that she'd never let it happen. And she kept her word.'

'But – but what happened later? I mean – didn't your fiancé arrange another date?'

Kathy shook her head. All the time they had been talking, Katy's gaze had been on her baby. She was drinking in the sight of him, not knowing when she would see him again. If ever. 'Tony had been called up.

The wedding was on the Saturday and then he was at the hospital until the Sunday evening and then – and then he had to report on the Monday morning. That's why the wedding had been arranged so hastily. Not because I was pregnant – because I wasn't. Not then.' She blushed at the memory of their lovemaking, but not for one moment did she regret it. The result of it lay in her arms. How could she regret bringing such a perfect little being into the world, even though it was breaking her heart to part with him?

'But couldn't you have been married later? When he came on leave? I'm sure if the authorities had known they would have granted your fiancé – Tony, is it? – ' Kathy nodded – 'compassionate leave.'

'He – he doesn't know about the baby.'

'Doesn't know?' Now Mrs Wainwright was shocked. 'But – but why?'

'He went away. He wrote to me once. But he wrote to his mother every other day.' She spoke flatly, without emotion, but the pain and disappointment – the betrayal almost – was plain to see on her face. 'It was never going to stop, was it? She was always going to be there between us. He would always put her first. And then . . .' Her eyes softened as she gazed at the child. 'I didn't want anyone to think he'd been forced to marry me.'

'If you don't mind me saying so, my dear, I think you should have fought a bit harder. My goodness!' She clapped her hand over her mouth, her eyes wide. 'What am I saying? If you had, I wouldn't have my adorable boy.' Now there was fear in her eyes as she added, 'You – you won't take him away from me, will you?'

Kathy shook her head. 'No – I won't. I promise.'

'But when your fiancé comes home on leave . . . ?'

Kathy pressed her lips together, trying to stem the tears that were never very far away. Huskily she said, 'He's never coming back. He was a fighter pilot and I've heard that he was shot down. Missing, presumed killed.'

'Oh my dear – I'm so very sorry. I don't know what to say.'

'Could I just ask you one thing?'

Mrs Wainwright nodded warily.

'I know I haven't any right to ask, but may I write to you? Would you write back to me and let me know how he is? Perhaps you could send me a photograph now and again if I give you my address in Lincoln.'

The woman relaxed and smiled. 'Of course. It's the least I can do.'

And that was all Kathy could ask, but it was more than she'd ever dared to hope for.

The train journey from Saltershaven on the east coast to Yorkshire, where their next performance was to take place, was long enough for Kathy to meet the other members of the concert party. Ron Spencer made the introductions, reminding her, 'And from now on call me "Ron". No more of this Mr Spencer lark. We're a friendly crowd and we're going to be spending a lot of time together. Now, this is Martin. He's an actor, but he also doubles as our stage manager.'

'Yes, we met before.' Kathy smiled and held out her hand. He was still as fit and healthy-looking as he had been and she couldn't help wondering immediately why he had not been called up already. Ron's next words explained. 'And we'll have to make the most of him because he'll likely be called up next year. I shall apply for a deferment for him, of course, but whether I'll get it is another matter.'

Martin took her hand in his huge paw and shook it with a strong grasp. His smile crinkled his swarthy face.

Kathy smiled back. 'You look as if you're used to working out of doors. Have you worked on a farm?'

Martin gave a deep, rumbling laugh. 'No. I worked for a brewery.' He flexed his huge arms. 'Heaving barrels about all day. Now I heave stage props and scenery about, as well as a bit of acting now and again. And writing the odd sketch too.'

Kathy laughed. 'Is there anything you *don't* do?' Then she glanced from one to the other, puzzled. 'But don't the theatres we visit have their own stage managers? The cinema at Saltershaven did.'

'Yes, some of them,' Ron agreed. 'But you see we're not always in theatres or even cinemas with a stage. We go to factory canteens, shipyards, as well as to airfields and barracks – anywhere we can entertain. Even docks, if we hear of troops about to embark.'

'And we have to improvise with scenery,' Martin put in, 'build a stage sometimes. I'm the chap who begs, borrows and steals whatever we need.'

'Folks are very good. Martin asks around the locals and he always comes up with the goods.'

Kathy smiled up at the good-looking young man. 'With a smile like that, I bet he has them eating out of his hand.'

'Now, who's next?' Ron went on. 'Ah yes . . .'

The introductions continued until Kathy's head was dizzy with all the names. The only one she really remembered was Rosie, with whom she would be sharing a room in whatever digs could be found in the various places. She was a member of 'The Cinderellas', a group of three girl dancers. Like Melody, they all took part in the comedy sketches. Most of the men were Ron's age and too old to be called up, with the exception of Martin and one other. Lionel was pale and thin, with light brown hair and pale, hazel eyes. He was very serious and hardly ever smiled.

'He's failed his medical,' Ron whispered. 'And he's a bit cut up about it. Evidently he has a heart problem, but he's determined not to be an invalid.'

Kathy said nothing, but already she admired the young man, who was still determined to 'do his bit'. What a contrast to Tony's mother, she thought. 'What does Lionel do?'

'He's the comedian.'

'Really?' Kathy couldn't hide her surprise.

'Doesn't look like one,' Ron chuckled, 'but you wait till you see him on stage. He has the audience – and us – in stitches. He writes his own material and some of the sketches too, along with Martin and Melody. We're always wanting new material because we sometimes visit places more than once and they don't want to see the same old thing again. He's really very clever.'

As Ron brought them together, Lionel held her hand and gazed earnestly into her eyes. 'Can you act?'

'I – I don't know.'

'We'll try you out. You've a very pretty face. I could write some good parts for you.'

With that he turned away. Evidently, Kathy thought, Lionel was not one to engage in small talk.

But Rosie was, and so were the other two Cinderellas, Maureen and Joan. For the rest of the journey Kathy sat beside Rosie and the other two girls sat facing them. The carriage resounded with their chatter, now and again punctuated with shrieks of laughter.

In their merry company, Kathy felt her spirits lift. She would never get over the sadness buried deep in her heart, but from now on she would keep a smile on her face and hide her heartache. She would give herself over to entertaining others, trying to lighten the drudgery and hardship of wartime conditions. Many in the audiences, she knew, would have just as much grief as she did. If she could make people forget, even for a few moments, their heartache, then maybe she could forget her own for a little while.

The first show in which Kathy took part was in a factory canteen in Leeds.

'What do they make here?' Kathy asked innocently, as she pulled on the strapless evening gown and asked Rosie to fasten the single string of pearls that Tony had given her around her neck.

'Ooh, don't ask,' Rosie said. 'We never ask questions, wherever we go. Ron says it doesn't do. It might sound as if we're spies. Besides – ' she shrugged – 'I'd rather not know. If it's munitions or something dangerous I'd rather not be thinking we're all going to get blown to kingdom come any minute.'

Kathy laughed. To her surprise it was a genuine laugh that had come spontaneously. It was a long time since she'd laughed so readily. Impulsively, she turned and hugged Rosie.

'Whatever's that for? I only fastened your necklace.'

'Just – Oh, I can't explain, Rosie. It's just – just that I've been through a bit of a tough time since the war started and – and – well, you've all been so friendly and – and kind.'

'We're a nice bunch, I'll grant you that. Specially that Martin.' There was a sudden sparkle in Rosie's blue eyes.

Kathy found herself laughing again. 'I think you'll find that he's just a little friendlier towards you than to the rest of us. Not that he isn't, I mean,' she added swiftly.

Rosie grinned and her cheeks were pink. 'He's nice. I do like him, Kath. Do you think he likes me?'

'Ask a silly question, Rosie. 'Course he does. Now, come on, we'd better get down to the side of the stage.'

'The wings, you mean,' Rosie giggled.

'I'll never get used to all the names. Upstage, downstage – I still haven't got the hang of it.'

'Don't worry,' Rosie said, linking her arm through Kathy's as they left the draughty little room, no bigger than a cupboard, that served as their dressing room. 'When you go the wrong way, it all adds to the fun.'

Kathy took a deep breath as they neared the side of the stage and peeped through the curtains. 'Oh heck! There's hundreds out there. I was hoping for a small audience for my first time.'

Rosie looked out too. 'How many million times have I told you not to exaggerate? There's fifty at the most.'

'It looks like hundreds to me,' Kathy said nervously.

'You'll be fine. Everyone said what a lovely voice you've got when they heard you in rehearsal. Melody's quite envious.'

Kathy turned. 'Oh, Rosie, she's – she's not upset that I've come, is she?'

'Lord, no. It's given her the chance to do what she's really good at. Be a comic actress. And she's quite a good impressionist. I think Ron is thinking of giving her her own spot if she can come up with enough impersonations. Have you heard her do that woman off the wireless, the one that's in ITMA that says, "Can I do you now, sir?"'

'Mrs Mopp, you mean?'

'That's the one. Melody sounds just like her. Brilliant she is.' Rosie giggled. 'Funny thing is, when she impersonates Vera Lynn, she sings just like her. In tune and everything. Yet, when she tries to sing as herself, it's awful. Funny that, isn't it?'

'Mm,' Kathy murmured, her mind once again on the audience filing into the canteen. 'I do hope I remember all the words when I start to sing. At this moment, everything's just flown out of my head.'

Rosie squeezed her arm. 'You will.'

Ron, as compère, introduced all the acts, and when it came to Kathy's spot, he said, 'Now, today we have a young lady making her very first appearance with us. Please give a warm welcome to our very own nightingale, Kathy Burton.'

Taking a deep breath, she stepped out on to the makeshift stage that Martin had set up at one end of the canteen. She forced a smile as she neared the microphone. Still she couldn't remember the words, nor even what song she was supposed to be singing.

This is awful, she thought, as the butterflies in her stomach turned into vultures. I can't remember a word. I'm going to make a complete fool of myself and let Ron and all the others down . . .

The clapping died away and the pianist struck the first chord and played the introduction. Kathy opened her mouth and from somewhere the words came: 'I'm Gonna Sit Right Down and Write Myself a Letter . . . '

The applause at the end of the first song gave her a little confidence and as she finished her second song someone from the back of the room shouted in a cockney accent, 'Sing us "The Lambeth Walk".'

'Nah sing us, "On Ilkley Moor . . ."'

'But we're miles from home, mate. Let's 'ave "Lambeth Walk"?'

While the argument went on, with others joining in, Kathy turned to the pianist. 'Do you know either of them?'

Terry nodded. 'I think so, but I'll have to improvise a bit. Do you know the words?'

She laughed. 'Not all of them but I think I'm going to get some help, don't you?'

Terry grinned at her and struck the opening chord, and Kathy began to sing the opening line of 'The Lambeth Walk'. At once the group of workers sitting at the back of the room were singing loudly and swaying to the music. One or two of the women got up and began to dance, linking arms and kicking up their legs.

As the song ended with a resounding 'Oi', the pianist went straight into the second of the requests and now the rest of the audience joined in. Kathy only knew one or two verses of the song, so was left conducting the singing from the stage.

At last even the born and bred Yorkshire folk ran out of verses and tumultuous applause broke out. Some even stood up, whistling and cat-calling, as Kathy curtsied and left the stage to be met by a beaming Ron and an excited Rosie.

'That was terrific. You're a real trouper, Kathy. Go

on,' Ron added, giving her a little push. 'Go and take another bow.'

As she stepped back onto the stage the applause was thunderous, and when she finally returned to the wings, there were tears in her eyes.

For the ten minutes she had been on stage she had not thought about Tony or even little James.

At last she had found a way to bury her heartache, even if only for a few moments each day.

It was a start.

Thirty-Two

For the next four months, they toured the north of England playing in army camps, airfields, shipyards and factories.

At one factory Ron warned, 'You can't wear any jewellery, not even hair-clips or watches today.'

'Not hair-clips,' Rosie wailed. 'Why ever not?'

'They make high explosives here. Anything that might cause the slightest spark has got to be left behind.'

'Don't blame me if my hair's flying all over the place when we dance then,' Rosie said tartly, tossing back her thick mane of auburn hair.

'Don't worry, Rosie, the fellers'll love it.'

'Can't I – can't I wear my pearl necklace?' Kathy asked, her voice trembling a little.

Ron's eyes softened. He'd guessed how much the piece of jewellery meant to her. She was never without it.

'Sorry, love, but I'll keep it safe for you, if you like.'

The minor irritations of the unusual regulations were all forgotten when the performers heard the clapping and cheering and stamping feet of the enthusiastic audience.

'We don't often get concert parties coming to us,' the manager of the factory told them, 'so we really appreciate you coming here. You've really lifted all our spirits.'

The members of the company felt a warm glow on hearing his words. It made all the travelling on draughty trains and sleeping in hard, lumpy beds worthwhile.

'So, where are we off to now, Ron?' Rosie asked as they all boarded a train out of Manchester.

'Liverpool. We're to play to the lads awaiting embarkation. There's a ship leaving on the twenty-eighth.' He glanced round the carriage to make sure that there were no servicemen overhearing what he was about to say. 'It'll not be easy. They're just going to war. Young lads, most of them. Probably away from their homes and families for the first time. And a lot of them . . .' he paused before adding softly, 'might never come back.'

'Liverpool was blitzed earlier in the year. May, I think it was, when London got it so bad.'

There was silence now in the carriage, each member of the party lost in their own thoughts and quietly vowing to give the boys as good a send-off as they possibly could, despite the dangers. Nothing was going to stop them. Not even Adolf and his bombs.

Kathy chose her programme of songs very carefully. 'Should I keep it all bright and cheerful?' she asked Ron.

To her surprise, he shook his head. 'No, love. It might bring a tear or two to their eyes, but they like the odd sentimental ballad, you know. One or two that were popular in the last war might be appropriate. 'Pack up Your Troubles' . . . and 'Tipperary' . . . but also songs like 'Keep the Home Fires Burning' – that sort of thing.'

Ron was quite right. As Kathy stood on the draughty dockside, the soldiers gathered around her, lifting her bodily onto the makeshift stage that Martin had built. Within minutes, they were joining in the rousing songs, but the ballads were just as warmly received, sung softly and with feeling.

The cheers for Kathy were always the loudest, but no one in the company seemed to begrudge her the affection from the 'boys'.

'You're our "sweetheart",' one shouted from the front row as she began her final song. For a moment she thought she wasn't going to be able to sing for the lump in her throat. But she had to; this time 'Wish Me Luck' held a very special meaning for each and every one of them.

Kathy rested her aching head against the cool glass of the carriage window. It had been a late night, and maybe the hospitality of the NAAFI on the army camp where they'd played to an enthusiastic audience who'd whistled and stamped their feet had been just a little bit too much. But she could sleep on the train, she'd promised herself as she'd dragged herself out of bed to finish her packing before it was even light. She'd glanced at the other bed, which had not been slept in. Rosie was missing again. Kathy had sighed. She'd seen the romance blossoming between the young girl and Martin and now it seemed it had taken a more serious turn. She just hoped Rosie wasn't going to get herself into trouble like she had. It wouldn't be many weeks now before Martin received his call-up papers, and despite Ron's belief that he would be able to get deferment for the young man, Kathy very much doubted it. She would have liked to warn the young girl, but Rose was a chatterbox. Even if she confided in her, Kathy didn't believe she was capable of keeping a secret. And although Ron Spencer knew what had happened on her wedding day, he knew nothing about her baby. All he thought was that she had gone away to get over her broken romance with Tony Kendall.

She felt someone ease themselves into the empty seat beside her. To her surprise it was not Rosie, but Ron, who said, 'Do you know where we're going now, Kathy?'

'Mm,' she murmured sleepily. 'Not really. I just get up in a morning, catch the train, sing, act a little, and then go to bed. Next day, I do it all again. I've lost track of where we are or even what day it is.'

She'd been with the concert party for over five months and already the weather had a definite autumnal feel about it. Though her heart was still in Saltershaven, she had not regretted her decision to join Ron's troupe for a moment. The travelling and the performing and then more travelling were very tiring, but it kept her busy and her mind occupied.

Ron chuckled. 'Well, I'll tell you. We're going home.'

Kathy's head shot up. She was wide awake now. 'To Lincoln? You mean we're going to Lincoln?'

'That's right. We'll be there by mid-afternoon. We've got four days off and we all meet up again on Wednesday. Now, how about that?'

Kathy wasn't sure. She fingered the key she always carried in her coat pocket. The key that Jemima had pressed on her when she'd left.

'This is your home, Kathy. You're welcome back any time you want to come. You hear me. I'll keep the spare room bed aired and you're to regard it as your room.'

A sudden longing to see the brisk, no-nonsense woman again was overwhelming.

After all this time away, she hoped Jemima Robinson's promise still held good.

Ron suggested taking a taxi from the station. 'We'll treat ourselves. We're not dragging these heavy cases another inch. Let's arrive home in style.'

Kathy insisted on paying half the fare and, when the vehicle drew up in the street, the driver carried her case right to the front door of Jemima's house.

'Don't I get a hand?' Ron asked in a mock plaintive tone.

'You're not as pretty as her, sir.'

Ron laughed. 'Well, I have to agree with you there.'

Ron and Kathy waved to each other. 'See you Wednesday morning, lass. Don't be late. Train goes at eight thirty.'

'Want picking up?' the cheeky taxi driver asked.

'Good idea,' Ron said. 'Eight fifteen all right?'

'I'll get you there in time for the train, sir.'

With a saucy wink at Kathy, he walked back to his taxi. 'Though I wouldn't mind makin' that 'un miss the train.' He jerked his thumb back over his shoulder towards Kathy. 'I'd like to tek her home wi' me. Mind you,' he sniffed. 'I don't know what the missis'd say if I did.'

The three of them laughed and then, as the taxi was driven away, Ron and Kathy went into their homes.

As Kathy inserted the key into the lock and pushed open the back door, the familiar warm furry body wound itself around her legs and miaowed a welcome.

'Darling Taffy,' Kathy murmured as she bent to stroke him. He rubbed his face against her hand and purred ecstatically.

She carried her suitcase upstairs, the cat bounding ahead of her as if showing her the way. As soon as she opened the bedroom door, Taffy pushed his way into the room and took a flying leap into the middle of the bed, where he turned round three times, kneading the cover.

'Not on Aunt Jemima's second best eiderdown,' Kathy laughed, picking up the cat. She flung back the satin eiderdown and set the cat on the blanket underneath. 'You shouldn't really be on the bed at all,' she scolded him lovingly. 'But I'm so pleased to see you, you can stay while I unpack my clothes.'

The cat closed his eyes to satisfied slits and purred even louder.

A little later, Kathy scooped Taffy up from the bed and carried him down the stairs, stroking him and talking to him as she went.

'Now, let's see what's for your tea and then I'll find something to cook for your mistress when she comes home. Won't that be a nice surprise?'

The meal was cooked and sitting in a warm oven by the time Jemima was due. The cat was fed and sitting sleepily on Kathy's knee as she sat in the chair in the corner in the darkness, with only the light of the fire she had lit in the grate for company. She dozed, waiting for Jemima to come home, the warm weight of the cat on her knee a familiar comfort she had so missed since she had been away.

She didn't hear the back door open and so Jemima's

cry of surprise as she turned on the light woke both her and Taffy. The cat dug his claws into her leg in fright and then jumped down and fled towards the door and out into the night.

'Oh my, you gave me such a fright,' Jemima said, recovering a little and laughing. Kathy jumped up and the two women moved towards each other, arms outstretched. 'But how lovely to see you, my dear.' Jemima hugged her and then stood back, still holding Kathy by her shoulders. 'Let me look at you.' She paused and then added, 'You look tired. I expect Ron's been working you far too hard.'

Of course, Jemima knew all about her touring with the concert party. Kathy had written to tell her and, besides, Ron's wife would be keeping her well informed too.

'It's okay,' Kathy smiled tremulously. She was surprised how emotional she felt at seeing Jemima. She had told her nothing in her letters about her traumatic time at Willow House, the birth of her little boy and all that had happened since.

Time enough for that in the evening when they had eaten and were sitting together in the firelight.

Then she would tell Jemima everything that had happened to her.

'So,' Kathy began when they had washed up the pots together and were sitting close to the fire, Jemima in her chair, Kathy on the rug at her feet. The late September evening was surprising chilly and Jemima had insisted on lighting a fire in the front room. 'How is everyone? Uncle Ted and Auntie Betty and Morry? And have you heard from Amy?'

'Yes. I get a letter from her most weeks.' Jemima regarded Kathy over her spectacles. 'She's a better letter writer than you, Katherine Burton. You disappointed me. I had hoped you would keep in touch right from the time you left.' She reached out and patted Kathy's hand. 'I do care about you, you know. I wanted to know that you were all right.'

'I'm sorry,' Kathy said at once. 'It – it was difficult.' Her face was haunted as she was forced to remember her time at Willow House.

And then, like the flood gates opening, it all came tumbling out. She told Jemima about the harsh regime at the home for unmarried women and the almost inhumane treatment meted out to her when she had been in labour. And then, worst of all, how she had been tricked into signing away her baby.

'I never held him, never even saw him,' she said huskily.

Jemima's face twisted in sympathy. Her own plight all those years ago seemed as nothing compared to what Kathy had suffered.

'But you knew it was a boy?'

'I wouldn't have done, but one of the other girls told me.'

'I see. But you've never seen him.'

'Well, yes, I have. Now.' Kathy went on to explain how she had found the address of her little boy's adoptive parents and how she had even got to know Mrs Wainwright.

'Do you think that was wise, dear?' Jemima said, and then added swiftly, 'Oh I don't blame you. I don't blame you one bit and maybe I'm not the best judge. I've been lucky all these years; able to see my son and even have Maurice know who I am. But – but won't you always be drawn back to go and see him? And I'm so worried that while his mo— Mrs Wainwright might seem friendly enough now, there might come a time when she'd rather you didn't see him. When he becomes old enough to ask awkward questions . . .' Jemima's voice trailed away.

Kathy was not hurt or offended by the older woman's words. She knew the outspoken Jemima well enough by now to know that whatever she said was spoken with good intention, even if the words were not always what one wanted to hear.

'I know,' Kathy said quietly, 'and I'm ready for that happening. I'm trying to build a life without him, but, Oh, Aunt Jemima, it's so hard.' Suddenly, unable to hold back the tears any more, she buried her face in Jemima's lap. The older woman stroked her hair tenderly and gazed into the fire's flickering flames, for once quite lost for words.

A little later, when she was calmer, Kathy asked, 'Have you heard how my mother is?'

'She's fine. Betty keeps an eye on her. Of course, her life is hard, we all know that and short of leaving your father, it always will be, but Betty keeps her posted about you and . . .'

Kathy drew in a sharp breath. 'You mean – you mean she knows?'

Jemima shook her head. 'No, not about that. We wouldn't divulge such a thing unless you told us we could.'

'I suppose,' Kathy said pensively, 'I wouldn't mind my mother knowing, but then it puts her in a very difficult position having to keep it from my father, so it's – it's best she doesn't know. Not yet, anyway. Maybe one day, I'll be able to tell her.'

There was such a wistful longing in the girl's tone that Jemima's heart went out to her. Instead, she said briskly, 'It's best not. And she'd only worry more about you. Kinder that she doesn't know for the time being.'

'Have you heard how Mr and Mrs Kendall are?'

'Not good,' Jemima sighed. 'Poor George is heart-broken, though he still trudges to work and looks after Beatrice.'

'And Mrs Kendall?'

'Much the same.'

'I'd've thought it might – well – have made her worse. Much worse.'

'Killed her, you mean?' Jemima was as blunt as ever.

'To be honest – yes.'

'Mm,' Jemima was thoughtful. 'We've always thought her illness was put on, haven't we? Now I'm sure of it. If she really had a weak heart, news of the death of her only beloved son would surely have made her very ill or worse. Instead, it was poor George who had to take a fortnight off work when they got the telegram, but it was Beatrice who just lay there on the couch as always, weeping and wailing and playing the part of the bereaved mother to perfection.'

'How do you know all this?'

'Because I went to see them.'

'You did?'

Now Jemima looked embarrassed. 'To tell you the truth, Kathy, I was about to commit an unforgivable sin. I went with the intention of telling them that you had had Tony's baby . . .'

Kathy gasped and her eyes widened in surprise. She

was appalled that Jemima could even think of doing such a thing.

'But I didn't do it,' Jemima went on hastily. 'When I got there, I just couldn't betray you in such a way. And besides, I'm not sure it wouldn't have made matters worse. Poor George was shattered and struggling to keep going. I arranged for Beatrice to go into a nursing home for a week. Mr James paid for it, just to give poor George a rest.'

'Is he all right now?'

Jemima sighed sadly. 'He went away for a few days while Beatrice was in the nursing home. He looked much better when he came back. Though there was still that awful haunted look in his eyes. I don't suppose he will ever get over losing his only son. His only child.'

'And her?'

'Oh, she's all right,' Jemima said, with not a scrap of sympathy for the hypochondriac. 'Beatrice and her like will be all right, because, my dear Kathy, despite what she'd like the world to think, there's only one person she's ever cared about and that's not, as she would have you believe, her beloved son, but herself. Beatrice Kendall is the epitome of the very worst kind of selfishness.'

There was silence between them for a while until Kathy murmured. 'I'd like to go and see his dad.'

'I wouldn't, my dear, not this time anyway. Perhaps when you come home again.'

Kathy smiled up at her, tears in her eyes. It wasn't just the woman's kindness and understanding, it was the inference that Jemima's house was Kathy's home that brought a lump to the girl's throat and an overwhelming gratitude.

Thirty-Three

'Now I know the members of this concert party of Ron's do get paid a little, but it can't be much . . .' Jemima began on the Wednesday morning as they breakfasted together before Kathy had to leave.

'Aunt Jemima, it's very kind of you, but I couldn't possible take any more. You've already been more than generous.'

'Oh, phooey.' Jemima dismissed her protests with a wave of her hand, then her green eyes twinkled mischievously. 'So, I'm to take it you're rolling in it, am I?'

Kathy laughed wryly. 'Not exactly, but—'

'No more "buts". Take it.'

'You're too good to me,' Kathy said, her voice trembling.

'More than likely,' Jemima said crisply, but she was smiling as she said it.

Moments later, as she drove away with Ron Spencer in the taxi, Kathy looked back to see Jemima standing outside her front door with Taffy in her arms waving goodbye.

When they arrived at the railway station, Ron rounded up all the party and stood on a nearby seat to say, 'We're not going on the train. I've got a surprise for you all. Follow me.' He jumped down and led them all out of the station.

'What's going on?' Rosie asked.

'Search me,' Kathy said. 'He didn't say anything in the taxi.'

'Ooh, 'ark at her. Taxi, is it? Come into money, have we?'

Kathy grinned. 'Actually, we treated ourselves to a taxi home last week – Ron and me live in the same street. Well, this lovely driver took us home and promised to pick us up today. And do you know what . . . ?'

'He wouldn't let you pay this morning.'

Kathy's eyes widened. 'How did you know?'

'Because it's what a lot of them do when they know who we are and what we're doing.'

'Oh.' Kathy felt deflated and Rosie pinched her arm, laughing. 'I was only teasing you, you know. I don't care if you're a millionaire – I'd still be your friend.'

'If I was, we wouldn't be travelling about on draughty trains any more— Oh my!' She stopped short as the whole party came to a halt.

'It doesn't look as if we're going to anyway,' Rosie said, as they all saw Ron pointing proudly towards a single-decker bus with the words 'The Lindum Players' painted on the side. 'The local bus company have donated one of their old buses for our permanent use and, better still, one of their drivers who's just reached retirement age has volunteered to come with us. This, ladies and gentlemen, is Keith.'

The whole party cheered the man, who gave them a cheery wave. 'Hello, there. We'll get to know each other, but for now let's get you all stowed aboard and we'll be off.'

*

The concert party grew even closer now that they travelled together all the time, so every time someone was called up, the gap they left was even harder to fill. New members joined and were welcomed into the group, but those that had gone were still missed.

Ron's face wore a perpetually worried frown, and at the beginning of December 1941, even he began to lose heart.

'They're going to call up all single women between twenty and thirty,' he told the company dolefully. 'How are we ever to keep going if we lose all the young singers and dancers?'

Rosie put her arms around Ron, 'Then we'll all just have to get married,' she joked.

Ron smiled thinly but the anxious frown never left his forehead. 'I'm serious. How are we to hold the party together?'

'Can't you apply for deferment for us like you did for Martin? We're doing our bit for the war effort, when all's done and said.'

Ron's face lightened a little. 'I could try, I suppose. But whether they'll let you all stay . . .'

'It's worth a try, Ron,' Rosie and her fellow dancers chorused.

Ron's application was successful – at least for the time being. More and more the work of ENSA was being recognized as being a valuable part of the war effort. Entertainment of any kind, especially live shows, helped cheer troops and war workers alike, especially at Christmas for those who could not get home. And when America entered the war after the attack on Pearl Harbor, it was likely that there would soon be servicemen stationed in Britain who were thousands of miles from home. Keeping up morale was going to be more important than ever.

She knew she was part of something special, but Kathy still felt restless. She longed to go back to Saltershaven to see James. Despite her promise to write, Kathy had received no letter or photograph of her little boy from Mrs Wainwright and the passage of time only seemed to make her longing greater, not less. He would be a year old now. Was he walking yet? Had he said his first words? She so longed to know, but she was very afraid that Mrs Wainwright had changed her mind. Perhaps she'd told her husband and they'd decided that they should cut off all contact with their son's natural mother.

'We'll write a pantomime.' Ron interrupted her thoughts, knowing nothing of her inner torment. Kathy sighed and forced a smile. 'I want you to play principal boy,' he went on. 'You've lovely long legs and Melody can play principal girl. Yes, I know, I know, she can't sing, so that's why we've got to rewrite it. We'll make her part more comic and she can do some of her impressions. It'll be different and you can sing all the serious ballads. All right? Now, when can you help Lionel and Martin get to work on the script?'

'As soon as you like,' Kathy said summoning up enthusiasm. A new challenge would help take her mind off her son.

'That's the ticket.'

The party's rewrite of *Jack and the Beanstalk* was a roaring success and enjoyed by the concert party as well as by all their audiences. They kept it running for two months, over the Christmas period, altering the topical jokes to fit in with what was happening in the news, lampooning Hitler and his cohorts mercilessly. Early in the New Year they played to audiences of children when the camps invited the locals to the show. By February, they were back to their usual show, travelling by bus from city to city, airfield to army camp, from factory canteen to hospital wards. The routine continued through the spring. In the summer they made another fleeting visit to Lincoln and Kathy was appalled to hear from Jemima, and to see for herself, the damage that bombing had inflicted on the city. But she was pleased to see that, despite the shortages and the constant fear of the bombing, Jemima was coping well. And she was relieved to hear that all was fine at Sandy Furze Farm.

'Your mother's keeping well too, dear,' Jemima greeted her. 'Betty's roped her in to help out with war work in the village.' Jemima smiled impishly. 'Your father grumbled, but as it was Betty asking, there was nothing he could say. He doesn't want to fall out with Edward and Maurice. They're helping him out a lot on his farm because he flatly refuses to have land army girls. And evidently it's doing poor Edith the world of good getting out and meeting other folk. Like I always say, it's an ill wind that blows nobody any good. Oh, and there's a letter for you, dear. It arrived two weeks ago, but I didn't know where to send it on to and I didn't want it to get lost. Mabel said you were due back here this week, so I hung on to it. Maybe it's from your mother.'

Kathy took the letter eagerly, but the handwriting was not that of her mother. It was not one she recognized and the envelope felt stiff, as if there was something else in it besides folded pages of writing paper. Her heart leapt as she opened the envelope carefully and eased out the contents. There was a short letter on one sheet of notepaper, but it was the other item that captured her attention. It was a photograph of a dark-haired little boy, taken at about eighteen months old. He was beaming at the camera and raising one chubby little hand in a friendly wave.

Her legs gave way beneath her and she sank into a chair. 'Oh look,' she breathed, not taking her gaze from the snapshot she held in her trembling hand. 'Aunt Jemima – do look. It's him. It's James. Mrs Wainwright has sent me a letter.'

Jemima held out her hand for the photo and, almost with a reluctance that was quite unnecessary, Kathy handed it to her. While Jemima looked at it, Kathy read the letter aloud.

'*Dear Kathy, I hope this reaches you eventually, as I know you are travelling a lot. I hope you like the picture of James. He is such a sweet little boy and so good. He is walking, of course, and talking too. He is getting quite a chatterbox and is adorable. I know you'd like a photograph of him. The enclosed was taken about a month ago . . .*'

'He's a handsome little chap,' Jemima said truthfully. 'And there's no mistaking who his father is, Kathy.'

She took the photo from Jemima and gazed at it again. 'No,' she whispered. 'I wonder if I should—'

'No, you shouldn't,' Jemima said, reading her mind. 'It could be disastrous to reveal to Beatrice Kendall that she has a grandson. Goodness only knows what she might try to do.'

'You're right,' Kathy admitted. 'But I would so like Mr Kendall to know.'

'Perhaps in time,' Jemima said.

The letter and the photograph brought Kathy some comfort. Now she had an image of her son that she carried everywhere with her, yet she still yearned to hold him.

The door slammed behind Kathy as she sat at the dressing table applying her stage make-up. The sound made her jump and smudge her lipstick. 'I do wish you wouldn't do that, Rosie.'

'I hate him. I don't ever want to see him again.'

'*Now* what? Can't you and Martin go five minutes without a blazing row? Really! For a couple supposed to be madly in love, you take the biscuit.'

'I'm not madly in love with *him*. I wouldn't marry him if he was the last man on earth.'

'You wouldn't get the chance. You'd be killed in the rush.' Calmly, Kathy rubbed away the smudged lipstick and started again. 'What – is it – this time?' she asked, stretching her lips as she applied fresh lipstick.

'He's going to join up even though Ron got him a deferment for six months. He says he doesn't want folks thinking he's a coward.'

'They won't think that,' Kathy said.

'*I* know that, but try telling him.'

The door opened with a dramatic flourish.

'You don't know what it's like to be a fit young man and have people staring at you wondering why you're not in uniform,' Martin shouted.

'You just want to be a hero,' Rosie screamed. 'You're

doing a good job here else you wouldn't have been given a deferment.'

'There's no talking to you.' Martin turned and left, slamming the door behind him. But Rosie dragged it open and followed him across the corridor into his dressing room.

'Well, I don't want to talk to you if all you want to do is go and get yourself killed.'

She came back into Kathy's room and slammed the door again.

'That door is going to fall off its hinges if we're here much longer,' Kathy remarked mildly.

Rosie collapsed into the rickety armchair in one corner of the dressing room and dissolved into noisy weeping.

'Oh, Rosie,' Kathy sighed, getting up. 'I'm on your side. I don't want Martin to go either . . .' She paused, wondering whether to confide in the girl of her own loss, but decided it might only make things worse. Martin was the one she should tell that to, if anyone. As far as she knew, only Ron knew about the loss of her fiancé. Theoretically, he had still been her fiancé when he'd been killed.

'But you have to let the men do what they feel they need to do.'

'What would you know about it?' Rosie sniffed sulkily. 'You haven't even got a boyfriend.'

Softly, with a catch in her voice, Kathy said, 'I know more than you might think.'

Rose stared at her for a moment and then jumped up. 'Did you – have you – lost someone?'

She hadn't meant for it to come out, but now there was no point in lying about it. Biting her lip, Kathy nodded.

Rosie stood up and put her arms about her. 'Kathy, I'm so sorry. I didn't mean to upset you. But – but you must know how I feel, then.'

'I know exactly how you feel. But it's no use, Rosie love. If they want to go, there's nothing we can do to stop them.'

'I can have a jolly good try though. I'll go down fighting,' Rosie declared. The two girls stared at each other and then collapsed against each other laughing.

'Come on,' Kathy said at last. 'We'd better finish getting ready. The show'll be starting in ten minutes and you're on in the opening number. Just one more piece of advice: don't spend your last few days before he goes – if he does go – fighting. If . . . if anything did happen to him – and God forbid that it does – but if it did, you'd regret it.'

Rosie gazed at her. 'Is – is that what happened to you?'

'Not exactly, but – but I have a lot of regrets. Things I didn't do – things I . . . I didn't tell him that . . . that I should have done. And now I never can.'

Rosie's tears ran afresh, but now for a different reason, as she hugged Kathy again.

'Now, come along. Go and make up with Martin before the show starts or you'll both be looking as black as thunder all the way through and you know Ron— he'll pick up on it.'

Rosie smiled, rushed out of the door, across the corridor and into the dressing room opposite. Kathy saw Martin with his arms outstretched and Rosie flying into them. She turned away, the familiar lump rising in her throat and a physical ache in her arms at their emptiness.

The show began to tumultuous applause and Ron

smiled and nodded in delight. 'That's what I like to hear. A good audience from the off.'

At the end of every number there was rapturous applause, whistling and stamping feet. The audience was a mixture of servicemen and women from a nearby camp, factory workers after a long day's shift and munitions workers letting their hair down, released for a few hours from their dangerous work.

There was such a lot of noise that no one heard the sirens begin to wail until an ARP warden came rushing into the theatre, down the centre aisle towards the stage, shouting and waving his arms. The music petered out and the audience shuffled to their feet. Now, everyone could hear the sirens. The warden climbed on to the stage and grabbed the microphone.

'There's an underground shelter down the street,' he began, but Ron tapped him on the shoulder.

'Is it big enough to take all of us?' He swept his arm in a wide arc to encompass all the cast of the show and the audience too.

'Er – well – no, probably not, but . . .'

'Then we're staying here. The show goes on. We'll give those who want to go time to leave, but we're going on.'

His announcement, heard over the mike, was greeted with a huge cheer, and many of the audience who had stood up sat down again, settled themselves comfortably back in their seats and looked expectantly towards the stage.

'Get on with it then,' shouted a voice from the middle of the auditorium. 'Let's show old 'itler 'ee can't stop us having a bit of fun.'

Laughter rippled through the theatre and more people sat down again. In the end only a handful left, either to go home or to hurry to the shelter. The warden shrugged his shoulders and left the way he had come in, muttering darkly, 'On your own head be it then. And it probably will be. We'll likely be digging you all out in the morning.' He was greeted with catcalls and pelted with crumpled-up cigarette packets by those nearby who heard his words. But he ducked out of the door with a good-natured grin on his face. He was worried that his words would be prophetic, but, deep down, he admired the spirit of the players and those who stayed to watch. They were cocking a snook at the enemy and he liked that. It was what he did every night on duty.

The show went on; the quintet who served as the concert party's orchestra played Kathy's opening music and she went on stage to tumultuous applause. She sang her usual songs to end the first half of the show, but during the interval she sought out Ron and the pianist, Terry.

'Do you think it'd be a good idea to change the finale to our wartime songs? I'll lead the singing with the whole cast behind me?'

Ron glanced at Terry and they nodded together. 'Good idea, Kathy, and we'll keep going until the "All Clear" sounds, even if it takes all night.'

The word went round the cast of the change in their programme. The first half began again, sooner than normal. Without the music and the clapping and cheering, the occasional "crump" of a falling bomb was unnerving some of the audience. Though no one else left the theatre, everyone was relieved when the show began again to drown out the noise of the air raid.

As they began the finale, there was a loud thud close

by and the whole theatre seemed to shake, but Kathy stood in front of the microphone and belted out the words to 'It's a Long Way to Tipperary' without so much as a tremor. The audience clapped and cheered. Kathy waved her arms, inviting the audience to join in. By now the show was over-running by half an hour, but no one left. They stayed in their seats clapping and cheering and singing and ignoring the bangs and thuds outside. With perfect timing Kathy was singing 'When They Sound the Last All Clear' as the noise of the sirens began again and everyone heard the "All Clear" in reality.

As the song ended, a cheer rippled through the audience and Ron approached the microphone.

'Ladies and gentlemen, I'd just like to say thank you for your support . . .'

'No, mate, thank you,' a voice came out of the darkness, and the whole auditorium erupted in applause yet again.

When Ron could make himself heard again, he said, 'We'd like to end our show with 'Land of Hope and Glory', led by our very own soloist, Miss Kathy Burton.'

By the end of the song, there wasn't a dry eye in the house. As they always did at the end of the show, the cast went to the foyer of the theatre to stand in line and bid the audience good night as they filed out.

There were handshakes and hugs and kisses.

'Brilliant.' 'So brave to carry on.' 'Thank you.' 'God bless you.' 'You're doing a grand job.' The whole cast basked in the praise. Kathy, standing next to Rosie and Martin, seemed to receive the most plaudits, but it was pretty, blonde Rosie who got the admiring glances.

'You're a doll.' One airman in his smart blue uniform kissed her soundly on both cheeks. 'When are you going to let me take you out?'

Before Rosie could utter a gentle refusal, Martin butted in, 'Sorry, old boy, she's taken.'

The airman turned slowly to look Martin up and down. What he saw was a tall, fit young man old enough to be in uniform. He said nothing, but his scathing glance spoke volumes. He turned back to Rosie and shrugged. 'If that's what you prefer, honey, good luck to you.'

The young airman turned away to follow his mates, leaving Martin staring after him, his expression thunderous.

'That does it. I'm volunteering tomorrow.'

Thirty-Four

There was nothing anyone could say now to dissuade him. Within a week Martin had left the party to go home, pack his case and wait for his papers to arrive.

Rosie walked about in a trance, her eyes permanently swollen with weeping. But like the trouper she was, she insisted on carrying on with the show.

'I just need thicker make-up,' she remarked drily.

'That's the ticket, love,' Ron commended her as he patted her on the shoulder and winked at Kathy, who knew what he was hinting. She gave him a little nod that said a silent Yes, I'll keep my eye on her.

But who, she thought sadly, is keeping their eye on me? Ron knew about her loss, but not the whole of it. No one else here knew about her yearning to hold her tiny son again.

'What on earth are we going to do without Martin?' Ron moaned. 'It'll take about three people to do the work he used to do.'

'I thought you'd found a new stage manager,' Kathy said.

'I have, but he doesn't help write the scripts like Martin did, nor does he want to take part in the sketches.'

'There's still Lionel and Melody to write, and maybe

you'll find someone else to join us. Have you been in touch with ENSA? They might know of someone looking to join a concert party.'

Ron's face brightened. 'Now that's an idea, Kathy. Why didn't I think of that?'

'Because you've got a lot of other things on your mind, that's why.'

His sighed and his face fell into worried lines again. 'But I don't think we'll be able to write a pantomime for this year. It's a huge task. Have you any ideas?'

'Not for a pantomime, no. I presume you don't want to revive *Jack . . .*'

Ron shook his head. 'We'll be visiting some of the same places we did last year. They won't want to see the same old stuff again.'

'True.' Kathy was thoughtful before she said, 'Then why don't we put together a Christmas show? You know – seasonal songs with one or two sketches with a festive flavour. I'm sure Lionel and Melody could come up with one or two brand new scripts. They're used to producing new material all the time.'

Ron put his hand on her shoulder and at last he was really smiling. 'Now that *is* a good idea.'

'Well, there's nothing like rubbing it in, is there?' Rosie said bitterly, slamming the door of the bedroom she and Kathy were sharing in their current digs.

The Christmas-themed shows instead of a pantomime had worked well and the party had worked all over the festive season, not even getting home to see their families.

'All the lads and lasses in the forces have to be

away, so we can too,' had been Ron's suggestion. He wasn't surprised when everyone had agreed with him. Christmas was a tough time for those forced to be away from their loved ones. The least they could do was to bring a little laughter into their dull routine. Now they were into the new year of 1943. Kathy could hardly believe that another whole year had gone past. James would be two by now. She still only had the one photograph of him. She looked at it each morning when she woke and at night before she fell asleep.

Kathy's eyes widened. 'Why? What's happened?' Her heart began thumping painfully. Oh, surely nothing had happened to Martin?

'We're going to a hospital, would you believe, to entertain the patients?'

Kathy breathed a sigh of relief, but now she was puzzled. 'But – we've been to hospitals before. Why – why are you so upset about this one?'

Rosie bit her lip. 'We've always just played to an audience that could come to us in a big room in the hospital or a nearby hall. *This* time Ron wants us to go into the wards. There are some very – very sick lads there. Badly injured and – and – ' Tears filled her eyes. 'We might even see someone – someone *die*. And all the time I'll be thinking – it could be Martin.'

Kathy stood up and put her arms around her. 'Try not to think like that. Try to think that he'll be one of the lucky ones. That – that he'll come back.' Kathy's voice quavered and at once Rosie returned her hug. They held each other close. 'I'm so sorry. I was forgetting. I'm being selfish, aren't I, when there's countless other girls feeling just the same? You're right and we have a job to do. Martin – ' now her voice too was unsteady – 'Martin would be the first to say "the show must go on", wouldn't he?'

Next day, the whole party clambered into the bus to travel to the north of England, to a hospital in a town just south of Newcastle. Travelling was much more fun now with everyone together. There was laughter and banter and even singing throughout the journey. It left Kathy – and now Rosie too – less time to brood.

As they neared the town where the hospital was situated, Ron stood up at the front of the bus. 'Now listen, you lot. I understand that the hospital has kindly found accommodation for all of us. The girls are to go to the nurses' home and the boys are in a hotel nearby. It's where a lot of the parents, wives and so on stay if they come to visit the lads in the hospital. They do special rates for them and they'll do the same for us. The hospital administration says that visits like ours help keep up the staff's morale as well as the patients'.'

An appreciative murmuring at the compliment rippled through the bus and when, a few moments later, they turned into the driveway leading up to the hospital and drew to a halt at the front steps, they saw two nurses standing at the top. At once they came running down, smiling and waving. When Ron stepped down, Kathy heard a merry voice greet him.

'You must be Mr Spencer. I'm Brenda and this is Elsie. I'm to take the ladies to the nurses' home and Elsie will take you gentlemen to the hotel. It's only just there.' She waved her hand to the right of the hospital. 'Nice and handy. And you can park the bus round the back of the hospital.'

Ron shook their hands. 'Thank you. You're very kind.'

'It should be us thanking you,' Brenda laughed. 'We've all been looking forward to you coming so much. There was a raid in Newcastle last night and some of the bombs got a bit close. It's unsettled some of the patients, so you've come at just the right time.' She glanced up at the windows of the bus and saw Rosie's and Melody's young faces. Her own face sobered and she leant a little closer to Ron to say, 'We do have some very sick boys here. I – I hope all your party are – prepared.'

'I'll have a little word before we come into the wards,' Ron said quietly. 'Thank you for warning me.'

Brenda chattered all the way as she led the girls in the party to the nurses' home, situated to one side of the huge hospital. 'You'll have to sleep in a dormitory. I hope you don't mind. One or two have moved out temporarily so you can all be together. I hope we've prepared enough beds . . .' She did a quick head count. 'Oh yes, that's right. Five of you. That's what we were told. What do you all do? Sing? Dance? What?'

'I'm the female vocalist,' Kathy volunteered. 'Rosie, Maureen and Joan are dancers and Melody here, well, she's a very talented actress.'

'And she does some wicked impersonations too,' Rosie put in, while Melody blushed prettily.

'Sounds like a great show,' Brenda said, leading them up two flights of stairs and flinging open the door to a long, airy room with beds and lockers down each side, each one separated by a green curtain. 'Here we are. I hope you're going to be comfortable. I'll see you settled in and unpacked and then I'll take you down to the canteen. They've got a meal waiting for you.'

'Thank goodness for that,' Maureen spoke for the first time. 'I'm starving.'

The men of the party joined them in the canteen.

'Now,' Ron began when everyone had finished. 'We're going to build a bit of a stage at the end of the room there, but not all the patients can get here. Some are too ill, so, as you may know, Matron has asked that we take one or two of the acts into the wards. Our two vocalists – ' he nodded towards Kathy and Roly – 'and Lionel, of course, but it's not really possible for the dancers to do their routines in the wards. Sorry, girls, and we won't be doing the sketches in the wards either, but we thought perhaps Melody could do some of her impressions. All right, love?'

Melody nodded, though, glancing at her, Kathy thought she looked a little apprehensive.

The show in the canteen went well. Only the 'walking wounded' were there, with arms in slings and legs in plaster. 'They mostly have GSWs,' Brenda explained.

'What's that when it's at home?' Kathy asked as she brushed her hair. It had grown longer over the last few weeks and fell in shining waves and curls to her shoulders.

Brenda laughed. 'Oh sorry. Gun shot wound, but they're not serious. One or two have broken legs or arms but mostly—' She stopped when she saw Rosie's face turn pale. Concerned, Brenda touched the girl's arm. 'Are you sure you're up to this? I mean, one or two in the wards are much worse than this.'

Rosie pressed her lips together. 'Oh, yes. If you can look after them and face all – all that you have to, then I can certainly do a bit of high-kicking for them. That's nothing compared to what you must have to do day after day. Besides, I'm a dancer. If I want, I can chicken out of going into the wards.' Bravely, she forced a smile to her lips. 'But I don't want to. I'd like to go and talk to one or two, if we're allowed.'

'So would I,' Kathy put in at once, before she could change her mind.

'*Allowed!* That'd be fantastic. Some of the lads don't get any visitors. Their families live too far away. They'd be so glad to have someone to talk to other than us for a change.'

'Right you are then. Now – ' Rosie turned her back towards Brenda – 'make yourself useful. Fasten me up, will you? Goldilocks here's too busy fussing with her tresses.'

As they trooped into one of the wards a little later, Kathy took a deep breath and steeled herself for what she might see. Was this what had happened to Tony? Had he died in a hospital just like this one, far from home? Or had he been shot down and killed immediately? She shuddered inwardly, but determined to keep the smile on her face and her voice pure and steady when she sang.

'Right,' Ron said. 'Roly, you open this little mini show and then we'll have Lionel telling a few jokes, and close your ears, girls, because with an all-male audience he tends to get a little risqué. After that we'll have Kathy bring a little decorum back to the proceedings and then finish off with Melody's impressions.'

Roly sang some rousing songs in his rich baritone voice and Lionel was a great hit with his saucy banter, but it was Kathy's sentimental ballads that brought a tear to one or two eyes. And it wasn't just among the patients. The nurses too, sitting or standing by the beds, reached for their handkerchiefs. But despite the tears, the cheering and clapping told her that she had touched their hearts.

'Your turn, Melody,' she said, as she left the ward and returned to the corridor just outside where the young girl was waiting. Melody got up and pushed open the door into the ward. Something in the girl's face made Kathy turn and watch her through the glass panel in the door. She saw her walk to the centre of the room without glancing to left or right. Melody reached the spot that Kathy had just left. Then she raised her head but no sound came. Kathy held her breath.

'What is it?' Ron said, coming up behind Kathy.

'I'm not sure,' she murmured, 'but I think . . . Oh Lord!' She pushed open the door and walked towards Melody. She spread her arms wide and began to sing the famous Gracie Fields song that Melody always used to open her spot. It was always instantly recognized and the girl did a magnificent impression of the much-loved singer. But not tonight. Poor Melody stood transfixed by the sight of the wounded soldiers.

Kathy reached her and put her arm around her shoulder, trying to give the girl the strength to go on. But the younger girl gave a little sob, put her hand over her mouth and turned and fled out of the ward, crashing the door back against the wall in her desperate bid to escape. Without faltering, Kathy sang on, swiftly going into the second of Gracie's songs that Melody used. 'It's the Biggest Aspidistra in the World.' Though she couldn't emulate Gracie's distinctive voice, she managed to inject the singer's sense of humour, and soon she had the patients smiling and joining in the chorus. She ended with the song that Melody ended her act with, 'Sing As We Go'.

The clapping continued as Roly and Lionel joined her for a curtain call, even though this time there was no actual curtain.

'Is she all right?' Kathy muttered to Rosie as they came out of the double doors.

'Don't know. Ron's gone after her. He's asked us to stay and talk to the patients. You all right?'

'I'm fine,' Kathy said. 'Right. Let's do it.'

The four of them spent the next hour sitting by the bedside of those too ill or incapacitated to get to the canteen to see the full show.

'And this is Charlie,' Brenda said, trying hard to keep the laughter from her tone. The young man was lying face down. ' "Tail-end Charlie", we call him. He – er – caught it in the posterior, hence his prone position.'

'You can laugh,' he muttered morosely. 'How'd you like to be laid here like this all day long with nowt to look at but the bloody pillow.' Charlie twisted his head and looked up at Kathy. ' 'Scuse me not getting up.'

'That's quite all right,' Kathy said, sitting down near the head of the bed so that he could glance up and see her.

'My – you're pretty. Pity I couldn't see you when you were singing. You are the singer, I take it?'

'Yes.'

'Nice voice too. I say, there was a bit of a kerfuffle, wasn't there? I couldn't see. What went on?'

'It was nothing, really,' Kathy said airily. 'One of the young girls got a bit of stage fright, that's all.'

He looked up at her knowingly. 'Chap in the next bed told me the lass took one look at us lot and scarpered. Can't say I blame her.' He looked – and sounded – depressed.

Kathy bent down to him. 'Well, *we're* here, aren't we? You can't be that frightening.'

'How long are you staying?'

'I'm not sure. Three nights, I think. We do a full show in the canteen and then come to the wards.' She forbore to add: to entertain the bedridden.

'Right,' the young man said, with a new determination in his tone. 'Tomorrow I'll see if I can get on my feet and come to the show. I might have to stand at the back, but it'd be worth it to get a proper look at you.'

Kathy chatted a little longer, and as she was leaving, Brenda caught hold of her arm. 'What did Charlie say?'

'Oh, nothing much really. He didn't seem to want to talk about his family.'

Brenda's mouth tightened. 'Not surprising, poor love.'

Kathy was intrigued. 'Why?'

'No one's been to visit him, yet they only live in York. They could get here if they wanted. Rumour has it he's got a fiancée, but she's sent him a "Dear John" letter. You see,' Brenda bit her lip, 'we try to jolly him along and tease him about getting hit in his behind, but it's a bit more serious that that. He got it in the you-know-what's an' all, and I don't think he's much future as a husband, if you know what I mean.'

'Oh,' Kathy breathed. 'Poor chap. Oh, how awful. And how cruel of his fiancée.' Silently, she thought, I'd've cared for Tony for the rest of our lives no matter what injuries he had, if only he were still alive. Aloud she asked, 'But what about the rest of his family? His parents?'

'Seems they can't cope with the news either. Can't bring themselves to come and see him.'

Kathy stared at her. She was quite lost for words now. Whatever had happened to their son, she couldn't imagine any parents not wanting to rush to his bedside.

'There's some folk don't deserve to have children,' she muttered bitterly. 'While others . . .'

'You can say that again,' Brenda said with feeling.

Thirty-Five

On their last night at the hospital, after the show, Ron came to the small room near the canteen allocated to the girls as a dressing room. Kathy was alone there and one look at his face told her that something was dreadfully wrong.

'Oh no, Ron. Don't tell me it's Martin?'

Ron shook his head, seeming unable to speak. He pulled up a chair, sat down and took her hand in his.

'What is it? What's wrong,' Kathy demanded, her heart thumping, her mouth dry.

'My dear, there – there's been a bomb fall in our street.'

Kathy let out a squeak of alarm and her free hand flew to her mouth. Her eyes were wide with fear as she asked, 'Is – is anyone hurt or – or . . .' She couldn't bring herself to voice her greatest fear. Aunt Jemima. Was she badly hurt or killed? And Ron's wife? What of her?

'Mabel's safe. It was her rang here to the hospital. She always knows where we are,' Ron said quietly. 'She was out at the time, thank God, but . . .' he chewed at his lip for a brief moment before adding, 'But Miss Robinson's house took a direct hit and – and no one can find her. They're still digging but . . .'

'But there's not much hope?' Kathy said flatly.

Ron shook his head. 'They found her cat. He was

on top of the washhouse roof, howling pitifully. Mabel tried to take him home with her – at least, to where she's staying with some friends. Our house was badly damaged too, but old Taffy keeps escaping and going back home. He just sits on top of the rubble, she says, miaowing.'

'When did it happen?'

'Yesterday, some time. I don't know exactly when.'

'Friday,' Kathy mused. 'Well, in the daytime, she should have been at work and if it was evening, Friday's one of her WVS nights. Are they absolutely sure she's not gone to a friend's, maybe even to her brother's in the country?'

Ron was shaking his head sadly. 'Mabel's been asking all round but no one seems to know anything. And besides,' he added, 'she wouldn't have left old Taffy, would she?'

The hope in Kathy's eyes died. 'No,' she whispered hoarsely. 'No, she wouldn't. But they are still digging? They're still looking?'

Ron nodded but there was no hope left in his eyes. 'I'm so sorry, love.' There was a pause before he asked, 'Do you want to go home? We can manage for a night or two, though it won't be the same without you,' he added hurriedly. 'The audiences love your songs.'

'I – I don't know. I mean, do her family know yet?'

Ron lifted his shoulders. 'I've no idea. I expect the authorities will inform them as soon as – as soon as they have some definite news.'

'When they've found her – her body, you mean?'

He nodded.

'Poor Ted and Betty. And Morry – oh, poor Morry,' she added, though she didn't confide in Ron just why her heart went out to Morry.

'Fond of his aunt, was he?' Ron asked kindly, but Kathy could only nod, her throat too full of tears to speak.

'I didn't tell you before the show. There's nothing you could have done. You do understand, Kathy, don't you?'

Briefly, a sarcastic retort sprang to her lips, castigating him for having kept the news to himself until the show was over. Oh, nothing must get in the way of 'the show going on', must it? she almost said. Instead, she bit back the words. She had seen for herself how their concert party helped others, how it brought a little brightness into the dull lives of those trapped in the daily drudgery of wartime Britain. It even had the power to keep people in their seats all the way through an air raid.

'You were right,' she said huskily. 'I wouldn't have been able to go on if I'd just had that news and it's what Aunt Jemima—' she smiled fondly at the thought of her – 'would have expected me to do.'

Kathy spent a restless night, and both she and Rosie got up the following morning tired and bleary-eyed. They breakfasted, packed their belongings and stripped the beds they had occupied in the nurses' dormitory.

'Are you gong home?' Rosie asked as, lugging their suitcases, they walked towards the bus parked at the rear of the hospital's main building.

'Yes, I'm going to ask Ron if I can catch a train to Lincoln this morning instead of coming to Leeds with you all. He did say he didn't mind.'

They reached the bus and stood with some of the party until everyone else arrived.

'I can't imagine life without Miss Robinson,' Kathy murmured. 'My home was with her and now it's gone.'

'Have you lost much? Possessions, I mean?'

Kathy shrugged. 'Not really. I didn't have much.' She didn't care about material things, but sadly she realized that the people she cared about most in the world, apart from her mother, were being taken away from her one by one. Even though she was surrounded by her friends in the concert party, Kathy still felt very lonely.

Ron and the rest of the party arrived. 'Everyone here? Right then, we'd better be off . . .'

'I say, wait a minute. Wait!'

They all turned to see Brenda running across the car park towards them. 'Anybody here by the name of "Burton"?'

'Y – yes. Me,' Kathy stammered.

'Phone call for you,' the nurse panted. 'Long distance. In the matron's office. Come on, I'll take you.'

Kathy's heart leapt in her chest. She dropped her suitcase and ran after Brenda. Inside the matron's office, she picked up the receiver with shaking hands. Ron had followed her and was standing uncertainly just inside the doorway.

'H – hello?'

'Kathy, my dear, it's me. I though you might be worried—'

Tears flooded down Kathy's face as she spluttered, 'Oh Aunt Jemima, Aunt Jemima – you're safe. Thank God!' She turned to see Ron beaming from ear to ear. 'She's safe,' Kathy cried. 'She's safe.' Ron smiled and lifted his hand in acknowledgement, then disappeared to tell the others of Kathy's good news.

'Where were you? Are you hurt? Where are you now?'

'I was in the cupboard under the stairs. I'd just got home when the raid started and I could already hear bombs dropping. It was too late to go out again to the nearest communal shelter, so I dived for the cupboard.'

'How long were you there?' Kathy shouted into the instrument. The line was crackling.

'Oh, hours, all night and half the next day,' Jemima said cheerfully. 'And it's only thanks to dear old Taffy that they found me. I could hear him miaowing and one of the rescue party told me afterwards that it was because of him they'd kept digging. They were sure he knew I was under there.'

'Are you all right?'

'A few cuts and bruises, but we're both safe and we're at Edward and Betty's now. I couldn't ring you before, dear girl. I couldn't find out where Mabel was to get the telephone number from her. Are you there tonight?'

'No, we're about to leave to go to Leeds, but I was coming straight home from there.'

'Shouldn't bother, dear. There's no home to come to at the moment. Of course you can come here if you like, but there's no need to if you want to stay with the party.'

'Are you sure you're all right?'

'We're fine. Truly. You carry on. You're all doing such a fine job.'

'All right, I will then, if you're really sure?'

'I am,' were Jemima's final words as the line went dead. Kathy replaced the receiver and sighed with relief. Ron had come back and was standing just outside the office, waiting for her. 'Well, are you going or staying now she's safe?'

'I'm staying,' Kathy told him with a grin.

'That's the ticket.'

There was one piece of news that caught up with Kathy about a week later. They were due to stay in Leeds for a full week. Mabel had given Jemima the address of the theatre so that she could write to Kathy and reassure her that both she and Taffy were now safely at Sandy Furze Farm and that she was not to worry.

There is one piece of sad news, which I ought to tell you though, my dear. In the same air raid in which you and I lost our home, poor Stella was killed. Although she lived in a village outside the city one or two stray bombs dropped there and their house took a direct hit. Her parents were killed too . . .

Kathy sat on the edge of the bed staring into space, remembering the young girl with whom she'd worked for a few months.

'We never did get that trip to the cinema I promised you. And you were so looking forward to it,' Kathy whispered aloud to the empty room. 'I'm so sorry, Stella.'

At the end of that week, Ron called the members of the company together.

'There's been a slight change of plan. The canteen of the factory where we were due to play next has been bombed, and as the theatre there is closed for the duration, we've been asked to go back to Saltershaven. We're going to play for the RAF boys billeted in the town. We'll be there a week.' He looked around and caught Kathy's gaze. 'You'll be singing in the cinema where you were usherette, lass. That be all right?'

Kathy felt her heart leap. It'd be more than 'all right'. At last, she might have a chance to see James. She'd certainly try. She could hardly wait.

As the bus drew into the town, it was like coming home, except that her memories of the place were very mixed. The dreadful nightmare of her time at Willow House, the heartbreak of having her baby snatched from her, but then the joy of holding him in her arms at last. And the kindness of the woman who was now her son's mother. She would never forget that. But now she was back here, she was apprehensive. Seeds of doubt had been sown in her mind. Perhaps Mrs Wainwright would not be so welcoming this time. She'd had time to think about things and perhaps she'd come to the conclusion that it would be better if Kathy had nothing to do with the boy. In the two years since she had last seen her son, there had only ever been that one letter from his adoptive mother. Kathy had written regularly, but no further word had come back to her. Kathy had made all sorts of excuses in her mind. Perhaps the woman's letters had been lost in the post or had arrived after the concert party had moved on. Perhaps she hadn't managed to get any photographs taken. Perhaps . . . Kathy dreamed up all sorts of reasons to comfort herself, but now she was back here in the town, she was scared about what she would find.

There was no opportunity for her to go to Sea Bank Road that first day. The party had to settle in at their digs and then meet in the cinema for a rehearsal before the concert started at seven thirty.

But the following morning, Kathy was up early, unable to sleep for excitement. Today she might be able to see her darling boy. With gentle fingers she wrapped the toy rabbit she had knitted so lovingly during her idle hours sitting in dressing rooms and digs.

'Who's that for?' Rosie had asked.

Kathy had felt a blush creeping up her neck as she was forced to lie. 'It's – it's for a friend of mine.' But was it really a lie? she'd asked herself later, because James was Mrs Wainwright's child now. Not hers. The thought broke her heart all over again.

But today she might see him. For a few brief moments perhaps she could hold him and play with him and pretend he was still hers. Clutching the knitted toy, she set off on the long walk to the Wainwrights' house.

There was a cold wind off the sea as she walked the long road to the outskirts of the town, turned left past the golf course and then turned right into the road that ran parallel with the sandhills. She glanced briefly to her right at the houses, but her gaze came back time and again to the house standing at the end of the row. As she drew nearer, she frowned. There was something not quite right about the house. It looked different. As she walked closer, her hands felt clammy and her legs were weak. As last she stood in the gateway, staring at the house in horror. Half of it was gone, reduced to a mound of rubble and leaving rooms, still with furniture in, gaping open to the elements. Wallpaper was half torn from the walls and fluttered pathetically in the breeze.

For a moment Kathy thought she would faint as she staggered and leant against the rough brickwork of the gatepost. Wildly, she looked about her, but the place seemed deserted. The shattered house was empty and forlorn, the once neat garden neglected and overgrown. James, her baby boy! What had happened to him? She glanced at the neighbouring house and saw a movement through the window.

Galvanized into action, Kathy ran up the drive, her heart beating erratically. She banged on the side door, shouting, 'Please, please help me. What happened?'

The door opened and a woman stood there, frowning slightly at the noise. 'Whatever's the matter?'

'I'm sorry,' Kathy panted. 'But please tell me, what happened to the people next door? To Mrs Wainwright and – and her little boy?'

'Who are you?'

'I – I'm a friend. Of Mrs Wainwright. I've been away. On tour. With a concert party. I didn't know . . . Please . . .' She was begging now.

'Then I'm very sorry to have to tell you that your friend was killed.'

Kathy gasped and felt the colour drain from her face. Her knees began to buckle and she clutched at the doorframe. 'Oh no.'

'You'd better come inside and sit down a moment,' the woman said briskly. 'I don't want you fainting on my doorstep.'

She took Kathy's arm and almost pulled her into her kitchen and pushed her into a chair near the table. 'I'll make you a cup of tea.'

'The child?' Kathy burst out. 'What about James?'

'He wasn't hurt, thank God. He was in the nursery upstairs on the far side of the house, but Beryl was downstairs in the kitchen on this side and, as you can see, she didn't have a chance.'

Now Kathy felt faint with relief, but she took a few

short panting breaths and her head stopped spinning. 'Where is James now?'

'I've no idea. With Mr Wainwright, I suppose.' She smiled. 'Funny, I always called him that. I knew Beryl well, but not him so much. He was always "Mr Wainwright".'

'Do you know where he is? I – I'd like to see him.' Whether the 'him' Kathy referred to was Mr Wainwright or James, the neighbour was not to know.

'I've no idea where they're living now, but I expect they're still in the town somewhere. Mr Wainwright wouldn't leave his job. Very important work he does.' She smiled again. 'At least he seems to think so. But you'll know all about that.'

Kathy bit her lip. If she wasn't careful, she was going to let slip that she didn't know the Wainwrights as well as she was trying to make out. Surely a friend of the family would know what he did. But Kathy had no idea. Mr Wainwright had hardly been mentioned in her conversations with his wife. She chewed her lip and asked. 'Was there other damage in the town?'

The woman shrugged. 'Not much. They say it was a lone raider who offloaded his bombs as he flew back out to sea. The swimming pool and several houses in the town were damaged. There were one or two more killed besides Beryl. Poor Beryl,' she mused. 'I've never seen her so happy as she's been these last two years since she got that baby. And poor little mite. What'll happen to him now, I don't know.'

Kathy's heart missed a beat. She had to take a risk. She had to push the woman to tell her more. 'What do you mean? Won't – won't Mr Wainwright look after him?'

The woman glanced at her, a question on her face, but Kathy smiled and, mentally crossing her fingers, said, 'I'm a bit like you, I didn't know him awfully well. It was Beryl I was friendly with.'

The neighbour nodded, 'Mm, yes, well, I know what you mean. All I know is that his job was everything to him. He thought this town would fall to pieces if he didn't put in an appearance in his office at the Town Hall all day and every day.' Her tone was a little scathing. 'That's why I say "poor little mite". Goodness knows who he's been palmed off with to look after him.'

Kathy's heart leapt. The Town Hall, the woman had said. Mr Wainwright was 'something important' in the town and he worked at the local council offices.

The woman set the cup of tea down in front of her and Kathy sipped it gratefully. She was feeling a little better now. James was obviously safe, though where he was she would have to find out. But now she knew where Mr Wainwright worked, she could see him there. Make an appointment, do it properly. With a restraint she didn't know she possessed, she continued to sit in the kitchen and listen to the woman relating the details of the bombing. 'We were lucky not to get more damage than we did. All our windows were broken and part of the roof damaged. We were both out at the time, but when we got back, oh the mess. There was soot everywhere that had been blown down the chimneys . . .' On and on the woman went and Kathy sat there, hiding her impatience to be gone. At last she felt she could stand up, thank the woman for her kindness and the tea and make her escape.

She walked back down the drive, stood a moment longer to look at the Wainwrights' home and then turned and walked back towards the town. There was nothing more she could do today, and tomorrow was Sunday, but on Monday morning she'd be outside the Town Hall waiting for the offices to open.

Thirty-Six

'Do you have an appointment?' the severe-looking receptionist asked. 'Mr Wainwright can't just see anyone who turns up unannounced, you know. The town clerk is a very busy man. What is it about?'

'It's a personal matter.'

'Personal? To whom? You – or Mr Wainwright?'

Kathy was about to say 'both', but then realized the implication. She took a deep breath and said, 'He might not know me, but I was friendly with his wife. And I just . . .'

'Can't you write him a letter of condolence?' the woman snapped. 'I'm sure he doesn't want to keep being reminded. Especially when he's at work.'

'I realize that, but – but I just wanted to ask him about his son. How he's coping and – and if I could be of any help.'

The receptionist's eyes narrowed as she regarded Kathy with a steady, calculating stare. 'Mm,' she said noncommittally, but then seemed to come to a decision. She picked up the receiver of a telephone on her right and dialled a number.

'I have a woman here in reception asking if she might see Mr Wainwright. She says she was a friend of his wife's and that she's anxious to see if she can be of any help with the baby. You know what the situation is, I just wondered . . .' There was a pause while Kathy felt herself scrutinized again. The woman lowered her voice to say into the mouthpiece, 'Well, she looks all right. Very presentable, in fact. I mean, we both know he's looking for . . .' She broke off and then added, 'Oh, has he? I didn't know that. Anyway, do you think he'd see her? She's brought a little gift for the child.' There was quite a long pause until she said, 'Right,' and then replaced the receiver.

'Mr Wainwright's secretary will be down in a moment.'

Kathy beamed at her. 'Thank you. Thank you very much.'

Kathy sat on the edge of a chair to wait. People walked through the reception area, their feet clattering on the tiled floor. After what seemed an eternity but was in fact only a few minutes, a young woman appeared out of one of the doors. She came towards Kathy. 'Miss – er . . .'

Kathy jumped up. 'Miss Burton.'

'If you'd come this way, Miss Burton, Mr Wainwright will spare you a moment. It won't be long, though, I'm afraid. He has a meeting at ten.'

The secretary led the way up polished oak stairs, along corridors, until they came to her office. She bade Kathy sit down a moment and then went to another door, which led into an inner office. The layout reminded Kathy poignantly of Tony's office, with Miss Foster sitting guard in the outer office, deftly fielding all unwelcome calls upon her boss's valuable time. After a moment the young woman returned and, with a smile, ushered Kathy into the office of the town clerk of Saltershaven.

The man who rose from behind his desk was older than Kathy had anticipated. He was thin, but not very tall. The word 'dapper' sprang to her mind as she shook the hand he held out to her. He was immaculately dressed in a pinstriped suit with a white shirt and sober tie. His hair was thinning and his eyes, behind the round, steel-framed spectacles, were as cold as the grey waters of the North Sea.

'I'm so sorry to hear about your wife. She was a lovely lady.'

'Thank you. Please sit down. What can I do for you?'

'I just – I just wanted to give you this for – for James.' She held out the carefully wrapped parcel. 'It's nothing much, but I made it myself and I – I so wanted him to have it.'

'That's very kind of you.' He placed the gift meticulously on the corner of his desk. 'I'll certainly make sure he receives it.'

'How – I mean – where is he? Is he with relatives?'

Mr Wainwright shook his head. 'No. Sadly, my wife and I have few relatives and certainly no one living close.'

'Then – then you have a nanny for him?'

'No. He's gone back to Willow House!' Kathy gasped, but he didn't seem to notice and went on. 'I'm putting him back up for adoption. I really can't cope with a young baby.'

'Adopted? You're going to have him adopted?' Kathy was desperate. At least at the moment she knew where her baby was. If he were to be adopted again, then she would certainly lose touch with him. She couldn't bear it. 'But – but couldn't you employ a nanny to look after him? A live-in nanny?'

'I suppose I could. But it was my wife who wanted a child. Not me. I only agreed to it to keep her happy.

And I'd need a bigger place. I'm living in a one-roomed flat at the moment. It's totally unsuitable for a young child and my house is uninhabitable.'

'I know. I've seen it.'

He spread his hands helplessly, though to Kathy he was far from being a helpless man. 'Then you see my position.'

'But you'll get another house?'

He nodded, 'Oh yes. I'm in negotiations now with one of the estate agents in the town, but it might be a while . . .'

'But you haven't actually signed any adoption papers yet?'

'Well, no, I haven't, but . . .'

'Oh please don't, Mr Wainwright. It's not what your wife – what Beryl – would have wanted, is it?'

It seemed as if, at last, she had touched a nerve. His face crumpled briefly and he passed his hand across his brow. But in moments he was in control of himself again. He doesn't love James, Kathy thought shrewdly, but he did love his wife. He leant his arms on his desk and sighed heavily. 'I've felt guilty enough about my decision, but I didn't know what else to do.' He stared at her. 'Just who are you and how did you know my wife?'

Kathy licked her lips. She could tell the truth, but not all of it. 'I was walking one day along the road where you live and Beryl was out pushing the pram. We got talking and then I met her again and she invited me in to see the baby. We – we became friends.' Kathy made it sound as if the friendship had gone on over a period of time and was deeper than it had been. 'She – she didn't mention me to you?' Kathy held her breath, fearing that if his wife had told him that she'd met the girl who was James's natural mother, Mr Wainwright might very well now put two and two together very quickly and realize exactly who she was.

'I don't think so,' he murmured, wrinkling his brow. 'What's your name again?'

'Burton. Kathy Burton.' Now Kathy felt a little easier. She couldn't remember ever giving Beryl Wainwright her name.

'No – no, I don't recall hearing her mention you, but then,' he gave a wry, rather sad smile, 'I'm afraid I was guilty of not always listening to my wife's chatter about domestic affairs.' He looked up and seemed to be appraising her again.

'You live here? In Saltershaven?'

Kathy avoided answering directly. 'I've been away touring with a concert party. We're affiliated to ENSA and we entertain servicemen and women, factory workers, hospitals.'

'Really?' Mr Wainwright's eyebrows rose fractionally. 'That sounds very commendable. And what do you do?'

'I'm a singer. A soloist.'

There was another pause before Kathy asked tentatively, 'Won't you consider employing a nanny? He's your son. Surely . . . ?'

He smiled a little wearily and said flippantly, 'Are you applying for the job?'

Kathy gasped in surprise. It was more than she'd dared to hope for. 'Yes. I am. I'd like nothing better than to care for Beryl's baby as she would have wanted.' She felt no guilt in ruthlessly exploiting the man's one and only weakness, if it meant she could be close to James.

He nodded slowly. 'I'll think about it. I promise I will give it serious thought. You're right about one thing. Beryl wouldn't have wanted me to give him back for adoption. She loved the little chap.' It was almost an admission that he did not. 'I presume you're still with the concert party at the moment?'

Kathy nodded. 'Yes, we're here for the whole week. At the theatre. But I could stay. I needn't go with them. The cast aren't under any kind of contract. It's all voluntary.'

'I see.' He was thoughtful again. 'Of course, I'll have to find out what the position is regarding your eligibility for call-up. At the moment, I presume you're classed as doing valuable war work. I'm not sure that becoming a nanny for one child would be viewed as such. However, I'll make some enquiries. Come and see me at the end of the week some time on Friday. Check with my secretary for a suitable time and I promise I will have an answer for you by then.'

He rose and Kathy knew herself dismissed. She shook hands with him again and left his office, not quite sure if her trembling legs were going to carry her safely down the stairs and outside the building before she could give way to the tears that welled up inside her.

She was close, oh so close, to being with her baby. To holding him, feeding him, dressing him, loving him – to being able to spend every moment with him. But then common sense intervened and she tried to calm herself and not get too hopeful. After all, if Mr Wainwright felt very little affection for the child, why would he want to keep him at all? At the moment, he felt an obligation to the wife he had loved and lost. It would have been her wish, but as time went on and his grief lessened he might view bringing up a child that wasn't even his as a burden he could well do without. Kathy decided she would tell no one within the company until she knew Mr Wainwright's decision.

Thirty-Seven

How she got through the rest of the week, Kathy didn't know. The time seemed to crawl and she passed the days in a trance. She could sleep, yet she didn't feel tired. She was buoyed up with hope and excitement. She was bursting to confide in someone, yet she dared not. She felt that if she voiced her hopes aloud, her dream would be shattered.

Friday came at last and she was once more waiting outside the council offices for her early appointment with Mr Wainwright. The moment she stepped into his office she knew the news was good. He rose from behind his desk and came towards her with his hand outstretched to shake hers.

'Good morning, Miss Burton,' he smiled. 'Please sit down. Now, let me tell you straight away that I have decided to give you a month's trial in the post as James's nanny. In fact, to give us both a month's trial.' He sat down at his desk again, rested his arms on its surface and linked his fingers together. 'I went to Willow House to see James. He's being well cared for, but it's a grim place. I – Beryl wouldn't have been happy to think he was back there.' He paused, remembering his wife. 'Anyway, we'll give it a try, but please understand, I am not making a long-term commitment at this stage. I – I really don't know if I can. And like I said before, you may be called up. But for the moment,' he went on briskly, adopting his business-like manner once again, 'let's discuss practicalities. I have agreed a price on a house, and though they're hurrying things up as much as possible, I can't move in for two weeks. You won't be expected to do very much in the way of heavy housework, though perhaps you wouldn't mind cooking the occasional meal? I have a daily help, Mrs Talbot, where I'm living now. She's good in her way,' he added wryly, 'but she is burdened with an idle, good-for-nothing husband who resorts to illness as a means of having a few days off work. But domestics aren't easy to come by these days so I shall be keeping her on when I move.'

'Of course I wouldn't mind helping out.'

'Good. Now, in the meantime, perhaps you could give me the name of two people. I like to take up references; it's the way we do things here. But I'm sure it's only a formality, so, if you'd like to make arrangements with the concert party to leave in two weeks' time and return here then?'

Kathy nodded, her eyes shining. No matter what the future held, at least she would be able to spend a month with her little boy. It wasn't much, but it was better than nothing.

'I'll be here,' she promised.

'A nanny? Whatever do you want to become a nanny for? Have you any experience with children?' Ron was aghast. 'Of course I'll give him a reference . . .' Ron was one of the two names she had given Mr Wainwright, the other being Mr James Hammond, which had seemed to impress him. 'But I can't understand why you want to leave us to look after someone else's child. My dear,' he took her hand and patted it gently. 'It won't be a substitute for your own, you know. I know you had a dreadful time but one day you will meet a nice young man and . . .'

Tears filled Kathy's eyes as she shook her head. 'You don't understand. This is something I have to do. Something I want to do – more than anything else in the world.'

Ron stared at her. 'Why, Kathy?' he said softly. 'Just tell me why? We're going to miss you so much in the party and you bring such pleasure to the audience. A pretty girl – a very pretty girl – with a beautiful voice and you want to bury yourself away here to devote yourself to just one child. Oh my dear, don't cry. I'm sorry. It's none of my business, but I just can't understand it. I thought you enjoyed being with us. You get on with all the other members in the party, don't you?'

Kathy nodded wordlessly.

'Then . . .'

Kathy sighed. This man had been so good to her, so kind. He deserved to hear the truth, even if it cost her a good reference. But she knew instinctively that she could trust him. He was a devout man who would not betray her confidence.

'If – if I tell you the real reason, will you promise me that it'll remain just between us?'

'Of course, but . . .'

'Then please sit down, Ron. This is going to take a while . . .'

She told him it all, starting right back at the beginning with her life of drudgery at home and how she had longed to escape. 'If my father hadn't hit me that day, I'd probably still have been there.' She smiled wryly. 'Dreaming of the bright lights, no doubt, but still there milking cows at the crack of dawn.'

Ron smiled. 'I always wondered how come you were so good at getting up in a morning to catch the early train. I almost have to drag some of the others out of bed, but there you were, bright and early and with a smile on your face . . .'

Her story went on. How the Robinson family had taken her in and how Jemima had found her a job.

'That was how I met Tony. And then – and then . . .'

'And then the wedding that didn't happen.'

She nodded and went on huskily, 'But there's something you don't know. After – after Tony had gone away, I – I found I was pregnant.'

'Oh, my dear girl.' There was no censure in his tone, just sympathy and understanding.

'I came here to a home for unmarried mothers and babies. I – I wanted to keep him but I was tricked into signing adoption papers and they took him away from me. They never even let me see him or hold him . . .'

She went on with the whole story, right up until the previous day when Mr Wainwright had offered her the post of nanny.

'It's my little boy. James is my little boy, Ron. Do you see now why? I just have to grab this chance to be with him. Even if it's only for a little while.'

'Of course I do. But, Kathy love, are you sure you're not just building up further heartache for yourself? What if, at the end of the month, this Mr Wainwright decides he doesn't want to keep the child? What if he decides to put him up for adoption again?'

'I don't know,' Kathy said bleakly. But then she lifted her chin with a new determination. 'But I'm not going to live on "what ifs". I'm just going to take each day as it comes.' She paused and then, putting her head on one side, added wistfully, 'I don't suppose you feel like giving me a reference now, do you?'

'My dear, dear girl,' Ron said, surprising her by pulling her to him and hugging her. Though a kindly man, he was not given to displays of affection. 'Of course I'll give you a reference. A glowing one. What better "nanny" could that little boy have than his own mother?' He pulled away and looked into her eyes. 'And you need have no worries. Your secret is safe with me.'

'Thank you, Ron,' she said simply.

The two weeks passed surprisingly quickly. There were four engagements for the party. They played in and around Nottingham: in a factory canteen, the NAAFI of an RAF station near Newark and two hospitals. This time, with help and encouragement, Melody took part in the show in a hall attached to the hospital, but she did not visit the wards. After Kathy's final performance, Ron organized a leaving party for her. She was touched by the gifts she was given. Perfume, handkerchiefs, a pretty scarf, and from the comedian in the party, a pair of earplugs. 'That's for when he cries too much.'

They all laughed and Rosie pressed her gift into Kathy's hands. 'That's from me and Martin. I know he's not here, but he'd want to join in. I know he would.' It was a children's picture book. 'I don't know whether I envy you or think you're mad.' She laughed. 'I want children of my own one day, but I don't think I could ever look after someone else's.'

Kathy smiled and deliberately avoided meeting Ron's glance. 'Thank you, Rosie. It's lovely,' was all she said, neatly avoiding commenting on the girl's statement.

And then she was on her way to Saltershaven. Soon now, she would see her little boy again.

'Can you go to Willow House to pick him up?'

Kathy's heart missed a beat. How could she? They might recognize her!

'I – yes, of course,' she said boldly. 'But – but do you think they'd hand him over to me? I mean – I could be anybody.'

'Mm. I hadn't thought of that. I'll write a note. Better still, I'll get my secretary to type it on headed paper. That way they'll know it comes from me.'

'Wouldn't you – like to fetch him yourself?' Kathy ventured, trying to make it sound as if it was an occasion he ought not to miss.

'I really haven't the time,' he said and pressed the buzzer on his desk that brought his secretary into the room.

He dictated the letter he wanted written and then scribbled on a piece of paper the address of the house he had just moved into and which was to be Kathy's new home. 'Get yourself settled in first,' he said. 'Make sure you have everything you need for the boy and then you can fetch him tomorrow.'

Kathy took the piece of paper from him and waited in the outer office until his secretary had typed the letter. As she left the Town Hall, she was still wondering how on earth she was going to take James out of Willow House without being recognized. And if she was, she was sure the matron would lose no time in telling Mr Wainwright just who his new nanny was.

The new house Mr Wainwright had bought was situated on a road at the opposite end of the town to the one where he'd lived with his wife. It was a grand house, set high on a ridge of land that ran parallel with the shore and overlooking the sea. She was surprised that he had chosen one that had such a similar setting and view to his old home. But perhaps, she thought, he wanted to live with his memories and wanted to be reminded of his wife. She let herself in with the key he had given her and wandered through all the rooms until she came to the one that had been decorated and furnished as a nursery. The workmen he had employed must have worked very hard to have everything completed so quickly. She crossed the room to the connecting door and found herself in the neighbouring room, which was obviously to be hers. Fresh flowers had been placed on the dressing table, by the daily help, Kathy presumed. She couldn't imagine the career-minded Mr Wainwright taking the time to get the flowers himself, much less arrange them in a vase and place them in her room.

Mrs Talbot, the "daily", turned out to be a jolly round little woman who lived two streets away. She arrived later in the afternoon to prepare Mr Wainwright's dinner and to see that the new nanny had everything she needed.

'Ee's told me you're going to fetch the little one.'

'Yes, I'm going tomorrow morning.'

'Like me to go with you?'

Kathy hesitated. She had formed a plan. A daring one, certainly, but she hoped that with her new-found acting skills, learned while taking part in the numerous sketches which were part of the concert party's show, she could pull it off. But Mrs Talbot would undoubtedly think it strange and would more than likely mention it to her employer.

Kathy smiled widely at her. 'That's awfully kind of you, but if you wouldn't mind being here and having something ready for him to eat.'

'Oh aye, that's mebbe for the best. Let's see, how old is he now?'

Kathy knew to the minute, but she pretended uncertainty. 'Er – I think he's about two years old.'

'I'll make him one of my special egg custards. Little ones love my egg custards.' She winked and tapped the side of her nose. 'And made with fresh eggs, let me tell you. But don't ask me how, 'cos I aren't telling.'

Kathy laughed. It seemed they both had secrets they were not about to share, though she liked Mrs Talbot. In some ways she reminded Kathy a little of Auntie Betty.

'The mester said you was to take a taxi tomorrow morning. It's a long way out to Willow House. D'you know where it is?'

'I think so,' Kathy made the pretence of sounding doubtful.

'Well, the taxi driver'll know anyway.'

But Kathy had already made up her mind that she would walk there, because first there was somewhere else she had to call.

Thirty-Eight

'Well, well, fancy seeing you here again. Come for your old job back, Kathy? We've got a vacancy for an usherette. You can start tomorrow and I don't need references.'

'Thank you, Mr Johnson, but I have a job.'

'Shame. You were a good lass. I haven't had one since who's prepared to do all the jobs you didn't mind turning your hand to, I must say. Anyway, what can I do for you?'

'I've come to ask a favour. I – I've been invited to a fancy dress party and – and I wondered if I could borrow some props.'

Larry Johnson waved his arm in the direction of the room where the props were kept. 'Help yourself. Mrs Jervis isn't here at the moment, but I'll square it with her. Mind you let us have whatever you borrow back though. Costumes are hard to come by.' He adopted a comic sarcasm. 'There is a war on, you know.'

'I had noticed.' Kathy giggled.

Kathy found what she wanted and, alone in the dressing room she had shared with Rosie, donned the black wig and the spectacles. The false hair hung to her shoulders, and she covered it with a wide-brimmed felt hat, which she pulled down low over her forehead. She decided to wear her own clothes, but now she was wearing a smart, tailored suit and looked nothing like the waif in a cheap cotton dress who had presented herself at the door of Willow House seeking admittance. She found some gloves that almost matched her suit and regarded herself in the mirror. Well, she looked the part. Could she now play it?

She picked up her handbag and the copious shopping bag she had brought with her. She walked out of the dressing room and along the passageway towards the stage door that led to the street behind the theatre. Luckily, there was no one about backstage and, once in the street, she let out her breath and began to walk briskly away.

She took a taxi from the town out to Willow House. She didn't want any delay in her getaway. At the gate of the home, she hesitated for just a moment to look up at the forbidding building. The next few minutes would certainly decide her fate one way or the other. Taking a deep breath, she walked up the driveway and knocked boldly on the door. It was answered a few moments later by a heavily pregnant girl. Kathy's heart went out to her and she longed to smile warmly and talk to her, but she had a part to play. The most important part she would ever undertake in her life.

Feeling like a traitor to her own kind, Kathy looked the young girl up and down disdainfully and saw her cringe. Her courage almost failed her, but instead she took a deep breath and said in an affected, upper-class tone. 'I have come to collect the child, James Wainwright. Whom do I have to see?'

'Come in, please, ma'am,' the girl said and pulled open the door. 'If you'd just wait here in the hall, I'll tell Matron.'

The girl walked away with that peculiar rolling gait

reserved for the heavily pregnant towards the door of the matron's office.

Kathy remained in the shadowy hall, praying that she would not be invited into the woman's office, where she knew she would be obliged to stand facing the bright light from the windows.

But the matron came bustling out of her room. 'Oh good morning, Miss – er . . .'

Kathy felt panic twist her stomach. She hadn't thought of a false name. But then, she thought, I have to use my own. Mr Wainwright will have used my real name in the letter. Oh, how foolish she'd been. She was about to be discovered and all because she hadn't thought soon enough to use a pseudonym.

Deciding that the best form of defence was attack, she said in imperious tones that implied that giving her name to such a woman was beneath her, 'You have the boy ready?'

'Oh, yes.' The matron seemed quite flustered and so unlike the woman Kathy remembered that she almost laughed out loud. 'Mr Wainwright telephoned this morning. Everything is in order.'

Kathy made no attempt to hand over her letter of authority from Mr Wainwright and, silently, she blessed him for having taken the trouble to contact the home in person.

'You, girl—' The matron now spoke in the manner that Kathy remembered so well. She shuddered inwardly, but managed to keep her authoritative composure. 'Go and bring the child here. Mind you bring his belongings with him. Get one of the other girls to help you.'

The girl hurried away as fast as her bulk would allow her.

'Would you care to wait in my room?' the matron asked with an obsequious smile once more.

'No, thank you,' Kathy replied stiffly, avoiding meeting the woman's eyes. She gazed at the staircase, willing the girls to hurry, but she knew the poor creatures would be unable to do so in their advanced condition.

'You're to be Mr Wainwright's nanny, I understand?'

'That is correct.'

'He's a lovely boy. You do know he's adopted?'

'So I understand.'

'He came from here. His natural mother was a lovely girl, but you know how it is. The best of them can make mistakes.'

Kathy almost laughed aloud to hear the kindly understanding in the matron's tone, when she knew how very different the reality was. Oh, how she'd love to wipe that false smile off her face.

'Such a tragedy, Mrs Wainwright being killed like that, but I'm so pleased to hear that Mr Wainwright has decided to keep the child. Ah, here they come . . .'

Kathy held her breath as two girls now descended the stairs, the first one leading the little boy by the hand as he carefully negotiated each step, the second carrying a bag of his belongings.

'There we are . . .' The matron took hold of the child's hand from the girl and passed him to Kathy. Deliberately, she avoided meeting the matron's glance and kept her gaze fixed on her child. At last, she had him back where he rightly belonged. No matter that no one knew he was hers, just so long as she could be with him.

'Do you need any help? The bag's quite heavy.'

'I have a taxi waiting . . .' Kathy snapped and turned towards the door, anxious to make her escape. The matron herself opened the door. 'Bowen, carry the child's bag out to the taxi for Miss – er . . . for the lady.'

Kathy was out of the door and down the steps and willing herself to walk sedately down the drive to the waiting vehicle as she matched her step to the child's. But all the time she felt a prickling sensation down her back as she felt the matron's gaze still upon her. Any moment she expected to hear a shout, ordering her to stop. But she walked on and with every step she breathed a little more easily.

The taxi driver leapt out of the vehicle and, taking the bag from the girl, opened the door for Kathy to lift the child in and then climb in beside him. As the girl lumbered back up the drive, the driver started the engine with a twirl of the starting handle and then climbed into the driver's seat.

'Eh, it's grand to see another little chap leaving that place. He's not yours, I suppose, is he? He's older than the ones I usually have in my taxi. Not meaning to pry, like, but I just wondered if he was actually yours and you'd come back for him.'

Kathy decided that it was better to keep up the pretence a little longer. The fewer people who knew the truth, the better. You never knew, she thought, in a small town like this just who knew who. If she were to confide in the taxi driver, he might well turn out to be Mrs Talbot's second cousin twice removed. You just never knew.

Although she wanted to shout it from the rooftops. Yes, he's mine. Of course he's mine. Instead she said, 'His mother was killed in the air raid . . .'

'Oh, poor little chap.'

'But from now on, yes, he's mine.'

'Then his luck's changed, madam, if you don't mind me saying so.'

'Thank you.'

In the back of the taxi, Kathy removed her black wig and the glasses. She pulled the hat back on and tucked her own blonde hair beneath it, hoping, at the last ditch, that the taxi driver wouldn't notice the sudden dramatic change in his passenger's appearance.

He didn't. When the vehicle pulled to a halt outside the house, James started to whimper and the driver quickly helped her out and carried her bag up the drive to Mrs Talbot waiting at the door. He hardly gave Kathy a second glance as she handed the child to the daily help and then paid her fare.

At last, the door closed on the outside world and they were safely home.

'Isn't he a little love?' Mrs Talbot cooed. The child's tears dried instantly and he smiled, his whole face lighting up as he beamed and chuckled. 'I bet you're hungry, aren't you? I bet they've not fed you right at that horrid place. Now, you come with me and we'll see what we can find for you in my kitchen.'

Kathy smiled. She had her son back. She could be with him all day and all night too. For the moment, she was quite content to let Mrs Talbot fuss over him. Time enough for her to cuddle him and get to know him when they were alone.

He had Tony's eyes and his dark hair too. Even his nose had the makings of being the same shape. As she bathed him that night, Kathy examined every inch of him, touching him with gentle, loving fingers, revelling in the smooth skin, the rounded arms and legs. She kissed his forehead, his feet and his hands.

'Oh, my darling boy,' she murmured. 'I'll never let you go again. Somehow, I'll find a way to stay with you.'

And James smiled his beatific smile.

Mr Wainwright had certainly not misled Kathy in his attitude towards his adopted son. He hardly saw the child. Though he made sure that Kathy had everything she needed for him and for herself, he wanted nothing to do with little James. That first evening, Kathy brought him down to the dining room where Mr Wainwright was eating his meal alone at one end of the polished mahogany table.

'We've come to say "Goodnight",' Kathy said.

Mr Wainwright looked up, a startled expression on his face. 'Oh – er – yes – right.' He made no move to get up but just gave a curt nod and said, 'Goodnight then.'

Kathy stared at him for a moment and then looked down at the child standing quietly beside her. He was gazing at the man with a blank look, as if he was a complete stranger.

'That's your daddy,' Kathy said.

Mr Wainwright set his spoon down in the empty dish. 'Er – I've never liked the term "Daddy". I always called my father by his proper title. "Father". And I'd be obliged if you would teach James to use that name for me.'

Again Kathy stared at him. What a cold, unfeeling man he was. But she smiled dutifully and said, 'Of course. Is there anything else I should know? I mean, when would you like to spend some time with him?'

'I wouldn't,' Mr Wainwright said bluntly. 'He's your responsibility – entirely. Please ask me for anything you need and I'll see you get it – if possible, of course, in these difficult times. But – I don't want to have anything to do with him. I – I'm not good with babies or toddlers. Perhaps when he gets a little older. School age, perhaps, then I might find him a little more interesting.'

'I see.' Kathy tried very hard to keep any note of disapproval out of her tone. She didn't want to do anything that might endanger her position here. But she couldn't resist the urge to say, 'Don't you even want to see him in the evening, just – just to say "Goodnight"?'

For a moment Mr Wainwright regarded the child thoughtfully. James beamed and waved his chubby hand at him. ''Night, 'night,' he said, endearingly. Kathy saw the man's expression soften a little.

'Very well, then,' Mr Wainwright said at last. 'Just at night, when I've finished my dinner, you may bring him to my study.'

'Thank you, Mr Wainwright.' As she turned to go, he said, 'Oh, Miss Burton, please feel free to use the sitting room whenever you wish. I shall be spending very little time in there. More often than not I shall be working in my study in the evenings. And please use the radio whenever you wish, though I'd be glad if you'd keep the volume turned low so that it does not disturb me.'

Kathy was tempted to say that it was unlikely she'd have the radio playing so loudly that she would not be able to hear James. Instead she thanked him politely and carried the little boy up to his cot in the nursery. Clutching the knitted rabbit, he settled down at once and his eyelids closed as soon as she had tucked the covers around him.

She set the nightlight and tiptoed into her own room and glanced around it. It had been furnished as a bed-sitting room. The bed was in one corner, with a bedside table and lamp on it. Nearby was a dressing table and wardrobe, but near the window that looked out over the back garden of the house, an easy chair and low coffee table had been placed. There was even a book-case to one side, filled with a variety of books. Kathy ran her finger along the titles and smiled. There was a battered copy of *Pride and Prejudice*. She took it from the shelf, sat down in the chair and opened the book. On the flyleaf, in scrawling handwriting was written, 'To dear Beryl on her fifteenth birthday from her loving Aunt Mary'.

Kathy smiled. By the appearance of the book, it had been a treasured and much-read possession. Something else she had in common with Beryl Wainwright.

Thirty-Nine

The Wainwright household settled happily into a routine. Mrs Talbot did most of the housework and cooked evening meals during the week for the master of the house. Kathy had usually eaten by the time Mr Wainwright came home, for it coincided with James's bedtime ritual. On the days Mrs Talbot did not come – at the weekends – Kathy cooked for both Mr Wainwright and herself and they both ate a little earlier, at six o'clock instead of seven. For the first two weeks Kathy ate in the kitchen with James while Mr Wainwright took his meal alone in the dining room.

On the Sunday evening of the third weekend, Mr Wainwright came into the kitchen. Kathy jumped to her feet at once. 'Is there something—?'

He put his hand out, 'No, no, please, don't get up. I was just thinking—' He paused and eyed James sitting quietly in his chair, his brown eyes regarding Mr Wainwright solemnly. 'Is he a good boy? I mean, at mealtimes? At the table?'

Carefully Kathy said, 'Usually, yes. I'm trying to teach him the way to behave. I – I don't think one can start too young.'

Mr Wainwright looked pleased and nodded. 'Quite right. To be honest, Beryl was a little lax with him at times.' A pause and then he went on. 'What I was thinking was that it seems a little silly for you to be sitting in here and me in there – on my own. In the week, of course,' he added hastily, as if not wanting to give away too much of his privacy, 'it's better to keep to James's routine, but at weekends when you do the cooking – for which I'm very grateful incidentally, as that was not part of our original agreement.'

'I don't mind. I enjoy it. And James sits in his chair watching.'

'I was thinking we might all eat together in the dining room at weekends.'

'That would be very nice. Thank you, sir.'

'Of course, if I have guests . . .' He never entertained, so Kathy couldn't understand him even mentioning it, but dutifully she said swiftly, 'Of course. A proper dinner party is no place for a child.'

He nodded. 'Right, that's settled then. And – er – please call me "Henry".'

So a slightly altered routine was established. During the week, Mr Wainwright – or rather Henry as Kathy now must think of him – ate alone, and the only time he encountered his son was when Kathy took him downstairs, bathed and dressed in his pyjamas. At weekends, the three of them ate in the dining room together, Henry at the head of the table, Kathy at one side with James's chair beside her. For the first three weeks things passed calmly enough, but on the Saturday night of the fourth weekend, James was fractious. He was whimpering as Kathy sat him in his chair, and as she tried to feed him with a spoon his cries increased and he turned his head away.

'Is something the matter with him?'

'Perhaps he's getting another tooth.' It pained her to admit it even to herself that she wasn't sure at what age children cut their various teeth. 'See how red his cheek is?'

'Are you sure that's all it is? He hasn't got a temperature, has he? He looks awfully hot.'

'That's because – if it is a tooth coming through – his gums are hurting and he's cross.'

She tried James with another spoonful but he screwed up his face and pushed her hand away, spilling the food from the spoon on to the carpet. Kathy mopped it up at once with her napkin, but it left a dark, wet stain on the floor.

Henry's face was thunderous. 'Perhaps this wasn't such a good idea after all.'

Kathy rose, leaving her own meal untouched. 'I'll take him upstairs.'

'But what about your own meal?'

'I'll just put him in his cot and come back.'

'Very well.' Henry carried on with his own meal and didn't even speak to or look at the child as Kathy carried him out.

She laid him in his cot. 'Poor little man,' she murmured. 'Is that nasty old tushypeg hurting, then? I'll be back in a jiffy. I must just go down and clear our plates away. I'll be right back.'

She ran lightly down the stairs and went back into the dining room. 'I'm so sorry about that,' she said. 'I'll mind not to bring him to eat in here if he's fractious.'

She began to pick up her plate and James's dish.

'Aren't you going to sit down and eat your dinner?'

'He's crying. I must get back to him.'

A look of annoyance passed over Henry's face. 'Let him cry. It won't hurt him for once.'

'No,' Kathy said quietly, hoping that defying her

employer would not bring about her instant dismissal. 'It's not naughtiness. If it was I'd be the first to let him cry out his paddy, but he's got toothache.'

'As you wish,' Henry said stiffly. 'I see now that you're as soft as Beryl when it comes down to it.'

'Not when it's naughtiness, I assure you. Only when he's so obviously in pain.'

With that, she gathered the dishes and left the room, returning only to move James's chair back into the kitchen.

Henry Wainwright continued his meal in stony silence, a churlish look on his face. Kathy was smiling as she ran back up the stairs. If that same look had been on James's face, she would have classed it as mardy.

They continued to dine with Mr Wainwright when James was sunny-natured and well-behaved. If he showed the slightest sign of 'playing up', as Mrs Talbot fondly called it, they ate in the kitchen. Kathy still waited on her employer, serving him his dinner and then clearing away and washing up after James was in bed and asleep.

One evening about ten o'clock, when she was putting away the last cup and saucer in the cupboard, Henry wandered into the kitchen carrying two brandy glasses. He held out one towards her. 'A nightcap.'

She smiled and took it. 'Thank you.'

'Is the child asleep?'

'Yes.'

'Let's go into the sitting room.' He turned to lead the way, but Kathy hesitated. She didn't want to anger

Henry – he seemed in a particularly mellow mood – but she couldn't be sure of hearing James if he cried.

As if reading her thoughts, Henry said over his shoulder, 'You can leave the door ajar. You'll be able to hear him then.'

Breathing a sigh of relief, she followed him into the room and sat, a little self-consciously, on the sofa while he took his usual armchair by the fire. He swirled the brandy around in the glass and looked across at her through narrowed eyes. 'Tell me about yourself.'

Kathy's heart missed a beat. It was the sort of question she'd dreaded him asking. She'd begun to feel safe here. Henry Wainwright seemed so wrapped up in his work, with little interest in his adopted son and even less in her, that she had been lulled into feeling secure.

'I – there's not much to tell, really. I was brought up on a farm but I wanted to see a bit more of life, so I went to work in Lincoln.'

'So how did you come to join the concert party and end up visiting this town?'

Unwittingly, he had made it so easy for her. Put another way, the question could have been impossible to answer truthfully. As it was, she could say honestly. 'Mr Spencer, who formed the concert party, used to be the conductor in a choral society I belonged to in Lincoln. He asked me to join him.' It was the truth, if not the whole truth.

'And are you quite happy here? I mean, it doesn't seem much of a future for a pretty young girl like you just to be looking after one child.' He paused and eyed her keenly. 'I mean, what about marriage? Wouldn't you like to get married one day? I thought that was the ambition of every young woman.'

'Perhaps one day,' Kathy said carefully, but her heart was hammering painfully. The questions were getting a little too personal and any moment she expected him to ask something that would trap her.

'Have you never had a young man?'

'I . . . there was someone, but – but he went into the RAF. He – he was a fighter pilot.' She knew her face looked bleak, her eyes haunted.

'So,' he said softly, 'you've lost the one you loved too, have you?'

Wordlessly, she nodded.

'I'm sorry to hear it, Kathy. Very sorry.'

Life might have continued in much the same way in the Wainwright household if the concert party had not returned to Saltershaven in June. Kathy saw the advertisement in the local paper, and on the afternoon of their first concert she wheeled James in his pushchair to the cinema knowing the cast would be rehearsing for the evening performance.

'Kathy, my dear girl.' Ron greeted her with open arms as she walked down the aisle towards the stage carrying James in her arms. 'Hello, young man.' He beamed at the child, and tickled him under the chin to be rewarded with a wide smile from James. 'He's a handsome little chap, isn't he?' He lowered his voice and winked at her. 'But then, of course, he would be, wouldn't he? How's it all going? Are you happy?'

'Yes, Ron, I am. I get to be with him all the time. Mr Wainwright isn't very interested in him. It seems it was his wife who really wanted children. I think Mr Wainwright is married to his job, if you know what I mean.'

Ron laughed. 'I do. I've met a few like that in my time. Oh well, my dear, as long as you're happy.'

'Have you seen anything of Miss Robinson?'

'Mabel gets a letter now and again. But I expect you do, don't you?'

'Yes, we write to each other regularly, but I miss *seeing* her. Do you think she'll ever go back to Lincoln?'

Ron shrugged. 'I doubt it. They've laid a few off at Hammonds. Business for them just isn't the same as it was before the war. You can't expect it to be. Folks haven't got the money – or the coupons! I don't think she'll even try to go back there. She's still with Ted and Betty. She seems happy enough.'

And why shouldn't she be? Kathy thought. She's with her son too.

Forty

'Kathy, I have something to ask you.'

Ron was standing in the kitchen of Henry Wainwright's house, twirling his hat nervously in his hands. On the day she had been to the theatre to see him, he'd promised to come and see her before the party left town and now here he was. But she hadn't expected this.

'What is it?'

'I wondered if you'd come back to the party . . .' As she opened her mouth to refuse, he put up his hand. 'Don't answer straight away. Hear me out – please.'

'Sit down, Ron. I'll make a cup of tea.'

'If you're sure. It's a long walk here.' He sat down gratefully but then added, 'What about the little feller?'

'Mrs Talbot's gone into the town shopping and she's taken him in his pushchair.'

'Ah, that's all right then.'

When they were both sitting at the table with a cup of tea in front of them, Ron cleared his throat. 'Now, I'll quite understand if you say "no", my dear, but I would just like you to think about this very carefully. We've been asked to give a series of very special concerts and I'd really like you to come with us. It'd only be for a couple of weeks, I promise.'

'I thought Melody had taken my place with her impressions?'

'That's right,' Ron said carefully. 'But she's very young and – and – well, I don't think she'd cope with the circumstances very well, seeing as what happened at that hospital near Newcastle. You remember?'

'Oh, I see. It's another hospital, is it?'

'Yes, but a very specialized one. Have you heard of Archibald McIndoe?'

Kathy stared at him. 'Yes,' she said slowly. 'I read an article in the paper only the other day. He's the plastic surgeon who's helping solders and airman with – with facial disfigurements, isn't he?'

Ron nodded. 'Especially – fighter pilots.'

'Oh Ron . . .' Kathy didn't know whether to laugh or cry. 'That's a low blow. You – of all people – resorting to emotional blackmail.'

'Sorry, my dear. But I so want you to come. We've been asked to go to the Queen Victoria Hospital in East Grinstead and also to the convalescent home where the airmen go between their many operations. You could cope – you've already proved as much – with whatever we're going to see. It won't be easy, but I know you could hide any – any embarrassment you might feel. We all need to go in there and take absolutely no notice of their terrible injuries and the operations they're undergoing. There are some weird and wonderful methods being used, so I'm told, but the marvel of it is they're working. These poor fellows have a future, thanks to a very clever and dedicated man.'

'I'd like to but – but I don't see how I can leave James. I mean, you know how very much this job means to me.'

'I know. I've been thinking about that. You told me that Mr Wainwright isn't all that interested in your – I mean – his son?'

Kathy nodded. 'He wouldn't want to be left with him. That I do know. He'd get someone else and I – I couldn't bear that, Ron.'

Ron patted her hand. 'I know that. But if you explained the situation to Mr Wainwright, said what it was all about, would he let you take young James out to the Robinsons' farm? They'd look after him for you, wouldn't they? Just for two weeks?'

Kathy thought of Betty and couldn't help smiling. 'Of course they would. Betty would love it.'

'So – do you think Mr Wainwright would agree to let the boy go there?'

Kathy shrugged. 'I can only ask.'

'I don't see why not.' Henry seemed unconcerned. 'I presume you know these people well?'

'I've known the family all my life. They lived on the neighbouring farm.'

'And they really wouldn't mind having a young boy in the house?' His tone sounded as if he could hardly believe there were such people.

'No, they wouldn't. They've already got an evacuee. So, do I have your permission to write and ask them?'

He shrugged. 'Yes, if that's what you want. How long would it be for?'

'About two weeks.'

'It's all right by me, if you're sure they wouldn't be put about.' He sounded as if he couldn't imagine anything worse than having a young child – and a stranger at that – foisted on him for two whole weeks. 'Now, if you'll excuse me, I have some work to do . . .'

*

As she had known they would, the Robinsons replied by return that they'd be delighted to have James. Kathy decided to take him there and then return to pack her own suitcase and travel down south by train to meet up with the concert party. She would stay at Sandy Furze Farm overnight and see James settled in.

'Oh, isn't he a lamb?' Betty cried, opening her arms wide to pick him up. Beaming, James held out his chubby arms and went happily to her.

'They always know when someone loves them,' Betty said. 'Now, my little man, what has your Auntie Betty got in her kitchen for you?'

'Pudding?' James said, smiling hopefully as Betty bore him away.

'My dear girl.' Jemima appeared and hugged Kathy. 'How good it is to see you. And look, here's Taffy to greet you. Just look at him. He's getting quite fat. He's spoiled rotten here. As, indeed, am I.'

Kathy had been concerned that the shock of losing her home and all of her possessions might have made Jemima thin and ill. But far from it, she looked fitter and happier than ever she had in the city. 'Now let me help you with your things. You must have had a tiring journey. It's not easy travelling with a little one.'

'The train was full of troops, but James had a great time being made a fuss of by all the soldiers. Have you heard from Amy? How is she?'

'She's fine. She's found herself a young man. A petty officer in the Royal Navy. He's been here with her once. He's a very nice young man, but . . .' Here Jemima glanced quickly at Kathy and bit her lip.

Kathy smiled sadly and murmured, 'I know, I know. But she's got to grab what chance she's got of a little happiness. I – I don't regret any of it. Not any more.'

'No,' Jemima said with her usual spirit that Kathy remembered so well. She leaned closer as she whispered, 'And neither do I, my dear. Neither do I. Now, let's get you settled in upstairs. And you must meet little Susan. She'll be home from the village school soon.'

'Susan? I thought it was a boy evacuee they had?'

'He went home. And now we've got Susan.'

Kathy smiled. Was there no end to the Robinsons' kindness?

It was a merry gathering that sat down to supper than evening with James the centre of attention sitting in an old battered child's chair that Betty had dug out of the loft the moment she had heard of the little chap's imminent arrival. Susan was a merry child of ten or so with blonde, unruly curls and bright blue eyes. She sat at the table close to James and talked non-stop to him in her cockney accent. The little boy watched her with wide eyes, beaming and reaching out to tug her curls. Later, when both children were sound asleep after a tiring day, Morry sought out Kathy.

'Are you happy, Kathy, because from what you say about this bloke, he might not object to the little feller being adopted? What I mean is, if – if you wanted, we could . . .'

'Oh Morry, dearest Morry, don't. Please don't. I know what you're going to say and I love you for it, but it wouldn't be right.'

Morry looked crestfallen once again, but he smiled. 'Oh well, it was worth a try. But I hope you know I'm always there for you if you ever want – well – anything.'

'I know,' Kathy said huskily. 'And I don't deserve you, Morry. I really don't.'

Now Morry really did blush.

Kathy arrived back in Saltershaven late on the Thursday evening. She was to travel south on the Friday and meet up with the concert party for their first show on the Saturday evening.

'Mr Wainwright's asked that you wait for him to get home tonight and have dinner with him, seeing as how you haven't got the little boy to look after,' Mrs Talbot greeted her.

'Oh, right – thank you. Then I'd better get my packing done before he gets in.'

By the time Mrs Talbot called up the stairs, 'Right, I'm off now, love. Your dinners are in the oven. I'll see you in a couple of weeks, then, shall I?'

Kathy hurried to the top of the stairs. 'Yes. Goodbye, Mrs Talbot. Thank you.'

By the time she heard the front door open and close and knew that Henry was home, Kathy was all packed and ready for her early start in the morning.

'I've brought some wine. I hope you like red. Mrs Talbot said it was beef tonight, though I hope it's not as stringy as the last lot we had. I'll open it. Let it breathe a little . . .'

Kathy served the main course and they sat down at the table, Henry in his usual place at one end of the table, Kathy on his left-hand side. But tonight there was no James on her left.

They ate in silence for a while until Henry opened the conversation. 'You do know what you're letting yourself in for, don't you?'

Kathy nodded. 'We played a lot of hospitals when I was with the concert party. Some of the injuries we saw then were pretty horrific.'

'I suppose so,' he murmured. There was a long silence before he burst out, 'You will come back, won't you? I mean, it really is only for two weeks?'

She stared at him in surprise. 'Yes, of course I'll come back. I love my job and – and I – I've grown to love James.' She was treading on dangerous ground, but she wanted him to know that there was no way she was leaving for good. Then another thought struck her. A terrible thought that made her heart pound anxiously.

'You – you do want me to come back?'

'Of course I do.' The swiftness of his answer surprised her. 'In fact . . .' He hesitated then added, 'Look, let's go into the sitting room. There's something I want to ask you.'

'I'll clear away . . .' she began, getting up.

'No, leave it.'

She sat on the edge of the sofa in the sitting room, feeling strangely apprehensive. Was he going to tell her that he'd decided to have James adopted again after all? It seemed to take him an age to pour out two brandies and to hand one to her. Then he sat down.

'Kathy, I've been thinking about this for some time. I have a sort of proposition to put to you. I've got used to having you around the house. You're quiet and seem to understand my need to work in the evening. Something Beryl didn't always seem to understand.

That's why I gave in to her overwhelming desire to adopt a child when we found we couldn't have any of our own.'

Kathy waited, becoming more alarmed at the way this conversation was going. He'd never wanted James and now he was going to say that he'd thought it through and decided he didn't want a lifetime of responsibility, however much his late wife might have expected it of him. She felt the lump begin to grow in her throat. Was she, once again, going to have her happiness snatched away from her?

'For myself,' he went on and her heart plummeted even more. 'For myself, I would give the child up for adoption again. He should have two parents, not one, but I know that's not what Beryl would have expected of me. I – I feel duty bound to honour what I know her wishes would have been. Kathy, what I'm trying to say in a very roundabout and clumsy way is – will you marry me and be a mother to James?'

Kathy stared at him and knew her mouth dropped open. She was in such a state of shock that she scarcely heard his next words.

'It would be a marriage of convenience. I do realize that you were very much in love with the young man you lost and I – well – I still feel Beryl's loss very keenly. I mean, if you wanted it that way, it would be a marriage in name only, though I would hope that perhaps in time . . .' He broke off, leaving the implication hanging in the air.

She couldn't understand it. Oh, she knew well enough what he was suggesting, but why? That's the part she couldn't understand. He was saying quite bluntly that he didn't have feelings for her, that he knew she hadn't for him. If he'd loved the boy and had been suggesting their marriage to safeguard the continuity of the same two people in his life, safeguarding against a procession of nannies, then she could have understood it. But he didn't love the boy. He'd made that very clear. So, why . . . ?

'I need a woman about the place. I miss Beryl running the home. Oh, Mrs Talbot's all very well but she's not always reliable. I mean, that idle husband of hers has only got to stop off work a day and she sends a message that she can't come. I do so like everything to be just so. I like my life ordered in a strict routine. I do *not* like disruption.'

So, thought Kathy, that was his reason. He wanted a built-in housekeeper and nanny for James.

'And I thought it might help you too. I managed to get a temporary deferment for you, but I doubt I can for much longer. But if you were to be a married woman with our child to care for, then it would be a different matter. So, while you're away, will you promise to think about it?'

Kathy opened her mouth to retort that she would never entertain such a preposterous idea. It was almost immoral. In her eyes anyway. But then she closed her mouth. If she refused, what about James? Henry might well decide to have him adopted and look around for a suitable woman to be his housekeeper so that his well-ordered life could continue without the encumbrance of a child. A child who wasn't even his and who he'd never wanted in the first place. He'd only ever agreed to the adoption to keep his wife – the perfect housekeeper – happy.

'I – will think about it,' she said and stood up. 'But now, if you'll excuse me, I have an early start in the morning.' As she reached the door, he said, 'Oh, do you think you could cook my breakfast in the morning before you go? Mrs Talbot's husband has one of his famous stomach upsets.'

Keeping her face straight, Kathy inclined her head and said, 'Of course.'

Surprisingly, Kathy slept well and it wasn't until she was sitting on the train heading south that she had time to think once again about Henry's strange suggestion.

Well, if that's not about the most unromantic proposal a girl's ever had, she thought. But it had caused her a dilemma. If she accepted, she could be with her son always. True. But there'd be a price to pay. She'd be an unpaid housekeeper and, possibly, something of a concubine – though a married one – in the future. Men, she knew, even cold-hearted ones like Henry Wainwright, had their needs. And it seemed that eventually he would expect her to behave in every way like a wife should. He'd hinted as much.

On the other hand, if she refused him, she suspected that he would at once put James up for adoption and dismiss her. She would be parted again from her son and this time, there would be no way of finding out who his new parents were.

Of course, there was another solution.

As the train sped on the clattering wheels seemed to say, 'Marry Morry, marry Morry.'

Forty-One

Ron was waiting on the platform for her when the train drew in.

'How did you know what time I'd be arriving?'

'I didn't. We're staying not a hundred yards from the station, so I've been meeting all the trains since midday.'

'Oh, Ron!' She was touched by his patient thoughtfulness. 'How is everyone? How's Rosie?'

'She's fine – apart from fretting about Martin. Now he's flying on bombers she's worried sick, poor girl.'

'Bombers? As a pilot?'

'No – no. He's a tail-end Charlie – a rear-gunner – I'm afraid. Very dangerous. I'm just hoping she'll be able to cope with seeing these poor injured fellows.'

Kathy smiled sadly. 'I – I often wonder how poor Tony died. Whether he – he—'

Ron's face fell. 'Perhaps I shouldn't have asked you, lass. I'm sorry.'

But Kathy put on a brave smile. 'No, Ron. I'm glad you did. I'll feel I'm doing my bit for Tony.'

'Sure?'

'Absolutely.'

'That's the ticket,' Ron said, picking up her suitcase. 'Right, then, let's get you settled in. I want a bit of rehearsal tonight. The hotel's got a function room they'll let us use and we've got our first concert at the hospital tomorrow night.'

As they walked out of the station and along the road towards the guesthouse where most of the concert party were staying, Kathy linked her arm with Ron's. 'Oh, it's good to see you again.'

'How's that little boy of yours?' he asked softly.

Now Kathy smiled widely. 'He's wonderful, Ron.'

'And – and it's working out? You looking after him?'

'Yes – yes, it is.' She wrinkled her forehead. 'Of course, I've been worrying constantly that Mr Wainwright is going to change his mind and put him up for adoption but then, last night – he – he—' She paused, still unable to believe it had happened and wondering for a brief moment if she had dreamt the whole thing.

'He what?' Ron's tone was concerned. He'd heard about young nannies being seduced by their employers. Had the man made advances to her?

'He asked me to marry him.'

Ron breathed a sigh of relief. But guardedly, he asked, 'And did you accept?'

'Not – not yet. You see, it was a business proposition.' She laughed wryly. 'It certainly wasn't a romantic proposal, that's for sure.'

'So – he didn't profess to be in love with you?'

'No. Not at all.'

'What about your feelings for him?'

'I'm certainly not in love with him,' she said bluntly. 'I – I don't think I'll ever love anyone but Tony. He was the love of my life, like poor . . .' She stopped and bit her tongue. She had been about to say 'like poor Aunt Jemima', then she realized just in time that Ron Spencer knew nothing of Jemima Robinson's secret.

They'd reached the guesthouse, but paused outside before going up the steps. Ron turned to face her. 'So why exactly is he asking you to marry him?'

'He – he needs a wife to run his home and look after James.'

'But why,' Ron persisted, 'if – as you say – he has little interest in the boy, that they only adopted him because his wife wanted a child, why is he keeping him? Why doesn't he let him be adopted by another childless couple?'

Kathy's face was bleak at the thought. 'Because – because he believes it's what Beryl – that was his wife – would have wanted him to do. To keep James as his son and bring him up.'

'Mm.' Ron was thoughtful. 'So . . . he's marrying to get a built-in housekeeper and mother for the boy and you – well, if you do agree to it – you're marrying him just to be with your son?'

Kathy bit her lip and nodded. 'Put like that it does sound a bit – a bit calculating.'

'Oh it is, Kathy. It is. All I would say to you, my dear, is think very carefully about it before you give him your answer. Just think, what's going to happen when James grows up and leave home? What then, eh? Do think about it, Kathy.'

'I will, Ron. I promise. I've got these two weeks and by then I'll know what I should do.'

Everyone in the concert party welcomed Kathy with open arms, and Rosie was ecstatic.

'I've missed you so much. There's no one else I can talk to like I can talk to you. Have you heard? Martin's on bombers now and I'm so terrified . . .'

'I know, love. I know,' Kathy comforted her, but she couldn't in all honesty voice the words that the young girl wanted to hear. She couldn't reassure her that he would be all right, that he would come through. The life expectancy of anyone flying in bombers wasn't good, and for a rear-gunner it was even worse.

'How've you been? How's that little boy you've been looking after? Are you enjoying it? I really can't imagine why you'd want to look after someone else's child.'

Kathy smiled. If only you knew, she thought.

The rehearsal went well, and Kathy slipped back into the routines as if she'd never been away. 'I just daren't risk taking Melody,' Ron said. 'These boys need to be treated just as though there's absolutely nothing wrong. They'll be ultra-sensitive to people's expressions when they first meet them. Do you think you can manage it, Kathy? I mean, I'd rather you said now if you feel you can't.'

'I'll be fine, Ron. Really. I'm prepared for it.'

'Well, you're a good actress. You've been brilliant in some of the sketches in the past. But I'll warn you now – you're going to need all your acting skills when you walk into that place.'

The following night the members of the concert party were all subdued when they set off in the rattling bus to take them to the hospital. They were all thinking about how they were going to react and hoping that they would be able to greet the terribly injured men with respect and sympathy that was not overly gushing.

However much they'd thought about it and steeled themselves, not one of them was prepared for the sight of the ghastly injuries the airmen had suffered. And the skin grafts they were undergoing were just as strange and frightening. But Kathy walked on to the makeshift stage with a broad smile and looked out over the sea of disfigured faces with a calmness she had not expected to feel.

In the interval the cast congregated in a room that the hospital had set aside for their use. There were cups of tea and biscuits on a side table. As Kathy took a cup and poured milk and tea into it, Ron came to stand beside her.

'All right?'

She nodded. 'I'm fine. I'm coping better than I thought I would. I knew I wouldn't show revulsion, but I thought I wouldn't be able to hide my sympathy for them. I guess that's almost as bad.'

'You did wonderfully well. I was watching. In fact, everyone's been marvellous and we've got the worst over now. I don't think even meeting them later will be so bad. You do know we've promised to mingle after the show, don't you?'

Kathy nodded. That part had worried her the most, but now she felt she could do it.

'Some of the operations and treatments they're receiving look almost as bad as the original injuries,' Ron remarked.

'But isn't there a wonderful atmosphere? They laugh and tease each other,' Kathy marvelled. 'And they make jokes against themselves. I heard someone shout out something when we were doing that second sketch and he was poking fun at himself.'

'I know, but you know what, this chap McIndoe, he doesn't profess to be able to do the impossible and give them back their former looks, but to the lads here he's already working miracles. He's giving them hope for the future and that means everything to them. Everything, Kathy. They have such faith in him, it's humbling to see it.'

'They're so brave. They must be in terrible pain sometimes.'

'Of course they're brave. That's why they're here, because they were brave enough to go out and fight a war for us. You'd be amazed at the number of DSOs and DFCs that are in this room right now. See that tall chap standing near the window with his back to us? He's a DFC. They say his plane was shot down and on fire and instead of baling out as he could have done, he stayed with it until he was clear of a village and over open fields before he jumped. By then, of course, he'd been badly burned himself. That's what I call bravery, Kathy.'

Kathy set down her cup and saucer and smiled at Ron. 'And now it's up to us to show our appreciation. Do you think my usual finale is okay? All those patriotic wartime songs? Do you think they'll like them?'

'They'll love them.'

They did. The audience, which was mostly men with just a few female nurses standing at the back, clapped and cheered and catcalled for encores, and Kathy had to sing 'We'll Meet Again' twice and 'Land of Hope and Glory' three times before they would let her leave the stage.

As she walked back to the room where they'd all changed she was smiling, though her smile was tinged with sadness. This war had changed her life, and part of her wished she was still touring with the concert party, feeling she was doing her bit for the war effort and lifting the spirits of servicemen and women and war workers. But she couldn't leave James; she couldn't bear to be parted from him again. She might lose him forever. She might never see him again. A cold shudder of fear ran through her at the mere thought.

She sighed. In two weeks' time she must return to Saltershaven. And then she must give Henry Wainwright his answer.

During the fortnight, the concert party played other venues as well as the hospital, but they returned there several times, on each occasion playing to a slightly different audience. Each time they mingled with the patients afterwards, drinking tea and talking.

Kathy moved among them, laughing and chatting, each time looking straight into the patients' eyes whenever she could. She ignored their facial wounds, their scarred and misshapen hands, and their slurred speech when it was their mouth that was affected. As she moved away from a young man from Liverpool who had been shot down over the Channel during the Battle of Britain, she glanced around the room and saw a tall young man standing alone by the window. It was the same man Ron had pointed out to her a few days earlier. The airman was watching her, but as soon as she caught his eye he turned away and looked out of the window.

Kathy's heart skipped a beat. There was something about the tilt of his head and the way he moved that reminded her so heartbreakingly of Tony. He was even the same height. Drawn irresistibly to him, she threaded her way through the throng until she stood just behind him.

'Hello,' she said softly. 'Did you enjoy the concert?'

He remained standing perfectly still, looking out of the window. He didn't move, didn't turn round and didn't even speak.

She could only see a little of the left-hand side of his face. It was badly damaged and his left ear was gone. Perhaps he can't hear me, she thought. Gently she touched his arm. He started and spilt tea from the cup he was holding.

'Oh, I'm so sorry.' Kathy was contrite, gently taking the cup and saucer from his hand and setting it down. 'I didn't mean to startle you.' She moved to the side and leant around him so that he could see her face. Perhaps he could lip-read. Perhaps . . .

The man turned his back on her again.

'Can you hear me?' she asked softly. She saw him stiffen and knew that he could. He just didn't want to face her.

'My name's Kathy. What's yours?'

Again, an uncomfortable silence.

Kathy sighed. 'I'm so sorry. I didn't mean to intrude. I just wondered if you'd enjoyed our performance?'

'Yes,' he mumbled. 'It was – wonderful.'

Now it was Kathy who caught her breath, staring at the back of his head, at the broad set of his shoulders. His voice! Though it was muffled through swollen lips, the timbre of it was the same.

'Tony,' she whispered. 'Oh, Tony. It *is* you. Oh, dear Lord, please say it's you.'

Forty-Two

Slowly, oh so slowly, while Kathy held her breath, he turned towards her.

The left-hand side of his face was cruelly injured, but now that she could see the right-hand side, she knew it was him.

'Tony,' she breathed, drinking in the sight of him. Tears filled her eyes. 'Oh, Tony, why?'

She only needed to say that one word for him to understand exactly what she meant.

He stared at her for a moment. His left eye was half hidden by a drooping, scarred eyelid. His cheek was disfigured and raw. His mouth, that had kissed her so gently, so passionately, was twisted out of shape. But, strangely, the flames that had engulfed him had hardly touched the right side of his face. His right hand was whole, while his left was misshapen and clenched into an unusable fist.

'Isn't it obvious?' he asked harshly. 'I wish you hadn't come. If I'd only known, I wouldn't have come to the concert that first night, but I never dreamed for one minute—' He sighed and swept his good hand through the wispy hair on the right side of his head. 'And then – when I knew the party was coming again, I – I couldn't resist just one more sight of you. Please, Kathy, just go. Leave me . . .'

She stepped towards him, so close that she could

feel his uneven breath on her face. 'I'm going nowhere.' She touched his face with tender fingertips. 'Darling, why didn't you tell me you were alive?'

'Looking like this?'

'Looking like *anything*! I've been heartbroken, believing you dead.'

'But – but you went away. You left Lincoln. Mother said . . .'

'Ah yes, your mother,' Kathy said bitterly. 'But for your mother, we'd have been married.'

'I know.'

'And you didn't write . . .'

'I know.'

'Is that all you can say, Tony?'

'I don't know what else to say. If I could turn back the clock, believe me, I'd do it all so very differently, but it's too late now.'

'What – what do you mean? Too late now?'

When he didn't answer, her heart felt like stone. 'You – you mean you've met someone else?' She tried hard, but now, she couldn't help her voice from breaking. The last few days, seeing all these poor boys, had been emotional enough, but now finding that Tony was alive, was just too much. Her head dropped and the tears flowed. She buried her face against his shoulder and wept.

'Oh, my darling, don't cry. Please don't cry.' With his good hand he stroked her hair. 'Just go, Kathy, and forget all about me. Please. For the sake of the love we once had for each other, please just go.'

She pulled away and stood in front of him, dabbing self-consciously at her eyes, aware that others in the room were watching her. Ron pushed his way towards her and took her arm.

'Kathy, we should go now.' His voice was stern. He thought that she had let him down, that she had not been able to hide her pity for the injured airmen.

'You don't understand, Ron. This is Tony. My Tony. I thought he was dead, but he isn't. He's here. He's alive.'

Ron stared at the young man.

'I'm sorry, young feller,' Ron said, smiling and putting out his hand to shake Tony's. 'I didn't – ' he stopped, cleared his throat and changed what he had been going to say – 'realize.'

Tony smiled a little lopsidedly and murmured ruefully, 'You didn't recognize me, you mean.'

Ron looked embarrassed for a moment, but Tony laughed and said, 'It's all right. You couldn't be expected to. Besides, I've been trying to stay out of the way all evening. I – I didn't want Kathy to see me.'

Before he could bite back the words, Ron echoed Kathy's feelings. 'Why ever not?'

Tony groaned with mock irritation. 'Not you as well, Mr Spencer. Isn't it obvious?'

'Not to me, young feller. This lass here's never stopped loving you, despite what happened and then there's—'

'No, Ron. Don't . . .' Kathy butted in, afraid that he was about to divulge her secret.

Ron glanced at her and looked shamefaced. 'Sorry, lass,' he muttered and turned away. 'I'll leave you to sort it all out, but the bus'll be here in half an hour. We'll have to go then.'

He moved away, and despite the crowded room, the two young people felt as if they were alone.

Kathy had recovered a little and was able to say more calmly now, 'You've got someone else?'

'Of course I haven't,' he said impatiently, as if talking to a stupid child. 'How could you think that? There's never been anyone else but you . . .'

With a sudden lift in her heart, Kathy was even able to tease him gently and say, 'You mean, *since* you met me? There were a few before, if I remember rightly.'

He groaned and closed his eyes. 'Oh, don't remind me.'

Then her face sobered again and she shook her head. 'But you still don't want to marry me?'

'How can I? How can I expect you to live with – this?' He gestured angrily towards his damaged face.

For a moment, she wasn't quite sure how to handle the situation, how to answer his question. Deliberately, she put her head on one side and appraised him. 'You always did have an over-inflated opinion about your own good looks,' she said bluntly. It was not the truth and he knew it, and he realized too what she was trying to do. '*I* don't see so very much difference.' Then she softened her tone and touched his arm. 'You're – you're still my Tony. Still the man I love, and I'll tell you something, Tony Kendall. You won't escape so easily this time. This time, you're going to marry me whether you like it or not.'

'Did you tell him?' Ron asked quietly without preamble as he sat down next to her in the bus. Above the noisy engine, the rattling of the windows and the chatter of the rest of the party, no one could hear what they were saying. 'About James?'

Kathy shook her head and said huskily. 'I couldn't. I didn't want him to think I wanted to marry him because of James.'

'I know what you're thinking,' Ron said mildly. 'If you go back to Wainwright and tell him the truth that he'll be only too happy to hand the boy over to you.'

Kathy stared at him. 'How did you know?'

Ron smiled. 'Because it's what I was thinking. From what you've told me, it's a possibility. But no more than that. It's not a certainty by any means. And I don't want to see you getting your hopes up for a perfect ending to all the unhappiness when, my dear, it might not happen. I don't want to see you getting hurt all over again.'

'But – but I can't marry Mr Wainwright.' She paused and smiled at herself. The very fact that she still referred to the man who had proposed to her as 'Mr Wainwright' said it all. 'Not now. Not when Tony's still alive. Oh, he's still saying he doesn't want to tie me to him, but I know I can persuade him. Given time.'

Ron sighed. 'Are you sure? When he leaves here, won't his mother want him back to look after him?'

'I . . .' Kathy began and then stopped. Carried along in a fervour of happiness because Tony was alive, imagining them being married and living with their son, she had not stopped to think of all the things – or rather people – who still stood in the way of their happiness.

She groaned, closed her eyes and leaned her forehead on the cool glass of the bus window. Why, Oh why, was she so impulsive? Why did she never stop to think things out?

Then she raised her head and turned to look straight into Ron's worried eyes. 'I do know one thing, Ron. No matter what, I'm going to marry Tony and I will fight for my child. Our child.'

Ron nodded. 'I wouldn't have expected anything

less, my dear. Not from you, but I really think you should tell Tony the truth before you marry him. He deserves that at the very least.'

It was three days before the company were due to appear again at the hospital and Kathy felt unable to break her commitment with the party. She sang and acted, but now her heart wasn't in it. She wanted to rush back to the hospital to see Tony.

On the day the of next concert, Kathy sought out Ron. 'We're not rehearsing today, are we?'

'No. I thought we all need a bit of a break before the show tonight.'

'Good, then you won't mind if I go over there to see Tony and meet you there tonight?'

'No, of course not, dear. Break a leg.'

Kathy giggled. 'Thanks.' Then she winked. 'It might be one way of getting into bed beside him.'

'You little minx!' Ron chuckled. 'Get away with you.'

As Kathy walked up the driveway to the hospital, her heart was hammering and her knees were trembling. She couldn't remember when she had felt so nervous, except perhaps the time she had been waiting for Henry Wainwright to make his decision over whether to employ her or not.

She'd been so sure that Tony would want to marry her, but now she realized she'd bulldozed him into it. She hadn't given him the chance to tell her how he really felt. She'd taken it for granted that he'd been thinking of her, that he hadn't wanted to saddle her with marriage to an invalid. Goodness knows, he knew enough about invalids and what it could do to a marriage! And now, today, she was going to tell him the whole truth and perhaps *he* wouldn't want to marry *her* then. Perhaps he would think she was pushing him into marrying her so that they could adopt James . . .

He was waiting for her in the garden, sitting on the fallen trunk of a tree.

'It's shady here,' he explained after they had greeted each other. 'Sorry, but I can't stand the sun on my face.'

'Of course.'

There was a silence and then they both began to speak at once.

They smiled and then Tony said, 'After you.'

'There's something I have to tell you, Tony.'

'Ahhh.' He let out a long sigh. 'I thought so. You've changed your mind. I don't blame you, Kathy . . .'

'Will you let me finish? No, I haven't changed my mind at all. I want to marry you more than anything in the world, but, in fairness, there's something you should know first and when you've heard it – well, it might be you who wants to change your mind.' She grinned ruefully. 'I did act rather like a Churchill tank the other day. I'm sorry.'

He laughed. 'Maybe it's what I need. But go on. What is it? Is there someone else in your life?'

'Yes, but not the way you think. At least . . . Look, let me tell you everything from the beginning.' She took a deep breath. 'After the wedding and you went away, you only wrote the once.'

'I know,' Tony said, shamefaced. 'I tried so often and then screwed them up. I just didn't know what to say. How could I ever get you to forgive me for what had happened? And then, when I came home after training, I was coming to see you to sort it all out face to face, but Mother said you'd left.'

Kathy shook her head at the depths of deceit to which the woman was prepared to stoop to keep her son bound to her. She sighed. No doubt Beatrice Kendall would be even more of a formidable foe now that her precious son was so hurt. She would want to take him home and care for him herself. Perhaps it would even make her get up from her own sickbed, thinking that now she had him to herself forever.

Only she was reckoning without Kathy. Kathy was no longer the innocent country girl. She had been through a lot in the last few years and she was stronger. Oh, so much stronger. Now she would fight all the way for what she wanted.

'I left on the first of April—' She pulled a wry face. 'I thought it very appropriate at the time. So – when did you come home?'

'The beginning of April, I think.'

Kathy nodded. 'I probably would've been gone by then, but I doubt if your mother knew that. Not many people did at first. Didn't you go to Aunt Jemima's to make sure?'

Tony stared at her. 'You mean – you mean Mother *lied* to me?'

Still not wanting to hurt him, Kathy said gently, 'Truthfully, I don't know. It's all a matter of timescale.'

He nodded slowly, a bleak look in his eyes. 'She must have done. Like you say, she couldn't have known you'd gone. I was home for three days and then I went to fighter pilot training. I – I never got home again, because this – ' he pointed to his face – 'happened.'

She looked straight at him, examining the extent of his injury. 'Is Mr McIndoe helping you?'

'Oh, yes. He's marvellous.' Suddenly there was a light in his eyes, hope in his voice. 'It'll never look perfect, of course, but I'll feel able to face the world.' He gave a grin that was lopsided because of his disfigurement. 'As long as the world is able to face me.'

'You're not the only one, and as time goes on, most people will know about what's happened to you and all the others. They'll understand then.'

'I hope so. There are some poor chaps in here far worse than I am. Mr McIndoe is having to rebuild faces completely in some cases.'

'I know,' Kathy said quietly. 'I saw.'

There was silence between them for a moment, then Tony said softly, 'Go on.'

She met his steady gaze and held it, wanting to see his immediate reaction to what she had to say next. She pulled in a deep breath. 'The reason I left Lincoln was because I found I was pregnant.'

He stared at her and then burst out, 'Oh, Kathy! Oh, my darling! If only I'd known. Why – why didn't you write and tell me?' His reaction was genuine. Loving, concerned – hurt, almost. It was Kathy who felt embarrassed and a little foolish. She should have trusted him more.

'I – I didn't want you to marry me just because of the child. After what had happened . . .' Her voice trailed away in apology.

'It was all such a dreadful misunderstanding, wasn't it?' He paused briefly and then, to her surprise, there was a bitter note in his voice. 'And all because of my selfish, possessive mother.'

She stared at him but said nothing.

'I see it all now. How everyone – including you – must have been able to see her for what she was. Everyone but me and my poor old dad.'

With gentle fingers, she took hold of his hand, deliberately choosing the damaged one. 'It must have been difficult for both of you. Being so close to her. I do understand.'

'And the baby?' There was eagerness in his voice, but Kathy's eyes clouded. As she continued with her story, Tony's eyes too mirrored her sadness, suffered with her the trauma of her baby being snatched away. When she had told him everything, even up to Henry Wainwright's strange proposal, he let out a long, deep sigh.

'What can we do? Do you think – if you told him everything now, told him the truth – he'd agree to us adopting him?'

'He might, but – oh Tony, do you mean it? Do you still want to marry me?'

'There's never been any doubt about that,' he told her solemnly. 'Where I went wrong was being so soft over my mother.'

'But what about your mother now? I expect she can't wait to get you home and look after you herself.'

Tony stared at her. 'Of course, you won't know, will you?'

'Know? Know what?' She stared at him and then breathed, 'Has – has something happened to her?'

'No.' His tone was suddenly hard. 'No, she's fine.'

'Your dad? Oh, not your dad?'

He shook his head. 'No, he's fine. I do hear from

him and he's been down here a couple of times, but it's difficult for him to come all this way. I understand that.' He paused and then went on haltingly, as if even he couldn't believe the words he was saying himself. 'My mother doesn't want to see me like this. She can't bear it. She – she's cut me out of her life as if . . . as if I was dead. She even tells everyone I was shot down – which is true, of course, but she implies I was killed.'

'Well, you were posted missing presumed killed, weren't you?'

'Briefly, at first, yes. But it wasn't very long before they were informed that I had survived. If you can call it that,' he added bitterly.

Kathy raised his injured hand to her lips and kissed it gently. 'Don't you ever dare talk like that again in my hearing. Not ever.'

He leant against her. 'Oh Kathy, darling, it's so good to have you back. You'll never know how much I've missed you.'

'About the same as I've missed you, I expect.'

They gazed at each other and she leaned forward and kissed him tenderly on the mouth. 'That – that doesn't hurt you, does it?'

'No, not a bit.' He smiled as he added, 'And even if it did, it'd be worth it.'

They sat close together for a long time, not saying much, just holding hands and revelling in having found each other again.

'So,' Tony said at last. 'When am I going to see my son?'

'I'll go back and tell Mr Wainwright everything. We – we'll just have to hope and pray that he'll let us adopt James.'

Forty-Three

Kathy felt torn in two. She didn't want to leave Tony but she had to get back to Saltershaven, and yet she feared what awaited her when she did.

There were two more concert dates and then she could leave. The time dragged, and it seemed much longer than three days until Ron was loading her suitcase onto the train and thanking her profusely for joining the party for the very special concerts.

'It's me who should be thanking you, Ron,' she said, kissing his cheek. 'If I hadn't come, I wouldn't have found Tony again. I'd probably have spent the rest of my life thinking he was dead.'

'Kathy,' Ron said seriously, taking both her hands in his, 'can I ask you something?'

'Of course you can.'

'If you hadn't found Tony again, would you have married this Mr Wainwright?'

'You want me to be truthful?'

He nodded.

'It sounds awful . . .'

'Go on, my dear. This is just between you and me.'

'Then – truthfully – I don't know. I'm just so grateful that now I don't have to make that decision. I'm going to marry Tony.'

'Even if it means losing your child? You have thought that Wainwright might turn awkward?'

'Yes,' she said hoarsely. 'It's my worst nightmare, but I have to face it.'

'Then – break a leg, my dear, in fact, break two.'

She went straight back to Saltershaven, arriving at the house just before Henry was due home from work. Mrs Talbot was just putting on her hat and coat to leave as Kathy opened the door.

'How lovely to have you back. I thought it was today you were coming home, so there are two dinners keeping warm in the oven. Have you had a good time?'

'Oh yes, Mrs Talbot. Very good, thank you.'

'Well, you look as if you have, love. There's a light in your eyes I haven't seen before.' She put her head on one side and regarded Kathy with knowing eyes. 'Might it have something to do with coming home to a certain gentleman?'

'If you mean, James, then yes,' Kathy replied impishly, knowing exactly who Mrs Talbot meant.

The woman shrugged. 'Oh well, I can only try. I'd like to see the master settled again with a good woman. I just thought . . . But maybe it's a bit too soon yet. The poor man's got to have time to grieve.'

Kathy said nothing, but silently she thought that to her mind, Henry, despite his protestations about how much he had loved his wife, wasn't exactly the typical grieving widower.

'I'll get off, love,' Mrs Talbot said, realizing that her attempt at matchmaking was falling on deaf ears. 'My Dan will be wanting his tea.'

Left alone, Kathy was jittery, anxious for Henry to arrive home so that she could say what she had to say. Waiting was making her even more nervous. She kept glancing at the clock, but the hands seemed to be crawling round. At last, she heard his key in the door and ran lightly down the stairs to meet him in the hallway.

He smiled as he closed the door and held out his arms to her. 'Does this mean what I think it means? What I hope it means?'

Kathy froze. How could she have been so stupid? Rushing to meet him like that had given him the wrong impression entirely. She had been so full of her own hopes, she hadn't stopped to think of his.

'I'm sorry,' she blurted out. 'No, it doesn't. Oh dear, I didn't mean to say it like that.'

His smile had vanished and his arms dropped to his sides. 'I see.'

'No, you don't. Look, let's have our dinner and I'll tell you everything. You go up and change.' She knew he liked to change out of his pinstriped suit when he arrived home. 'And I'll have it all ready when you come down.'

Henry sighed. 'Very well, then.'

They ate in silence, though Kathy was only picking at the food on her plate. Though she hadn't eaten since early morning, her appetite had completely deserted her. But it wasn't until he had eaten both his main course and pudding that Henry laid down his spoon and looked across the table at her.

'So – what is it you have to tell me?'

'I'll make the coffee and bring it into the sitting room. It – it might take some time.'

Henry raised his eyebrows but did not demur. He rose, dropped his napkin on the table and left the room. For a moment, Kathy stared at the crumpled napkin that he had discarded so carelessly. That would have been my life, she thought. Just acting as his slave.

Clearing up after him, pandering to his every whim. Having to do everything just the way he demanded. She shuddered, thinking what a narrow escape she had had. Now it was a decision she didn't have to make any longer.

But there was still James. What was to happen to her darling boy? Was Henry, as both Tony and Ron had feared, going to turn awkward because she was refusing to marry him?

As she handed Henry the cup of coffee, he said, 'You're trembling. My dear girl, there is no need to be frightened of me. Whatever it is you have to say to me, I'm sure we can talk it through like sensible adults.' He gave a dry, humourless laugh. 'It isn't as if our emotions are engaged, now is it? And no one else knows about this. At least, I hope they don't.'

Kathy smiled weakly and sat down on the sofa. She set her own coffee on the nearby small table and then clasped her hands in front of her. 'There's something I have to tell you. I – I haven't been entirely honest with you.'

'Oh dear,' he said, with a slightly mocking air. He too set his coffee down beside him and got to his feet. 'I think I'd better pour us both a brandy.'

Another few minutes of waiting, while Kathy grew more agitated by the minute. When he handed her the bulbous glass, she took a grateful sip. He sat down again and leaned back in the soft armchair, swirling the liquid around the glass cupped in his hand.

'Now, off you go. What is on your mind?'

'I did meet your wife and I hope she counted me as a friend, but I – I wasn't as close to her as perhaps I made out.'

'Go on.'

'You see, I sought her ought deliberately. I found out your address from the files at – at Willow House.'

Henry was listening intently and Kathy could see that his mind was working swiftly. No doubt he was already way ahead of her. But he said nothing. He just sat watching her and swirling the brandy round and round.

'James is my son. It was a difficult birth and they took him away from me without even letting me see him or hold him or . . .' Her voice cracked, but she cleared her throat and pressed on. 'They'd tricked me into signing adoption papers when I was admitted. Of course, we're not supposed to know who adopts our babies, but I found out and I walked along your road so many times in the hope of just catching a glimpse of him.' She turned pleading eyes towards him. 'I want you to believe me that I meant no trouble. Though I never wanted to part with my baby, once I'd met your wife, seen how she adored him and how she was looking after him, then – then I had to admit he was in the best place, even though it broke my heart.'

'Did you tell Beryl who you were?'

'Not at first. And I never would have done. I swear I meant no trouble . . .'

He nodded and said quietly, 'I believe you. Go on.' But she couldn't tell from his expression or from his tone how he was reacting to her revelations.

'I was standing outside the house one day – after we'd already met, I mean – and she came out and invited me in to see the baby. It – it was when I was holding him that she guessed. She suddenly said, "You're his mother, aren't you?" I admitted I was, but I begged her not to say anything. I told her what had happened, that I just wanted to hold him – even if it was only once. She understood and she – she was very kind to me. Obviously, she never told you. She sent me a letter and a photograph of him when he was about eighteen months old.'

Henry sighed. 'Well, she wouldn't. Obviously, she'd taken a liking to you and didn't see you as a threat.'

'I wasn't.'

'And she probably thought that if she told me, I'd have reported you.'

Kathy looked down at her hands. Her heart was thudding painfully. There was a long silence before he asked, 'Why exactly are you telling me this? I had assumed, from what you said when I arrived home, that you are refusing my proposal.'

'I'm sorry, but yes, I am.'

'But you don't want to be parted from the boy?'

Kathy bit back the angry retort that sprang to her lips. His name is James. Call him by his name. But she said nothing, realizing that she must do nothing to antagonize him. Instead, she said quietly. 'No, I don't. But there's more to it now than just that.' The words came out in a rush. 'I've found him again. I've found Tony – the man I was engaged to. James's father. He's not dead after all. He was badly burned when his fighter plane was shot down. He's at Mr McIndoe's hospital receiving treatment.'

'And you're going to marry him?'

Kathy nodded.

Now he understood. 'I see. And you want to take your boy back?'

Again, all she could do was nod and watch his face.

'Mm.' Again the liquid twirled in the glass. There was a long silence before he said, 'So, after persuading me to keep him so that you could take the post as his nanny, you're now asking me to hand him back to you?'

Her voice was a hoarse whisper. 'Yes.'

Another long silence.

'Well,' he said at last, 'You've been very honest with me—' He smiled wryly. 'At least, now. And in turn I will be very honest with you. I've no interest in the child. It was Beryl who yearned for children, not me. And now she's gone, there's really no reason for me to keep him. You might think me a cold fish, Kathy, but I'm not completely heartless. I loved my wife dearly. She was the perfect wife for me and I indulged her in her desire for a family. And I thought you were right when you said she would've wanted me to keep the boy and bring him up, but what I *now* think is that she would want you to have him. You and his real father. She wouldn't want me to stand in your way.'

Tears were coursing down her face. 'Oh thank you, thank you . . .'

Henry swallowed his brandy in one gulp and got up. 'Please – don't cry,' he said coldly. 'I can't abide women's tears.'

Kathy scrubbed at her face with the back of her hand and sniffed. 'I'm sorry, but I can't thank you enough.'

'There's no need. If I'm honest you're relieving me of an encumbrance I never really wanted in the first place.'

Kathy stood up. Mindful of his position in the community, she said, 'You – you'll want it done properly though, won't you? Legally?'

He nodded. 'Of course. I'll instruct my solicitors in the morning.'

'There's no need for Willow House to be involved, is there? I don't want him to go back there. Please – don't send him back there.'

'I wouldn't think so for a moment. Besides, if what you've told me about that place is true – ' he held up his hand as she opened her mouth – 'and I've no reason to disbelieve you, then I think I might ask my solicitor – who is a good friend of mine – to look into the place. It sounds to me as if it's not being run properly. Whether they're doing anything against the law, I'm not sure, but it ought to be looked into. I can't have something like that going on in my area.'

Kathy almost laughed aloud. It was his reputation he cared about, not the welfare of the unmarried mothers and their children. But she said nothing. At least if it got the authorities to look at Willow House, it didn't matter how it came about – just that it happened.

'So – so what about James?'

He shrugged. 'You keep him. Just let me know your address so that I can send the papers through for you to sign. I expect it would be better if you and your fiancé were married first. Is that possible? I mean he's not too ill?'

'No, no. We can be married straight away, and I'm sure the people who've looked after James while I've been away won't mind keeping him a little longer. That's if you're sure . . . ?'

'Oh, I'm sure.' Henry laughed and there was an undoubted look of relief on his face as he added, 'And you're welcome to take all his belongings too. All the nursery furniture too, if it's of use to you.'

'That's most generous of you.'

He shrugged and added, 'It's of no use to me.'

He turned and left the room, heading across the hall towards his study. Kathy watched him go, feeling a fleeting stab of pity for the man. It probably wasn't needed. Henry Wainwright would be happy enough in his career and maybe, some day, he'd meet someone else who'd fit his exacting requirements in a wife. But now . . .

Kathy's legs suddenly gave way beneath her. She sank down on to the sofa and gave way to tears of thankfulness.

Forty-Four

Kathy spent the following morning packing up all James's clothes to take with her. She would arrange for the nursery furniture to be collected when she knew where she was going to be. Then she called a taxi, thankful that Mrs Talbot was not due to come that morning. She didn't want to get involved in lengthy explanations to the woman, yet, if she'd been there, Kathy couldn't have left without a word. The woman had been kind to her. Silently promising herself that she would write to the housekeeper, Kathy carried her cases out to the taxi when it drew up at the gate.

The driver helped her to load them and Kathy climbed in. She took one last look at the house where she had spent the last few months. As the taxi drove away, she did not look back.

'Is James all right?' was her very first question. 'Oh, I can't wait to see him.'

'He's fine, my dear. He's asleep just now, but let me have a look at you first.' After their first greeting, Jemima held her at arm's length and scrutinized her face. 'You look wonderful, Kathy,' Jemima greeted her, kissing her cheek. 'The change has done you the world of good.'

'Oh, Aunt Jemima, more than you could begin to

guess. I've so much to tell you, but – ' she hesitated and the light in her eyes was suddenly overshadowed – 'if you don't mind, I ought to tell Morry first. I owe him that much.'

There was an unspoken question in Jemima's eyes, but she nodded. 'Of course, my dear. You'll find him in the cowshed. It's almost time for evening milking.'

Morry was herding the cows into the byre for milking when Kathy pulled on the spare pair of wellingtons that always sat by the back door and crossed the yard towards him.

'Kathy!' The delight showed plainly on his round, beaming face.

'Morry,' she said softly and submitted to his bear-hug and a kiss on her cheek. Impulsively, she kissed him back and then wondered if, yet again, her impetuosity was giving out the wrong signals.

'Morry – dear Morry. I want you to be the first to know, Tony's alive. I've found him.'

'Alive? Oh Kathy, that's marvellous. Wonderful news.' He gripped her hands and his smile was even wider, if that were possible. Kathy searched his face anxiously but there was not a trace of disappointment or resentment, either in his eyes or in his voice. He was genuinely happy for her, and so glad to hear that the young man was not dead after all.

'Oh, Morry,' Kathy whispered again as tears filled her eyes and she leant her face against his shoulder. 'You're so good.'

'There, there.' He patted her back. 'You know I only want you to be happy, Kathy love. That's all I've ever wanted.' Unbidden, the image of Muriel's face came into her mind. She and Morry were so alike in their unselfishness.

And her tears flowed even faster.

'Now, come along, this won't do. I want to hear all about it, but you'll have to come into the milking shed with me. Some of these poor creatures will burst their udders if I don't get to them.'

Kathy drew back and dried her tears. 'I'll help you. I don't think I've forgotten how to do it.'

Morry laughed. 'I'm sure you haven't. It's like riding a bike.'

They followed the beasts into the long shed and herded them into the stalls. Then they sat back to back to milk a cow each so that they could talk. The cow-shed was warm and cosy, the only sounds the contented chewing of the animals, the occasional swish of an impatient tail and the staccato sound of the milk spraying into the buckets.

She told him everything and when, at last, she fell silent, Morry didn't speak for a few moments.

'I can't understand why Tony's mother doesn't want to see him. Like you, I'd've thought she'd have wanted nothing more than to take him home and care for him.'

Kathy shook her head. 'I don't understand it either, and I think poor Tony's bewildered and hurt by it too. His father writes regularly and he's been to see him, but his mother doesn't want to know.'

Morry gave a wry laugh. 'Well, like Aunt Jemima always says, "It's an ill wind that blows nobody any good." Mrs Kendall's not going to ruin your next wedding, is she?'

Kathy turned on her stool to stare at him for a moment and then she burst out laughing.

*

Jemima and the rest of the Robinson family were just as genuinely thrilled as Morry had been. She went through the whole story again while she cuddled her son on her knee. She could hardly drag her gaze away from him, and she couldn't believe the incredible turn in her fortunes. She had found the man she loved, they were to be married and they had been given their son back.

'We'll get married down south,' Kathy told them. 'Tony has another operation coming up so he won't be able to leave hospital for several weeks. Maybe even months. I shall take James and get lodgings near the hospital and we'll be together.'

'What a lovely ending, cariad,' Betty said, wiping tears from her eyes. 'Well, almost. I still can't help feeling sorry for his poor mother. I know she's been spiteful and possessive, but she must be in shreds. And as for his poor father, he must be torn in two. Wanting to be loyal to his wife, yet desperate to see his son. Poor, poor man.'

Three days later, Kathy walked up the drive to the hospital.

'My, but you're heavy,' she chuckled to the child in her arms.

It was a bright, warm day and she knew most of the mobile patients would be out in the grounds. And she knew just where to look for Tony. In his favourite spot, sitting on the fallen tree trunk in the shade. She had almost reached him before he heard the soft sound of her footsteps on the grass. He turned, the right side of his face towards her, and for a fleeting moment it was the old Tony, the handsome unblemished face of the man she loved, turning to her, standing up and holding out his arms. And now she saw his whole face, saw the ravaged left-hand side and knew she loved him even more if that were possible.

She stood before him and, with a catch in her voice, said, 'This is your son. This is James.'

The look of incredulous joy and wonder on his face swept away any lingering doubts Kathy might have had. All the misunderstandings, all the heartache was forgotten. They were together at last and whatever the future held for them, they would face it – together.

Forty-Five

Over the weeks that followed their poignant reunion, Kathy was carried along on a tide of ecstasy. She scarcely knew what was happening in the war, she was so totally wrapped in her own little world of happiness – a happiness she had never expected to find. But somewhere in the back of her mind lurked a feeling that all was still not quite right. That her happiness was not as complete as she had expected it to be.

They were married quietly in the local church, the congregation made up, almost entirely, of patients from the hospital. To crown their happiness, Tony's final operation was a success and the great man declared that there was really nothing more he could do for him. His face would always be scarred and he would never regain the full use of his left hand, but, as Tony himself said, he was better than a great many.

'We can go home,' he told Kathy. 'Back to Lincoln.'

Suddenly, Kathy realized what had been niggling at her. Tony's parents. Betty's words had stayed with her. The generous woman could still find it in her huge heart to feel pity for the lonely, twisted woman. But why? Why didn't Beatrice want to see her son any more? He had come back and yet she was still acting as if he was dead, as if she *wanted* him dead.

Understanding came to her as she was bathing James on the last evening before they were due to travel north back to Lincoln. Gently, as she soaped his smooth skin, she revelled in its perfection. She watched him splash in the warm water, listening to his happy chuckles. He was growing to be just like his father. He was going to be so handsome, so good-looking . . .

The realization came slowly, seeping into her mind. Now she understood. Beatrice had so loved her perfect boy that she couldn't bear to see him injured, couldn't cope with the tragedy of his marred good looks. All her life she'd wanted perfection. She'd been born into the wrong branch of the Hammond family. Though spoiled by her wealthy uncle, she'd still been the poor relation. In her eyes, her husband had disappointed her and now her son, on whom she'd pinned all her hopes, had failed her too. Beatrice was a bitter and twisted woman, but gazing now on her own son, feeling her love for him overflow, at last Kathy began to understand.

As she lifted the slippery, wriggling child out of the water and wrapped him in a warm, fluffy towel, she whispered, 'We're going home tomorrow, my precious boy. And do you know what? You're going to meet your grannie and granddad.' Her smile broadened as another thought entered her mind and she murmured, 'And what your other grandparents will say, I daren't think.'

But in her heart she already knew. Her father would grumble and grouse for a while, but then the realization would dawn on him. He had a grandson. A boy! At last, he had an heir for his family's farm. Kathy's smile was tinged with sadness. Perhaps, for once in her life, she had done something that would please her father. And as for her mother? Well, the moment James was placed in her arms she would feel a happiness she hadn't known existed. No, the problem – as always – was Beatrice Kendall.

Their long journey took them to Sandy Furze Farm, where Tony was welcomed into the warm and loving Robinson family. Even Morry shook his hand warmly, slapped him on the back and joked, 'Just look after our Kathy, else you'll have the whole of the Robinson family after you.'

They stayed for a week, during which time Tony and Kathy travelled backwards and forwards to Lincoln to find somewhere to live. 'And if you think I'm going to live in a flat on Mill Road, you can think again,' Kathy teased him.

They found a small terraced house on one of the streets leading off Monks Road, not far from where she had lived with Jemima, and signed the contract to rent it for a year. Then they went into Hammonds' store and sought out Mr James. He was in the office that had once been Tony's.

The shock and then the delight that spread across the older man's face touched Kathy. 'Anthony! You're alive! My God! This is wonderful. Come in, come in, sit down. How are you?'

He ushered them into his office, sat them down and sent his secretary scurrying to unearth a bottle of champagne. 'This calls for a celebration. And if I'm not mistaken, there's another reason, isn't there? You're married?'

Shyly, Kathy nodded. She glanced at Tony and gave a slight nod, silently giving her permission for the rest to be told.

Tony cleared his throat and said with a mixture of

embarrassment and pride in his voice. 'We – er – we have a son. His – his name is James.'

The man stared at them for a moment and then threw back his head and laughed aloud. 'You've named him after me?'

'Well – to be honest, not exactly,' Kathy said. 'It's a long story.'

'Let's hear it then.' Mr James stood up as his secretary returned with a dusty bottle and three glasses. As he popped the cork and poured it out, Kathy explained.

'I'm so glad it's ended happily for you both – for the three of you, I should say. But there's only one thing that disappoints me,' he added, looking directly at Kathy. 'That you didn't come to me. I would have helped you, my dear. But perhaps, then, you didn't know me well enough. I expect I was just Mr James, owner of Hammonds, and rather aloof?'

Kathy blushed and nodded.

'Then I'm sorry because, truly, I would have stood by you.' Now he looked sternly at Tony. 'And as for you, young feller, well, you're damned lucky to get a second chance to put the fiasco of that wedding right.'

'I know,' Tony said simply.

Mr James was smiling again. 'Just one thing,' he said wagging his finger at the pair of them. 'I insist on being the boy's godfather. Oh, and by the way,' he added with deliberate casualness, 'when can you start back to work?'

Tony and Kathy gaped at him.

'You mean – you mean you'll employ me? Looking like this?'

'Why ever not?'

*

They had been living in Lincoln for a month. Tony had settled back into his position at the store and James Hammond had given him more responsibility than ever, happy to return to his privileged life of golf and fishing.

'I think most people are getting used to me now. One or two customers still stare a bit. I suppose I shall always have to put up with that.' He smiled lopsidedly. 'The kids are the best though. They're so open and unafraid. They just come up to me and say, "What's the matter with your face, mister?" It's the parents who are embarrassed and try to shush them.'

He sat in silence, lost in his own thoughts. Kathy took a deep breath. 'Talking of parents, we should go and see yours. We should take James to meet his grandparents.'

The bleak look in Tony's eyes as he glanced at her twisted Kathy's heart, but she was resolute.

'They – they don't want to see me.'

'That's not quite true, is it? I'm sure your father does.'

'But Mother doesn't.'

Kathy sat on his knee and put her arm round his neck. Gently, she said, 'No, but she'd like to see James, now wouldn't she?'

He rested his cheek against her breast. 'You really mean you'd risk taking him to see her?'

'What do you mean, "risk"?'

'She'll want to take him over. Replace me with him. He's very like me. Like I used to be,' he added wistfully.

Kathy slid off his knee and knelt in front of him. With gentle hands she cupped his face and looked straight into his eyes. 'Tony Kendall, after all I've been through, do you really think I'm going to let anyone – *anyone* – take away my son from me again?'

Tony grinned sheepishly. 'No, I don't.' He was thoughtful for a moment before he nodded slowly, 'All right. We'll go. But on your own head be it.'

The following Sunday was a fine, bright day as they walked up the hill to the Kendalls' home, Tony carrying James in his arms. Kathy rang the front door bell and they waited, glancing at each other a little nervously until they heard George's slow and heavy tread approaching on the opposite side. The door opened and the man standing there stared at them, his glance going from one to another and then coming to rest, finally, on the child in Tony's arms. His expression softened and tears welled in his eyes.

'Hello, Dad,' Tony said at last. 'Aren't you going to invite your grandson in?'

Wordlessly, as if for the moment he had quite lost the power of speech, George pulled open the door and gestured to them to step inside.

'Is Mrs Kendall in the front room?' Kathy asked, taking the lead.

George nodded.

'Then I'll go and see her on my own first. You take James into the kitchen and introduce him to his grandfather properly.'

Without waiting for a reply, Kathy opened the door to the left of the hall and went into the room.

Beatrice Kendall was lying on the sofa, looking for all the world as if she hadn't moved a muscle since the last time Kathy had seen her. Except, Kathy recalled, the very last time she had seen the woman had been in the church, feigning a heart attack.

At the sound of the door opening and closing, Beatrice opened her eyes and lifted her head. She squinted against the light from the window to see who had entered.

'You! What on earth do you want?'

Kathy sat down in the armchair. 'I've come to see you. *We've* come to see you.'

Beatrice caught her breath. 'Anthony? Anthony's here?'

Kathy nodded.

The woman put her hand over her eyes in a dramatic gesture. 'I don't want to see him,' she wailed. 'I can't.'

'All right. You don't have to. But wouldn't you like to meet your grandson?'

There was a stillness in the room, the only sound the ticking of the bracket clock, the crackling of the logs on the fire.

Slowly, her hand dropped away from her eyes and she stared at Kathy. 'My – my grandson?'

'Yes, he's called James and he'll be three in November.'

'You mean – you mean he's illegitimate?'

'No. Because we're married and as I understand it, even if a child is born out of wedlock, when the parents marry the child is legitimized.'

'You're married?' Beatrice almost spat out the question.

'Oh, yes,' Kathy said airily. 'We're married.'

Beatrice pulled herself up and thrust her face towards Kathy.

'When?' she demanded.

'Six weeks ago.'

'Six weeks?' Beatrice's mouth twisted. 'Then how

do I know it's really Tony's child? It could be anybody's.'

Anger surged in Kathy's breast. Resentment and bitterness towards this woman welled up inside her. Beatrice hadn't changed. Not one bit, but Kathy bit back the sharp retort and with a serenity that surprised her, she said, 'Oh, I can assure you that he's Tony's son. You'll soon see for yourself.'

There were conflicting emotions flitting across the woman's face as she struggled to come to a decision.

'Bring him in,' she muttered at last. 'Just the child. Not – not Tony.'

'Oh no,' Kathy said firmly. 'James won't come without his daddy. It's both – or nothing.'

The two women stared at each other in a battle of wills. It was Beatrice who was the first to lower her eyes and submit with a brief nod.

Kathy rose and left the room, returning a few moments later. Tony followed her into the room, carrying the little boy. George hovered nervously in the doorway.

Beatrice's gaze was fixed on the child. Deliberately, it seemed, she avoided looking into her son's face. She didn't even greet him. Her whole focus was on the little boy. Tony bent forward and set the little chap in her lap. James looked up into her eyes and reached out to touch her face.

'Hello, Grannie,' he said, just as Kathy had taught him.

Tony stepped back to stand beside Kathy. She sought his hand and held it and together they watched. George too, from the doorway, watched. Before their amazed eyes, a change came over Beatrice. They saw it. All of them saw it for themselves, though had they not, not one of them would have believed it if it had been told to them.

The woman's face softened, seemed to grow younger even. She smiled, and her eyes were alight with a tenderness they had not shown in years.

'Anthony,' she breathed. 'My little Anthony. You've come back to me.' But it was not the grown man standing nearby to whom she spoke. It was the child.

Kathy moved then and knelt beside her. 'Mrs Kendall, it's not Anthony, but it is his son. This is your grandchild, but that – ' she gestured towards Tony – 'is your son.'

Slowly, with what seemed like a great effort, Beatrice raised her eyes and looked at Tony for the first time. He didn't flinch, didn't even turn the injured side of his face away, but met her gaze steadily.

'Oh – Oh – my – darling – boy,' she gasped at last and the tears flooded down her face. She held out her arms and, for a moment, the child on her knee was forgotten.

Kathy picked James up and carried him from the room, whispering to George as she passed close to him, 'I think we'll leave them together for a while, don't you?'

George followed her out. In the kitchen he took his grandson into his arms for the first time and held the boy close. In an unsteady voice, he murmured, 'You really have the most remarkable mother.' His gaze rested upon Kathy. 'Thank you,' he said simply. 'Thank you for your generosity of heart, lass.'

Kathy smiled and touched her baby's cheek as she said softly, 'I can understand her so much better. Now that I know what it's like to be a mother.'

Wish Me Luck

ACKNOWLEDGEMENTS

Many people have helped me in my research for this novel. I am especially grateful to Mick Richardson for his generosity in lending me the private papers and flying log book of his father, Sergeant W. J. Proffitt, the wireless operator of a Lancaster bomber, who was killed whilst on a bombing mission in March 1944.

My thanks also for his help to my brother-in-law Peter Harrison, who flew thirty missions as a wireless operator during the Second World War; to Mrs Lillian Streets and Mrs Barbara Brooke-Taylor for sharing with me their memories of their time in the WAAF; to Mike Smith, Curator of the Newark Air Museum, for answering my questions; to Fred and Harold Panton at the Lincolnshire Aviation Heritage Centre at East Kirkby for all the marvellous displays and wealth of information that have helped me so much, and to Michael Simpson, head of exhibitions at the Imperial War Museum North, Trafford Park, Manchester, for his advice and help.

I have also consulted numerous books in the course of my research, but special mention should be made of *A WAAF in Bomber Command* by Pip Beck (Goodall, 1989) and *Square-Bashing by the Sea (RAF Skegness, 1941–1944)* by Jack Loveday (J. Loveday, 2003).

Very special thanks to the members of my family who read and commented on the script: Robena and Fred Hill, and David and Alan Dickinson. As always, my love and thanks to all my family and friends whose support and encouragement means more than I can say. And not forgetting Darley and his Angels at the Darley Anderson Literary Agency and Imogen Taylor, my editor at Macmillan. To all of you – you're always there when I need you – thank you!

One

APRIL 1941

Fleur Bosley stepped down from the train, hitching her kitbag onto her back. The platform was in darkness, the blackout complete. She moved forward carefully. It was like stepping into the unknown. Behind her someone else jumped down from the train and cannoned into her, knocking her forward onto her knees. She let out a cry, startled rather than injured. At once, a man's voice came out of the darkness. 'Oh, I'm sorry, miss. I didn't see you.'

His hands were reaching out, feeling for her to help her up, but she pushed him away. 'I'm all right,' she said, feeling foolish.

A thin beam of torchlight shone in her face. She blinked and put up her hand to shield her eyes. 'D'you have to do that?' she asked testily, but the only answer coming out of the darkness was a low chuckle. 'I just wanted to see if whoever I knocked over was worth picking up.' A young man's voice, deep with a jovial, teasing note in it.

'Well, you needn't bother trying to pick me up.' She emphasized the words, making sure he knew she understood his double meaning.

His only answer was to laugh out loud. 'Come on,

the least I can do is buy you a nice cuppa. Let's see if there's a cafe or a canteen open somewhere nearby.'

'Shouldn't think so at this time of night,' she said, slightly mollified by his offer as she bent to feel around for her kitbag. Fleur hadn't had anything to eat or drink since midday and her throat was parched. Travelling from the south of the country had taken all day. There'd been delays all along the line because of air raid warnings and now she was stranded in Nottingham with no promise of further transport for the last leg of her journey. Fleur was hungry, thirsty – and cross!

'Here, let me . . .' The man shone his torch and picked up her bag, then ran the beam of light up and down her.

'Snap!'

'What?'

'You're a WAAF.' He turned the light on himself and she saw he was wearing RAF uniform. 'Come on, you can't refuse a cup of tea with me now, can you?'

In the darkness, she smiled. 'Oh, go on then.'

Minutes later, as she was sitting at a table whilst he went to the counter to fetch two teas, she was able to study him. Tall, with fair, curly hair; bright, mischievous blue eyes; a firm, square jaw and the cheekiest grin she'd ever seen. As he came back, set the tea on the table and sat down opposite her, she knew that he, in turn, was appraising her.

She took off her cap and laid it on the chair beside her. Shaking out her soft brown curls, she returned his gaze steadily with a saucy sparkle in her dark brown eyes. 'Will I do then?'

He took in her smooth skin, her small, neat nose and

perfectly shaped mouth that was delicately enhanced with just a touch of pale pink lipstick. 'Oh, you'll do very well, miss. It's usually little grey-haired old ladies I knock over, not pretty young ones. My luck must be changing.' He held out his hand across the table. 'Robert Rodwell, at your service. But my friends call me Robbie.'

She was about to answer tartly, 'How do you do, Mr Rodwell.' But something in his open face made her put her hand into his warm grasp and say instead, 'Fleur Bosley. Pleased to meet you – Robbie.'

As they drank their tea, he asked, 'So, where are you heading? Here in Nottingham?'

'No. South Monkford. It's a small town not far from Newark.'

Robbie nodded. 'Yes, I know it.' A slight frown line deepened between his eyebrows. 'I think we used to live there years ago, but my mother never talks about it much and we came to live in the city when I was little. But I seem to think my father – he died before I was born – ran a tailor's shop there.'

Fleur wrinkled her forehead. 'Can't think of a tailor's shop there now. There's old Miss Pinkerton's; she's a dressmaker and—'

'That's it. That'll be the one. Mother said once that a woman who was a dressmaker had taken it over.'

'Her and her sister run it. They sell women's clothes.' She giggled. 'They call it "Pinkertons' Emporium", would you believe? They're sweet old dears, but they're both a bit doddery now. And their shop is so old-fashioned. It's like stepping back in time when you walk in.'

'All corsets, wool vests and big knickers, eh?'

Fleur laughed and pretended to be coy. 'Really, sir, saying such things to a lady. And when we've only just met too. I do declare!'

They laughed together, feeling already as if they had known each other far longer than a few minutes.

'So – were you hoping to get to South Monkford tonight?' Robbie asked.

Fleur pulled a face. 'I was, but it's doubtful – there won't be a train out of here now. I could ring up and get my dad to fetch me, but I don't like to ask him to come all this way at this time of night. And using his precious petrol.'

'You've got a car? *And* a telephone?'

Fleur grinned. 'Yes. The car's called Bertha. It's a 1923 Ford and it's seen more "active service" down dirt tracks and across fields than many a tank. As for the phone – we live on a farm in the middle of nowhere. My mum insisted it was essential.' Her brown eyes twinkled. 'But I think it's just so that we've no excuse for not letting her know exactly where we are and what we're doing.'

'And do you?'

'What?'

'Let her know exactly where you are and what you're doing?'

Fleur laughed. 'Not likely!'

Trying to sound casual, but failing, Robbie asked, 'Er – who's "we"?'

'My brother, Kenny, and me. And Dad too. She likes to keep us all close.' There was an edge of resentment in her tone as she added, ' "Tied to her apron strings" is the phrase, I think.' Her face clouded and a small frown puckered her smooth forehead. She didn't know why, but for some reason she felt she could confide in him. The words were out before she'd even thought to stop them. 'She . . . she didn't want me to volunteer. It . . . it's caused a lot of rows at home.'

'That's a shame,' he said gently. 'How long have you been in?'

'Oh, right from the start. I volunteered as soon as I could.'

His blue eyes twinkled. 'Me too. The day after Mr Chamberlain's "we are at war" broadcast.'

They stared at each other and then smiled, amazed that they'd both felt the same.

'Are they calling up women yet?'

'Don't know,' Fleur replied cheerfully. 'I didn't wait to find out.'

'And you live on a farm? You could've applied to be classed as a reserved occupation, couldn't you?'

Fleur grimaced. 'I know. That's why my mother was so put out. I could quite legitimately have stayed at home for one reason or another, but I didn't want to. I . . . I wanted to "do my bit" as they say.'

'But you're not regretting it, are you?'

'Not for a minute.' Her reply was swift and genuine. 'But it's still – well – difficult when I go home.' She sighed. 'But I'll have to go. I've just been posted and I've got three days' leave before I have to report there. It might be a while before I get any more.'

'Where are you going?'

She opened her mouth to reply and then hesitated, her smile causing two deep dimples in her cheeks as she said impishly, 'I'm not sure I should be telling you. Careless talk and all that.'

'Well, I'll be terribly careless and tell you exactly

where I'm going. Wickerton Wood just south of Lincoln. It's a new airfield. Parts of it are still being built, so they say, but it's ready enough to start flying.'

Fleur's eyes widened and she couldn't prevent a little gasp of surprise. Chuckling, he leant forward to say softly, 'Don't ever volunteer for special operations, will you? Your face gives you away. That's where you're headed too, isn't it? Wickerton?'

Feeling reprimanded, she nodded and murmured, 'Oh dear.'

'Don't worry,' he said cheerfully. 'Your secret's safe with me.'

'Is . . . is that where you're going now?'

'Yes, the day after tomorrow, but first I'm going home to see Ma.'

'What are you going to do at Wickerton Wood?'

'Ah, now that *would* be telling.'

'You're right. I'm sorry,' she said at once.

He laughed with a deep chuckle that was infectious and somehow endearing too. Don't be silly, Fleur, she told herself firmly, you've only just met him. He could be anybody. But already, she realized he wasn't just anybody. He was someone she'd like to get to know so much better. The thought surprised and shocked her.

Fleur regarded herself as a no-nonsense type of girl: down to earth and with no foolish romantic notions, especially now that they were plunged into war and all its uncertainties.

'I was only teasing.' The sound of his voice brought her back and she saw that his eyes were suddenly serious. 'You know,' he went on and now there was a note of surprise in his tone. 'It might sound daft, but I feel I could tell you anything.' Then, as if fearing he was sounding soppy, the mischievous twinkle was back and he leant towards her again. 'You're not a spy, are you?'

Now Fleur laughed. 'No. Like you say, I'd give the game away all too easily. Too honest for my own good, that's me.'

'Mm, me too.'

She hesitated, but then asked, 'Where've you been up till now?'

His face clouded. 'Down south. It's been pretty rough for the past few months, especially between July and October last year. The Battle of Britain, as Churchill called it.'

'Is that what you are?' she asked, filled with a sudden dread. 'A fighter pilot?' She knew all too well the average number of ops a fighter pilot was expected to survive and then . . .

But Robbie was shaking his head. 'No – no. I'm on bombers.' His smile crinkled his eyes. 'I'm a wireless operator.'

But Fleur wasn't comforted. She shuddered. 'Don't . . . don't wireless operators have to – have to fill in for other crewmembers if . . .' Her voice trailed away.

He was looking at her keenly. 'If one of them gets injured?'

Wordlessly, she nodded.

'I'm trained as an air gunner too. And yes, sometimes it happens, but not often.' He paused and then asked, 'How do you know so much?'

She took a deep breath. He'd know soon anyway if they were both going to be working on the same station. 'I've just finished training as an R/T operator. That's what I'm coming to Wickerton to do.'

'Ah,' he said, understanding. 'A radio telephone

operator? Yes, I'd heard a lot of WAAFs are being trained for that. One of the chaps was saying he thinks it's because a woman's voice is more high-pitched. Comes across the airwaves better.'

Fleur pulled a comical face. 'At least you know what we do. Most people just look blank when I tell them.'

'Will you be in Control?'

'I . . . I don't know yet. Maybe.'

He smiled. 'It'll make a nice change to have a lovely girl to talk us down when we come back from a raid . . .' He paused a moment and then added softly, 'Or who waits up all night for us if . . . if we're late?'

A lump came into her throat as she remembered how they'd all been warned during their training that that was exactly what they'd be expected to do. Wait and wait into the small hours until there was no more hope. 'Are you fixed up with a crew?'

'Oh yes. We met up at Operational Training Unit. They put us all together in a huge briefing room and left us to sort ourselves out. It's a very informal way, but it seems to work.' He laughed. 'That way, it's unlikely you end up flying with a chap you can't stand the sight of.'

Fleur nodded. 'I'd heard that's what happens at OTU, but . . . but doesn't it make it more difficult? Flying with people who become your friends?'

Robbie's face sobered as he shook his head. 'Strangely, no. I expect it's a bit like the "pals' regiments" they had in the last war. There's just something about going into battle with a "brother" at your side.' He paused and then added, 'I've been lucky. Tommy Laughton, the skipper, is a great bloke. You can't help but like him and the rest of the crew – well – I'll soon be getting to know them a lot better. But they seemed OK. We'll be flying Hampdens, we've been told. With a crew of four.' Robbie grinned, trying to lift the mood that was getting all too serious for his liking. 'We shouldn't be talking like this.'

'No.' She forced herself to return his smile. 'There's more than likely a policeman hiding behind the counter over there ready to spring out and arrest us for careless talk.'

As the cafe was now otherwise deserted – even the girl behind the counter had disappeared – they laughed together at the likelihood of anyone overhearing them. That they perhaps should not trust each other never occurred to either of them for a moment.

'What did you do? Before the war, I mean.'

'Worked in a bank.'

'Oh, very posh!' she teased.

He grimaced. 'It was a good job, I have to admit, but it was a bit too staid for me. I was always getting told off for cracking jokes or laughing with the customers. We're supposed to be very polite and formal. I agree with the polite bit, but—' He cast his eyes to the ceiling in mock despair. 'The formality got to me in the end. I couldn't wait to get out.'

'But there's lots of rules and regulations in the RAF surely. It can be very "formal". All that saluting officers and calling them "sir".'

'True, but most of them have earned the right to be treated with that degree of respect.' He leant forward. 'And there's always the compensation of nights out with the lads, *and* – best of all – flirting with a pretty WAAF.'

Fleur arched her eyebrows sardonically, but smiled nonetheless.

'So? What are you doing for the night then?' he asked.

'Bed down in the station waiting room,' she replied promptly. 'It won't be the first time I've done it.'

'Oh no, I won't hear of it. You're coming home with me. You can have my bed. I'll sleep on the sofa.'

Fleur suddenly remembered just how short a time she had known this rather nice young man. Her face sobered, but he read her thoughts at once. 'Of course, I've got an ulterior motive.' He pretended to leer at her, but then added, 'But there's not much a chap can do with his mother in the next bedroom. And my grandfather lives with us too. We'll be well chaperoned.' He pulled a comical expression, displaying mock disappointment. 'More's the pity.'

'But it's an awful imposition on your mother. Bringing a strange girl home in the middle of the night.' Impishly, she added, 'Or is she used to it?'

'Sort of. One or two of the lads have bunked down at our place when they've been stranded, but this'll be the first time I've taken a *girl* home. She'll not mind a bit, though. She helps out at the WVS and she's always picking up waifs and strays from the forces, taking them home and feeding them.'

'Well, if you're sure . . . ?'

'I am,' he said firmly as he got up and picked up her kitbag as well as his own. 'We've got a bit of a walk, though. Hope you're up for it?'

'Now if my drill sergeant could hear you even asking me that – I'd be on a charge!'

Laughing together, they stepped into the blacked-out street.

Two

'Let's get inside quickly,' Robbie said as he unlocked the front door of the terraced house. 'Our warden has got eyes like a hawk and if he sees the tiniest chink of light, he's down on us like a ton of bricks.'

Fleur giggled. 'That's an unfortunate turn of phrase, isn't it?'

Through the darkness, she heard his chuckle. 'Yes, I see what you mean. We might get a ton of bricks on top of us literally if Jerry sees a light when he's flying over.'

They were still laughing, his hand cupping her elbow as he guided her into the strange house in the darkness. 'This is Ma's best front room.' The door from the street had opened directly into it. 'Be careful, because she—' he began when the inner door opened and a light streamed in.

'Robbie? Is that you?'

'Hope so, Ma,' he called out cheerily, 'else you've got burglars.'

'Oh, you rogue! Come on in and let me see who you've brought home this time.'

Fleur drew in breath sharply and was about to kick his shins for having lied to her, but as he led her into the light of the next room, she saw the surprise on his mother's face and knew it was genuine.

'Oh! A WAAF!' The woman smiled a welcome and held out her hands. 'And what a pretty one too.'

'I bumped into her in the blackout, Ma. Knocked her over getting off the train as a matter of fact.' He put his arm about Fleur's shoulders with an easy familiarity that she was amazed to realize she didn't mind. 'You could say she fell for me there and then.'

Now Fleur did retort, muttering beneath her breath so that only he could hear, 'You should be so lucky!'

She heard – and felt – his laughter rising from deep within his chest. She glanced up to find him looking down at her, his face so close that she could feel his warm breath on her cheek. In just that brief moment she noticed the way his eyes crinkled at the corners when he laughed and the tiny, stray hairs at the end of his eyebrows. And his smile – oh, his smile – such white, even teeth with tiny spaces between them. She'd only to stretch just a tiny bit and she could've kissed his mouth . . . At the unbidden thought, she felt the blush rise in her face.

'The least I could do was bring her home,' Robbie went on smoothly as she felt him squeeze her shoulder. For one foolish moment she wondered if he could read what was in her mind. 'She can't get transport tonight to where she wants to be,' he went on, explaining to his mother. 'I couldn't let her sleep in the station waiting room, now could I?'

'Dear, dear,' Meg Rodwell tutted. 'Certainly not. Come in, love, and make yourself at home. You're very welcome.'

Now that Fleur's eyes were becoming used to the bright light after the darkness, she saw that Robbie's mother was slim and youthful looking. Her shoulder-length red hair, showing not a trace of grey, was swept back over her ears in curls and waves. Her green eyes smiled a welcome. She was wearing a fashionable patterned cotton dress with short sleeves and padded shoulders, its hem only just covering the knees of her shapely legs. Fleur couldn't help smiling at the contrast between this woman and her own mother, who, as a busy farmer's wife, had little time for 'titivating', as she would have called it. Fleur's mother wore her greying hair drawn back into a bun at the nape of her neck and dressed in plain blouses and skirts that were usually covered with a paisley overall. And sensible shoes were a must about the farm. At the thought, Fleur looked down at Mrs Rodwell's dainty feet. It was no surprise to see the high-heeled shoes with a ribbon bow at the front.

But the woman was smiling so kindly at her, drawing her further into the room and towards a chair beside the warm fire burning in the grate of the old-fashioned kitchen range. Fleur gave a start as she suddenly noticed a bent old man with a crocheted shawl around his shoulders sitting on the opposite side of the hearth.

Robbie let his arm slip from about her and moved towards him, putting his hand on his shoulder. 'Now, Pops. How are you?'

The old man looked up and reached out with a hand that was misshapen with arthritis, the knuckles swollen and painful. 'Mustn't grumble, lad, mustn't grumble.'

'You never do, Pops.'

To Fleur's surprise, the old man's eyes watered as his fond gaze followed Robbie's mother while she bustled between kitchen and the back scullery, setting food on the table. 'No,' he said in a quavering voice. 'Because I know how lucky I am.'

Meg came into the room carrying two laden plates. 'Come and eat. You must be starving. I'll just go and change the sheets on your bed, Robbie . . .'

Fleur roused herself. The warm fire was already making her drowsy. 'Oh, please, don't go to any trouble on my account. I can sleep on the sofa—'

'I wouldn't hear of it—'

'Certainly not—'

Robbie and his mother spoke together and the old man laughed wheezily. 'There you are, lass, outnumbered.' He tapped the side of his nose. 'And if you take my advice, you won't argue with m'lady here. Rules the roost, she does.'

'Now, Dad.' Mrs Rodwell stepped towards the old man, tucked the shawl cosily around him and planted a kiss on his white hair. 'You'll have this nice young lady thinking I'm a regular tartar.'

Robbie pulled a comical face. 'Well, you are.' He winked at Fleur. 'We'd better do as she says before I get my legs smacked.'

As Robbie towered over his mother by at least eight or ten inches, Fleur could not suppress a giggle at the picture that sprang into her mind of the grown-up young man hopping from one foot to another to avoid the chastising hand. They were all laughing now.

'Come and eat.' Robbie urged her to take a seat at the table. 'And then it's night-nights for you. You look as if you might fall asleep in the gravy.'

*

'What did you say her name was?' Meg Rodwell asked her son the following morning as she cooked breakfast.

'Fleur,' Robbie replied, his mouth full of fried bread. They had both been so tired the previous evening that, once they had eaten, Meg had shown Fleur to Robbie's bedroom and he had headed for the sofa set against the wall in the cluttered front room which his mother used, working from her home as a dressmaker. Despite the austerity of the war – or more likely because of it – there were still many calls on Meg's talents with her sewing machine. 'Make do and mend' was the order of the day. Whilst much of her work was now altering and re-styling second-hand clothes, it was a matter of pride to Meg that she was still able to support her family. And now that Robbie contributed some of his RAF pay whenever he came home on leave, she didn't have to work long into the night these days. Though she would gladly have worked around the clock if it meant keeping her boy safe.

Smiling brightly as she determined not to spoil their few precious hours together with her darkest fears, Meg turned to greet the young WAAF her son had brought home as the girl appeared in the kitchen. She looked rested this morning, but still a little self-conscious and perhaps feeling awkward now at having allowed herself to be taken home by a complete stranger.

'Come and sit down, love,' Meg greeted her warmly. 'What would you like to eat? I'm sorry I've no eggs—'

'Please, don't apologize. I don't want you to go to

any trouble. I feel very embarrassed, descending on you like that in the middle of the night and eating your rations.'

'Don't mention it. We were glad to help. Sit down, do.'

'What about the old gentleman?'

Meg laughed. 'Oh, he doesn't get up until later. You're not taking his place or his breakfast – I promise.' She returned to the stove in the scullery, but left the door open so that she could talk to them as they sat at the table. Dropping a single rasher of bacon into the frying pan, she said, 'Now, have your breakfast and then Robbie will walk you back to the station. Where is it you're going?'

Fleur sat down at the table. 'South Monkford.'

Meg was suddenly very still, staring at the girl. 'South Monkford,' she murmured, her eyes misting over. 'Fancy.'

'Robbie mentioned that you used to live there.'

Meg nodded slowly. 'A long time ago,' she whispered. 'A long time ago now.'

'My father had a tailoring business there, didn't he?' Robbie put in. 'And didn't you say someone called Pinkerton took the shop over from you? Well, Fleur says they're still there. Two old dears – sisters – running it.'

'Fancy,' Meg murmured again, prodding absent-mindedly at the sizzling bacon.

'Maybe you know Fleur's family. Her surname's Bosley—' Robbie began, but he got no further as his mother turned sharply, catching the handle of the frying pan. It clattered to the floor, spilling hot fat and the precious piece of bacon over the tiles and splashing her legs. Meg's hands flew to her face and her eyes were wide, staring at Fleur. She swayed as if she might fall.

'Ma? Ma, what is it?' Robbie was on his feet and moving swiftly to catch hold of her. He helped her to a chair, whilst Fleur hurried to the tap in the scullery to get a glass of water.

'Here,' Fleur said gently. 'Drink this.'

Meg took the glass with shaking hands and sipped it. 'I'm sorry. How stupid of me.'

The young couple glanced at each other and then, concern on both their faces, looked back at Meg, but neither asked the questions that were racing around their minds. It had been Fleur's name – her surname – that had startled Meg so.

'I'm sorry,' Meg said, placing the glass of water on the table and taking a deep breath. 'It was just . . . hearing your name.' She looked up into the open face of the lovely girl standing in front of her, so smart, so confident in her WAAF uniform.

And now she looked more carefully she could see the likeness. The rich, brown hair and deep, dark brown eyes, watching her at this moment, with such concern.

'How is he?' Meg asked softly. 'How's Jake?'

Now it was Fleur who sank into a chair, staring at Robbie's mother. 'My dad? You . . . you know my dad?'

Meg nodded.

'He . . . he's fine.' Fleur waited a moment but Meg volunteered no more. 'How d'you know him?'

'I—' Meg hesitated. It was an ironic and cruel fate that had conspired against her to bring these two young people together. The past that she wanted to keep buried was doing its best to catch up with her. She must say nothing. It was not her place to be telling this girl things that perhaps her parents had never told her and most likely didn't want her to know. After all, she hadn't told her own son, had she?

Meg shuddered, and Robbie sat down beside his mother too, chafing her hand that was suddenly cold between his warm ones. He was willing Fleur not to ask any more questions that were obviously upsetting his mother. 'Are you all right, Ma?'

Absently, as if she had only just become aware of the pain, Meg rubbed her leg. 'The fat splashed, but it's nothing.'

'You ought to put something on it.'

'Don't fuss, Robbie,' she said sharply, her spirit returning, the colour coming back into her face. 'I'm all right.' Now she turned to Fleur. 'I'm sorry, my dear. How silly of me.' She was back in control of her feelings now and of the situation. But inside she was still quaking. I must be careful what I say, what I ask, she was thinking. Forcing a brightness into her tone, she said, 'It was just hearing the name after all these years. Of course I knew your father when we lived there. Both your parents.'

The two young people were aware that there was much more to it than just that. They glanced at each other, wanting to ask more, but afraid of distressing Robbie's mother again.

But in her turn and despite her desire to let secrets stay hidden, Meg could not stop herself asking, 'Are they still at Middleditch Farm? Still working for the Smallwoods?'

Fleur hesitated but, seeing Robbie's slight nod, she answered, 'Dad owns the farm now. The Smallwoods both died about eight years ago and they left the farm to my father and mother.'

Meg gasped and before she could stop herself, she blurted out, 'Not – not to their daughter?'

Fleur was puzzled. 'I didn't know they had a daughter.'

Meg closed her eyes and shook her head. 'I'm sorry, I shouldn't have said anything.'

Again Fleur and Robbie exchanged a glance, but their attention was brought back to his mother as she asked one last question. Was it Fleur's imagination or was there a slight hardening of her tone as Meg asked, 'And your mother? How is Betsy?'

Three

'So – what do you make of all that then?' Robbie said as he pulled the front door shut behind them and shouldered Fleur's kitbag. They began to walk side by side along the street towards the station.

Fleur frowned. 'I honestly don't know.'

'There's more to it than she's letting on,' Robbie said.

'Well yes, I thought so too, but I didn't like to say. I mean, it's none of our business, is it? Certainly not mine.'

He touched her arm. 'I'd like it to be. I'd like to see you again. We're going to be on the same camp. It shouldn't be too difficult. I mean – that is if . . . if you . . . ?' He was suddenly boyishly unsure.

She smiled up at him, surprised that he even needed to ask. 'Of course I want to see you again. That's if you want to be seen with a lowly ACW, Flight Sergeant Rodwell?'

'Mm,' he murmured absently as if the matter of rank was the very last thing on his mind at this precise moment. He squeezed her elbow. 'It's strange, but I feel as if I've known you years.'

'I know,' she said simply and without being conscious of what she was doing, she slipped her arm through his and they walked closely side by side, matching their strides.

They didn't speak again until they were standing on the platform. Robbie had put her kitbag in the carriage and now they stood facing each other. He put his hands on her shoulders, smiling down at her. 'I'll see you soon then?'

She nodded and now she did what she'd been wanting to do almost since they'd first met. She stood on tiptoe and kissed him. Not a chaste kiss on the cheek, but on his wide, generous mouth.

As she drew back, he laughed softly and murmured, 'You hussy . . .' Then his arms were tightly around her, his warm mouth on hers. Her arms wound themselves around his neck, her body pressed to his.

A whistle sounded and a merry, gruff voice said, 'Break it up, now. Train's leaving if you're catching it.'

They broke apart and turned to see the guard with the whistle in his hand, grinning at them. 'Sorry, folks, but the train can't wait.' The man's craggy face softened. 'Not even for you.' In his job he saw so many partings, so many tears. He often wondered what happened to all those youngsters whose poignant goodbyes he witnessed. Did they meet again or did those tears of 'sweet sorrow' become a deluge of grief?

But these two were laughing and blushing, and the older man guessed their love was new and young, just on the threshold . . . But his train couldn't wait – not even for love.

Fleur scrambled aboard and leant out of the window, clasping his hands. 'Come out to the farm later,' she invited rashly, 'and bring your mother.'

'I'll be there. Can't vouch for Ma, but I'll be there,' he vowed.

He stood watching the train out of sight, marvelling that in the space of a few hours he had found the girl he wanted to spend the rest of his life with. However long or short, he thought soberly, that life might be.

'I wish you'd've let me know you were coming. I could've come to fetch you from Nottingham last night.' Jake Bosley frowned worriedly. 'I don't like the idea of you going home with a complete stranger. Even if he is in the RAF, he could be anyone.'

Fleur grinned as she dropped her kitbag to the floor, returned her father's bear hug and then dutifully kissed her mother's cheek.

Betsy sniffed. 'It's nice of you to remember you have a home.' There was a pause before she added, 'When are you going back?'

Deciding to ignore the barbed remark, Fleur responded gaily, 'Good old Mum. You always say the same thing. It sounds as if you can't wait to get rid of me again.'

Betsy's mouth tightened. 'You know very well that's not the case. We never wanted you to go in the first place. But you had to have your own way, didn't you? Couldn't wait to get away. Anyone would think—'

'Now, now, Betsy love. Don't spoil the precious time we've got with her,' Jake said, trying as he always did to quench the sparks that so easily flared between mother and daughter.

'I'm sorry, Mum. I was only teasing.' Fleur kicked herself mentally. She ought to know by now that her mother rarely took teasing from anyone – unless, of course, it was Fleur's younger brother, Kenny, doing the tormenting.

Fleur turned back to her father. He was still frowning anxiously. He was a good-looking man and middle age was being kind to him, for there were only a few flecks of grey in his thick, brown hair. His build was stocky and strong from years of farm work even though he walked with a stiff leg – the result of a wound in the Great War that everyone had believed would 'end all wars'. How wrong they had all been! But she saw now that the laughter lines on his face were deepening into anxiety and the look in his dark brown eyes troubled her, for she knew she was the cause.

He hadn't wanted her to join up. Neither of them had. Her mother had cried and stormed and demanded that she stay at home, whilst her father had gone about his work on the farm with a worried frown permanently on his face.

'You don't have to go. You're doing important work here on the farm,' he'd tried to insist.

'You'll be killed,' Betsy had wailed dramatically. 'I know you will.'

'Oh, Mum, girls don't fly. I'll just be on an aerodrome. In the offices or the canteen or – or something.'

'Airfields get bombed,' Betsy had persisted. She'd got Fleur dead and buried already before she'd even signed up. But for once Fleur had stood her ground. She wanted to do her bit, wanted to see something of life away from the farm, though of course she didn't tell them that.

'Kenny's still here.' She'd tried to soften the blow. 'He's too young to go.'

'That depends on how long this wretched war goes on,' her mother had said bitterly. 'He's seventeen now.'

'Only just,' Fleur said.

'What if it lasts another two years?' her mother

persisted. 'He'll get called up when he's nineteen. And I bet,' she added bitterly, 'it won't be long before they lower the age for call up.'

'But he'll work on the farm. Dad can apply for a deferment for him. He won't have to go,' Fleur had argued.

'But he *will* go.' Betsy's voice had risen hysterically as she'd said accusingly, 'Because he'll copy you. He idolizes you. You can't do anything wrong in his eyes.' There was more than a tinge of jealousy in Betsy's tone. It was she who idolized her son, and she made no effort to hide her possessiveness. Miraculously, the boy himself was unspoilt by her favouritism and Fleur enjoyed an easy, bantering relationship with her brother.

'It's the mother–son and father–daughter thing,' he'd once said laughingly, showing a surprising insight for one so young. 'You're Dad's favourite.'

But Fleur wouldn't allow that. 'No, he doesn't have favourites. You know that. But maybe he's a bit more protective of me because I'm a girl.'

Kenny had grinned. 'Nobody's ever going to be good enough for his little girl, eh?'

Fleur had laughed. 'Something like that.'

It hadn't mattered then – there'd been no young man she'd been serious about. But now . . . ? Well, now it was different.

'As a matter of fact,' she said carefully, 'the young man I went home with wasn't a complete stranger.'

Jake's face cleared. 'Oh, it was someone you know?'

'Not exactly,' she said carefully. 'Someone *you* know, or at least, used to know.'

The frown was back, but this time it was a puzzled look rather than a worried one that creased Jake's craggy features. And, strangely, there was a touch of wariness in his eyes.

'Do you remember someone called Mrs Rodwell and her son Robbie?'

Before Jake could answer a cry escaped Betsy and, her eyes wide, she pressed her hand to her mouth. And then to Fleur's utter amazement, Betsy began to scream. 'No, no, not her. Oh, not her. I thought she'd gone for good. I thought—' She clutched wildly at her daughter, her fingers digging painfully into Fleur's arm. 'You're to have nothing to do with him. Do you hear? He's a bad lot.'

Jake moved forward at once and put his arms about his wife. 'Now, now, Betsy love, don't take on so. Surely, after all this time—?'

Betsy twisted to face him. 'Leopards don't change their spots, Jake. She'll never change and her son'll be like her. Self-centred, devious, spiteful.' She rounded again on Fleur. 'What did she say? Does she know who you are?' Betsy was still like a wild thing, screaming questions at her daughter. Fleur stared at her. She'd seen her mother in some tempers, but never – in all her life – had she seen her quite like this. Completely out of control.

'Mum—' She reached out but Betsy slapped her hands away as if her daughter's touch was suddenly abhorrent.

Fleur let her arms fall to her side. 'Actually,' she said flatly, realizing that the tentative romance that had already begun between her and Robbie was doomed. 'She was as shocked as you are when she heard my surname, but she . . . she didn't react quite as . . . as . . .' Fleur faltered and her voice dropped to a whisper. 'Well, not like this.'

'She took you in, you say?'

Fleur nodded.

Betsy's voice hardened. 'So – what was in it for her?'

'Mum!' Fleur was appalled. She'd liked Robbie's mother. She couldn't believe the things her own mother was saying about her. Mrs Rodwell had been so kind, so welcoming. And the old man; she hadn't had much of a conversation with him, but he'd seemed a dear old boy.

Fleur sighed and said flatly, 'I don't know what you're getting at, Mum. But there was nothing "in it" for her, as you put it. She was just nice to me. Cooking breakfast for me. Apologizing because she had no eggs when there I was – a complete stranger – taking their rations.'

'But you're not a stranger.'

'I was then. She was doing all that before she knew my name. And Robbie says she works for the WVS. That she's always taking home waifs and strays. And she looks after the old man—'

'Ah! I knew it! She's got another poor old boy in her clutches.' Betsy was scathing now. 'Well off, is he?'

'An old man?' Even Jake was curious now, but Fleur was startled by the sudden bleak look in his eyes. 'Who was he? Her husband?'

'I . . . I don't think so. Robbie called him "Pops". And . . . and . . . yes, she called him "Dad".' Fleur looked from one to the other, puzzled and more than a little alarmed by their reaction. 'He must be her father.'

'Her *father*!' Now Jake was shocked. 'My God!' he murmured, and he was obviously stunned. 'Her father.'

'Huh!' Betsy pulled her mouth down at the corners. 'It'll more likely be a fancy man who's old enough to *be* her father.'

But Fleur was watching the strange, thoughtful look in Jake's eyes.

Betsy's voice was still high-pitched, demanding, 'I want to know what she *said*.'

'She asked how Dad was.'

'I bet she did. Oh, I bet she did!'

Fleur blinked under the vehemence in her mother's voice. She glanced at her father, but he was far away, lost in his own thoughts. She looked back at her mother, hoping to placate her. She couldn't know that it was entirely the wrong thing to say as she added, 'And she asked about you, too.'

'Wanted to know if I was still around, I suppose. Hoping I wasn't. Hoping I was dead and in my grave.'

'Mum!'

'Betsy!'

Jake and Fleur spoke together, shocked by Betsy's hysterical outburst. Jake went on, 'Now that's enough. You've no call to—'

'No call? No call, you say? Look at the lives she ruined with her . . . with her carryings on.' The venom was spitting out of Betsy's mouth. 'But you still love her, don't you? All these years you've never stopped loving her, and if she so much as crooked her little finger you'd go running.'

Fleur gasped and felt the colour drain from her own face as she listened to her mother's terrible accusations.

Jake's face was dark with anger, any sympathy and understanding gone from his expression. His wife was pushing him just a little too far now. 'That's not fair,

Betsy, and you know it. I've always loved you and our children. I've done my best to be a good husband and father, haven't I?' He turned his head slightly and now his question included his daughter. 'Haven't I?'

Fleur moved swiftly to his side and linked her arm through his, hugging it to her. 'Oh, Dad, of course you have.' She turned towards her mother. 'Mum—'

'You stay out of this.' Betsy's voice was still high-pitched. 'It's nothing to do with you.'

'Well, as a matter of fact, I think it has. You see – I'm sorry – but I invited Robbie to come out here to tea this afternoon. And . . . and I said he could bring his mother if . . . if he wanted.'

For a moment Betsy stared at her. Then she let out a chilling scream and began to pull at her own hair like someone demented. Jake released himself from Fleur's grasp to take hold of his wife, but she struggled against him, beating his chest with her fists, crying and screaming, even kicking out at him. Jake winced as the toe of her sturdy shoe caught him on the shin.

'Dad?' Fleur raised her voice above the noise her mother was making. 'Shall I fetch the doctor? Shall I call Dr Collins?'

There was a sudden silence in the kitchen as the screaming stopped abruptly. But then Betsy began to laugh – a hysterical sound that was more chilling than her crying.

'Oh yes, oh yes. Call Dr Collins – and his wife. Let them all come. Let them all meet. I'm sure Dr Collins would like to meet his—'

To Fleur's horror, Jake suddenly clamped his hand across Betsy's runaway mouth. 'That's enough,' he bellowed in a tone that brooked no argument.

Four

Middleditch Farm lay five miles from the small town of South Monkford amidst gently rolling countryside. Robbie – and his mother, if she came – would have to take the Nottingham to Lincoln train, get off at the Junction and catch the little train that the locals called 'the Paddy' out to South Monkford. Fleur hadn't dared to ask her father to meet the train. Not now. So, from the town railway station they would have to hitch a lift out to the farm. That afternoon Fleur walked down the lane some distance from the farmyard gate to waylay Robbie and – more importantly – his mother. Fleur frowned as she went over in her mind every little detail of her own mother's frenzied outburst. Her father was tight-lipped about it all. He would explain nothing.

Jake had released his hold on his wife, glared at her for a moment, then turned on his heel and gone outside into the yard, slamming the back door behind him. Betsy had stared after him, pressing trembling fingers to her mouth.

Fleur had stepped towards her, holding out her arms. 'Mum—?' But Betsy had let out a sob, turned her back on her daughter and run upstairs to her bedroom, slamming the door just as Jake had done.

Fleur had winced and stood alone in the kitchen, biting her lip. After a moment, she'd followed her father outside and found him leaning on the gate, staring with unseeing eyes at the spread of land before him that was now all his. She'd stood beside him, resting her arms on the top of the gate.

'Dad—?'

'Leave it, Fleur.' He'd sighed heavily, his anger dying as swiftly as it had come. 'It all happened a long time ago and it's best left buried. It's over and done with.'

'It doesn't sound like it as far as Mum's concerned,' she'd retorted. Immediately she regretted her words when she saw the bleak expression that flitted across her father's face.

'Oh, Dad,' she'd said, putting her hand on his arm and trying her most cajoling tone. 'Won't you tell me what it's all about?'

His hand had covered hers as he'd replied softly, 'I . . . I can't, love. They're not my secrets to tell.' And he'd refused to say any more.

For mid-April, it was surprisingly hot and still in the lane, sheltered from the light breeze by hedges on either side. Fleur spread her greatcoat on the grass and sat down beneath the shade of two huge trees, the branches rustling gently above her. She leant back against one of the trunks, her gaze still on the corner of the lane. She wanted to see him again – even wanted to see his mother again. She'd liked her. But part of her wanted them to stay away. For, if they did come, how was she going to explain that they weren't welcome at Middleditch Farm? She certainly couldn't risk taking them home. She didn't want her mother throwing another fit. Nor did she want to see that terrible haunted look on her dad's face.

Fleur loved her dad – loved both her parents, of course, but she was fiercely protective of her father. She didn't really understand why – couldn't have put it into words – but for as long as she could remember she'd sometimes seen a strange, sad, faraway look in his eyes and, even as a little girl, she'd felt the instinctive desire to shield him from hurt. Only the touch of her tiny hand in his had brought him back to his happy present, as he'd hugged her to him or ruffled her hair affectionately. As she'd grown older she'd thought his moments of melancholy were because of Betsy's preoccupation with Kenny, believing her father felt neglected and excluded. It had drawn her even closer to him.

But now, she wondered, was that sadness, buried deep, to do with Robbie's mother? If it was, the reminder of it had made her own mother hysterical . . .

There was something tickling her nose. Drowsily, she brushed it away, and then she heard his soft chuckle and opened her eyes.

'Sleeping Beauty,' he teased. He was lying beside her, leaning on one elbow and tickling her with a piece of grass.

She gave a startled cry and sat up. 'I must have fallen asleep.' She blinked and rubbed her eyes as she looked around her. 'Where's your mother?'

'She hasn't come.' For a moment, his eyes clouded. 'Said it wouldn't be right.' He shrugged. 'I don't understand why though.'

'I do,' Fleur said promptly. 'At least, part of it. I think I know why she hasn't come.'

She lay down, leaning on her elbow so that they were facing each other. 'There's something gone on in the past between them all. I don't know what it is – they won't tell me – but it must be something pretty awful 'cos my mum threw a ducky fit.'

'A what?' He was laughing in spite of himself.

Now Fleur grinned too. 'Sorry. It's something one of the girls I met while training was always saying. It must be catching.'

'I take it your mother wasn't best pleased?'

'That's an understatement if ever there was one. I've never – in my whole life – seen her act like that. Oh, she gets a bit het up about things. Fusses and flaps about anything and everything – usually about our Kenny – but this morning she was screaming and shouting and hitting out at my dad when he tried to calm her down.'

'Good Lord!' Robbie frowned thoughtfully for a moment and then said slowly, 'My mother was sort of – well – odd. Not hysterical or anything, but you saw how shocked she was when she heard your surname.'

Fleur nodded. 'Did she explain why?'

Robbie shook his head. 'No. Shut up like a clam. She went very quiet and seemed lost in a world of her own. I couldn't reach her, if you know what I mean.'

'Oh, I know exactly what you mean. I bet it's the same sort of look my dad sometimes has. As if he's lost in the past.'

'That's it. That's it exactly.' They stared at each other for a moment before Robbie said slowly, 'You . . . you don't think there was – well – something between them, do you? Between your dad and my mother? Years ago?'

Fleur nodded. 'There must have been because . . . because in amongst all my mum's shouting and hysterical crying she said, "All these years, you've never stopped loving her." '

'And you think she meant my mother?'

Again, Fleur nodded, but now she said no more. She couldn't for the heavy feeling growing within her chest, a feeling of ominous foreboding.

Robbie blew out his cheeks as he let out a long sigh. 'Crikey! Now I see why Ma wouldn't come with me today and why you're waiting for me in the lane.' His blue eyes were dark with disappointment. 'I take it I'm not welcome at your home?'

She shook her head, not trusting herself to speak for the lump in her throat.

He sighed again and sat up, resting his arms on his knees and linking his fingers. His back was towards her as he said flatly, 'So, you don't want to see me again?'

Fleur sat up too and touched his arm. Slowly, he turned to face her. They gazed at each other for a long moment before she said, 'I *do* want to see you again. I mean – that is – if you want to see me.'

'Of course I do.'

She smiled and felt a warm glow at the swiftness of his reply. 'But,' she went on, 'we've just got to realize what we might be getting ourselves into. We won't be able to visit each other's homes.'

'You can come to mine. Ma won't mind.'

'Are you really sure about that?'

'Well . . .' She could see the sudden doubt on his face.

'She was very kind to me last night,' Fleur went on, 'and even after she knew who I was, but that doesn't mean she'll want to see me again. Have me visiting, reminding her . . .' There was a long silence before Fleur said, 'So do you see why I say, "as long as we realize what we're getting ourselves into"?'

'Yeah,' Robbie's mouth tightened. 'Right into the middle of a Shakespeare play by the sound of it.'

Fleur laughed, stood up and held out her hand to pull him up. 'Just so long as you know I've no intention of committing suicide over you like Juliet.'

He stood close to her, still holding her hand and looking down into her dark brown eyes. 'And that's another thing.'

'What is?' she whispered, suddenly frightened by the serious look in his eyes.

'Death. Not by suicide, of course. But I face it every time we take off on a bombing run. And you're not in exactly the safest job there is, are you? Airfields are constant targets for the enemy.'

'I know,' she said quietly. 'But we're only in the same boat as thousands of others. We . . . we've all got to take our happiness when we can, haven't we?'

Robbie nodded. 'Damn right we have. And damn the past and all its secrets. We're living in the present.' Though he didn't speak the words aloud, as he took her into his arms and bent his head to kiss her Robbie was praying silently: Dear Lord, grant me a future with this lovely girl. Don't let me end my days in a burning plane, or her buried beneath a pile of rubble on a bombed-out airfield. Let us grow old together, with our grandchildren at our knees . . .

Five

'There's something else I want to ask you.'

'Fire away,' Robbie said, resting his elbows on the small table in the cafe where they were sitting. They were determined to spend the afternoon together, even if they were not welcome at Middleditch Farm, and had walked back to South Monkford, hitching a ride on a farm cart for part of the way.

'Who's the old gentleman who lives with you?'

'Pops?'

Fleur nodded.

'My grandfather.' There was a pause before Robbie asked. 'Why?'

Fleur stirred her tea, even though, with wartime rationing, she had stopped taking sugar in it. She avoided meeting his gaze. 'Your mother's father?'

Robbie nodded.

'Has he always lived with you?'

Robbie wrinkled his forehead. 'No. I must have been about eight or nine when he arrived out of the blue. I think – no, I'm sure – before that there was just me and Ma. My father died before I was born. I told you that, didn't I?'

'Mm.'

Slowly, as if he was reliving a memory he'd not thought about in years, Robbie went on, 'There was a knock at the door one day and I ran to answer it. You know how when you're a kid, you love to be the one to answer the door?'

Fleur nodded but did not speak. She didn't want to break his train of thought.

'This chap was standing there. I thought it was an old tramp asking for food. He was wearing scruffy clothes, had a full straggly beard and long greasy-looking hair.' He grinned. 'Mind you, it wasn't the first time I'd seen a gentleman of the road knocking at our door or sitting in our kitchen being fed.' He laughed. 'They reckon tramps leave signs for one another pointing the way to a house where they'll likely get a meal.' The smile faded and the thoughtful frown returned. 'But when Ma saw this particular chap, I thought she was going to faint. I do remember that. Then she hustled me away – sent me to my bedroom. Next morning the old boy was still there. Clean clothes, shaved, hair neatly trimmed. Ma's a dab hand with her scissors around hair as well as material. He was sitting in the chair by the fire just as if he'd taken up residence.' Robbie laughed again. 'And he had. He patted my head and said, "I'm your grandad, son." '

'And he's lived with you ever since?'

'Yup.' She felt his searching gaze on her face. 'Why all the interest?'

He'd seen through her. She laughed self-consciously. 'I can't hide anything from you, can I?'

'Nope.' His wide smile was back.

'It was just – well – when I mentioned him at home, my dad seemed flabbergasted.'

'Oh? I wonder why.'

'Mm. So do I.'

They sat in thoughtful silence drinking their tea,

until Robbie, leaning forward, whispered, 'Don't look now, but there's a woman over there who can't seem to take her eyes off me.'

Fleur giggled. 'Must be the uniform. There are some women who'll do anything for a man in uniform.' She held up her hand, palm outwards. 'And before you say it, I'm not one of them.'

Laughter crinkled his face and his bright blue eyes danced with merriment. 'Shame,' he murmured and his glance caressed her. She felt as if she were wrapped in his arms even though the table separated them. A pink tinge coloured her cheeks but she returned his gaze boldly. Fleur was no shrinking violet who simpered and tittered under a man's admiring eyes. She'd been a WAAF long enough to fend off ardent advances, but she had no wish to fend off Robbie Rodwell.

If only . . .

'Look out,' Robbie muttered suddenly, 'she's coming over.'

As the woman approached, Fleur looked up and then she smiled. 'Why, it's Aunt Louisa.' She jumped up and kissed the woman's cheek before pulling out a chair and inviting her to join them.

As she introduced her to Robbie, the young man stood up and held out his hand. Louisa gazed up at him as if mesmerized, allowing him to take her limp hand in his broad grasp. 'I'm pleased to meet you.'

'She's not really my aunt but I've always called her that. She's Mrs Dr Collins.' Fleur laughed. 'That's what folk call her, isn't it, Aunt Louisa?'

'Yes,' Louisa mumbled weakly, still unable to drag her gaze away from Robbie's face.

'And this is Robbie Rodwell. We only met last

ni . . .' Her voice faded away as she watched Louisa's face turn pale. The older woman seemed to sway and sink down into the chair Fleur had placed for her. But, still, she was staring up at Robbie.

'Aunt Louisa – what is it? Whatever's the matter?'

'Rodwell,' Louisa murmured. 'You're – you're Meg's boy, aren't you?'

Robbie, too, sat down. 'Yes, I am, and I'm very sorry if meeting me is distressing you in some way. It seems—' he glanced up at Fleur, seeking her permission to say more. Fleur gave a tiny nod and he turned back to face Louisa. 'It seems there are a lot of things that Fleur and I don't know about.'

Louisa was regaining her colour now and some of her composure, though her hands still trembled. 'Oh yes,' she said, a bitter edge to her tone. 'There are a lot of things you don't know. But I'm not the one to tell you.' She struggled to her feet and, automatically, Robbie and Fleur rose too. Robbie put his hand out to steady her, but she snatched her arm away as if she couldn't bear him to touch her. She stared at him for a moment and then said, 'You ask your mother, if you want to know. Yes, you ask her. Ask her . . .' She made a gulping noise that sounded suspiciously like a sob. 'Ask her about your . . . your *father*.' Then she swung round towards Fleur. 'But don't you go asking your dad anything – and certainly not your mother. Don't you go hurting my little Betsy. Not again.'

With that, Louisa turned and hurried from the cafe, her shoulders hunched and holding a handkerchief to her face. The young couple stared after her, concerned by the woman's obvious distress yet still mystified.

'Seems everyone knows what this is all about – except us,' Robbie said.

'Yes,' Fleur agreed slowly. 'It does, doesn't it?'

Robbie caught hold of her hand. She turned to face him and he put his hands on her shoulders. Looking down into her face, his expression was serious. 'You . . . you won't let this come between us, will you? Whatever it is?'

Fleur was anxious too, but she said firmly, 'No, I won't. *We* won't.'

And there, in the cafe, oblivious to onlookers, he bent and kissed her. Those around them who noticed merely smiled and turned away a little sadly. So many partings, they were thinking. So many young couples snatching brief moments together before the war tore them apart again. Not so long ago, such a public display of affection would have been frowned upon, but now no one said a word.

They walked back to the railway station, their arms around each other. It felt quite natural, even though they had only known each other such a short time. They were living in strange times – times when happiness had to be grabbed whenever and wherever it happened.

'There's only one thing I can think of.'

'I know.'

'It must be that your father and my mother were in love.' Robbie was the one to voice aloud what they were both thinking. 'Or at least that your dad was in love with my mother and your mum was . . . well . . .' He didn't like to say the word, but Fleur finished the sentence for him. 'Jealous.' She was quiet for a moment before whispering, 'Do you think they had an affair?'

Robbie wrinkled his forehead and blew out his cheeks. 'Who knows? Let's face it, they lived through the last lot, didn't they? Maybe they met in the last war and . . . and felt just like we do now.' He turned and brushed his lips against her hair. 'Oh, Fleur, Fleur. I'm so glad I met you.'

'But my parents were married then. I was born just after the war ended.'

'So was I. Well – in the following June to be precise.'

Now they stopped and turned to face each other.

'You don't suppose—' Robbie began, as an appalling thought crept its way into his mind. So in tune with each other were they that Fleur ended the sentence yet again.

'That we're half-brother and sister?'

They stared at each other, stricken. They had promised each other that nothing would keep them apart. Nothing that had happened in the past was going to come between them. But now, with growing horror, they realized that there was something that could do just that.

'But my mother would've said if it had been that.' She paused and then asked doubtfully, 'Wouldn't she?'

'I don't think so. You said she was hysterical – like you've never seen her before?'

'Yes.' Fleur's voice was low.

'And she forbade you to see me again?'

'Yes.'

'And that woman in the cafe. She knows something.

She reacted just the same as my mother and your mother did.'

'But surely my dad would have said—'

Robbie shook his head. 'I bet your dad idolizes you, doesn't he?'

Fleur nodded.

'Then do you really think he'd want you to find out something like that about him?'

Mutely, Fleur shook her head.

'And there's something else too,' Robbie said solemnly. 'Something I should have realized before.'

'What?'

'Your dad's name? It's Jake, isn't it?'

Fleur nodded.

'That's my middle name. I'm Robert *Jake* Rodwell.'

'Oh no!' Fleur whispered.

He put his arms around her and held her close, trying to lessen the pain his words would bring. 'I really think we'd better find out what all these secrets are, don't you?'

Against his chest, he heard her muffled 'Yes.' Then she raised her head. 'But how are we going to find out?'

Robbie's face was grim. 'We'll have to ask them. I shall tell my mother that we've fallen in love.' For a moment he stroked her hair tenderly and kissed the end of her nose. 'And that we need to know. We have a *right* to know.'

'Would it be best if I asked my dad?'

He pondered for a moment. 'No, I'll ask my mother first. We've always been close. I think she'll tell me the truth. Your dad might . . .' He hesitated, not wanting to say what was in his mind, but uncannily she knew.

'You mean, he might not tell me the truth for fear of hurting my mum?'

Robbie nodded.

'Yes, you're right.'

'So I'll ask my mother. Don't worry, darling. I'm sure there's a simple explanation.'

But when they parted they were still both anxious and the kiss they shared was tentative, as if they were each holding back. Just in case . . .

Six

Louisa Collins sat in the darkness of her sitting room in the big, double-fronted house that was both their home and her husband's medical practice. The room to the right of the central front door was their private sitting room, whilst across the hall was Philip's surgery and dispensing room. Patients waited in the spacious hallway and Louisa, acting as her husband's receptionist, welcomed them with words of comfort and reassurance and ushered them into his room when their turn came.

The blackout curtains were drawn and the only light in the room came from the fire in the grate of the ornate fireplace, the flickering flames casting eerie shadows around the room, glinting on the heavy, old-fashioned but lovingly polished furniture. The light settled for a brief moment on the oil paintings on the wall and the delicate china in the glass cabinet and then flitted away again.

She sat perfectly still, yet her mind was busy with darting thoughts and fleeting memories and dark suspicions that refused to be buried any longer. She hadn't thought about all that for years. Only now and again when she saw Jake and Betsy was she reminded, but even then, as the years had passed, she had managed to stop her thoughts dwelling on those times they had all shared but never spoke of now.

She had loved Philip, body and soul, ever since she

had first met him. There had never been anyone else for her but him. Her only regret was that she had never been able to give him children. The sob rose in her throat and she pressed her fingers to her lips to stop the sound escaping, even though there was no one else in the house to hear. She had shed many tears over it through the years, mostly alone, but sometimes against her husband's shoulder whilst he held her and patted her and told her it didn't matter. They were happy, weren't they? Just the two of them? They had each other and more than likely it was all his fault anyway. Being gassed in the Great War had left its mark on him and he was sure that could be the reason. But Louisa knew that he was trying to be kind, trying to spare her the dreadful burden of being barren – of not being able to give him a child.

And now, today, she'd seen Meg's son. And – of all people – he'd been with Fleur. She'd seen the way they'd looked at each other and she shuddered. If ever she'd seen two people on the brink of falling in love, it had been those two. Then, stupidly, oh so foolishly, she had lost control of her emotions. She'd said far too much to them, far more than she should have done. A fresh panic swept through her. They would be sure to ask questions after the way she'd acted. He would ask Meg and – despite her plea – she was sure that Fleur would ask her parents too.

Now she groaned aloud to the empty room and dropped her head into her hands.

'Oh, what have I done?' she whispered. 'What *have* I done?'

*

At Middleditch Farm, Betsy, too, was sitting in the dusk beside her bedroom window. There was no light in the room behind her so the blackout blinds were not drawn. She looked down into the yard, watching Jake finishing the evening milking and driving the cows out of the byre, through the gate and down the lane back to the field.

She should have been helping him. With Fleur gone, he was always short-handed nowadays, even though Kenny lent a hand whenever he could. And that was another worry. Where was Kenny? He should have been home from school hours ago. They had persuaded their son to stay on at school into the sixth form, with the hope that he might go on to university afterwards. Anything to try to keep him out of the war for as long as possible.

Betsy craned her neck, trying to see further up and down the lane through the gathering gloom. She opened the window and leant out, straining to hear the sound of his whistling. Kenny was always whistling as he rattled homewards on his bicycle. She'd hear him long before she saw him . . . But the evening air was still, the only sounds the occasional bark of their dog as he helped herd the cows along the lane.

And Fleur – where was she? She'd not come back since going out to meet that boy. Meg's boy. Betsy had watched her go from this very window – had seen her walk down the lane. Watched her turn the corner until she was out of sight.

The very lane that Meg had walked down all those years ago as she left with her baby. The day that Jake had said 'goodbye' to her for ever. The day he had chosen to stay with Betsy and their daughter, and they had stood together in the yard and watched Meg walk away.

Betsy sank back into the chair, her arms resting on the sill, and dropped her head onto her arms. It was as if the intervening years had never happened. As if all the love and care Jake had lavished on his children and, yes, on her too, she had to admit, had never happened.

It seemed like only yesterday that she'd stood beside him as he'd waved goodbye to Meg.

'I'll drop you at the main gate for you to book in at the guardroom,' the driver of the RAF lorry that had met them at Lincoln railway station told them, as he drove through Wickerton village and turned into the gateway of the RAF station. Robbie and Fleur had met up on the Nottingham to Lincoln train as they had planned and travelled the last few miles together.

'Here we are, then,' the driver said as he slowed the vehicle to a halt just in front of the barrier. Whilst they waited for the sentry to approach them, he added, 'You'll need to report in at the main guardroom here first, but all the living quarters are set well away from the actual airfield itself. The Waafery's that way, miss.' He pointed along the road to the left. Fleur giggled inwardly at the nickname given to the WAAF buildings.

'That's where you need to go and they'll tell you where to go from there, but you, sunshine' – he nodded at Robbie – 'will have a bit of a walk.' His grin widened as he added, 'I reckon they've built the fellers' quarters as far away from the lasses as they can.'

Robbie laughed. 'I shouldn't wonder!'

'Over there, see.' The driver jerked his thumb to the right, towards several buildings of all shapes and sizes, scattered across a vast area some distance away. 'That's the men's quarters. There's the CO's quarters, officers' mess, sergeants' mess, airmen's mess, NAAFI, gym, chapel and the sick quarters. Let's hope you don't see much of that place, though.' He winked at Robbie. 'I wouldn't mind meself. There's a couple of nice nurses there, so I've heard.'

Robbie jumped down and held out his hand to help Fleur. 'Home for the next few months at least.'

As the lorry drove off further into the camp with a series of splutters and bangs, they looked about them.

Fleur shaded her eyes against the setting sun beyond the distant airfield, its huge, camouflaged hangars black silhouettes against the golden glow. A little nearer several aircraft stood in a silent row.

'What are those?' Fleur asked. Though she'd studied pictures of various aircraft, she'd never been so close to one.

'Hampdens,' Robbie murmured. 'I wonder if one of them's ours.'

Fleur gazed at the planes and shuddered. Soon Robbie might be flying night after night in one of them. And she would be left watching and listening and waiting.

'Come on,' he said, picking up his belongings and Fleur's kitbag too. 'We'd better do as we've been told and then I suppose we'll have to go our separate ways.' The regret in his tone mirrored her feelings.

'But we'll see each other, won't we? About camp, I mean?'

He grinned at her through the gathering dusk. 'Just

let 'em try to stop us.' But his hearty tone was forced now. The worry was still in both their minds. Should they even be meeting at all?

When they'd reported in, they stood together for another few minutes, in the middle of the road, both reluctant to make the final move to part.

'There doesn't seem to be anyone about,' Fleur said. 'I thought the place'd be teeming with activity.'

'You'd think so, wouldn't you? Maybe it's supper-time or something.'

'That'd explain it.'

'Or maybe they're flying . . .'

Again, a silence, but neither of them moved.

Robbie nodded towards the WAAF buildings. A few were obviously still under construction. 'I'd heard this was a newish station. Looks like it's not finished yet.'

Fleur looked about her and then said reluctantly, 'We . . . we'd better go, hadn't we?'

Robbie grinned. 'Trying to get rid of me already, are you?'

'Course not.' Fleur pretended indignation that he could even think such a thing. 'I just don't want you in trouble on your first day. I . . . I'm not quite sure how they'll view the men and women mixing, especially different ranks. You know . . . ?'

Robbie laughed aloud. 'Shouldn't think they'll be able to stop it even if they try.' His blue eyes twinkled at her through the gathering dusk. 'Not with us they won't. Will they?'

'Not likely,' Fleur grinned, then she sighed. 'I'd better report in at the Waafery.'

'And I'd better go and find the rest of the chaps, I suppose,' Robbie said and handed over her kitbag. 'So – this is it then?'

Fleur nodded and tried to smile. 'Looks like it. I . . . I'll see you around, then.'

'You most certainly will even if I have to break into the Waafery at night.'

'Don't you dare . . .' she began and then realized he was teasing. Instinctively, she knew he wouldn't do anything that would get her into trouble, even if he didn't mind for himself.

As she moved towards the WAAF buildings, Fleur glanced over her shoulder and waved as Robbie's long strides took him along the road in the opposite direction further and further away from her. At the same moment, he turned and raised his arm in the air and then strode away, quickening his pace.

With a small sigh, Fleur shouldered her heavy kit-bag and walked towards the Waafery. As she did so, a WAAF came out of the nearest building, slamming the door behind her. As she drew nearer, Fleur could see that she was short and round, her uniform buttons straining to stay fastened across her ample bosom. She was a good few years older than Fleur and her plump cheeks were florid, her small eyes almost lost in the fatness of her face.

The woman – a Flight Sergeant – would have walked straight past without even glancing at her had not Fleur said, 'Excuse me. I've just arrived. Could you tell me where I have to go?'

The WAAF stopped, looked Fleur up and down, and then snapped, 'Name?'

Fleur reeled off her number, rank and name.

'You're late. Supper's nearly finished, but you'd best go to the dining room.' She nodded towards the building she had just left. 'You might get something.' She didn't sound very hopeful and seemed to care even less. 'Find Morrison. You're billeted with her. In the village. And report to Flight Sergeant Watson in Control in the morning. They work a system of shifts in the watch office: a four-hour and then an eight-hour, times varying of course, so between all the operators, the twenty-four hours are covered, with always at least two on duty. More sometimes, when they're flying. The rota's posted on the board in the office. Because you work a twelve-hour day and often through the night, the time off is very generous.' It sounded as if she heartily disapproved of the WAAFs being given any time off. No doubt she was a great believer in the 'idle hands' saying.

'Thank you,' Fleur said carefully.

The older woman eyed her critically. 'Your hair's too long. It's touching your collar. Either mind it's tied up properly under your cap or get it cut.' Then she turned and marched away.

'Well,' Fleur murmured as she watched her go. 'I hope the other girls are a little friendlier than you!'

Seven

As Fleur entered the dining room, the noise of chatter and laughter hit her. She stood, blinking in the bright light, and looked around her, not sure what to do.

Catching sight of her, a plump, merry-faced girl with unruly fair curls rose from her seat at one of the long tables and came bouncing towards her. 'Hello there. Come and sit with us and I'll get you something to eat. Leave your gear there. We'll sort it out in a mo.'

She caught hold of Fleur's arm and pulled her towards the place where she'd been sitting. 'Budge up, you lot. Room for a little 'un. Sorry about the squash. We're having to make do with trestle tables at the mo, though they keep telling us that proper dining tables and chairs are on order.' Then she rushed away towards the counter where the food was being served.

As they shuffled along the bench seat to make room for her, the other girls smiled at her. 'Just arrived, have you?'

Fleur nodded. 'Yes. Thanks,' she added, as she squeezed into the space they'd made for her. The girl who'd greeted her arrived back carrying a plate of cheese on toast and a mug of tea. 'There. Get that down you. Bet you're hungry. Come far, have you?' She hardly paused for breath as she sat down again.

'I'm Ruth Morrison, by the way, and you'll be with me. We're billeted in the village. Most of the girls are.' She nudged Fleur and winked. 'Don't reckon they trust us to stay on the camp with the fellers.'

'It's nothing of the sort,' a fair-haired girl sitting opposite retorted. 'Don't listen to her. I'm Peggy Marshall.' She held out her hand across the table and Fleur took it.

'Fleur Bosley. Hello.'

'And don't believe a word our Ruth tells you. Truth is, they haven't got the sleeping quarters finished yet, so most of us are billeted out . . .'

'Not all of us.' A dark-haired girl further down the table remarked. There was a distinct note of resentment in her tone, though, as Fleur glanced at her, the girl winked. 'Some of us,' she went on dryly, 'have to put up with sleeping in a draughty hut on hard biscuit beds and eat forces' fare whilst the rest of you languish in feather beds and are plied with delicious home cooking by the locals.'

There were cries of derision and someone threw a dry biscuit at her, but the girl just smiled, her dark eyes sparkling with mischief.

'That's Kay Fullerton, by the way. As you can see, she's a corporal,' Ruth said. 'The rest of us are just lowly ACWs.'

Fleur nodded. 'Me too.'

Ruth nodded towards Kay as she added, 'She doesn't mean it – about the sleeping arrangements, I mean.'

'Oh yes I do. Why should all the newcomers get the best billets, I'd like to know?'

Fleur looked up and met the girl's belligerent expression. 'Well, I don't mind sleeping here if you want to swap,' she offered.

Kay stared at her for a moment until someone else put in, 'Kay's all talk. She'll not leave camp – she's already got her eye on one of the new pilots that's just arrived.'

The remark was greeted by loud guffaws and even Kay smiled sheepishly. 'No, you're OK, but – thanks for the offer.'

As there was a general movement to get up from the table, Kay came up to Fleur and held out her hand. 'You're the first one to do that.'

Closer now, Fleur could see that the girl had the most unusual dark blue eyes – so dark they were almost violet. Her skin was smooth and flawless, and her black hair was so shiny it seemed to glint in the light as she moved. She was really very pretty.

'She gives all the new ones a hard time over it,' Ruth explained, 'just to see how they react.'

Kay laughed. 'Most of them go all red and embarrassed, but none of them have ever offered to swap. You're all right, Fleur Bosley. In my book anyway.'

Now it was Fleur's turn to look a little embarrassed at the unexpected compliment.

'Not one to hold back is our Kay. You'll get it straight John Bull from her,' Ruth said. 'If she likes you, she'll tell you so. And if she doesn't – well, she'll tell you that an' all.'

'What job will you be doing? Do you know?' Kay asked.

'R/T operator.'

Kay's eyes lit up. 'Oh, then you'll be with me in Control. That's good. Welcome aboard, Fleur.' Then she spun on her heel, adding, 'Must go. Things to do, people to see. See you tomorrow.' And before Fleur could say a word, she had marched down the long room and out of the door.

Ruth spluttered with laughter. 'She's a caution, that one, as my mother would say.'

Fleur smiled. She was feeling very much at home already. She liked Ruth and had taken to the girl she now knew would be working with her. She wondered if she'd be working with Ruth too. 'What do you do, Ruth?'

'I'm in intelligence. I help at briefings and then debrief the crews when they come back from a raid.'

'That must be tough,' Fleur murmured sympathetically.

Ruth's hazel eyes clouded for a moment. 'It is a bit. An RAF intelligence officer usually asks the questions and I write down their answers. But if it's been a rough one and the crews are dog tired, sometimes their stories take a lot of unravelling. Still, it's an interesting and – I think – worthwhile job. Though you're right, it's harrowing at times.'

Fearing she had touched on something sensitive, Fleur changed the subject swiftly. 'So – how do I find this billet we're sharing?'

Ruth's expression lightened at once. 'I'll take you. I'm not on duty for a couple of hours or so when the first planes start coming back.'

'There's a raid on tonight then?'

'Mmm. Not a very big one, just a gardening run . . .' She grinned. 'Mine-laying, you know, but we still have to go through the routine, of course. Come on. Let's get your gear. We're only a few yards down the road on the outskirts of the village. With a widow.

She's a nice old dear. Fusses a bit, but then I think she's lonely. Her husband died a few years ago and all her chicks have left home. Oh, you'll get the full family history within the space of ten minutes, believe me.'

As they walked out of the main gate and along the road, following the pencil-thin beam from Ruth's torch, she chattered. 'I'm from Lincoln. I live with me mam and dad and two sisters. They're younger than me and keeping their fingers crossed that the war's going to last long enough for them to join up.' She pulled a face. 'Selfish little devils – fancy anyone wishing such a thing!' But Fleur heard Ruth's soft chuckle through the darkness. The girl linked her arm through Fleur's as she confided, 'Mind you, it could be my fault. I'm always telling them what a great time we have and how we're surrounded by all these handsome chaps.' Then her voice faltered as she added sadly, 'I can't bring myself to tell them the truth, see. Of course, we do have fun, but . . . but it's no fun, is it, when you wave all the bombers off at night and know what they're going to face? And then, when they come back, counting them all. One by one. Only they're never all there, are they? They never *all* come back, do they?'

Fleur shook her head. 'Not very often.'

Ruth squeezed her arm and forced jollity back into her tone. 'Hark at me, getting all serious. As if I need to tell you. You've worked on another operational bomber station, haven't you?'

Fleur nodded. 'Yes, down south, but I applied to remuster as an R/T operator and hoped I'd get a posting a bit nearer home and here I am.'

'Me too. I was up north for a while straight after training and I've been very lucky to get a posting so near home. What about you? Did you manage it?'

'What?'

'To get a posting nearer home?'

'Oh yes. I live at South Monkford. Do you know it?'

'Near Newark, isn't it? Well, you should be able to get home on leave easily enough. Even on a forty-eight-hour pass. You might have to hitch, but we're really lucky. Some of the girls are hundreds of miles from home. Peggy's from Newcastle. And Kay's from London. They can really only get home about once every three months.'

At the mention of Kay, Fleur remembered what had been said at the table. 'Has . . . has Kay got a boy-friend here then?'

'Yes, she has,' Ruth said with a snort that sounded very much like disapproval. 'Silly mare!'

'Why do you say that? Haven't you got one?'

'Me? Oh no. Fancy free, me. And I mean to stay that way.' Again there was a sniff. 'It doesn't do.'

Alarmed, Fleur said, 'What do you mean? Isn't it allowed?'

'Well, you have to be careful, but they can't stop it, even if they'd like to. No, what I mean is, you're stacking up a load of heartache for yourself if you let yourself get close to anyone.'

Fleur thought she detected a note of real pain in the girl's tone and she was about to ask gently if she had lost someone close to her, but before she could form the words, Ruth said brightly, 'Here we are. Rose Cottage. "Home, Sweet Home".'

She pushed open the wooden gate and they crunched up the narrow cinder path.

'Watch yourself. The garden's so overgrown the

long grass falls onto the path. When it's wet, your ankles are soaking by the time you reach the door.'

In the wavering torchlight, Fleur caught glimpses of the neglected front garden. The grass looked so long it would need a scythe to cut it now, she mused. As if answering her unspoken question, Ruth said softly, 'Poor old dear loves her garden. Her old man used to keep it immaculate, she says, but since he's gone it's got topside of her. She's got a huge back garden with an orchard at the end of it. Used to grow veg and all sorts. But she's got arthritis, see, and can't cope with it. But she won't move. Says she came to this cottage as a young bride and she'll die here.'

Briefly, Ruth flashed the torch over the low, oblong shape of the cottage. 'Typical "roses-round-the-door cottage" we all dream of, eh? But she really got it.'

'Mm,' Fleur murmured. 'No wonder she doesn't want to leave it.' Even before she had met Mrs Jackson, she knew she was going to be a sweet old lady who'd lived a lifetime of love in her little cottage. Fleur had a sudden mental picture of a young bride being carried over the threshold to start a long and happy life with her groom in the idyllic little house. However, the image in her mind's eye was not of the unknown Mrs Jackson but of herself and Robbie.

'I'm surprised the authorities haven't been on to her about her garden,' Fleur said, dragging herself back to the present. ' "Dig for Victory" and all that.'

'I think they did try. Got some local boy scouts to come and dig the back garden, but they made a right pig's ear of it.' She giggled in the darkness. 'There was even talk of them building her an Anderson shelter, but after a couple of spadefuls, they gave up, so she says.'

'Not got a shelter and living so close to an airfield!' Fleur was shocked. 'Well, we'll have to see about that.'

'Come on, then,' Ruth urged. 'We'll go round the back. Tell you the truth, the front door's stuck and she can't open it.'

They followed the narrow path round to the back, brushing through long wet grass so that by the time they arrived in the unevenly paved back yard their ankles were quite damp, just as Ruth had predicted. She shone the torch and nodded towards a brick building a few steps across the yard from the back door. 'That's the lav.' She leant closer and whispered, 'It's a bit basic. No indoor facilities, but the old dear cooks like a dream.' Ruth patted her stomach. 'Makes up for a bit of discomfort in other areas. 'Sides, she provides us with a potty under the bed so we don't have to come tripping out into the back yard in the dark.' Ruth giggled again as she added, 'She calls it a "jerry". I always imagine I'm piddling on Adolf's head if I use it in the night.'

Fleur laughed softly. 'Home from home, Ruth. It's what I'm used to. We've no inside lav either.'

Ruth's eyes widened. 'But I thought you said you lived in South Monkford? It's a town, isn't it?'

'A small one. But I live on a farm about five miles from the town itself. Right out in the wilds.'

'You're a country girl, then?'

'Born and bred.' Fleur moved carefully across the cobbled yard towards the rickety little gate leading into the back garden. As her eyes became accustomed to the darkness, she could see the shapes of trees silhouetted against the night sky. Ruth came to stand beside her and shone the torch and now Fleur could see that the whole area was as overgrown and choked with weeds as the front one.

'There's raspberry and gooseberry bushes and all sorts down the bottom there. The old dear said they even had a strawberry patch once. And you can see the fruit trees. There's a lovely old apple tree with a little bench seat under it. It's where her and her Arthur used to sit on a summer's evening, she said.'

'You know,' Fleur suggested, 'we could help her in our spare time.'

'Hey, hang on a minute. I'm a city girl. Born and bred in Lincoln. That's why I chose the WAAFs instead of the Land Army. You're welcome to go grubbing about in Mother Earth but don't ask me to join you.' The words could have been tart and dismissive, but they were spoken with such a warm humour that Fleur laughed.

'We'll see,' she teased, as Ruth grabbed her arm and pulled her towards the back door. As she pushed it open, it scraped and shuddered on the uneven floor.

'Coo-ee, Mrs Jackson. You in?' She turned and whispered. 'She hardly ever goes out, 'cept to church on a Sunday and sometimes as far as the village shop, but her legs are getting that bad, poor old thing. She walks with a stick as it is, though she can move about the house without it. Come on in. Mind the blackout curtain. It's a bit long and trails on the floor. It gets caught under the door if you don't watch out.'

They moved through the back scullery, which housed a deep white sink and wooden draining board with shelves of pots and pans above. There was also a cooker to augment the range that Fleur knew would be in the kitchen. Ruth flung open the door into the kitchen-cum-living-room where an elderly lady was struggling to lever herself up out of her armchair in the far corner of the room beside the black-leaded range that Fleur had expected to see. A fire burned in the grate and a kettle stood on the hob. It really was just like home, Fleur thought.

'Don't get up, Mrs Jackson,' Ruth was saying. 'I've brought another lodger for you. This is Fleur Bosley. She's just come to work in the watch office.'

The old lady sank back thankfully into her chair, but she beamed up at Fleur with such a wide smile that her rounded cheeks lifted her spectacles. She was a plump little woman, with her white hair pulled back and wound into a roll at the nape of her neck. She wore low-heeled lace-up shoes and lisle stockings, and her striped blouse and navy skirt were almost hidden by a paisley overall. Fleur smiled. It was identical to the one her mother wore. This woman could be Betsy in thirty years' time, she thought, though she couldn't imagine her mother welcoming complete strangers into her home the way this woman was doing. Her mother wouldn't even make someone she knew welcome, Fleur thought wryly, thinking of the uncomfortable last few hours she had spent at home. It was a sad fact – and it hurt even to think it – but she'd been glad to get away.

Fleur quickly scanned the room, taking in the other armchair on the opposite side of the range and the table with its white lace runner and two chairs set against the wall. On a small table beside the old lady sat a wireless with a polished oak cabinet, silk front and black Bakelite controls. It seemed out of place in the old-fashioned cottage, yet Fleur knew that the wireless had become almost a necessity in the homes of those anxious for news of the war.

Fleur crossed the room to stand on the pegged

hearthrug. 'Hello, Mrs Jackson. I'm pleased to meet you.'

'You're very welcome, lass,' the old lady said, her faded blue eyes smiling up at Fleur. 'Mek yourself at home. Ruth'll show you your room upstairs. I can't get up there now.'

'Mind your head,' Ruth warned, as she led Fleur up the narrow staircase to the two attic bedrooms under the eaves. 'There's only us here. We have a room each. I'm in the bigger room with the double bed and you'll be in here . . .' she said, opening the door into a small room that only had space for a single iron bedstead, a wardrobe and narrow dressing table. But the bed was covered with a cheery patchwork quilt and there was a pegged rug beside the bed to step onto instead of the cold floor.

'Do you mind?' Ruth glanced back over her shoulder.

Fleur smiled reassuringly. 'Course not. Don't be daft. It's fine. It's not much smaller than the one I have at home. Honest.'

'The old dear sleeps downstairs in her front parlour now. Bless 'er. I'll show you when we go down.'

As Ruth helped her unpack her belongings, hanging her clothes in the narrow wardrobe with a creaking door, she pulled a face and said, 'At least staying here we don't get those dreadful kit inspections every morning. Mind you, I'll warn you now. Ma'am has eyes like a hawk so it pays to keep your uniform spick and span. And she has been known to make an unannounced inspection of our billet now and again.'

'Is she very strict?'

Ruth turned surprised eyes towards her. 'Who? Mrs Jackson? Heavens, no!'

'I didn't mean her.' Fleur laughed. 'I meant the WAAF CO. I mean, are we allowed to meet the RAF lads?'

Ruth stared at her for a moment. 'Well, of course we meet them at work. And there's the dances on camp, usually in the men's NAAFI or sometimes in the sergeants' mess. Then there's the Liberty Bus on a Saturday night.'

'What on earth is the "Liberty Bus"?'

Ruth grinned. 'A bus laid on to take us into Lincoln. To dances or the pictures.'

She was silent a moment, watching Fleur sort out her underwear and put it away in one of the drawers in the dressing table. Then Ruth said quietly, 'Why all the questions? Do you know someone on camp? Someone – special?'

Fleur felt the blush creep up her face and knew she couldn't hide the truth. 'Well, sort of. I've only just met him. We bumped into each other – literally – on Nottingham station. He's just been posted here an' all. That's how we met.'

'Oh, Fleur!' Ruth flopped down onto the bed. The springs protested loudly, but neither of the girls noticed. 'Don't get involved with someone – with anyone. Not if he's a flier. He is, I take it?'

Fleur nodded. 'He's a wireless operator on bombers.'

Ruth groaned and then sighed heavily, regarding her new-found friend with a hangdog expression. 'I don't suppose anything I say's going to make any difference, is it?'

Fleur grinned. 'Not a scrap.'

Ruth heaved herself up. 'Well, my shoulder's ready when you need it.'

'Don't you mean "if"?'

Ruth stared at her for a long moment before she said seriously, 'No, love. I'm sorry, but I do mean "when".'

Eight

As Fleur approached the control tower early the following morning, her heart was beating faster. Although she had been thoroughly trained and had been briefed on how to cope with every emergency possible, she was still a little apprehensive. This was her first posting as a fully fledged R/T operator and she knew that 'the real thing' would be very different. Mistakes in training hadn't mattered. Now they did.

She stepped into the ground floor of the watch tower. The concrete steps leading to the upper floor were on her right, but first she was curious to see what else the building housed. The first room on the left was the met office, with maps spread out on the waist-high table against the wall. A WAAF sat at a telephone switchboard; another stood in front of a teleprinter, which was noisily chattering out a message. A nearby desk was cluttered with telephones, a black typewriter and papers. Next door to the met office was the duty pilots' rest room. It was empty and silent, newspapers flung down untidily amongst the battered easy chairs. Dirty mugs, an overflowing ashtray and dog-eared books littered the table almost hiding the telephone. It seemed, even here, there was no escaping the call to duty. Near the door was the compulsory sand bucket – the ever-present reminder of the war and all its dangers.

Fleur climbed the stairs to the upper floor. The smell from the freshly painted cream and green walls reminded her that this was a new station, still in the process of being built. She peeped into the signals' room with its wirelesses, typewriters and teleprinters. For a moment she stood listening to the morse code blips that filled the room, mentally translating a few words in her head. Directly opposite the signals' room was the rest room, but Fleur ignored this for the moment and, taking a deep breath, moved to the end of the narrow passageway and opened the door into the watch office.

This was the largest room in the building. Directly in front of her was the long desk where the R/T operators sat. In one corner the duty officer sat at his desk, overseeing all that was happening. Flight Sergeant Bob Watson was in his mid forties, Fleur guessed. He was tall and thin and had dark, Brylcreemed hair and the usual moustache that was fast becoming the trademark of the RAF. Fleur was to notice that he stroked it continuously when the tension mounted in the watch office and that he would pace up and down behind the operators as the aircraft took off one by one and again when they landed.

As she entered the room, Bob Watson greeted her informally with a friendly smile. 'You must have made an impression already. Fullerton has already asked if you can work with her.'

Fleur smiled and felt a faint blush creep into her cheeks. 'I'd like that, Flight, if it can be arranged. I think we'd work well together.'

He eyed her keenly. 'You think so? Some of the younger girls find her – well – a bit abrasive. She doesn't suffer fools at all – let alone gladly, as they say. Mind you,' he said arching his eyebrows, 'neither do I, but I suppose they expect it from me.'

Fleur remained silent. He stroked his moustache thoughtfully. 'Well then, I'll adjust the rotas so you work with Fullerton. And in that case, you'll be on from tonight, but only if they're flying. Come on duty a bit early and we'll show you the ropes – how we do things in this watch office.'

'Thank you, Flight.'

So, she thought, as she went down the steps, I've the rest of the day off. I wonder what Robbie's doing.

Ruth brought her the news in the NAAFI at midday. 'I don't think you'll see much of him for the next few days. The new crews are getting to know one another. They might even get a few practice flights in to make sure they gel before they're sent on a mission. Mind you, they could be flying tonight if Tommy thinks they're ready. He's done quite a bit of flying on Hampdens already evidently and . . .' But Fleur was no longer listening. She was far too wrapped up in her own disappointment that she wouldn't be able to see Robbie and – worse still – there would be no chance for him to get home on leave for quite a while. No chance for him to ask his mother some very delicate – yet to them very important – questions.

With time on her hands, Fleur went back to the cottage and changed into civvies – a pair of old trousers and a thick sweater.

'Are you hungry, dear?' Mrs Jackson asked as Fleur came downstairs.

'No, thanks. I ate in the NAAFI, but I wouldn't mind a cup of tea, if you can spare one.'

'Of course. I get extra rations with you two here.'

'I'll make it. You sit down.'

The old lady sank thankfully into her chair and took up her knitting. 'Socks for the troops.' She smiled. 'A nice WVS lady brings me the wool and collects them. It gives me something to do and I feel I'm helping.'

'You're helping a lot already, putting up with us two.'

Mrs Jackson's face creased into smiles and her spectacles wobbled. 'Oh, that's no hardship, dear. I enjoy the company.'

Fleur set a cup of tea on the small table beside the old lady. She was about to sit in the chair on the opposite side of the hearth when she paused and asked quietly, 'Is it all right for me to sit here?'

There was the slightest hesitation before Mrs Jackson said, 'Of course, dear. My Arthur would have been tickled pink to think that a lovely young WAAF was sitting in his chair.'

Fleur sat down, balancing her cup carefully. 'When . . .' she began tentatively, thinking that this was as good a time as any to broach the subject of the garden, 'When did your Arthur . . . ?'

The old lady's face dropped into lines of sadness. 'Three years ago next month. Very sudden. Heart attack. Out there in the garden.' She smiled fondly. 'But it was just the way he'd've wanted to go. With a spade in his hand, doing what he loved best.'

'And the . . . er . . . um . . . garden?'

Mrs Jackson sighed deeply. 'It makes me so sad to see it like that. Poor Arthur. All his hard work overgrown and so quickly too. Who'd have thought it could've gone wild in only three years?'

'Would you mind if I worked on it when I'm off duty? I mean, if you'd rather I didn't,' she began, fearing she might have upset the old lady, but Mrs Jackson's face was alight with joy.

'Oh, my dear, that would be wonderful. Really wonderful.' Her face clouded. 'But do you really want to? I mean surely a young lass like you wants to be out enjoying herself. And besides, I mean, do you know much about gardening?'

Fleur laughed. 'Born and bred on a farm, Mrs Jackson. What I don't know already my dad will tell me.'

The old lady laughed along with her. 'Well, you won't have to go very far for a bit of advice, love. Old Harry next door will be only too pleased to help. In fact' – she smiled – 'you'll have a job to stop him.'

'Right then,' Fleur said jumping up, glad to have something physical to do. With her first duty looming and maybe with Robbie flying with his new crew for the first time, she needed something else to concentrate on. 'No time like the present.'

Mrs Jackson's garden shed in the back yard was cluttered; there was hardly room to step inside it.

'Another job for a rainy day,' Fleur murmured as she unearthed some rusty gardening tools. There was a sickle but no scythe, and cutting the grass at the front of the cottage and the overgrown kitchen garden would be a long and back-breaking task on her hands and knees.

'Mrs Jackson?' she said, going back into the house. 'Do you know anyone who's got a scythe?'

The old lady washing up at the deep sink in the small scullery turned in surprise. 'Whatever do you want a scythe for?'

'To cut all the overgrown grass back and front. If

I get it dug over there's still time to plant some vegetables.'

Mrs Jackson's eyes were filling with tears. 'D'you know, when Arthur was alive I never 'ad to buy vegetables all year round.'

'You'll have to tell me what he used to grow,' Fleur said gently. 'I'm sure he'd be pleased to think we'd got it like it used to be.'

'Oh, he would, he would.' Mrs Jackson wiped the corner of her eye with the back of her hand and sniffed, but she was smiling through her tears. 'A scythe, you say? Harry next door might 'ave one or 'ee'd know someone who has.'

'Right then.' Fleur began to turn away but then paused to ask, 'What's his surname, Mrs Jackson? I can hardly call him "Harry".'

The old lady chortled. 'Oh, Harry wouldn't mind. He's a one for the pretty lasses.' Her face fell into sad wrinkles. 'He's on his own like me now. His wife, Doris, died two years ago. His name's Harry Chambers.'

Fleur went through the front gate and along the lane to the next-door cottage. She walked round to the back and as she turned the corner of the house, she gasped in surprised delight. The layout was the same as Mrs Jackson's cottage and garden, but there the similarity ended: beyond Harry Chambers' back yard lay a lovingly tended kitchen garden. But after her initial pleasure, Fleur frowned. If he could do his own garden, why didn't he help the old lady next door? The way Mrs Jackson had spoken of her neighbour, they were friendly, so why . . . ?

As she lifted her hand to knock tentatively on the

back door, Fleur bit her lip, wondering, after what Mrs Jackson had said, just what she was going to have to deal with. But she needn't have worried. When Harry Chambers opened the door, she saw that he was as old and bent as her landlady, yet there was a mischievous twinkle in his rheumy eyes and a wide, toothless smile.

'By heck – have I died and gone to heaven? A pretty young lass knocking at my door. Come away in, lass.' He turned away and shuffled back into the kitchen. Smiling inwardly, Fleur followed. Now, the question in her mind was not why he didn't help his neighbour, but how on earth did he manage to keep his garden so immaculate? As she stepped into the kitchen, she saw the answer. The inside of his home was like a rubbish tip. The range was dirty, the floor filthy and every surface was littered with newspapers and unwashed pots. The old man swept aside a pile of clothes on a chair. 'Sit down, sit down,' he insisted, beckoning her forward.

Thankful that she was wearing her old trousers, Fleur sat in the rickety chair. The old man let himself down into the dusty armchair near the range and beamed at her. 'A' you one of them lasses at Mary's?'

'Yes. I only arrived yesterday. I'm just getting settled in, but I'd like to make a start on getting the garden in order for her.'

'Aw lass . . .' To Fleur's horror, tears filled his eyes. But at his next words she realized they were tears of joy too, just like Mrs Jackson's had been. 'That'd be wonderful for 'er. I'd've liked to have kept it right but I've more than I can manage with me own bit.' He wiped the back of his hand across his face. 'Her ol' man, Arthur – we was mates.' He laughed wheezily.

''Cept when it came to the village show and we was both entered for the biggest marrow competition. Then it was "gloves off" time. Eee, lass, but I miss him. You don't know how much I miss our little chats over the fence.'

Fleur smiled but didn't know what to say so she let the old man ramble, reliving happier times. But he was laughing along with his tears. At last, he came back to the present.

'So what can I do for you, lass?'

'Mr Chambers, have you got a scythe I can borrow?'

He gaped at her. 'A scythe, lass? Aw now, I don't know if I should let a young lass like you loose with a scythe. Them's dangerous things if you don't know what you're doing . . .' He leant towards her, screwing up his eyes in an effort to see her better. Then he chuckled. 'I can see by the look on your face – you *do* know, don't you?'

Fleur nodded, her eyes brimming with mischief. 'If my dad could hear you, Mr Chambers, he'd say, "No daughter of mine's going to grow up without knowing how to use a scythe." I was born and brought up on the farm.'

The old man blinked. 'Then what are you doing here? In the WAAFs? I'd've thought they'd've needed you at home.'

Fleur sighed as she felt a sudden stab of guilt. 'They do,' she admitted, 'but I wanted to get away. To see something of the world outside me dad's stackyard. I still want to do my bit, but . . .'

The old man watched her for a moment as she bit her lip. 'I can understand that,' he said gently. 'I volunteered for the last lot even though I could have stayed safely at home 'cos I was getting on a bit for service life. My Doris begged me not to go, but I would have me own way.'

'So did my dad. I think he understands why I wanted to join up, but me mum . . .'

'Aye well, she's your mother, lass,' was all he said as if it explained everything. There was a moment's silence between them and then he began to chuckle. 'And now here you are, wanting to dig up Mary's garden. Seems you can't get away from it, eh, lass?'

Fleur spluttered with laughter. 'Just serves me right, doesn't it?' And they rocked with merriment.

'Ee lass, you've done me a power of good. I don't know when I last laughed so much. It's the best medicine, they say. I'll be throwing all me pills away if you're staying long.'

'I'm staying.' Fleur nodded as her thoughts turned to Robbie. 'Oh, I'm staying, Mr Chambers.'

'Right then, lass,' he said as he levered himself up from the battered chair. 'Then you'd best start calling me "Harry". I don't know who on earth you're talking about with all this "Mr Chambers" business. Now, let's go and see if I can find this 'ere scythe for you.'

When he opened the door of his shed, Fleur could not prevent a gasp of surprise escaping her lips. All the gardening tools were neatly stacked against the walls or lined up in order along the shelves or hanging from hooks. Each item had been cleaned and oiled before being put away. She almost laughed aloud to see the contrast between the old man's garden shed and the state of his house. But, she reflected, the smile dying on her lips, this was his domain; the house had been his wife's and he'd lost her.

''Ere we are,' Harry said, carefully unhooking the

huge scythe from its nail. 'It's a big 'un, lass. Sure you can manage one this size?'

Not wanting to sound boastful, Fleur said, 'I think it's the same size as me dad's.' She took it from his hands, feeling the weight. 'Yes, I'm sure it is. Anyway, I'll soon know.'

'Just you be careful, lass.' Harry was still anxious.

'I will,' she smiled. 'And thank you.'

'Don't mention it. There'll be no one more pleased than me to see old Arthur's garden looking a picture again. I just wish . . .' His voice faded away and a sad, faraway look came into his old eyes as he glanced back towards his own house.

'What do you wish, Harry?' Fleur prompted softly, but he sniffed and forced a smile. 'Nothing, lass, nothing at all.'

But as she walked past the open back door and saw again the cluttered state of the old man's kitchen, she thought she knew what he had been going to say.

Of course, as she thought might happen, Harry leant on the fence between the two gardens to watch her taking the first few sweeping strokes. Soon she was into a steady rhythm. When she paused for a breather, she looked up to see him nodding at her.

'Aye lass, you're right. You can do it. Never seen a lass frame so well, I haven't. In fact' – his expression was comical – 'I can't say I've ever seen a lass scything afore.' He levered himself off the fence. 'Well, can't stand here all day chatting. I'd best be getting on with a few jobs mesen.'

'Harry, before you go, could you pass the sharpening stone over? I'm going to need it.'

'Right you are, lass. Ah, and here comes Mary with a cuppa.' Fleur turned to see Mary Jackson tottering along the mud path down the centre of the garden. Laying down the scythe, Fleur hurried towards her. 'Oh, you shouldn't have bothered,' she scolded the old lady gently, but reached with eager hands to take the mug. 'Mind you, it's thirsty work. I'm ready for it.'

'Any left in the pot, Mary?' Harry called out and the old lady chuckled.

'Course there is, Harry. Think I'd forget you?' And she turned to walk stiffly back towards the cottage.

'Don't you be struggling out again, lass,' Harry called. 'I'll come round.'

Fleur stifled her giggles to hear the old lady called 'lass', but maybe they'd lived side by side for years and that's how he still thought of her.

Before long the two elderly people were sitting on a couple of old stools in the back yard chatting amiably – Harry's jobs forgotten – whilst Fleur worked herself into a sweat cutting the long grass. She was still at it when Ruth appeared round the corner of the cottage.

'Well, it's all right for some. 'Ello, Harry – Mrs Jackson.' She shaded her eyes and looked down the garden. 'What on earth is she doing?'

'Cutting the grass. Mekin' a good job of it an' all,' Harry said with a note of pride, almost as if he had trained Fleur himself.

'Then what's she goin' to do?' Ruth turned wide eyes on Harry. 'She's never going to dig that lot?'

Harry began to chuckle and Ruth cast her glance skywards. 'Don't tell me! She is.'

At that moment, Fleur, red faced and breathing hard, paused and looked up. Seeing Ruth, she waved.

'I've got a message for you,' Ruth shouted. 'From

Flight Sergeant Watson and . . .' Her eyes were full of mischief. 'From lover boy.'

Fleur dropped the scythe and pushed her way through the long grass, her eyes anxious. 'What is it? There's nothing wrong is there?'

Ruth shook her head. 'Far from it. Flying's cancelled tonight. Low cloud over the target.' She pulled a face. 'Wherever that was. So he's got the night off.' She grinned. 'And so have we, 'cos we're not needed if they're not flying. A gang of us – including your Robbie – are going to the Mucky Duck in the village.'

Fleur's eyebrows rose. 'The Mucky Duck? What on earth is that?'

She heard Harry's deep, rumbling chuckle and saw Mrs Jackson's smile. 'It's the locals' name for our pub – the White Swan. It's been called the Mucky Duck for as long as I can remember.'

'Right,' Fleur said. 'I'll just clean the scythe and—'

'No, no, lass,' Harry said, pulling himself up off the stool. 'I'll see to that. You get off and enjoy yourself.' He seemed about to say more, but then cleared his throat and, instead of whatever he had been about to say, added, 'You've earned it.'

'Thanks, Harry. Can I borrow the scythe next time I get some time off?'

'Course you can, lass. Any time. Just come round and help yoursen out o' me shed.'

'And I'd better get you girls a bite to eat if you're going out.' Mary was struggling to pull herself up. Ruth and Fleur held out their hands to haul the old lady to her feet. 'Thank you, my dears. Now off you go and make yourselves pretty.'

'That won't take too long to do,' Harry laughed. 'Pretty as a picture already, they are.'

'By the way,' Ruth said. 'Sorry, but we have to wear uniform. Ma'am's orders.'

Fleur shrugged. 'I don't mind. I'm proud to wear my uniform.'

'You might change your mind when you see all the local girls in their pretty dresses being chatted up by all the fellers.'

'There's only one I want to be chatted up by and he'd better not be looking at other girls while I'm around – uniform or no uniform.'

The two girls laughed and hurried into the house to wash at the sink in the back scullery and change their clothes.

The two old people watched them go. Quietly, Harry said what he had stopped himself from saying earlier. 'Aye, let 'em enjoy themselves, eh, Mary? While they can.'

Nine

The moment Fleur and Ruth stepped into the public bar of the pub, she spotted Robbie with three other airmen. Kay and Peggy were already sitting with them. Robbie must have been watching the door for he rose at once and threaded his way around tables to reach her. He didn't kiss her, but took her hands in his and squeezed them warmly. 'Come and meet the rest of the crew. They're great lads.'

He pulled her behind him, weaving his way through the crowded bar room, and made the introductions. He reeled off the names. 'This is our skipper, Tommy Laughton. And these two reprobates are Alan Hardesty and Johnny Jones.' Then Robbie waved his arm to encompass other airmen sitting in small groups around the bar room. 'We'll no doubt get to know a lot of the other chaps on our Flight in time. They all seem a great bunch.'

Tommy unfolded his lanky frame and shook her hand warmly. He was thin faced with sharp eyes that missed nothing and he sported a moustache that stuck out on either side of his upper lip like a stiff, bristly shaving brush.

It was a merry evening. The beer flowed as did the conversation and laughter. They talked about anything and everything. Everything, that is, except the war.

But Fleur was acutely aware that perhaps the jollity was a little forced, the laughter just a little too hearty.

'Fleur, you must meet Bill Moore, the landlord.' Tommy Laughton, the pilot of the newly formed crew, got up and held out his hand to her. 'Come on. You can help me get the next round in and I'll introduce you.'

Fleur glanced at Robbie, who stood up to let her move past him.

'Bill,' Tommy called to the middle-aged man behind the bar. The landlord was dressed casually in a collarless striped shirt, the sleeves rolled up above his elbows, and a black waistcoat. His strong arms pulled pint after pint effortlessly. What hair he had left was dark, yet the pate of his head was bald, and he sported a black moustache that drooped over the corners of his mouth.

'This is Fleur Bosley. She's come to work in Control. She's the lovely voice we'll hear when we're coming home. And a very welcome voice it'll be too, I can tell you.'

'Of course, it could be mine,' Kay chipped in. 'You'd better be able to tell the difference or there'll be trouble.'

As Tommy grinned briefly over his shoulder at Kay and winked, Fleur realized that the newly arrived pilot that Kay had 'got her eye on', as Ruth had said, must be Flying Officer Tommy Laughton.

'Pleased to meet you, love.' Bill Moore enveloped her hand in his huge paw. She felt the calluses on his work-hardened hands – strong, capable, reliable hands. The sort of hands you could trust . . .

'Pleased to meet you, Mr Moore.'

'Eh now, lass. None of that there "mister" stuff. Bill's the name.'

Standing behind the bar amongst the pumps, the bottles and the glasses sparkling against the polished wooden surface of the bar, Bill Moore was master of all he surveyed. Fleur smiled. The man was just like Harry had been when they had first been introduced. No standing on ceremony. What a friendly bunch these locals were. Actually, she was surprised. She would have thought that the locals would resent having the airfield quite so close to their village. Despite the custom that came the pub's way and maybe to the local shop too, she was sure the disadvantages of noisy aircraft day and night and the danger of attacks, not to mention having a lot of strangers milling about the place, would far outweigh any advantages.

But it seemed she was wrong. The locals – young and old alike – were mingling freely and in a friendly manner with the RAF boys. Especially, Fleur noticed with a wry smile, the local lasses, who were being very friendly with the handsome RAF lads in their smart, blue uniforms. And the only looks of resentment were on the faces of one or two local youths not in uniform and obviously feeling that their noses had been pushed very much out of joint.

As Fleur began to ferry the drinks back to their table, Johnny jumped up and said, 'I'll give you a hand, Fleur.' He went to stand beside Tommy, but at once a young blonde girl in a short-skirted dress sidled up to him and tapped him on the arm.

'Hello, Johnny.'

'Hello, Kitty. Would you like a drink?'

'Ta. Don't mind if I do.'

Johnny bought her a drink and they stood at the bar chatting.

'I reckon we could have trouble from one or two of the local lads,' Fleur whispered to Robbie as she took her seat beside him again. 'See that lad in the white shirt and sleeveless green pullover? Over there – near the fire.'

Robbie glanced casually around him. 'I see him. What about him?'

'Well, just keep your eye on him for a few moments. He's watching Johnny talking to that lass, and if looks could kill, Johnny would be feeling decidedly ill.'

Robbie didn't seem perturbed. 'I expect the girl old Johnny's chatting up is the lad's girlfriend.'

'Did you ought to warn Johnny, 'cos I don't think he's noticed?'

Robbie chuckled. 'No. He's otherwise occupied, isn't he? And Johnny can take care of himself. Besides, there's plenty of us here if—'

As if on cue, the youth in the corner got up and brushed back the flop of hair from his face. Then he stumbled his way between the tables, knocking against a chair and then someone's arm.

'Watch it, young 'un. You're spilling me beer.'

But the young lad took no notice. His eyes, bleary with drink, were fixed on the girl who was now sitting with Johnny and cuddling up to him quite openly.

'I really think you should do something, Robbie,' Fleur muttered.

Robbie put down his beer and unfolded his tall frame. He held out his hand. 'You're right. I should get you out of here before any trouble starts.'

'I didn't mean that. I meant—' Fleur began, but at that moment the landlord's thunderous tones cut through the chatter and laughter. 'Now then, young Alfie. I want no trouble in my pub.'

Alfie stopped in his tracks and stood swaying unsteadily in the middle of the bar-room floor.

'Go home, lad, an' sleep it off. Kitty's doing no harm. She's only being friendly, like.'

'A bit too – friendly,' the lad slurred his words. 'Kitty! You're my girl. You come here this minute.'

Now all eyes were turned towards Alfie or on Kitty sitting with her blonde head against Johnny's shoulder. She raised it briefly and waved her hand towards Alfie as if brushing him away. 'Oh, go home, little boy.'

Incensed by her dismissive taunt, Alfie launched himself towards the pair, knocking over drinks and tables.

'Steady, lad.'

''Ere – watch what you're doing.'

With one accord, the rest of the crew – including Robbie – rose to their feet and moved together. Tommy and Alan caught hold of the youth's arms and Robbie grasped his kicking legs.

'Calm down, mate, calm down,' Johnny said. 'No offence meant. If she's your girl, then—'

'I'm not his girl,' Kitty piped up. 'Only he'd like to think so. Tek no notice of him. He's nowt but a kid. Ought to be in uniform, he did. He's old enough.'

There was a brief silence whilst the locals glanced at each other uncomfortably.

'Now, now, Kitty,' Bill said gently. 'No need for that sort of talk. The lad works on a farm. He's doing a good job.'

Kitty said no more, but her lip curled disdainfully.

'So why aren't *you* in uniform?' Alfie spat back at her, struggling to free himself, but the young airmen were holding him fast. 'Like that lass there.' He nodded towards Fleur, who felt embarrassment creep up her face. 'Or are you "doing your bit" another way?'

His crude meaning was obvious to everyone listening and a gasp rippled around the room. But Alfie turned his attention to the young men holding on to him. He glared into the face of each one of them and then, slowly and deliberately, he said, 'And I hope your bloody plane crashes.'

Now there was a shocked silence through the whole bar. For a moment, no one moved. Then Fleur leapt to her feet, her eyes blazing. 'That's a wicked thing to say!'

'Steady on, lass. He doesn't mean it—'

'Oh yes, I do,' the youth muttered.

'He's had one too many – he dun't know what 'ee's sayin',' Bill said and moved from behind the bar to step between the airmen and take firm hold of Alfie himself. The burly man held the lad quite easily. 'Time you was going home, Alfie Fish. You've said quite enough for one night. More than enough. Now, I don't want to 'ave to bar you from my pub, but if you can't behave ya'sen, I will. Mek no mistake about that. These lads' – he nodded towards Robbie and the rest – 'and those lasses there an' all' – now he included Fleur and the other girls too – 'are all here for a very good reason. They're fighting this war for us. They're in the front line, as it were. Now, to my mind, we're all doing our bit. You're working on the land, providing us all wi' food. I'm doing my bit, giving these young 'uns a bit of fun on their time off. So, we're all doing our bit one way or another. Everybody here.' Now he swept his arm wide to include everyone sitting in the bar room. 'So let's have no more fighting amongst oursens. We've got enough on, fighting old Adolf. And as for Kitty – well – you're hardly going to keep her with this sort of behaviour, now a' ya?'

Suddenly, the fight seemed to go out of the young man and he slumped against Bill. The older man took his full weight and the airmen released their hold. With a shake of their heads the locals resumed their conversations and took a swallow of their beer, whilst Bill helped Alfie from the bar room out into the night.

As Bill returned, he nodded towards Robbie and the others. 'Sorry about that, lads. Just give him a minute or two to get hissen down the road home afore you leave.' He winked at them meaningfully. 'I 'aven't got so much authority on the public highway and PC Mitchell's nowhere to be seen when you want him.' He laughed heartily. 'Mind you, it's a good job sometimes if I'm a bit late closing.'

After about fifteen minutes, Tommy said, 'We'll have to get going, chaps, else we'll be late back at camp. 'Specially if we've to escort these lovely young ladies back to their billets.'

'No need,' Ruth said brusquely. 'We'll be fine.'

'And I, of course,' Kay remarked dryly, 'am going the same way as you lot anyway. Back to my biscuit bed in a draughty hut.' She cast a mock resentful glance towards Ruth and Fleur, who merely grinned in return, refusing to rise to her bait this time.

'Right then. Time to go,' Robbie said, standing up and holding out his hand to Fleur. As they moved towards the door, calling 'goodnight' to Bill, and out into the darkness, none of them noticed the three youths who had been sitting with Alfie in the corner rise to their feet and follow them out.

The youths came at them out of the blackness,

launching themselves at their perceived enemies with the same ferocity as any trained solder with a bayonet in his hand.

'Look out!' Fleur's cry came too late and, as she found herself pushed to her hands and knees on the rough road, Robbie and the rest were under attack.

It was an unequal fight, even though it was four against four. Alfie too had appeared out of the shadows. The airmen, though fit from drill and gymnastics on camp, were no match for the brawny strength of the young farm workers. Fists flew and solid punches found their mark. Grunts and shouts filled the night air, whilst the four girls peered through the gloom, watching helplessly.

'Ouch! You little sod!'

It was Robbie's voice that galvanized Fleur. 'Stop it! Stop it this minute!' she cried and then launched herself at the youth attacking Robbie. She clung to his back and wound her arm around his throat. Suddenly, all the play-fights she had ever had with her younger brother came back to her. She hooked her leg round Robbie's attacker and pulled him backwards so that he lost his balance and fell to the floor.

'Ruth!' she yelled. 'Come and sit on this one.'

'Attagirl!' Ruth whooped and threw herself bodily across the prone figure, satisfied to hear his weak groan of futile protest as her weight knocked the last ounce of breath from his body.

Squinting through the darkness, Fleur saw that Tommy was taking a real battering.

'Come on.' Now she heard Kay's voice at her side and together they launched themselves against Tommy's assailant. A moment later, he too was lying on the ground with Kay sitting astride him.

With both Robbie and Tommy now free, Alan and Johnny's attackers were soon dispatched. They fled into the darkness and only then did Ruth and Kay release their captives.

Panting heavily, the airmen and WAAFs stood in the lane listening to the pounding feet growing fainter in the distance.

'Now we'll be for it,' Tommy muttered. 'Fighting with the locals. We'll be on a charge and no mistake.'

Ten

'Well, I'm going to say I fell over in the dark. That'll explain my laddered stockings,' Ruth declared next morning. 'What about you?'

Fleur bit her lip. She'd never liked telling lies. She'd always owned up to any misdemeanour either to her parents or to her teachers. But now, others were involved and she didn't want to get anyone else into trouble. 'I wonder how the lads are faring.'

'It's a clear forecast for tonight – so Peggy was saying,' Ruth told her as they left the dining room together after breakfast. 'They'll be flying for sure. I doubt a word will be said as long as no one from the village makes trouble. And I don't think they will. You heard what Bill Moore's attitude is. And I reckon most of the villagers feel the same.' She laughed wryly. 'More likely those lads will get a leathering from their dads for being such idiots.' She nodded wisely. 'The station brings a lot of trade to this area to say nothing of the little treats that find their way from our NAAFI onto the tables of the villagers.' She tapped the side of her nose. Fleur laughed, hoping fervently that Ruth was right.

As she climbed the steps to the watch office that evening, Fleur found her heart was hammering inside her chest and she felt sick. Already, the vehicles were ferrying crews out to their aircraft as she took her place beside Kay. Although she'd spent four hours earlier in the day familiarizing herself with how things were done in this particular flying control, this was her first time on duty during a mission. Kay was a good teacher, brusque and to the point as was her manner, but in no way irritable or impatient. Fleur, meticulous as she had always been since the day she'd signed up, welcomed the other girl's professional attitude. Bob Watson was on duty that night. He smiled and nodded at Fleur as she took her seat, rearranged her writing pad and pens in readiness for the notes and lists she would be required to jot down through the busy night. She adjusted her headphones and the microphone around her neck for comfort as, behind her, other members of the team readied themselves too.

On the walls around the room were maps and clocks, and blackboards giving local weather conditions and target information. The most interesting one to Fleur was the operations blackboard with 'WICKERTON WOOD' painted in white at the top. Beneath it, the station's call sign 'Woody' and the numbers of the two squadrons operating from Wickerton Wood with their respective call signs, Lindum and Pelham. In the centre of the board was the word 'RAID' with a space for the name of the target to be chalked in each time. Below that was a white painted grid where Peggy was already filling in all the details of each aircraft and the pilot's name for tonight's raid. As each one took off she would fill in the time. And then, lastly, there was the blank column that everyone watched most anxiously: 'RETURN'.

Fleur glanced over her shoulder to see Peggy writing

in Tommy Laughton's name. Now there could be no mistake. Robbie was definitely on tonight's raid.

She glanced out of the window, criss-crossed with tape, in front of the long desk where the R/T operators sat with all their instruments and telephones overlooking the airfield's runways. Her heart skipped a beat. In the distance she could see the airmen climbing into their planes. She strained her eyes but could not pick out Robbie. Good luck, darling, she said silently. Safe home.

One by one, dozens of engines burst into life, their throbbing filling the night air and almost shaking the ground as they taxied from the various dispersal points, forming up to take off at orderly, timed intervals. At the end of the runway each aircraft waited for the controller's red light to switch to green before, revving its engines, it began its cumbersome, breath-holding take-off. One by one the Hampdens, heavy with fuel and bombs, lumbered down the runway.

On take-off and until the aircraft reached the target there was radio silence, unless in a dire emergency. Landing back at base, when security no longer mattered quite so much, was when the girls in the watch office would have radio communication with the aircraft. But they were all on duty for take-off, listening in, ready to help if needed.

'Right, ladies and gentlemen,' Bob Watson said. 'Let's see these lads into the air.'

There was a clatter of footsteps outside and the door burst open. A breathless Ruth came to attention in front of Bob's desk. 'Permission to go up to the roof, Flight?'

With a small smile, Bob nodded and Ruth rushed out of the room.

Fleur blinked and turned questioning eyes towards Bob Watson, who said shortly and with a trace of sarcasm, 'Your friend seems to think it vital that she waves off every mission from the roof of the watch tower. Some silly superstition of hers. She comes in even when she's not on duty herself and, if she's on leave, she makes someone promise to do it for her.'

Fleur said nothing. She understood about superstition and 'good luck' charms that the airmen carried. Why, at this moment, one of her initialled handkerchiefs nestled in the breast pocket of Robbie's uniform. No, she didn't blame Ruth one bit for her 'silly' superstition.

It was a long night. Once the flurry of activity of watching all the aircraft get safely airborne was over, there was nothing for the team in Control to do but wait.

'You girls can take it easy for a while. It'll be several hours before they're back,' Bob said. 'Get a cup of tea in turns . . . er . . . write letters, knit or do some . . . er . . . mending . . .' Fleur noticed that Bob was looking hopefully at Kay, who was studiously avoiding his eyes.

Fleur chuckled. 'I think Flight has a job he'd like you to do, Corp,' she said, pretending innocence.

'Then he can think again,' Kay said tartly, but Fleur caught the twinkle in the girl's eyes and she sent Fleur a surreptitious wink. She was toying with Bob, who looked crestfallen. Suddenly Kay swivelled round on her chair. 'What is it this time? Socks? Shirt buttons?'

'Actually – it's a button on my jacket . . .'

'Oh, now that is serious,' Kay mocked. 'Just think

if you were called to the CO's office with a button missing on your jacket. Tut-tut.' She winked at Fleur. 'You any good with a needle, Fleur?'

Fleur caught the mischief in Kay's eyes and shook her head. 'Terrible! My mother despaired of me.' She could hardly stop the giggles that were welling up inside her from spilling out. The truth was that Betsy had brought her up to sew, mend and make do. She was quite expert with her needle and thread and no slouch with a sewing machine either.

Now the two girls dissolved into laughter whilst Bob stood looking at them helplessly. Peggy joined in the conversation. 'You're rotten, you two.' She turned to Bob. 'I'd offer, but I really am useless at needlework. I bet that one' – she jabbed her finger at Fleur – 'is pulling your leg. She's been brought up on a farm and I bet she could knit you a jumper straight off a sheep's back.'

Fleur wiped the tears of laughter from her eyes, thankful that for a few moments she had been able to put aside her anxiety over Robbie. 'Not quite, Peggy, but I am teasing. Yes, I can sew. My mother would have a ducky fit if she heard me denying all her teaching. Hand it over and I'll see what I can do.'

As she fished in her bag for her 'housewife' with, amongst other items, its sewing needle, blue thread and tiny pair of scissors, Bob brought his uniform jacket to her, holding out the shining button in the palm of his hand. 'Lucky I didn't lose this.'

'Well, on your own head be it, Fleur,' Kay remarked. 'Don't say I didn't warn you. Word will go round this place like wildfire that you've set up as the camp seamstress. You'll have all these ham-fisted fellers beating a path to your door.'

'I should be so lucky!' Fleur quipped as she threaded her needle.

'There's just one thing,' Bob said seriously. 'Don't let the CO catch you. He's a stickler for the rulebook.'

'Then you'd better keep an eye out.' She grinned up at him. 'At least while I'm doing *your* jacket.'

'I'll get us some tea,' Peggy offered, whilst Kay turned back to study her notes and the jottings she had made during take-off.

The hours of waiting seemed interminable, especially on the eight-hour night watch, but Fleur was glad to be here. It helped her to feel closer to Robbie, even though she had a hollow, sick feeling in the pit of her stomach that she knew would not go away until he had landed safely. But tomorrow she could look forward to a day off after the long night duty. She hoped Robbie would have some time to spend with her.

As the time drew near for the aircraft to return, the relaxed atmosphere in the watch office disappeared and became businesslike once more. Just as the voice from the first homecoming aircraft came crackling over the airwaves, a red air-raid warning came in and at once the runway lights went out. Hurriedly, but with surprising calm, Kay gave warning to the homecoming crew about what was happening.

Though her hands were shaking, Fleur managed to speak calmly into her own microphone, warning each aircraft as it called in of the danger. They were all given the command to orbit at a certain height, though several were already low on fuel and wouldn't be able to circle for long. Fleur bit her lip, her ears tuned for the call sign of Robbie's plane, D-Doggo.

Then they heard the incendiary bombs falling.

Thud! A silence and then another thud. Closer now. Another, even closer, and then came a thunderous boom very close to the control tower. The whole room seemed to shake and the glass rattled, but Kay continued to speak calmly into her microphone. 'Hello, G-George, this is Woody receiving you, strength niner, over . . .' Then she wrote rapidly on her notepad, her hand moving smoothly over the page, without any telltale shake.

Fleur took a deep breath. 'Hello, P-Poppy, this is Woody . . .' She was gratified to find that her voice was level and calm too, but her heart was pounding so loudly in her chest, she was sure they could hear it over the airwaves.

They waited for the next bomb to fall, convinced it would be a direct hit on the watch office. Well, there's one thing, Fleur thought irrationally. If I'm to die so soon, my mother will have been proved right!

But no more bombs fell and in a few moments the all-clear was declared.

'Just a lone raider dropping a stick of bombs, I expect,' Bob said, smoothing back his hair, which had become distinctly ruffled during the last few minutes. The landing lights came on and, as soon as the runway was declared damage free, instructions to land began at once.

Later Fleur was to learn from Ruth that one or two aircraft had landed on almost empty tanks.

One of the last aircraft to land was D-Doggo. Finally, Fleur could breathe again. Robbie was safely back.

If every night was going to be as bad as this one had been, Fleur wondered how she would cope. But cope she would; she had to for Robbie's sake. It wouldn't help him if she let him see how dreadfully anxious she was. And yet she needed to let him know how very much she cared for him, how very much – already – she loved him.

She smiled. But he knew that, just as she knew how much he loved her.

There were no doubts between the two of them about their feelings for each other. If only he had been able to talk to his mother . . .

Eleven

'Hi, Sis. Thought I'd bike over and see how you're getting on.'

'Kenny! What are you doing here this time of the morning? Whatever time did you set off?'

He was waiting for her as she came off duty after the long night. She wouldn't see Robbie until later – they both needed to sleep. Kenny had arrived at the guardroom at the main gate and a message had been sent to Fleur.

'There's nothing wrong at home, is there?' Fleur was still anxious.

Kenny grinned. 'No more than usual. Mum's still going on about you joining up and me following you. I shan't wait till I'm called up, though. I shall volunteer as soon as I can.'

'Oh, it'll all be over by the time you're old enough,' Fleur said, hoping she sounded more convincing than she felt.

'Hope not,' Kenny said cheerfully with the thoughtlessness of youth. 'I want to see a bit of the action myself.'

Fleur sighed heavily but couldn't prevent a smile. 'And you know who'll get the blame if you do "see a bit of the action"?'

'You will.' He grinned, draping one arm around her shoulder and wheeling his bicycle with the other hand as they began to walk down the lane towards Rose Cottage. Although five years younger than Fleur, he was already a head taller.

'Exactly!' she said with wry humour, but then her tone sobered. 'But seriously, Kenny, I couldn't bear it if something happened to you. No more than Mum and Dad could. You do know that, don't you?'

He gave her shoulder a squeeze. 'Course I do,' he said softly, but then teased, 'now don't start getting all soppy on me. But I'll tell you now, if the war is still going on, I shall join up. I'm not having anyone calling me a coward.'

'Oh, Kenny, they wouldn't. Farming's acknowledged as a reserved occupation.'

'I know, and *I* don't blame those who stay, but you've seen for yourself the looks that young, unmarried fellers get.'

Fleur was silent, thinking of Kitty's scathing remark about Alfie. She'd seen for herself now how hurtful such comments could be.

'And it's not your fault either. I'd've gone anyway, whether you had or not, and I shall tell Mum so when the time comes.'

Fleur slipped her arm around his waist and laid her head against his shoulder as they walked side by side.

'It makes no difference whether Mum blames me or not, love. I shall blame myself.' There was a pause and then she said, 'I just wondered why you're here so early, that's all.' She sighed. 'It's a sign of the times. I immediately thought something was wrong.'

'I just thought I'd like to spend the day with you. I've no school today and Dad said he'd manage the morning milking on his own, so I set off at the crack of dawn.'

'How long does it take you?'

Kenny wrinkled his forehead. 'Couple of hours, I suppose. Bit more, p'raps. I use all the back roads and lanes, cutting across country. It's quicker.'

'Well, it's great to see you,' she said, giving his waist a quick squeeze.

As they rounded the last corner towards the two cottages, Fleur glanced up and saw Robbie waiting by the gate, arms akimbo, watching them approach. His fair hair was ruffled by the breeze, his jacket and shirt collar undone, his tie hanging loose. She pulled in a sharp breath and Kenny looked down at her.

'What is it, Sis?' Then, as he saw the brightness in her eyes, he followed the line of her gaze. 'Oho,' he said softly, 'so this is the feller all the trouble's about, is it?'

'Yes,' Fleur breathed. 'That's him. That's Robbie.'

'Then you'd better introduce me and I can report back to Mum.'

'It won't make any difference,' Fleur murmured sadly. 'There's something that happened in the past, but we don't know what and no one will tell us. Look, Kenny, be a dear. Don't say anything in front of Robbie, will you?'

'Course not if you say so.'

They were too close now to be able to say more without him hearing, so, releasing herself from Kenny's arm, Fleur ran towards Robbie.

'What's this?' he said, smiling down at her. 'A rival already, have I?'

'Absolutely! This is the man I've loved all his life. Robbie – this is Kenny, my . . . my brother.' For a brief moment her voice faltered and they exchanged a stricken glance.

What if . . . oh, what if . . . ?

But then Robbie had mastered his expression and was turning towards Kenny, his hand outstretched. 'I'm very pleased to meet you,' he said warmly, but Fleur was still battling to control her runaway emotions. What if she were at that moment introducing half-brothers to each other?

A shudder ran through her and it was Robbie's arm that now tightened around her, silently encouraging her to stay strong.

Kenny held out his hand. Although he favoured their mother's colouring – fair hair and blue eyes – there were times, like now, when his face creased in smiles just like their father's did when he laughed. 'Pleased to meet you.' The younger man looked Robbie up and down. 'Smart uniform, though I was thinking of the army mesen – when the time comes.'

'You'll probably see more of the world than I will stuck up there in a plane. But I fancied the flying.'

Kenny nodded. 'Yeah. Now you come to mention it,' he said thoughtfully, 'it must be thrilling, though I think I'd prefer fighter planes. Bit more exciting, that one-to-one stuff.' And they laughed together, comrades already.

Fleur stepped between them and linked her arms through theirs. 'Right, now I'll take you to meet Mrs Jackson and Harry – if he's about. And Ruth should be home soon.'

'Well, I'd come to tell you that I'll give you a hand this afternoon with this overgrown garden you were telling me about,' Robbie said. 'I felt like some fresh air and a bit of real work when I've had a few hours' kip.'

'Me too,' Fleur agreed. She was delighted to see

Kenny, but after the long night of anxiety she felt she could fall asleep standing up.

'But I needed to come and make sure you were all right after the air raid.'

'Air raid? What air raid?' Kenny asked at once before Fleur could even reply.

'Oh, it was nothing, just a lone raider dropping a stick of incendiaries,' Fleur said airily, as if it was a daily occurrence and nothing to get excited about. She squeezed Robbie's arm, warning him not to make too much of it.

Catching on at once, Robbie adopted a light, bantering tone. 'Well, it was just an excuse to see you really.'

Kenny glanced at Robbie above Fleur's head and, despite Robbie's affected nonchalance about the raid, Kenny could still see the worry in his eyes. The young man knew that they were both trying to make light of the incident in front of him.

Softly, he said, 'You can tell me the truth, you know. I won't go running home to tell Mum. I know an airfield's a dangerous place.' He looked down at Fleur. 'You've been on duty all night, haven't you? And you,' he said, glancing up again at Robbie, 'have been flying?'

Robbie laughed softly. 'Seems there's no keeping any secrets from this brother of yours, darling.'

Fleur smiled ruefully. 'No,' she said wryly. 'I don't think there is. Not about anything.'

'So, you both need to get some sleep,' Kenny began, but Fleur cut in saying, 'Well, yes, but don't go. I've the rest of the day off. In fact, I'm not on duty until the afternoon shift tomorrow.'

'And our aircraft's out of action until tomorrow. We encountered flak coming back across the coast and there are a few holes here and there.' Again, he was trying to make light of it. 'We'll just need a couple of hours and then we can spend the afternoon with you, Kenny.'

'Right-o,' Kenny said cheerfully. 'In the meantime, I can maybe make myself useful. What's all this about a garden?'

Fleur laughed. 'Careful – I might set you on.' Swiftly, Fleur explained about the state of the old lady's garden. 'It must have been a wonderful kitchen garden when her old man was alive, but now . . .' She shrugged. 'Well, you'll see the state of it for yourself. I scythed about half of it yesterday and then it'll want digging over. There's a lot of work, but it'll be worth it if I can get it right. And it's still only April. There'll be time to plant a few veggies.'

They went in by the front gate and around the corner of the house and then moved to the little gate leading into the back garden. The two men stood looking at the neglected ground.

'Grow a lot of stuff, that would,' Kenny mused. 'And the government's shouting for us all to use every spare bit of ground. I'm surprised they haven't sent a couple of sturdy Land Army girls to do it for her. Dad's got two coming, since you left.'

Fleur laughed. 'Now there's a compliment! Takes two to replace me, does it?'

Kenny grinned. 'That's about the size of it, Sis.'

'It's a lot to tackle on your own,' Robbie said. 'Is Ruth helping?'

'She's a city girl. Wouldn't know a 'tatie from a

turnip. Mind you' – Fleur's eyes sparkled with mischief – 'I've got another little job lined up for her – though she doesn't know it yet.'

'Well, I don't mind lending a hand when I'm off duty. Be good to get my hands dirty for once,' Robbie promised.

'Maybe I could bring you some tools—' Kenny began, but Fleur shook her head. 'No need. What Mrs Jackson hasn't got in her shed, Harry'll lend me. Come on in and meet my landlady.'

Fleur led the way into the kitchen and watched the old lady's eyes light up at the sight of the two handsome young men. The introductions over, Fleur made tea whilst Robbie sat down opposite Mrs Jackson with Kenny next to her. From the back scullery, Fleur heard them all laughing. It was the first time she had heard the old dear laugh aloud and when she carried the tea tray into the room and set it on the table, she saw that Mary's face was pink with pleasure.

'Coo-ee, it's only me,' a voice shouted as the back door was thrown open and Ruth appeared like a whirlwind. 'Why didn't you wait for me—?' she began as she stepped into the kitchen, but she stopped short as she saw the two young men. She'd met Robbie during the evening at the local pub, but her eyes widened as she spotted Kenny. Her mouth twitched with amusement as she said with mock severity, 'Well, I can see why now. Wanted to keep this handsome pair to yourself, did you? I call that greedy, don't you, Mrs Jackson?' She stuck out her hand towards Kenny. 'Hello. I'm Ruth. Fleur's very *best* friend.'

Kenny scrambled up, the colour rising in his face. 'H-hello. I'm Kenny. Fleur's brother.'

Fleur watched with mixed feelings as her little brother – not so little now, she noticed with a pang, for he towered over Ruth – took the girl's hand in his, his gaze fastened on her pretty face. Ruth smiled, the dimples in her round cheeks deepening. She took off her cap and shook her wayward curls. 'Nice to meet you, Kenny.'

She let go of his hand and turned towards the table. 'Any tea in the pot? I'm parched.'

Kenny sank back down into the chair, but his gaze never left Ruth as she busied herself freshening the pot and pouring herself a cup. She sat in a chair near the table, crossed her shapely legs and smiled round at everyone.

They sat chatting for several minutes until a knock came at the back door, which then opened. 'You there, lass?' came Harry's voice. 'I saw you come in. I've brought you the scythe round.' He reared the implement against the wall and stepped into the house. 'Oh, sorry. Didn't realize you had company.'

The old rascal, Fleur thought. If he saw me come home then he must have seen the lads with me. He's just come round to see what's going on. Then, remembering how lonely the old boy must be, she introduced him to Robbie and her brother.

Harry nodded at them in turn. 'How do?'

'How d'you do?' Robbie said, getting up. 'You must be Mr Chambers. Fleur has told me about you.'

'Call me 'Arry, young feller. Everybody does.'

'Well then, pleased to meet you, Harry.'

'Well,' Fleur gave an exaggerated sigh. 'I'd best get me head down for a couple of hours and then into me gardening clothes. You're a hard taskmaster, Harry, an' no mistake.'

'No, no, lass, if you've got company, I'll take the scythe back again.'

'It's OK,' Kenny said at once. 'I'll have a go while Fleur has a sleep. I'll do all the grass under the fruit trees and bushes at the bottom of the garden. Have you got a sickle I could use as well, Mr Chambers?'

'I have, lad, and I'll fetch it round for ya, but only if you call me "Harry".'

'And I'll be back this afternoon,' Robbie promised. 'And we'll all do a spot of digging.'

Kenny, red to the roots of his hair, said, 'You know I could bike over now and again and lend a hand, if you like, Sis.' But she noticed that his eyes went to Ruth as he made the offer.

Struggling to keep a straight face, Fleur said, 'That'd be great.'

'Well, young feller,' Harry put in, 'if you're as handy with me scythe as your sister, you should get that grass cut by the end of the morning.'

'You're on, Harry.' Kenny grinned.

That afternoon, Robbie returned. As he took off his jacket and hung it on a nail in the shed, he glanced down the garden to where Kenny was mowing the last patch of long grass, with Ruth sitting on the bench under the old apple tree, watching him.

'You know,' he said softly to Fleur, 'I think your little brother is smitten with Ruth.'

'Mmm, I noticed. But he's not so little now, is he?' she added wistfully and felt a shudder of apprehension at the thought that in the short space of a year her beloved Kenny would be old enough to enlist. 'Come on,' she said, determined not to let thoughts of the war spoil this sunny afternoon. 'Let's go and help.'

'What do you want me to do?'

Fleur grinned at him. 'How are you at digging?'

Twelve

It was a happy afternoon. Robbie and Kenny tackled the digging – a tough job, for the ground was hard and the grass and weeds had taken a firm hold – whilst Fleur finished the last bit of scything.

Harry sat in the house, chatting to Mary Jackson in between making little forays into the garden to see how the work was progressing, whilst Ruth kept everyone supplied with tea.

'The old dears have fallen asleep,' Ruth said about the middle of the afternoon. 'Harry's snoring with his mouth wide open. But they look so sweet,' she added fondly. 'You'd think they were an old married couple instead of just neighbours.'

Kenny, his face red from exertion, took a breather leaning on his fork. 'Thanks,' he said, the colour on his face deepening as he took the mug of tea from Ruth.

Hands on her hips, Ruth surveyed their work. 'Well, I feel like a spare part. But I wouldn't know where to start.'

Fleur rested on the scythe for a moment. 'You could rake this grass up if you like, but mind you don't get near me.'

'Huh! Not likely when you're wielding that thing.'

'Well, you're doing a great job keeping us supplied with tea for today. It's thirsty work.'

'I'll stick to that then. Mind you, I suppose I could do a bit of raking. Seems easy enough.' She was about to move away to rummage in the conglomeration of Mrs Jackson's shed to find a rake when she turned back and eyed Fleur suspiciously. 'What did you mean "for today"? Sounds as if you've got something else lined up for me. I told you, I'm a city girl.'

'I know – but how are you at housework?'

Ruth's eyes lit up. 'Oh, I'm a dab hand at that. I like everything spick and span.'

'I know,' Fleur said ruefully. 'I've seen your bedroom.' She was having a hard time keeping her own room as neat and tidy as her fellow WAAF's.

'We live in a council house back home,' Ruth went on. 'And me mum keeps it like a little palace.' She frowned. 'But Mrs Jackson's cottage is spotless. I don't see—'

'I wasn't thinking of here.' She paused, leant towards Ruth and lowered her voice. 'Have you seen Harry's place?'

Ruth stared at her and shook her head. 'Harry's place?' she repeated. 'No, I've never been inside.'

Fleur laughed. 'Well, take my word for it. It's a tip.'

'But – but he keeps his garden immaculate.'

Fleur nodded. 'I know, but I reckon that was his domain and the house was his wife's, and since she's gone . . .'

'Oh, I get you. Not much of a housewife, is he?'

'That's an understatement, love,' Fleur said wryly.

'But – but how can I offer to help? I mean, I don't want to hurt the old boy's feelings. He's a pet.'

'Go back into the house and say you feel a bit – well – a bit useless out here.'

'Oh, thanks!'

'You know what I mean. You've got to lay it on with a trowel.'

'I told you – I'm no good with trowels.'

They laughed, sparring with each other, until Ruth nodded and said, 'I'll go in and ask Mrs Jackson if there's anything she wants doing. I know she'll say "no" 'cos I've asked her before and there's only so many times I can clean my bedroom from top to bottom. And then I'll turn to Harry and ask him if he wants any ironing doing or the washing up. That'd be all right, d'you think?'

'Perfect,' Fleur grinned.

'Right.' Ruth took a deep breath. 'Here we go, then.'

The grass forgotten, Ruth headed for the cottage and a few moments later she emerged, her arm linked through Harry's. Behind his back she gave Fleur the 'thumbs up' sign and called, 'Mrs Jackson's taking over tea-making duties. Let her know when you want another.'

At the sound of her voice, Kenny looked up. 'Where's Ruth going?'

'Just next door. Give Harry a bit of a hand. She's not one for the outdoor life, it seems.'

'Oh.' His disappointment was clear to see. 'Will she be back before I have to go?'

'I expect so, but if not, you can nip next door and say "cheerio".'

The grin was back on his face as he attacked the solid ground with his fork. Unseen by Kenny, Robbie winked at Fleur just as Mrs Jackson appeared in the back doorway with a plate of scones in her hand to go with the tea Ruth had brought out.

As they stood leaning against the outer wall of the cottage, drinking tea and eating scones, Robbie declared, 'D'you know, I'm a townie like Ruth, but I have to say I'm enjoying a bit of physical work.'

'You'll suffer for it tomorrow.' Fleur grinned. 'You'll ache in muscles you didn't know you'd got.'

Robbie pulled a face. 'Quite likely, but it'll be worth it. It's good to get away from camp and to concentrate on something other than what we've got to do at night. And that reminds me.' He glanced at his watch. 'I'll have to go in about half an hour. There's a final briefing in an hour's time and even though I'm pretty sure our crew's not flying tonight, I'd better be on hand just in case.'

'Yes, and I'll have to report in too. Someone might have gone off sick and I'll be needed to take their place. Ruth too.'

As she collected the cups and plates, Kenny said, 'Look, you two go off – for a walk or summat. Have a bit of time to yourselves. I'll carry on with the digging here. I can stay till you have to go, Sis.' He glanced at the cottage next door.

'Right you are, Kenny. Thanks.' Deliberately casual, she said, 'And don't let me forget to give Ruth a shout. We'll both need time to get back into our uniforms.'

Kenny grinned. 'No, I won't forget.'

'I bet he won't.' Robbie laughed softly as they walked, hand in hand, out of the squeaking gate and a little way down the lane to where the houses stopped and the countryside began. They headed for a little copse at the edge of a field that would afford them a bit of privacy. Climbing over the gate, they headed for the shelter of the trees.

Robbie took her in his arms, but Fleur was stiff, afraid to respond. 'Oh, Robbie,' she whispered, tears filling her eyes. 'Did we ought to?'

He sighed heavily and rested his cheek against her hair. His arms were still about her but comforting rather than desirous. 'Darling, I'll try to speak to Ma as soon as I can. I promise. Maybe I could wangle a day's leave on compassionate grounds. I got a letter from her this morning and she says Pops has a very bad cold and it's gone on his chest. She's quite worried about him, I think.'

Fleur pulled a face. 'I doubt you'll manage it unless the weather gets bad and you can't fly.'

So much taller than Fleur, Robbie kissed the top of her head. 'Then we'll just have to pray for snow.'

Fleur laughed, despite the worry clouding their time together. 'What? In April?'

'It's been known. Pops reckons he remembers it snowing in the middle of May in nineteen hundred.'

'Really?'

'So he says.'

They stayed for the half-hour, just happy to be together, and yet they dared not kiss – it felt wrong until they knew for sure.

'Oh I wish we knew. I wish we knew the truth,' Fleur moaned as they walked back to Mrs Jackson's cottage. Robbie squeezed her hand. 'I'll find out as soon as I can. I promise.'

The snow that they'd wished for didn't arrive and there were operations on each of the following three nights. The watching and waiting didn't get any easier and Fleur breathed a sigh of relief each time D-Doggo landed safely. On the fourth night, however, there was a weather report of bad visibility over the target area that cancelled the mission. All aircrews were stood down and Robbie went at once to see Tommy Laughton.

'Skip, is it absolutely definite that we won't be flying? Because, if it is, I could do to nip home for twenty-four hours.'

'It's definite, old boy, so it should be OK. Mind you fill in a two-nine-five.' Tommy reminded him to submit the usual application form. 'But can you be sure to be back by thirteen hundred tomorrow? If there's flying tomorrow night, briefing's likely to be at fourteen hundred.'

Robbie nodded. 'I'll hitch if the trains don't fit up. Folks are very decent about picking up servicemen.'

Tommy stroked his bristly moustache thoughtfully. 'Tell you what, nip along to MT. They might have a lorry going your way.'

'Thanks, Skip. I will.'

When he went in search of Fleur, it was to find that she too had been given permission to go home for a brief visit because there was no flying that night. He squeezed her arm. 'I've got a lift all the way to Nottingham. I'll ask the driver if he can take you too.'

They parted in Newark.

'Could you drop me outside Castle Station, please?' Fleur asked. 'I rang home and my father had to come into Newark anyway today so he said he can pick me up there.'

'What if he sees me?' Robbie asked worriedly.

The WAAF driver smiled knowingly, but made no comment as Fleur said cheerfully, 'I don't care if he does. You've got to meet each other some time.'

The lorry came to a halt and Fleur leant over and kissed Robbie's cheek before climbing down. As the vehicle pulled away, she turned towards the station to see Jake standing beside his battered Ford. She caught her breath. He must have seen Robbie. When she got closer she was shocked by the look on her father's face. Even though he was tanned by the outdoor life he led, the colour had drained from his face and his eyes were haunted. He looked as if he had just been dealt a devastating blow. The thought terrified Fleur. Had her father believed he was looking at his own son for the first time?

Her voice shook as she said, 'Dad? What is it? What's the matter?'

He was breathing heavily. 'Is that him? Is that Meg's boy?'

'Yes,' Fleur said hesitantly. 'He . . . he couldn't stop now. He's on his way home. His grandfather's ill. He—'

'Are you *sure* it is his grandfather?' There was still disbelief in Jake's tone.

'Yes. I asked him. It's his mother's father.'

Jake shook his head as if he couldn't believe what she was saying. 'You do surprise me,' he murmured, but he was speaking more to himself than to her.

Fleur took a deep breath and put her arm through her father's. 'Dad – Robbie and I – well, we've fallen in love, and unless you tell me that there's a good reason why we can't see each other—'

'Isn't upsetting your mother good reason enough?' he demanded harshly.

Fleur kept her voice calm. 'No – not on its own. I'm sorry, but it isn't.'

'Don't you think she's got enough to worry about

with you gone and Kenny just waiting for the day when he's old enough to join up without you taking up with someone – with someone – unsuitable?'

'But *why* is he unsuitable, as you put it? If only you'd tell me then perhaps I could understand.'

Jake's mouth was a hard, unyielding line. 'I've told you once and I won't tell you again.' It was as if she were small again and he was chastising her for some childish escapade. 'It's not my secret to tell.'

'Are you sure?' Fleur cried passionately, no longer able to stay calm. 'Are you quite sure it has nothing to do with you?'

The bleak look on her father's face tore at her heart and when he pulled himself free of her grasp, picked up her bag and marched towards the car, she knew it would be fruitless to ask any more questions.

'I just hope Robbie's having better luck with his mother,' she muttered angrily as she followed Jake.

They drove all the way from Newark to South Monkford in an uncomfortable silence. As he drew the vehicle to a halt in the yard, Jake said, 'Not a word to your mother about all this. You hear me?'

If she didn't want to spoil her leave completely, Fleur gave the only answer she could. 'Yes, Dad.'

Thirteen

'Oh, it's you.'

'Well, that's a nice greeting, Mum, I must say.'

'What do you expect?' There was no smile from Betsy, not even a hug. 'It was bad enough you leaving us in the lurch, but now Kenny's taken it into his head to come cycling over to see you every spare minute instead of helping your father.'

'Mum, he's been over *once* . . .'

But Betsy was in no mood to listen. 'He *says* it's to help some poor old dear with her gardening.' She gave a disapproving click of her tongue. 'But there's more to it than that.' She wagged her finger in Fleur's face. 'He's done nothing but talk about a girl called Ruth. Who is she, I'd like to know?'

Fleur took off her uniform jacket and hung it up on the back of the door. The teapot – as ever – was standing on the hob in the range. She picked it up, moved to the table and poured herself a cup of tea.

'Well,' Betsy demanded impatiently.

Fleur sighed as she sat down at the table. 'She's the other girl in the billet with me and the old lady is our landlady. She's a sweet old dear, but she's crippled with arthritis. Her husband used to keep the garden lovely, but since he died three years ago, it's been neglected. I just thought I'd help tidy it up in my spare time, get some veggies growing. You know, like the government's always telling us to do.'

'It's here you should be helping.' Betsy prodded her forefinger towards the floor. 'Not digging some stranger's garden *and* enticing your brother away from his duty too.'

'I didn't *entice* him, as you put it,' Fleur said wearily. 'I didn't even ask for his help. He came over to visit me and saw what I was doing.'

'Huh! And I expect you're trying to set him up with this Ruth girl? He's far too young to be thinking about girls. He's still at school, for heaven's sake.'

'Only because you've made him stay on. Still want him to go to university, do you?'

'No,' Betsy said promptly. 'Agricultural college.'

Fleur raised her eyebrows. 'That's a new idea. I've not heard that before. When did you think that one up?' Her eyes narrowed thoughtfully as she stared at her mother. 'Oh, I get it. You think it will keep him out of the war, don't you?'

Betsy wriggled her shoulders. 'Can't blame a mother for trying.'

Fleur was about to say, No, though you're trying much harder to stop Kenny going than you ever did with me. But she bit back the retort. It was the mother/son thing. She knew that. She sipped her tea in the tense silence.

Almost as if she had read her daughter's thoughts, Betsy blurted out, 'I'd've thought you'd have done what your dad wanted, even if you'd take no notice of me. But no, you had to go, didn't you?' Tears filled Betsy's eyes. 'And now there'll be no stopping Kenny.' Her voice rose hysterically. 'He'll go and it'll be all your fault. If you'd stayed here at home, he would've done an' all. But now . . .'

Fleur set down her cup with deliberate care. 'I know you won't believe me, Mum, but I've asked him not to go. But I don't think anything any of us can say will make any difference. And – and he said he'd go anyway – that it has nothing to do with me . . .' She saw her mother's sceptical glance but ploughed on. 'He doesn't want to be thought a coward. He says he gets some funny looks even now because he's not in uniform – because he's so tall for his age.'

Now Betsy leant over the table towards Fleur, almost menacingly. 'I'd rather him be thought a coward,' she said slowly, emphasizing every word, 'put in prison for it even – if it keeps him alive.'

'Oh, Mum!' Now Fleur's eyes filled with tears as she felt an overwhelming pity for her mother. 'That's not our Kenny. Can't you be proud of your son that – that he wants to do his duty for his country?'

Betsy banged the table with her fist. 'His duty's here. Helping his father on the land. Why else would the government make farming a reserved occupation? He'll be helping his country just as much. More, if truth be known, than becoming cannon fodder.' Fleur gasped as her mother ranted on. 'I've been through all this before, you know. Your father was in the last lot. Oh, he married me before he went – so that I would get his pension.' Her face twisted. 'His pension! What good is a pension compared to a lifetime of loneliness?'

'But Dad came back.'

'Aye, he did. I was lucky . . .' For a moment her eyes glazed over and she was lost in the past. 'I was lucky he came back – that he came back to *me* – that he stayed with *me*.'

Fleur felt as if ice-cold water was running down her spine. 'Mum – what d'you mean – came back to *you*?'

Betsy blinked, back in the present. 'Eh? Oh – oh nothing. Nothing.' She bit her lip and turned away, murmuring, 'Yes, you're right. I was lucky.' And then adding ominously, 'That time.'

The atmosphere lightened noticeably when Kenny breezed in from school, slung his satchel in the corner, hugged Fleur and then lifted his mother in a bear hug and swung her round. Betsy laughed and slapped him playfully. 'Oh, you bad boy! Put me down, put me down. I've your tea to get . . .'

She bustled about the kitchen and scullery with renewed vigour, a smile on her face now that her beloved son was home. She placed an overloaded plate of hot food before him, fussed around him, stroking his hair and patting his shoulder.

How does he put up with it? Fleur thought, gritting her teeth, realizing that she was glad she was not her mother's favourite if that was what she would have to put up with. She glanced across the table at her father, but Jake was eating his meal, outwardly placid, his face expressionless. But she wondered what exactly he was feeling inside.

'How's Ruth?' Kenny mumbled, his mouth full of meat and potato pie.

Before Fleur could answer, Betsy, sitting down next to Kenny, said, 'Don't talk with your mouth full and never mind about her. Did you see the careers master today? Did you ask him about agricultural college like I told you?'

Kenny stopped chewing and laid his knife and fork

down on his plate, though his meal was only half eaten. He swallowed.

'Mum,' he began, his face unusually serious. He put his arm along the back of her chair and touched her shoulder. 'I don't want to go to college or university or anywhere. Not yet. When I leave school, I'm going to join the RAF. I want to be a pilot. A fighter pilot.'

For a moment there was complete stillness in the room until the air was rent with Betsy leaping to her feet, pointing at Fleur and screaming. 'See? See? I told you. It's all your fault. If it hadn't been for you, he'd never even have thought of the RAF. If – if he's killed, it'll be your fault. All your fault.' She swung round towards Jake. 'And you're no better. You should have forbidden her to go. But you're too soft, too – too . . .' Betsy couldn't find the words to describe what she felt about Jake. She sank back into her chair, covered her face with her hands and broke into noisy sobbing.

'Oh, Mum, don't.' Kenny hugged her awkwardly, but it was to no avail.

Above the noise, Jake said, 'Betsy, now that's enough. You know I won't interfere with what either of them wants to do. I went myself last time, didn't I? I can hardly start playing the heavy-handed father this time round. Besides, if you want the truth, I'm proud of them. Proud of them both that they want to do their bit.'

Fleur and Kenny gaped at him, a mixture of emotions on both their faces. Gratitude for his understanding and because he'd spoken up in their defence, but at the same time shock because it was the first time they'd ever heard him criticize their mother. At least, in front of them. What perhaps passed between their parents in private they weren't to know.

Betsy's sobs subsided and she let her hands fall away from her face. In a flat voice she said, 'Then you don't care if they get hurt or even killed?'

'Of course I care.' Jake's voice was rising in anger now. 'How can you accuse me of not caring? But the whole country is in the same boat. Every mother's son is in danger.' He looked at Fleur and added, 'And a lot of fathers' daughters too.'

'I don't care about anyone else,' Betsy said and now her quiet tone was more frightening than her screaming. 'I only care about my own.' And she leant towards Kenny to emphasize just where her concerns lay.

'Then that's very selfish of you, Betsy.' Jake pushed back his chair and rose. As he was about to turn away, his wife said, 'I bet *she's* only bothered about her own precious son.'

Jake was very still and Fleur held her breath. Slowly he turned back to look down at Betsy. There was sadness on his face, a sorrow that was far deeper than disappointment in his wife's attitude. He was struggling to hold his tongue, to end the argument, but he lost the battle as he said quietly, 'He's a fine boy.'

Betsy stared up at her husband, her eyes wide with shock, whilst Fleur and Kenny could only watch in silence, mystified by what was being said. 'You've seen him?' she whispered. 'You – you've met him?'

'No, but I saw him – at a distance.' Without thinking, his glance went automatically to Fleur. It was enough for Betsy.

'He was with her? At the station? You saw him there? Today?'

Jake sighed. After all his warnings to Fleur, it was him who'd let the secret out. 'Yes, he was.' His eyes were hard as he held his wife's gaze. 'He's a fine-looking boy, Betsy.'

'I bet he is. Oh I bet he is.' Tears ran down her face once more. 'I expect he's just like his *father*!'

There was a breathless pause before Jake said, with surprising calm now, 'Yes, Betsy, he is. He's the spitting image of his father.'

Fourteen

'I seem to say nothing but "I'm sorry, darling", don't I?' Robbie said ruefully.

They had arranged to meet in Newark and travel back to Wickerton Wood together.

'So – I take it you didn't get to ask your mother?'

Robbie shook his head. 'I felt very guilty asking for compassionate leave when the old boy had got no more than a cold, but in actual fact, when I got home, he was in hospital. Pneumonia, they say.'

Fleur gasped. 'Oh no! Will he be all right?'

'I hope so. Ma will be devastated if anything happens to him. Specially now with me . . . You know?'

There was no need for him to say more: Fleur knew exactly what he meant. If anything happened to Robbie, then the old man was the only person his mother would have to cling to.

Interrupting her thoughts, Robbie said, 'I just couldn't worry her at the moment.'

'Of course you couldn't.' Fleur was quick to reassure him. 'But there is a glimmer of hope.'

'Really?' His eyes lit up.

Over their tea, Fleur recounted the strange, mystifying argument between her parents. 'And when Mum said she expected that you're just like your father, Dad said, "Yes, he is. He's the spitting image of his father."' She reached across the table and clasped his hands, leaning towards him to say earnestly, 'But you're nothing like my dad. You're fair and he's dark. He's starting to go a bit grey now, but he has brown hair. You've got blue eyes – really bright blue eyes – and his are brown. You're tall. He isn't particularly. So, where's the resemblance? I can't see it. Admittedly, your face creases up when you smile, a bit like his does, but then so do a lot of people's.' She paused and laughed. 'Old Harry's does, for a start.'

Robbie's face creased as he chuckled. 'Yeah, but he's got a lot more laughter lines on his face than I've got at the moment.'

'At the moment'. How poignant that simple phrase was. In these dangerous days how many handsome young men would never grow old enough to have a wrinkled face like Harry's?

Fleur deliberately tried to lighten their thoughts. 'Laughter lines, you call them?' she quipped. 'Nothing's that funny!'

Returning to the comparison between Robbie and her father, she went on, 'You've got a much squarer jaw than my dad and . . .' Suddenly, her voice faded away as she stared across the table at Robbie.

'What? What is it? Grown another nose, have I?'

Fleur shook her head, but she was still staring at him. 'You know, you do remind me of someone. Not my dad,' she added hastily, 'but someone . . . But for the life of me, I can't think who.'

Robbie grinned. 'Some handsome film star, I've no doubt.'

Fleur laughed out loud so that one or two folk at nearby tables smiled fondly. It was good to see two young people in uniform enjoying themselves.

'Of course,' Fleur teased. 'That must be it.'

They rose from the table, put a tip beneath the plate for the waitress and left the cafe, their arms about each other, suddenly a little freer to let their feelings show. And yet, they wouldn't be certain, not absolutely certain, until Robbie had spoken to his mother. Not until then would they allow themselves to be real girlfriend and boyfriend. Until then, they must act like the brother and sister that – God forbid – they might really be.

'You really are a grand pair of lasses to be helping us old folk like you are,' Mrs Jackson said as she shuffled across the room to set the table in time for an early tea. Both Ruth and Fleur were due to report back to camp for the evening shift. The lads – including Robbie – were flying tonight.

'It keeps us out of mischief,' Ruth laughed. 'I mean, if we weren't doing that we'd only be down the pub—'

'Or dancing—'

'Or shopping—'

They glanced at each other in mock horror.

'What *are* we thinking of?' Ruth said and Fleur giggled.

Ruth put her arm round the old lady's ample waist. 'Don't you fret, Mrs Jackson. I'm one of these strange people who actually enjoy housework. And – if I'm not mistaken – Fleur is going to get a lot of satisfaction when she sees leeks and potatoes and whatever else she's going to grow in that garden of yours.'

Fleur nodded. 'I've got it all planned out. I was asking my dad for advice when I was home at the weekend and he's given me a list of what to plant and when to plant it. I've written it all down in an old diary. I'm going to plant carrots, potatoes and cauliflowers, maybe leeks and onions too. And that rhubarb patch we unearthed when we cut the grass needs looking at. And I'll start a compost heap in the far corner. And in the other corner, I'm going to build you an Anderson shelter, Mrs Jackson.'

'Oh, don't worry about that, love. I don't think I could get there quick enough anyway. Someone did come a while back, but I told 'em I'd go round to Harry's if we got a bad raid.'

The two girls stared at the old lady. 'But . . . but Harry hasn't got a shelter either,' Ruth said.

Now Mrs Jackson looked suddenly sheepish. 'No, I know. He wouldn't accept any help from anyone and he promised the authorities he'd build one himself.'

'But he never did.'

Mrs Jackson shook her head. 'I don't think he ever intended to, the awkward ol' devil!' She smiled fondly.

'Well, you really ought to have one,' Fleur said firmly, 'especially living so close to the airfield, so we'll build one for the two of you. We'll put it in the corner of your garden nearest his and cut a hole in the fence for him to get through and you can share it. All right?'

Mary Jackson smiled. 'If you say so, dear.'

'Right – that's settled then,' Fleur said firmly. 'I'll make enquiries as to how to get hold of what we need to make one.'

'The local ARP people might know,' Ruth suggested.

'That's a good idea. Only thing now is – I could do to find a farmer nearby with a lot of pigs, and maybe cows and chickens as well.'

'Pigs!' Ruth exclaimed. 'You're not thinking of keeping pigs at the bottom of the garden, are you?'

'Mr Clegg at Top End Farm keeps pigs,' Mrs Jackson put in. She was smiling as if she'd already guessed what Fleur was talking about. 'All the villagers keep their scraps for pigswill for him. He collects two or three times a week.'

Fleur's face lit up. 'Great!'

'But what do you want them for?' Ruth persisted. 'You're not seriously thinking of having some here, are you?'

'I don't actually want the *pigs*, I just want what they produce. For the garden.'

'What they—?' Ruth's face was a picture as realization dawned. 'Oh my! Well, now I've heard it all!'

The bombing mission that night was a difficult one and the planes encountered heavy flak both over the target and along the route home, especially near the enemy coast. Fleur was careful to hide her anxiety as the bombers limped home, some with aircraft so badly damaged that it was a miracle they got back at all.

Anxiously, she waited for the call sign of D-Doggo. At last, she heard, 'Hello, Woody, this is Lindum D-Doggo. One engine u/s and wounded on board . . .'

At once, Bob Watson was standing behind the operators. 'Kay, call up number four and tell him to overshoot. Fleur, tell D-Doggo he has straight in approach. Corporal—' Bob called to the airman who manned the internal telephone. 'Call up the ambulance and fire tender.'

Fleur took a deep breath. 'Hello, D-Doggo, you are

number five to land, straight in approach, runway two-zero . . . switch to channel B.'

Calmly, her instructions were repeated and then they heard the drone of the aircraft as it approached the runway.

'His other engine doesn't sound too healthy,' Bob said. Everyone was holding their breath, trying to see out into the darkness. The aircraft touched down, the noise fading as it ran towards the end of the runway.

The radio crackled again. 'Hello, Woody, this is number five. Turned left off runway, but second engine now u/s. Over.'

From the clipped message, Fleur knew that the aircraft had been able to turn off the runway, but now it seemed that the second engine had given up on them and the plane could taxi no further under its own power.

'Help is on its way, number five,' she said into her microphone. 'Well done. Out.'

Now Fleur could breathe easily again and at once began to call up the aircraft waiting to land. It had been a close call for Tommy Laughton and his crew. The rear gunner was injured, but at least they were all home. Five planes failed to come back. Debriefing revealed that one had been seen to crash in enemy territory.

'I did see parachutes, though,' one of the pilots told Ruth.

Three aircraft had ditched in the sea, though the fate of the crews was unknown and one plane couldn't be accounted for at all.

D-Doggo was badly damaged and would be out of commission yet again for two or three days whilst the mechanics worked on it frantically. Several more planes in the same squadron needed extensive repairs before they would be airworthy.

'I've got a seventy-two, so I'm going home. And this time, I really will speak to Ma,' Robbie promised Fleur. 'What about you? Can you get any leave?'

She shook her head. 'No. Sounds like there's a big op on for tomorrow night. We're on duty.'

A fleeting look of regret crossed Robbie's face. 'And I'll miss it,' he murmured. Fleur looked at him incredulously, shaking her head slowly. She said nothing, but she was wondering just what it was about these young men that made them want to be in the thick of danger. Was it the excitement? And was that excitement all the more thrilling because it was dangerous? She didn't know. All she knew was that Kenny craved that same kick.

Robbie put his arm about her waist. 'I'm sorry you can't get leave too. We could have met up. Spent some time together.'

'I know,' she said softly, anguished at the thought of not being able to spend every precious minute with him. 'But maybe it'll be worth it if you do get a chance to talk to your mother.'

'I'll make sure I do this time. I promise.'

Fifteen

Fleur attacked the gardening work with a vigour born of anxiety and frustration. Anything, to keep her mind from wandering to Robbie and what was being said between him and his mother.

She double dug an area down one side of the garden ready for planting potatoes, then levelled an area nearby to plant carrots and cauliflowers. After that she carefully weeded the rhubarb patch. Then she marked out the oblong shape for the Anderson shelter and began to dig out the hole. The ground was hard and the effort back-breaking.

Taking a break about mid morning, she went into the house to find Mrs Jackson standing at the kitchen table rolling out pastry. Beside her was a container of shrivelled-looking rings.

'What on earth are those?' Fleur asked.

Mrs Jackson chuckled. 'Dried apple rings.'

'Dried? I've never heard of doing that.'

'Oh, they come out quite well if you soak them and then use them in a pie.'

'My mum always bottles all her fruit. She's got a cooker as well as the old range and she uses a huge metal container. A big box-like thing . . .' Fleur demonstrated its size with her hands. 'It holds about eight bottles at once. And she packs all the fruit into them with syrup and then boils them for – oh, I don't know how long.'

Mrs Jackson was nodding. 'Yes, I used to do something similar in the oven with Kilner jars, but since Arthur went I haven't had the heart. Truth is, I found it too hard to get the fruit picked.'

Fleur put her arm around the old lady's shoulders. 'Well, this year we'll harvest it all and we'll see what we can do then, eh?'

Mary Jackson smiled. 'That'd be lovely, dear. My Arthur would be so thrilled to think all his hard work hadn't been wasted. He planted those fruit trees, y'know, when we was first married. There's two apple trees and a Victoria plum as well as raspberry canes and gooseberry bushes. Just before our Eddie was born, it was. And he built that bench under the apple tree so's I could sit down there with the pram.'

'Eddie? Who's Eddie.'

The old lady's face fell into lines of sorrow. 'Our boy. Our son. Our *only* son.'

'And – er – where is Eddie now?' Fleur held her breath. For some reason she feared the answer.

'He was killed in the last war. On the Somme.'

'Oh, Mrs Jackson, I am sorry.' She paused, before asking tentatively, 'Have – have you any other children?'

'Two daughters. Phyllis and Joyce.'

Fleur waited for Mrs Jackson to volunteer the information herself. 'Phyllis is married and lives down south. She . . . she doesn't get home much, but she writes every week.'

Fleur nodded. She had seen the letters arriving regularly and had posted replies for the old lady, although she hadn't known they were addressed to Mary's daughter.

'And . . . and Joyce?'

Mrs Jackson was silent for a moment, concentrating on rolling out the pastry for the apple pie. Her voice was husky with sadness when she did answer. 'Joyce was only seventeen when she started courting a lad from the village. She . . . she got herself into trouble.'

Fleur said nothing, knowing that in such a small community the gossips would've had a field day.

'They got married but . . . but she died having the bairn. She was only just eighteen.'

Fleur's eyes filled with tears. 'Oh, Mrs Jackson, how sad. I'm so sorry. And . . . and what happened to her baby?'

'A little boy, it was, but his daddy – the whole family, in fact – moved away. They've kept in touch and I've seen him a few times while he's been growing up. I've always sent him a little something at Christmas and on his birthday.'

How sad that must be for the old lady, Fleur thought. The boy's birthday would also be the anniversary of his mother's death.

'He . . . he's seventeen now.' Mrs Jackson's expression was suddenly anxious. 'I expect he'll be called up when he's old enough. If . . . if it's not over by then.'

'Same age as Kenny.'

'That's right. Your Kenny reminds me of Simon in some ways. Same cheeky grin.' Now she smiled fondly.

'Do you mind Kenny coming here? I mean, I wouldn't want it to upset you if he reminds you—'

'Mind? Heavens, no, dear. I like him to come. He's a lovely lad.'

'Has Phyllis any children?'

Mary laughed fondly. 'Oh yes. Four. Two boys and two girls. Clever, wasn't she?'

Fleur laughed too, glad to move on to a happier note. But still, even with her other grandchildren, it seemed Mary had worries.

'One of the girls is in the WAAFs like you and the other is in the Land Army. The eldest boy is a fighter pilot. We were very worried last year when the Battle of Britain was going on. He was in the thick of it. But he's all right, thank the Good Lord. And the youngest boy, well, he's only thirteen. I hope it'll all be over by the time he reaches call-up age.'

'Oh, my goodness, let's hope so,' Fleur said fervently.

There was a silence between them as Mrs Jackson shaped her pastry to fit the pie dish.

'Has Harry any family?'

'Not now. They only had one child – a boy – and he was killed an' all in the last lot. Ypres, I think it was.'

Fleur couldn't think of anything to say. How sad it was for these lonely old people and now they were being plunged into another terrible war. Hearing about Mrs Jackson's loss and old Harry's made Fleur understand her mother's fears a little more. What she couldn't understand was Betsy's vehement hatred of Meg and her son. Surely, in such troubled times past animosities and feuds should be laid aside, forgotten and forgiven. Whatever could have happened to make her mother so bitter and resentful against Robbie's?

Outside again, Fleur eyed the area she had marked out for the Anderson shelter with a frown. She'd made a start but was getting tired now, and she had to remember that she still had a full eight-hour night shift to do.

'I'll do a bit in the front garden,' she decided. 'The ground might be a bit softer there.'

She hadn't been digging for many minutes when she heard the familiar, 'Hi, Sis.'

Fleur looked up at the sound of squeaking brakes as Kenny slithered to a halt at the gate. He jumped off his bike, reared it against the fence and straddled the gate without bothering to open it. Fleur grinned and leant on her fork. 'Hello. What brings you here?'

'To see my sister, of course.' Kenny grinned and the twinkle in his eyes told the rest.

'Really?' Fleur teased with a wry note of disbelief in her tone. Then she capitulated and laughed. 'It's good to see you – whatever the reason. But shouldn't you be at school?'

'Nope. Our school's sharing with another that got bombed out. So we go in the morning and they have the afternoons. And before you say anything – yes, I have taken this morning off to get here, but don't tell Mum, will you?'

'You bad lad!' Fleur laughed again, but Kenny knew she wouldn't give him away.

'What are you going to do here?' He changed the subject, pointing to the newly turned earth at her feet.

'I thought runner beans. I'll get them planted and then build a frame from canes for the plants to climb. I've seen a bundle in Harry's shed.' She lowered her voice. 'And Mrs Jackson said that her Arthur always used to grow her a row of sweet peas. They're her favourite flowers. I'd love to grow some for her, but I don't think I dare.'

Kenny frowned thoughtfully. 'Wait a minute. What

about . . . ?' He moved to the corner of the cottage furthest away from Harry's cottage and pointed at the end wall. 'Down this narrow border here. It's not much use for anything else, and behind that big bush she's got there near the fence, it won't be easily seen from the road. I reckon you could get away with it there. And if the authorities say anything . . .' he shrugged. 'Then you'll just have to rip 'em up again.'

Fleur beamed at him. 'You clever old thing. That'd be perfect. It'd just take a narrow frame, wouldn't it?'

'And it'll get a bit of sun,' Kenny added. 'Not much, but enough. Mind you, you're a bit late now for getting sweet peas sown, aren't you?'

'Dad's got some seedlings, hasn't he?'

Kenny's face cleared. 'So he has. I'd forgotten. I'll bring you a trayful next time I come.'

'Meantime, I'll get that narrow border dug over and a cane frame built, but not a word to her.'

'Won't she see it?'

Fleur shook her head. 'Doubtful. She only comes out once a week to go to church and then she walks round the other end of the cottage and down this front path.' She stood a moment and glanced towards the other end of the building. 'No, she'll not see it. Not unless she goes that end deliberately – and I don't think she will.'

'Mum's the word then, until you present her with a bouquet of sweet peas.'

Fleur hugged herself. 'I can't wait to see her face.' Then her expression sobered. 'Talking of "mum" – is everybody all right at home?'

Kenny laughed. 'Right as they'll ever be. She's still adamant that if I apply for college, I won't be called up, and nothing we say will persuade her any different.'

He pulled a face. 'I reckon when the time comes, she'll march into the nearest recruiting office and tell them I'm not going and that's it.'

Fleur wasn't laughing. 'You know,' she said seriously, 'she might very well do just that.'

'Eh?' Kenny looked scandalized. 'I was only joking. Oh, Sis, she wouldn't really, would she?'

'She'll do anything to stop you going. Anything she can. She'll use the "reserved occupation" argument and anything else she can think of. She certainly might apply to the local War Agricultural Executive Committee for your exemption.'

'But it wouldn't work, would it? I mean – they wouldn't take any notice of a chap's mother, would they?'

'If she makes a proper application as your employer, then, yes, I think they might.'

'Does she know that?' he asked worriedly.

Fleur shrugged. 'If she doesn't yet, she'll soon make enquiries and find out. You can be sure of that.'

'Fleur, I want to go. Just like you.'

'Oh, don't say that, Kenny.' Fleur groaned. 'You make me feel so guilty.'

Kenny shook his head. 'That's not what I mean. I'd go anyway – I've told you that already – even if you hadn't volunteered.'

Fleur looked at him, wanting to believe him but not sure she could. She had set an example to her younger brother and he didn't want to be outdone by her. If anything happened to him . . .

'Right then, where do you want me to start?' Kenny interrupted her maudlin thoughts with his ready grin and willing pair of hands. 'By the way,' he added, trying to sound nonchalant, 'Ruth here, is she?'

'She'll be home later. She should be back before you go. But, yes, I would be glad of your help.'

Kenny grinned. 'More digging? I thought you'd've got it finished by now.'

'It is – more or less – but I want to build an Anderson shelter that both Mrs Jackson and Harry can share. Down the bottom of the garden. I've made a start, but the ground's so hard.'

'Right-o. I'll help you dig out the foundations.'

'Actually, there's something else I'd rather you helped me with today, if you would.'

'Oh yes. What's that then?'

'I've made arrangements to go up to Top End Farm and see about some manure. If I can get some for this afternoon, I was hoping to get it dug in tomorrow. I'll be off all day after tonight's shift. In fact I'm not on again until the day after tomorrow in the afternoon, so I'll get a good long go at it. But now you're here.' She smiled archly at him. 'You could help me dig it in this afternoon. I was going to ask Robbie, but his plane's grounded for repairs and he's gone home to see his mother, so I thought I might twist Ruth's arm to lend a hand.'

Kenny guffawed loudly. 'I don't think you'll get either of that pair of townies to deal with a pile of—'

'Careful, Kenny,' Fleur laughed. 'Mrs Jackson's a lady. It's "manure" to her.'

Her brother's grin widened. 'I'll try to remember, Sis. She's a sweet old dear. I wouldn't want to upset her. She reminds me of Gran.'

They were both silent for a moment, remembering

with affection their father's mother who had lived with them for the last two years of her life.

'She is a bit, I suppose. Gran had arthritis just like her.'

'And she's round and waddly – just like Gran.' After another brief pause, Kenny said, 'Right then, what about this – manure? How are we to get it here?'

'I saw the farmer. Mr Clegg. He said if I went up today, I could have one of his horses and his cart. I've to do the loading up that end and the unloading this end and take the horse and cart back before I go on duty.'

'Sounds as if it's a good job I've come then.'

'Bro, you don't know how glad I am to see you.'

'You only want me for my brawn,' Kenny teased, flexing his muscles.

'Absolutely!' she retorted, but brother and sister smiled at each other with deep affection.

They walked the half-mile through the village until, a short distance after the houses ended, Fleur pointed to a rough track leading down a slight incline towards a farmhouse and outbuildings nestling in a natural shallow vale. Kenny glanced around him. 'Is this what they call the Lincolnshire Wolds?'

'I'm not sure. I think they're a bit further east. More in the centre of the county. And then there's the Lincoln Edge. Not so flat as people think, is it? I think it's flatter to the east – towards the sea and in the south of the county.'

'Oh yeah. What they call the fens down there, isn't it? Mind you, you can see why it's ideal for all the airfields they're building, can't you? I heard someone call it "bomber county" the other day.'

'Really?' Fleur was thoughtful for a moment. 'Well,

yes, I can see why they might call it that. Right,' she said more briskly as they reached the farm. 'Now, where is Mr Clegg?'

'Well, there's his horse and cart standing over there near that pile of . . .' He grinned. 'Manure. And if I'm not mistaken, someone's already started loading.'

As he spoke, a forkful of manure flew up in the air and landed with a thud on the growing pile in the back of the cart. As they approached, Fleur stroked the horse's nose and patted his neck. 'Now, big feller,' she murmured.

Hearing her voice, the man at the back of the cart straightened up. 'Na' then, lass. Thought I'd mek a start for ya.'

The farmer was a big man, tall and broad with iron muscles standing out on his arms. He wore heavy workaday boots, dark green corduroy trousers that had seen better days, a striped, collarless shirt and a checked cap. Mr Clegg nodded towards Kenny. 'Brought reinforcements, I see. Yar young man, is it?'

'My brother.'

'Pleased to meet you, young feller.'

Kenny stuck out his hand, 'Kenny Bosley, sir. Pleased to meet you, an' all.'

The farmer blinked down at the young man's outstretched hand. 'Oh, I don't think I'd better shek yar hand, lad. Not with my mucky 'un.'

Kenny laughed. 'We're used to it, Mr Clegg. Born and bred on a farm. Never afraid of good, clean dirt, our dad always says.' He nodded comically towards the manure heap. 'And especially not this that's going to do Mrs Jackson's garden a power of good.'

The big man laughed loudly. 'Ah well, in that case, lad, put it there.' And the two shook hands.

'It's very good of you to let us have it,' Fleur said.

'Pleased to get rid of some of it. I keep pigs, cows an' chickens so there's plenty to go at. Mind you, you'd be surprised at the number of folks asking for it nowadays. Now then, if I can hand over to you, I must get on wi' me other work. Just mind you have old Prince here back for 'is tea, else 'ee's likely to get a bit cussed and take off on his own. Trouble is,' he added, laughing, 'he knows 'is way home so 'ee won't think twice about it.' He paused and eyed Kenny again, his gaze running up and down him as if assessing him. Bluntly, though not unkindly, Mr Clegg said, 'Home on a spot of leave, a' ya, lad?'

The flush rose in Kenny's face at once. 'Well, no, actually . . .'

'Ah, reserved occupation, is it? On yar dad's farm?' Now there was the tiniest note of disapproval in his tone.

Fleur caught and held the big man's gaze. Quietly, she said, 'Kenny's only seventeen, Mr Clegg.'

'I'll be joining up next year,' Kenny put in. 'Soon as I can.'

Mr Clegg smiled. 'That's the spirit, lad. Pleased to hear it.' His face sobered. 'Same as me own boy. He joined up, though his mam wanted him to stay wi' me on the farm. But I was in the last lot. Two years in the trenches, I was, and never a scratch.' He paused before saying in a low voice, 'I was lucky, though. I know that.'

Fleur nodded. 'Our dad was too. He was wounded and has a stiff leg, but at least he came back.' She bit her lip before she added quietly, 'A lot from the town never did.'

'Aye,' the big farmer sighed heavily. 'Bad business,

it was. And now they've no more sense than to get us involved in another one.' He sighed. 'Aye well, I wish you luck, young feller. When you go. Good luck to you.'

Kenny nodded. 'And I hope your son's – all right.'

'Aye, so do I, lad. So do I. He's all we've got. If owt happens to him, the missis will never forgive me.' His voice was low as he added, 'Won't forgive mesen, if it comes to that.' Then briskly he shook himself and smiled. 'Aye well, let's not dwell on all that. Not when there's work to be done. Look, I tell you what, you carry on here now loading up and if I've got me own work done, I'll see if I can come with you. Give you a bit of a hand, like.'

'Oh, Mr Clegg. Are you sure? You must have such a lot to do, 'specially if you're on your own now.'

'Aye, there is. But I'm never too busy to help a neighbour. Old Arthur Jackson used to work for me, see? Good man, he was. Worked on this farm most of his life – well, the latter part of it anyway. I'd like to help his widow.'

Fleur and Kenny grinned at him. 'Then we'll gladly accept your offer,' Fleur said.

'Right you are, then. Come and find me when you're ready to go. In fact, come to the back door of the house. I'm sure the missis will find you a drink and a bit of summat to eat.'

'There you are, you see,' Kenny said, as the farmer moved out of earshot. 'What did I tell you? Even a nice man like Mr Clegg questions why a big lad like me isn't in uniform.'

'Yes, but you soon will be, won't you?'

'Yeah,' Kenny said, firmly. 'And the sooner the better.'

At that moment, a cloud crossed the sun and a sharp breeze brought a chill to the bright day. Fleur shuddered, then snatched up the fork and attacked the pile of manure as if her life – and Kenny's too – depended upon it.

'By heck, you've done a grand job with this back garden,' Mr Clegg said three hours later as he stood surveying all their hard work.

'My sister's done most of it,' Kenny said and then, as Fleur walked away from them to fetch mugs of tea, he added slyly, 'when she's not on duty at the airfield.'

The farmer's eyebrows rose. 'Yon lass? She's in the forces?'

Kenny nodded. 'She's a WAAF. She's an R/T operator. Talks to all the aircraft when they land. That sort of thing.'

Mr Clegg pulled a face. 'Tough job. Specially if you get to know the airmen, like.'

'There's one she's particularly close to,' Kenny confided.

'Not the best place to be then,' the big man murmured, but as Fleur came back their conversation ceased.

'How are we going to get it all round to the back?' she asked, handing out the mugs of tea.

'Tell you what,' the farmer suggested. 'I'll take it round into the field at the bottom of her garden and tip it there. It'll be easier to chuck it over the fence.'

Fleur eyed the grass field where cows grazed contentedly. 'Will the farmer who owns that field mind, d'you think?'

The big man laughed. 'Shouldn't think so. Them's my cows and it's my field.'

When Ruth arrived home, she stood staring in astonishment at the farmer on top of a pile of manure in the neighbouring field, rhythmically flinging forkfuls over the fence into the garden. Then at Fleur and Kenny, who were moving it and spreading it over the surface of the garden and digging it into the earth. All three of them were red faced and sweating, but they worked on as a team.

Kenny looked up and grinned at her. 'Hi, Ruth. Come to lend a hand?'

Fleur looked up and grinned mischievously. 'There's another fork over there.'

'Not on your nelly!' Ruth was horrified. She wrinkled her nose. 'Pooh, what a pong.'

Fleur closed her eyes and breathed in deeply. 'Nothing like it. Best perfume in the world.'

'Dead right there's nothing like it, but I don't know about the last bit. *Eau de cochon*? No thanks! Count this townie out. Tell you what, though, I'll make you all a nice cuppa. Will that do?'

There was a heartfelt unanimous chorus of 'Yes, please', and Ruth held up her hand, fingers spread out. 'Give me five minutes to get out of my uniform.'

'Sounds heaven,' Fleur called.

The promised minutes later, they stood in the tiny back yard, drinking tea, eating scones and admiring their handiwork.

'What a' ya thinking of planting, lass?' Mr Clegg looked to Fleur as the leader of the venture.

'Potatoes, carrots, leeks, cabbages. Runner beans in

the front garden. Oh don't let's forget to take some of the manure round the front.'

'It'll cost you a fortune to grow all that lot,' Ruth exclaimed.

'Dad's promised me some seeds.'

'Now mebbe I can help you there,' the farmer put in. 'I'll have a word with the locals and see if we can put a bit of a collection together. Not money, lass,' he added hastily. 'But a few seed 'taties, an' that.'

Fleur's eyes filled with tears. 'Oh, how kind of you. That'd be wonderful.'

'Aye well,' the man said gruffly, touched by her gratitude, 'we've all got to pull together. All got to do our bit. There is—'

And they all chorused together, '. . . a war on, you know.'

Sixteen

Later the following morning, after a few hours' sleep, Fleur reluctantly returned to digging out the foundations for the Anderson shelter. She'd managed to dig the oblong shape to a depth of about a foot when the curved sheets of corrugated steel arrived for the shelter.

'Ya'll need to be another three foot down, luv,' the man who made the delivery advised, nodding his head towards the hole.

'I know. It's harder than I thought. This ground hasn't been dug over for some time and certainly not four-foot deep.'

'Ah, well, I wish I could give you a hand but I've still three more shelters to deliver today. I'd best be getting on . . .'

'Would you like a cup of tea?' Fleur asked.

'Nah, lass, ah'm all right. Had one at the last house.' He set off back along the narrow garden path, having deposited his delivery near where Fleur was working. 'Good luck, lass. I reckon you're going to need it.'

'Thanks!' Fleur muttered wryly but she gave him a cheery wave.

She'd dug for another ten minutes and then sat on the edge of the hole for a breather when she heard the chugging sound of an engine that sounded vaguely familiar. 'Can't be,' she muttered. The noise died away and she shrugged, stood up and, with a sigh, picked up her spade once more.

She'd dug five more spadefuls when a voice said, 'You look as if you could use a little help, love.'

Fleur stopped, looked up and then dropped her spade with a squeal of delight. She flung her arms wide as she scrambled out of the hole. 'Dad! And Kenny too! Whatever are you doing here?' Her face clouded. 'Oh, there's nothing wrong, is there? Is Mum all right?'

'She's fine,' Jake laughed as he gathered his daughter, earthy hands and all, into a bear hug.

'Then why are you here?'

'A little bird told me you were planning to put up an Anderson for the old folk to use and finding the digging a bit tough.' He shrugged. 'So, here we are. We thought a little help wouldn't come amiss.'

'Come amiss!' Fleur echoed. 'You're heaven sent!'

'Right,' Kenny grinned. 'I'll go and get the tools out of the boot while you take Dad to meet Mrs Jackson. And I've no doubt Harry will be popping his head over the fence any minute now . . .'

Right on cue, as they moved towards Mrs Jackson's cottage, the old man appeared round the corner with his usual greeting, 'Now then, lass.'

Fleur and Kenny leant against each other, unable to stem their laughter, but Jake merely smiled broadly and moved towards the old man, his hand outstretched. 'You must be Harry. I've heard a lot about you. I'm Jake Bosley, Fleur and Kenny's dad.'

Harry beamed as he shook hands. 'I'm real glad to meet you. You've a fine couple o' bairns, Mr Bosley.'

'Jake – please.'

If it could, Harry's beam widened even further. 'Have you met Mary yet?'

'No. We were just on our way in to say "hello" before we get digging.'

'Ah. Come to give the lass a bit of a hand have you. It's a big job on her own and I'm afraid I'm past that sort of digging mesen else I'd've . . .'

'Of course,' Jake said and put his hand on the old man's shoulder.

'Well, come and meet Mary. I'll introduce you. She'll be glad to meet you an' all. Thinks a lot of yon lass, an' that lad o' yourn an' all. Tells me he can't wait to join up.'

Jake's face sobered. 'Aye.'

Harry stopped on his way towards the back door of the cottage and faced Jake in surprise. 'You don't sound too pleased about it.'

Jake sighed. For some reason he couldn't at this precise moment fathom, he felt he could confide in the old man. 'It's not me, it's his mam. She . . . she wants to keep her chicks safely at home and because we live on a farm she can't understand why they even want to go.'

'Were you in the last lot?'

'Aye. I volunteered.'

'Then *you* know why they want to be involved?'

Jake nodded. 'Oh yes. I know why.'

'We lost our lad in the last war. Nearly broke my Doris's heart when the telegram came. But we were still proud of him. To this day, I'm proud of him. The only sad thing is that these youngsters have got to do it all again now. Don't seem right, does it?'

'No. It doesn't. But they'll do it. They'll do it all right.'

'Oh, I know that. Whilst we've got young 'uns like yourn there . . .' He nodded towards Fleur and Kenny. 'And that young feller of hers, then we'll win. No doubt about that. It's just – well – what we might lose along the way, eh?'

Now Jake couldn't speak for the sudden fear that arose in his throat, so he just gently squeezed the old man's shoulder.

Harry nodded understandingly and then opened the door and called cheerily, 'Hello, Mary, love. Got a visitor for you. Fleur's dad.'

Mrs Jackson was standing at the kitchen table, her hands floury as she rolled out pastry. She looked up and smiled a welcome as Harry opened the door and ushered Jake into the room.

'Sorry I can't shake hands but come in, do. You're very welcome.' She glanced beyond him. 'Is your wife with you?'

'Er – no. She stayed to mind the farm. But Kenny's here.'

Mrs Jackson's beam plumped up her cheeks so that her glasses rose. 'He's a lovely boy. So helpful. Please, Mr Bosley, do sit down. I'll make a cup of tea.'

'No, no, don't trouble just now. We've come to help Fleur with the shelter for you both.'

Mrs Jackson gasped and pushed up her glasses to wipe a tear away, leaving a smudge of flour on her face. 'How kind you all are.'

At that moment Kenny pushed open the back door and deposited a box on Mrs Jackson's table. 'Just a few eggs and a bit of butter from our dairy. And I think there's a chicken in there.' He grinned. 'Plucked and dressed with my own fair hands.' He nodded towards Harry. 'It's for you both. And we killed a pig last week. Dad's got a licence, of course. So there's some sausages and a piece of pork. Oh, and a couple of rabbits as well, but I haven't had time to skin them. But Fleur can do them for you.'

'Oh, I don't know what to say. I really don't.' Mrs Jackson was lost for words.

'You're looking after Fleur for us, Mrs Jackson. It's the very least we can do,' Jake said softly. 'Now, where's that pick we brought, Kenny? We'd best get cracking.'

The earth yielded willingly to Jake's experienced wielding of the pointed pickaxe. When he paused for a breather, Kenny shovelled out the broken-up earth whilst Fleur ferried mugs of tea down the path. The hole sank steadily deeper. 'Don't make yourself late, Dad. You ought to get home before milking time.'

'Just a few minutes more, luv, and I think it'll be deep enough. Can you manage to put up the shelter?'

'Yes, Robbie and Ruth will give me a hand with that as soon as they can.'

'Where is Ruth? Is she due back soon?' Kenny asked, pausing for a breather and mopping his forehead.

'No, sorry, she's on duty.'

Kenny's face fell. 'Oh well, give her my love, won't you?'

Jake climbed out of the hole and brushed the earth from his trousers. 'There. I think that'll do.'

As they gathered the tools together to take back to the car, Fleur said, 'Where've you built one at home?'

'I haven't.' Jake laughed. 'I can't see us getting bombed in the middle of nowhere, can you? It's different for these folk here, though. They're likely to catch a few stray bombs being aimed at the airfield.'

'Oh, Dad, I think you should build one. You never know.'

'But we can't even hear the sirens, love. Only very faintly in the distance and then only if we happen to be outside. If we're in bed asleep, we'd never hear them anyway. Besides, your mam'd never use it. "Can't waste my time sitting in here when there's work to be done," she'd say. You know she would.'

'You might have to build one if you're going to have Land Army girls.'

'I don't think I need them. Old Ron says he'll lend a hand when he can.'

Old Ron, as Jake now called him, and his family had lived in a cottage on Middleditch Farm for as long as Fleur could remember. He'd worked for her father and for the Smallwoods before that until his retirement a few years earlier. He was still fit and healthy and liked to help out at lambing and at harvest time.

'You will when I go, Dad,' Kenny said, throwing the spades into the back of the car.

Jake sighed. 'Aye well, I'll think about that when the time comes.'

'You off, then?' Harry hobbled round the corner of the cottage and stood beside Fleur as they all said their goodbyes.

'Well, I think so, unless you can come back with us, Fleur? Kenny said he didn't think you were on duty until tomorrow afternoon. Will it be all right? We could be sure to get you back tomorrow morning.'

Fleur forced a smile. Part of her didn't really want to go home, didn't want to face more antagonism and censure from her mother, yet she could see that both Jake and Kenny wanted to snatch another few hours with her. 'I'll risk it. I'll just get my things . . .'

As she ran upstairs she was thinking: at least it might keep my mind off Robbie; but in her heart she knew it wouldn't. Oh I wonder if he's asked her yet, she couldn't help thinking as she slipped out of her workaday clothes and back into her uniform. I wonder if he knows already . . .

Seventeen

'Mother dear . . .' Robbie began, using the more formal address he'd adopted as quite a young boy when he was trying to wheedle his way around her.

Meg smiled archly at him. 'Oho, and what is it you're wanting now?'

He took her hand and led her to sit on the sofa in front of the fire. 'I need to talk to you.'

He'd been at home for two days and was due to return to camp the next morning. He was glad to have been there for he'd been on hand to help his mother bring his grandfather home from the hospital. The old man was much better, glad to be home and tucked up warmly in his own room upstairs. And now was Robbie's last chance to talk to his mother.

'Oh dear, this sounds serious,' Meg said gaily. 'What have you been up to now? Have I got to write an apologetic letter to your commanding officer – just like I had to so many times to your headmaster?'

Robbie forced a laugh, though at this moment he didn't feel like laughing. His mother, sensitive to her beloved son's feelings, said softly, 'What is it, love? Something's troubling you, I can see that.'

'Ma – I want to ask you about my father.'

He heard her pull in breath sharply and her green eyes were suddenly round, dark pools of anxiety.

My God, Meg was thinking. He's heard something.

They've told him something. It must have been that day just after he'd first met her. He must have gone to the farm, met Fleur's parents . . . They must have said something.

I should have tried to stop him seeing Fleur, she thought in panic. But how could I, she asked herself, her mind in a turmoil, when they're stationed on the same camp? She licked her dry lips and said unsteadily, 'What about your father?'

'There's no easy way to put this, Ma, so I'll just come right out and say it.'

'Don't you always?' she murmured, though her heart was thumping madly in her chest. Her son was one of the most honest, reliable and straightforward people she had ever known in her life. Even more so than Jake.

Jake, oh Jake! What did you say to him? Are you still so bitter after all this time that you would wreak such a revenge on me?

Clasped in his huge, warm hands, Meg's own hand trembled. Robbie felt it. 'It's all right, Ma. I don't want to upset you, dearest, but I have to know. It's important to me. To me and Fleur.'

Meg's head shot up. 'You – and Fleur?'

'Uh-huh. We . . . we want to go on seeing each other, but there's something going on that we don't understand. That we don't know about. Ever since we met, it's . . . it's been very . . .' He sought for the right word. 'It's been very strange. In fact, it started that very first day when you were so surprised to hear Fleur's name.'

Meg tried to pull her hand away from his, but he held her fast, though gently. She gave a huge sigh and sagged against his shoulder. She closed her eyes for a moment and two tears squeezed their way out from under her eyelids and ran down her face, making a salty rivulet down her carefully applied face powder.

'Oh, Ma, don't cry. I hate to do this, but we *have* to know.' Gently, he wiped her tears away. It was so like Jake's tender gesture all those years before – the very last time she had seen him – that her tears just flowed all the harder. 'And then when you thought it best if you didn't go with me to Fleur's home. And you were right. When I got there – well, to tell the truth, I didn't even get as far as the farm. Fleur met me in the lane and said that when she'd told her parents about me, her mother had become hysterical, shouting and screaming and saying all kinds of – well – odd things. Things that Fleur couldn't understand.' He paused but his mother was silent, trying to put off the dreaded moment for as long as possible.

I'll lose him, Meg was thinking. If he finds out the truth, he'll have nothing more to do with me. Oh, and I've tried so hard over the last few years to make amends for all the wicked things I did. I've tried so hard, Jake, I truly have. She took a deep breath and said, 'All right. What is it you want to know?'

'Was . . . was Percy Rodwell my real father?'

Meg raised her head slowly and looked into his eyes – her dearest, darling boy who'd been conceived in a few moments of passion with a man she now realized she'd never truly loved. A man who, though infatuated with her, had been too afraid of losing his standing in the eyes of the community. A man who'd deserted her when she had needed him most. There was only one man she'd ever really loved in her whole life, only she had been too blind, too grasping, too afraid of living a life of poverty, to recognize it. And now this son of hers, who'd grown up to be such a wonderful human being, the son whom she had almost given away to that dreadful woman, was going to find out all about her. All her sins were going to be revealed and she would have to pay the price. This was to be her punishment.

She was going to lose him.

His hands tightened around hers until he was hurting her. 'Who is my father, Ma?' he demanded harshly. 'Is it Fleur's dad? Are we . . . are we half-brother and sister?'

'Jake!' The relief flooded through Meg. So this was what it was all about. 'Oh no, no, it wasn't Jake.' She laughed, light-headed with relief.

He was still holding her hand tightly, but now she didn't mind. 'Is that really true? We're not related in any way? Me and Fleur, I mean?'

Meg shook her head. 'No, you're not.'

His grip on her relaxed and he let out the longest sigh she'd ever heard as if releasing all the tension inside him.

She swallowed and tried to ask casually, 'Whatever gave you that idea?' She was regaining her composure now enough to pretend offence. 'And fancy thinking such a thing of your mother.'

'Oh, Ma, I'm sorry.' He drew her into his bear hug and she stayed there, closing her eyes with thankfulness. 'It's just . . . it's just some of the things Fleur's mother said when she was having her "ducky fit" as Fleur called it.'

An inner voice was telling Meg to let it lie, to ask no more, but before she could stop the words coming out, she'd said, 'What did she say?' And when he told her, she closed her eyes again. Was it true? Had Jake loved her all these years, just as she had loved him? But Robbie's voice was dragging her back to the present and now his words filled her with dread once more.

'And there was something else funny happened. We met a woman in a cafe in the town and she seemed about to pass out at the sight of me. Fleur called her "Aunt Louisa". She was the local doctor's wife.'

'My dear, what is it? You don't seem yourself? Are you ill? I could prescribe something for you if—'

'Don't fuss, Philip. I'm perfectly all right.'

Philip Collins blinked. It was so totally out of character for his wife to snap in such a way. Louisa was usually so calm, serene and in control of herself. She was the perfect wife for a doctor, for any man, if it came to that. And yet . . . He sighed inwardly. She was beautiful. She dressed elegantly and was a perfect receptionist for his patients. She soothed them and marshalled them with a gentle hand. She smoothed his path through life and had supported him in everything he had ever done.

So why, oh why, could he not forget the red-haired firebrand with whom he'd once fancied himself in love? He'd almost given up everything for her; his infatuation for the passionate, persuasive young woman had nearly been his downfall. But he'd not had the courage, if that was the right word to apply to what would have been such an act of betrayal. Betrayal of his wife, his upbringing and his vocation. It would have meant the end of his career as a doctor, and he'd realized that he loved that more than any human being. More even than *her*.

So he had turned his back on his mistress and her son and for the last twenty-two years he'd lived a model life as the caring doctor, the dutiful husband with a perfect wife. There was only one thing that disappointed him and now it was never spoken of between them. It was the tragedy of their lives that he and Louisa had never been blessed with children. Was it a punishment, he had so often wondered, because he had not been man enough to shoulder his responsibilities, as a man of honour would have done?

He had always loved Louisa – of course he had, ever since he'd met her when she was a lowly schoolmarm, struggling to support her widowed mother. But he had to admit now that he'd never quite loved her with the unbridled passion he'd felt for—

Louisa was reaching out to him across the dinner table. 'I'm so sorry, Philip dear. I didn't mean to be snappy. It's just this war. All the privations, the anxiety I see on the faces of all your patients, especially those with husbands or sons or sweethearts in the services. I . . . I . . .' She hesitated, about to touch on something which had always been a painful subject between them. 'I never thought I'd say it, Philip,' she whispered. 'But I'm almost glad we didn't have children, if that's the heartbreak it brings.'

Philip patted her hand and smiled thinly. His blue eyes were kindly yet shadowed with hidden thoughts and memories, but he said nothing. Whatever he was thinking, he kept it to himself.

She couldn't tell him the truth, the real reason for her bout of bad temper; she was worried sick in case he ever came face to face with the young man she'd seen with Fleur Bosley. Robbie Rodwell. Meg's boy. What would happen if Philip saw him? She felt sick at the thoughts that tumbled around her mind in a riot of fear. Would he see the likeness? Of course he would. It would be like turning the clock back and looking into the mirror of his youth. She wondered if he'd always known. She remembered Meg coming to the house once with the child in her arms, but what had passed between doctor and patient remained a secret behind the surgery door.

Had Philip known Meg's boy was his son? Perhaps he had and he'd kept the secret from her, his wife, all these years. So, Louisa thought bitterly, the whispered gossip all those years ago had been true. There had been something between Philip and Meg. It was obvious now and, surely, neither of them could deny it any longer. You only had to look at the boy to see the truth.

She wasn't sure which hurt her the most. The fact that her husband had been unfaithful to her, had had a son all this time, or the fact that he had never told her about any of it.

So, Meg was thinking at that very same moment, Louisa has seen him. Mechanically, she tucked her father in bed and saw that the lamp and the glass of water were in easy reach on the bedside table, but her mind was elsewhere. She was so thankful her father was home from hospital and out of danger, but he'd need careful nursing for some time. Kissing the old man's forehead, she turned off the light and went downstairs. Robbie was in bed and sleeping soundly now that she had given him the answer he wanted. He'd be up early in the morning and on his way back to camp, back to the girl he loved. Fleur Bosley.

Meg sat down in front of the dying embers of the fire. She kicked off her shoes and sighed heavily. Why Fleur? Why *Jake's* daughter? Of all the people in the world, why did Robbie have to meet her? And fall in love with her?

Fate had played a dirty trick on Meg. Yet, she was honest enough now to admit that perhaps she deserved it. She wasn't proud of some of the things she'd done as a girl, yet she'd tried to make amends. From the moment of Robbie's birth she had changed. For the first time in her life she'd loved someone more than she cared about herself. From the moment he'd stared up at her with those bright blue eyes, she had adored him, worshipped and idolized him. She'd never loved anyone quite like that before. Not even Jake, though she now knew that he'd been the love of her life up until the time her son had screamed his way into the world and wound himself around her heart.

She stared into the glowing coals. How strange life was, she mused, that her son and Jake's daughter should meet and fall in love. How ironic. And how catastrophic, for she knew without a doubt that Betsy would never agree to such a union. And yet she hadn't been able to lie to her son. It would've been so easy to tell him that, yes, they were half-brother and sister, that they couldn't – mustn't – be together. Yet she couldn't do it. She'd had to tell him the truth. There'd been enough lies and deceit in the past. It was time now for the truth to be told, whatever the consequences might be.

Much as she might have wished it all these years, Jake was not Robbie's natural father. But then, neither was her dead husband, Percy Rodwell. She shuddered afresh as she remembered Robbie's final words.

'We met a woman in a cafe in the town and she seemed about to pass out at the sight of me.'

Well, she would, wouldn't she? Meg closed her eyes and groaned aloud. Louisa would see the likeness at once.

Robbie's likeness to her own husband.

Eighteen

With trembling fingers, Louisa reached for the telephone receiver. Her heart was racing. What she was about to do was unethical, and if Philip were to find out . . . But she had to know. Years ago, when she'd heard the gossip about her husband's frequent visits to the little cottage near the church, she had dismissed them. She'd trusted Philip completely. But seeing Meg's son – the image of Philip as a young man – she feared now that the rumours had been true.

Louisa bit her lip, pulled in a deep breath and began to dial the first number on the list in front of her.

When a woman's voice answered, Louisa said, 'I'm sorry to bother you. This is Dr Collins' wife from South Monkford. My husband . . .' She faltered for a brief moment over the deliberate lie she was about to utter. 'My husband has asked me to try to trace a former patient of his. She left the district without informing us and we . . . we still have her medical records here. We know she moved to Nottingham . . .' Louisa was babbling now, a nervous note creeping into her voice. She tried to calm herself again.

The woman's voice on the other end of the telephone was stiff and uncooperative. 'The usual way is for the new doctor with whom the patient has registered to send for their records.'

'Yes, yes, I know, but . . .'

The woman unbent a little. 'Well, I will have a look and see if the patient has registered with us. Of course, there are several other doctors in the city.'

Louisa glanced down at the rather long list on the desk in front of her, hoping it wouldn't prove necessary to phone every one of them. 'Yes, yes, I realize that,' she said.

'What name is it you're looking for?'

'Meg Rodwell. Mrs Meg Rodwell.'

'Hold on one moment.'

There was a lengthy silence whilst Louisa grew more and more agitated. She glanced nervously towards the window. Philip was out on his morning rounds, but that didn't mean he might not arrive back home at any moment.

'I'm sorry.' The woman's voice sounded again in her ear. 'But we have no one of that name recorded with us.'

'Thank you for your time,' Louisa said. 'Goodbye.'

She tried four more numbers and was met with a similar reluctance to give out information. Two even refused to look for the name in their records. 'I couldn't possibly divulge such information. You could be anyone ringing up . . .'

Louisa almost slammed the receiver back into its cradle in her frustration.

On the sixth attempt a young girl's voice answered merrily, 'Good morning. Dr Gough's surgery.'

Louisa repeated her request and gave Meg's name.

'Hold on. I'll look for you.' The girl voiced no concern and Louisa felt a sudden stab of guilt that she might be getting her into trouble. But within moments the girl was back on the line. 'Yes, we have a patient of that name.'

Louisa held her breath, willing the girl to give her Meg's address without her having to ask outright for it, hoping the young receptionist wouldn't realize that Meg had been their patient for years and the story of the 'lost notes' was nothing but a ruse.

As if the gods were now smiling kindly, the girl rattled off the name of the street and even the number of Meg's home in the city.

'Thank you, thank you very much,' Louisa said weakly. As she was about to replace the receiver, the girl said, 'So you'll send her notes through to us, will you? Have you got our address?'

'Oh – oh yes. Yes, I have it here.' It was on the list in front of her. 'Thank you for your help.'

'Don't mention it,' the girl said gaily, oblivious to the fact that she had given out confidential information to a stranger.

Louisa replaced the receiver slowly. She had not even bothered to write down Meg's address. She would remember it only too well.

When Meg opened her door, it was perhaps one of the biggest shocks of her life to see the woman standing on her doorstep.

'My God!' she breathed. 'Louisa.'

The two women stared at each other until Louisa said calmly, 'Good morning, Meg. May I come in?'

Meg looked nervously up and down the street. Robbie had gone into the city, but he could be back at any moment. The last thing she wanted was for him to run into Louisa. He might start asking more awkward questions. But neither could she make Louisa unwelcome.

'Oh yes, I'm sorry. Of course.' Meg pulled the door wider and gestured for Louisa to step inside straight into the front room of the terraced house. 'Please excuse the mess. This is my workroom – as you can see.'

Louisa looked around her. The room was strewn with paper patterns, materials and pins. On the table in the centre of the room stood a Singer sewing machine.

'I make my living as a dressmaker,' Meg explained, gesturing nervously with a hand that still shook from the surprise. She tried to calm her whirling thoughts.

'So,' Louisa was saying smoothly. 'Your husband taught you well, did he?' She was much more in control. But then it was she who had chosen to come here. She had had time to marshal her thoughts and her emotions.

'May I offer you a cup of tea?' Meg said, ignoring the remark and playing for time. But she guessed the reason for this visit. 'Please come through to the back room. We'll be more comfortable there.' She led the way through and Louisa seated herself in front of the range whilst Meg went through into a back scullery.

As she listened to the rattle of cups and saucers, Louisa glanced about her. There was little in the room that gave any indication of Meg's former life. No photographs, no obvious relics from Percy Rodwell's house. Perhaps the only thing she had kept had been his sewing machine. No doubt, Louisa thought bitterly, it wasn't her own husband whom Meg wished to remember.

Meg came back into the room and set the tray on the table. She poured a cup of tea and offered her visitor a biscuit.

'They're rather dry, I'm afraid.' She pulled a face. 'The war, you know.'

Louisa smiled thinly and shook her head. 'No, thank you. The tea is fine.'

Meg sat down opposite, but she was still on edge, listening for any sound that heralded Robbie's return. As they sipped their tea the two women regarded each other. They each saw in the other's face the changes the years had brought.

They were each thinking that the years had been kind to the other. Louisa was dressed in smart clothes, well tailored and expensive. Whilst Meg wore a fashionable dress, she had made it herself from a length of material bought on a market stall. Louisa's complexion was smooth and well cared for. She was the epitome of a doctor's wife – serene and sweet and caring. Her hair, still black, was smoothed into a chignon and showed no sign of grey.

And Meg's too belied her age. Her luxurious red hair was swept up into waves and rolls and her figure was still slim; her legs beneath the short hem of her dress were shapely and she wore silk stockings. I wonder how she can afford those, Louisa thought uncharitably.

She was the first to speak. 'I met your son recently.'

Meg felt a sudden flush through the whole of her body and her heart was pounding so loudly she was sure Louisa must hear it. 'Oh?' Her voice was unnaturally high and she fought again to control her feelings.

'He was in a cafe in South Monkford with Fleur. Fleur Bosley.' She laid emphasis on the name.

'Oh yes.' Meg forced a smile and set her cup and saucer on the tray. She was so afraid that her trembling hands would give her away. 'Robbie brought her home. They'd bumped into each other – literally – on the station. In the blackout. She . . . she couldn't get transport home that night so . . . so Robbie brought her here.'

'What a coincidence!'

'Yes, wasn't it?'

There was an uncomfortable pause before Louisa, staring hard at Meg, said, 'He's a very good-looking young man.'

Meg managed to hold down the fear climbing into her throat and said, 'I think so, but then I could be biased.'

And then the question she had been dreading came.

'He's not like Percy, is he? Or you. So who does he take after?'

Louisa was looking directly into her eyes, holding Meg's gaze. It was so obvious that she had seen the likeness to her own husband in the young man's features. As he had grown, Robbie had become even more like his natural father. It had been Meg's ever-constant fear that one day someone from South Monkford would meet her son. And of all people it had to be Jake's daughter.

What a cruel and devious mistress fate was.

Meg felt suddenly calm. She knew what she must do. She had thought she could tell the truth now and, as the saying went, 'shame the devil'. But she found she couldn't do it. Once Robbie had the answer he wanted, he hadn't pushed to learn more. And now, Meg doubted he would. So, for all their sakes, she must tell the biggest lie of her life and she must make Louisa believe it. She smiled, serene now in her decision. 'He's like my father.'

Louisa looked startled. 'Your father?'

Meg nodded, growing more confident with each minute that passed and warming to her story. 'Yes. He was fair haired and blue eyed, just like Robbie. Of course,' she added, feigning innocence, as if she had just realized, 'you never knew my father, did you? He lives with us now.' She gestured to the room above them. 'But he's very frail. He doesn't get up until dinnertime. Mind you.' Meg forced a laugh. 'You'd be hard pressed to see the likeness. He's white haired and crippled with rheumatism. And he's just home from the hospital. A nasty bout of pneumonia. We're lucky he's survived it.' Silently, she prayed that her father would not choose this morning to get up earlier. There was no likeness to see between grandfather and grandson. Never could have been. Her father, Reuben, had had brown hair and eyes.

'No,' Louisa was saying, 'I never met him.' She was surprised to hear that the old man was living with his daughter. Had Meg really forgiven him – the man she had vowed never to see again? My goodness, Louisa thought, Meg really must have changed. She was tempted to ask more, but it was Meg's son who interested Louisa. If what Meg was telling her was true, then perhaps she'd been wrong. Perhaps the gossip about Philip's friendship with this woman all those years ago was unfounded. Maybe he'd been what he always said he'd been to Meg. Just a friend.

Louisa set her cup down and clasped her hands in her lap. The whiteness of her knuckles was the only sign of her inner turmoil. Her voice was quite steady as she said, 'We never had children, you know. It has been a great disappointment to us both, especially to Philip.' She stared directly into Meg's eyes as she added deliberately, 'He'd have loved a son.'

Meg returned her gaze. 'I'm sorry,' she said gently. In those simple words there was a world of apology for everything that had happened in the past between them. All the misunderstandings, all the hurt. In the briefest of moments there passed between them a flash of understanding of the truth, though they both knew that neither of them would ever voice it. And Meg emphasized this again as, choosing her words carefully so that she gave nothing away but implied everything, she added, 'It has always been my greatest sorrow that poor Percy did not live. *Robbie's father would have been so proud of his son.*'

They stared at each other for what seemed an age, before Louisa dropped her gaze and said, 'Yes, I . . . I'm sure he would.'

After a few moments, she stood up and took her leave. The two women kissed each other's cheek awkwardly. At the door, Louisa said solemnly, 'Goodbye, Meg.' Then she turned and walked up the street, her head held high. From the doorway, Meg watched her go, knowing it was unlikely that they'd ever meet again. Nor would she ever meet Philip again. Louisa would see to that.

Louisa's step was lighter. She would never tell Philip about her meeting with Meg. She knew, in her heart, that Robbie Rodwell was Philip's son, but Meg had given her a credible story: a story she herself would use if it were ever needed to confound the gossips. But strangely the truth was easier to deal with than the terrible doubts. Not knowing had been far worse.

Louisa smiled. Now she knew what to do. When

the war ended – and surely the end must come soon – she would encourage Philip to take a well-earned retirement and move away.

The south coast perhaps, Wales or Scotland. She would let him choose. Just so long as it was miles away from South Monkford.

Nineteen

Fleur was counting the hours until Robbie got back from his leave and praying that, this time, he would be able to talk to his mother.

The first night had passed quickly enough as she'd been on duty and now, on the second night, she had come home with her father and Kenny, and the time seemed to tick by so slowly. She said nothing to her parents, did not even mention Robbie's name, but she was edgy and distracted, her thoughts miles away. Her forced gaiety, punctuated by long, uneasy silences, alerted both Jake and Betsy.

'She's still seeing him. I know she is.' Betsy was threatening to become hysterical again.

Jake tried to calm her. 'Maybe so, love. But there's nothing we can do to stop it. And you know what they say, the more parents try to stop their offspring doing something, then the more they'll want to.'

'Don't I know it? Just look at them both. Won't listen to a word we say, will they? What's the world coming to, Jake? Just think what it was like for us as kids. They don't know they're born today.'

They exchanged a glance. Their shared past was something they never spoke of – not even their children knew anything about their parents' childhood.

Jake sighed. 'It's not easy for them, love. Not with this war on.'

'We lived through a war, didn't we? We had to cope. You with the terrible life in those trenches. Me worrying every minute of every day, dreading the telegram or seeing your name in the casualty lists in the paper.'

'I know. But this one's different. It's so much closer to home with the bombing. In the last lot most of it happened abroad, but this time it's on our doorstep.' He forced a smile. 'Come on, Betsy love, let's not spoil the precious few hours we have with her. We'll both take her to the station in Newark tomorrow morning and see her off. Then you can do a bit of shopping afterwards, love. How about that, eh? Time you had a trip out and a bit of a treat. Now, let's get the supper on the table and have a nice evening – all of us together, eh?'

'Well, maybe we could,' Betsy said tartly, 'if only Kenny would come home when he's supposed to. Where is he now, I'd like to know? Dashed off out as soon as you all got home. He's missed helping you with the evening milking again. I'll clip his ear for him when he gets back.'

'It's all right, love. Fleur helped me tonight. I think she quite enjoys keeping her hand in when she's on leave.' It was the wrong thing to say and Jake could have bitten his tongue off the moment he'd said it, for it prompted his wife to say tartly, 'She'd have been better "keeping her hand in" all the time instead of swanning off to become an officer's ground-sheet.'

'Betsy! I won't have you talking about our Fleur like that or any other WAAF, if it comes to that. They're a grand lot of lasses.'

Betsy pursed her lips and said no more but the loud

clattering of dishes in the scullery left Jake in no doubt of her feelings.

Supper was ready on the table by the time the back door opened and Kenny burst into the house, his face wreathed in smiles. 'I've done it! I've joined up!'

Betsy gave a little scream, covered her mouth with her hand and sat down suddenly, staring at him with wide, fearful eyes, but Jake and Fleur stared at him in puzzlement.

'What are you talking about, lad? You're not eighteen till next year.'

'I know.' Kenny was still beaming.

'But . . . but they won't take you till you're at least eighteen,' Fleur said.

Kenny's grin widened even further – if it were possible. 'No – but the Home Guard will. They'll take you at seventeen. I've joined the South Monkford Home Guard.'

Everyone in the room relaxed and Betsy was so overcome with relief that she almost fell off the chair. 'You bad boy – giving me a fright like that.' She pretended to smack him and then was hugging him and kissing him.

'Leave it out, Mum,' the young man said, red in the face whilst Jake and Fleur, relieved too, smiled at his embarrassment.

'So,' Betsy said gaily as they all sat down at the table and she began to serve out the rabbit pie, 'you won't need to join the forces now, will you? If you're in the Home Guard, you can stay here.'

There was a moment's silence as Kenny glanced at Jake and Fleur. 'It . . . it doesn't work quite like that,

Mum,' he told her quietly. 'I'm still going to volunteer for the RAF when I'm old enough.'

The plate Betsy was holding trembled slightly, and though she said no more, the light that had been in her eyes died instantly.

Determined to change the subject, Jake said, 'I think Blossom's going to calve any day now and I reckon she's carrying two.'

Robbie saw the three of them standing together at one end of the platform. Quickly, he shrank back into the carriage lest Fleur should glance in his direction. He sat well back, watching them. Strangely, it wasn't Fleur who captured his interest this morning, but her father. So this was the man who had perhaps loved his mother. He narrowed his eyes, trying to see him clearly, but the distance between them was too great. Robbie sighed. He'd dearly love to meet Fleur's dad, but . . .

The whistle sounded and uniformed men and women from all the services jostled each other good-naturedly as they rushed to board the train. Last farewells were said, hugs and kisses exchanged. Robbie stayed back until he saw Fleur look up and down the train, deciding which carriage to climb into. Then he moved to the open door of the carriage and leant out, calling her name and waving to attract her attention amongst all the hustle and bustle. She glanced round and, seeing him, hurried along the platform towards his carriage. Her father, carrying her bag, followed. Robbie held out his hand to her and hoisted her up into the carriage and then leant down again and held out his hand to take her bag. In that brief instant, he looked into the dark brown eyes of Fleur's father. Recognition was instant. Jake knew who he was. Robbie saw the older man catch his breath as, almost in a trance, he handed up the bag.

Fleur, standing beside Robbie, leant out too. ''Bye, Dad.' Then she waved to the woman standing like a statue on the platform, her gaze fixed upon Robbie. Fleur's wave faltered as her heart sank.

Her mother had seen him too.

The guard was moving along the platform, slamming doors and blowing his whistle. As the train began to move, there was no answering wave from her mother, nor, to Fleur's disappointment, from her father either. Though not together, they were both standing quite still, their gaze on Fleur, yet neither of them waved goodbye.

She ducked back into the carriage and sat down suddenly, her eyes filling with tears. Robbie sat beside her and took her hand.

'They didn't even wave,' she gulped.

'Darling – I'm so sorry. I should have stayed back out of sight. But . . . but I so wanted to travel with you. I couldn't wait a moment longer to tell you . . .'

Fleur's head shot up and her eyes widened as she saw that he was beaming, it seemed, from ear to ear.

'Oh, Robbie,' she gasped. 'Is it . . . is it really all right?'

He nodded and then she was in his arms, and behind them in the carriage there were whistles and catcalls and ribald laughter. But neither of them cared. They were laughing and crying and hugging each other.

As the train gathered speed and passed by the waving onlookers on the platform, through the window Jake saw it all. He sighed. Whatever Betsy wanted, he thought, nothing was going to keep those two apart. For a fleeting moment, he'd seen the joy on his daughter's face when she'd first caught sight of Robbie and hurried towards him.

It was the same joy he'd always felt when he saw Meg. And, deep in his heart, he knew that if she were to step onto the platform right this minute he would feel it again.

'What did you say to her? What did *she* say?'

As the train sped through the countryside towards Lincoln, Fleur was anxious for a verbatim report.

Robbie, all his anxiety gone now, laughed. 'This is like a debriefing. You sound just like Ruth.'

'True,' Fleur said, trying to adopt a stern tone. 'So get on with it Flight Sergeant Rodwell.'

He gave a mock salute. 'Yes, ma'am.'

Robbie recounted, word for word, what had passed between him and his mother. 'She pretended to be a bit indignant that I'd even thought such a thing of her, but I could tell she was only teasing me. It was strange,' he mused. 'When I first broached the subject she was very edgy, but when I asked her straight out who my father was – was it your father – she laughed. Yes, Fleur, she actually laughed, and like I said she pretended to be indignant.'

'But she denied it?'

'Oh yes – and it was the truth. I could see it was. But there was still – well – *something*.'

Fleur patted his hand. 'Maybe she doesn't like to be reminded of your father. Perhaps his death still affects her,' she said gently, referring to Meg's husband.

'Mmm. Maybe.' Robbie chewed his lower lip thoughtfully. 'She doesn't very often talk about him, come to think of it.' Then he smiled, determined to put it all out of his mind. They had the news they wanted – why worry about anything else? 'I'm sure you're right, sweetheart,' he murmured and, oblivious to the other passengers, he kissed her firmly on the mouth.

Twenty

Two weeks later, Fleur was busier than ever with the garden. The Anderson shelter had been constructed with the earth from the hole they'd dug placed back on top of it.

'Mek it a good thick layer, lass,' Harry had advised. 'And then you can plant summat on top.'

'Can I?' Fleur had eyed it sceptically.

'Aye, you can,' Harry had nodded. 'Lettuce or marrers. Summat that doesn't need a great depth of earth to grow in.'

So the area on top of the shelter was drawn in on Fleur's plan of the garden that she'd sketched out and kept on the shelf of the little table beneath Mrs Jackson's precious wireless.

The gifts of seed and small plants from the old lady's neighbours had been overwhelming, and now Fleur was anxious to get everything planted as soon as possible. 'These plants'll shrivel up if I don't get them in the ground,' she'd said, and had been working in the garden every minute of her spare time. Robbie still joined her whenever he could, but when a longer bit of leave came due, he said, 'Darling, I must go home and see Ma and Pops.'

'Of course you must,' Fleur said at once. 'And I should go home too, but I just can't leave here until everything's planted. I'm late with some of it now and it'd be so unfair to all the people who've been so generous not to use it all. Plants and seeds are very precious just now.'

'I'm sure your mum and dad will understand.'

Fleur grimaced. 'Dad will, but I'm not so sure about Mum. Mind you,' she added as an afterthought, 'Dad did promise to come over sometime and see what I'm— Sorry' – she grinned – 'what *we're* doing.'

'I should think so too!' Robbie pretended indignation. 'Like you said I would, I'm still aching in muscles I didn't know I'd got.' His face sobered. 'But I hate not seeing you for days on end.'

They gazed at each other, their love spilling over. 'I know,' Fleur said, 'but we're luckier than most. We see each other nearly every day.'

'I know, I know. I shouldn't grumble. I'm not doing really, it's just . . .'

Now it was Fleur's turn to say, 'I know. I know just how you feel.' She reached up to touch him, but then, realizing her fingers were grubby, she smiled ruefully and dropped her hand.

'I can't bear to be away from you – not even for a moment. Fleur,' he said impulsively, grabbing her hands, oblivious of the earth clinging to her fingers. 'Fleur – let's get married. Now. Let's not wait any longer. Oh, darling, do say "yes".'

Fleur's eyes widened and she gasped in surprise. 'Are you – are you proposing?'

'Of course I am. Oh, I'm sorry – it's not the most romantic setting, but . . .'

Fleur's eyes filled with tears. 'Oh, darling, it is, it is.'

He dropped to one knee, not caring if his uniform

got dirty. 'Darling Fleur, I love you with all my heart. Will you marry me – please?'

'Oh yes, yes!' She flung herself at him, knocking him over so that they rolled on the ground together, laughing and crying and hugging each other.

''Ere, 'ere, what's all this, then?' Harry's voice came over the fence. 'Well, I nivver. I know the ground wants a bit of a roll when you've planted seeds, but I've never seen it done that way afore.'

Fleur and Robbie buried their faces against each other and roared with laughter.

'Come on,' Robbie said at last, still spluttering with mirth. 'We can't lie here all day.' Then he murmured against her ear, 'Much as I'd like to.' He got up and held out his hand to her to pull her to her feet, then drew her into his arms and kissed her tenderly. He turned towards the old man, still leaning on the fence.

'You shall be the first to know, Harry. This lovely girl has just consented to be my wife.'

The old man nodded and Fleur was touched to see tears shimmer in his eyes. 'That calls for a celebration, lad. You go and tell Mary to get the glasses out. I'll be round in a jiffy . . .'

'What's he up to now?' Fleur wondered.

'I don't know, but we'll do as he says.'

They went towards the house, hand in hand. In the back scullery, Fleur washed her hands quickly whilst Robbie brushed down his uniform. Before she could step into the kitchen to speak to Mrs Jackson, Harry was opening the back door with Ruth on his heels. She had been in his cottage ironing the old man's sheets.

'What's going on? Harry's dragged me round here

just when the irons are hot.' Ruth looked disgruntled. 'What's all the excitement?'

'Here we are then, lass,' Harry interrupted. 'Last bottle of my elderflower wine. Sparkling, it is. Nearest I can get to champagne.'

'It'll be better than champagne, Harry. But are you sure you want to use it? I mean . . .'

'Course I am.' He winked at her. 'Been looking for an excuse to open it up. I can always mek some more. I used to enjoy me wine making, but to tell you the truth, I haven't had the heart since Doris passed away. But now, well, I feel I might have another go. Now this lass has got me all straightened out in the house, I can see the wood for the trees, as they say. Come on, has Mary got the glasses ready?'

'I haven't had time to tell her yet.'

'Will somebody please tell me what's going on?' Ruth asked again, but Harry still ignored her, saying to Fleur, 'You go in and tell Mary and get the glasses ready. Come to think of it, I'd best open this outside. It might make a bit of a mess. Bring a glass, lass. Don't want to waste any . . .'

'What *is* going on?'

Shyly, Fleur said, 'Robbie's asked me to marry him and I've said "yes".'

Ruth stared at her. 'Oh no. You can't,' she burst out. 'Not now. Not while there's a war on. Oh Fleur!' She gripped Fleur's arm. 'Think about it. Please. What if—'

Fleur blinked. 'I don't need to think about it, Ruth,' she said stiffly, hurt that her friend didn't seem to be pleased for her. 'I love him and he loves me.'

'But . . .'

Squashed together in the tiny scullery, Harry could not help but overhear all that was being said. Gently, he touched Ruth's arm. 'Listen, love, I know what's troubling you. You're afraid that if anything should happen to that young man out there . . .' Harry jerked his head towards the back yard, where Robbie was still trying to remove the earth stains from his uniform. 'That she'll be terribly hurt. You're trying to protect her from that, aren't you?'

Ruth bit her lip and tears filled her eyes. 'I tried to warn her when we first met.' She glanced at Fleur. 'Didn't I?'

Fleur nodded. 'But it's too late for that now. It was even then. We'd already fallen in love. It happened so fast, I can still hardly believe it myself.'

Ruth sighed deeply as old Harry put his arm round her shoulders. 'Terrible times we live in, lass. I know that, but if you get a chance of a bit of happiness, you've got to take it. Grab it with both hands, 'cos you never know when you're going to get the chance again. Or . . . or . . .' He hesitated to say more, but it had to be said, 'Or how long it'll last.'

'I'm sorry, Fleur,' Ruth said contritely. 'It's just . . . it's just . . .' She took a deep breath. 'A few weeks before you came I got to know a bomber pilot. Got rather fond of him to tell you the truth and . . . and . . .'

She didn't need to say any more – both Fleur and Harry guessed what had happened. 'Oh, Ruth!' Fleur put her arms around her. 'Why didn't you tell me?'

'I'm not the only one,' Ruth said sadly. 'It's happening to countless wives and sweethearts. I just . . . I just wanted to stop you getting in too deep.' She smiled tremulously, the tears still shimmering on her eyelids. 'Seems I was too late. Oh, Fleur – of course I wish you every happiness. There's just one thing . . .'

'What?' For a moment, Fleur was apprehensive again.

'Can I be your bridesmaid?'

'Of *course* you can.'

Five minutes later it was a merry little party drinking Harry's sparkling elderflower wine in Mary Jackson's kitchen.

'Oo, it smells lovely, Harry,' Fleur said. 'Just like perfume. I don't know whether to drink it or dab it behind me ears.'

'So when are you getting married then?' Harry asked, his cheeks beginning to glow pink. His home-made wine was strong.

Robbie laughed and put his arm around Fleur's shoulders. 'I don't know. I suppose I'll have to ask her old man's permission.'

The words were said jokingly and everyone in the room laughed. All except Fleur. She was not smiling.

In the excitement, the joy of Robbie asking her to be his wife, she had not given a moment's thought to what her parents would say at the news.

Twenty-One

'I don't care what you say, Fleur.' Robbie was adamant. 'We're going to do this properly. I'm going to see your father.'

'Not without me, you're not,' Fleur retorted. 'There's no knowing what might happen. 'Specially if my mother's there – which she will be.'

'You really think he'd withhold his permission?'

Fleur pressed her lips together to stop them trembling. 'Yes, I do. Not because he wants to,' she added swiftly. 'But because Mum will be against it. Dead against it. And . . . and he'll not want to upset her.'

'I see,' Robbie said thoughtfully.

'Did you tell your mother?'

Robbie had just returned after a brief visit to Nottingham when ops had been cancelled because of poor visibility over the target. He shook his head. 'No. I didn't think it right until I'd spoken to your father. As soon as I – as soon as we – have seen him, then I'll try to see her. I want to tell her myself. I don't want to write to her. Not with this sort of news.'

'Will she . . . will she mind, d'you think?'

'Good heavens, no. She'll be tickled pink.'

'Really?' Fleur still wasn't so sure.

'Well, can we both wangle a forty-eight next weekend?'

Fleur nodded.

'Then we'll go together. First we'll go out to South Monkford and face your parents together and then – if there's still time – we'll go to Nottingham.'

'No – no, it'll be easier to go to Nottingham first and then come back here from South Monkford,' Fleur suggested. 'If the trains don't fit up, it might be easier hitching from there back to Lincoln.'

Robbie frowned. 'Yes, you're right. But I wanted to do it properly. To ask your dad first.'

Fleur smiled thinly. Much as she wanted to marry Robbie and as soon as possible, the days until the following weekend were filled with dread and, when the time came, she could not stop trembling and the nerves fluttering in her stomach made eating impossible. Fate, or perhaps the weather, smiled kindly upon them. There was no flying and they were both granted leave.

'There's no need to worry about Ma and Pops,' Robbie tried to reassure her for the umpteenth time as they stepped off the train and began to walk towards his home. 'I bet she offers to make you a wedding dress.'

'That's the least of my worries,' Fleur said. 'Besides, most people these days are getting married in uniform.'

'The fellers, yes. But I want to see you in the full works. Long white dress, veil and a huge bouquet of red roses from Harry's garden.'

Fleur stared at him. 'Harry hasn't got any roses in his garden. It's all vegetables.'

Robbie laughed. 'Haven't you been round the far side of his cottage?'

Fleur paused to think. 'Well, no, actually I haven't.'

The paths to the two neighbouring cottages were

side by side. Fleur had never had need to go to the other side of the old man's cottage.

'Ah, there you are then. Harry's got a bed of red roses at that end. Well hidden from the road, it is. He says they were his wife's favourite flowers and no way was he going to dig them up, not even for Potato Pete. He's already tending them with extra loving care so they're just right for your wedding day.'

'Really!' In spite of the ever-present worry, Fleur laughed. 'And does he know when that's to be then? Because if he does – he knows more than me!'

'Roses last a fair while. He reckons they'll still be in full bloom by the time we tie the knot.'

As they arrived at the end of the street where Robbie's family lived, Fleur pulled in a deep breath. 'Well, here goes then.'

They were welcomed with open arms by Meg, and the old man by the range smiled and nodded his pleasure at the sight of them both.

'How long have you got?' Meg asked, bustling about to set the table for a welcome home meal.

Fleur giggled, anxiety making her nervous. Meg paused, glancing from one to the other. 'What? What did I say?'

Robbie, too, looked at Fleur.

'Nothing – nothing,' she said hastily. 'Honestly. It's just that my mother always asks, "When are you going back?" The way you ask just sounds so much nicer. It . . . it sounds as if you really want us here . . .' Her voice trailed away. She was explaining herself badly and sounding very disloyal to her mother too.

Meg smiled gently. 'I'm sure your mother doesn't mean it to sound the way it does. We just want to know how to make the very best of the time we've got with you.' She turned away swiftly and hurried out to the scullery, but not before Fleur had heard the catch in her voice and seen tears in her eyes. Meg Rodwell might be putting on a very brave face, but she was just as desperately anxious about her son as any other mother.

When she came back into the room, Robbie got up and put his arm about her shoulders. 'Ma, come and sit down for a moment. We've got something to tell you and Pops.'

Meg's eyes widened and the colour drained from her face. Fleur felt a tremor of fear. Had she really told Robbie the truth or had she lied to cover up her shameful past? Robbie must have noticed her reaction too, because he glanced at Fleur as he drew his mother to sit down. Still holding both Meg's hands in his, he knelt down on one knee beside her chair. 'Ma, Fleur and I are going to get married.'

Meg looked from one to another. Her mouth dropped open and she gave a little gasp of surprise, but it was relief that flooded her face. Relief and then a growing delight.

'Oh, how wonderful!' She flung her arms around Robbie's neck and kissed his cheek. Then she held out her arms to Fleur. 'It's wonderful news. Wonderful!'

In his corner by the range, the old man smiled and nodded and wiped away a tear running down his wrinkled cheek.

Gently, Robbie said, 'You looked frightened to death for a moment there, Ma. What did you think we were going to say?'

'I—' Now embarrassment crept up Meg's face. 'I just expected bad news,' she rushed on nervously. 'Nowadays – you know – I thought perhaps – there was bad news from—' She glanced at Fleur. 'From home. That . . . that Jake . . . I mean that someone in your family.' She pulled her scattered wits together and smiled brightly. 'But I never guessed it would be that. I mean, you've only known each other just over a month.' She looked at them both again, searching their faces. And she could see the love there, knew they were right for each other and – because of the frightening times they were living in – knew they couldn't wait. A month, a year – ten years? When had love ever taken notice of time?

'You are pleased, Ma?'

'I'm thrilled. I—' Now she allowed tears of joy to run down her face. Gently, Robbie wiped them away with his finger. Then Meg looked across at Fleur again. 'Will you let me make your wedding dress for you?'

Fleur and Robbie exchanged a look and then both burst out laughing. 'I told you, didn't I?' Robbie spluttered. 'I told you so.'

'Well, that was easy enough,' Robbie said as they climbed on the train the next morning back to South Monkford.

'Yes,' Fleur said dryly. 'Now comes the difficult bit.' As they settled themselves in the carriage, she added, 'You know, your mother never asked if we'd told my parents, did she?'

Robbie, having stowed their small overnight bags on the rack, sat down next to Fleur. 'She asked me later. When you were out the back.'

'What did she say?'

'Just asked if we'd told them yet and I said, "No, but we're going to tomorrow." '

'And?'

'She just said, "Well, I wish you luck," but it was said with a sort of wry smile.'

'Mm,' Fleur nodded. 'She knows, doesn't she? She knows how they're going to react.' She paused a moment and then bit her lip. 'Robbie – you are absolutely sure she told you the truth. Don't get me wrong,' she added hurriedly. 'I love your mother – I think she's great – but, well, I just wondered if she'd been protecting you.'

Robbie smiled, put his arm around her and kissed her hair. 'I know what you mean.'

Fleur closed her eyes, marvelling at how understanding Robbie was. He reminded her so much of her father . . . Her eyes flew open in horror. It was still there. Would it always be there? This terrible fear that perhaps . . . She dragged her thoughts back to what Robbie was saying.

'I really don't think, Fleur, that my mother would have been so delighted to hear that we're getting married if there was the remotest possibility that your father is mine too. Now, seriously, do you?'

'Well – no – but . . .'

He hugged her to him. 'We've got to put all that right out of our minds.' He frowned. 'There *is* something in their past, though. That's obvious – but I don't think it affects us.'

Fleur was silent. She wasn't so sure.

As they walked along the lane towards the farm, Fleur's heart was thumping in her chest and her hands were clammy. As she pushed open the yard gate, she heard Kenny's voice.

'Hey, what are you two doing here?' He loped across the yard to envelop his sister in a bear hug and to shake Robbie's hand. 'Come on in. Mum and Dad'll be pleased to see you.' He paused and then, with a wry grin, added, 'Well, Dad will be.'

He led the way across the yard, flinging open the back door and shouting. 'Mum? Mum? Look who's here.'

They stepped in through the wash house and into the kitchen just as Betsy turned round from the sink, drying her hands on a towel. For a brief moment, she began to move towards her daughter, but then her glance took in Robbie standing behind Fleur in the doorway. Betsy dropped the towel and she gave a little cry. Then she opened her mouth and screamed. 'Jake! *Jake!*'

'Mum—' Fleur began, taking a step towards her and holding out her hands. 'Please . . .'

'Don't touch me. Don't come near me. And get . . . him,' she panted, 'out of here. Out of my house.'

Kenny was shocked, glancing helplessly between them. He'd heard Betsy ranting about Robbie, but he'd never seriously thought she would take it this far. To forbid the young man's entrance to her home.

'Mum . . .' he began helplessly but, at that moment, Jake opened the door that led from the kitchen into the living room, a newspaper in his hand. 'Whatever's the matter?' Then he spotted Fleur and, behind her, Robbie. 'Ah.'

'Dad – please . . .' Fleur began. 'We just want to . . .'

'Of course you do,' Jake said easily. 'Come in and sit down. Betsy, make us all a nice cup of tea, love, will you?'

'Tea? Tea? You want me to make tea?' Betsy's voice rose hysterically. 'You think a cup of tea's the answer to everything?'

'Now, Betsy.' Jake's voice suddenly held a note of firmness, a tone that all his family – including his wife – recognized at once.

Jake was an easy-going man. He liked a contented, peaceful life and rarely did he raise his voice or insist on things being done just his way. But once in a while, when he felt strongly about something, he put his foot down very firmly and all his family knew that he meant it. There was no arguing with Jake when his mouth was a firm line and his jaw hardened. Even his dark brown eyes lost some of their velvet gentleness.

He held out his hand to Robbie and shook his hand, indicating his own easy chair near the range for the young man to sit down.

'Thank you, sir,' Robbie said. There was a tension in his voice and a slight flush to his face.

Betsy stood a moment, staring at her husband, then at the young airman. Then, with a sob, she turned and fled from the room. They heard her footsteps pounding up the stairs and then the slam of the bedroom door.

'I'm sorry,' Jake said, his eyes troubled.

'Whatever's got into Mum?' Kenny was mystified.

No one answered him. Fleur just muttered, 'I'll make that tea.' And Jake sat down opposite Robbie, who leant forward, resting his elbows on his knees and linking his fingers together.

'Mr Bosley, I'm sorry to have distressed your wife. I wouldn't have come here at all, but . . .' He glanced at Fleur busying herself between scullery and range. 'We – I – have something to ask you. Something important and it wasn't fair to expect Fleur to do it.'

There was a moment's silence in the kitchen, and then Kenny let out a guffaw of delight. 'I know why . . .' he began, but earned himself a light punch on the shoulder from his sister.

'Shut up, our Kenny.' But she was smiling as she added, 'Let Robbie do it properly.'

So Kenny sat down on a chair near the table, folded his arms and looked backwards and forwards between his father and Robbie, a huge grin on his boyish face. 'Get on with it, then.'

Robbie cleared his throat and said formally, 'I'd like to ask for your daughter's hand in marriage, sir.'

Kenny tried to stifle a laugh but failed. 'Don't you want the rest of her?'

Fleur punched him again, but her gaze was on her father's face.

Jake stared at Robbie for a moment. Then slowly, his gaze came to rest upon Fleur's anxious face. 'Well, well,' he murmured at last, after what seemed an age. 'Meg's boy and my girl. Who'd ever've thought it?'

Fleur was holding her breath. She moved closer, beseeching him with her face. Their eyes met and held for a long, long moment. And then she saw the smile begin to twitch at the corner of his mouth. He rose and she flung herself against him, wrapping her arms around his neck, laughing and crying, 'Oh, Dad! Dad!'

Robbie rose to his feet as Jake held out his hand. 'It's not going to be easy, lad,' he said softly. 'I think you know that, but you have *my* blessing.' No one in the room could fail to hear his accent on the word "my".

Kenny sprang to his feet and slapped his future brother-in-law on the back. 'And mine. As if it makes any difference,' he added wryly.

'Of course it makes a difference,' Fleur cried, turning from her father to hug her brother. 'You might be the one to bring Mum around.'

There was an awkward silence until Kenny broke it by saying, 'Dad – what is up with Mum? She can't not like Robbie. She's never even met him before, has she?' He glanced at the other two. 'Has she?'

Fleur shook her head and looked to her father for an explanation. An explanation that she and Robbie needed too. But Jake shook his head. 'Don't you worry about it. I'll talk to her. Try to get her to see reason.' It should be the happiest day of their lives and Betsy was trying to rob them of their joy. He glanced sadly at the young couple as he added, 'But I can't make any promises.'

Twenty-Two

'I shan't go to the wedding, Jake, so you needn't expect me to. I don't know what you're thinking of – giving your permission. If you'd told her "no" she might've had the sense to think again.' Betsy sniffed. 'Mind you – I doubt it.'

'It was just a courtesy to ask, love,' Jake said mildly. His anger was gone now, but replaced by disappointment that Betsy refused to join in the happiness that such news should have brought. 'They don't need to. They're both over twenty-one.'

Robbie and Fleur had left and now only the three of them – Jake, Betsy and Kenny – sat around the supper table.

'Mum – why don't you like Robbie?' Kenny asked innocently. 'He seems a good bloke and he's besotted with our Fleur. And her with him. Why—?'

'It's nothing to do with you, Kenny. You're too young to understand . . .'

The young man flushed but he was not about to cave in. 'Mum – if I'm old enough to fight for my country, then I'm old enough to understand why—'

'You're not old enough to fight for your country.' Betsy's voice began to rise.

'Leave it, there's a good lad,' Jake said softly. There was no censure in his tone – just an infinite sadness.

There was a morose silence between them. Betsy's

blue eyes flashed from one to the other. She was rarely angry with Kenny, but now even he was included in her malevolent gaze. At last Jake said, 'You don't mean it, Betsy love, do you? You wouldn't really stay away from your daughter's wedding. Your *only* daughter's wedding.'

Tight-lipped, Betsy muttered, 'If she marries *him*, then, yes, I shall stay away.' Her eyes narrowed as she glared at her husband. Slowly and deliberately she added, 'And if you go, I shall never speak to you again.'

Shocked, Jake stared back at her. Slowly, he rose to his feet and stood looking down at her. Sadly, but firmly, he said, 'Then this house is going to be very quiet, Betsy, for I intend not only to attend the wedding but also to give my daughter away. No one – not even you – is going to deny me that.' He began to turn away, but Betsy sprang to her feet and caught hold of his arm.

'I'm not just thinking of myself, though God knows if I never saw Meg Rodwell again as long as I live, it'd be too soon. No – I'm thinking of Fleur. He'll break her heart. He'll be devious and ruthless and selfish, just like *her*. But you can't see it, can you? Where Meg Rodwell's concerned, you're blind. Always have been.'

Jake shook his head. Quietly, and with a patience that the watching Kenny – for once – believed his mother did not deserve, Jake said, 'I'm well aware of all Meg's faults, Betsy. But I do believe that when Robbie was born, she changed.'

Betsy snorted derisively. 'How do you know? You've not seen her since . . .' Her eyes widened as she added accusingly, '*Have* you?'

'No, of course I haven't.' Now, even Jake's composure was wearing thin. 'Don't you trust me better than that?'

'It's her I don't trust. No man's safe around her. What about him? What about Robbie's father? His *real* father? He couldn't be trusted, could he? Poor—'

'Betsy!' Jake thundered. 'We don't talk about that.'

Guiltily, Betsy glanced at Kenny as if – for a brief moment – she'd forgotten his presence. She had the grace to drop her head. 'No,' she whispered. 'You're right, Jake. I'm sorry. I don't want to hurt—' She bit her lip. 'Innocent people.'

But then her head shot up again and she tightened her grip on Jake's arm. 'But I meant what I said. If you go to their wedding, I'll never forgive you. Never!'

He stared at her for a long moment whilst Kenny held his breath. Then Jake shook himself free of his wife's grasp, turned on his heel and strode from the house, leaving both Betsy and Kenny staring after him.

'It's the last thing I wanted,' Robbie said as they sat together in the train, holding hands. 'To upset your family.' They'd been lucky. There was one bound for Lincoln just as they reached the station.

Fleur sighed. 'I know. But there was no other way to do it.' A faint smile touched her lips. 'Unless we eloped.'

He smiled too. 'Now, there's an idea. Why on earth didn't I think of that?'

She touched his cheek as she said seriously, 'Because you wanted to do it properly, and besides, we couldn't hurt your mum and Pops like that.'

'No, I wouldn't do that.' He sighed heavily. 'But it looks as if I've really caused trouble amongst your folks. The annoying thing is' – his eyes clouded – 'I don't know how or why. I wish I did. Just why is your mother so . . . so vitriolic against my mam? You see, Fleur, having seen her for myself now, I don't think it is actually against *me* personally. It's my mother.'

'I don't think we can worry about it any more. Dad said he'll come to the wedding and I know Kenny will.'

'And your mother?' Robbie's bright blue eyes were clouded with anxiety.

Fleur sighed. 'I don't think for a moment that she will come.'

Robbie's eyes widened. He was shocked. 'Not come to her only daughter's wedding?'

Fleur said nothing but just shrugged her shoulders.

'My God!' Robbie breathed. 'It must be something serious.'

For the rest of the journey, they were both silent, each lost in their own thoughts, yet those thoughts were much the same.

Just what on earth could have been so serious that Betsy's bitterness was so deep, her hatred of Meg so strong, that she would refuse to attend her own daughter's wedding?

'There's a notice on the board about a dance in the sergeants' mess on Saturday night. There's rather a shortage of females on station – so all ranks are invited. You going?'

'You bet!' Fleur grinned.

Ruth rolled her eyes. 'As if I needed to ask! And I expect you'll monopolize one particular chap all night and not give any of the rest of us girls a look in.'

Fleur grinned again. 'Of course. But there'll be plenty left for you.' She paused, wondering if she dare raise a rather delicate subject. 'Anyone in particular you've got your eye on?'

'Who me? Never! Safety in numbers. That's my motto,' she said, with a forced gaiety, and her mouth tightened as she added, 'now.'

'There's one thing,' Fleur said lightly, trying to steer the conversation away from thoughts that were painful for Ruth. 'At least we'll all be in uniform. We won't have all the civilian girls in their pretty dresses to contend with.'

Ruth laughed. 'You're right and there won't be any local yokels getting jealous either.'

Fleur pulled a face as she remembered the recent fracas at the Mucky Duck. 'You know we were lucky to get away with that. We could all have been in serious trouble if anyone had reported us. Especially Tommy.'

'I don't think they would. I think all the locals – apart from young Alfie and his mates – are friendly towards all of us.'

'Maybe you're right. They've certainly been generous giving me stuff for Mrs Jackson's garden.'

'You've done a grand job, Fleur. It's coming on a treat. Do you know, Mrs Jackson was in tears the other day?'

Fleur gasped. 'Tears? Oh no, why? Have I upset her?'

'No, no. Tears of joy, silly. She's so happy to see the garden like her Arthur used to keep it. Only thing she misses, she says, are her precious sweet peas.'

Fleur smiled. 'You haven't told her then?'

'Course not. And I've sworn old Harry to secrecy.

Mind you, when he comes round now, he uses the little gate you've made through the fence near the shelter. Not round the front path like he used to.'

'But he does know about them?'

Fleur had planted a row of sweet peas close to the sunny wall on the south side of the cottage, and the plants were already growing well and climbing the cane frame.

'Yes, but he'll not say a word,' Ruth reassured her.

'Do you think she'll see them before they're ready?'

'I doubt it. She hardly ever goes out now. She can hardly get across the back yard to the lavvy some days, her arthritis is that bad. Poor old dear. Harry says she used to love going to church every week but she hasn't even managed that the last two Sundays. Shame, isn't it?'

'Mm,' Fleur said thoughtfully. 'I wonder if we could get hold of a bath chair. We could wheel her to church.'

'You'd never get a bath chair down that narrow path, would you?'

'We could take her out of the front door.'

Ruth laughed. 'Her front door is jammed shut. Just like Harry's. I bet neither of them have used their front door in years.'

'How are you getting on with Harry? I was round there the other day taking some tools back he'd lent me and he took me into his kitchen. You've got it looking like a new pin.'

'Yeah, the house is clean from top to bottom now. There's still a lot of clutter I'd like to turf out, but I can't be too hard on the old boy. Do you know, he's still got all his wife's clothes hanging in the wardrobe? And she's been dead for two years, he was telling me.'

Fleur sighed. 'I expect he can't bear to part with them. Perhaps it helps him to feel she's still close. Still around, even.'

'Maybe. But nobody would ever want to wear them again. Not now, even though there are some lovely things amongst them. They pong to high heaven of mothballs. No, I've given that up as a bad job. But there's just one thing I haven't managed to do yet.'

'What's that?' Fleur asked innocently, and then dissolved into helpless giggles at Ruth's answer.

'Get that tin bath that's hanging in his shed on the hearth in front of the fire and get Harry in it!'

The dance was a great success. It was the first that Fleur had been to on the camp, though Ruth said there had been one or two before Fleur's arrival. Half the fun for the girls was getting ready together in their bedrooms at the cottage. There was much to-ing and fro-ing across the tiny landing.

'Have you got any shoe polish?' Fleur called.

'Only a tiny bit, but you can have it. I've done mine.'

'Have you got any Brasso? My buttons look a bit dull . . .'

And then, from Ruth, a mournful, 'I'm down to my last pair of silk stockings. Do you think it's worth risking them getting ruined?'

'That's up to you, but don't let Brown catch you or you'll be on a charge. Silk stockings aren't exactly classed as regulation uniform, y'know. I'm saving mine for a rather special occasion . . .' Fleur smiled at the thought. 'So I've only got my be-ootiful lisle ones.'

'Right then. Silk, it is. Even if only to show you up.'

'Thanks, *friend*!'

'Don't mention it,' Ruth called back gaily. A pause and then, 'Do you want this lipstick? It doesn't suit me. I'm better with paler colours, but it might suit you.'

Fleur trotted across the landing. 'Let's see. Ooh, yes. That's lovely.'

'You can keep it . . .'

Fleur grinned. 'No, tell you what. I'll borrow it. And I'll borrow it on my wedding day. That can be my "something borrowed".'

They went down the stairs, laughing and chattering, their spirits high at the thought of being able to forget the war for a few hours and into the kitchen for Mrs Jackson's inspection.

'It was just like listening to my girls getting ready when they were going out on a date. Now, have a good time, my dears, won't you?'

Impulsively, they both kissed her on her cheek. It was like having a loving granny watching out for them.

'Oh, she is an old duck,' Ruth said as they walked through the darkness back to camp.

'She is,' Fleur agreed readily, 'but with her arthritis so bad, I just don't know how we're going to get her to the wedding.'

'Oh, she'll get there. By hook or by crook. You'll see. She was only saying the other day that she'll manage it somehow, if she has to get all the village lads together to carry her.'

Ruth couldn't know how much her remark touched Fleur. To think, she mused, that an old lady who had only known her a few weeks was prepared to make the painful effort to get to her wedding, when her own mother was flatly refusing to attend.

'Here we are,' Ruth said, interrupting Fleur's troublesome thoughts as they walked into the large hall, where the tables and chairs had been cleared away. The air was filled with cigarette smoke and the smell of beer. Chatter, laughter and music shook the rafters. Already couples crowded the floor, dancing to the band.

Robbie, standing near the bar, had been watching for them and at once threaded his way around the edge of the dance floor, Johnny following in his wake.

'May I have the pleasure . . . ?' they chorused as Robbie held out his arms to Fleur and Johnny bowed courteously to Ruth.

'It was so nice,' Fleur commented as she and Ruth walked home through the darkness, their arms linked as they followed the tiny beam of Ruth's torch, 'to be just RAF personnel and weren't the band fantastic?'

An RAF band had been formed on camp – the girls had often heard the lads practising in a hangar, the music echoing around the silent aircraft.

'Mmm,' Ruth murmured. 'A pity though.'

'A pity? Why d'you say that?'

'There was a very good-looking lad on the drums, but of course he couldn't come and dance.'

Fleur spluttered with laughter. Ruth had been as good as her word. She'd not danced with the same man twice all the evening, yet had never been short of partners.

'What were you trying to do? Dance with every man there?'

'Something like that,' Ruth chuckled.

'Well, I was happy with just the one.'

'We noticed!'

Fleur smiled to herself in the darkness. It really had been a lovely evening. She'd been able to spend the whole time in Robbie's arms quite openly. The rumours of their engagement were already flying around the room. There'd been slaps on the back for Robbie and chaste kisses for Fleur.

Strangely, only Bob Watson had been disapproving. Fleur had tackled him about it at once. 'Do you mean I won't be able to carry on as an R/T operator after I'm married?'

He'd shaken his head. 'No, it's not that. I just don't hold with wartime marriages. 'Specially not with fliers. When he goes missing, it'll be the rest of us who have to mop up your tears.'

Fleur had been dismayed by his bluntness. And the worst of it was he had said 'when' not 'if'. That, more than anything, had shocked her. He was as bad as – worse than – Ruth. At least her friend was no longer disapproving, or if she was, then she was hiding it very successfully.

'Well, I'll tell you something, Flight, here and now. *If* it does happen,' Fleur had replied heatedly, emphasizing the word deliberately, 'then I promise you, you'll never see me cry.' And with that, she'd turned on her heel and gone in search of Robbie, who was at the bar getting drinks for them. By the time he returned to her, she'd calmed down and was able to smile and enjoy the rest of the evening.

But climbing into bed that night, Bob Watson's words came back to haunt her. Ruth seemed to have come round to the idea. She was her friend and, if the worst did happen, Fleur knew she could count on her, but there were still others who viewed a wartime wedding with scepticism and disapproval.

Including her mother. But that, of course, was for a very different reason. Whatever that reason was. Fleur only wished she knew the answer.

Twenty-Three

'I've got a darky,' Kay said calmly.

Fleur's heart skipped a beat. An aircraft in trouble. Bob sprang into action, issuing orders for the landing lights to be switched on and the crash crew to be alerted.

'Better let sick quarters know too,' he instructed Peggy, whilst Fleur threw aside her sewing and took her seat beside Kay.

Kay was speaking reassuringly to the aircraft in trouble. 'Hello, B-Beer. This is Wickerton Wood. You are cleared to land. Runway two-zero. QFE one zero two zero. Switch to channel B. Over.'

Faintly, everyone in the control room heard the intermittent noise of an engine.

'He's in real trouble,' Bob murmured, as Kay continued to talk the aircraft down. The spluttering noise came closer and closer and the crash crew, fire tender and ambulance were already moving as close as they dared to the runway. The black shape appeared suddenly, low over the perimeter hedge.

'God – he's only just missed it,' Bob muttered, straining his eyes through the darkness and pulling nervously at his moustache. 'I hope he doesn't block the runway just before all our lads are due back.'

Fleetingly, Fleur thought Bob was being callous, but then she realized the tough realism behind his remark.

With the runway blocked by a crash, their own returning aircraft would be endangered. Low on fuel, they might not be able to make it to another airfield.

Everyone seemed to be holding their breath, whilst Kay kept up a serene conversation with the stricken aircraft.

Lower and lower the plane came until, with a squeal of rubber, it touched the runway, bounced once and then stayed down, trundling past the control room where every head turned to follow its progress. When the aircraft slowed and came to a halt at the far end, there was a unanimous sigh of relief as the crash crew and fire tender raced after the plane.

'I think he's OK,' Bob said, still watching. 'Well done, Fullerton. Couldn't have handled it better myself.'

'Now there's a compliment,' Kay drawled. 'Could I have that in writing, Flight?'

As the crippled aircraft was towed away, the first call came from Wickerton Wood's own squadron and the control team swung into their practised routine.

'Coming to the pub tonight?'

It had been a busy week. The weather had been good and there had been flying almost every night. With one R/T operator off sick, Fleur and Kay had been required to work extra shifts and it wasn't until the Saturday, when there was no flying, that the friends had an evening off.

Fleur stared at Kay in surprise. 'Do you think we should?'

Kay, with a little smile on her mouth, shrugged. 'Why ever not? It's a free country.'

They glanced at each other, aware that that was the very reason they were all here. Fighting to keep that freedom.

'What about the locals? I mean we . . . we don't want to antagonize them any more. We might not get away with it next time.'

There had been no repercussions from the fracas outside the White Swan – much to the surprise of everyone involved.

Kay's little smile became a smirk. 'Johnny's planning something.'

Fleur's eyes widened in fear. 'Oh no! He's not planning to round up a . . . a posse, is he?'

Kay laughed, her dark violet eyes twinkling with mischief. 'Johnny? The responsible navigator of a Hampden? Really, Fleur. The very idea!'

'Then – then . . . ?'

'Ah, now that would be telling. If you want to find out, you'll just have to come along, won't you?' She swung back in her chair to face her desk, adding, with a touch of sarcasm, 'Or are you chicken?'

'Is Robbie going?'

'Of course.'

'Then so am I.'

As she heard Kay's soft chuckle, she swung round and marched out of the room. There was half an hour before she needed to be at her desk to complete her morning shift. She wanted to find Ruth.

'What do you think Johnny's planning? Trouble?'

Ruth screwed up her face thoughtfully. 'Shouldn't think so. He doesn't seem the type to me.'

'Doesn't he?' Fleur was not so sure. Johnny had had no compunction in flirting with a local girl and causing her boyfriend to be jealous.

'Well, I'll come along too. Tell you what though. At the first sign of trouble we're out of there and I don't care if they do think we're chicken. I'm not incurring the wrath of the owd beezum for anyone else.'

Fleur laughed. She knew Ruth was referring to Flight Sergeant Brown rather than the Squadron Officer Davidson, who was the most senior WAAF officer on the station. Ruth was Lincolnshire born and bred, and though her dialect was not broad there were times when it came out strongly.

'What on earth is an "owd beezum"?'

'An old hag.'

Fleur laughed louder. 'Oh, that's priceless. I must remember that.'

'Well, don't let her hear you calling her it. You'd be on a charge for sure.'

Chuckling, Fleur returned to the control room. Only a few more hours, she was thinking, and she'd be with Robbie.

Later, as Fleur brushed her uniform and polished the buttons on her jacket until they sparkled, she felt butterflies of apprehension begin to flutter in her stomach. Downstairs she found Ruth and Mary Jackson listening to the wireless. Fleur stood quietly for a moment, holding her breath. Was it more bad war news? Then she let out her breath with relief. It was only one of Mrs Jackson's favourite programmes, *In Town Tonight*.

'Oh, sorry.' Catching sight of her, Ruth jumped up. 'Ready?'

'When you are.' Though Fleur was anxious to meet Robbie, part of her would have liked to stay here safely in the cottage, listening to Mrs Jackson's wireless.

'Now, you promise to go to the shelter if the sirens start, don't you, Mrs Jackson?' Ruth said.

'I don't think I could manage the path in the dark, my dears.'

'Harry's said he'll come and fetch you. Now I want your promise. Please.' Suddenly, Ruth bent down and kissed the old lady's wrinkled cheek. 'We don't want anything happening to you, you know.'

Tears filled Mary Jackson's eyes. 'You're such dear girls. All right, I promise I'll try.'

As the two girls walked down the dark lane, arms linked and following the thin beam of Ruth's torch, she murmured, 'I suppose that's the best we can hope for. That she'll try. But I very much doubt she'll venture down that path in the dark on her own.'

'But you said Harry had promised to go round.'

'Oh, he will, he will.' Ruth laughed wryly. 'He'll go round all right. But I bet they'll just sit there listening to Mrs J's wireless and gossiping while the bombs fall around them.'

'So all that digging was a waste of time, was it?'

'Not at all. We've tried. At least it's there.' She sighed. 'Now it's up to them. But we can't make 'em go in it if they really don't want to.'

They walked on in silence until they saw the blacked-out shape of the pub looming up in front of them.

'Now then, girls,' was Bill Moore's friendly greeting. 'The lads are already in the corner over there.'

Fleur glanced round and her heart skipped a beat as

she saw Robbie, but it was Johnny who rose to his feet from his place beside Peggy and came towards them. Draping his arms around their shoulders, he said, 'Now, girls, what are you drinking? I'm in the chair.'

As Johnny ordered the drinks, Fleur looked around her trying hard not to make it obvious that she was looking for someone. Then she let out a sigh of relief. There was no sign of Alfie Fish and his cronies. Fleur carried her drink across the room to sit beside Robbie.

'Hello, darling. All right?'

She nodded. She was feeling a little easier, but not entirely relaxed. It was early. There was still time for the local lads to make an appearance. And when Johnny came back and sat down, her fears increased again. He positioned himself so that he sat opposite the door and every so often he glanced up at the entrance.

He's watching for them, Fleur thought in horror. He really is planning trouble. Her heart began to pound and her hand, held warmly in Robbie's, trembled a little.

'Darling?' he said at once, full of concern. 'What is it?'

Fleur opened her mouth to blurt out the truth about what was worrying her, when she caught Kay's eyes. There was a gleam in those violet eyes. A gleam that seemed to say, I thought as much – I thought you were a scaredy cat.

Fleur closed her mouth and lifted her chin with a new determination. Right then. Let them come. Let them all come. She'd show 'em. She'd wade in with the rest of them and hang the consequences. It would likely be promotion out of the window, but what the hell?

She smiled brightly at Robbie and said, 'Nothing. It was just . . . just a bit cold walking here, that's all.'

As it was a warm May night, her excuse was feeble. Robbie looked deep into her eyes and such was their closeness already that he seemed to be able to read her very thoughts. He leant close and whispered against her hair so that no one else should hear. 'It's all right. I promise. Don't worry.'

As he drew back, he squeezed her hand. She gave him a small smile, not in the least surprised that he'd guessed what was troubling her. The time ticked on, with much laughter and jollity in their corner. The drinks flowed. Tommy sat with his arm around Kay. She snuggled up to him and Ruth was engaged in a verbal sparring match with the ebullient Johnny, while Peggy – the quiet one of the group – listened and smiled but did not join in the banter. Thankfully, the local girl, Kitty, was nowhere to be seen and neither – to Fleur's huge relief – was Alfie.

There was only half an hour left until closing time and Fleur was beginning to relax. Surely, the local lads wouldn't come in this late. She was laughing at something Johnny had said when, behind her, she heard the door to the public bar open and saw him glance towards it. She knew by his expression that this was the moment he'd been waiting for all evening.

They were here. She knew it. Without even turning round to see, she knew it. Alfie Fish and his pals were here.

Johnny rose and moved out from behind the table and towards them. Involuntarily, Fleur gripped Robbie's hand tighter. He returned it with a comforting squeeze, but Fleur found no reassurance in the gesture.

She leant towards him. 'Can't you—?' she began, but to her surprise, he put his finger to his lips and whispered, 'Just wait and see.'

Fleur glanced at Kay but her eyes were afire and a small smile played on her lips. The chatter in the bar room had fallen silent. Everyone was watching now. Sighing inwardly with resignation for whatever was about to happen, Fleur turned round slowly to see Johnny walking towards Alfie and his mates, his hand outstretched in greeting, a broad grin on his face. Then her eyes widened and she gasped in surprise, not just at Johnny's unexpected gesture, but at the sight of Alfie.

The young man and all his friends were dressed in Home Guard uniform.

'No hard feelings, lads,' Johnny was saying. 'I'd no idea the young lady was your girlfriend, Alfie. As far as I'm concerned, she's strictly out of bounds from now on.'

He still stood with his hand outstretched, waiting for Alfie to accept his apology and shake on it.

One of Alfie's friends guffawed. 'She ain't his girl. He'd just like to think so.'

His remark cost him a sharp nudge in the ribs from another in the group. 'Shut it, Tony.'

The smile on Johnny's face never wavered nor did his hand drop. 'That's as may be, but I meant what I said. I've no wish to upset any of you local lads, especially' – he laid emphasis on the words – 'fellow comrades in uniform.'

Alfie glared. 'Are you 'aving a laugh?'

For a moment Johnny's smile faltered. 'A laugh? No. Course I'm not. What d'you mean?'

'A' you 'aving a go at us 'cos we're not in the proper services?' His mouth twisted in a sneer. 'Not one of the Brylcreem Boys?'

Slowly Johnny let his hand drop now. It seemed Alfie had no intention of shaking it. His smile faded too. 'From what I hear,' he said in a last-ditch effort to heal the breech, 'the Home Guard is doing a great job. You – and all your mates – are doing just as much as us. Let's face it.' He nodded towards all of them. 'If old Hitler does get here, you'll be the ones on the front line. You'll be the ones fighting on the beaches and in the hills, like Mr Churchill warned. And we – well – if it gets to that, we'll have failed, won't we? So, no, I wasn't having a go.' He turned away from them to go back to his seat, but over his shoulder he called, 'Bill, set 'em up for these lads, will you? Maybe a drink'll make 'em realize there's no hard feelings. At least, not on my part.'

Johnny returned to his seat, picked up his glass and drained it. Near the bar the youths stood in an uncertain, embarrassed group.

'What'll it be then, lads?' Bill asked easily, though Fleur could see he was keeping a close eye on the undercurrent of tension still in the room. Then the one called Tony ordered himself a pint, and the atmosphere relaxed a little as the rest of the group followed his lead, until there was only Alfie who had not taken up the well-meaning offer. He was still glaring malevolently across the room at Johnny – indeed, at all of them, Fleur thought, quaking inwardly, though she was careful not to show apprehension on her face.

Bill had just pulled the second pint when the familiar wail of the air-raid warning siren sounded.

'Right, everyone in the cellar,' Bill roared above the din, but the Home Guard lads slammed their pints down on the bar and made for the door, Alfie in the lead, as the first bomb landed with a thud that rattled the windows and shook the doors. The rest of the locals were diving towards Bill's cellar.

'We'd best get back to camp,' Tommy said, taking the lead. 'Are you girls going down the cellar?'

Ruth glanced at Fleur. 'We ought to get back to Mrs J's. Her 'n' Harry are never going to go down the garden to the Anderson. I know they're not. Not unless we're there to drag them into it.'

'Right you are, then,' Fleur said at once. Strangely, she'd been more worried about a fight breaking out between the RAF lads and the local boys than she ever was about a few bombs falling.

'And where do you think you two are going?' Robbie said as Ruth and Fleur rose and began to head towards the door.

'Back to the cottage,' Fleur said. 'Those two old dears won't venture down to the shelter in the dark on their own.'

'Wouldn't they be safer to stay put?' Another thud, further away this time but nevertheless a warning. 'Now it's started.'

The two girls looked at each other. 'I still think we should get back to them. Be with them for once.'

'All right. I'll come with you,' Robbie said and as Fleur opened her mouth, he added, 'and no arguments.'

'Come on then,' Tommy said, 'whatever you're doing, we'd best get moving and let Bill here get down into his cellar.'

They all turned to the landlord, who was calmly clearing up, washing glasses and wiping down the smooth, polished bar top.

Another crump, a little closer again this time.

‘’Night, Bill,’ Johnny called. ‘We’ll let you get down the cellar.’

‘Oh, I don’t bother,’ the big man said calmly. ‘Jerry didn’t get me last time an’ I doubt he will this.’ He nodded towards them all. ‘’Night all. You tek care, now.’

They glanced at one another, shrugged and, chorusing ‘Goodnight’, went out into the noise of the air raid overhead.

Expecting to see the streets deserted whilst the enemy bombers wrought their havoc, they were startled to see figures running this way and that, illuminated by flames that were billowing from a building a little way down the lane opposite the pub.

Silhouetted against the bright orange flames licking the night sky was the black shape of a square tower.

‘That’s the church,’ Ruth gasped. ‘Oh, how terrible. A lot of the villagers use the crypt as a shelter.’

‘Come on, lads,’ Tommy said. ‘We’ll go and help. You girls go down to the cottage. You too, Kay. Don’t try getting back to camp on your own. Not in this.’

But Kay shook her head. ‘No, I’ll come and help too.’

‘We’ll come back,’ Ruth added, ‘once we’ve got the old folk into the shelter.’

Robbie took hold of Fleur’s arm. ‘I don’t suppose it’s any good me asking you to stay in the shelter, is it?’

‘Not a chance,’ she retorted and grinned up at him, the light from the burning building flickering eerily on his face.

He squeezed her elbow swiftly. 'Take care, then. Give my love to the old folk. We'll all meet back here at the pub . . .' And then he plunged after Tommy, Johnny and the others.

Twenty-Four

'Come on, Fleur. Let's get the oldies into the shelter and then we can get back here. Else we'll miss the fun.'

Fleur swallowed a hysterical laugh. It was not quite what she would call fun, she thought, as she began to run down the lane after Ruth.

Bombs were still falling with a frightening regularity, but they were further away from the village now.

'That's the airfield,' Ruth panted as they ran.

'I know,' Fleur gasped. 'I just hope everyone's all right.'

'They'll be going for the aircraft on the ground and the runways to put the whole station out of action.'

They reached the cottage and pounded down the path round the end of the house and into the back yard. Opening the back door, Ruth called, 'Mrs Jackson? Are you there?'

There was no reply.

'Come in, Fleur, and shut the door before I open the one into the kitchen. If there's a light on, the last thing we want to do is attract Jerry's bombs here.'

With the back door safely shut, Ruth opened the door leading from the scullery into the kitchen. Light flooded out and they stepped into the room to see Mrs Jackson still sitting in her chair in the corner near the range and Harry sitting in the visitor's chair. Between them the wireless blared out a music hall programme. The two old people looked up guiltily.

'I thought as much,' Ruth said, as she stood on the hearth rug, her hands on her hips, looking down at them. 'Now come on, you two. We're going to get you down to that shelter Fleur's spent so much time digging and then we've to go. But we're not going anywhere till we know you're both safe. Come on, no arguments.'

She put out her hands and grasped Mrs Jackson's. With a sigh of resignation, the old lady allowed herself to be hauled to her feet. 'We'd better do as she says, Harry, else I'll never hear the end of it.'

With a chuckle, Harry levered himself out of his chair. Fleur picked up the emergency box containing candles and matches, a bar of chocolate and a bottle of fresh water, which Ruth religiously changed every day. In the box there was also a first aid kit which everyone hoped would never be needed, but it was there – just in case. It was kept in the scullery near the back door for just such an occasion as this.

'I'd better get you a couple of blankets,' Fleur muttered. 'You go on, Ruth. I'll catch you up . . .'

They lurched their way down the narrow garden path. It was a short but tortuous journey in the darkness, Ruth only daring to show the tiniest light from her faithful torch.

'Where are you two going? Back to camp? Can't you stay with us?' Mrs Jackson quavered as they got her settled on one of the battered old armchairs they had put in the shelter.

'No. We're going to help out down in the village. The church has been hit. It's on fire.'

'Oh no! Not the church. Oh Harry, that's where my Arthur and your Doris are.'

'They'll be all right, lass,' he said, reaching for her hand in the darkness. 'They'll be safe.'

As Fleur and Ruth climbed out of the shelter and pulled the sacking cover across the entrance, they heard the old lady say, 'And I'm missing *Music Hall*. It's one of my favourites.'

Giggling, the two girls hurried back along the pathway.

'What she'd do without that wireless of hers, I dread to think,' Ruth said.

'It's a pity we can't take it down to the shelter with her. It'd keep her happy.'

Ruth stopped suddenly and Fleur cannoned into the back of her. 'Now what?' she said a little crossly as she'd bumped her nose on the back of Ruth's head.

'Well, we can.'

'Eh? Can what?'

'Take her wireless down there. It's a battery-operated one.'

'Do you think she'd want us to?'

'It's probably the only thing that'll keep her down there.'

'Come on then. Let's make it quick . . .'

A few minutes later as they left the Anderson once more, it was to the sound of dance music blaring out into the night, accompanied by the distant sound of falling bombs.

The fire at the church had been put out, but at the west end of the building was a gaping, smouldering hole in the roof.

The fire-fighters, together with members of the ARP, the Home Guard and villagers, their faces and clothes blackened and smutty, took a breather as the all-clear sounded. As the noise faded away, the RAF and WAAF contingencies found each other and made their way back to the pub, where Bill had opened his doors and was serving beer again as if nothing had happened.

'It's after hours,' Johnny said, picking up a welcome pint and taking a long drink before adding, 'won't you be in trouble with the local bobby?'

Bill laughed and nodded his head towards a figure sitting in the far corner of the bar room, his face blotched with smuts, his eyes wide with weariness, his uniform rumpled and his helmet missing. 'PC Mitchell turns a blind eye on such occasions.' Bill's deep chuckle rumbled again. 'Besides, he were first in the queue.'

'You look a sight,' Kay remarked, looking Ruth and Fleur up and down.

They grinned back as they retorted, 'So do you.'

Kay grimaced. 'I expect we're going to be on a charge when we get back.'

'Depends,' Ruth murmured.

'On what?'

'What's been happening there. I reckon there's been a lot of bombs fallen on the airfield. I expect that was their target.'

'That or Lincoln,' Tommy put in and, draining his glass, added, 'We'd better get back.'

'I just want to pop down the lane and see if the old folks are all right,' Fleur said to Robbie. 'But you go with the others. We'll be all right now.'

'Aren't you staying at your billet?'

Ruth and Fleur glanced at each other. 'No,' Ruth said. 'We might be needed on camp. We'll come back.'

'All right,' he agreed as he kissed her. 'Perhaps I'd better go with the lads, if you're quite sure . . .'

'I am,' she said firmly.

They were all moving towards the door when it burst open and Alfie and his cronies crowded in. For a brief moment the two groups stood staring at each other. Alfie's glance sought out Johnny and he took a step towards him and held out his hand, a wide grin breaking out over his boyish face. 'Thanks for your help tonight. Put it there, mate.'

With a laugh Johnny grasped the outstretched hand. 'Gladly.'

There were suddenly handshakes and back-slapping all round before Tommy said regretfully, 'Sorry we can't stay to have another drink with you lads, but we'd best get back to camp. We reckon it's taken a bit of a battering. We might be needed, but we'll see you all again as soon as we can.'

'Right you are,' Alfie said with a nod. 'And the drinks are on us next time.'

'You're on.' Johnny grinned.

'Oh, I do hope they're all right,' Fleur fretted as she and Ruth hurried back down the lane towards the two cottages. They were thankful to see that there was no damage to the two properties.

'They'll be back in the house, I bet,' Ruth said as they rounded the corner into the back yard and moved towards the back door. Her hand was already on the doorknob when she became still.

'Listen!'

Through the darkness the sound of dance music drifted from the Anderson.

'They're still down there. Come on, we'll help them back into the house and then go.'

But as they lifted the sacking over the entrance, above Billy Cotton's music on the wireless, they heard Harry's loud snoring.

Clutching each other and stifling their helpless giggles, they tiptoed away in the darkness.

They signed in quickly at the main gate.

'Do you know what's happened?' they asked the young airman on duty in the guardroom. His face was white, his eyes fearful. He's incredibly young, Fleur thought. He looks younger than our Kenny.

'Not really. I've been stuck here. It . . . it was pretty frightening. I think the runway's been hit and one or two buildings, but I don't know what.'

'I wonder where we'd better go,' Ruth wondered aloud. 'Where can we help?'

People were running to and fro and vehicles were rushing about putting out fires that still burned here and there.

'That's an aircraft.' Ruth nodded. 'I wonder how many we've lost.'

Fleur sighed. 'One or two I expect. But at least the crews will be safe.'

It was always annoying to lose aircraft on the ground. It seemed such a futile waste when they weren't even in battle, but it did mean the airmen were unharmed to fight another day, though they hated losing their aircraft. Some pilots and crews became attached to their own particular plane like a talisman.

'Come on. Let's see if we can find Kay.'

They found her eventually in the NAAFI, sitting at a table with her hands cupped round a mug of coffee, staring into space looking stunned.

'Kay? What is it? What's happened?'

Her eyes still didn't focus properly on them. 'She's dead,' she murmured hoarsely.

Ruth and Fleur glanced at each other.

'Get us a tea, Fleur. I'm parched.' The young girl behind the counter was calmly dispensing tea and coffee as if nothing had happened. She was even singing softly to herself. It was a particular kind of courage that Fleur always admired. Carrying on, no matter what.

When she returned to the table with two cups of tea they both sat down opposite Kay.

'Now,' Ruth said firmly, but not unkindly. 'Tell us what's happened? Who's dead?'

It was strange to see the outspoken Kay looking lost. The girl blinked and suddenly seemed to see them for the first time, to recognize them.

She took a deep breath as if trying to rally herself. 'Flight Sergeant Brown – the one you call the owd beezum. She was in the sergeants' mess and . . . and it took a direct hit. There's her and three of the fellers killed and one or two more injured.'

'Why on earth didn't they go to a shelter? There's one near the mess.'

'There wasn't time. The bombs started falling almost as soon as the siren started.'

'That's true. They did.' Ruth nodded.

'What can we do to help?' Fleur touched Kay's hand.

She shook her head. 'I – don't know.'

'Then we'll go to the watch office. Bob might be there. He'll know what we ought to do.'

Ruth and Fleur drank their tea quickly and stood

up. 'You coming?' Ruth said to Kay, who hadn't moved.

'What? Oh – oh, yes, I suppose so.'

As they moved out into the darkness, Fleur whispered to Ruth, 'Do you think she's all right? I mean, she looks stunned. Sort of – lost. I wouldn't have expected it of her. I mean, she's always so . . . so . . . well, I don't quite know what to call it, but you know what I mean. On top of things. I mean, when we had that raid when I was on duty with her, she was magnificent. She was calm as you like.'

'I don't know, but we'll keep her with us. She'll be all right. Maybe it's just shock.'

The three of them ran to the control room. Bob Watson was there ranting at the enemy.

'Would you believe it?' he raved. 'It's going to take days to put this lot right.' He flung his arm out to show them the glass littering the floor and paperwork scattered everywhere.

'Right,' Fleur said, as if metaphorically rolling up her sleeves. 'Let's get stuck in, girls. Kay, you fetch a sweeping brush. Ruth, you make some tea. Flight here looks as if he could do with a cup and I'll start sorting all this paperwork out.' She glanced at Bob. 'You here on your own? Where're the others?'

He sighed and sank down into a chair as if thankful to hand everything over to Fleur. 'Sick quarters. They both got cuts from the glass.'

'They're not badly hurt, are they?'

He shook his head. 'But I expect there'll be a few that are. Have you heard? I've been here all the time.'

Fleur nodded and repeated what Kay had told them.

Bob Watson shook his head sadly. 'That's a shame.

Poor old Brown. I know she was a bit of a tartar to you girls, but she was doing her duty as she saw it. She had your best interests at heart really, you know.'

Fleur was thoughtful for a moment before she nodded slowly and said, 'Yes, yes, you're right. I think she had.'

Twenty-Five

There were five fatalities that night on the airfield – three airmen, Flight Sergeant Brown and a young WAAF who had been running across the airfield to the nearest shelter but hadn't made it in time. The dead were buried side by side in the local churchyard. It was sad and touching to see the five coffins all being buried at the same time. Fleur, Ruth, Kay and seven other WAAFs formed a guard of honour around the coffins of Flight Sergeant Brown and the young WAAF. It was a grey, miserable day befitting the mood of those attending the funeral, made all the more poignant by the gaping hole in the roof at the end of the nave. A cold, damp breeze filtered into the church, chilling the mourners. It was even colder standing in the graveyard.

Afterwards, as they were about to turn away towards the pub for something to warm them, Fleur said, 'You two go on. I just want a word with someone.'

'OK. You know where we'll be,' Ruth said and linked her arm through Kay's as they walked on.

Others moved away until there was only a couple standing forlornly by the graveside of the young WAAF – and Fleur. She gave them a few moments before moving quietly towards them.

'I just wanted to say how sorry I am,' she said

softly. The man turned to face her. There were tears on his face, yet he managed a smile. 'Thank you, miss. That's kind of you. Were you a friend of our Joyce's?'

'I'm afraid I didn't know her well,' Fleur said evasively. In truth, she couldn't even remember having met the girl at all. There were several WAAFs she only came into contact with on parade. She knew them by sight, but not by name. Perhaps Joyce had been one of them. Billeted off camp, Fleur really only knew the girls with whom she worked.

'She'd only just finished her basic training a month ago. This was her first posting,' his wife said, her voice tremulous. But she, too, was smiling. 'It's such a shame – a waste, but we were so proud of her for joining up—'

'We still are,' the man said quickly. 'I wouldn't want you to think we'd have it any different, even though this . . . this has happened.' His voice broke and he blew his nose loudly on a large handkerchief.

His wife glanced at him and then turned back to say, 'She volunteered on her eighteenth birthday, you know?'

Fleur didn't, but she nodded anyway. 'Are you coming across to the pub? Bill – the landlord – will have laid on refreshments . . .'

'That's very kind of you, miss, but we'd best be catching the bus back to Lincoln and then the train home. We've a long way. I don't expect we'll be home before nightfall.'

'Where—?' Fleur began, and then stopped. She had been about to ask where they were from. But then, she realized quickly, they would know she hadn't really known their daughter. She cleared her throat and swiftly changed what she had been about to say.

'Where will you get something to drink and eat? You ought to have a cup of tea at least.'

The man and woman exchanged a glance. 'All right, miss. You're right. We could do with something – even if it's only a cuppa.'

But half an hour later, Fleur was pleased to see them tucking into the sandwiches that Bill's wife always managed to produce when there was a particularly harrowing funeral. And today's certainly fell into that category, Fleur thought sadly. A little later she saw the couple onto the bus for Lincoln. The man – she still didn't know his surname – shook her hand warmly.

'It's been nice to meet you, miss, though I could have wished for happier circumstances. But it's a comfort to the missis and me to know that our girl had lovely friends like you. You've made today a lot easier. Thank you.'

Fleur couldn't speak for the lump in her throat. She would probably never meet these people again, but if she had helped ease their pain at all, then the little white lie that she had known their daughter was surely forgivable. As a salve to her own conscience she said impulsively, 'While I'm here, I'll look after Joyce's grave for you. Keep it tidy and that. I promise.'

The woman leant forward and kissed her cheek. 'How kind,' she murmured and dabbed away her tears.

'We'll arrange for a headstone. Perhaps you could see that it's done nicely?'

'I will,' was Fleur's parting promise to them.

Later that night, in Ruth's bedroom at the cottage, Fleur told her what had happened after the funeral and the promises she had made. 'And there's something else . . .' Her voice dropped to a whisper. 'When we were in the graveyard I noticed poor Mrs Jackson's husband's headstone has been broken in two. The top half's lying on the ground. I bet the bomb did it.'

'Oh, crumbs, she'll be upset. It was the first thing she thought of when we told her the church had been hit. Are you going to tell her?'

Fleur shook her head. 'No, but I'm going to see if I can get it repaired for her. Maybe she won't need to know. I'll ask my dad. He'll know what to do.'

It was several days after the bombing before Fleur got a chance to go home for a brief, overnight visit.

'Dad?'

'Ssh, listen!' Jake was sitting in his chair near the range, his head against the wireless that sat on a shelf next to the range. 'Listen!'

Fleur bit her lip, waiting impatiently, until Jake reached and turned off the wireless. 'They've got the *Bismarck*. Can you believe it? Our lads have sunk the *Bismarck*!' Jake's face was alight with triumph for a moment, then he sobered swiftly. 'It's a great victory for us, but you can't help thinking about all those poor boys drowned or shot to pieces. They reckon there must be over a thousand men lost.' He shook his head sadly. 'And I bet half those young lads don't know what they're fighting for. You know, Fleur,' he said heavily, 'lots of folks wouldn't agree with me, but I reckon the ordinary German bloke doesn't want this war any more than we do. They've just been swept along in a tide of patriotism by a fanatic who's just bent on ruling the world.'

Fleur sat down beside him and touched his arm in a

gesture of understanding. 'You're right, Dad. And the loss of life on both sides, well, it's just sinful, isn't it? But what can we do? We've got to stop Hitler. We can't let him achieve his terrible ambition, now can we?'

'No, love, of course we can't.' He sighed heavily. 'But it's just so sad that all these innocent young lives are being wasted in the process. And only twenty years after the last lot. Another generation of young fellers.'

They sat in silence for a moment, until he pulled himself together and said, 'What was it you wanted, love?'

Fleur explained about the air raid and the damaged gravestone.

'Tell you what, love, I'll take you back tomorrow and see what I can do.'

'Oh, Dad, would you really? That'd be lovely – but not a word to Mrs Jackson, mind. We haven't told her. I'm just hoping no one else does before we can get it mended.'

'Aye, we'll have a family outing. Mebbe your mum'll come too. And Kenny.'

But Betsy was determined to play the spoilsport. 'I've too much to do to go gallivanting about the countryside. And you shouldn't be using petrol to go jaunting.'

'I've enough petrol to take my daughter back to camp without endangering the war effort and to do a favour for an old lady,' Jake replied, keeping his tone deliberately mild.

'You shouldn't be having to take your daughter anywhere. She should be here at home doing her duty. And now, because of her, I've likely got to put up with having strangers living here. Land Army girls, indeed.

And townies! What are they going to know about life in the country, I'd like to know.'

Betsy went back into her kitchen still muttering darkly, whilst Jake winked at Fleur. 'Well, I tried. She can't say she wasn't asked to come, now can she?'

It was a merry little party that set off in Jake's boneshaker of a car the following morning. Just the three of them – even Kenny had not been able to persuade Betsy to come along.

'You shouldn't be skipping school,' she admonished. 'Not if you want to get into agricultural college . . .'

Kenny opened his mouth to retort that he had no intention of going to college and never would have, but, guessing his intention, Jake cut in, 'Half a day won't hurt, love. And I really need his help.'

They bowled along, singing at the top of their voices, above the chugging of the noisy engine, but when they arrived at the churchyard their spirits sobered as they viewed the damage and saw the five freshly dug graves, side by side.

Kenny put his arm around Fleur's shoulders and gave her a quick hug. He said nothing, but his action spoke volumes. That could have been you, Sis, he seemed to be saying.

Jake cleared his throat and became suddenly brisk and businesslike. 'Right then. Where's old Arthur's grave, Fleur?'

She led them around the end of the church that had been damaged. They paused for a moment looking up at the gaping hole in the roof. 'That's going to take a bit longer than a day's work,' Jake declared. They moved on to stand before Arthur Jackson's headstone.

'Well, there's one good thing,' Jake said, after he

had examined it carefully. 'It's a clean break. I reckon a bit of cement will sort that out. You'll still see the crack, I'm afraid, but that'll maybe weather in time.' He glanced up at Fleur. 'Do you think she'll know yet?'

'Only if someone's told her while I've been away. Ruth won't, but Harry might if he finds out.'

'Right then, we'll see what we can do.' He straightened up and began to move back towards the car. 'Give us a hand, Kenny, will you?'

They carried all the paraphernalia that Jake had brought with him in the boot of the car through the gateway and set it all on the grass beside the grave.

'See if you can find us some water, Fleur. There's usually a tap somewhere in a churchyard.'

Fleur picked up a bucket and set off in search of water. She'd walked all the way around the church and arrived back at the main door when the vicar appeared from inside the church.

'Oh, hello, Vicar. Where can I find some water?'

'For flowers?' Revd Cunningham asked.

Fleur shook her head. 'We're trying to repair Mr Jackson's headstone. It got broken the other night and I know it'll upset poor Mrs Jackson if she finds out about it. I've just been home on a couple of days' leave so my father's brought me back and come to see what he can do.'

The man, who had led the most difficult funeral service only a few days earlier, beamed at Fleur. 'How very kind of him – and of you to think of it. The tap's over there, my dear, near the wall a little way along from the gate. I'll go and have a word with your father.'

Fleur followed the line of his pointing finger and saw the tap. 'Thanks, Vicar.'

When she returned, it was to find the three men talking and laughing together as if they had known each other for years.

'What a great bloke,' Kenny said when Revd Cunningham had excused himself and left them to their repairs. 'I thought all vicars were stuffy and superior. But he's a smashing chap.'

'He gave a lovely service last week,' Fleur said. 'At the funerals, I mean. It can't have been easy for him. But he seemed to know just what to say somehow. I can't remember a word he said now, but I know it was both moving and comforting at the same time.'

Jake had finished the mix of cement and had smeared it on top of the broken edge. 'Right, Kenny. Help me lift this up and when we've got it in place you can hold it whilst I put a couple of iron strips on the back of the headstone. Cement alone won't hold it. I don't know what it'll look like, but it's the best I can do.'

A little later they all stood back to assess Jake's handiwork. 'I'm afraid the crack still shows badly.'

'At least Arthur's got his headstone back,' Fleur said as they gathered everything up and reloaded the car.

'Now, do you think your Mrs Jackson could find us a cup of tea and one of those delicious scones she makes before we set off back?'

'Of course, she will. But not a word about what we've been doing.'

'Actually, love, I think we should tell her now. She's bound to hear about it and it'll soften the blow, perhaps, if we tell her what we've tried to do.'

Fleur sighed. 'Yes, I expect you're right.'

Mary Jackson not only made them a cup of tea, but

also insisted that they should share the stew she had made.

'We can't take your precious rations,' Jake insisted at first, but then from the back seat of the car he carried in a box of a dozen eggs, half a pound of butter and a wedge of cheese.

'How very kind of you,' Mrs Jackson said. 'Now I insist you stay for your dinner. Besides, Harry would never forgive me if I let you go without him seeing you again. Ah, that'll be him now. Come away in, Harry. We've got visitors.'

After the meal, whilst Fleur cleared the pots away and washed up in the scullery, Jake sat beside the old lady and, taking her hand in his, explained gently the reason for his visit.

'We've done the best we can, my dear. I'm afraid I can't say it's as good as new, though.'

Mrs Jackson dabbed her eyes with the corner of her apron, but she was smiling through her tears. 'How kind of you to come all this way to do that for me. You really shouldn't have, but I am glad you did. Thank you, Jake. Thank you very much.'

Twenty-Six

The next few weeks were a flurry of excitement, marred only by Betsy's obstinate mood. Meg, blithely ignorant of the depth of the trouble within Fleur's family, offered to make not only the bride's gown but also a bridesmaid's dress for Ruth. When the girls couldn't get to Nottingham for a fitting, Meg travelled by train and bus to the village where they were billeted, lugging a suitcase full of paper patterns and material samples with her.

Fleur hurried down the path to meet her. 'Oh, this is so good of you. Neither of us can get leave at the moment.'

'Don't mention it, love. It's nice to get away for a while.' She laughed gaily. 'Oh, don't get me wrong. I love Pops dearly, but with working at home as well I never seem to see anything but those same four walls.'

'I can guess what you mean. How is Pops? Is he better now?'

'As good as he'll ever be. He's got a bad chest and he's only to pick up a cold and it's bronchitis or even pneumonia. Hence the stay in hospital. Still, he's much better now the warmer weather's here. Edie, next door, is keeping an eye on him today. She'll fuss round him and he'll enjoy that.'

'Here, let me take that case for you . . . Goodness!'

Fleur exclaimed. 'Whatever have you got in here? It weighs a ton.'

Meg chuckled. 'You'll see.'

'Come along in and meet Mrs Jackson. She's a sweet old dear and getting so excited about the wedding. Did Robbie tell you, we've booked the church here for Saturday, the sixth of September? And we've both applied for a week's leave.'

Following Fleur down the narrow path and round the side of the house, Meg asked quietly, 'Don't you want to be married in South Monkford?'

Fleur paused, her hand on the back doorknob, and turned to glance back at Meg. 'No,' she said quietly. 'It'll . . . it'll be easier here. We're resident in this parish and . . . and . . . well, it'll be better all round. Dad and Kenny can get here and . . .'

Meg was staring at her. 'What d'you mean? Your dad and Kenny? What about your mother?'

Fleur kicked herself mentally. She hadn't meant to tell Robbie's mother yet. Of course, she'd find out eventually but . . . Anyway, she'd said it now. She sighed and said flatly, 'She won't be coming.'

'Won't – be – coming?' Meg was scandalized. Then, after a moment's thought, she pursed her mouth. 'That's because of me, is it?' She sighed and shook her head in disbelief. 'I wouldn't have thought that Betsy's bitterness went quite so deep. So deep that she won't come to her own daughter's wedding.'

Fleur stared at Meg for a moment before she took a deep breath. 'I don't understand it at all. What *is* she so bitter about?'

Meg lifted her padded shoulders, but she was avoiding Fleur's candid eyes as she forced an offhandedness. 'My dear, I really have no idea.'

And there – for the moment – Fleur had to let the matter drop. She didn't want to risk upsetting Robbie's mother. She knew Meg was lying, or at least avoiding the truth, but she couldn't question her – not as much as Robbie would be able to do. And even he hadn't wanted to press matters any further than he already had done. He had his mother's reassurance that he and Fleur were not related and that was all he needed – or wanted – to know. As long as he could marry his lovely Fleur, that was all that mattered to him. So, Fleur took her lead from him, and instead of asking the awkward questions that still tumbled around her own mind, she smiled brightly and opened the back door. 'Come in. Mrs Jackson's so looking forward to meeting you. She's very fond of Robbie.' Fleur leant towards Meg to whisper. 'She gets all girlish when he's around.' She forbore to say that it was more that Mrs Jackson mothered him, perhaps remembering her own lost son.

Meg laughed. 'Well, he's a handsome boy, even if I say it myself.'

The awkwardness of a few moments ago was pushed aside, if not quite forgotten. At least, Fleur had not forgotten. Silently, she promised herself: one day I will find out what all the mystery is.

Very soon the old lady's kitchen table was spread with paper patterns and scraps of material.

'Now then,' came Harry's voice as he knocked on the back door, opened it and came in. 'What's going on here?'

'Harry,' Fleur called, winking at Mrs Jackson. She guessed the old man had seen Meg arrive and the sight of the pretty, smartly dressed stranger had aroused his lively curiosity. 'Come on in and meet my future mother-in-law.'

Harry stood just inside the doorway and stared at Meg. He stroked his white moustache and chuckled. 'You can't be young Robbie's mother. You're not old enough.'

Meg's eyes sparkled mischievously as she held out her hand. 'I assure you I am. And you must be Harry? I've heard a lot about you from Robbie – and from Fleur too. I'm very pleased to meet you.'

'Likewise, Mrs – er . . .'

'Meg.' Her eyes twinkled merrily at him. 'Please call me "Meg".'

Unbidden, her mother's words came into Fleur's mind. 'It'll be some poor old fool she's set her cap at.' Quickly, she pushed aside the unjust thought. She must not allow her mother's prejudice to influence her.

Bringing her thoughts back to the present, Fleur sighed as she fingered the pieces of silk and satin that Meg had brought. 'But how am I to raise enough coupons for any of these fabrics?' Fleur murmured. At the beginning of June clothing coupons had been introduced.

'Don't you worry about that,' Meg said. 'I've a trunk in the loft at home full of old dresses I've collected over the years. You know, when people have been getting rid of them. There are at least three silk dresses up there. I'm sure I can turn one of them into something for you if we can't raise enough coupons for new material. Only trouble is,' Meg said with disappointment, 'they're not white.'

'You can have my clothing coupons, dear,' said Mrs Jackson. 'I won't need them all.'

'And mine,' Harry put in. 'You can have all mine. Long as me good suit'll still fit me for the big day, I don't need no coupons for new clothes.'

Meg smiled at him archly. 'You'll have to try your suit on, Harry, and let me know if it needs any alteration.'

The old man chuckled, his eyes sparkling. 'Well now, I'm sure it'll need summat doing. It's a long time since I wore it.'

Fleur shuddered as once again her mother's words pushed their unwelcome way into her thoughts. Stop it! she told herself sharply. She's only being nice to the old boy. We all have fun with Harry. Even Mary Jackson teases him and Ruth positively flirts with him.

But now, Fleur could not help thinking, Ruth might have a rival for Harry's affections.

'That's very generous of you,' Meg was saying, pulling Fleur's thoughts back to the moment. 'But it's not only the coupons, it's finding the right material too.'

'Er . . .' Mrs Jackson seemed suddenly hesitant. 'Er . . . there is my wedding dress. It was white. You – you could have that, dear.'

Fleur stared at her. 'Oh, Mrs Jackson, no, I couldn't. It must hold such memories for you. I wouldn't want to . . .' Her voice faded away as Harry moved forward and put his arm around the old lady's ample waist. 'There now, Mary, that's a kind thought. A very kind action. And I'll match it. They can have my Doris's things, an' all. Time we stopped clinging to the past, eh, and let the young folks mek what they can of the present.' He wiped a tear from the corner of his eye. 'I reckon they're earning it, don't you? Besides' – he chuckled and winked at Fleur – 'Ruth'll be pleased to hear I'm getting rid of some more rubbish.' And they all laughed.

'You're right, Harry. My Arthur would agree and I know your Doris would have turfed all her old clothes out ages ago.'

The old man laughed again. 'She would that. I bet she's up there shaking her fist at me for letting the house get in such a mess. Anyway, thanks to young Ruth, it's bright as a new pin now. Doris'd've been pleased to help you, lass.' He nodded towards Fleur.

'And wouldn't Arthur be chuffed with his garden?' Mary Jackson was not quite finished with her reminiscing yet. 'And I owe that all to you, Fleur dear. So, yes, if Mrs Rodwell here . . .'

'Meg,' Meg interposed.

Mrs Jackson smiled. 'If Meg here can do anything with my wedding dress, you're very welcome to it.'

'And I'll get young Ruth to sort out all Doris's clothes and let you have them.'

Mrs Jackson was already moving stiffly towards the front room of the cottage that was now her bedroom. 'It's in here. In a trunk . . .'

But when they unearthed Mary's wedding dress, it was sadly yellowed and moth-eaten. The old lady fingered the material with tears in her eyes. 'What a shame. Such a happy day we had.'

Meg glanced at Fleur and at Ruth, who had now arrived home. Then she put her arm around the old lady's shoulders. 'It's a good job our memories last better than material, isn't it?' she said gently.

'But I thought it'd help Fleur . . .'

'Don't worry,' Meg reassured her. 'I know just what we can do. We'll scrape together enough coupons for Fleur to have a brand new dress.' She looked at Ruth.

'And I'm sure I can alter one of the dresses I've got, or one of Doris's, into a bridesmaid's dress for you. And some of the lace on this dress of yours, Mrs Jackson, is perfect. I can dye it to match whatever dress we decide on for Ruth.'

'Pink,' Fleur said.

'Blue,' Ruth insisted and fluffed her blonde curls. 'I look all wishy-washy in pink.' She made a moue with her mouth.

Meg regarded her thoughtfully. 'You know, Fleur, I think blue would suit her better, if you don't mind me saying so.'

Fleur smiled. 'Of course I don't. To tell you the truth, I don't care what anybody wears as long as Robbie turns up.'

They all laughed now, but Meg said very seriously, 'Oh, he'll turn up all right, I promise you that.' Though it was not spoken aloud, the thought was in everyone's mind. Just so long as he's able.

Twenty-Seven

'I'm here again,' Meg trilled as she opened the back door of Mary Jackson's cottage.

'Come in, love, come in,' Mary said, struggling to her feet.

'Please don't get up, Mrs Jackson,' Meg said as she heaved the huge suitcase through the back door. As the old lady sank back thankfully into the armchair, Meg added, 'But I could do with a cuppa. Mind if I make one?'

'Of course not, love. Help yourself.'

'I don't like using your precious tea.'

'Don't worry. The girls bring supplies from the camp. They're allowed to,' she added hastily, 'seeing as they've had to be billeted off the camp.'

Meg nodded. 'How're they getting on with building the WAAFs' quarters?'

Mrs Jackson smiled. 'Slowly.'

Meg chuckled. 'But I can see you don't mind about that.'

The old lady shook her head. 'Those two lasses have changed my life.' Her smile widened. 'And I'll be seeing a lot more of your boy too after they're married, I expect. He's a grand lad.'

Meg nodded. 'I think so,' she said earnestly, and then added with a smile, 'but then I could be biased.'

She glanced out of the window overlooking the back garden.

It was the third week in June already and all Fleur's hard work was beginning to pay off. Lettuces and radishes were sprouting up on top of the Anderson shelter and rows of green ferny leaves had appeared where she'd planted carrots. In the front garden, runner beans were climbing their frames, as too, unbeknown to Mrs Jackson, were the sweet peas at the end of the cottage.

'She's working so hard,' Mrs Jackson told Meg. 'Every spare minute she's out there dressed in her old clothes and her woolly hat when it's windy. And your boy, too, he comes whenever he can. They both helped me yesterday to bottle some gooseberries and make some strawberry jam. Harry's got a strawberry bed and he gave us some of the fruit. Don't forget – before you go – I'll give you a jar.'

'Oh, how lovely! Home-made jam. That will be a treat. Didn't you find it tiring? You mustn't overdo it,' Meg added with concern.

Mrs Jackson laughed. 'Oh, they did it all.'

Meg's eyes widened. 'My Robbie? Jam making?'

'Well, under Fleur's instruction. I didn't have to do much. I just sat here and topped and tailed the gooseberries. Her mother must have trained her well. She knew just what to do.'

Meg's eyes darkened as she said, 'Yes, I expect she did.' Her tone – though unnoticed by Mrs Jackson – hardened a little as she added, 'I expect her mother is the perfect farmer's wife.'

'Fleur's even saying,' Mrs Jackson went on, 'that she can't be away too long on honeymoon because a lot of the fruit and vegetables will be ready in September.'

Meg laughed. 'Well, I think Robbie might have something to say about that, don't you? But I can understand what she means. She doesn't want all her hard work – and the produce – to go to waste.'

'Oh, I think we can manage for a week. Harry will come round and do what he can and even Ruth's promised to help.'

Meg's voice was dreamy as she murmured, 'Perhaps Jake would come over.'

'I expect he's got enough to cope with on the farm,' Mrs Jackson said, knowing nothing of Meg's inner thoughts. 'But Kenny will cycle over, I don't doubt. We – Harry and me – think he's got his eye on Ruth.'

'So,' Meg said, turning away from the window. 'When will the girls be home?'

Mrs Jackson's face sobered. 'I don't know. There's some sort of flap on at the camp. I . . . I . . .' She hesitated to worry the young airman's mother, but she couldn't lie. 'I think there's a big raid on tonight. We're not supposed to know, but because so many of the personnel are living in the village at the moment, we . . . we sort of get the feel that something's going on. They don't say anything, of course. Not a word. But we've got to know how to read the signs.'

'I see,' Meg said quietly. 'So . . . so you think the girls might not be back today at all?'

Mrs Jackson shook her head.

Meg bit her lip. 'Well, I can't stay. I have to get back because of my father.' How she would love to have stayed – to have been here when the girls got home whatever time it was. To know at once that

Robbie was safely back. But she couldn't impose on Mrs Jackson and, more importantly, she couldn't leave her father for all that time. Since his spell in hospital, he was even frailer and needed a helping hand to climb the stairs to his bed. 'But I'll leave the dresses here. They can try them on and help each other with the fitting. Tell them I'll come back a week today and if they still can't be here, then they must pin them carefully and leave me instructions. We've still over two months to the big day, so there's plenty of time.'

Mrs Jackson nodded. 'You'll be surprised how fast the weeks go and with the girls working different shifts it's difficult for you to meet up with them. But I'll be sure to tell them what you've said. The big day will soon be here.'

Meg nodded, unable to speak. She was too busy praying that Robbie would be there.

She kissed the old lady's wrinkled cheek and let herself out of the back door. As she walked down the narrow path between the two cottages, she heard Harry's voice.

'Now then, lass. All right?'

She glanced up, and despite her sober thoughts, couldn't help smiling. To hear the old man call her, a woman of over forty, 'lass' always made her laugh. But, she supposed, to him she was 'no' but a lass'.

'Mustn't grumble,' she answered.

'Doesn't do any good if you do,' Harry chuckled. 'Nobody listens.'

He moved closer and leant on the fence running between the two pathways. 'I saw you arrive. I was just coming round. Are you off again?'

Meg nodded. 'Mrs Jackson doesn't think the girls are going to be home today.'

'Ah,' Harry nodded knowingly. 'So she said when I popped round this morning . . .' The idea of old Harry 'popping' anywhere, made Meg smile again. 'I'm very fond of them lasses, y' know. They're like me own.'

'Have you any family, Harry?' Meg asked, trying desperately to get her thoughts away from her own son and, for a few moments, to concentrate on someone else.

'Aye. Not now, lass,' his face clouded. 'Me an' Doris only had the one son and he were killed in the last war.'

'I'm sorry,' Meg murmured.

'What happened to Robbie's father then?' Harry asked, with the bluntness that old age seemed to believe it had a right to.

Meg gave a start and stared at him for a moment, then swallowed nervously. It was an innocent question. Of course, Harry couldn't know anything. This wasn't South Monkford . . .

'My husband,' Meg said carefully, 'was quite a few years older than me. He was too old for the last war, but he died in the influenza epidemic just after.'

Harry nodded sympathetically. 'Aye, I remember that. Took a few from this village. It were a bugger, weren't it? All them lads surviving the trenches to be hit by the flu when they got home. Bad business. Bad business.' He eyed her keenly. 'And you've brought that lad up on yar own?'

Meg smiled. 'It wasn't difficult. He's a good boy. And then my father came back – came to live with us. He worked a little at first. Here and there – just odd jobs, you know. And I've always been kept busy with my dressmaking.'

‘’Spect you’re in demand now with all the shortages,’ Harry nodded.

‘Well, yes, I am. And I expect it will get worse – or better’ – she smiled – ‘depending on your point of view. Now they’ve brought in rationing, women want the clothes they’ve got altering to be a little more fashionable. Keeps their spirits up, you know.’

Harry looked her up and down. ‘You always look so pretty and smart. Now I know why.’ He paused, then cleared his throat and stroked his moustache with a quick nervous movement. ‘Did you find anything useful amongst Doris’s things?’

‘Oh yes.’ Meg was enthusiastic. ‘There was a lovely long silk gown I’ve been able to make into a bridesmaid’s dress. And it was blue – just the colour Ruth wanted.’

Harry nodded. ‘Aye, I remember that.’ His eyes misted over briefly. ‘Doris looked a picture in that.’ Then he chuckled. ‘You might not think looking at me now, but I used to be quite a good dancer. Loved dancing, did the wife, and she always liked to dress up if we went to a proper dance.’ He cleared his throat. ‘Well, I’m real pleased if her things were some use to you. Ruth sorted ’em all out for me. She was real good, didn’t make me part with anything I didn’t want to, but she’s right, it’s high time I let go. Doesn’t mean I’m going to forget my Doris just because I let her old clothes go, does it?’

‘Of course not,’ Meg agreed gently. ‘And I’ve been able to make use of those two nice suits of your wife’s. It was such good material. I’ve altered one to fit Mrs Jackson for the wedding. They must have been almost the same size. I hope you don’t mind. I mean, it won’t upset you, will it, seeing her wearing it?’

'I'll not let it,' Harry said stoutly. 'I'll just remember that my Doris would have liked that. They were big pals, y'know. 'Er and Mary Jackson. Big pals. Allus in and out of each other's kitchens. Borrowing sugar and a bit of flour. And swapping recipes. No, lass, she'd have been thrilled. And so will I be.'

Twenty-Eight

Life at Wickerton Wood had been fairly mundane for several weeks, if being involved with bombing raids could ever be described as mundane, but on the day that Meg came to visit a bigger mission than usual had been planned for that night and everyone on the airfield was tense.

Take-off, with more than the normal number of aircraft taking part, went smoothly and everyone in the watch office heaved a sigh of relief as the last bomber lumbered into the air and disappeared into the deepening dusk. The airfield was strangely silent after the drumming of dozens of engines. Yet for some reason the staff were unable to relax into their usual diversions for the waiting hours. Peggy made copious cups of tea until Fleur said, 'Do you know, when this war's over, I don't think I'll ever drink tea again.' She was trying to lighten the atmosphere, but failing. 'It's my landlady's cure-all and we seem to drink gallons of it here too.' Fleur, more than anyone, was feeling jittery. When she'd pricked her finger twice sewing a button on her blouse, she gave up and tried to read. But the words on the page blurred before her eyes and the light romantic novel seemed out of place when she was in the middle of a real-life drama.

The aircraft were late – all of them – and Bob began his restless pacing as he always did. At last, the first call sign came over the airwaves and one by one the planes limped home. And many of them had some damage. Several were landing on almost empty tanks. One plane had a damaged undercarriage and slithered off the runway to land on its belly on the perimeter track, the crash crews and fire tenders screaming out to it at once.

Then there were only three left to return, but the airwaves were silent. Fleur glanced up at the blackboard. Her heart missed a beat and then began to thump wildly.

Beside Tommy Laughton's name, the space was blank.

The minutes seemed to turn into hours whilst they all waited. The wireless crackled and a voice requested permission to land. But it wasn't Tommy and Robbie's aircraft. Kay snapped her answer. It was the first time Fleur had ever seen her colleague show any sign of stress whilst on duty.

The aircraft landed safely and then – there was silence once more. The tension in the watch office mounted. No one spoke as the minutes ticked by.

At last, when they were almost ready to give up hope, the radio crackled into life once more, and Fleur almost fainted with relief as she heard, 'Hello, Woody, this is D-Doggo calling . . .'

Fleur flew into his arms, not caring who saw them, not caring if she was reprimanded.

'I thought you weren't coming back. I thought we'd never get married. I thought . . .'

Though exhausted, with heavy dark rings under his eyes, Robbie could still raise a smile. 'Hey, what do you take me for?' He put his arm about her as they continued walking towards the debriefing centre. 'I'm not the sort of chap who leaves his girl standing at the altar. Not even Adolf is going to stop that.'

'Oh, Robbie . . .' She was crying openly now.

He paused a moment and turned to face her, taking her face between his hands. 'I have to go now, darling. You know that. But I'll see you tomorrow.'

She nodded. 'Get some sleep. You look all in.'

His eyes clouded. 'It was a bad one, Fleur. Our plane is badly damaged. But the one good thing is we won't be flying tomorrow. So I'll see you tomorrow night and you can tell me how all the plans are going. Love you . . .' He kissed her soundly on the mouth and turned to follow his weary crew into debriefing.

Suddenly, the tiredness washed over Fleur. Anxiety for Robbie had kept her going, but now that he was safe, the sleepless hours finally caught up with her. By the time she had walked to the cottage – it would be a while before Ruth could come home – Fleur had scarcely the strength to climb the stairs and fall into bed. So it wasn't until the following morning that Fleur heard from Mrs Jackson that Meg had visited.

'I told her I didn't think you'd be home yesterday, so she didn't wait, but she left the dresses for you to try on . . .' Mary Jackson repeated Meg's instructions about the fitting. Then she added anxiously, 'Fleur, I'm sorry, but I told her I thought there was something big going on at the airfield. I hope I didn't worry her.'

Fleur stared at her. She opened her mouth to say, *Of course you'll have worried her. You shouldn't have said anything. You shouldn't have said a word . . .* But seeing the troubled look on the old lady's face, her swift anger melted and instead she said, 'Robbie's back safely. I'll let her know somehow.'

'Don't send her a telegram,' Ruth said, her mouth full of porridge. 'That'll scare the living daylights out of her.'

Fleur bit her lip. 'But how can I let her know then? I can't go in person, we're on duty again tonight, aren't we?'

Ruth nodded. 'But Robbie probably won't be flying. His plane won't be ready for tonight.' She glanced up at Fleur. 'Did you see it?'

Fleur shook her head.

'Badly shot up, it was. One engine out of action and holes all down the fuselage. It was a miracle they got back at all, and even more miraculous not one of them was hurt.'

Fleur shuddered and sent up a silent prayer of thanks.

'I'll ring Mr Tomkins at the shop on the corner. He's the only one with a telephone in our street, but he doesn't mind taking messages for folks. 'Specially not now. And his little lad positively longs for the phone to ring.' Robbie laughed. 'The little tyke gets a few coppers from anyone he delivers a message to. More, if it's good news he brings.'

'I hadn't the heart to tell Mrs Jackson off, but she really shouldn't have said anything.'

Robbie pulled a face. 'Ma knows the score, I doubt she's any more worried than usual. But I will ring. There might be something on the wireless about it being a bad raid. Then she will worry.'

'Let's walk down to the phone box and do it now,' Fleur insisted. Although it wasn't her fault, she felt guilty that Meg had been burdened with extra anxiety. Though the worry would always be present, miles away in Nottingham she was usually unaware of exactly what was happening. But not this time.

As they walked down the lane, arm in arm, Robbie said, 'At least I've a bit of good news. My leave for the whole week after the wedding has been granted.'

Fleur grinned up at him. 'Mine too. I heard yesterday.' She hugged his arm. 'So where are you taking me on honeymoon?'

'Ah – now I haven't quite decided. But I'll tell you one thing. One of the chaps is lending me his sports car for the week, so as long as I can scrounge enough petrol we can go anywhere you like.'

'I don't care. Just as long as we're together.'

They reached the phone box and Robbie got through to Mr Tomkins. 'Just get your Micky to nip down the street and tell Ma and Pops I'm OK.'

'Right you are, lad . . .' Fleur, squashed into the box alongside him, heard the shopkeeper's voice faintly. 'Glad to hear you're OK. All ready for the big day, a' yer? All the best from me and the missis.'

'Thank you, Mr Tomkins,' Robbie said and turned to Fleur. 'Did you hear that?'

Fleur nodded as Robbie bent his head to kiss her. 'Oh, I'm ready for the big day all right.' Only the sharp rapping of someone on the glass window, anxious to use the telephone, finally disturbed them.

On a warm day towards the end of June, Fleur was at the end of the cottage tending the growing row of sweet peas. She sprayed the plants with water and then pinched out the side shoots. Pulling up one of the plants where the leaves had turned yellow, she said, 'You're not going to give Mrs Jackson any pretty flowers, are you, poor thing?'

'Fleur, Fleur – where are you?' She heard Mrs Jackson calling from the back door. Not wanting to give away what she was growing in secret along the wall, Fleur quickly moved into the front garden, paused a moment to inspect the row of runner beans and then went around the house by the pathway.

'Did you call?' she asked innocently as she rounded the corner.

'Oh, there you are, dear. Come in and listen to this on the wireless. We can't believe it!'

'What is it? What's happened?'

Mrs Jackson beckoned. 'Come and listen – you'll never believe it.' The old lady turned and hurried as fast as her legs would take her back to her seat beside the wireless. Harry was sitting in the chair on the other side and, as Fleur took off her boots and stepped into the kitchen, she saw the old couple, one on each side of the wireless, leaning towards it, straining to hear every word the news announcer was saying.

'What's happened?' Fleur asked again, to be answered with a 'Shh' from both of them.

Fleur listened but could make no sense of the final words of the bulletin and, as Mrs Jackson switched off the wireless, Fleur glanced at them in turn, the question on her face.

'Old Adolf's invaded Russia.'

'Russia?' Fleur was shocked. 'Whatever for? I thought he'd signed a non-aggression pact with Stalin?'

'He did. But he's broken it.'

Fleur sank down into a chair. 'But why? Russia's a massive country with an army of millions. How can he hope to beat Russia?'

''Cos he's a madman, that's why. Mind you, it'll probably be his downfall and while he's busy fighting that lot he won't be bothering us so much, now will he?'

Fleur wrinkled her brow thoughtfully. 'Maybe not.'

'If he tries to keep all his fronts going, he'll be spread too thin, see.' Harry stroked his moustache and beamed. 'What we want is for the Yanks to come in. Then we'd really see the end of Hitler.'

'I don't think they will. It's not their war, is it? You can't really expect them to do any more than they're doing,' Fleur said reasonably. 'I mean, I know we weren't exactly being attacked when war was declared, but we were certainly on his agenda, weren't we?'

'Aye, aye, I see what you mean, lass. It's just that – to my mind – with the might of America behind us, we couldn't lose.'

Fleur grinned at him. 'We can't anyway.'

Harry smile was tinged with poignancy. 'No, lass,' he said and his voice was husky with emotion. 'No, not whilst there's youngsters like you about, we can't lose.'

'Well, this won't get the hoeing done,' she said getting up. 'We're all going to a dance in Lincoln tonight, so I'll need a bit of time to get my glad rags on.'

As they climbed aboard the 'Liberty Bus' to take them into the city that evening, the chatter was all about the invasion of Russia and how it might affect Britain.

'It's got to take the heat off us, surely.'

'Well, I don't mind a bit of a breather, 'specially in September,' Robbie remarked, putting his arm around Fleur's shoulder. His statement was greeted with whistles and catcalls until Fleur blushed.

'Where are we all going?' she said, trying to divert attention from herself. 'It's too nice to sit in a cinema or a smoky dance hall, isn't it?'

'How about,' Robbie suggested, 'a row on the Brayford?'

'That's a good idea,' Tommy agreed. 'We could have a race.'

'Well, I'm popping home to see my folks,' Ruth said. 'But only for an hour or so. I'll meet you down there later.'

'Aw, come on, Ruth. Your folks won't mind for once, will they?' Robbie tried to persuade her.

'I won't be long, I promise.'

Robbie seemed disappointed. 'Where do you want the bus to drop you, then?'

'Monks Road near the school. I'll walk down to the Brayford from there. I'll only be about an hour.'

'My goodness,' Fleur exclaimed as they arrived beside the Brayford Pool. She shaded her eyes against the sun setting over the smooth expanse of water, the tall warehouses silhouetted against the golden glow. Sitting on a wall, three young boys dangled home-made fishing rods in the water. 'I've never been down here before. Oh, and look at all the barges. It's lovely.'

Boats were hired and soon everyone was out on the wide pool and heading towards where the Pool narrowed into the Fossdyke.

There was much shouting to one another and laughter and banter. A race of sorts developed until the airmen rowing decided the competition wasn't worth the risk of aching muscles the next day and they all rowed leisurely towards a pub set a little way back from the bank.

'We should have waited for Ruth,' Fleur said regretfully. 'She won't bring a boat out on her own.'

'Don't expect she'll be on her own,' Robbie said cheerfully.

'Really? Why? Do you know something I don't?' Fleur felt a little miffed. Ruth was her friend. Her best friend. Surely . . . ?

'You'll see,' was all Robbie would say.

Fleur lay back in the prow of the boat and trailed her hand in the water that shimmered with a myriad of colours in the setting sun. Through half-closed eyes she could see the fields on either side of the water and the cathedral standing proudly on the hill bathed in golden light.

The war and all its turmoil seemed miles away.

'There's a boat behind us.' Fleur shaded her eyes but couldn't make out just who was in the craft.

'That'll be Ruth,' Robbie said. He stopped rowing and rested on the oars. 'We'll wait for them to catch up.'

'Them?' Fleur teased. 'So you do know something.'

As the boat drew nearer, Fleur let out a gasp of surprise. 'Kenny! It's Kenny.'

Robbie's grin broadened. 'I know. I fixed all this up with him last time he was over to help you with the garden. He was to keep out of sight and meet us at the Brayford. And then Ruth had to throw a spanner in the works by going home to see her parents.'

Fleur laughed. 'I wondered why you were trying to persuade her not to go. You rogue! Trying your hand at a bit of match-making, are you?'

'Something like that.'

'Well, it won't work. Not with Ruth.'

'Oh, I don't know,' Robbie said, glancing across at the other boat where Ruth was waving excitedly and Kenny, though rowing hard to catch up with them, had a huge grin on his face.

The evening was a merry one, the landlord of the pub friendly and the regulars welcoming, and it was with reluctance that the party rowed back to the Pool as dusk settled over the waterway.

'Did you see?' Robbie was triumphant. 'Ruth sat with Kenny all night and he had his arm round her. And look at them now – laughing and talking as he rows her home. And I heard him insisting there was no room for anyone else in their boat when we all set off.'

'Mmm.' Fleur watched her brother and her best friend. She would've liked nothing more than to see them happy together, but soon Kenny would join one of the services, and the way he was talking these days, it sounded as if he was determined to become a fighter pilot.

And Ruth did not get close to fliers.

For a few hours they had been able to get right away from the war and all its anxieties, but now it was back with Fleur with a vengeance.

Twenty-Nine

Through July the bombing raids went on from Wickerton Wood, but now their targets were the docks and ports on the coast of France. These were being used by the enemy's shipping which was patrolling the seas around Britain in an effort to sink the convoys bringing vital food supplies to the country.

At the beginning of August the day came that Fleur had looked forward to: the day she could pick a huge bunch of sweet peas and present the bouquet to Mrs Jackson.

The old lady was dozing in her armchair, her cheeks red from the heat of the day, little beads of sweat on her forehead. Fleur crept into the room and stood on the hearthrug. As if feeling her presence, Mrs Jackson opened her eyes. For a moment, she blinked rapidly as if she couldn't believe the sight before her, and then tears flooded down her face.

'Oh, Fleur! How beautiful! They're just like Arthur used to grow for me. Wherever did you get them?'

Fleur chuckled. 'From the end of your cottage.'

'Eh?' Mrs Jackson was puzzled until Fleur explained what she had been doing. 'I didn't think you ever went round that end and it wasn't suitable for growing much else. Runner beans, perhaps, but I've got those in the front garden. So – I thought I would grow you your favourite flowers. I'm sure the authorities won't clap me in irons for it.'

Mary Jackson clasped her hands together. 'Oh, I hope not, dear. I do hope not. You don't know what pleasure you've given me. They'll remind me so much of Arthur.' She started to struggle to her feet, but Fleur said quickly, 'Don't you get up. Just tell me where I can find a vase and I'll stand them on the table where you can see them.'

Minutes later, as she went back into the garden, Fleur left the old lady smiling gently at the delicate blooms and reliving her happy memories.

'Mum? You didn't really mean it about not going to Fleur's wedding, did you?' Kenny asked as he sat down to supper in the farmhouse, three weeks before the date in early September that had been set. Jake was in the scullery washing his hands before coming to the table.

'Oh yes, I did. And if you and your father really care about me, you won't go either.'

'But why? What on earth have you got against Robbie?'

Betsy was silent, struggling against blurting out the truth. 'I've got my reasons,' she said tartly at last.

'What?'

'You're too young to understand . . .' She glanced towards the door leading into the kitchen from the scullery and lowered her voice. 'Maybe I'll tell you one day. Oh yes, maybe when you're a bit older I'll tell you it all. But . . .'

At that moment Jake stepped into the kitchen and Betsy fell silent. Jake looked from one to the other, sensing that something had been said. He sighed. 'Now what's going on?'

Kenny avoided meeting his father's eyes, picked up his knife and fork and attacked the plate of food in front of him.

'Nothing,' Betsy said, but her tight lips and the angry sparkle in her eyes told Jake far more than a thousand words.

'I see,' he said as he sat down heavily. 'Like that is it? Getting in practice for three weeks on Saturday, when you won't be speaking to either of us forever more.'

Betsy slammed down Jake's plate in front of him, spilling gravy onto the pristine white tablecloth.

'You think it's a joke, don't you, Jake? Well, let me tell you—'

But Jake cut her short, raising his hand. 'No, Betsy. I don't want to hear whatever it is you've got to say. I've heard enough. More than enough. And if you think your attitude is going to stop either of us going to Fleur's wedding, then you'd better think again. Because it won't. Now, sit down and eat your supper and let's see if we can hold a civil, pleasant conversation for once.'

Betsy stared down at him for a moment. Then she gave a little cry, pressed her hand to her mouth, turned and rushed from the room.

'Obviously not,' Jake muttered as he took his first mouthful.

Kenny said nothing and they continued the meal in silence.

*

The evening before the wedding, Ruth tugged the tin bath from Mrs Jackson's shed into the kitchen and set it on the hearth, as she had done every Friday night since coming to live in the cottage.

'Like me to fill it with water for you, Mrs Jackson?'

'No, no, I can manage now.'

The hot water came from a tap at the side of the range, and the old lady was used to filling the bath with a jug before undressing in front of the warm fire and stepping into the water. She had done it all her life. The only thing she couldn't manage any more was bringing the bath from the garden shed into the house.

'Do you know,' Fleur said. 'I quite fancy a soak in there myself tonight. It'd . . . it'd remind me of home. It's what we did every Friday night. There's something very comforting about sitting in hot water in front of the fire. Would you mind, Mrs Jackson? After you, of course.'

'That's all right, dear. There's plenty of water. You can empty it after me and have some fresh.'

'What about you, Ruth?'

'Oh, I had a bath up at camp as usual. No, actually . . .' Ruth paused and a wicked gleam came into her eye. 'I was thinking of going next door. I've got the perfect excuse now.'

Mrs Jackson and Fleur exchanged a puzzled glance. 'An excuse? What for?'

Ruth's smile widened mischievously. 'To get Harry in a bath.'

Mrs Jackson and Fleur stared at her for a moment and then they both burst out laughing.

'I'll believe that when I see it,' Fleur spluttered.

'Oh, I don't think he'd let you watch!' Ruth

chuckled. 'But, you see, I've promised to trim his hair for him. Make him smart for tomorrow. His clean clothes are all ready for the morning. All laid out in his bedroom. Now all he needs is a bath.'

'You are good to him, dear.' Mrs Jackson was still laughing. 'But I don't think you'll get him to bath. Doris used to have a job. He's a "stand at the sink and wash up and down" sort of chap is Harry.'

'He'll love it – once he's in.'

'Ah – but that's the point,' Fleur laughed. 'It'll be *getting* him in!'

'Right then.' Ruth was determined. 'I'm going to give it a go. Wish me luck.'

'You're going to need it,' Fleur said.

They left the back door open. In the warm stillness of the September evening, they heard Ruth dragging the bath across the yard into the cottage. There was a moment's silence before they heard Harry come out of his back door as if a swarm of hornets was after him.

'Nah, lass. I dorn't need a bath. Only dirty folks need baths. You tellin' me I'm a mucky beggar.'

Fleur and Mrs Jackson stood together, peeping out of the scullery window. They could see Harry standing in the neighbouring back yard, his hair ruffled in panic. Mrs Jackson chortled.

'Eh, this is just like the old days. The times I've seen poor old Doris chasing him round the back yard on a Friday night to get him in the bath.'

Ruth appeared in the doorway of Harry's cottage, her arms akimbo. 'Harry, it's a special day tomorrow. A big day . . .'

'I knows that. Don't you think I knows that but—'

'But nothing, Harry. You said you'd let me cut your hair—'

'Me hair – yes. I dorn't mind that, but—'

'Well, when I've cut it, it'll look nicer if it's washed.'

'Aye – well – mebbe,' Harry agreed reluctantly, then added, with a gleam of hope, 'But old Bemmy never said to wash it after.'

'Old Bemmy? Who's old Bemmy?'

'Feller who used to cut me hair. Lived in the village, he did. Used to cut all the fellers' hair.'

'So do you want him to do it for you? But you've left it a bit late now.'

Despite his agitation, Harry laughed. 'Much too late. He's been dead nigh on six years.'

'Ah!' Ruth paused a moment and then said, 'Aw, come on, Harry. All that lovely hot water in front of a blazing fire. Height of luxury, I call that.'

'Well, you're welcome to use it. I don't mind, duck.' Harry's eyes were twinkling now. 'I'll scrub ya back for ya.'

Ruth laughed. 'I bet you would.' Then her eyes glinted. 'Right, you're on. You can scrub my back if you let me scrub yours.'

'Eh!' Now Harry looked positively frightened. 'I was only kidding. I didn't mean . . .'

Ruth fell against the door frame, laughing helplessly, whilst Mrs Jackson and Fleur, still watching from the scullery, stifled their laughter as they heard Ruth say, 'I'm only teasing you, Harry, you old dear. But I am serious about you having a dip. I'll fill it with lovely hot water and then make myself scarce. I'll cut your hair first and then you can wash it.'

Harry made one last plea. 'Can't I just have me hair washed? At the sink in the scullery?'

Ruth shook her head firmly. 'No, Harry, it's all or nothing.'

Suddenly, Harry capitulated disarmingly. He smiled and his eyes twinkled. 'D'you know, lass. It's just like having my Doris back.'

Ruth crossed the space between them and linked her arm through the old man's. 'That's the nicest thing anyone's ever said to me, Harry,' Fleur heard her say as they disappeared into the house.

She turned back from the kitchen window to say in surprise. 'Do you know, Mrs Jackson, I really think she's managed it.'

'Wonders never cease,' the old lady murmured, smiling as she began to ready herself for her own bath.

By the time Ruth returned from next door, Mrs Jackson was tucked up warmly in her bed and Fleur was sitting in the bath in front of the glowing fire.

As Ruth flopped into Mrs Jackson's empty chair, Fleur, soaping herself, asked, 'And did he let you scrub his back?'

'Yes, and wash his neck. It was just like dealing with a grubby little boy. He chuntered and grumbled the whole time. But I think he enjoyed it really – once he got in. He even let me cut his toenails for him.'

Fleur blinked. 'You're kidding me.'

'Nope. I had to go out into the scullery whilst he got undressed but once he was in, he shouted me in. Do you know, Fleur, it was a lovely cosy time we had together. He told me all about his family. He was born in that little cottage, y'know. He was one of ten kids. Where the heck they put 'em all, I can't think.'

'So, has he got a lot of family left?'

'No. Sadly. He was one of the youngest and there's only a sister left and she's in Canada.'

'And then he and Doris lost their only son, didn't they? How sad.'

There was silence in the kitchen, the only sound the ticking of the little clock on the mantelpiece and the coals settling in the fire. Ruth stirred and moved to kneel beside the bath. 'Here,' she said gently, 'let me soap your back for you.' Fleur leant forward whilst Ruth gently smoothed soap over her back.

'You've got a lovely skin, Fleur,' she said. 'I'm quite envious. My back's all spotty.'

It was warm and cosy and the two girls were feeling drowsy. 'Oh well, I suppose I'd better get out and empty this bath . . .'

'Well, you can get out and get yourself dry and up to bed, but I'll see to the bath.'

'Oh, but . . .'

'No "buts". I'm your bridesmaid. Remember? I'm supposed to look after you. And if I want to pamper you a bit, then I've every right.'

'Yes, ma'am.' Fleur grinned and gave a mock salute. As she stood up carefully, Ruth wrapped a warm fluffy towel that had been warming on the fireguard around her. As she did so, she held Fleur close and whispered, 'You do know I wish you every happiness, don't you?'

Fleur rested her head against the other girl's shoulder. 'Course I do.'

'I didn't mean to be hard on you when . . . when you first told me you'd got a boyfriend and when you said you were getting married. It's just . . .' She bit her lip, unable to continue for the lump in her throat.

'I know, I know,' Fleur sympathized. 'I didn't understand then, but I do now. You'd just been through it, hadn't you?'

'I let myself get very fond of Billy. I vowed I wouldn't. Right from coming into the WAAFs, I promised myself

I wouldn't let myself get fond of anyone, but then I had to meet Billy.'

There was another long silence before Fleur, pulling back a little, looked into her friend's face glowing in the dancing light from the fire and asked gently, 'Tell me honestly, do you wish you'd never met him?'

Ruth blinked and then slowly, with sudden understanding, shook her head. 'No,' she said huskily. 'No, I don't. "Better to have loved and lost" and all that, you mean?'

'Well, I didn't want to get all poetic on you, but, yes, I suppose that's what I do mean.'

'You're right.' Ruth sighed heavily. 'But – oh, Fleur, it hurt so much. So much. I just didn't want – you know.'

'Yes, I know.'

'But seeing you with Robbie – well, I suppose I've changed my mind a bit. Whatever happens, you'll have such happy memories. No one can ever take them away from you and . . . and despite everything – the war and even the trouble it's caused in your family – oh, everything, I still bet you don't wish you'd never met Robbie, do you?'

'No, I don't,' Fleur said emphatically.

Thirty

Fleur woke up on the morning of her wedding with a strange fluttering in her stomach. She lay a moment, trying to quell the unaccustomed nerves, and then she smiled and mentally castigated herself. What on earth am I nervous about? I've no doubts about marrying Robbie. So why? But she knew why. Today might mean the end of any sort of relationship with her mother. If Betsy did not attend the wedding, as she had threatened, then Fleur knew that her mother would carry out her threat to the letter. She would never speak to her daughter again. As she rolled out of bed, Fleur sighed. She just hoped her mother would not carry out the threat that extended to her father and brother.

For herself, she could cope with it. The relationship between herself and her mother had always been a strained one. Kenny had always been their mother's favourite; Betsy had never even tried to hide it. Luckily, it had not affected the love Fleur had for her brother, nor his for her. And Jake had always made up for Betsy's lack of demonstrative affection towards her daughter. Fleur just hoped that today was not going to cause a rift between herself and her father and brother. If they bowed to Betsy's demands and stayed away from the church today, then Fleur's day would be spoilt.

That – and only that – fear was what was causing her to feel nervous.

The service was set for midday, but Fleur was dressed and ready and standing nervously in Mrs Jackson's kitchen by eleven-thirty.

'My word,' Ruth teased. 'You don't intend letting him get away, do you?'

Fleur smiled nervously.

'You look fantastic,' Ruth said, standing back to take a final check on the bride's appearance. Mrs Jackson too nodded her approval.

'You look wonderful, my dear.' She stepped nearer and reached up to kiss Fleur's cheek and then dabbed a tear from her eyes. But the old lady's tears were tears of happiness. 'Now, I'll leave you. I'll go round to Harry's. He's borrowed a bath chair to take me to church.' She hesitated and then said, a little nervously, 'You – er – don't mind if he comes round? I know he . . . he wants to see you before you leave for the church.'

'Of course I don't,' Fleur said and almost added, I might have to ask him to give me away if Dad doesn't turn up. When the old lady had closed the back door behind her, Fleur burst out, 'Oh, Ruth, they're not coming, are they? They promised to be here by now.'

'Aren't they meeting you at the church?'

Fleur, pressing her lips together to try to stop the tears flowing, shook her head. Her voice was shaking as she said, 'No. Dad said he'd come here to take me to church.'

'He'll be here, don't worry.' Ruth tried to make her tone reassuring, but even she had begun to have doubts. 'And Kenny,' she added, hoping that Fleur's handsome brother, young though he was, would have the guts to stand up to his mother.

They heard a sound in the back yard and Fleur's heart leapt, but it was Harry who passed the window and opened the back door. He stood in the doorway. 'Eh, lass, you look a picture.'

Fleur raised a smile. 'Thanks, Harry.'

'But where's your bouquet, lass? You can't get married without a bouquet.'

'Well, flowers are so hard to come by. I thought I'd just carry a prayer book. You know . . . ?'

With a flourish as dramatic as any seasoned actor, Harry produced a bouquet of red roses from behind his back. 'I made it mesen,' he said proudly. 'Cut all the thorns off, lass, so's you don't prick yasen, and I begged a bit of fern from Mester Clegg to finish it off.'

'Oh, Harry. It's beautiful! I don't know what to say. Thank you – oh, thank you.'

Tears threatened again but Ruth was quick to rush forward and dab her eyes. 'Oh, Harry, you old dear. They're lovely, but if you make her ruin her make-up I'll chase you round the yard again.'

Laughing wheezily, Harry backed out of the door. 'In that case, I'll be off to get Mary to the church. See you there, girls.'

They heard his footsteps go round the end of the cottage and down the cinder path and then there was silence. The minutes ticked by and slowly the colour drained from Fleur's face until it was almost as white as her dress.

'What about Robbie's mum? Is she coming here?' Ruth asked, trying to turn Fleur's thoughts away, even if only for a few moments, but failing.

'No – she's going straight to the church. She . . . she said she . . . she didn't want to make matters worse by bumping into my family here.' Fleur's eyes filled with tears now. 'Looks like it wouldn't have mattered.'

'Look, love . . .' Ruth began, but at that moment they heard the sound of a noisy engine spluttering to a halt outside the cottage. The two girls stared at each other for a moment before Fleur's eyes shone. 'That's them. That's Bertha.'

'Bertha! Who the hell's Bertha?'

Fleur laughed. 'Our car. It's an old banger of a car. Now I know why they're late. Bertha's been playing up.'

'Mebbe your mother jinxed it?' Ruth laughed as she opened the back door and Jake, flustered and red faced, rushed in followed by a grinning Kenny.

'Fleur – I'm so sorry—' Jake began, but then he stopped short and his mouth fell open as he stared at his daughter in her wedding finery. 'Oh, Fleur,' he whispered. 'You look – beautiful.'

Now her tears spilled over and Ruth rushed to dab her cheeks with a clean handkerchief. 'Stop that – you'll wreck your make-up.'

Kenny grinned. 'Who is it, Dad? Surely it's not our Fleur? Where's her trousers and her woolly hat?' His teasing broke the poignant moment and they all laughed. Then Kenny held out his arm to Ruth.

'Come on, pretty lady. We'd better go ahead and see if the groom's been daft enough to turn up.' For a moment his glance lingered fondly on Fleur. 'You look great, Sis,' he said softly. 'We'll see you in church.'

As Kenny and Ruth left the cottage to walk the three hundred yards down the lane to the little church,

Jake stood once more just staring at his daughter, drinking in the sight of her.

'You look lovely, Fleur.'

'Oh, Dad,' Fleur said, now a little more in control of her emotions. 'Don't set me off again.'

'I just wish—' Jake began and shook his head sadly. 'I just wish your mother could see you. Maybe . . .' His voice trailed away.

'She . . . she's not come then?'

'No, love. I'm sorry. Nothing we could say made any difference.'

Fleur put her arm through his. 'But you and Kenny are here. Thank you for that and I'm so sorry if it's made things difficult at home. But I'm not going to apologize for marrying Robbie.'

Jake looked deep into her eyes. 'As long as you love him, Fleur, and you're sure he loves you . . .'

'I am.'

'Then that's all I need to know. And now, if Bertha can manage to carry us another few yards, we'd best be going.'

Bertha spluttered and coughed her way down the lane, pulling up to a thankful halt outside the gate of the old stone church, with its gently leaning square tower and arched porch. The path was so narrow that they had to walk in single file until they reached the door where Ruth awaited them. Adjusting Fleur's headdress and veil and straightening her gown, Ruth then fell into step behind the bride and her father.

'Ready, love?' Jake asked, huskily.

Fleur's eyes glowed as she turned to smile at him with unmistakable joy. Her love for Robbie shone out of her, and as Jake led her into the church and they turned together to walk down the aisle, he saw Robbie standing tall and handsome and proud at the altar steps.

Beside the groom stood Tommy Laughton, resplendent in his uniform, and behind them both, in the second pew back, were the other crewmembers from D-Doggo. And to Jake's surprise, the church was almost full. There were a few other RAF and WAAF personnel, but then all the spare seats were taken up by villagers. They'd come to see a pretty wedding, to try to forget the war, just for a few hours, as they turned their backs on the gaping hole in the roof at the back of the church and watched the beautiful bride and her handsome groom.

Jake's attention came back to the young man who was about to become his son-in-law. He saw the love in the young man's eyes as he watched his bride coming towards him and Jake was left in no doubt now. Fleur was doing the right thing. Whatever Betsy's feelings were, there was no mistaking this couple's love for each other. As they neared the steps, Fleur had eyes for no one but Robbie, but Jake could not stop his gaze roaming over the few guests in the front pews.

And then he saw her. For the first time after half a lifetime apart he saw Meg again.

Thirty-One

The service was over and Fleur and Robbie had stood just outside the porch as all the guests and villagers had filed past them, shaking Robbie's hand and kissing Fleur. Then the pictures had been taken with a great deal of laughter and amusement at the elderly photographer, who kept disappearing beneath the black cloth covering the square box camera which teetered precariously on a spindly tripod.

'Just look at him!' Kenny spluttered with mirth. 'Trampling all over the graves to get his antiquated camera in the right place. Is he allowed to do that?'

Robbie and Fleur were almost helpless with laughter.

'Well, I don't think the folks he's walking over are going to say much,' Robbie chuckled.

'I just hope there's none of their relatives watching though,' Fleur said, ever sensitive to the feelings of others. 'They might feel it's a bit . . . a bit – oh, what's the word?'

'Sacrilegious?'

'Something like that.'

'Well, I don't think there's anyone left much to notice.'

Fleur glanced around her. Most of the villagers who'd been in the church had gone, and only a few were left peering over the church wall to watch the goings on.

'Now I wonder where they've all rushed off to?' Kenny mused. 'You'd've thought they'd have stayed to watch the comedy. Mind you,' he added, nodding towards the little man waving his arms about to position his subjects and looking as if he were directing traffic, 'I reckon he's done it before. He seems to know just where he wants us to be.'

'You sure about that?' Robbie murmured.

'Smile please,' trilled the photographer and they all tried to straighten their faces into sensible smiles rather than wide, toothy grins and fits of giggles.

As the photographer declared, 'That's it, folks,' Robbie turned to Fleur. 'And now, Mrs Rodwell, we're off on our honeymoon. Your carriage awaits, m'lady.'

'I'll just have to go back to the cottage and get changed. I can hardly travel in this . . .'

'Why ever not?' Robbie pretended surprise as he bent to kiss her. 'I want the world to see my beautiful wife.'

'Now then, plenty of time for that later, you two lovebirds.' Harry hobbled up to them and held out his arms. 'I haven't kissed the bride yet.'

There were tears in the old man's eyes as Fleur leant forward so that he could kiss her on both cheeks. 'Eh, lass, but you're bonny an' no mistake. You're a lucky young feller . . .' he added, holding out his hand to shake Robbie's.

'Thank you, Harry.'

'Right then, we're all off to the pub. You will let me buy you both a drink before you go, now won't you?'

Fleur and Robbie exchanged a glance. They couldn't wait to be alone together, yet they didn't want to appear ungrateful to Robbie's mother, who had worked so hard on Fleur's gown and Ruth's dress, nor to Jake and Kenny, who had defied Betsy to be here. They owed it to their guests, to Harry and Mrs Jackson too, to spend a little time with them.

'Of course we will,' Robbie said. 'That's very kind of you, Harry.'

The old man beamed. 'Right.' Harry raised his voice. 'Everyone across to the Mucky Duck.'

There was a ripple of laughter.

'The what?' Kenny blinked.

Ruth hooked her arm through his. 'It's the White Swan, really, but all the locals call it the Mucky Duck. Come on, you can escort me. I'm supposed to walk with the best man – handsome devil, isn't he, in that uniform – but his girlfriend's here and I don't want to spoil the little bit of time they've got to spend together.'

'It's my pleasure,' Kenny said gallantly and the faint flush on his face told her that indeed it was.

The crew of Robbie's aircraft and six WAAFs, Kay and Peggy amongst them, formed a guard of honour down the pathway. Handsome young men in their smart blue uniforms that not only set the hearts of the young women in the village aflutter, but caused several of the older women to smile fondly and wish themselves forty years younger.

Then Harry led the way from the church across the road, pushing Mrs Jackson in the borrowed bath chair. 'Come on, folks, follow me,' he called, his excitement bubbling over as the wedding party fell into step behind them, with the vicar bringing up the rear.

'Dear old Harry,' Ruth murmured. 'He's loving this, isn't he?'

Kenny was thoughtful. 'D'you know, I reckon he's up to summat.'

'Eh?' Ruth's eyes widened. 'What d'you mean?'

'I dunno. Maybe he's got them a special present that he can't wait to give them. But there's something going on behind those twinkling eyes. And there's something else funny too.'

'What?'

'Well, I'd've thought there'd've been crowds to watch my beautiful sister come out of church, but there's hardly anyone about now. In South Monkford, I know it's a town and we've got a big church, but the street's usually lined with folk when there's a wedding going off. Anybody's wedding – it doesn't matter whose. They just like to have a nosy.'

'Mm,' Ruth mused. 'Funny that. Mind you, most of them were in church. Maybe they've seen all they wanted to.'

Harry was rushing on ahead as fast as his bent old legs would carry him and wheezing a little as he pushed the bath chair in front of him. Arriving at the main entrance of the pub, he parked the chair outside and helped Mary Jackson to stand up and walk inside. But instead of disappearing, he threw open the double doors and stood just inside, beaming at the bride and groom walking towards him.

As they approached, Bill Moore, dressed smartly in a black suit, white shirt and black bow tie, came to stand beside Harry to usher the wedding party inside.

As Fleur and Robbie stepped into the dark interior of the public bar, a huge cheer threatened to shake the rafters. It seemed as if the whole village was crammed into the room.

Fleur gasped and gazed around, stunned by the

applause that greeted them and the cries of 'Congratulations' and 'Good Luck' on every side.

'So that's where they all disappeared to.' Kenny laughed.

'Come through, come through,' Harry said, leading the way into a large room just beyond the bar. He stood to one side and waved his arm to show them a table at the far end, laden with food. In the centre stood a magnificent wedding cake, complete with bride and groom figurines on the top.

'Everyone in the village has contributed. The women have been baking all week and . . .'

'Oh, Harry!' Now the tears flooded down Fleur's face. The kindness of all the villagers, some of whom she hardly knew, was overwhelming. Even Robbie had tears in his eyes. He held out his hand and shook Harry's hard. 'Thank you, Harry. This is wonderful. I really don't know how to thank everyone.'

'It's us who wanted to say "thank you", lad. To you and your lass here. To all of you really . . .' He nodded his head to include the best man in his RAF uniform and Ruth in her bridesmaid's dress. 'That's fighting this war for us. It's our way of showing our gratitude. But 'specially to you two and Ruth for all you've done for me an' Mary. You're . . . you're like family to us. No disrespect to your own families, like.'

'None taken,' Jake, standing just behind Fleur, murmured. He was touched by the villagers' obvious fondness for his daughter and for Meg's boy, as he still called Robbie in his own mind. He only wished Betsy was here to see all this and hear what was being said. Perhaps it would melt even her hard heart.

But he doubted it.

Robbie was nodding his thanks, but unable to speak for the lump in his throat and Fleur was still trying to stem her tears. But they were tears of happiness.

Just for a few short hours they could all forget the war and its tragedies and celebrate a happy occasion. A very happy occasion.

Of course the moment had to come. The moment when Jake and Meg came face to face for the first time in twenty-two years.

As the guests milled around, helping themselves to the food, chattering and laughing, Meg made her way through the throng to stand behind him.

'Hello, Jake. How are you?'

He heard her voice and, slowly, he turned to face her. The breath caught in his throat. She was even more beautiful than he remembered. He didn't see the tiny lines around her eyes; to him the years fell away and there before him was his flame-haired Meg with her heartbreaking smile.

He cleared his throat but his voice was still a little husky as he answered, 'Fine, Meg. And you? You . . . you look – wonderful.' He couldn't stop the compliment escaping his lips, even though he felt disloyal to the absent Betsy the moment the words were said. But Meg was smiling up at him, her green eyes gently teasing him. 'So do you.'

Jake pulled a face. 'I don't know about that. I've a lot more wrinkles and grey hairs.'

Meg's gaze never left his face. 'No,' she said softly. 'You haven't changed. You're still my – still Jake.'

There was an awkward pause before she went on,

making her tone deliberately light. 'Who'd've thought it, eh? Your girl and my boy. Must be fate taking a hand, Jake.'

Jake sighed. 'That's one way of putting it, I suppose. But is it a kind fate or a cruel one?'

Meg glanced across at Robbie and Fleur, who were touring the room, making sure they spoke to each and every person there to give their thanks.

'He's not like me, Jake. Just in case you're worried. He's got none of my badness. He loves Fleur dearly. He won't hurt her like I . . .' Her voice trailed away and Jake saw the tears shimmer in her eyes.

'Oh, don't cry, Meggie, I couldn't bear it,' he whispered and fished out the spotless white handkerchief from his top pocket. 'Here.' His use of the pet name he'd always had for her all those years ago was almost her undoing. For a moment the tears threatened to spill over.

'Thanks.' Meg dabbed carefully at her eyes. Then she handed him the handkerchief, which he stuffed back into his pocket.

'You weren't bad,' he told her softly. 'Just . . . just very young and you'd been so hurt by – well – by life. I said some very harsh things to you then, Meggie. I'm sorry.'

'I deserved them, Jake,' she said simply. 'But I want you to know, I've changed. Ever since that day when I nearly lost Robbie, when that dreadful woman tried to snatch him away from me, I've tried to make up for all the terrible things I did. I know I can't change the past, but I've tried to be a better person. Truly, I have.'

'Don't be so hard on yourself, Meggie. We . . . we all make mistakes. We've all done things we maybe shouldn't have.' She looked at him keenly, but he was avoiding her gaze now. 'Can I ask you something, Meg? Don't answer, if you don't want to.'

She knew a moment's panic, but then remembered. This was Jake she was talking to: Jake, who knew everything there was to know about her. She had no secrets from him. Nor did she want any. If there was one person in the whole wide world whom Meg could trust, it was Jake.

'Is it true that you have your father living with you?'

Meg laughed with relief. 'Yes, but I can see why you're surprised.' She smiled impishly now. 'That's all part of my reformed character, Jake. How could I continue to bear a grudge against him when I did things that were just as bad, if not worse?'

Jake pursed his lips. 'Well, it was because of what *he* did that made you like that. You were only searching for security. For someone to take care of you. You couldn't wait for . . .' His voice trailed away.

Meg shook her head. 'Don't try to excuse me, Jake. I . . . I should have had more faith.' Her voice was almost an inaudible whisper as she added, 'More faith in you.'

'How did he come back into your life?'

'Just turned up at my door one day. He'd been living rough. He was in a terrible state. How could I turn him away?'

'What happened to Alice Smallwood? The girl he ran off with?'

Meg shrugged. 'She'd found a bigger fish. Ran off with someone with money. Pops has never talked about her much, but I gather he tried to follow her, and the feller she'd taken up with got some of his cronies to beat Pops up. Nearly killed him. He'd still got a lot of the bruises by the time he found me.' She paused and then added softly, 'He's spent every day since trying to make it up to me and he's been wonderful for Robbie.' She glanced across fondly at her son. 'That's one thing I'm never going to apologize for, Jake. Having Robbie. Though I could have wished that his father—'

'Don't, Meggie, don't say it.' He reached out and took her hand. 'It shouldn't be spoken of. Not today of all days.'

'No, you're right.' She smiled up at him, her tears dried now. 'Today's a happy day. Let's just enjoy it. Let's just enjoy seeing each other again because I gather' – she looked around the room – 'that this might be the only chance we'll ever get.'

'Yes,' Jake said sadly. 'I'm afraid it probably is, Meggie.'

Thirty-Two

'Fleur,' Robbie whispered close to her ear so that no one else could hear. 'Don't look now, but your dad is holding my mum's hand.'

'Eh?' Startled, Fleur looked round quickly, her gaze seeking out Jake and Meg.

'No, no, don't look. Don't – spoil it. In a minute or two as we move round the room, take a look though. There's something between them. You can see it in their faces. Just look.'

Fleur tried to concentrate on what the woman in front of her was saying. 'My dear, you look lovely,' the little woman who helped her husband run the village bakery gushed. 'It's done us so much good to have such a pretty wedding in the midst of these dark times. Everyone in the village has loved planning this little surprise for you both. Of course, it was Harry's idea, but we've all chipped in. I made the cake. I'm so sorry it's covered with a cardboard decoration instead of real icing.'

'You've all been wonderful. You've made our day even more special. And the cake looks wonderful. You'd never know until you get right near it that it's not real. But the real cake underneath tastes delicious,' Fleur said and, impulsively, she leant forward and kissed the woman's cheek.

'Lots of people gave me fruit for it,' the little woman

went on, blushing a little. 'And Mr Clegg gave me the eggs.'

'How very kind everyone has been.'

Then, at last, Fleur was able to move away and take a surreptitious look across the crowded room towards her father and Meg. What she saw made her catch her breath in a gasp of surprise.

Close beside her, Robbie murmured, 'See what I mean?'

'Yes.' Fleur nodded slowly. 'Yes, I do.'

Jake and Meg were standing close together looking into each other's faces as if there was no one else in the room. They were oblivious to the chatter and laughter around them, completely lost in their own little world.

Fleur made an involuntary movement towards them, but Robbie touched her arm and said softly, 'Don't spoil it, Fleur. What harm can it do? Just this once. This may be the only time they'll ever have.'

Fleur bit her lip. Even from the other side of the room, she could see the raw emotion on her father's face, could see Robbie's mother's eyes shimmering with tears, and her tremulous smile.

'Yes, but what about my mum? What about her?'

'She was the one who chose not to come today.'

'Yes – and now we can see why, can't we?'

Robbie sighed. 'But if she had come, darling, that' – he nodded towards the couple – 'wouldn't be happening, now would it?'

'I suppose not,' Fleur agreed.

'I don't expect they'll ever meet up again. Let them just have these few moments, eh?'

Fleur nodded, a lump in her throat. She felt torn by divided loyalties: loyalty to her mother and yet now she understood a little more the reason behind the faraway look she had so often seen in her father's eyes.

'Kenny'll put a stop to it, though, if he sees.'

Robbie laughed softly. 'He's got eyes for no one but Ruth, darling. I don't think he'll even notice. Now, come along, I think we can be on our way without it looking too rude to all these kind people.'

They made another circuit of the room, saying goodbye to everyone and repeating their thanks.

Kenny pumped Robbie's hand. 'Look after my big sister, else I'll be after you.'

Robbie laughed. 'I will and thanks, Kenny, for today. I know it hasn't been easy for you.'

Kenny pulled a face. There was no need to pretend he didn't know what Robbie meant. 'It's Dad I feel sorry for. It's not long before I can join up and, believe me, I'm off the moment I can. But Dad'll be left there on his own with her.' He shook his head. 'I really don't know what's got into her. She never used to be like this. But maybe once this is all over, she'll settle down a bit. Come to terms with it, you know.'

'I hope so,' Robbie said, but as he turned away to go towards where Jake and his mother were still standing engrossed in each other, he thought, *but I doubt it.*

Meg and Jake broke apart, almost guiltily, as Robbie and Fleur arrived beside them at the same moment.

'You off now?' Jake said heartily. He held out his hand to Robbie. There had been no official speeches by the father of the bride or the best man. Only Robbie had stood up and thanked everyone present for the marvellous surprise reception. So now was the moment for Jake to say, 'I'm proud to have you as my son-in-law. Take care of each other . . .' He seemed about to say more, but his voice cracked and he swallowed as if having difficulty in holding back the tears.

Meg broke the moment by kissing Fleur on both cheeks and saying, 'And I already love you, my darling daughter-in-law. And I can't wait for you to make me into a granny.'

The tension was broken by Robbie saying, 'Hey, steady on, Mum.' But he enveloped Meg into his arms, giving her a bear hug. 'Look after Pops and we'll see you as soon as we get back.'

'Where are you going?'

'Now that's a secret. Even Fleur doesn't know. But I'll ring Mr Tomkins when we get there. I promise.'

After a lot more handshaking and hugs, Fleur and Robbie finally made their escape, running hand in hand down the lane, laughing together.

'I thought we'd never get away,' Robbie said.

'I know, but wasn't it a lovely surprise? How sweet of everyone.'

'It was. The perfect send off.'

Back at the cottage, Fleur changed quickly into her best outfit and Robbie loosened his tie and flung his cap into the back of the borrowed sports car as he stowed Fleur's battered suitcase in the boot space. He opened the passenger door for her to climb in and then he vaulted over the door on the driver's side.

'Ready?' He grinned at her and Fleur giggled, deliciously anticipating the week ahead. A whole seven days alone and away from the war.

As they passed the pub, a shower of confetti cascaded over them, thrown by the villagers who lined the lane. With shouts of 'Good Luck' ringing in their ears, they roared out of the village.

It was strangely quiet after the sound of their car had faded away, an anti-climax after all the frivolity. The villagers began to drift away back to their own homes, carefully carrying some of the food that had been left. It was too precious to waste. Jake and Meg stood awkwardly together, knowing the moment of parting had come. As Kenny came bounding towards them, Meg held out her hand.

'Goodbye, Jake. It's been lovely to see you, and Robbie will look after her, I can promise you that.'

Jake nodded. 'I know,' he said huskily. 'And . . . and you take care of yourself, Meggie.'

'Ruth's had to rush off. She's on duty later. So—' Kenny glanced from one to the other. 'Are you ready, Dad?'

'Just coming, just coming, lad,' Jake replied, yet he made no move.

It was Meg who turned to Kenny, held out her hand and said, 'It's been good to meet you, Kenny. Take care.'

'Can we give you a lift anywhere, Mrs Rodwell?' the young man asked.

'That's very kind of you.' Meg smiled. 'But I'll be fine.'

Then, before either of them could stop her, she turned and walked away from them without looking back. Jake stood a moment watching her until Kenny touched his arm and said gently, 'Come on, Dad. Time we were going home.'

*

'What's this, I'd like to know?'

Betsy thrust Jake's large white handkerchief towards him, shaking it under his nose. Even before he could look at it properly, she shrieked, 'Make-up, that's what it is. A woman's make-up. Whose is it, might I ask? As if I didn't know.'

Jake blinked and stared at the smear of pink on the white cotton. Keeping his face expressionless, he said mildly, 'It's Fleur's. Whose do you think it is?' He stared her straight in the eyes. 'She had a few tears, the lass did. And why do you think that was, eh?'

For a moment, Betsy was disconcerted. 'Over me, you mean?'

'Of course over you, Betsy. Doesn't every girl want her mother with her on her wedding day?'

'How would *I* know?' Betsy said bitterly. 'I never had a mother. At least, not one I can remember very well.'

'Then all the more reason why you should've swallowed your own resentment and thought of her – for once. But you'll just have to live with it now, Betsy, won't you? That you didn't go to your only daughter's wedding.'

Jake turned on his heel and slammed out of the house, leaving Betsy – for the first time – feeling a twinge of guilt.

Thirty-Three

They drove to the east coast, to Skegness, where they walked along the sea front and viewed with sadness the lovely scene scarred with rolls of barbed wire. Areas of the wide expanse of sandy beach were mined. Even there, the war could not be forgotten entirely.

'There's a lot of RAF chaps about. I wonder why?' Robbie mused. In the bar of the guesthouse where they were staying, they found out.

'It's a training centre,' the landlord, Jim Spriggs, explained and winked. 'Good place for square bashing, ain't it? All that drill along Grand Parade and Tower Esplanade. They're even using some of the quieter streets, an' all. It's a sight to see.'

'We saw them this morning,' Robbie said. 'We were trying to get on the pier, but couldn't. I wanted to see it from the ground.' He smiled. 'We often come over this way when we're setting off across the North Sea and Johnny – that's our navigator – uses your pier as a guide. Reckons he knows what course to set then.'

'Aye, I've heard that said afore,' Jim nodded. 'They've built an assault course near the pier and another in an overgrown area at the end of North Parade that the locals have always called "The Jungle". The RAF lads are billeted in the empty hotels on the sea front and their officers' mess is in one of the bigger hotels, the NAAFI in another.' He pulled a face. 'But I reckon a lot of the hotels are closed for the duration – to holidaymakers that is. Oh, we get a few, like yourselves, but not like we used to afore the war. The kiddies can't play on a mined beach, can they? There's even a gun position in the Fairy Dell.' His mouth tightened. The fact seemed to hurt him personally. 'But it's not the RAF being here we mind,' he said, as if fearful he might have given offence to his guests. 'We like having 'em, and, of course, we've got the Royal Navy just up the road. Taken over Billy Butlin's holiday camp. HMS Royal Arthur, they call it. Oh, there's a lot going on in Skeggy, I can tell you, but it's just this bloody war's altered everyone's lives, hasn't it?' He eyed them curiously. 'What about you two . . . ?' Then, guessing correctly, a broad smile spread across his face. 'Ah, honeymooners, eh? A wartime wedding?'

Robbie grinned back at him. 'That's right.'

'Oi, missis,' the man raised his voice. 'We've got a couple of honeymooners here, love.'

His wife appeared from the kitchen, drying her hands on a towel. 'Oh, how lovely. I'll cook you something special tonight, my dears . . .' And with a smile and a nod, his 'missis' disappeared back into her kitchen.

'Now, mebbe I shouldn't be telling you this,' Jim said with a teasing smile, 'seeing as you're honeymooners, but there is a very good show on this week at the local theatre.' He reached under the bar and pulled out the local paper. Opening it up, he jabbed his finger. 'Aye, here it is. "All Clear" they call it. Some clever acts, so I've been told. And then there's two very good cinemas in the town.' He sniffed with annoyance. 'Used to have three we did until the Luftwaffe decided to bomb one of ’em last January. The Central and then there’s the Parade on the sea front.’

‘We saw it this morning. It was advertising a Henry Fonda film, I think.’

‘That’s right. *Chad Hanna*. It’s got Dorothy Lamour in, an’ all. I like her. Bit of all right, she is.’ He glanced archly at Robbie. ‘Mind you, you’ll not be noticing, will ya, lad?’

‘Of course not,’ Robbie said gallantly.

Fleur grinned saucily and said, ‘Well, I don’t mind you looking, as long as you don’t touch.’ To which remark the two men laughed heartily.

‘Then there’s *Pygmalion* on at the Central with Leslie Howard and Wendy Hiller . . .’ Jim went on.

‘I’ve seen that,’ Fleur said.

‘So’ – Robbie grinned – ‘Dorothy Lamour it is, then.’

The variety show they saw at the Arcadia Theatre later in the week was slick and professional, with a silent comedy routine, a witty comedian, and a clever dancing act. To top it all, the female singer, Elsie, each night picked a serviceman from the audience to assist her in her song ‘Arm in Arm Together’.

Robbie, sitting three rows back, in his smart RAF uniform, the silver buttons sparkling in the lights, was a sitting duck. He cast a rueful grin at Fleur, who dissolved into helpless laughter to see him taken up on stage to be greeted by rapturous applause from the audience. At the end of the song, Elsie brought him back to his seat and planted a kiss on his cheek, leaving a perfect impression of her mouth in lipstick.

'I thought I told you you couldn't touch,' Fleur spluttered and Robbie spread his hands in mock helplessness.

They had a blissful week before they had to return and be plunged once more into the middle of the war.

'I've missed you so much.' Ruth hugged her the moment she walked through the door. 'The girl they brought in to work in the watch office whilst you've been away is thick as pig whatsit. Kay's never stopped grumbling about her and can't wait for you to get back.' She pulled a comical face. 'Eh, hark at me getting all countrified. And you'll never guess what?'

Laughing, Fleur shook her head. 'Go on, tell me.'

'Harry's even had me gardening out there.' She nodded towards the back garden. 'Said I'd got to keep it in shape for you and that stuff needed gathering and it'd go to waste otherwise and then all your hard work'd be wasted.' She held out her hands, palms upward, fingers spread. 'Just *look* at my hands.'

'I just hope you've not pulled out all the plants and left the weeds.'

'Oh no. Harry was there, leaning over the fence, telling me what was what. Actually,' she added, self-consciously, as if she was quite surprised at herself, 'I've quite enjoyed it.' For a moment her eyes were haunted. 'It . . . it gets your mind off this bloody war for an hour or two.'

'Has . . . has it been bad?'

Ruth bit her lower lip as she nodded. 'Mm. We've lost eight planes during the last week.'

Fleur gasped. 'And the crews?'

Ruth lifted her shoulders in a helpless shrug.

And suddenly, the war with all its catastrophes was back with a vengeance.

Ruth linked her arm through Fleur's. 'Now, come and see what else I've been up to – with Mrs Jackson's permission of course.'

Fleur stared at her. 'What . . . what do you mean?'

'Come upstairs. I'll show you.'

Mystified, Fleur followed her up the narrow stairs.

Instead of turning to the small back bedroom where Fleur normally slept, Ruth flung open the door of the large front room that had once been Mrs Jackson's and her husband's but was now Ruth's room.

'This is your room from now on. Yours and Robbie's, when he can get away from camp.'

'But . . . but it's your room.'

'Not any more, it isn't. I've moved into your room at the back. I' – she let out a wistful little sigh – 'have no need of a double bed.'

'But you might. You might meet someone and—'

Now Ruth pursed her mouth and shook her head vehemently. 'No, I've told you. I made the mistake once of getting fond of someone and he got killed. I'm not putting myself through that pain again.' She glanced ruefully at Fleur. 'Sorry, love, I don't mean to put a damper on things for you. It's . . . it's just how I feel for myself, that's all. Maybe it's me that's being stupid.'

'No,' Fleur said gently and touched her friend's arm. 'I can only guess how you must have felt, but I do know that if anything happened to Robbie, I wouldn't want to take up with anyone else. So, if you'd really fallen for this chap, then . . . then . . . I do understand.'

'Oh, it was only early days with Billy. Nothing serious. We weren't engaged or anything. Hadn't even got as far as discussing marriage before he – before he . . .'

'But you had the feeling that that's where it might have led?'

Again Ruth bit her lip as tears filled her eyes and she nodded. But then she wiped her eyes and smiled. 'Come on in and see what I've done.'

They stepped into the bedroom and Fleur gazed around her. 'I don't remember it being like this.'

'It wasn't.' Ruth laughed now. 'I've painted it. Or rather, Kenny did.'

Fleur's eyes widened as she stared at Ruth. 'Kenny? Kenny's been here?'

'Oh yes. Cycled over three times, bless him. He's been great. He did all the painting and your mother-in-law has made the curtains and bedspread. Aren't they pretty?' She grinned widely. 'It's the best we could do in the time to create a bridal suite for you both.'

'Oh, Ruth, it's wonderful.' Slowly Fleur turned and took in every detail. Then she glanced at Ruth again. 'Did Kenny say – how things are at home?'

'Not as bad as they'd expected. It's a bit frosty, but at least she's speaking to them both.'

'And . . . and me?'

'He's not said. Sorry.'

Fleur sighed and turned her thoughts away from her mother and back to the present. 'I don't know how to thank you for all this. I don't know how you've managed it and keeping up with the garden an' all.'

'Think nothing of it. It's been fun doing it. We've had a lot of laughs, me an' your little brother.'

'I think a great deal of it, Ruth,' Fleur told her. 'And I can't wait to tell Robbie.'

For a few idyllic weeks, the front bedroom in Mary Jackson's tiny cottage became their little hideaway from the war even though it was still going on so close to them. But then Ruth came home with news that threatened their love nest.

'The WAAF quarters are finished. We've to move onto camp.'

Fleur stared at her in horror. 'Oh no! Really?'

Ruth nodded.

'What about—?' she began but, not wanting to sound selfish, went on, 'What about Mrs Jackson's garden and old Harry? He'll never manage to keep his house straight without you, Ruth.'

Ruth bit her lip. 'We'll just have to come whenever we can. We'll go and talk to ma'am. She's a good sort. I'm sure she'll let us come down here on our time off duty. Especially if we tell her about your garden. After all, that's part of the war effort, isn't it? As long as we don't take advantage of it.'

'Could we get hold of a couple of bikes, d'you think? It'd only be a few minutes on a bike.'

'We could try, but bicycles are in short supply just now. Everybody's riding them to get about camp.'

'I've got one at home. Maybe I could get it here somehow.'

'Perhaps Kenny would ride it over and hitch back.'

Fleur laughed. 'I'm sure he would – if *you* asked him.'

'Mission accomplished, then.' Her face sobered. 'But what about you and Robbie? It'll put paid to . . .'

She pointed upwards to the floor above and the bedroom that they had made their own.

Fleur nodded but could not speak.

But Mary Jackson, it seemed, had other ideas. 'You can come here whenever you can. As long as you look after the rooms – wash the sheets, an' that.'

'But won't you want the rooms for other lodgers. Evacuees maybe?'

Mary Jackson laughed softly and shook her head sadly. 'I'd've liked nothing better, my dears, than to have a couple of youngsters here, but I couldn't look after them, now could I?'

'They might want the accommodation for a mother with a baby or a young child,' Fleur said, still unable to believe that nothing stood in the way. 'They send the mothers too sometimes. They did at the beginning of the war.'

'They might,' Mary agreed. 'But I think it unlikely now. The evacuation seems to have slowed down. In fact, a lot of children are going back to the cities.'

'That's true,' Ruth said. 'Though I think the parents are daft. Old Hitler might choose any big city to have a go at. Look what he did to Coventry. Why Coventry, for heaven's sake?' She paused and then clapped her hands. 'That's settled then. As long as we can get permission, we'll come here every spare minute. Stay the night whenever we can. Fleur and Robbie can do your garden and I can still help old Harry.' She beamed. It all seemed so easy. 'Now all we've got to do is persuade ma'am.'

Squadron Officer Caroline Davidson was, as Ruth had put it, 'a good sort'. When the two girls asked to see her, she welcomed them into her office and heard what they had to say without interruption. She was thoughtful for a few moments whilst Fleur and Ruth waited anxiously. Then she smiled. 'I don't see why not. Just so long as you're very careful never to be late back on duty, otherwise it would have to stop immediately.'

Both girls nodded at once. 'Yes, ma'am. We'll make sure of that.'

As they saluted smartly and turned to leave, she added, 'And I'll have a word with Flight Sergeant Rodwell's commanding officer. Just to make sure he's aware of the situation. How very valuable Robbie's help is for the old lady's garden on his time off. We're very anxious to help in the local community whenever we can, you know.'

Fleur turned back to stare at her and was rewarded with a broad wink.

'Thank you, ma'am,' Fleur breathed.

Thirty-Four

The last weeks of September passed in a haze of busy hours on duty and, in a way, even busier off-duty time. Kenny brought Fleur's bicycle over and the following week he came again, pedalling one that Jake had unearthed from the barn for Ruth.

'It's a bit of a bone-shaker,' Kenny said, 'but I've cleaned it and oiled it.'

'As long as it gets me from A to B, I don't mind. Thanks, Kenny. I'll give you a kiss at Christmas.'

Though a flush crept up the young man's face, he was at ease enough with Ruth now to say, 'I'll keep you to that! And now, are you going to help me pick those apples down the bottom of the garden? That poor tree is so laden down, you can hardly see the bench underneath it.'

Ruth chuckled. 'Fleur often sits there for a bit of a rest. Her and Robbie.' For a moment, Ruth's eyes misted over. So often, just lately she had seen them sitting there under the apple tree, talking or just holding hands and watching yet another glorious Lincolnshire sunset. It always brought a lump to her throat. Half of her envied her friend, but deep in her heart she feared for her too.

But now she smiled brightly at Kenny as she added, 'But I haven't seen them sitting there lately. I reckon they're afraid of getting clouted on the head with falling apples.'

'Well, we can soon put that right. The fruit are well ready for picking – I had a look at them last week. It's a shame to let them fall off and get bruised; they don't store so well then. And then they can have their love seat back. Where are they, by the way?'

'Having dinner in the NAAFI. They'll be here in a bit.'

Kenny had only just reared the ladder up amongst the branches, when Fleur and Robbie rounded the corner of the cottage.'

'Need any help?'

'Hi, Sis. Well, I suppose if you can find another ladder, we'd be done in half the time. I could do this side of the tree and Robbie the other.'

'Harry's got one in his shed.'

'I'll fetch it.'

Robbie was back in a few minutes with Harry following in his wake.

'Now mind how you handle them apples. They bruise easy.' The old man stood looking up into the tree and stroking his moustache. 'Fine crop you've got there. How're you going to store them?'

'Lay them out on newspaper under the beds,' Fleur said.

'Aye, mind they're not touching an' you'll be all right. Just unmarked ones, mind. Any fallers, Mary can use straight away or dry them.'

'I'm going to help her bottle some this year,' Fleur put in. 'She can sit down to peel them and I can do everything else.'

'Mum's busy doing it at the moment. I picked all ours earlier in the week.'

For a moment, Fleur felt a pang of longing to visit her home again. To see her dad and – yes – her mother too.

'Harry – Harry!' Mrs Jackson was calling him from the back door. 'Come away in and leave them youngsters to it. They know what they're doing . . .'

With a comical smile, Harry shambled back up the pathway and disappeared into the house.

'They'll be sat either side of the wireless now,' Ruth smiled. 'Listening to—'

'The news!' the other three chorused and they all laughed.

'It'll be *Workers' Playtime* in a bit.'

'Well, we've no time to be playing. Let's get cracking . . .'

With the beginning of October, summer was over.

'By heck, it's nippy this morning,' Ruth shivered as they hurried towards the NAAFI. 'We ought to see if we can get Mrs Jackson any more coal. This weather won't do her arthritis any good.'

'I know. Have you seen her poor knuckles? They're so swollen. I didn't want her to peel all those apples when we were bottling last week, but she insisted.'

'Mind you she's that proud of her shelf of bottled fruit, I think it was worth it for her. Made her feel useful again.'

'Oh, she's doing her bit, all right. She's still knitting for the troops and it must be painful for her hands.'

As they walked into the dining room for breakfast, the air was thick with chatter, more animated than usual.

'Hello,' Ruth remarked, glancing round. 'Summat's

up. Let's find Kay. She'll know. I reckon she sleeps with the wireless on all night so she doesn't miss the news.'

They took their places at one of the new tables that had recently been delivered – a table for four that they shared with Kay and Peggy. They were already there, eating breakfast, but talking rapidly too.

'What's up, Corp?' Ruth demanded, sitting down opposite with her loaded plate and reaching for the sauce.

'He's advancing on Moscow. That'll be the end of him. Fancy trying now! In October! Doesn't he know what the Russian winter is like?' Kay was excited by the thought. 'If Napoleon couldn't do it, I doubt Adolf can.'

'Well, if he's got other things on his mind, maybe he'll leave us alone for a bit.'

It did seem a little quieter at Wickerton Wood, but whether that was because the Germans were busy elsewhere or because of the atrocious winter weather that lay over the whole country, no one could be certain. But everyone was thankful for a little respite, whatever the reason. Life settled into something of a routine, with off-duty times for Ruth, Fleur and Robbie spent at Mrs Jackson's little cottage. Kenny still cycled over at weekends whenever he could, but now Jake never came and Fleur missed her father more than she ever admitted to anyone.

The weather worsened, the temperature dropped and a cold winter was forecast.

November fog caused disruption to flying. No one

minded too much if raids were cancelled, but the worst situation was if, after take-off, a swirling mist shrouded the airfield by the time the aircraft were due back.

'I hate it when they're all diverted,' Fleur muttered quietly to Kay on one such night as they waited in the watch office, the runway only a few yards in front of them completely blotted out. 'I like to know that D-Doggo is back – that they're all back safely,' she added hurriedly, in case she'd sounded selfish.

For once, Kay did not respond with a tart retort. Instead, she sighed. 'I know just what you mean. It's daft, but I feel just the same.'

'Do you?' Fleur couldn't stop the surprised question escaping her lips.

Kay smiled wryly as she glanced behind her to make sure that Bob Watson was out of earshot. 'Oh, I know I sound as if I don't give a damn most of the time, but inside – I do care.' Her voice was suddenly husky. 'I care very much. A lot of my . . . my attitude is just an act, Fleur. Bravado, if you like . . .' Her voice trailed away and then, suddenly, she was brisk and efficient and razor sharp as ever, 'But if you ever tell a soul I've said this, I shall deny it hotly. OK?'

'Naturally, Corp,' Fleur said and, though she gave a playful salute, her tone was sincere. The two girls, bound by their concern for the safety of the same aircraft, exchanged a look of complete understanding.

'Now, we'd better get ready for telling these boys that they can't come home tonight . . .'

Later, as they clattered down the steps from Control, they were met by the eerily silent fog-bound station. They stood a moment, listening, but there was absolutely nothing to hear. Fleur shuddered. 'Come on, let's get to bed. I hate it like this. It's . . . it's ghostly.'

'Mm,' Kay, in a strangely pensive mood, pondered. 'Makes you think, doesn't it? I wonder if the ghosts of all the boys we've lost come back here? To their station?'

'Oh, don't! I don't even want to think about it. Come on, Kay, let's see if we can find the WAAF quarters in this lot. I tend to lose my sense of direction in fog.'

After taking a couple of wrong turns and ending up near the main guardhouse, they found their quarters and fell into bed. Fleur was exhausted, but sleep eluded her for over an hour. She knew D-Doggo had landed safely at another airfield, but it wasn't the same as knowing he was sleeping only a few hundred yards away in the airmen's quarters. If only they'd hurry up and get the married quarters built, it'd be even better.

The squadron had been forced to go on to land at an airfield in Yorkshire, many of them dangerously low on fuel. Only one didn't make it and had to crash land in a field. Luckily, the crew only suffered cuts and bruises and came back to Wickerton Wood the following day indignantly travelling in the back of a RAF lorry. The rest of the aircraft flew in throughout the morning. Other than the unwelcome diversion, it had been a successful mission and all the crews were safe.

'Talk about brass-monkey weather,' Fleur shivered as she joined the other three at breakfast. 'D'you know there were icicles on the *inside* of the window this morning? I wish I was back at Mrs Jackson's in her nice feather bed.'

'It'll be even colder in Russia. It's the first of December tomorrow,' Kay remarked, wagging her fork towards Fleur. 'If Hitler doesn't take Moscow in the next few days, his troops'll never survive the winter.' Her interest in the news never waned. 'And I'll tell you something else I've heard on the grapevine. All single women between the ages of twenty and thirty are to be called up. So – we'd all have been in the services soon even if we hadn't volunteered.'

For a moment Fleur felt a rush of relief. Her voluntary entry into the WAAFs had been vindicated, but at Kay's next words she felt a shudder of apprehension.

'And they're lowering the call-up age for men to eighteen and a half and raising it to men aged fifty.'

So in roughly a year's time, Kenny – he would be eighteen next March – would have to go anyway. And what about her dad? He was still under fifty – just. Would he be called up? She had a sudden picture of her mother sitting at the table filling out numerous forms to stop her menfolk being sent to war.

Then Fleur remembered. Her dad still limped from an injury in the last war. He wouldn't be classed as fit enough now.

But Kenny would. Oh yes, Kenny would be A1 fit.

'We don't need a bloody wireless when you're around, Corp,' Ruth was saying, dragging Fleur's thoughts back to the conversation around the table. 'But could you give us a little light entertainment too, d'you think? Can you imitate Tommy Handley or sing like Vera Lynn?'

Kay enjoyed the banter. Both Fleur and Ruth gave

her back as good as she gave out, but Kay never 'pulled rank' though, as a corporal, she could have done. Only Peggy was the quiet one of the four and just listened to the sharp exchanges with a placid smile.

But a few days later everyone was appalled by the news that was going round.

'Oh, they've done it now.' Kay was jubilant. 'That's America in the war for certain now.'

'But it's Japan that's attacked them. They'll concentrate on them, won't they?'

'It's a world war now. They'll just fight everybody.' Kay grinned as she added, ''Cept us. Good to have a mighty friend on our side, isn't it?'

Fleur shook her head. 'But why? Why have Japan attacked Pearl Harbor? They must know they'd reap the whirlwind.'

'Don't ask me. I'm just glad we're on the right side of the whirlwind.'

A few days later, the news guru said, 'I told you so. I told you didn't I?'

'You tell us a lot of things, Corp,' Ruth remarked dryly. 'To which particular piece of your undoubted wisdom are you referring?'

'Oh well, if you don't want to know, then . . .' Kay retorted but then she caught Ruth's wink. 'Oh, you . . . !'

'Tell us, then,' Fleur said.

The three of them were sitting at their usual table in the dining room for dinner. Peggy was away on leave.

'The Russians are chasing Adolf out. They've recaptured some of the places that the Germans had taken and now Adolf's boys are on the run. I told you the Russian winter would defeat him – his troops can't withstand the cold. Can't get supplies through either, I shouldn't wonder. But the Russians know how to cope, don't they? They're used to it.'

'Do you think he'll try again? Next spring?' Fleur, too, was caught up with the staggering news of the last few days.

Kay shrugged. 'Not if he's any sense.'

'But he hasn't, has he?' Ruth put in, her mouth full of stew and dumplings.

'What?'

'Any sense.'

They were silent, each concentrating on their meal, until Ruth asked, 'So? What are we all doing for Christmas, then?'

'Oh, crumbs, I haven't got as far as that yet,' Fleur said.

'You still haven't come down off cloud nine since your wedding,' Kay teased, and gave an exaggerated sigh. 'Ordinary life has to go on for the rest of us. Like planning Christmas.'

'Have we got leave?'

Ruth pulled a face. 'Shouldn't think so for a minute. I think – though I don't know – that leave will be granted to those whose homes are a long way off. After all – to be fair – we do get home a lot because our families live relatively near. I mean, we can get home and back on just a twenty-four, can't we?'

Fleur nodded. 'I see what you mean.' She was silent for a moment. 'I wonder if they'd let us do something on camp to celebrate? Those of us who don't go home?'

'Oh, I'm sure there'll be a dance in the sergeants' mess and—'

'No, I meant something a bit more than that.' She

leant forward across the table towards the other two. 'I tell you what I'd really like to do.'

'What?'

'Throw a Christmas party for all the evacuee kids in the village – and the village kids an' all, of course.'

Ruth stared at her for a moment and then her face lit up. 'Fleur – that's a brilliant idea. Who do we have to ask?'

'Er – well, we could start with ma'am . . .'

Fleur's idea was taken up enthusiastically by everyone on camp and the date was fixed for the afternoon of Christmas Eve. A few days beforehand, willing hands – even those who would not be there on the day because they'd be on leave – helped to decorate the sergeants' mess.

'There's a bloke at the main gate asking for Fleur,' Johnny called from the doorway.

'Oho, Robbie,' Tommy shouted from the top of the ladder, where he was hanging paper chains across the ceiling. 'Got a rival already, old boy. Have to watch her.'

Johnny, grinning in the doorway, said, 'Well, he's a nice-looking bloke, I'll give you that, but he is old enough to be her father . . .'

Fleur gasped and her eyes widened. 'Dad? Here? Oh – I wonder what's wrong?' Before Johnny could say any more, Fleur had gone out of the mess and was running along the road towards the main gate, her hair flying loose, her jacket undone. She was lucky she didn't encounter any WAAF officers in her headlong flight, or she might have been on a charge and missed the children's party for which she'd worked so hard.

Jake was standing talking amiably to the guard commander as Fleur dashed up.

'What's wrong, Dad?'

'Oh, sorry, love, I didn't mean to worry you. Nothing's wrong. I've just brought you a Christmas tree. Kenny said you're throwing a party for all the kids in the village and I thought—'

'Oh, Dad, that's wonderful. We've only got a pathetic-looking thing made out of wire and green paper.' She turned to the guard commander. 'May he drive round to the sergeants' mess?'

Permission granted, Jake was greeted at the mess with open arms, quite literally, for Ruth ran towards him as he struggled through the door with the Christmas tree. 'Mr Bosley, you darling! We've got all these lovely tree decorations from Mrs Jackson, Harry and Bill Moore at the pub and no tree to put them on. Oh, that's perfect.' She clapped her hands. 'Now, where shall we put it?'

Already, Robbie, Tommy and Johnny were moving forward to help. 'How about over here in the corner? And then we can put all the presents for the kids under the tree.'

'Presents? My word, you have been busy,' Jake said.

'We've collected round the camp and we've managed to buy one present for each child.'

'And the CO has promised to dress up as Father Christmas.'

'Fleur,' Jake said softly, 'I tried to get your mam to make some extra puddings and a cake, but . . .'

'Don't worry, Dad,' she said, slipping her arm through his and hugging it to her side. 'This is absolutely great – you couldn't have brought anything better. And . . . and it's lovely to see you. I . . . I've missed you.'

His dark brown eyes regarded her soulfully. 'Why don't you come home any more? Surely you must have had a couple of days' leave some time since your wedding?'

Fleur ran her tongue round her lips. 'I . . . I wanted to. At least, if I'm honest, *part* of me wanted to. The other part – well – I didn't want to make matters worse than they already are.'

Jake sighed heavily. 'Well, they're not going to get any better unless you do come home from time to time and try to heal the breach.'

'All right, Dad. I will come. I promise.'

His face was bleak for a moment. 'Kenny's going in March, don't forget. He'll be eighteen then and he still seems determined to go even before he really has to.'

'I know,' Fleur whispered. She was hardly likely to forget that. It blighted her waking hours and some of her sleeping ones too.

'Have you heard?' Robbie's face was ecstatic. 'Tommy's just told the crew.'

'Father Christmas has landed on the runway?' Ruth volunteered.

'Better than that!'

'The war's over?'

'It soon will be now. We're getting the new Lancasters and they're arriving on Christmas Eve.'

All eyes turned to look at Robbie and then the excited questions began. 'How many?' 'Will we get a chance to train on them?' 'How many crew do they need?' 'What bombs can they carry?'

'Whoa, whoa there!' Laughing, Robbie held out his hands, palms outwards, fending off the volley of questions. 'We'll find out soon enough.'

The arrival of the new aircraft was amazing. Every vantage point was lined with station personnel and Fleur and Kay, on duty in the watch office, held their breaths as the first of the magnificent planes approached the airfield and landed smoothly.

'My word, what a beauty!' Kay said, her mouth open in wonder as she stared at the lines of the aircraft, strangely elegant in such a powerful machine.

'What a Christmas present!' Fleur laughed as another approached the airfield and she heard the wireless burst into life. 'Hello, Woody, this is J-Janie calling . . .'

And in they all came, one after another until they were all safely landed.

'And now we're going to party,' Kay said as they clattered down the steps from the watch office and headed towards the sergeants' mess.

The party was a great success, even though one or two children over-indulged at the sight of so much food and promptly threw up. 'Father Christmas' played his part and earned a new respect from those under his command.

'D'you know,' Johnny said later, 'I always thought the CO was a miserable old devil, but he was really good with those kids. Did you see? And he was great on Christmas Day too, wasn't he?'

The station had followed the usual tradition of all

the officers serving the lower ranks with their Christmas dinner. They had entered into the spirit of the occasion with great aplomb and accepted the ribbing with equanimity.

'No, he's a good bloke,' Robbie said. 'But, y'know, I think I'd be a miserable old devil in his position. I don't envy his responsibilities one bit. Sending crews off night after night, not knowing how many are going to come back. And just think of the dreadful letters he has to write when they don't.' Robbie gave a shudder. 'God – it must be a nightmare.'

Johnny's usual cheerful face sobered suddenly. 'Yeah, you're right, mate. I hadn't looked at it like that.' Then, his face crinkling once more into its usual grin, he punched Robbie's shoulder. 'Come on, let's go and play with our new Lanc.'

There would be no operations for a while from Wickerton Wood.

'We've to go on a course at a heavy conversion unit,' Robbie told Fleur. 'It'll be for about six weeks.'

'Six weeks! D'you mean I won't see you for six weeks?' She was staring at him in horror, but Robbie was grinning.

'It's only near Newark.'

Fleur let out a sigh of relief. 'That's all right then. You think you'll get leave now and then?'

Robbie shook his head. 'Probably not, but you should. There'll not be much going on here until we come back, I shouldn't think.'

Fleur pulled a face. 'I wouldn't bank on it. They'll find something for us to do, I've no doubt.'

The six weeks passed surprisingly quickly whilst the newly formed crews of seven instead of four underwent their training on the new aircraft: take-offs, circuits, landings and even flying across country at different heights to familiarize themselves with how the aircraft, heavier than they had been used to with its four mighty Merlin engines, performed. Whenever they met up, Robbie talked of nothing else.

When they all returned to Wickerton Wood, Robbie was enthusiastic about his new instruments.

'It's all right for you, you jammy devil,' Alan, the rear gunner, complained. 'You've got the hottest seat in the house.'

Robbie laughed, but Fleur was anxious. 'What's he mean?'

'He means it's the warmest place in the aircraft.'

'Oh, I . . . I thought he meant it was the most dangerous.'

'No. Actually, it's probably one of the safest places to be. I'm right behind the skipper and the back of his seat is armour-plated.'

'Really?'

'Yes, really.' He kissed her on the end of her nose. 'So stop worrying. It's a great aircraft.'

'It's the best Christmas present ever. Now we can get at 'em,' was the opinion of everyone.

Thirty-Five

'You know, you really ought to go home, Fleur. For a visit. Try to make it up with your mother,' Robbie murmured as they lay in each other's arms in the pale light of dawn after a blissful night of love. He kissed her hair. 'I don't like being the cause of a rift between you.'

It was February already and neither of them had been able to get home over Christmas or at New Year or since. Robbie because of the training course and Fleur because heavy falls of snow had given her the perfect excuse to stay at Wickerton. It was surprising that the crews had managed to complete enough flying hours on the course, but somehow they had.

Despite her father's plea, Fleur was still putting off the moment. 'I suppose you're right.' She sighed. 'But I don't want to miss any time with you.'

'Well, we're not always off duty at the same time,' Robbie pointed out reasonably.

'Mostly we are. Because . . . because when you're flying, I'm usually in the watch office.' There was a pause before Fleur suggested, 'We could go together.'

'No, I don't think that's a good idea. Rather fuelling the flame, don't you think?'

'I suppose so.'

'Tell you what, next time we get a decent leave I'll

go and see Ma and Pops and you go to Middleditch Farm.'

'All right.' Fleur sighed again, knowing he was right, but feeling she would much rather visit the tiny terraced house in Nottingham with him. She would receive a warmer welcome from Robbie's mother than she ever would from her own.

'Good,' he said as he began kissing her. 'And now, Mrs Rodwell, before we have to get up and face the day . . .'

'Hello, Dad,' Fleur said softly, leaning on the top of the bottom half of the cowshed door. 'I thought I'd find you here.'

Jake straightened up from the milking stool. 'Fleur, love.' His smile was warm and loving. He picked up the bucket of milk and came towards her. 'Good to see you.' He looked into her eyes. 'I don't need to ask if everything's all right. I can see it is.'

'Oh, Dad, if only it wasn't for this wretched war, then life would be perfect.'

'Aye,' Jake's face clouded. 'Aye, it would.'

'But then, if it hadn't been for the war, I might not have met Robbie.'

'True, true,' Jake murmured absently.

Fleur glanced behind him into the shadows of the cowshed. 'Where's Kenny? Isn't he here? Helping you with the milking?'

Jake shook his head. Fleur searched his face. 'What is it, Dad? What's wrong?'

'He's gone. Kenny's gone.'

'Gone? Gone where?'

'Into the RAF. Seems he volunteered a while back

and he got his papers the day before yesterday and off he went.'

'But . . . but . . . he's not old enough. He's not even eighteen yet.'

Jake shrugged. 'He is next month. Seems it doesn't matter. He's in and that's all he cares about.'

There was a pause before Fleur said, 'He'd've been better in the army. Maybe they wouldn't send him abroad straight away, but the RAF. I mean once he's done his training he – they . . .'

'I thought it was the army he wanted too. It was – at first. But it seems . . . it seems as if he was influenced by – by . . .' His voice fell away as if he couldn't bring himself to say any more.

'By Robbie, you mean,' Fleur whispered.

Her father nodded. They stood awkwardly for a moment, neither knowing what to say. At last Jake said haltingly, 'You'd best go in. See yer mother.'

'No, no, I'll help you finish here.'

'You'll get yerself mucky,' he said, glancing at her uniform.

She pulled in a deep breath. 'Then I'll go in and find some old clothes. Unless, of course, Mum's thrown them all out.'

'No, no.' Jake sighed. 'Your room's just as you left it.'

'I won't be a mo, then.'

'Fleur—' Jake began but she was gone, running across the yard towards the back door. As she stepped into the scullery, her mother looked up from the sink.

'Oh, it's you. Well, I hope you're satisfied. He's gone. Joined the wonderful RAF.'

'Mum – I'm sorry. But it's not all my fault. He was determined to join up somehow.'

'It's your fault he's joined the RAF, though. Yours and – and *his*.'

Stung to retort, Fleur snapped. 'His name's Robbie.'

'Oh yes, I know what his name is all right. And his bloody mother's. Oh, I know *her* name all right. As if I could ever forget it. I wish to God I could.' Betsy slammed down the plate she was washing onto the wooden draining board with such force that it cracked in two. 'Now look what you've made me do. I've broken one of me best plates.'

'Mum,' Fleur said tiredly. 'Won't you tell me what all this is about? Don't you think we have a right to know? What has Robbie done for you to hate him so? You don't even know him.'

Betsy didn't answer but picked up the shattered pieces and dropped them into a bin at the side of the sink. 'It's not him. It's his mother.'

'Then why take it out on Robbie if it's not his fault?'

Betsy glared at her and avoided answering. Instead, she asked another question. 'Were they together at the wedding?'

Fleur frowned. 'Who? Robbie and his mother?'

Betsy gave a tut of exasperation. 'Your dad and her?'

Fleur blinked. 'Well – yes – they talked.'

Betsy held Fleur's gaze, as if daring her to look away. Fleur stared back boldly but her heart was thumping madly. She didn't want to lie to her mother, but neither did she want to admit that her father and Robbie's mother had stood close together holding hands and gazing into each other's eyes.

'Did they – did they go off together?'

Her heart rate slowed a little. 'Go off together? Of course not.'

'Hm.' Betsy sounded doubtful. She folded her arms in front of her and stepped closer to Fleur. 'Tell me – and I want the truth mind – did your father wipe your face with his handkerchief?'

Fleur gaped. 'Wipe my face? I don't know what you mean.'

'There was a woman's make-up on his handkerchief. He said it was yours. That . . . that you'd shed a few tears and he'd mopped your face. Is that true?'

Fleur's gaze didn't flicker, but she felt her heart begin to pound again. Slowly, she nodded. 'Yes, yes, he did. When he first got to the house. He was late and I thought he wasn't coming . . .' Her voice trailed away and she held her breath. Was her mother going to believe her? It was true she'd cried. It was true that someone had dabbed her face with a hanky. But that someone had been Ruth – not Jake.

After a moment, Betsy nodded. 'Very well then. But they did meet and they did talk?'

Fleur forced a laugh. 'Well, yes, of course they did. They could hardly avoid each other, now could they? But it was only at the pub afterwards and—'

'But you weren't there all the time, were you? You went off on your honeymoon. You don't know what happened after that, do you?'

'Well, no, but Kenny was still there.'

'Oh yes, Kenny. But he was so taken up with this . . . this Ruth that he wouldn't see what was going on under his nose.'

'Ruth had to go back to camp straight after we left. Kenny wouldn't have wanted to stay on then.'

'Oh.' Betsy was thoughtful for a moment then she turned away. 'Anyway, what have you come for?'

'I came to see if I could put matters right between you and me, Mum.'

'Well, I'm sorry you've had a wasted journey. While you're married to that lad and seeing his mother, I don't want owt to do with you. And now Kenny's gone . . .' She left the accusation hanging in the air.

'Then I'm sorry, Mum, very sorry. But I love Robbie and he loves me and if no one will tell us what this . . . this feud is all about, then there's nothing either of us can do. And I'm sorry about Kenny too. He would have gone somewhere – the army or somewhere – but yes, I agree, it is my fault he chose the RAF and I'm just going to have to live with that, aren't I?' Then she turned and fled upstairs, rushed into her old room and slammed the door behind her, leaning against it. She closed her eyes and groaned. Now she had two people she loved to worry about. Robbie – and Kenny too.

Ruth's reaction to Fleur's news that Kenny had joined the RAF was predictable.

'Stupid little bugger,' she railed. 'Why on earth didn't he stay out of it? He'd got the chance living on a farm and being in a reserved occupation. All quite above board. Why on earth does he want to play the hero?'

'Mum says it's all my fault. Because I joined up, he doesn't want to be left behind and have everyone thinking him a coward.'

Ruth let out a very unladylike snort. 'No one's going to think that. At least, not anyone with any sense.'

There was a pause before Fleur asked gently, 'Then

why did you join the WAAF? You could have done your bit some other way – in a factory or something.'

''Cos I was just as stupid when it all began. Fighting for my country and all that tosh.'

'So you wouldn't mind if Hitler walked in then?' Fleur said with deceptive mildness.

Ruth sighed heavily, her anger dying. 'Yes, of course I would. Oh, I know we've got to stop him. I know we've got to stop him coming here and we've got to help all these other poor folk he's already trampling over, but . . . but – oh, Fleur – you should understand if anyone does – what with Robbie and now Kenny too in danger every day.'

'Oh, I do,' Fleur said grimly, thinking of the sleepless nights she was having even when she wasn't on duty. The only time she felt at peace was when Robbie was lying beside her. But even that was spoilt because now she had Kenny to worry about. She didn't even know where he was or what he was doing. She didn't know which was the worst: knowing – or not knowing.

'I'm sorry.' Ruth put her arms around Fleur. 'It must be awful for you. And with your mum making it worse by blaming you. How's your dad taking it?'

'He's worried. Naturally.'

'But – but does he blame you?'

'I don't know. He hasn't said except to say that Kenny had joined the RAF because of Robbie. He'd never say outright, but . . . but maybe deep down . . .'

Ruth hugged her harder. 'Come on, girl. Chin up. Let's just pray they'll both stay safe, eh?'

Fleur rested her face against Ruth's shoulders and screwed up her eyes, trying to stem the tears.

She'd pray all right. Oh, how she would pray. But it was a lot to ask.

Thirty-Six

Towards the end of March, the RAF began a round-the-clock bombing campaign against the German arms' factories. Night after night the airmen at Wickerton Wood and their new Lancasters were involved, often escorted by Spitfires.

On a rare night off Fleur and Robbie spent the time at Mrs Jackson's cottage. Flying was still going on, so Ruth was on duty.

Robbie lay back on the bed, still in his uniform, his tie loosened, his hair ruffled. He closed his eyes with a weary sigh. 'Oh, Fleur, when is it all going to end and we can find our own little cottage with roses round the door and an apple tree we can sit under to watch the sunsets?'

She sat on the bed beside him, took his hand and kissed each finger. 'I don't know, but we're all doing our best to end it quickly. You especially.'

'But the end's nowhere in sight. At least, it doesn't seem to be. Two and a half years and we don't seem any nearer. In fact, it just seems to have got worse. What with Japan and America in it too now. Oh, darling, I just feel so . . . so tired. I . . .'

Fleur leant forward to kiss him, but then she hesitated. Robbie was asleep. She put the eiderdown over him and then undressed quietly and slipped into the bed beside him. But sleep evaded her.

She was worried. She had never heard Robbie talk like that. With a defeated air. He was always so positive with a 'get up and get at 'em' attitude. But tonight he'd seemed – well – beaten.

He's just so tired, she thought. He'll be all right tomorrow. And tomorrow, she reminded herself, is his very last mission. The four men from the original crew would have completed a full tour of duty and deserved a well-earned break. But one worry ate away at her. With the newly formed crews, would they want to break them up? Would they make Tommy and the other three carry on? She wasn't sure of regulations and Robbie refused to discuss it. It was as if he was superstitious about discussing the elusive thirtieth op. Only very few aircrews survived to even reach it and to mention it seemed like tempting fate . . .

The following morning, they rose late and ate a leisurely breakfast, which Fleur had gone downstairs in her dressing gown to bring up to their room.

They set the tray aside and Fleur climbed back into the bed.

'Feel better this morning?' she whispered.

'Yes. I'm sorry about last night. I don't know what got into me.'

She stroked his hair. 'You're tired. You're all tired. But only one more mission tonight and then . . .'

'I know. Maybe that's what's getting to me. What'll happen then, d'you think? D'you think we might get split up? Posted, even?'

'Oh, I hope not!'

Robbie grinned wickedly and took her in his arms, 'But we'd better make the most of this morning, just in case . . .'

'Fleur? Fleur, dear, are you there?' It was Mary Jackson calling from the foot of the stairs.

Robbie let out a groan and Fleur stifled her giggles against him, before she was able to lift her head and shout, 'Yes, Mrs Jackson. What is it?'

'Kenny's here, dear.'

'Kenny! How lovely! Oh—' She turned back to Robbie. 'I'm sorry, darling.'

Robbie smiled and kissed her. 'It's all right. Let's go down and see him.'

They dressed quickly and hurried downstairs. Fleur flung her arms round her brother, tall and resplendent in his RAF uniform.

'I've just got a spot of leave,' he said excitedly. 'Basic training'll soon be finished. Then it'll be passing out parade and I'm volunteering for fighter training . . . So, in the meantime . . .' He saluted smartly. 'Aircraftman Bosley reporting for duty, ma'am. Digging fatigues, is it?'

Fleur hugged him. 'We'll have a lovely day together, but we're on duty tonight. It's Robbie's last mission for a while.'

Kenny grinned and slapped his brother-in-law on the back. 'And there I was hoping to be escorting you in my Spitfire one of these days.'

'Oh, you'll get the chance. I've no doubt we'll be called on to do another tour before long.'

Fleur felt her heart plummet. Naively, she thought that Robbie's flying days would be over, that he'd be given a nice, safe desk job somewhere. In her wilder moments she'd even imagined him being in charge of the watch office, that they would be working together. But of course that would never happen. He was a trained wireless operator. Of course he would have to fly again . . .

But for today, she had both of them safely with her. They would make the most of today. 'So,' she said, forcing a bright smile onto her face. 'What are we going to do?'

'Well, I thought I'd help you in the garden a bit this morning – if you want me to, that is – and then this afternoon, I thought we'd go into Lincoln,' Kenny said. 'I'll treat you to a slap-up tea in Boots cafe. How about that?'

'You're on. A celebration tea.' She glanced at Robbie. 'Do you know what day it is?'

Robbie blinked. 'Er – Wednesday?'

Fleur smiled. 'Well, yes it is, but I meant the date. It's exactly a year ago today since we met.'

'Is it really? Fancy me forgetting.'

She reached up and kissed him lightly. 'You're forgiven. You've rather had other things on your mind just lately.'

'I'll make a stew for all of us for dinner and an apple pie,' Mrs Jackson said, struggling to her feet.

'We don't want to put you to any trouble, Mrs Jackson.' Robbie turned to her.

'No trouble, love.' The old lady patted his arm and chuckled. 'It'll make me feel useful.'

'Oh, I almost forgot, Mrs Jackson,' Kenny said. 'Dad's sent you some eggs and butter. I'll get them.'

As he opened the door, Ruth was coming round the corner of the cottage. Kenny's eyes lit up. 'Just the person I'd hoped to see. We're going into Lincoln this afternoon for tea.' He gave an exaggerated bow. 'Would madam care to join us?'

'Hi, Kenny. Fancy seeing you here. Got your wings yet?'

'Not quite, but I start training soon. Can't tell you where, of course.' He tapped the side of his nose. 'Careless talk, and all that, but it's somewhere down south.'

Fleur giggled. 'Oh, I think we're allowed to know where, Kenny. Else how will Mum know where to address all those food parcels she's bound to want to send you?'

He blinked and his young face wore a comical expression. 'Oh yes. I suppose so. I'm just not used to all this sort of secrecy. They dinned it into us so much that we mustn't say this and mustn't say that, that I'm not exactly sure what I can say and what I can't.' He grinned. 'So I thought it best just to say nothing.'

They all laughed, but Fleur said, 'I know what you mean. I felt that way too at first, but you soon find out what it's safe to say. You can tell your family where you're stationed but not the details about missions and so on.'

'But I'm going to train as a fighter pilot. That's a bit different, isn't it? We get scrambled when enemy aircraft are approaching, don't we?'

'I expect so.'

'And I suppose that's why I'm being sent down south. That's where the Battle of Britain went on, isn't it?'

Fleur felt a cold shudder of apprehension run through her as she imagined her baby brother up there above the clouds chasing after enemy bombers as they thundered towards England to rain death from the skies. She quelled the feeling swiftly and smiled up at him. 'Let's hope there's not so much going on now. Old Hitler seems to have other things on his mind.'

'Good job he has,' Kenny said with feeling. 'We were lucky he didn't invade in 'forty, y'know.'

'I do know. If he had done . . .' She said no more, but the same thought was in all their minds. If Hitler had pressed home his invasion plans in September 1940, what would life be like right now in Britain? It didn't bear thinking about.

'I wish Mum would see it like that,' Kenny murmured.

'How is she?'

Kenny pulled a face. 'Cross and then weepy. Hardly speaking to me one minute and then crying all over me the next.'

'Poor Mum,' Fleur said. 'It's not easy for her, Kenny.' She punched his arm gently. 'And for heaven's sake, take care of yourself. And, now,' she added briskly, 'this garden isn't going to dig itself.'

Ruth yawned. 'I'll just grab a couple of hours on my lovely soft feather bed upstairs and then I'll nip round to Harry's.'

The day passed all too quickly and then they were waving Kenny goodbye on the train back home. 'Well, I'll be off back tomorrow and then I'll soon be up in the clouds alongside you, Robbie. Wish me luck.'

The two men shook hands and Fleur hugged her brother hard. 'Oh, we do, we do. Good luck, darling bro.'

And then Kenny turned to Ruth. 'Goodbye, Ruth,' he said and suddenly he was boyishly shy.

'Good luck, Kenny,' Ruth said, giving him a bear

hug. As she drew back, she touched his cheek tenderly and looked into his eyes as she added earnestly, 'And take care of yourself.'

'I will. I'll . . . I'll see you soon.'

Then, with a last wink to Fleur, he boarded the train and leant out of the window waving until they could no longer see him. For several minutes, Fleur stood watching the receding train until Robbie put his arm around her shoulders and said softly, 'Come on, love, time we were all getting back. Last trip for a while – I can't wait for tonight to be over.'

Fleur shuddered. It was the first time she'd ever heard Robbie talk like that. He must be wearier than even she had realized.

In the control tower, Fleur stood alone staring at the blackboard with the names of the aircraft chalked up as they returned. There was one blank space left. One plane had not returned from the operation.

Robbie Rodwell's bomber.

Fleur lost track of the time she stood there, just staring at the blackboard, willing the radio to crackle into life, praying to hear the call sign. 'Hello, Woody, this is Lindum T-Tommy calling . . .'

But the radio was silent, the space left blank. She couldn't even have Ruth with her. She was already on duty at the debriefing. But she knew that T-Tommy had not come home. Maybe, at this very moment, Ruth was hearing what had happened to Robbie and the others. It had seemed a good omen at the time, that the call sign given to the new Lancaster they were now flying had, by coincidence, the same name as its skipper. Now, Fleur wasn't so sure.

Kay, too, had remained in the control room, hunched over her radio but unable to meet Fleur's eyes. Bob Watson carried on with all the necessary duties he had at the end of a mission, his face grim. He was studiously avoiding looking at either of the girls.

The room was silent, the airfield outside the window silent too in the early morning light. Though she strained her ears, there was no welcome sound of a damaged aircraft limping home.

She heard the door open behind her and for a moment her heart leapt. She spun round, her face suddenly alight with hope. There'd been a mistake! T-Tommy had landed and they'd missed it. Robbie had been safely home all the time . . .

It was her heart speaking, not her head. Control never missed a plane landing. It simply didn't happen. They were all too professional, too thorough. But terror and hope are strange bedfellows and forced the mind to play strange tricks.

Of course it wasn't Robbie who had stepped into the room, but Squadron Leader Tony Harris, whose aircraft had been the last to land. His face was sombre and her heart plummeted as she saw the sympathy in his eyes.

'I'm sorry, Fleur. One of the other pilots has reported at the debriefing that he saw a bomber with two of its engines on fire going down just off the coast. It looks like it could have been T-Tommy. It's the only one that hasn't come back this time.'

It was a good night's work. Even Fleur had to acknowledge that. Only one bomber missing. But why, oh why, did it have to be Robbie's?

The lump in her throat threatened to choke her, but she managed to ask, 'Did they see any parachutes?'

'It was too dark to see.'

'Thank you for letting me know, sir,' she said, shakily.

'There's still a chance, Fleur. We don't give up hope until we know for definite, do we?' Like her, the squadron leader was forcing an optimism he didn't really feel deep inside. He was not relishing the thought of the difficult letters that he would have to write to all the families of the missing crew, should the worst be confirmed. Fleur nodded, now not trusting herself to speak.

'I'll see Caroline – your commanding officer.'

If she hadn't been so distressed, Fleur might have smiled at the squadron leader's use of ma'am's Christian name. Rumour on camp had it that they were seeing each other on the QT. As it was, Fleur was quite lost in a flood of grief that she scarcely noticed. She couldn't allow herself false hope. She'd already seen too much of it. 'I'll see if she can arrange a spot of leave for you,' he went on. 'I expect you'd like to go home. See your own folks. And . . . and his mother. She's in Nottingham, I understand.'

Fleur nodded and managed to whisper huskily, 'Thank you.'

He moved across the room to have a word or two with Kay, who was still sitting in front of her microphone. He put his hand on her shoulder and bent down towards her, but Kay didn't speak, didn't even respond to his kindly gesture.

After he'd left the office, Fleur stood for a few moments longer just staring at the blank space on the blackboard. A space that would never now be filled in.

'Fleur . . .' She heard the scrape of a chair on the floor and heard Kay's voice, but she held out her hand, palm outwards. She closed her eyes for a moment and shook her head. She couldn't cope with sympathy – however well meant – at this moment. She was about to turn away, to run away as far as she could go, to deal with her anguish on her own, but then, even through her own pain, she remembered.

Tommy – Kay's Tommy! Of course! He was missing too. How could she have been so thoughtless, so selfishly wrapped up in her own grief that she had not given a thought to Kay?

'Oh, Kay – Kay . . .' She held out her arms and the two girls flew to each other, holding their friend tightly and crying against each other's shoulder. Quietly, his work finished, Bob Watson left the room.

The man felt guilty. There was nothing he could say. It would sound hypocritical. He'd never hidden his disapproval of wartime romances, let alone a wartime wedding. And now his fears had been realized and there was nothing he could say – or do. Not for the first time he silently cursed this blasted war!

After a few moments, Kay pulled herself free of Fleur's clinging arms. 'Right. This won't do any good. It's not what they would have wanted. Come on, get a grip, girl.'

Fleur was still hiccuping, overwhelmed by her grief, wallowing in a deluge of loss, despairing as to how she was ever going to cope with tomorrow and tomorrow and tomorrow. A lifetime of loneliness stretched bleakly before her. She raised her head and stared through her tears at Kay. She couldn't believe that the other girl was already being so callous.

With a sob she tore herself free and rushed from the control room. Once outside the building, she began to run and run until she felt as if her lungs would burst. Only when she could run no more did she sink down near the perimeter fence and lie, face down in the long, cold grass and weep.

'Oh, please, let him be alive,' she prayed wildly. 'I'll do anything, give anything – everything – if only you'll let him be alive.'

His poor mother, she was thinking. How is she going to take it? And his grandfather? News like that might . . .

I must go and see them, Fleur told herself. Once there's been time for the authorities to have informed them, I'll go.

She shivered; the damp coldness of the ground was beginning to seep through. She sat up and dried her eyes, but fresh tears trickled down her face. She couldn't stem the flow.

'Fleur? Fleur – where are you?'

Distantly across the open ground, she heard Ruth's anxious voice. She scrambled to her feet and through the pale morning light she could see her friend running up and down, calling her name. She waved and called weakly, 'Here. Over here.'

At once, Ruth was running towards her, 'Oh, Fleur – Fleur. I've just heard at the debriefing. I so hoped they'd just be late . . . But . . . I came as soon as I could . . .' She almost threw herself against Fleur and wrapped her arms around her, holding her tightly. 'It's my fault. It's all my fault,' Ruth was babbling against her shoulder. 'I didn't wave them off like I always do. After final briefing, Serg wanted me to deal with some paperwork. I lost track of time and, by the time I got down to the edge of the runway, most of them had taken off. Oh, Fleur – I'm sorry. I'm so sorry . . .'

Fleur clung to her, unable to give her friend any comfort, unable to exonerate her. She was drained, trembling with shock and weak with anguish. Deep in her heart, she knew it would have made no difference if Ruth had waved them off. It was just another superstition, but at this moment she was incapable of voicing it.

Against her, she felt Ruth draw in a deep breath. Somehow, the other girl found the strength to say, 'Come on, Fleur. You can't stay out here in the cold. Let's get you to the NAAFI . . .'

'I can't – I can't face anyone.'

'Don't be daft, Fleur,' Ruth said with brusque kindness. 'Everyone knows. Everyone understands. Most of us have been there at one time or another. You need to be with people who understand.' Ruth was saying almost the same as Kay, but somehow the words were not so harsh. She felt badly about Kay now. It was just her way. She must be hurting inside every bit as much as Fleur. For a moment, Fleur despised herself for her weakness. She wished she could be as strong as . . .

'Kay? Have you seen Kay?'

Ruth nodded. 'She came to find me. To tell me that you'd run off.'

'I'm sorry. She was only trying to help . . .'

'She understands. She was concerned for you, that's all.'

'She's so strong,' Fleur murmured. 'Look at me. I've gone to pieces. I'm a wreck. I'm – weak!'

'No, you're not. And Kay's not as tough underneath as she likes to make out. She'll be sobbing her socks off in bed tonight, you mark my words.' There was a pause before Ruth added shakily, 'And she won't be the only one. I feel so guilty. But we shouldn't give up hope. Not just yet.'

Sadly, Fleur shook her head. 'But someone saw a plane go down. It must have been them. And they didn't see any parachutes . . .'

Now Ruth had no answer.

Fleur sniffed. 'I . . . I want to go home. I want to see my dad.'

'Course you do. Let's go and see ma'am. I'm sure she . . .'

'Squadron Leader Harris came into the control room. He said he'd see her. Ask her if I could have some leave.'

'That's OK then. Let's go.'

'I can't. Looking like this.' She brushed ineffectually at the front of her uniform, blotched with wet grass stains.

'I'm sure she'll overlook it for once. You're usually the smartest of the lot of us.' Ruth took Fleur's arm firmly and urged her towards the buildings. 'You can't stop out here. You'll catch your death.'

With a laugh that was bordering on hysteria, Fleur said, 'You sound like my mum.' And at the thought of her mother, Fleur's tears flowed even harder.

Thirty-Seven

'Dad! *Dad!*'

Two days later, Fleur went home. Despite his disapproval of wartime marriages and romances, Bob Watson had quietly rearranged the rotas so that both Fleur and Kay were not on duty for four days following T-Tommy's failure to return. Kay went to her home down south, adding on a couple of days' ordinary leave that she was entitled to, and Fleur travelled to Middleditch Farm. She could not yet face Robbie's mother.

Dumping her bag near the back door, she ran round the yard, peering into the shadows of the cowshed then running into the barn, calling, 'Dad, where are you?' She didn't want to see her own mother, either. Not yet. She had to find her father. Fleur wanted her dad.

But it was Betsy who appeared at the back door, drying her hands on a tea towel. 'Whatever's the matter? Fleur? Is that you?'

Fleur stood a moment amidst the straw on the floor of the barn, summoning up the courage to answer her mother. She moved slowly to the doorway but she did not cross the yard. The two women stared at each other across the space between them and then Fleur saw her mother's hand flutter to her face to cover her mouth. Slowly, Fleur began to walk towards her.

'Well, Mum,' she said harshly as she neared her. 'You got your wish. He's gone. Robbie's—' She bit hard down on her lip to stop the tears. 'Robbie's missing, presumed killed.'

'Oh, Fleur, how can you think that of me? I didn't want you married to him. To have anything to do with him. But I wouldn't have wished him any harm.'

Fleur's eyes filled with the tears that were never far away. 'I don't know what to think. How can I when you won't tell me anything? What on earth can possibly have happened in the past to make you so – so – vitriolic against him? You didn't even know him.'

The bitterness of years was in Betsy's eyes again. Then she sighed deeply and gave a little shake of her head. Flatly, she said, 'Like I said before, it wasn't against him personally. Just his mother.'

'Why? What happened?'

Betsy's mouth tightened. 'She was a wicked woman. Devious, manipulating and utterly – utterly – selfish.'

'How? What on earth did she do?'

Betsy turned away. 'I don't want to talk about it. I *won't* talk about it.'

'You really hate her, don't you? Well, if you wanted some kind of . . . kind of revenge on her, then you've certainly got it now. She's lost her son. Her only son.'

Betsy just stared at her, her face expressionless, saying nothing.

'You really won't tell me?' Fleur tried again.

Betsy shook her head.

'Then I'll ask Dad. I'll ask him this very minute.'

'Perhaps it is time you knew,' her mother murmured and nodded, as if answering an unspoken question she was asking herself. At last she dragged out the words reluctantly. 'He's . . . away up the . . . fields with . . .

the sheep. You . . . you'll find him in Buttercup Meadow.'

Fleur gave a brief nod and moved towards the back door. She picked up her bag and made to step into the house, but her mother didn't move aside. It was as if she was almost barring Fleur's way.

Fleur stared at her. 'I'll just change my clothes.' Her uniform was still a mess from her spasm of weeping in the wet grass the night she had heard that Robbie was missing. It would need sponging and pressing before she went on parade again. She would change into her old clothes before she went tramping through the fields to find her dad.

Betsy blinked. 'Can't you go as you are?'

'No, I can't. I need to change.'

'Well, you can't. I mean – you can't come in. There's . . . there's someone here that . . . that I don't want you to see. That you didn't ought to see.'

'What on earth are you talking about, Mum? What's going on?'

'Nothing. Nothing. I just don't want you to see her. Not just now. It'll be – awkward.'

'Who? Who is it you don't want me to see?'

Betsy bit her lip. 'You don't understand. I mean – I don't want *her* to see *you*. Not just this minute.'

'Who?'

Fleur was getting angry now. What was all the mystery and why – when Fleur was suffering the worst moment in the whole of her young life – was her mother acting so strangely? 'Mum – just tell me who it is you don't want me to see?'

Betsy sighed. 'Louisa. Your Aunt Louisa.'

'Aunt Louisa? Why on earth shouldn't I see her?'

'It's . . . it's complicated. It's all to do with . . . with

Robbie and his mother. You don't understand,' she finished lamely.

'No, I don't.' Now, Fleur pushed her mother aside. 'But I'm jolly well going to find out.'

'No, Fleur. Please don't. You don't understand – Fleur . . . !' Betsy tried to grab her daughter's arm, but Fleur shook her off and marched into the kitchen where Louisa was sitting at the table drinking tea.

'Fleur, my dear, how lovely . . .' Louisa began as she rose and held out her arms to hug Fleur, who submitted a little stiffly to the embrace. Then she stood back. 'My dear girl. What is it? What's wrong?'

Fleur stared into the older woman's eyes for what seemed a long time but was in fact only seconds.

'It's Robbie,' Fleur whispered at last. But before she could say more, Louisa took a step back. Her hand fluttered to cover her mouth and her eyes widened in horror. 'Oh, no!' she breathed. 'Don't say it – oh, don't say it!'

Fleur was puzzled. Despite the sorrow that anyone might feel to hear of a young airman's death and the sympathy Louisa, as a friend of the family, would naturally feel for the young bride so cruelly widowed, the woman's reaction was extreme.

'Aunt Louisa,' Fleur began, reaching out to take Louisa's hands. 'What is it? Whatever's the matter?' But Louisa snatched her hands away.

'No, no, don't. I must go. I can't stay . . .' She cast a beseeching, almost frantic look at Betsy who had followed her daughter inside. Then she snatched up her handbag and scarf and fled from the room. As the back door slammed behind her, there was silence in the room until Fleur moved woodenly and sank down into her father's chair by the range.

'What is it, Mum? What's it all about?'

Betsy sighed heavily and flopped down into the chair on the opposite side of the hearth, as if suddenly all the energy had drained out of her.

'Go and find your father,' she said flatly. 'Ask him,' was all she would say.

With sudden renewed vigour, determined to get to the bottom of the mystery, Fleur sprang to her feet. 'Then I will. I'll go now. This very minute.' She stood a moment, staring down at her mother, willing her to say something – anything. But Betsy was silent, just staring into the fire. She didn't move as Fleur hurried upstairs to change her clothes. When she returned, her mother had not moved. She was sitting just as Fleur had left her, staring silently and sadly into the flames.

'Mum?' Fleur said tentatively, but Betsy made no move, no sign that she had even heard her.

Fleur left the house and stood a moment outside the back door. She pulled in a deep breath. It helped to calm her, but nothing could assuage her terrible grief. She felt as if she would never smile or laugh ever again. The sun had gone out of her life. She thrust her hands deep into the pockets of her old coat and trudged across the yard, out of the gate and down the lane towards the field where she knew her father would be.

Even before Jake saw her, Bess, the black and white sheepdog, barked and came scampering across the field towards her.

'Bess!' Jake roared angrily, as the sheep scattered in fright. Then he saw Fleur and he grinned and began to walk towards her. But as he neared her, his smile faded. 'Aw lass, don't tell me. Is it Robbie?'

Tears choked her and all she could do was nod as

he limped towards her and put his arms around her, holding her close. 'Aw love,' he said huskily.

They stood for a long time until he said gently, 'Come on, let's go back to the house. Let's—'

'No, Dad. No. I want to talk to you. I *need* to talk to you.' She drew back, her eyes brimming with tears.

For a moment, he studied her face. Then he gave a deep sigh and nodded. 'All right. But first, tell me what's happened.'

'He . . . he didn't come back from a mission the night before last. It's so ironic – so cruel. It was their thirtieth mission. A full tour, Dad. They'd done a full tour. At least, the four of them had.'

'Those lovely boys at your wedding? They're all missing?'

Fleur nodded. 'They – some of the other pilots – told Ruth at debriefing that they'd seen a plane go down with two of its engines on fire just off the coast. Tommy's a wonderful pilot, but . . .'

'Was that the one who was the best man?'

'Yes. But . . . but even he wouldn't be able to do much if . . . if it was on fire.'

'Was it near our coast?'

She nodded.

'Then—' Jake began, with a tiny hope, but Fleur shook her head sadly.

'No one saw any parachutes. And there's been no word. We'd've heard by now if they'd been picked up.'

'Are you sure? There's been some dreadful bombing down south again. They reckon it's in retaliation for this round-the-clock bombing we've been doing.'

'It's no good having false hope, Dad. I've worked in the control room long enough, seen enough missions, to know that, nine times out of ten, when they don't come back that night then – then they don't come back at all. Oh, sometimes they do. The lucky ones. Their plane limps home late or lands at another airfield or they've parachuted out of the plane and been picked up. Even become prisoners of war, if it was over enemy territory. But . . . but this wasn't. It was over the sea.' She pulled in a deep breath. 'I've got to face it, Dad. He's gone. I've lost him.'

Jake shook his head, as if unable to believe the dreadful news, and yet it shouldn't really have come as a shock. Every day young men were dying for their country. Young men just like Robbie, young men just like Kenny.

'Have you . . . have you seen his mother yet? Have you seen Meggie?'

Fleur shook her head. Even now, she noticed he used the pet name for Robbie's mother that she'd never heard anyone else use apart from Pops. Meg's father called her that too. Maybe that's what she'd been called as a girl . . .

'But you will?' Jake was pulling her thoughts back to the present. 'You . . . you'll be going to see her?'

'Of course.'

'Then . . . then tell her I'm so sorry, won't you?'

Fleur raised her head and stared into his face. For a moment a shudder ran through her. The haunted look was back in her father's eyes and now it was ten-fold in its despair.

'Of course I will, Dad,' she said softly. There was a moment's silence before she added, 'Dad, will you please tell me what all the mystery is? Don't you think I have a right to know?'

Jake closed his eyes, sighed and shook his head.

'They're not my secrets to tell, Fleur love. If they were, then of course I would tell you. But . . .'

'But Robbie's gone. It . . . it can't hurt him now, can it?'

'No,' Jake said sadly. 'It can't and I can't tell you how sorry I am that that's the case. Poor Meggie. To lose her boy . . .' He wiped the back of his hand across his eyes and coughed to clear the emotion catching his throat. He sighed. 'Well, if I do tell you, you must promise me one thing first, Fleur.'

'Anything, Dad. I just want to know. I want to understand.'

He sighed heavily. 'You might not understand even when I've told you it all.'

'I'd like the chance to try. Mum and I have always clashed – you know that – but I don't want us to carry on like this – like we are now. It . . . it's tearing our family apart.'

Jake sighed. 'To be perfectly honest, I don't think your knowing about the past will help that. It's more this business with Kenny that's coming between you and your mum now.'

'What about you, Dad? Do you blame me for Kenny joining up?'

His answer was swift and certain. 'No, love, not for a minute. Like I've said before, I'm proud of him – and of you – even though I'm worried sick about you both. But your mother just wants to keep you safe. She doesn't even want to see the wider picture.' He gave a wry smile. 'I think she'd even rather Hitler marched in unhindered than lose either of you.'

Fleur shuddered. 'Well, I don't think any of us would last long if he did, do you? Can you imagine his jackbooted cohorts tramping through Britain?'

Jake shook his head. 'No, I can't and I don't even want to try. It doesn't bear thinking about.' He glanced at her, their faces almost on a level and so close. 'We can't let that happen, Fleur, and it's up to you and Kenny and all those wonderful young people just like you to stop it. Whatever it costs.'

'Yes,' she whispered. 'Whatever it costs.' Already it had cost her everything. It had taken away her future. There was no future for her now that Robbie was gone. Yet she had to summon up the courage to continue the fight Robbie had believed in so passionately. What would happen after the war was over, she dared not think. She couldn't face the thought of the empty years stretching ahead without Robbie.

Jake was speaking again, pulling her thoughts back to the present. 'I want your promise that even if you go on seeing his mother now and again – as I'm sure you will – you'll never breathe a word to her about what I'm going to tell you. It's not something she'll want to talk about or even like to think you know about. I don't want to hurt Meg any more than she's going to be hurt now. This is going to devastate her, Fleur. Oh, love—' He touched her arm. 'I don't mean to minimize your grief. But you're young. You've a whole life ahead of you—'

Fleur closed her eyes and groaned. 'But it means nothing without Robbie, Dad. Don't you see?'

'I know it feels like that now, but . . . but in time—'

'No, Dad. You're wrong. Eternity wouldn't be long enough. I'll never get over this. He was all I ever wanted. The only man I'll ever love.' She lifted her head and stared him straight in the eyes. 'And now I want you to tell me about the past. I swear I won't breathe a word to his mother. But I have to know. I have to try to understand what it is that makes Mum so bitter that she can hardly bring herself to say she's sorry he's dead.'

Jake blinked as if that shocked even him. Then he sighed again as he said heavily, 'All right, then. I'll tell you. But you must promise me not to say anything to Meggie. Not a word. Not ever.'

'I promise, Dad,' Fleur said solemnly.

'I'm being dreadfully disloyal to her.' His eyes were full of pain at the thought, though Fleur wasn't sure if her father was referring to his wife or to Meg Rodwell.

There was a long silence before Jake, haltingly at first, began to speak.

'I'll go right back to the beginning. It's time you knew a few other things besides matters that concern Robbie. It's high time you knew about your mum and me too.'

He paused again and pulled in a deep breath as if he was about to launch himself over a precipice. Perhaps that's how it did feel for Jake to talk about things that had not been spoken of for years.

Thirty-Eight

They leant on the gate, watching the sheep, whilst Bess lay panting beside them, as Jake began to speak. 'You know the big building on the outskirts of South Monkford?'

'The one that used to be a workhouse? It's some kind of convalescent place for the forces now, isn't it?'

Jake nodded. 'That's where I was born. And your mum came into the workhouse as a young girl when her mother died.'

'You were both in the workhouse?' Fleur was shocked. She would never have imagined that the successful farmer owning Middleditch Farm and all its acres, the man who was well liked and respected in the neighbourhood, could have been born into such lowly circumstances. Then another thought struck her. 'But . . . but you had a mother. Gran.' She spoke of the woman who had lived with them for the last few years of her life.

'Yes.' Jake's voice was husky. 'But I didn't know I had until . . . until – well, all the bother happened.'

'All the bother?'

'Mm.' He was silent again.

Though she was impatient for him to continue, Fleur held her tongue. Quite literally, for she had to hold it between her teeth to stop all her questions tumbling out.

'All I knew as a lad was that I'd been born in the workhouse,' Jake went on as he gazed out across the rolling fields that were all his now. But he was seeing, Fleur knew, pictures and events from the past. 'I thought I was an orphan. A feller called Isaac Pendleton ran the place. He was what they called the master of the workhouse and the matron was his sister, Letitia Pendleton. *Miss* Letitia Pendleton.'

'But that was Gran's name. Except – well – I always thought it was *Mrs* Pendleton. I never knew that she was a . . . a "Miss". She was always just "Gran". I'm sorry, Dad. Go on.'

'As a young girl she'd fallen in love with Theobald Finch.'

Now Fleur gasped and before she could stop herself she interrupted his tale again. It was impossible not to show surprise or ask questions, so she gave up trying. 'The Finch family who live at the Hall?'

'Aye, but there's only Miss Clara Finch left there now. Mr Theobald' – he paused over the name, still unable to refer to the man in any way other than the name by which he'd always known him – 'died a while ago.'

'I do vaguely remember seeing him in the town. I think Mum pointed him out to me once.' She glanced sideways at her father but his gaze was still far away. 'Dad, was he – Mr Finch – your father?'

Slowly, he nodded. 'My mother loved him,' he said simply, 'but his family didn't think her good enough for him. At the time, Isaac – her brother – was running the workhouse with his wife. But she left him – so the rumour went. Isaac took me in as an orphan and Letitia became matron.' He smiled wistfully. 'She took the job so that she could be near me, yet she was not allowed to acknowledge me openly.' Now his smile broadened. 'As a lad I always wondered why she favoured me. She saved me many a beating from Isaac.' Now he chuckled. 'Though I still got plenty.'

'Oh, Dad!' Fleur rested her cheek against his shoulder, tears filling her eyes. Jake put his arm about her shoulders and held her close.

'Don't cry, love. It's all a long time ago now.'

'I know, but I can't bear to think of you as a poor little boy, believing yourself an orphan and being beaten and growing up in a *workhouse*. I mean, I know it's a magnificent building, but it was still a workhouse. Why, even now the old folk in the town fear it, don't they?'

'Oh yes. We all still live in the shadow of the workhouse. Those of us who grew up there.' He smiled gently. 'And even some of those who didn't. It's still a threat hanging over us all even if it isn't a workhouse any more.'

Fleur wound her arms tightly around his waist and nestled her head against his shoulder. She said nothing. The lump in her throat wouldn't let her, but her actions implied: you'll never go back in the workhouse, Dad. Not while I'm around.

'There, there,' Jake murmured, feeling her compassion. 'I was a tough little tyke. And then' – he smiled fondly – 'Meggie arrived at the workhouse. And she changed my life.'

He didn't need to elaborate. By the tone of his voice, Fleur could tell he remembered that time as very special. That Meg was very special.

'She was so – so *alive*,' he went on. 'So spirited and . . . and full of daring. D'you know, Fleur, I'd lived in that place all my life and I was— Let's see, I'd be about fifteen by the time she came and in all that time I'd never ventured out. Never asked to go out to seek work, never really gone out of my own accord. Oh, I knew *how* to get out. Several of the others did. There was a hole in the wall. And once or twice I went through the gates, but I never went more than a few yards.' He laughed aloud now. 'Not until she came and took me out with her one day. She went looking for her dad.'

'The old man? Pops?'

'Well, he wasn't old then, love. He was a young man and a bit of a rascal, by all accounts.' He gave her shoulder a squeeze. 'We were all young once, lass. Even me and Meg.'

'Oh, I think she still looks young, Dad. She looks years younger than Mum.' The words were out before she could stop herself. 'I'm sorry. I didn't mean . . .'

' 'S all right, love. There's only you an' me here.' He glanced down at the dog, dozing at their feet. 'And Bess won't say owt, now will she? But just think a minute. Your poor mam's a busy farmer's wife. She can't dress like Meg and wear those flimsy shoes, now can she?'

'No, of course not,' Fleur said hurriedly. Privately, she was thinking that her mother could still make a little more effort even if it was only now and again. 'But I don't think Robbie's mum's had it that easy. The front room at their house is her sewing room. She's worked to keep them all. Herself, Robbie and the old man.'

Again, Jake had a faraway look in his eyes as he continued with his tale. 'Her father, Reuben Kirkland – the old man as you call him – worked for the

Smallwoods and so did Meg. She worked in the dairy. And then, Meg's father had an affair with the Smallwoods' daughter, Alice.'

Fleur was shocked. 'Pops did?'

'Yes. Pops.' Jake was adamant. 'Of course, they dismissed him and his daughter, Meg, and then turned the whole family out of their tied cottage – the one old Ron lives in now. Reuben took his family – his pregnant wife Sarah, Meg and her little brother Bobbie – to the workhouse, promising to return to get them out when he'd found other work.'

Fleur was ahead of her father, guessing what had happened. 'And he never came back for them? He ran away with Alice?' She paused, taking in all the startling revelations. Then she asked, 'Did Meg know?'

'Not then. Not when she first came into the workhouse. She believed him, trusted him. She told everyone that they wouldn't be there long. That he'd come back for them. She didn't know why they'd been dismissed. For a while I think she blamed herself.' He smiled fondly again. 'She was a cheeky little tyke and she thought the missis – Mrs Smallwood – didn't like her friendship with her daughter.'

'*Her* friendship? Meg was friendly with Alice too?'

'Yes. Complicated, isn't it? So, you see, when she did find out about their affair, she felt doubly betrayed. By her father *and* by her best friend.'

'So how did Meg find out?'

'Her mam gave birth to a stillborn child in the workhouse and Meg went in search of her father to tell him. Of course, she didn't know about her dad and Alice then. She just went to try and find him to tell him about her mam. And she took me with her. We went to the racecourse. She thought her father might be trying to find work there. He was good with horses.'

Fleur nodded. South Monkford racecourse was famous, though sadly neglected since the war had begun.

'Did you find him?'

'Oh yes.' Jake's face was grim. 'He was with her. With Alice. Bold as yer like, walking round the racecourse with his arm around her.'

Fleur gasped. 'Oh, poor Meg!'

'Yes,' Jake said thoughtfully. 'D'you know, as far as I can remember, it was the only time I ever saw Meggie cry.' Again, he used the pet name as he spoke of her fondly. 'She was heartbroken and vowed never to forgive her father. Said she'd cut him out of her life for ever.'

'Well, she can't have done because he lives with her now.'

'She's changed. But back then, she swore that she'd never forget and never forgive.'

'Did she?' Now Fleur was surprised. 'She doesn't strike me as being like that.'

'No. Like I say, she's changed since then. Life changed her. I know now that she's sorry for everything she's done. I could see that when I met her at your wedding. I asked her about her father and she said, "How could I turn him away, when I'd been just as bad?" '

'But she hadn't done anything, Dad. It was her father's fault,' Fleur said, mystified. She still couldn't reconcile the picture of the sweet old man sitting by the fire in the little house in Nottingham with the heartless womanizer who'd dumped his family in the workhouse and run away with his mistress.

'I'm coming to that, love. But I want you to see the whole picture. And to do that, you have to hear what led up to – well – what Meg did.' Even now, though he had promised to tell her everything and had begun the tale, there was reluctance in his tone. He still didn't want to speak ill of Meg. Not even after all these years.

'Whatever did she do, Dad, that was so bad?'

He was silent for a moment, lost in memories in which Fleur had no part. Now, in short staccato sentences, he answered her question, explaining everything. 'After she found out about her father and Alice she became very bitter. The tragedies didn't end there. Her little brother, Bobbie, died. Then Isaac Pendleton – he was a one for the ladies, an' all – he took up with her mother. And that was the last straw for Meg. She never forgave her mother – called her some wicked names. And Meg herself became hard and calculating. There was only one person she cared about then. Herself. She left the workhouse and got a job working for Percy Rodwell.' Now Jake's mouth suddenly became a hard line. 'She wound him round her little finger and he fell for it. Poor sod!'

Fleur twisted to look up into her father's face. She saw his pain and, yes, now there was anger and disgust there too. 'Were you in love with her, Dad? Were you in love with Meg all those years ago?'

Jake stared down into his daughter's eyes. 'Oh yes. I loved her then and—'

There was a breathless silence until Fleur whispered, 'And you love her now, don't you, Dad? You've always loved her.'

'Fleur, love.' He squeezed her shoulders again. 'I know you feel now that you'll never love again. That

Robbie was the love of your life – and maybe he is. Who's to say? But you may well meet someone one day, fall in love, get married—'

'Never! I could never love anyone the way I love Robbie.'

'Listen to me, love.' Her father gave her a gentle shake. 'No, not in the same way, maybe you won't, no. I can understand that. He was your first love and that's very special. But you might love someone else differently. There are all kinds of love, Fleur. Passionate, overwhelming and for life. Then there's infatuation that seems like love, but isn't and dies as quickly as it flared. And then . . .' He paused again and took a deep breath before he said, 'And then there's the way I love your mother. After Meg went, I left the workhouse and I came to work for the Smallwoods here. Their daughter had gone, of course, and they never heard from her again as far as I know. A year or two later, Betsy came to work at the farm too. In fact, I sort of got her the job there. She'd spent several years in the workhouse. She was a shy little thing and I always felt protective towards her. The Smallwoods treated us both as their own and Betsy grew and blossomed. She was a pretty lass and – well – that's how it happened. I married her before I went to the war, and when I came back you were born and then Kenny.'

There was a long silence whilst Fleur digested all that he had told her.

'There's a bit more you ought to know,' Jake said at last.

'More!' Fleur forced a smile.

'When Meg went to work for Percy he was engaged to Miss Clara Finch – had been for years – and when he married Meg Clara sued him for breach of promise.'

Fleur gasped. 'Never!'

'Oh yes. There was a big court case and it was the talk of South Monkford for weeks.' His mouth twitched. 'You see, the judge found in Miss Finch's favour, but he awarded her damages of one farthing.'

Fleur stared at him for a moment and then burst out laughing, but Jake's face had sobered now. 'Clara was a bitter, dried-up old spinster, and after Percy Rodwell died, she tried to force Meg to hand over her baby – Robbie – because she believed in her twisted mind that the child should have been hers. Hers and Percy's. When Meg refused, Clara had her turned out of the shop and her home – the Finches owned both properties – and she tried to kidnap Robbie and have Meg thrown back in the workhouse. With the power the Finches wielded in South Monkford then, I doubt Meg would ever have seen the light of day again if . . .' He stopped and was silent.

Intuitively, Fleur whispered. 'You helped her, didn't you, Dad? You helped her get out.'

'She was locked in the punishment room and her boy was missing. We found him – Robbie – in the dead room in a coffin. Clara, in her twisted mind, had had him hidden there until she could take him home. Just think.' Jake tried to inject a note of lightness into their conversation. 'Your Robbie might have been a toff and brought up at South Monkford Hall.'

The dead room. The punishment room. Fleur shuddered. It all sounded like another world from the safe and happy childhood she had known.

'It was then I found out about my own mother –

just who she was. Maybe if all that hadn't happened, I might never have known.' For a long moment, Jake was silent, then he came back to finish his telling of the story. 'That was when Meg changed from her hard and calculating ways. Almost losing her son had jolted her because there was never any doubt about her love for him. After that . . .' Jake sighed softly. 'She left the district and I . . . I never saw her again. Not until your wedding day, Fleur.'

'I suppose poor old Clara Finch wanted something of her sweetheart's,' Fleur said with understanding. 'She wanted Percy's son.'

'Ah,' Jake said, 'but that's the irony of it all. You see, love, Robbie wasn't Percy's child.'

Her eyes wide, Fleur stared at him wordlessly. Surely, after all, her father wasn't about to tell her that he was, in truth, Robbie's father too?

'Perhaps you can't see it like I can, because you wouldn't remember his father as a young man.'

Her voice was husky as she asked hesitantly, 'Dad, just tell me. Who was Robbie's father?'

'The man you call Uncle Philip. Dr Philip Collins.'

'I can't believe it. I mean, how—?'

Despite the seriousness of their talk and all the long-held secrets he had just revealed, Jake laughed. 'Now surely I don't need to be explaining the facts of life to you, lass, do I?'

Fleur smiled briefly and shook her head. 'I mean, when did it happen? Before *he* married Aunt Louisa?'

Sadly, Jake shook his head. 'No, love, nothing so above board as that, I'm sorry to say. They had an affair.' His mouth hardened again. 'While Percy was ill with the influenza that killed him. Of course, Meg was able to make out the child was his, but there's no hiding it now. Not for anyone who remembered Philip in his younger days and then . . . saw your Robbie.'

'Oh, Dad.' Fleur clutched his arm. 'Auntie Louisa saw him. I introduced them. In a cafe in South Monkford. Just after I'd met him. You know – the day I invited them out to the farm and—' She bit her lip. 'Aunt Louisa seemed – well – odd. Now I know why. She . . . she must have guessed.'

Slowly, Jake nodded. 'I wondered at the time if she suspected. Poor Louisa, specially as she's never had any family herself.'

'Did Uncle Philip know he had a son?'

'I've no idea. But knowing Meg as she was then, I've no doubt she told him. Maybe—' He began to say something and then stopped himself. 'No, that's not fair to speculate. I shouldn't judge her.'

'No, none of us should. I certainly won't. She's Robbie's mum and she's been kind to me and . . . and she's suffering now. Whatever she did in the past, Dad, she's paying for it now.'

'Aye, love,' Jake said sadly. 'I know she is.'

And once more the haunted faraway look that Fleur had so often seen on her father's face was there again. But now, she understood exactly what caused it.

Thirty-Nine

'Oh, Philip – I'm so sorry. I shouldn't have . . . I mean . . . I wish—'

'Now, now, my dear. What's the matter?'

Philip took her arm calmly and led her into the front sitting room. The huge room was cold; no welcoming fire burned in the grate. They were trying to economize on coal and only lit the fire when the room was to be used for a lengthy period. Otherwise, they now sat in the two easy chairs in the corner of the kitchen, close to the wireless on which Philip loved to hear the latest war news.

Louisa clung to him. 'Forgive me, Philip, oh, say you forgive me.'

'I'm sure I shall, darling, if only I knew what it is I'm supposed to be forgiving. Here, sit down. Let me make us both some tea.'

'No, no, I should do that. That's my job.'

'Not just at this moment. I can see you're upset. Sit down whilst I make it and then we'll talk about it. Whatever it is.'

'But . . . but you've got surgery, haven't you?'

'There's no one out there at the moment. My patients are remarkably healthy today, it seems.' He smiled at her archly, trying to lighten her mood. 'I must be a better doctor than I thought.'

'Oh, Philip, you're a wonderful doctor.' Her eyes

filled with tears. 'A wonderful man. I don't deserve you. I . . .'

'There, there, my dear. Please, don't upset yourself. We'll sort it all out – whatever it is.'

Philip was becoming increasingly worried about his wife. From being a calm, serene, perfect doctor's wife, she had in recent weeks become nervy and irritable and weepy. Had she been one of his patients, he would by now have diagnosed a nervous breakdown. And whilst he could scarcely believe – didn't want to believe – that that was what might be happening to his wife, ethics aside, it would be better for her to be treated by someone else. He was no expert in psychiatric cases.

He shuddered at the thought, but if that was the case, then it would have to be faced. She was such a tender-hearted person and even though they weren't experiencing particular hardship themselves, nor the loss of a close relative, still the community as a whole was being badly hit. And Louisa felt it, he knew. As he set her cup of tea on a small table beside her, he sat down opposite, leant forward and took her hands in his. 'Now,' he said in the kindly but firm tone he adopted when speaking to a distraught patient, 'tell me what is troubling you.'

Fresh tears spilled down her cheeks.

'Oh, Philip – he's dead.'

'Who's dead, my love?'

She raised her red-rimmed eyes to look into his face as she whispered, 'Meg's boy. He's – he's missing, believed killed.'

She felt his hands holding hers twitch involuntarily and saw the colour drain from his face. They stared at each other for long moments before, haltingly, Louisa broke the silence. 'You . . . you do know who he really is, don't you, Philip? Who . . . who his father is?'

The colour flooded into his face and she had her answer without him saying a word. Before he could speak, she rushed on. 'I wish you'd told me. I wish you'd had enough faith in my love for you to have told me the truth at the time. I presume you've always known?'

Wordlessly, Philip nodded.

'I know – I know you wanted to spare me the hurt.' Now it was she who was giving comfort. 'The fact that you'd been unfaithful to me – and with Meg of all people. But don't you see, if only you'd confided in me, perhaps, all those years ago, we could have adopted him? Brought him up as *our* son. Oh, Philip, I wish you'd told me then.'

He shook his head as he said heavily, 'No, my dear, it would never have worked. You . . . you say you'd have forgiven me, but you're speaking now with the benefit of hindsight. Back then, you didn't know that we'd never have children of our own. You didn't know that someone else's son could have filled the void in our lives—'

'But he was *your* son, Philip. I could have loved him, I could have—'

'Could you really, Louisa, have loved *Meg*'s son? Be honest now, since we're talking honestly. Let's be absolutely straight with each other.'

When she didn't answer, he added softly, 'No, I thought not.' He smiled wryly. 'Besides, Meg wouldn't let Clara Finch have him, would she?'

'Of course she wouldn't,' Louisa cried now. 'Meg knew – though Clara Finch didn't – that he wasn't

Percy's son. But if *you'd* wanted him, she'd've let him go.' Her lip curled. 'Remember how selfish she was, how self-centred? Oh, she'd've let you have him like a shot. Been glad to be rid of him, I dare say.'

'I think you're wrong, my dear. Whatever Meg may have been – and yes, I admit, she did some reprehensible things—'

'Reprehensible? Reprehensible, you call it. Unforgivable, I'd call it. Seducing poor Percy. Yes – yes – she seduced him, Philip. Poor, bumbling Percy Rodwell didn't know what had hit him when she batted her eyelashes at him and smiled so winningly.'

'My dear,' he said softly. 'We've all made mistakes. Especially me.'

Louisa held his gaze as she asked, 'Do you regret it, Philip?'

His answer was swift and he hoped that it sounded sincere. 'Of course I do. I wouldn't have hurt you for the world. Louisa, I've always loved you and I always will. You must believe that. Meg was just – was just a stupid, stupid mistake. An aberration. Please – please say you forgive me?'

'Oh, Philip!' Tearfully, she threw her arms around his neck. 'Of course I do. It's a long time ago. And . . . and you haven't seen her since. Have you?'

'No, no. I swear it.' That part, at least, was true. As for the rest, deep in his heart he couldn't be sure. He buried his face against his wife's neck and hugged her tightly, trying to block out the memory of that vibrant red-haired girl who had brought such passion into his life. Even though the affair had been brief, he'd never been able to put her completely out of his mind. And never a day had gone by through all the years since that he had not thought about the son she had borne him and wondered what he looked like.

And now he would never know.

‘So now you know, do you?’ Betsy asked, her mouth tight, as Fleur came back into the house. ‘Heard the whole sorry story?’

Fleur sighed and said flatly, ‘Yes. If that’s what you like to call it. Yes, I think I’ve heard it all.’

‘Well – it is a sorry tale. Your father loved her. I expect you’ve guessed that now, haven’t you? Even if he hasn’t admitted it.’

‘He did admit it, Mum,’ Fleur said simply. ‘He loved her *then*. Not now. Not since he fell in love with *you* and married *you*.’

‘Oh well, if that’s what you like to think.’

‘Look, Mum. Let’s have all this out – once and for all. Just what is it that upsets you so much? Do you think Dad had an affair with her? Maybe you think it’s been going on all these years. I mean, with all your insinuations you had us – me and Robbie, I mean – thinking that we were half-brother and sister.’

‘*Wha-at!*’

‘Oh, you can sound surprised, but look at it from our point of view. That first day you were screaming at Dad that he was in love with her and that he’s loved her all these years. And you were so . . . so vitriolic towards Robbie’s mother. And him. It was something terrible. It was all we could think of.’

Betsy wriggled her shoulders. ‘Well, I don’t know, do I? Maybe they did have an affair. Maybe it has been going on all these years. He’s had plenty of chances. All those supposed trips to market. How do I know where he *really* went?'

Fleur shook her head. It saddened her to think that, perhaps for the whole of her married life, Betsy had lived with the torment of imagining her husband was being unfaithful to her. For the first time, Fleur pitied her mother.

'Do you want to know what I think?'

'Does it make any difference?' Betsy snapped, recovering some of her spirit. 'I'm no doubt going to hear it anyway.'

'Dad was in love with Meg, yes, when they were kids in the workhouse.' She saw her mother flinch at the word that obviously brought back dark, unhappy memories. 'He owed her a lot. She had spirit. She gave him the courage to get himself out of there. To seek work here.' She pointed down at the ground, indicating their home, the farm, everything he now owned. Fleur paused a moment, letting her words sink in. And driving her point home she added, 'Just think, Mum, if he hadn't done that he – and you – wouldn't have everything you have now. Where would you have been, eh? Still in the workhouse?'

'It closed in 'twenty-nine,' Betsy murmured, but her protests now were without substance.

'But you wouldn't be here, would you? You wouldn't have been taken in and treated like the Smallwoods' son and daughter and left their farm because their own daughter had run away.'

A spark of sudden interest ignited in Betsy's eyes. 'Is it really her dad that lives with her?'

Fleur sighed inwardly. Still, her mother could not bring herself to speak Meg's name. 'Yes, it is. Evidently the girl he ran off with – Alice, was it?'

Betsy nodded.

'She left him and went off with someone else. He tried to follow her, but this chap got his cronies to beat him up.'

Betsy sniffed and her mouth hardened. 'Serves him right. And her? What happened to Alice Smallwood?'

Fleur shrugged. 'No one knows.'

'She was a bad 'un.'

'As bad as Meg?' Fleur put in slyly.

''Bout the same,' Betsy answered, refusing to give any quarter. 'Made a good pair, they did.'

There was a long silence before Fleur said softly, 'Meg's changed, Mum. She's not the girl you remember any more. Not, by all accounts, since she had Robbie. Having a baby changed her. She made some mistakes, did some terrible things. I see that now and I do understand how it must have hurt you to think that Dad loved her. But he chose *you*. He married *you* and he's stayed with *you*.'

'And that's supposed to comfort me, is it? When all the time I think he's been hankering after her.'

Fleur took in a deep breath. Although she knew that what Betsy said was perhaps true, she had to try to get her mother to get over it and move on. 'I think "hankering" is perhaps the wrong word. I think he remembers her with fondness. I . . . I suppose you never forget your first love.' Her voice broke a little, but she carried on bravely. 'But it was a love between children, Mum. What he has with you is different. Very different.'

Betsy gave a sad smile. For once she knew her daughter was trying to help her, trying to get her to let go of the bitterness and resentment she'd held all through the years. But it was impossible. She couldn't expect the young girl who'd only loved and known the love of one man to understand. To understand the heart-wrenching pain of knowing that the man you love and live with is, every day, thinking of someone else. Living your whole life believing yourself to be second best. It was a pain that Betsy had lived with all of her adult life – an anguish that Fleur would never understand unless she experienced it for herself. There was only one person who might understand.

She wondered if Louisa Collins had suffered the same wretchedness.

But Fleur was living her own agony. A sharp, intense pain that would never quite go away, but would, Betsy believed, lessen in time even if Fleur could not believe it now.

With a supreme effort Betsy said, 'I'm sorry about Robbie. Truly. I can't help how I feel about his mother, but I wouldn't wish that on anyone. Not . . . not even on her.'

Fleur sighed deeply. It was no use. She couldn't get through to her mother. Betsy would never change.

Forty

Fleur had to face Robbie's mother, but she didn't know how she was going to do it. She almost wished now that she had not bullied her father into telling her the secrets of the past. Perhaps they would, as both Jake and Betsy had tried to tell her, have been better left buried. It had changed her view of Meg; she couldn't help but look at her differently now. It was difficult to imagine the pretty, smiling woman as a scheming temptress who had seduced two men and ignored the man who had always loved her. What puzzled her, though, was why her parents hadn't told her the truth from the outset when she had first met Robbie. If they had maybe—? No, Fleur was honest enough to answer her own question. No. Nothing they could ever have said would have stopped her. She had fallen in love with Robbie at that very first meeting on the station platform in the blackout and from that moment she'd known – they'd both known – that they had to be together.

The next morning, Fleur packed and came downstairs, ready to leave. She had sponged and pressed her uniform and washed her underwear the previous evening. Now she was ready to go back and get on with fighting the war. The war that had taken away everything she had ever wanted and yet, if it hadn't been for the war, it was unlikely she'd ever have met Robbie.

But she knew that to get back into the thick of it would help. It would help her to feel close to him still.

But, first, there was something else she had to do. She must go to Nottingham. She couldn't avoid it any longer.

'So, you're going back are you?' Betsy said to her as they sat at breakfast.

'I'll take you, love,' Jake began, but Fleur shook her head.

'I'm going to Nottingham first. I'm not due back at camp until tomorrow, but I don't know when I'll get any more leave. Ma'am has been very good, but . . . but I'm not the only one . . .' Her voice cracked and she stopped.

Jake cleared his throat and glanced briefly at his wife before saying, 'Then I'll take you there.'

Betsy opened her mouth as if to protest, but then thought better of it. She got up, clattered the breakfast dishes together and moved away into the scullery, but her shoulders were tense with disapproval.

'It's all right, Dad,' Fleur said gently. 'The trains fit up quite nicely, but if you could just run me to the station in town so I can catch the Paddy to the Junction . . .'

When Meg opened the door to her, the two women stood staring at each other for a long moment. At first sight, neither looked any different. Meg was still prettily dressed, with her face cream and powder carefully applied. There was even a pale tinge of lipstick on her generous mouth. And Fleur was smartly turned out in her WAAF uniform.

It wasn't until they each looked closely into the other's eyes that they could see the undeniable grief they shared.

'Oh, Fleur!' Meg opened her arms and Fleur fell into them, hugging the older woman.

'Oh, Ma!' was all she could say, poignantly using Robbie's pet name for his mother that brought tears to their eyes.

'Now, now.' Meg, dabbing at her eyes, tried to smile. 'He wouldn't want us to be doing this. Come in, come in . . .' she urged as she drew Fleur into the warm kitchen.

'Where's . . . where's Pops?' she asked at once as she saw the empty chair by the range.

'In bed. He's taken it very hard and, of course, at his age . . .'

She said no more, but Fleur understood. For someone of his age grief was a strange thing. Some old folk took bad news in their stride. Not that they didn't feel it, but life had conditioned them to deal with tragedies and, if not exactly immune to them, at least they had learnt resilience. But for others, such news was the last straw as if they had no strength left to field another blow. Fleur understood. With each morning, when she awoke, the full horror hit her afresh and she wondered how she would get through the day.

'I suppose,' Meg said as she handed Fleur a cup of tea and sat down in the old man's empty chair opposite, 'that we shouldn't hope.'

Fleur bit her lip. How could she answer? How could she say that every moment of every day she prayed that a miracle would happen? I'll give anything, she kept promising, if only he's alive. 'They – they say not,' she said at last.

Meg sat down opposite her. 'I've had such a nice letter from Wing Commander Jones already. I was surprised. I . . . I thought Robbie would have put you down as his next of kin now.'

Fleur smiled wanly. 'I think he must have forgotten to get it changed. Besides, the CO's like that. I think he'd have written to you anyway.'

'And he sent me the names and addresses of the next of kin of all the other members of the crew in case I wanted to write to them. Do you think I should, Fleur?'

'Yes, I've got that list too. Maybe . . . maybe we could both write in . . . in a week or so.'

Meg nodded. 'Yes – yes, that's what I thought too. Let a bit of time elapse. But . . . but I thought I'd like to write to Tommy's family and Johnny's too. All of them really. They helped to make your wedding day so special, didn't they? Such lovely boys . . .' Her voice trailed away.

Fleur was staring at Meg – she couldn't help it. All the things that her father had told her about this woman were whirling around her brain. And Meg was staring back.

Softly, she said, 'You know, don't you? Jake's told you.'

Fleur blinked and said quickly – too quickly. 'Told me? Told me what?'

'Don't deny it, Fleur. Lying doesn't suit you.'

Fleur felt her cheeks grow hot. How could she have been so foolish as to let her feelings show so openly on her face? It had always been her downfall and now she had let her father down. He'd never forgive her. She tried to salvage the situation by saying, 'I don't know what you mean.'

'Dear Fleur.' Meg shook her head, smiling gently. 'You've got such an open, honest face. You really shouldn't be trusted with secrets.'

Fleur closed her eyes and groaned. 'Please – don't be angry with my dad. It . . . it wasn't his fault. I . . . I bullied him into telling me.' She sighed. 'And now I wish I hadn't. He swore me to secrecy. Made me promise that I'd never say a word to anyone – especially to you. And now—' Tears sprang into her eyes. 'You've guessed and he'll be so angry with me.'

Meg reached across and, though there was a wistful note in her voice, she said, 'It doesn't matter now, Fleur. Nothing matters now.' There was a long pause before Meg added softly, 'Do you hate me?'

Fleur's eyes widened as she stared at her. 'Hate you? Heavens, no!' and was touched as she saw Meg's tremulous, grateful smile.

'I couldn't bear it if . . . if I never saw you again,' she said. 'You're . . . you're all I have left of Robbie. I don't suppose—' Suddenly, her eyes were filled with a fresh hope. 'I don't suppose there's any chance you could be carrying his child?'

Fleur pressed her lips together and shook her head. 'No,' she whispered. 'I only wish I was.'

A week later Meg opened the door, half expecting to see Fleur standing there again. She had promised to visit as often as she could and had said that her commanding officer was being very understanding. The girl had already written twice to her during the week, trying to give comfort even though her own heart was breaking. Meg loved her for that.

But instead of her daughter-in-law standing there, there was someone she had expected never to see again. She felt as if she had been dealt a blow just below her ribs and the breath had been knocked from her body. She clutched at the door for support. 'Philip! Oh my God!'

'Hello, Meg.'

He, of course, had prepared himself for the sight of her, but she'd had no such warning. 'May I come in?'

'Yes – well – yes, of course. But – but—' She stepped back to let him into the house. 'Why are you here? Why have you come? Now, of all times. Why have you come now?'

'I should have come years ago, Meg. I shouldn't have abandoned you and . . . and our son so callously.'

Meg gasped at his open admission, but he wasn't finished yet.

'If I'd been more of a man, I'd've acknowledged him. Been a part of his life. And now – I've left it too late, haven't I?'

'Oh, Philip,' she said. 'We both made a mistake but . . . but you know, I won't ever say I'm sorry for having Robbie. He's been the light of my life. He—' Tears filled her eyes and spilled down her cheeks as Philip clasped her hands. 'He was a wonderful young man. You . . . you'd've been proud of him.'

'So Louisa has told me.'

'Louisa? She . . . she's talked to you about it?'

Philip nodded soberly. 'Yes. Come – let's sit down and I'll explain. Is there – is there somewhere we can talk alone? I understand you have your father living with you?'

'Yes, I do, but he's still in bed. He – since Robbie – he doesn't get up until the afternoon. It . . . it's hit him hard.'

'And you, Meg. I can see you're putting a brave face on it, but you're devastated, aren't you?'

And now the tears that she had tried so hard to keep in check ever since she'd had the telegram flooded down her face and she let out a howl of anguish like a wounded animal. She'd held herself together for her father's sake, for Fleur's sake, but Philip's kind and understanding words had opened the floodgates of her grief.

'Oh, Philip . . . how . . . am I to . . . bear it?'

He put his arms around her and held her close as she sobbed against his shoulder. Even in this dreadful moment, he felt again the stirring of the feelings he'd had for her all those years ago. And though he knew that for her all the passion that had once been between them was gone, he was honest enough to admit that if she had at that moment led him up the stairs to her bedroom, he would have gone willingly, like a lamb to the slaughter. He felt a surge of shame that after his lovely wife's generous forgiveness, he could even think of being unfaithful again. Was it really possible to love two women at the same time? Once upon a time he would have dismissed such a notion as ridiculous, branding it as a man's excuse for philandering. Yet now, he was not so sure. If it was love he felt for Meg, then, yes, it was entirely possible, for he knew he loved Louisa. He always had done. But theirs was the love that deepened and grew through their years together, based on true affection for each other and caring for each other.

Yet Meg had wielded such a seductive power over

him. He'd been helpless against the consuming passion he'd felt for her all those years ago that had made him embark on a dangerous affair with her. He had believed, when it ended, that no one but the two of them had been hurt. He knew that she had kept her counsel, that she had told no one, not even her own son, who his father was. But it seemed that fate had had other ideas. In making their boy the spitting image of his father, there was no hiding the truth from those who'd known Philip in his younger days and had, more recently, seen Robbie.

There had been no hiding it – not even from his wife.

He let out a deep sigh and, above her head, he closed his eyes in anguish. He felt her pain and, even though he had never known Robbie, his own grief was for the lost years, the lost chances.

He felt ashamed of the flare of passion he was feeling for this woman, but now, all she wanted from him was comfort in her grief for the loss of her son. Their son. He held her tightly and stroked her hair and his heart was full of regret.

If only, all those years ago, he had been braver.

'Come, Meg. Sit down.' He urged her gently towards a chair. 'Have you any brandy in the house?'

Meg gave a hysterical laugh as she dried her tears. 'You, a doctor? Prescribing brandy.'

'Very medicinal on occasions,' Philip remarked dryly.

'Under the sink in the scullery,' Meg instructed.

As she sipped the amber liquid a moment later, she asked, 'Why have you come?'

'Louisa was at Middleditch Farm visiting Betsy

when Fleur came home with the news that Robbie had been posted missing—'

'Presumed killed,' Meg ended flatly.

'They haven't said for sure though, have they?'

Meg shook her head and nipped her lower lip between her teeth.

'Then – then he might be all right. He might have—'

'Fleur doesn't think so,' Meg burst out. 'She's amongst it every day. She should know.'

'Well, yes, but even if his plane was shot down, maybe he baled out, maybe—'

'There were no parachutes.' She looked up at him, her eyes brimming with tears. 'And it was over the sea. I'm sorry – I know you're trying to be kind. But we have to face it, Philip.'

'Oh, Meg,' he said softly. 'Still as brave as ever.'

She smiled wryly. 'That's not a word I've heard used to describe me very often. Scheming, devious, wicked, a temptress. Oh yes.' She put up her hand as he made as if to argue. 'Yes, I was all those things, Philip. Once. But not any more. Not since the day that Clara Finch tried to kidnap my baby. I saw that as my punishment and if . . . if it hadn't been for Jake, I might really have lost him. It was Jake who found him.'

Philip stared at her. 'And it's Jake you've always loved, isn't it? I can see it in your eyes when you speak his name. You love him still, don't you?'

'Yes,' she said simply, too weary to hide the truth any longer. 'Oh, Philip, I was so wrong, so bad. To seduce poor Percy into marrying me just so that I had security . . .'

'Now, Meg, I won't have you blaming yourself for everything. Percy adored you and in the short time you were married to him, you made him very, very happy. You were loyal and . . .'

She raised her head and met his gaze. 'But not faithful, eh, Philip?'

'Well, no, but he never knew.'

She shook her head slowly. 'That doesn't excuse it.'

'Of course not, but – but what I mean is – you didn't hurt him.'

'But I hurt Louisa.'

'That was my responsibility. I betrayed my wife, not you. Meg, we share the blame for what we did. You don't carry the burden of guilt alone, you know. And, like I said, I should have behaved in a more gentlemanly way. I should have admitted everything at the time and stood beside you.'

Meg shook her head. 'No, no. You had everything to lose. Your career, your good name – and Louisa.'

'I might not have lost Louisa,' he murmured, as if thinking aloud. 'She says now that if I had told her at the time, she might have been willing to have adopted Robbie. It's been a great sadness to her that we have never had children.'

'But she didn't know that then, did she?'

'No – that's what I told her. It's how she feels now, but I very much doubt she would have felt that way back then.' He paused and then added, 'She told me she came to see you a little while back.'

'It . . . it was after she'd seen Robbie for the first time. In a cafe in South Monkford. It . . . it must have been a dreadful shock for her.'

'I wonder why she never said anything then?' Philip pondered.

Meg shrugged. 'I wouldn't admit that he was your son. I told her that my father had had fair hair and blue eyes, but I don't think she believed me. I think she had seen the truth only too clearly with her own eyes when she saw Robbie.'

There was a long silence between them before Philip said softly, 'And now she's regretting that she didn't give me the chance to meet my own son.' He caught and held Meg's gaze. 'Would you have let me see him, Meg?'

She was silent a moment more before saying slowly, 'Probably not. You see – I never told him the truth. Perhaps I should have done . . .' And she went on to tell Philip how Robbie, after meeting Fleur, had begun to ask questions. 'All he wanted was to know that Jake wasn't his father. And, of course, I was able to answer him honestly about that.'

'And he didn't probe any further?'

She shook her head.

'Yet someone or something must have put a doubt in his mind,' Philip said. 'About Percy not being his father, I mean.'

'It was Betsy. She became hysterical when she knew that Fleur had met Robbie and that they wanted to go on seeing each other. Wouldn't have him in the house and wouldn't say why. Naturally, the young ones wanted to know.'

'And so he asked you?'

'Mmm.'

'But you didn't tell him.'

'No. But Fleur knows now. Jake told her recently. Since . . . since Robbie was killed.'

'Why on earth has he told her now?'

Meg gave a small smile, thinking of her feisty

daughter-in-law and admiring her spirit. 'She said she bullied him into telling her the truth. She told him it couldn't hurt Robbie now and that she wanted to understand why her mother had behaved as she had.' Meg sighed. 'I don't blame her for wanting to know. I would have done in her shoes.'

Philip gave a wry laugh. 'You'd've found out months ago.'

And even Meg had to smile. 'I felt so sorry for her. She didn't mean to let it out that Jake had told her. He'd sworn her to secrecy. But I could see it in her eyes when she looked at me. Not disgust or anger or anything like that, but just . . . just something different. Just that – she knew.'

They sat together for several moments until Philip said, 'So – what now, Meg?'

'I don't understand. What do you mean "What now?" '

'What will you do?'

'Do?' She shrugged her shoulders helplessly. 'What can I do but carry on as best I can? Care for my father, hope that Fleur will still visit us now and again.'

'And Jake?'

'What about Jake?'

'Shall you – will you see him?'

'I very much doubt that I shall ever see Jake again. Betsy will see to that.' There was no bitterness or resentment in her tone, merely a calm acceptance of the inevitable, yet Philip could hear the desolation in her tone. She had lost her beloved son and the one man she had ever truly loved was also as good as lost to her.

As if seeing the sympathy written in his eyes, she reached out and touched his hand. 'I'm not the only one to lose my boy. There are so many of us – too many of us – all over the world grieving for the waste of young lives.'

'I know, I know,' he said gripping her hand. 'I'm just so sorry I never met him. But I'll tell you this, Meg, if by some miracle he is still alive, then by God I will see him. I will meet him and I will acknowledge him as my son. I promise you that. If I'm given a second chance, I will try to behave as a father to him.'

Forty-One

Fleur threw herself into her work. When she wasn't on duty she cycled down to the little cottage and attacked the garden as if it was personally responsible for Robbie's death. It was the only way she could think of to stop herself sinking into a dark abyss of grief and regret. Ruth was a tower of strength and even Mrs Jackson and old Harry played their part in helping her to cope.

'Time to plant carrots, love,' Harry told her, leaning on the fence between the two back gardens and jabbing the stem of his pipe towards the freshly dug ground. 'Fancy, it's a year since you came and started all this, lass. Least you haven't got all that grass and rubbish to get rid of this time, eh?'

'No, but I could do to go and see Mr Clegg again. See if his pigs are still producing what I need.'

Ruth came to the cottage too, as often as she could. She still helped keep Harry's house clean, his clothes washed and ironed. 'And he'll not have a bath from one month's end to the next if I don't personally drag the tin bath into that kitchen and push him into it,' she said as they were cycling down one afternoon.

The picture of Ruth pushing Harry into the steaming bath, probably fully clothed, made Fleur smile. She chuckled – the first time she had really laughed since

Robbie had been posted missing. 'It's only because he wants you to scrub his back for him.'

Ruth glanced at her friend, relieved to see a brief smile on her face. 'Well, at least now his hair's cut regularly. And his toenails. You should have seen them that first time I did them, Fleur.' She screwed up her face. 'Disgusting, they were. Almost curling round the ends of his toes!'

'No thanks,' Fleur said with feeling. 'I'll stick to my gardening.'

'Actually, if I'm honest, that sort of thing – Harry's mucky feet, I mean – doesn't bother me. My old grandad lived with us when I was a kid and the things my mam had to do for him – well, you don't want to know.' She shrugged. 'But she just accepted it and got on with it. Like ya do. And it was the norm for us kids.'

'You should've been a nurse,' Fleur remarked. 'You'd've been a good one.'

'Mm. Maybe you're right. Well, here we are again,' she said, squeezing the brakes on her bicycle to bring it to a squealing halt. 'You go and tackle Mrs J's garden and I'll tackle old Harry's toenails.'

Fleur laughed again. 'I call that a fair deal.'

Fleur had been working for a couple of hours under the warm sun. She straightened up, mopped her forehead, wet with sweat, and decided to take a breather. She dropped her fork and went to sit on the seat under the apple tree. Leaning her back against the trunk of the tree, she gazed out across the flat expanse of the airfield. It was silent today and she hoped it would stay that way. There hadn't been an air raid for a while now. They'd been lucky but there was an ominous kind of tension in the air as if any day they expected to see the Luftwaffe in the skies overhead again.

In the cottage, Ruth saw Fleur sitting beneath the tree. 'Breaks ya heart, doesn't it? To see her sitting there looking so lost and lonely.'

'It does,' Mrs Jackson agreed. 'And there's nothing any of us can do, is there?'

Sadly, Ruth shook her head. 'Not a thing. I'd go out and join her, but I think she'd rather be alone.'

'There are times when you just want to be by yourself,' the older woman said softly. 'Just to let go for a little while.'

'I know,' Ruth said, remembering only too well how she'd felt at Billy's loss and she hadn't even been married to him. She ached for the pain her friend must be feeling, yet she was helpless to comfort her. There was nothing she could say or do that would bring Robbie back and, right now, that was the only thing that would put a permanent smile back on Fleur's face. The only thing.

The days dragged interminably. Fleur couldn't believe that it was only just over a week since she had had news that Robbie was missing. And there was Kenny to worry about too. Now, he would be up there in the clouds, doing his training, hoping to be good enough to become a fighter pilot. Fleur sighed as she clattered down the steps from the control tower after another shift on duty.

I ought to go home again as soon as I can, she thought, but she shuddered at the thought of facing her mother. Betsy would be worried sick about Kenny and would turn her anger on her daughter. Yet Fleur knew her father would be feeling it keenly too. And she knew too that Jake would be sorrowful for Meg – a feeling he could never talk about with his wife. And I ought to go and see Robbie's mother again. See how the old man is too. It's what Robbie would have wanted me to do. But she shied away from the thought. Seeing Meg's grief only heightened her own.

As she was walking away from the control tower, she heard the dreaded sound of an air raid warning. Automatically, she turned to run to the nearest shelter, but then she remembered. She'd left Kay in the control room finishing off. She glanced back, hoping to see the girl emerging from the tower and running across the grass towards her. But there was no sign of the slim, dark-haired figure.

Fleur bit her lip. She was anxious about Kay. Since the loss of Tommy's plane, Kay had changed. She'd seemed very strong at first, but since she'd come back from leave, she'd been the one to sink into an abyss of misery. Fleur was constantly having to watch her at work to make sure she didn't make any mistakes, for Bob Watson had eyes like a hawk now and his disapproval of wartime romances was still evident every day.

Fleur turned and began to run back towards the watch office. She reached the foot of the steps as the first aircraft came swooping in, dropping incendiaries on the runway only a few feet from the control room.

'Kay! Kay!' Fleur shouted, but knew the girl wouldn't hear her above the noise. She almost fell into the room and then stopped in shock. Kay was standing in front of the long window overlooking the airfield, her arms outstretched, her head thrown back. She was laughing and crying hysterically and shouting, 'Come on. Get me! Get *me*! You've got him, now get me. Here I am . . .'

At that moment another plane screamed by, so low that Fleur fancied she saw the pilot sitting in the cockpit, could fancy she saw him press the button and pepper the ground with gunshot.

'Kay,' she screamed. 'For God's sake! Get down!' And she launched at the girl, bringing her to the floor and pushing her beneath the desk just as another aircraft dived towards them. The bomb landed just outside the tower, rocking its foundations, blowing all the windows into the room and showering the whole room with deadly shards of glass.

'Where's Fullerton and Bosley – I mean, Rodwell? Have you seen them?'

The raid was over, the all-clear wailing out and staff were emerging from their bolt holes. Bob Watson was first out, demanding of anyone nearby if they had seen 'his girls'. Bluff and disapproving though he might be of their private lives, nevertheless he secretly held them in high regard. Both were excellent in their work, and even though Fullerton had been a little preoccupied these last few days he'd found it in his heart to overlook it. Besides, he assuaged his duty-bound conscience, the other girl – Rodwell, as he must remember to call her – was emerging as the stronger of the two. He had noticed her keeping a keen eye on her colleague and leaping in to avert what could – in the hectic, tense atmosphere of Control – have been a disaster. Twice, to his certain knowledge, Fleur had prevented two aircraft being told to land at the same moment. Strange, Bob Watson couldn't help thinking to himself, how things turned out the way you didn't expect. He'd've laid money on it that the Rodwell girl would have cracked first, been a weeping wreck, whilst the outspoken Fullerton would have shrugged her shoulders, muttered, 'Well, that's war for you,' and moved on to the next handsome airman.

But it seemed, Bob was man enough to admit if only to himself, he'd been wrong.

Now, he was on the verge of panic himself as he realized suddenly just how fond he had become of those two girls, however much he tried to keep himself their aloof superior.

Ruth came running across the grass, shaking her fist in the direction the aircraft had disappeared.

'Bastards! Bastards! We'll get you. You wait till our fighter boys catch up with you . . .'

'Morrison,' Bob roared at the outraged girl. 'Have you seen Fullerton and Rodwell? Are they with you?'

Ruth stopped at once, her arm still in the air, her fist clenched. Slowly she let it fall to her side and turned to face him.

'Flight?' she asked stupidly and Bob repeated his question, watching her eyes widen in fear.

'No. I was in the shelter near debriefing. I thought – I mean – aren't they with you?'

'No.' Grimly, his glance went towards the tower. 'I left them in the watch office.'

The tower itself was still standing, but even from here they could both see that not a window was left whole in the building.

'Oh no!' Ruth began to run towards the tower, Bob Watson pounding close behind her. She flew up the steps and thrust open the door, the broken glass crunching beneath her feet, bracing herself for what she might find.

'Fleur! Kay!'

'Here. We're here – under the desk. Can you help me, Ruth? Kay's . . .'

She said no more but as Ruth bent down and offered her hand, she saw that Kay was as white as a sheet and shaking from head to foot. Tears were running down her face. Ruth's mouth dropped open. 'Kay?' she said in disbelief and again, 'Kay?'

'It's all right now, Kay,' Fleur was saying soothingly as Bob too arrived, panting heavily.

'Are they all right? Oh, good thinking,' he added as he saw they had taken shelter beneath the sturdy desk. 'Out you both come then. They've gone. Can't you hear the "all-clear"? But mind the glass, it's all over the bloody place.' He glanced round at the debris around him. Not only had the windows been damaged but radios and telephones. The blackboards hung drunkenly off the wall and papers had been scattered everywhere. 'Bloody 'ell,' he muttered. 'It'll take a month of Sundays to clear this lot up. And the runway's damaged. I reckon there won't be flying from here for a few days. Come on, you two, what are you mucking about at?'

'It . . . it's Kay. I think she's badly shocked,' Fleur said, crawling carefully out from under the desk. 'I can't get her to move.'

Kay was crouched beneath the desk, rocking backwards and forwards. 'Saved my life. She saved my life. Fleur saved my life,' she was muttering.

'Yes, yes, I'm sure she did, but come on out now,'

Bob snapped. Now he'd found they were safe, his patience was soon wearing thin.

'We'll sort her out, Flight,' Ruth suggested, standing up. 'Leave it with us. And we'll start and clear up here, if you like.'

'Ah well, yes. I ought to – er – yes, well. I'll leave you to it then.'

He left the room, and when they heard his footsteps clattering down the steps, Ruth breathed more easily. 'Right. Now he's out the way, we can sort her out.' She squatted down again and her tone softened, became cajoling, as she said, 'Come on, love. All over now. Give me your hand. Take her other hand, Fleur. Don't let her kneel else she'll cut her legs. God, what a mess!'

Whether Ruth was referring to the state of the control room or the state of their friend, Fleur could not have said.

'We'd best get her across to the doc's pronto,' Ruth muttered to Fleur and then again turned to Kay. 'Come on, love, that's it. There you go. Safe and sound.'

'Saved my life, she did.'

Kay emerged slowly from the makeshift shelter but she was still shaking visibly.

'It's the doc for you, Corp,' Ruth said, taking control. 'And you'd better come too, Fleur. You've had a shock an' all.'

'I'm fine. Honestly, but I'll help you take her across and then come back here.'

'Right-o. I'll come back and help you.'

The doctor – as they'd feared – was in great demand, but thankfully only for cuts and bruises.

No one, it seemed, had been killed or even seriously injured. The worst casualty seemed to be Kay and that was shock more than physical harm. She hadn't even a scratch though Fleur had cut the palm of her hand on some glass and had bumped her head as she'd dived for cover pushing Kay in front of her.

At last Kay was admitted to the sick quarters for observation. Ruth and Fleur, the cut on her hand bathed and dressed, returned to the control room to help tidy up. Already, there were plenty of willing hands sweeping up the glass, picking up pieces of paper and testing the radios. It would not take as long as Bob had feared to have the control room operational once more.

Fleur was very much afraid that it would take far longer for Kay to heal.

With the airfield out of action for a day or two, Fleur grabbed the chance of a couple of days' leave whilst repairs were carried out. Enough time to go home and to Nottingham.

For some reason she couldn't explain, this second visit to both places seemed more difficult than the first, but she couldn't put the moment off any longer. She ought to go to see Meg again and then she would have to go home. It was easier to get back to camp from her home than from Nottingham because if, for some reason, there was no train running at the time she needed one, her father would always bring her back.

But first she cycled down the road to make sure Mrs Jackson and old Harry were safe and unharmed. A few stray bombs had fallen in the village and she was anxious about the old couple.

But the two cottages looked unscathed and to her relief Harry was sitting drinking tea in Mary Jackson's kitchen.

'Now then, lass. All right?'

Although Harry's greeting was casual, Fleur could see her own relief mirrored in his eyes and Mrs Jackson said outright, 'Oh, love, I'm so glad to see you. We've been that worried. And Ruth? Is she all right?'

'She's fine. She'll be down to see you later, but I've got a forty-eight, so I'm . . . I'm going to see Robbie's mother and then going home.'

The old couple exchanged a glance and nodded. There was a pause before Harry, deliberately changing the subject, said, 'That there shelter in the garden you built for us came in handy.' He jabbed his finger towards Mary, teasing. 'And I got her in it, an' all. First time I've managed it on me own. But they was coming a bit too close for comfort yesterday. Don't mind admitting it.'

'We heard one or two had landed in the village. Was anybody hurt?'

Now Harry's face sobered and again he glanced at Mary Jackson. 'A couple of young lads playing down near the stream were killed. Fishing, I expect they were. Always been a favourite place for youngsters. Too busy to think of taking shelter, I dare say. Thought it would be just the airfield being targeted. Y'know?'

Fleur nodded. 'I'm so sorry,' she said.

'Three of Mr Clegg's cows were killed an' all. But that's nothing compared to the loss of a human life . . .' Old Harry's voice trailed away.

'No, of course it isn't,' Fleur agreed sadly. There was a pause and then she said, 'Well, if you're sure you're both all right, I'll be off. I'll come again as soon as I can.'

'Aye well, there's plenty to do in yon garden.' He jabbed towards the window with his pipe. 'There's a lot of planting to do and there's always hoeing needed. Weeds grow as fast as the plants, ya know.'

'Faster, if you ask me.' Fleur managed to raise a smile. 'But I'll be here.' Already she was looking forward to the peace and quiet of working alone in the garden. Of sitting under the apple tree – her quiet time to think about Robbie.

Forty-Two

Fleur hesitated outside the door, not really wanting to come face to face with Robbie's mother. Meg had seemed so strong when she'd seen her immediately after it had happened. But she'd seen now at first hand how easy it was for a seemingly strong person to crack. Who'd have thought Kay would be the one to end up a quivering wreck? Thankfully, she was already beginning to recover and, much to Fleur's embarrassment, was telling everyone how Fleur had saved her life.

Fleur took a deep breath and raised her hand, but before she could knock the door flew open and Meg was standing there, her face wreathed in smiles.

'Fleur! How lovely to see you. Come in, come in.' Meg reached out, grasped her arm and almost hauled her inside.

Fleur stared at her, anger welling up inside her. Well, she thought, it hasn't taken you long to get over your son's death. How can you be so cheerful? How can you be carrying on with your life as though nothing has happened?

'You got my message then?' Meg said as Fleur stepped into the cluttered front room and followed Meg's trim figure through to the back.

'Message? What message? No, I didn't get any message. All the lines have been down. We had an air raid the day before yesterday. No, I just came because . . .'

But Meg didn't seem to be listening. She was flinging open the door leading from the front room into the kitchen and announcing Fleur's arrival with a flourish and a beaming smile. 'Just look who's here . . .'

Perhaps she thinks I'm going to help raise the old man's spirits, Fleur thought. That's what all her cheerfulness is for. To try and buoy the old man up. Fleur tried to force a tremulous smile onto her mouth as she took a step forward past Meg and into the room.

The old man was indeed sitting in his usual chair, but there was someone else sitting in the chair on the opposite side of the hearth. Suddenly, the whole room seemed to spin. She swayed and clutched at the doorjamb. She felt the colour drain from her face and her legs felt as if they would no longer support her.

'Catch her, Ma. She's going to pass out. Damn this bloody leg . . .'

Fleur felt Meg's strong arms about her as she helped her to a chair near the fire. 'I'll get her some water . . .' were the last words Fleur heard Meg saying before everything went black.

Someone was bending over her and holding a glass to her lips. She opened her eyes and tried to focus on the beloved face close to her.

'She's coming round.'

Fleur felt clammy and cold and still dizzy, but she murmured, 'I'm all right now. It was just such a shock. I thought . . . I thought—' She reached up and touched Robbie's face, still unable to believe that he was really here. Her prayers had been answered. Robbie was alive and smiling down at her. 'I mean, I was told your plane went down in the sea.'

'It did.' Robbie was grinning at her. 'Hence this.' He tapped the plaster cast on his right leg.

'But no one saw a parachute.'

'No time. We were too near the water. But thanks to a brilliant bit of flying by our skipper, who managed some sort of belly flop with the plane – God knows how he did it – we all got out. We were picked up by the local lifeboat and here I am.'

'Yes,' Fleur said, grinning stupidly up at him. 'Here you are.'

Then she promptly burst into tears and clung to him, burying her face against him.

The rest of the afternoon was spent with laughter and tears, hugs and kisses. Tactfully, Meg left them alone with the excuse that she had a dress hem to finish.

'Now, come along, Dad. You can sit in the front room with me for a while. Let's leave these two young ones alone.'

Fleur watched as Meg helped her father to his feet and steadied him as he shuffled into the next room. 'Don't go without saying ta-ta to me, will you, lass?' he said in a quavering voice.

'I won't,' Fleur promised, a lump in her throat as she watched Meg's patient tenderness with the frail old man. Then she turned back to Robbie, still unable to believe the miracle that had really happened. 'Are you really all safe? Tommy too?'

'Yes, all of us. But, like I said, without Tommy's brilliant flying, we probably wouldn't be.'

'Oh, I can't wait to tell Kay.' Then she told him all about the air raid and Kay, and then for the rest of the afternoon they thought about no one else but themselves . . .

At five o'clock Fleur said reluctantly, 'I must go.'

'Darling, I wish I could come with you.' He grinned. 'But I really can't hop as far as the station and back – even on my crutches.'

'I'll be all right.'

'Just so long' – he tapped her playfully on the nose – 'as you don't let any strange young RAF types pick you up. Just remember, you're a married woman now.'

She wrapped her arms around him and held him close. 'I won't. I've got the only RAF type I want. And I'll come as often as I can. Are you staying here until your leg's healed?'

'I think so. They couldn't wait to ship me out of hospital as soon as they could. They needed the bed. Oh, darling.' His face sobered. 'I'm so sorry you've been worried. I can't understand why word didn't get through from Bournemouth.'

'Is that where you were? Bournemouth? Isn't that odd?' she murmured. 'Kenny's down south somewhere now.'

'Is he? Is he all right?'

'I hope so. He'll have started his flying training by now. He was so excited. Couldn't wait to start flying. Can't wait to get into the thick of it.'

'I hope he'll be all right,' Robbie said.

'I don't expect it's so bad for the fighter boys, is it? Not now? I mean – they did their bit in the Battle of Britain.'

Robbie smiled thinly and nodded. He couldn't bring

himself to disillusion her. That every day the fighter boys were in the air attacking incoming enemy bombers, trying to stop them reaching their targets.

Maybe Fleur hadn't heard the latest news and he didn't want to be the one to tell her. Hitler had issued orders for his air force to begin a series of attacks upon British cities. Exeter, Bath, Norwich and York had been targeted already and Robbie feared the German leader would turn his attention to the industrial cities of the Midlands next. But he said nothing of this to Fleur. Instead he said, 'I still can't understand why word didn't get through to you that we were all safe. I mean, I wrote to you from there myself, let alone the fact that the War Office should have let them know at Wickerton that all the crew were safe. I can't understand it at all. I think it must be something to do with the telephone lines being down. I tried to phone Mr Tomkins at the shop to let Ma know as soon as I could hop around again.' He tapped his leg again. 'And I tried ringing camp. But I couldn't get through to either of you.'

'Well, the lines are certainly all down now – since the raid. That is a fact.'

'And there I was thinking you were safe and sound.' He held her close. 'Oh, darling, do be careful.'

'I will,' she promised as she kissed him again and again, loathe to leave him. 'But I must go. I must go to Middleditch Farm. Dad will be so pleased to hear you're safe. And I must get back to camp first thing tomorrow morning.'

'Oh, I don't want to let you go,' he said, hugging her tightly to him as they stood at the front door saying their goodbyes. She laughed as she prised herself free and, planting a last kiss on his nose, began to run up the street, turning to wave once more before she turned the corner.

The house at Middleditch Farm was strangely quiet as she entered by the back door. The scullery was deserted, but as she stepped into the kitchen she saw her mother sitting motionless in the chair by the range, her head resting on her hand.

'Mum?'

Slowly, Betsy raised her head and stared for a moment at her daughter. Then with a low sound in her throat that sounded almost like a growl, she said, 'Get out! Get out of this house and don't ever come back.' Then she grasped the arms of the chair and pushed herself up. 'Don't ever show your face here again.'

'Mum—'

'Don't "Mum" me. You're no daughter of mine. I have no daughter. It's all your fault. He's gone because of you. My Kenny's gone. And it's your fault. All your fault.'

'Mum – I know he's gone. But he'll be all right. It's not like before when the fighter boys—'

'What d'you mean "He'll be all right"? He's gone, I tell you. Dead. Killed. His plane crashed when he was training. In *training*! He didn't even get to fly a Spitfire like he wanted.' Betsy shook her fist in Fleur's face. 'He's dead – and all because of you.'

For the second time that day, Fleur felt her legs give way beneath her. She felt as if the breath had been knocked from her body. The room swirled around her and she staggered forward towards her father's chair.

She sank down weakly, blinking and taking short, panting breaths, trying desperately not to pass out again.

'Oh no – no, you can't mean it. Not Kenny. Not my . . . little . . . brother.' The heartrending sobs came then, flooding out of her. She was shaking, feeling cold, so very cold.

Yes, her mother was right. It was all her fault. Kenny had only joined the forces because she had done so. He hadn't wanted to be outdone by his sister. But there was worse than that. Much worse than even her mother knew. Fleur had tried to bargain with God. What was it she had said? 'I'll give anything, if only You'll let him be alive.' So now, Kenny had been taken in his place.

Fleur was beside herself with anguish. From the heights of joy that Robbie was alive, she was plunged once more into the depths of despair. Her grief was a physical pain. She wrapped her arms around herself and rocked to and fro in the chair, sobbing in agony.

'Oh aye, you can shed tears now, can't you? Why didn't you think of that before? Why didn't you stop him going? Why did you ever—?'

'I did. I tried. I begged him not to go,' Fleur screamed. 'He'd've gone anyway, whatever I'd said or done.'

Neither of them heard the back door open and close, but suddenly Jake was in the room and hurrying towards Fleur. He knelt beside her chair and put his arms about her. Fleur hid her face against his shoulder, the sobs still racking her body.

'That's right. You comfort her. You comfort each other. But who's going to comfort me?'

Jake looked up at his wife, his own eyes bleak with

suffering, his face ravaged with loss. 'Fleur's had a double loss, Betsy love,' he said gently. 'First Robbie and now this. Can't you – just for once – feel for her?'

Betsy stared at them both for a moment, but instead of turning and running up the stairs as she usually did, she sank back wearily into her chair as if utterly defeated, without the will or the strength to argue any more.

Fleur raised her head slowly and whispered, 'No, Dad. That's . . . that's what I came home to tell you. Robbie's turned up. He's alive. The pilot managed to ditch the plane in the sea, just off our coast and . . . and they all got out. He's got a broken leg but—'

Betsy lay back in her chair and began to laugh and cry hysterically. 'Oh, that's good, that is. Her son is saved. It'd have to be *her* son that was saved, wouldn't it?'

Jake and Fleur stared at her, helpless to do or say anything.

Forty-Three

Early the following morning, before either of her parents were up, Fleur slipped away from Middleditch Farm. She hitched a lift into the town with an early milk lorry, but before going to the station Fleur slipped into the church in South Monkford. She sat down in a pew near the front and laid her cap, gas mask and bag on the seat beside her. She sat for a long time, just staring ahead at the altar. The tears ran silently down her face and she didn't even bother to wipe them away. She didn't pray. She didn't know how to now. She couldn't even bring herself to give thanks for Robbie's safe return. She didn't know what to say. Not now.

A man came out of the vestry. He crossed to the centre of the chancel, bowed to the altar and then turned and came down the steps towards her. He was dressed in a lounge suit, but in place of a shirt and tie he was wearing the collar of a clergyman. He wasn't the vicar she'd known since childhood: this man was a stranger. Old Revd Pennyfeather must have retired, she thought vaguely, but her mind was too numbed to even want to ask. The man hovered for a moment at the end of the pew where she was sitting. Then he sat down beside her, following the line of her gaze for a moment and staring, too, at the brass cross on the altar.

'You know it's a terrible thing to admit, but I really don't know what to say to people any more.'

Fleur said nothing.

He turned his head slightly to glance at her. 'But the good Lord will—'

Fleur held up her hand to silence him, but still she did not speak.

'Would you . . . like to tell me what's troubling you?'

She let her hand sink back down to rest on her lap, but she just continued to stare at the cross on the altar. Still she did not answer him.

'Would you like us to pray together?'

Still, there was silence until, haltingly, Fleur spoke in a hoarse whisper. 'I have no right to pray.'

She held her breath, expecting him to come out with some trite remark. To her surprise, he just said, 'Why?'

Another long silence before she dragged out the words. 'Because . . . I tried . . . to bargain with God. And lost.'

'Ah.' The sound held a wealth of understanding and sympathy. Fleur turned her head slowly and looked at the man for the first time.

He was small and white haired with a kind face. She could imagine that normally his face would be wreathed in smiles, that he would have a lively, almost saucy sense of humour, but at the moment, the lines on his face drooped with sadness. 'Would you like to tell me about it, my dear? Perhaps I can help.'

'No offence, Vicar, but I doubt it.'

'Try me anyway.'

Several minutes passed before Fleur could bring herself to speak. At first the words came slowly and then faster and finally in a flood as she poured out her anguish.

'My husband – we'd only been married a few months – was posted missing, presumed killed.'

'Oh, my dear, I'm sorry—'

'No – no – he's come back. That's the trouble, you see.'

The man was naturally puzzled. Fleur rushed on trying to explain in short, staccato phrases. 'I'm sorry. I'm not explaining this very well. We met by accident. On a railway station. In the blackout. We didn't know it then, but our parents – well, my parents and his mother – had known each other years ago. There were – well – complications, and when my mother found out who he was she refused to meet him. Refused to let him come to our home. She . . . she didn't even come to our wedding. And then . . . and then there was my brother, Kenny.'

Fresh tears welled in her eyes. 'He was younger than me. When I joined the WAAFs, he made up his mind he was going to volunteer too. As soon as he was old enough. And . . . and he did.'

'Why do you say "volunteer"? He'd've been called up sooner or later.'

Fleur shook her head. 'We live on a farm.'

'Ah,' the vicar said, understanding at once. There was no need for her to say more.

For a moment, Fleur covered her face with her hands. Then she straightened up, brushed away her tears, sniffed and went on. 'When my husband was posted missing, I prayed. Oh, how I prayed. And . . . and that's where I made my mistake. You see, I said, "I'll give anything if only You'll let him be alive." And now . . . now He's given Robbie back to me but . . . but He . . . He's taken my brother in Robbie's place. Kenny's plane crashed while he was training. He never even got to fight the enemy. And that was what he wanted to do most of all. He wanted to help save his country.'

The older man laid his hand gently on her shoulder and said softly, 'That's not how the good Lord works, my dear. We've all, in our time, been guilty of doing exactly what you've done. Promising anything so that we get what we want. God hears, He listens – but do you really think He's going to take a scrap of notice of our – well, as you put it – "bargaining" with Him? I think not.'

'I feel as if I'm being punished.'

'No, no, you shouldn't feel that. You really shouldn't. God has His reasons.'

'What reasons? How can there be a God when all this is happening? How can He let it happen? All these young men – a whole generation – being wiped out. Again. Just like the last terrible war. Why?'

'Don't you think we all ask that? But I see it as a test. A test of our faith.'

'Huh! Some test!'

'I know, I know. That's why it's called "faith". We have to believe without question, without being given answers or reasons why things happen. We just have to put our trust in God. And you see, to God, your brother isn't dead. None of these brave young men are. They're in a far better place than we are right now. In the arms of Jesus.' He paused a moment, before asking quietly, 'Do you believe that?'

'I . . . I'd like to, but it's hard.'

'Oh yes.' The vicar gave a wry laugh. 'It's hard. I'll grant you that. I have to admit, I sometimes feel weighed down with all the suffering and heartache I see every day. I've railed against Him, but somehow He keeps sending me the strength to carry on giving comfort where I can.'

'My mother blames me for Kenny joining up,' Fleur burst out. 'She'll never forgive me. She . . . she says she doesn't want to see me ever again.'

'I'm sorry to hear that,' he said and Fleur marvelled that, yet again, he didn't make any kind of trite remark, saying that given time she would come round. Slowly, Fleur turned to face him. 'You've been very kind and understanding,' she said and added simply, 'thank you.'

'Would you like to pray with me now?'

Fleur nodded and together they slipped to their knees. The vicar began to speak in a soft, deep tone, making up the words of a prayer to suit. He asked for forgiveness and understanding for Fleur in her sorrow and for reassurance that she bore no blame. He prayed, too, for Fleur's parents in their grief and especially for her mother who found her loss so hard to bear. He ended by inviting Fleur to join him in saying the Lord's prayer.

As she left the church a little later, Fleur was surprised to find she felt a great sense of calm settle on her. It would be some time before she would be able to forgive herself, but with the help of the kindly clergyman she had made a start.

'Come back and see me any time, my dear. I'm always here.'

'Thank you,' she said and, as she walked away from

him down the path, she was already giving thanks in her mind that she had met him.

As she entered the main gate, Ruth came rushing towards her. 'I've been watching out for you. We've only just heard. Isn't it wonderful? Everyone's so delighted for you. And Kay. You must go and see her. She's almost back to her old self. I think they'll be letting her out of the hospital tomorrow. Have you seen him? How is he?' Her face was wreathed in smiles, but then she became aware that Fleur's face was not so joyous. 'What is it? Is he badly hurt?'

Fleur shook her head. Flatly, with no hint of the turmoil of emotion inside her that she was trying, desperately, to hold in, she said, 'No. Only a broken leg. Once that's mended, he – he'll be back.'

Ruth blinked, staring at her friend's face. Then, slowly, thinking she understood, she nodded. 'Oh, I see. Once he's well, he'll be flying again. Is that it?'

Fleur lifted her shoulders in a helpless shrug. 'Partly, I suppose.'

Ruth stepped closer and put her arm around Fleur's shoulder. 'It's more than that. I can see it is. Fleur, tell me what's wrong?'

Slowly, Fleur looked up into her friend's eyes. Hesitantly, she dragged out the words she had prayed never to have to speak. 'It . . . it's Kenny.'

Close to her, she heard Ruth's sharp intake of breath, saw her eyes widen in shock and fear. 'Kenny? Oh no!' She shook her head, refusing to believe it. 'Oh no! Not Kenny.'

'He crashed while training. In *training*, Ruth. How unfair is that?'

'Silly bugger!' Ruth muttered, but her eyes filled with tears. 'The stupid, stupid bugger.'

Her arm dropped from around Fleur. Her head lowered and she covered her face with her hands, her shoulders shaking. Now it was Fleur who comforted Ruth.

'I knew I shouldn't do it,' Ruth wailed.

'Do what?' Fleur asked gently.

'Let myself like him. I put a jinx on people.' She let her hands fall away and raised her head. Her face was wet with tears. 'Oh, Fleur,' she whispered. 'I'm so sorry. It . . . it's all my fault.'

Despite her misery, Fleur smiled a little. 'Darling Ruth, if anyone's to blame, it's me. He joined up because I had. That's what my mother thinks. And, of course, I blame myself too.'

Ruth wiped her face with a quick, fierce action. 'It's this bloody war that's to blame. Nothing – and no one – else. Not you, not me. Just the war.'

'You're right. It's not our fault.' Fleur sighed and murmured, 'But I can't help feeling so guilty.'

Ruth, a little more in control of herself, said, 'You ought to ask for compassionate leave. You ought to go home to be with your mam and dad.'

Fleur shook her head sadly. 'I've been. Mum's more or less told me not to bother going home again. Besides, I reckon I've used up all my leave on compassionate grounds. Ma'am's been very good, but just about everyone on camp has a good reason for asking for leave. I can't expect any more for a while now.'

'But what about Robbie? Won't they let you go and see him?'

'I doubt it. But d'you know something, Ruth? I don't

mind going weeks without seeing him, if it means keeping him out of this war for a while longer.'

Ruth pursed her lips and nodded. 'Well, I'm with you there.'

They walked slowly towards the WAAF quarters. 'Tell me what happened to Robbie,' Ruth asked. 'All we know is that they were picked up by the lifeboat and all the crew are safe, though there are a few injuries between them.'

Swiftly, Fleur told her all that Robbie knew. 'He said it was all down to the skill of their skipper. But for Tommy, none of them would be here.'

Ruth smiled. 'Yeah. Tommy's a great bloke. All of them are. I'm so glad they're all safe.' Her voice petered out and they were silent, both with their own thoughts of Kenny, the one they had both cared for. The one who hadn't come back.

Forty-Four

Fleur was wrong about having used up her entitlement to compassionate leave. Two days after her return to camp, she was summoned to see the WAAF commanding officer.

'I'm glad to hear your husband is alive, but I understand you have suffered the loss of a near relative. Your brother?'

'Yes, ma'am,' Fleur answered quietly.

'I'm surprised you haven't requested leave to go home.'

'I—' Fleur began and then faltered. She was about to admit that she believed she wasn't wanted at home. She bit her lip and then altered what she had been about to say. 'I thought – I mean – I didn't think I'd be entitled to any more. Not for a while, ma'am.'

Caroline Davidson looked down at the papers on her desk, appearing to consult them. 'Your friend, Morrison, has offered to cover your duties. She was trained in R/T work before remustering to become an intelligence officer. She feels – though she has not betrayed your confidence – that there are special circumstances in your case why a further period of compassionate leave should be granted to you.' She looked up again, her clear blue eyes boring into Fleur's. 'I expect your parents would welcome your support at this time?'

Fleur licked her lips. Her heart was beating painfully. She didn't like telling lies, yet if she agreed with her superior and was granted extra leave, she could go to see Robbie. Even if she was found out and punished, it would be worth it for a few extra precious hours with him.

Concentrating on her father's feelings rather than her mother's, Fleur was able to say truthfully, 'Yes, ma'am, I'm sure they would.'

Caroline leant back in her chair and smiled, her blue eyes twinkling with a sudden mischief. 'And, of course, if your transport arrangements should have to take you via Nottingham . . .'

Fleur stared at her for a moment, speechless. Really, she was thinking, sometimes their superior officers were capable of showing their human side.

Caroline straightened up and shuffled the papers on her desk with a brisk, businesslike movement. 'I can't let you go for a couple of weeks, I'm afraid. The forecasters think we're in for a spell of good weather and you know what that means.'

'Yes, ma'am.'

'So – we'll see in a couple of weeks' time. Come and see me then.'

'Thank you, ma'am.' Fleur saluted smartly and left the office, still unable to believe her luck. But, she realized, it wasn't so much down to luck as to her friend, Ruth. She went to find her to tell her what had transpired. Ruth listened with a wide grin on her face, particularly when Fleur reached the part about the transport arrangements.

'She's a nice old stick, really, though she can be a tartar if you kick over the traces.'

'Old stick!' Fleur laughed. 'She can't be much older than us.'

Ruth wrinkled her brow. 'No, I suppose not when you think about it. I expect it's just her rank that makes you think she must be as old as the hills.'

They laughed together and then Ruth's smile faded. She eyed her friend keenly as she said, 'Er, we're not on duty until six. I – um – reckon we ought to cycle out to Mrs Jackson's . . .'

Before she had finished speaking, Fleur was shaking her head. 'Oh no, I can't face her. Not yet. She was ever so fond of Kenny . . .'

'I know,' Ruth said softly and touched Fleur's arm. 'All the more reason why we should go and see her. And old Harry. If they've heard, they'll wonder why we haven't been to see them. And if they haven't been told, then . . . then it's us that ought to tell them.'

Fleur sighed deeply. 'You're right. I know you're right. It's just – just . . .'

'I know, I know,' Ruth said softly. 'But we'll go together. I'll be with you.'

Fleur was touched by her friend's thoughtfulness. Despite her adamant declarations that she would not allow herself to get seriously involved with anyone whilst the war was on, Ruth had allowed herself to become fond of Fleur's brother. And whilst she was strong, the same sadness that was in Fleur's heart was mirrored in Ruth's. Yet she was still sensitive to the feelings of others who had known – and liked – Kenny.

'You're right,' Fleur said firmly, summoning up her own strength. 'We ought to go. In fact, we'll go right now before I chicken out.'

Ruth smiled. 'Oh, you're not one to do that.' She linked her arm through Fleur's as they went in search of their bicycles.

'Oh, my dears,' Mrs Jackson held out her arms, trying to embrace them both as they let themselves in through her back door and stepped into the kitchen. Tears ran down her wrinkled cheeks. 'Harry only heard yesterday. He told me last night. We're so very sorry. Your poor mother . . .' She patted Fleur's arm. 'Sit down, dear. I'll make a cup of tea.'

'I'll do it,' Ruth said. 'Then I'll nip round to Harry's. And you' – she wagged her forefinger in Fleur's face – 'can get down to a bit of digging when you've drunk your tea. Do you good.'

As they sipped their tea, Fleur asked tentatively, 'You . . . you had heard about Robbie? That he's safe?'

The old lady nodded and smiled. 'Yes. Harry heard that at the same time.' She sighed. 'Dearie me, what terrible times we're living in. We were thrilled to hear that, but then the awful news about that lovely boy . . .' She wiped the tears from her eyes with the corner of her apron. 'It doesn't bear thinking about.'

Ruth returned a few minutes later with Harry in tow. The old man patted Fleur on the shoulder and just said, 'Now then, lass,' but the tone of his voice and his action spoke volumes. His sympathy and understanding, though not put into words, were very real. 'Plenty of work in the garden, lass. Need any help?'

Fleur smiled tremulously. Robbie was out of action for some time and Kenny . . . Poor Kenny. She'd never hear his cheerful whistle and see his broad grin again.

Oh, how she would miss him and not just for his help in the garden.

'I'd better get on. I – we – can't stay long today.'

'I'll bring your tea out to you then.'

Minutes later Fleur was digging in the garden. So many times Kenny had been here beside her, helping her. She had thought that the memory, the poignancy, would be upsetting, but in fact she found it comforted her. She kept glancing up, half expecting to see him a few feet away digging alongside her. Involuntarily, her ears strained for his merry whistle. But there was only the sound of the wind rustling in the apple tree and the sound of bird song.

When Ruth brought out their tea, the two girls sat together on the bench beneath the tree.

'Robbie'll soon be back here with you, sitting under the apple tree.' They smiled at each other.

Fleur nodded, though just at this moment she could not share her thoughts with Ruth. There was another thought that had just crept its way into her mind. I wonder, she was thinking, if Dr Collins has heard that his son is still alive.

Louisa was waiting at the front door when her husband drew his car to a halt in front of the house and climbed wearily out of it.

Oh, he looks so tired, Louisa thought. This war's almost as bad for him as the last one. She had been waiting on tenterhooks for hours, ever since she had heard the two pieces of news. One would bring him further sadness. And the other? Well, of course he would be glad that Robbie was safe. But with that piece of news would come further complications.

Louisa knew he had visited Meg. He had told her on his return from the city.

'There are to be no more secrets between us, Louisa,' he had said, taking her hands in his. 'You have been a dear, dear girl in being so understanding and – and forgiving – and the last thing I want to do is to cause you any more pain, but—' Here he'd paused, not knowing quite how to continue, so Louisa had squeezed his hands and said softly, 'Philip – I do trust you. As long as you promise to tell me everything, we can deal with whatever happens – together.'

'Oh, my dear,' he had said, taking her in his arms and holding her close. 'I don't deserve you.'

Then she had laughed, trying to lighten the emotion of the moment, and teasing him had said, 'No, you don't.'

And then they had sat down together, the glow from the fire in the grate giving them the only light in the room, whilst he had told her of his visit to Meg. He ended by saying, 'I shan't see her again, Louisa, I promise you that unless . . . unless by some miracle Robbie comes back. Because . . . because I told her that if he did then . . . then—' Again, he had faltered not wanting to hurt her.

But Louisa was not only forgiving, she was compassionate and she finished the sentence for him. 'You'd want to meet him and get to know him.'

He nodded, but he had such a hangdog expression on his face, like a naughty boy that had been caught scrumping apples, that Louisa had laughed aloud and touched his cheek. 'Oh, my dear, of course you would. He's your son.'

'You – you wouldn't mind?'

She had shaken her head. 'Not now, no. Once I

would've done. Once I would have minded dreadfully. You were right when you said that my idea that we could perhaps have adopted him was foolish. I was, as you so rightly said, only speaking with the benefit of hindsight. I've thought about what you said a lot since we talked and I've admitted to myself that, no, at the time I would have been far too upset to have even thought such a thing. But . . . but not now. I'm older and I hope a lot wiser. What happened in the past cannot be changed. He's your son. There's no denying that. I saw it for myself. Of course, if we'd had children of our own then it might have taken a little more thinking about, for their sake. It would have been a shock for them to discover they had a half-brother, but since we haven't . . .' Her voice trailed away.

Philip had squeezed her hand. 'I . . . I don't think Meg would let us see him very often. I mean I don't think she would want him to become – well – part of our family.'

Louisa had smiled softly. 'If the Lord is good to us and he comes back, then I don't think she will have any say in the matter. He's a grown man and he will make his own decision.'

Philip had sighed heavily. 'Only if she agrees to tell him that I am his natural father.'

Louisa's eyes had widened. 'You . . . you mean he didn't know? She never told him?'

Philip shook his head.

'Oh,' was all Louisa had said then and silence had fallen between them. They'd not spoken of the matter again but now, as she waited at the door to greet him, she knew they had a great deal to discuss. The miracle – and all that it entailed – had happened.

He was coming up the path towards her now, smiling as he approached. 'Hello, my dear.' Then, as he became aware of her anxious face, he added, 'Is something wrong?'

'No – yes, well – oh, come in, Philip. Your supper's all ready. We'll talk later.'

He glanced at her, seeing she was on edge, but he said mildly, 'Whatever you say, my dear,' as she helped him out of his coat and took his medical bag out of his hand.

Louisa picked at the food on her plate, eating so little that at last Philip leant towards her across the table and said, 'I think, my dear, you'd better tell me now, else you're going to waste all this lovely food you've spent hours preparing. And' – he smiled – 'you're making me so nervous that my appetite's disappearing by the minute. Now, tell me. What has happened?'

Louisa laid down her knife and fork and looked up at him. 'Firstly, I must tell you that poor Kenny has been killed. In training, would you believe? Isn't that cruel? I've been to see Betsy today and she's in a dreadful state. Poor Jake too. He's like a zombie. Just going through the motions of work but . . . but they're both devastated.'

Philip's face fell into lines of sadness and he let out a long, deep sigh. 'Oh dear. I'm so very sorry to hear that.'

There was silence between them whilst they each spared a thought for the boy whose life had been so cruelly snatched away before Louisa added, 'But there is good news.'

Philip smiled bleakly as if nothing could be counted as 'good news' after what she had just told him.

Watching his face, she said softly, 'Robbie is alive.'

His head jerked up and she saw the spark in his eyes and knew that, whatever it cost her, she had to let him get to know his son.

'Alive? How – I mean – what happened? Do you know?'

'Jake told me. He didn't mention it in front of Betsy, but he followed me out into the yard to tell me. Robbie's plane came down in the sea only just off the coast and the local lifeboat rescued all the crew. He has a broken leg, but apart from that, he's fine.'

Philip let out the breath he'd been holding in a huge sigh of relief whilst Louisa went on. 'It seems that Fleur didn't know until she arrived at Meg's house in Nottingham. She'd been granted compassionate leave to go to see his mother only to walk in and find him sitting there. It seems they didn't even know on the station until just before she got back. There'd been an air raid and all the telephone lines were down. And then, when she was so happy, she went to Middleditch Farm on her way back to camp only to hear that Kenny had been killed.'

'Good news one minute and bad the next, eh?' Philip said. 'Poor Fleur.'

'Betsy's turned totally against her. She's blaming Fleur for it happening.'

'For Kenny volunteering, you mean?'

Louisa nodded.

He sighed. 'I'll have to go and see her. Betsy, I mean. See if I can talk to her. I might be able to help.'

'Philip – there's something else.'

He glanced at her, waiting.

'Jake told me that after Robbie was posted missing,

presumed killed, Fleur pressed her father to tell her about . . . about the past.' She ran her tongue nervously around her lips but Philip finished her sentence for her.

'And he did. He told her just who Robbie's father is?'

'Yes,' Louisa whispered.

'And you think she'll tell Robbie?'

'Well – yes.'

'D'you think Meg realizes Fleur knows?'

Louisa shrugged. 'Jake says he swore her to secrecy. Made her promise never to say a word to Meg, but, I mean, now he's come back . . .'

'Who's to know what will happen?' he murmured and, whilst his wife picked up her knife and fork to finish her meal, Philip sat lost in thought.

Forty-Five

Two weeks later, having been granted special leave, the thoughts that now occupied Philip's waking hours also slipped into Fleur's mind. She didn't like having secrets from Robbie, but as her father had once said to her they weren't their secrets to tell.

She went straight to Middleditch Farm, but her mother would not speak to her, would not even acknowledge her presence and deliberately turned her back on her. Fleur stayed only an hour, talking with her father in the yard and then begging a lift to the station to catch the train to the Junction and then on to Nottingham, arriving late in the afternoon at the terraced house. She had, of course, written every other day to Robbie, so he knew about Kenny, but she had not mentioned anything about what Jake had told her. Nor did she intend to. She had made up her mind. It was Meg's place to tell her son, not Fleur's. She wondered if she had already done so. Though Fleur knew nothing of Philip's visit and the quandary Meg now found herself in, she did believe that Robbie should know the truth. But it wasn't her place to tell him.

'Well, if it's not Long John Silver.' She grinned as the door opened and Robbie stood there.

'Darling! How wonderful,' he said, pulling her inside, shutting the door and enfolding her in a bear-like hug all in one movement. 'However did you wangle more leave?'

'Ma'am's been very good. She actually called me to her office. This is supposed to be compassionate leave for Kenny, but I'm not really wanted at home . . .' And then she could say no more, because he was kissing her hungrily.

Some time later, they emerged into the light of the kitchen. 'Look who's here,' Robbie said, limping into the room.

'As if I hadn't guessed.' Smiling, Meg got to her feet and hugged Fleur. 'Darling girl, we're so sorry to hear about Kenny. How are your mother and father?'

Fleur pressed her lips together. 'Not good.'

'Here, come and sit by the fire. I'll make some tea.'

'I've been to the farm today, but Mum won't even speak to me. She blames me, you see.'

'Yes, you said before. I'm sorry. I wish I could help, but . . .' She left the sentence unfinished but they all understood.

Fleur glanced towards the old man's empty chair beside the range. 'Where's Pops? Is he all right?'

'He is now Robbie's safe. He's in bed, but he always goes early. He's fine. Better than he was.'

Fleur smiled with relief and sat down in his chair.

'There, love, drink that.' As Meg handed her a cup of tea, Fleur looked up and met the older woman's gaze. There was no mistaking the look of pleading in her eyes. Don't tell him, she was asking silently. Don't say anything. Unseen by Robbie, who had hopped out of the kitchen into the scullery in search of something to eat, Fleur smiled and gave a little nod.

Meg bent closer and whispered, 'I shall tell him, Fleur. I just . . . just haven't had the right moment.'

'It's all right. I promise I won't say—'

'And what are you two whispering about?'

'I was just asking your mother if you've been behaving yourself.'

Robbie laughed and pulled a face. 'I'm bored out of my skull.'

Meg, straightening up, laughed. 'We're not very exciting company, I'm afraid. Just me and the old man.'

'I didn't mean that, Ma. I love being with you. It's just that it's all going on without me.'

'Just be thankful it is for a while,' Fleur replied tartly. 'It's giving us all a bit of a rest knowing you're safe. Think about us for once instead of being the hero.'

There was silence until Fleur covered her face and said contritely, 'Oh, I'm sorry – I'm so sorry. That sounded awful. It came out all wrong. I just . . . I just – what with you going missing and we all thought you were dead and then Kenny . . .'

'Darling, it's all right.' Robbie hopped towards her, rescued the cup of tea that was in danger of slipping out of her grasp and then sat down close to her and took her hands. 'I understand. I know it's worse for you and Ma and Pops when I'm up there. You see, we've all too much to think about when we're in the thick of it, but you're just all waiting – and fearing the worst. It must've been dreadful for you the night we didn't come back.'

Fleur sniffed. 'It was. I stood for ages just watching the blank space on the board.'

'It's worse for Fleur than for us in a way,' Meg said gently. 'She's on the spot seeing what's happening.'

'Do you think you should apply for a transfer?' Robbie suggested, but before he had finished speaking Fleur shot back, 'No! I want to be there. I want to be near you. I *have* to be near you, even if it is tearing me apart. I'm not the only one: there are several girls on camp with boyfriends or fiancés – even one or two more are married like us. It's the same for them.' She pulled in a deep breath and forced a tremulous smile. 'No, I've just got to keep going but – just for a while – whilst you're laid up, I've got a bit of a respite. And, now you've done a full tour, you . . .'

Her voice faded away at the rather sheepish look on his face. Her heart sank. Without him saying a word, she knew that Robbie would get back on operations as soon as he could. But she said nothing more. She didn't want to worry his mother. At least she could let Meg stay in blissful ignorance if only for a while. She forced a smile as she added, 'Now you're grounded, we can all relax.'

She looked up at him and he smoothed her hair back from her forehead. 'Except that you've lost Kenny,' he murmured.

'Yes,' she said heavily. 'I've lost Kenny.' She closed her eyes and leant against him. Perhaps one day she would tell him about the heavy guilt that lay on her. How she had bargained for Robbie's life. But not just now. She couldn't speak of it just now. It was all too raw.

The hours of her short leave were over all too quickly. Her goodbyes said, she left the house as the air raid warning sounded. Fleur hurried along the street. I hope Robbie and his mother and Pops go to the shelter. Robbie can hobble that far on his crutches, she thought. And if I can make it to the railway station, I'll be safe there . . . She could hear the drone of enemy aircraft yet no bombs seemed to be falling on this part of the city. As she hurried along she was sure she heard thuds in the distance, and saw the night sky to the north of the city illuminated by exploding bombs.

Some poor devils are taking a hammering, she thought, but at least it's not us tonight. Reaching the station, she found that the trains had been delayed.

'Air raid Newark way,' the waiting passengers were informed. 'No trains running until it's over.'

And even when it was and the all-clear sounded, the announcement came that the line had been damaged and no trains would be running that night.

'Oh Lor',' Fleur muttered. 'I'm going to be in trouble. I'll be late back at camp. And I'm not even supposed to be in Nottingham. Oh heck!'

'You stranded like us, love?' a merry voice called out and Fleur turned to see three young men in RAF uniforms standing together.

'Seems like it.' She smiled and moved closer. 'Where are you heading?'

'A place called Wickerton Wood.'

Fleur's smile widened. 'Me too. I'm stationed there.' She held out her hand and the four of them exchanged first names. Then Fleur suggested, 'Shall we share a taxi?'

'A taxi? That'll be awfully expensive, won't it?'

'Not if the four of us chip in.'

'Righto – I'll see if there are any outside the station, though they might all have gone by now . . .' The youngest-looking one of the three men dropped his kitbag and loped off in search of transport.

The others stood together, feeling awkward, smiling in that embarrassed way that strangers meeting for the first time do. In only a few minutes the airman returned. 'There's just one left,' he panted. 'Says he'll take the four of us.' His grin widened. 'And he'll only charge us for the petrol. He's got a lad in the RAF down south. A fighter pilot. He's glad to help, he says. Hopes someone'll do the same for his lad if he's stranded anywhere.'

'Righto. Come on, love. Need any help?'

'I'm fine.' Fleur smiled. 'As long as he gets us back to camp, I'll ride on the running board.'

They laughed but they all squeezed into the car, three squashed in the back and the airman with the longest legs taking the front seat beside the driver.

'Now then, mi duck, what are you doing out with these young rascals?'

Fleur laughed. 'I've only just met them on the platform whilst we were waiting for the train. I've just been home to see my *husband*.'

There was a unanimous groan and one of the airmen said, 'Just my luck! And there I was thinking I'd met the girl of my dreams.'

In the darkness, Fleur smiled to think that that was just how she had met Robbie.

There was laughter before another asked, 'Your husband? What does he do?'

'He's a wireless operator on bombers, but he's on sick leave. A broken leg.' She stopped herself saying more. These boys looked incredibly young. They were probably just out of training. Maybe this was their first posting. It wouldn't do to talk to them about crash-landings.

'How did that happen?'

Fleur chuckled. 'You seem to be asking an awful lot of questions. I'm not sure I should be telling you.' And again, the car was filled with laughter.

They chugged along, going at a steady pace through the blackout with only the pencil-thin beams from the partially blacked-out headlights to illuminate their way. It wasn't until the early hours that they reached the gates of the camp.

'Now for trouble,' Fleur muttered as she clambered out. 'I'm about four hours late.'

'So are we,' one of the airmen said cheerfully. 'But it's hardly our fault Jerry decided to drop a few bombs – just to make us feel welcome.'

'Right, tip up, chaps. Let's pay this kind feller for bringing us. At least we've got here. If we'd waited for the train it could have been a week on Tuesday!'

Fleur fished in her bag to find her money but the airman said, 'No, love. We'll sort it. It'll be nice for us to have a friendly face about the camp. This is our treat. All right, lads?'

'Yeah, course it is. Where is it you work, Fleur? Canteen, is it?'

Fleur smiled to herself. Why did all men take it that the only job women could do was to serve them their meals?

'No. I'm in Control. I'm an R/T operator.'

'Really? That's great. It'll be good to know we've got you watching out for us when we're up there.'

Did she imagine it, or was there a tiny note of apprehension in the young man's voice?

Fleur was allowed straight into the camp, but she had to bid the others farewell whilst they waited for their identities to be checked and all the formalities for new arrivals to be gone through. Thankfully, Fleur slipped away into the darkness towards the WAAF quarters and crept into the room she shared with Ruth.

'Oh, thank goodness!' Ruth sat up in bed at once.

'I've been that worried. Are you all right? I've been ringing your home, but it seems the lines are down.'

'I'm not surprised,' Fleur whispered. 'There's been an air raid in the Newark area, but I was in Nottingham.'

Ruth's chuckle came out of the darkness. 'Now why doesn't that surprise me? Good job you've got back when you have, else you'd've been for it. How did you get back? Are the trains running?'

'No. I met three RAF lads coming here, would you believe, and we shared a taxi.'

'A taxi? Heavens! Have you come into a fortune?'

'No,' Fleur giggled softly as she climbed into her single bed. 'They paid. But the driver was very generous. Didn't charge us the going rate as we're RAF. His lad's serving down south.'

Ruth sighed and lay down. 'There's still some nice people about.'

They lay in silence for a few minutes and Fleur was just about to fall asleep when Ruth asked tentatively, 'D'you think your folks are all right? I mean, you said the air raid was in the Newark area, didn't you?'

'Mmm,' Fleur said sleepily. 'They'd be after the airfield there, I expect. But we live several miles from Newark. Right out in the country. There's nothing there worth bombing.'

'But the telephone lines are down.'

Fleur yawned. 'Well, they will be, won't they? But they'll be all right. Our farm's miles from anywhere. Right out in the wilds. Dad didn't even build a shelter . . .' And with that, she fell asleep.

But for some reason she couldn't explain, Ruth was left wide awake staring into the darkness.

Forty-Six

Meg read the news in the paper the next morning and her blood ran cold.

> The bombing raid last night in the Newark area caused loss of life and severe damage to properties. Several of the bombs fell outside their target and a remote farmhouse some distance to the west of the town, which should have been considered relatively safe, received a direct hit. The farmer received extensive burns whilst trying to rescue his wife from the building, which was destroyed by fire. Sadly, his efforts were in vain and his wife perished. The man is in hospital and is thought to be in a critical condition. The names of the casualties have not yet been released as next of kin have yet to be informed.

'Robbie, oh, Robbie . . .' Meg was hurrying up the stairs to his bedroom, breathless as she pushed open the door. 'Oh, Robbie, it's Jake – it's Fleur's folks. I know it is.'

'What?' The young man sat up in bed and snatched the paper from her trembling hands. He scanned the newsprint whilst she sank down on the end of the bed, clasping and unclasping her hands in agitation.

He looked up at her. 'It doesn't mention South Monkford. It could be anyone. It doesn't even give the name of the farm. What makes you think it's them?'

Meg stared at him and pressed her hands to her bosom. 'But South Monkford is west of Newark. And I just know, Robbie. I feel it. In here. I know it sounds daft to you, but I just know.'

'Well, there's one way to find out,' Robbie said, swinging his legs out of the bed and hoisting himself upright. 'We'll ring the hospitals.'

'Oh, Robbie, can we do that?'

He looked down at her and tenderly touched her cheek. 'Anything, Ma, to take that devastated look off your face.'

Robbie spent half the morning in the phone box at the end of the street, feeding in coins one after another and hopping on his crutches between it and the corner shop for more change. After several calls – he lost count how many – he replaced the receiver slowly and pushed open the door of the box. As it swung to he leant against it briefly and his glance went to the front door of his home.

She was standing on the step, her hands clasped together, looking up the street towards him, but as he pushed himself away from the phone box and began to limp towards her, he saw her fingers flutter to her mouth. Then she turned and disappeared inside the house.

She knew already, from the droop of his shoulders, that he was about to bring her bad news.

The news was broken to Fleur by Caroline Davidson. How many more tragedies is this poor girl going to face? she was thinking as she said gently, 'My dear, we have just received information that your home was hit in last night's air raid.'

Fleur swayed momentarily, but remarkably she remained standing at attention. Silently, she was thinking, I was glad that it wasn't the city getting it last night and all the time . . . But aloud, all she said was, 'Are they dead, ma'am?'

'Your mother – I'm sorry – yes, but your father is in hospital. Evidently, he wasn't in the house when it was hit, but he tried to get into the burning building to save her. He's . . . he's very badly hurt, my dear, but he is still alive.' There was a pause and her unspoken words seemed to hang in the air. At the moment. 'He's in hospital in Nottingham. I need hardly say you are released from your duties immediately. I am issuing you with a seventy-two-hour pass on compassionate grounds . . .'

The journey back to Nottingham by public transport was impossible, but Caroline had pulled strings and arranged a lift for Fleur with an RAF vehicle due to go to the city that day. The journey seemed to take three times as long as normal. All the way, Fleur repeated the same prayer. 'Don't let him die. Oh, please don't let him die.'

This time she made no rash bargain with God, but just prayed simply and directly.

She reached the hospital late at night, and though their resources were already stretched the nurses found her a bed in an unoccupied side ward for the night.

'If we need it, we'll have to turf you out,' they told her cheerfully. 'Now, come along to the staff room and we'll get you something to eat.'

'How is he? Can I see him?' was all Fleur wanted to know.

'Best not tonight, love, he's sleeping now.'

'Can't I just see him? I promise not to disturb him.'

'I should wait until the morning, love.' The sister was gentle and understanding but there was a note of authority in her tone. 'You'll feel better able to cope after a night's rest.'

'Is he . . . is he . . . that bad?'

The woman's face sobered. 'He's not good, my dear. I can't lie to you, but the doctor will talk to you tomorrow.'

'Does he – my father, I mean – know about my mother?'

Sadly, the sister nodded. 'Yes.' More briskly, she went on, 'Now, a bite to eat, a sleeping pill and into bed with you, my girl.'

Exhausted by the journey, grieving for her mother and worried sick about her father, Fleur did not expect to sleep a wink. But the sister's pill knocked her out for a full ten hours and she might have slept even longer if a merry little trainee nurse hadn't bounced into the room, pulled open the curtains and woken her up.

'I've brought you some breakfast, miss,' she beamed. 'We don't do this for everyone, but your dad's a bit special.'

Fleur heaved herself up in the bed and rubbed her eyes. 'Oh?'

'Oh, yes. We've all been vying to be the nurse who looks after him.'

'Has he come round then?'

'He comes round for a bit and keeps apologizing for being such a trouble. But he isn't, miss, I promise you. Then he drifts off again. But he's a duck, ain't he?'

Despite her anxiety, Fleur smiled. She looked down

at the tray, not expecting to be able to eat a thing. To her surprise, she suddenly found she was very hungry.

'How is he?'

The little nurse's face clouded. She moved closer to the bed. 'It ain't my place to say, miss. You must ask the doctor or Sister, but' – she leant closer – 'he's still very poorly but I heard 'em say he's going in the right direction, if you know what I mean. But – please – don't tell 'em I said owt, will yer. I could get the sack.'

'Of course I won't. And thank you.'

'That's all right. See yer later.'

Fleur finished her breakfast, washed and dressed and stripped the bed. She knew it would have to be changed, and anything she could do to help the busy nurses she would do.

Now, she thought, taking a deep breath, I wonder if they'll let me see Dad.

He was in a small ward with three other seriously ill patients, each with their own nurse. Though she had tried to prepare herself, Fleur gasped when she saw her father swathed in bandages. She wouldn't have recognized him.

'He was badly burned,' the sister told her. 'But the medical profession are making huge strides in the treatment of burns. It's because of the war, you know. So many pilots, poor boys, get burned when they're shot down.'

Fleur shuddered. It could so easily have been Robbie she was coming to visit. Robbie lying in the bed . . .

She moved closer. 'Dad? It's me. How . . . how are you feeling?' It was a stupid question, but she didn't know what else to say.

He didn't answer her and she glanced up at the sister, a question in her eyes.

'Keep talking to him. We want to try to get him to regain consciousness fully. And you're the best person to get him to do that, Meg.'

Fleur stared at the sister. 'Why did you call me "Meg"?'

The sister blinked. 'Er – I'm sorry. I thought that was your name.' Obviously embarrassed, she looked first at her patient and then back to the girl.

'No, it isn't, but just tell me why you thought it was?'

'Er – it's the only name he's said when he's drifted in and out of consciousness.' The sister's face cleared. 'Oh, it was your mother's name, was it?'

Slowly, Fleur shook her head. 'No, as a matter of fact, it wasn't.'

'Oh dear, I am sorry. I shouldn't have said anything.' The sister was obviously upset and worried. 'I have put my foot in it, haven't I?'

The sister was only young for the post she held, little older than she was, Fleur thought. In all the forces, promotion came earlier and earlier and the nursing profession was every bit a fighting force as any of the others. They were all working round the clock for the same thing: the end of this war.

'It's all right.' Fleur touched her arm. 'Honestly. The thing is – I know who Meg is. And if he's calling for her then—?'

The sister nodded. 'Yes, if you could find her. It really might help him.'

'Oh yes,' Fleur whispered. 'I can find her.'

Forty-Seven

'Sit down, dear. There's something I have to tell you.'

'Oh no, it's not Fleur's dad, is it? You haven't heard something, have you, Ma?'

'No, no. Just – sit down, Robbie. Please.'

Robbie lowered himself into the old man's chair and waited whilst his mother settled herself on the opposite side of the fireplace. For a long moment, she stared into the fire, the flames dancing on her beautiful face. Robbie stared at her, marvelling at her smooth skin, at how young she still looked. It never ceased to amaze him that there wasn't a line of men beating a path to their door.

Slowly, she raised her head to meet his gaze. 'There's something I have to tell you. Something that – maybe – I should have told you years ago, but . . . but I couldn't bring myself to do it. I was so frightened of . . . of losing you.'

'Losing me!' Robbie leant forward, a little awkwardly because of the thick plaster on his leg still hampering his movements. Then he moved to sit on the hearthrug at her feet, taking her hands and holding them tightly. Earnestly, he said, 'Darling Ma, whatever it is, you couldn't lose me. Not ever. Not . . . not the way you're meaning.'

They stared at each other for a moment, each

knowing just how close they had come to Robbie being lost, but a different kind of 'lost'.

'When . . . when you were missing, Jake told Fleur and . . . and it's not fair of me to expect her to keep such a secret from you – from her husband.'

Robbie was silent, giving his mother time to tell her story. A story that was obviously difficult, maybe painful, for her to tell.

He stroked her hands tenderly. Those clever hands that had earned them a living all these years. Hands that had caressed him and nurtured him. Hands that lovingly nursed the old man now asleep upstairs.

Then slowly, haltingly at first, Meg began to tell Robbie about her past. Her shameful past. How she had once been a wilful, selfish girl, who had cared nothing for the feelings of others in her desire for security.

'You'll have to be patient with me, because I want to tell you everything. Right from the very beginning. I'll miss nothing out and then you can . . . can judge for yourself just what sort of a woman you have for a mother.'

He squeezed her hands encouragingly. 'I'm not going to judge you, Ma. Whatever it is.'

Meg lifted her shoulders in a tiny shrug. 'Well, we'll see,' she murmured.

Another silence before she took a deep breath and began. 'We were such a happy little family, Dad, Mam, Bobbie and me.'

'Bobbie? Who's Bobbie?'

Meg nodded and smiled a little. She was perhaps the one who was going to have to be patient with his interruptions. 'My little brother. You're named after him.'

'Your brother? I didn't know you had a brother.'

Meg nodded and her voice was husky as she went on. 'We lived in a small cottage on Middleditch Farm . . .'

Again Robbie could not keep silent. 'Middleditch Farm? But – but that's Fleur's home . . .' He stopped, realizing that the farmhouse now lay in ruins.

'Pops worked as a waggoner for the Smallwoods who owned the farm then. And I worked as a dairy maid for Mrs Smallwood.' A small smile twitched at her mouth as she added wryly, 'She was a tartar to work for. I was always in trouble with her. "You'll come to a bad end," she used to say to me.' Again she paused. 'Maybe she was right.'

'Oh, Ma, don't say that. You call this "a bad end"?'

'No, of course not. I'm content. At least . . .' She sighed inwardly. Was she about to jeopardize her contented life with her son when he heard the truth about her? Bravely, she pushed on. 'I was a bit cheeky and . . . and a bit of a flirt with the village lads. I was friendly with Alice Smallwood, their daughter. She was older than me and – if anything – it was her that was the flirt, but her mother thought *I* was the bad influence on *her*. Anyway, we jogged along quite happily, I thought, until one night my dad came home and said we'd both been dismissed without a reference and we were being turned out of our home too. It was a tied cottage, you see. It went with the job.' Meg bit her lip as if reliving the moment. 'I thought it was my fault. I thought I'd been cheeky to the missis once too often.'

'And was it?' Robbie asked softly.

Meg shook her head. 'No. It . . . it was Pops. He – well, I'll come to that in a minute. We had to leave the very next day and the only place we could go was the workhouse.'

'The workhouse?' Robbie was shocked. 'That big building on the outskirts of South Monkford?'

'You've seen it?'

He nodded. 'Oh, Ma,' he breathed sadly. 'You've lived in the workhouse?'

She smiled thinly. 'Dad took us there.' Talking of the times past, Meg referred to him by the name she had called him then, not 'Pops' as he was now known. 'Mam – she was expecting another baby – Bobbie and me. He left us there. Said he was going to look for work and that he'd come back for us . . .' Her voice trailed away for a moment, but then she took another deep breath and continued. 'But the weeks went by and he didn't come back. We had to work of course – in that place. Mam wasn't very well but they let her do mending and easy work. And they put me to work with the school marm. And for a while, I thought she was my friend. She was very kind to me. She was in charge of all the children and had to look after them all the time. One night, there was a little girl who was ill.' Meg glanced at Robbie. 'Actually, it was Betsy, Fleur's mum.'

Now Robbie was truly horrified. 'Fleur's mum was in the workhouse?'

Meg nodded. 'And so was Jake. He'd been born in there. So that's where I met them. Jake and I were friends even though we were segregated. Girls and boys, men and women. Poor Jake got a beating once for being seen with me.'

'And Fleur's mum? Were you friends with her?'

Meg ran her tongue round her dry lips. 'Not . . . not exactly. She was younger than us. Jake and me,

I mean. Anyway, this night she was ill, the school marm left me in charge of Betsy when Isaac Pendleton sent for her. He was the master of the workhouse – a lecherous old devil . . .' She paused and then put her head on one side thoughtfully. 'No, actually, that's not quite fair. And I am trying to tell you this very truthfully. He was a ladies' man, but he could be very kind.' She sighed. 'I didn't see it that way then, but now I have to admit that he was. In his own way. Well, at that time he had his eye on Louisa, the school marm—'

Again, Robbie could not help interrupting. 'That's not the woman Fleur calls Aunt Louisa, is it? Mrs Dr Collins?'

'Yes. She was working as the schoolmistress at the workhouse. I believe she had an elderly mother she was supporting. She was engaged to Philip Collins then, and was trying to avoid old Isaac as much as she could. So, this particular night, she left her watch with me and told me that after a certain time, I was to go and knock on his door and say that she was needed – that Betsy was worse. I did just as she said, but when we got back the watch was missing and she accused me of having stolen it. I hadn't, of course. Whatever else I may be, I'm not a thief. Anyway, it turned out that Betsy had it. She'd wanted to hear it ticking. It reminded her of her daddy, she said. Louisa apologized but I was impulsive and fiery in those days—'

'Must be the red hair,' Robbie teased and they both smiled.

'And I was unforgiving. Oh, Robbie, how unforgiving I was. I suppose, looking back, that was what caused all the trouble. If only I had been more willing to forgive and forget then maybe—'

'Go on, Ma,' he prompted gently as Meg seemed to get side-tracked. 'What happened?'

'I refused to work with Louisa any more. I couldn't forgive her for having accused me. And – quite wrongly – I bore Betsy a grudge too. I said I'd rather scrub floors than work with Louisa. And I did,' she added wryly. She sighed again and went on. 'Anyway, I'm getting a bit ahead of myself. Earlier that same day, my mother had gone into labour and the baby was stillborn.'

She saw Robbie wince but he said nothing.

'So a couple of weeks later I decided I should try to find my dad and tell him what had happened to Mam and the baby. And . . . and I just wanted to see him anyway. I got permission from the master to go in search of him, and Jake came with me.' Now she smiled. '*Without* permission.'

'Ooh-er,' Robbie said imagining the severe punishment he might have incurred.

'He didn't care. He wanted to be with me.'

'Did you find your dad? Pops?'

'Oh yes, we found him all right.' Meg's voice was suddenly hard as she relived that dreadful day. 'We went to the racecourse. He was so good with horses that Farmer Smallwood sometimes took Dad with him when he went to the races. And then we saw him, walking along, bold as you like, with his arm around Alice Smallwood.'

Robbie blinked. 'His arm? Alice Smallwood?'

Meg nodded and now there was no hiding the bitterness in her tone. 'My father had been having an affair with the daughter of his – of our – employers. They had found out and turned him and all his family out because of it. So, it wasn't my fault as I had feared. It was his.'

'Pops? I can't believe it.'

Meg raised a smile. 'Oh, Pops wasn't always the frail old man you see now.'

'Well, no. When he first came to live with us he was still – well – quite sprightly.'

'When he was younger, he was a fine figure of a man, I have to admit.'

There was a long silence before Robbie asked gently, 'So – what happened then?'

'I went back to the workhouse, but from that moment on I cut him out of my life and vowed I'd never forgive him. It was up to me to take care of my mother. I went out into the town to seek work and I found it. With poor Percy Rodwell in his tailor's shop.'

'Why do you say "poor" Percy Rodwell?'

Meg sighed. 'He was a lovely man. A kind and generous man and I . . . I seduced him.'

'Oh, Ma! Whatever next?' Robbie began to laugh, but seeing his mother's serious face, he stopped. 'Mind you,' he added. 'You're still a stunner, so I expect the poor bloke hadn't got a chance.'

For a brief moment Meg's eyes sparkled with mischief. 'He hadn't.'

She explained about his long-standing engagement with the sour-faced Miss Finch and how, when Percy jilted her to marry Meg, he found himself in court on a charge of breach of promise. 'Poor Percy,' she murmured. 'He really didn't deserve all the trouble I brought to his door.'

'What happened to your mother and to your little brother?'

'Bobbie fell ill soon after I'd found out about my father.'

Robbie was intrigued by the way Meg kept referring to the man he knew affectionately as 'Pops' as 'my father'. It was as if she, too, couldn't think of them now as one and the same person.

'And he died. D'you know?' she said, the sadness still in her tone even after all the years. 'We buried little Bobbie on my sixteenth birthday.'

'And . . . and your mother?'

Meg's mouth hardened even more. 'She became Isaac Pendleton's mistress. I disapproved and refused to see her ever again. Jake tried to persuade me to go to see her. In the end I did, but I was told she had no wish to see me. I think it was a lie – in fact, I know it was now. I did go, truly I did.' She met his gaze, pleading with him to believe her. He gave her hands another little squeeze. 'But she fell ill and died before . . . before I could make it up with her.'

'So why did you think all this was so very dreadful, Ma? I mean, I know it's a shame you didn't make it up with your mother, but you were young and . . .'

'I haven't finished yet.'

'Ah.'

'I married Percy and the following year Louisa and Philip were married. Then the war came. Jake volunteered in 1916 and he married Betsy before he went. Then Philip went too. They were lucky – they both came back, but then we got that dreadful epidemic of influenza. Percy caught it.' She bit her lip. 'And I called Philip – Dr Collins. I . . . I'd always known he . . . he was attracted to me and . . . and I was lonely. Percy was ill – dying – and I . . . I mean we—'

'You had an affair with Dr Collins?' Robbie said gently, without any note of censure in his tone.

Meg nodded and tears filled her eyes. 'It was wicked of me. I . . . I still felt resentment against Louisa for believing I could have stolen her watch. You see? I never forgave anyone. And yet I did worse things myself than ever they'd done. Far worse.'

'How long did the affair go on?'

'Not long. When Percy died, Philip had an attack of conscience. It finished, but by then, of course, you'd been conceived.'

Robbie raised her hands to his lips and kissed them gently. 'So – Dr Philip Collins is my natural father?'

'Yes,' Meg whispered. 'But I want you to believe me, Robbie, that whilst I do regret so many of the things I did, I do not regret having you. Not for one moment. And if I hadn't had the affair, I wouldn't have had you. But it wasn't really until after you were born that I changed.'

Swiftly she recounted what Jake had already told Fleur about Miss Finch and her twisted belief that she had a right to Meg's baby boy. 'Angry and disgusted though Jake was with me – oh, he knew all about me. There was no hiding the truth from Jake – he still came to my rescue when I needed him. I suppose,' she ended reflectively, 'that's why Betsy has hated me all these years. From what Fleur says, Betsy believed that Jake still loves me.'

'Maybe he does, Ma,' Robbie said softly. There was a long silence between them until Robbie said at last, 'And what about – my father? Does he know that I'm his son? Has he always known?'

Meg nodded. 'He came to see me when he heard

you'd been posted missing. He . . . he said that if . . . if a miracle happened and you came back that he wanted to meet you. Get to know you.'

'Did he indeed? And what would his wife say to that? Does *she* know, d'you think?'

'Yes. She does now. Perhaps – perhaps she's always suspected, but now she knows for certain. You . . . you're so like he used to be as a young man. Anyone knowing him then and seeing you now . . .'

'So *that's* why she looked so startled that day I met her in the cafe with Fleur. I thought she was going to pass out.'

'It must have been a shock for her. Specially when she found out just who you were.'

Again there was a long silence between them, before she asked tentatively, 'Do . . . do you want to meet him?'

'What do you want me to do?'

'Oh, it's not up to me. Not any more.'

'But will it cause you pain? I wouldn't want that, darling Ma.'

She looked down into his upturned face, his handsome, open, loving face, and tears filled her eyes. 'You . . . you don't hate me, then?'

'Oh, Ma!' Again he kissed her fingers. 'How could you even think such a thing?'

'I . . . I thought you might be disgusted. I . . . I wasn't a very nice person back then, Robbie.'

'You had a tough time.' He laughed gently. 'Because of that old rogue up there. Who'd have thought old Pops could do such a thing? The old rascal, him.'

Suddenly, Meg was frightened. She clung to Robbie. 'Oh, you won't say anything to him. Oh, please, Robbie, don't—'

'Of course I won't. If you can forgive him, then I certainly can.'

'And . . . and you forgive me?'

'There's nothing for me to forgive where you're concerned. I'm still me, whoever my father is.' He paused and cocked his head on one side. 'Did you love him very much, Ma?'

Meg bit her lip. 'That . . . that's the worst part. I don't think I loved him at all. I was just lonely and . . . and he was handsome and besotted with me.' She looked him straight in the eyes then, meeting his gaze as she said solemnly, 'There's only one man I've ever truly loved, but I was too blind, too ambitious and too selfish to see it. And I've spent the rest of my life regretting that – through my own stupidity – I lost him.'

Slowly, Robbie nodded. 'You're talking about Fleur's dad, aren't you?'

Meg nodded and whispered, 'Yes. Jake was the only man I've ever really loved. And – once upon a time – I know he did love me. But I lost him. I lost my beloved Jake.'

Forty-Eight

Fleur knocked on the door of the terraced house and then waited for what seemed an age. At last, thinking they must be out, she turned away, disappointed. But she had only taken a few steps when the door opened and Robbie stood there.

'Sorry, it takes me a while to get to the door. Fleur, darling, how is he?'

'Oh, Robbie!' She rushed to him and was enfolded in his strong arms. He held her tightly, believing the worst had happened.

'Darling, I'm so sorry,' he murmured against her hair.

'No, no, it's not that,' she said, her voice muffled against him. She pulled back a little to say, 'He's all right. Well, he isn't – what I mean is, he's still alive.'

There was puzzlement in Robbie's eyes and she knew exactly what he must be thinking: then why aren't you with him?

'I've come for your mother,' Fleur was babbling in her anxiety. 'He's asking for her.'

'Asking for my mother?' Robbie was startled.

'Yes – yes. She will come, won't she? Is she here?'

'Oh yes, she's here, but as for coming to the hospital—'

Fleur's eyes widened. 'She won't refuse to come,

will she? Oh, she can't. She must come. It might help him. It *will* help him. I know it will.'

'It's not that, Fleur. But she . . . she's not well herself. Come in and see for yourself. She's just sat by the fire, not moving. She's been like that ever since yesterday.'

He drew her into the front room and closed the door. They did not move further into the house, but stood just inside the door whilst Robbie whispered, 'We had a long talk the night before last. She told me everything. All about what your dad told you.'

Fleur nodded. 'I'm glad you know. It wasn't my place to tell you but I hated having a secret from you. You do understand that, don't you, Robbie?'

'Of course.' He ran his hand distractedly through his hair as if, at this precise moment, that was the least of his worries. 'But ever since then, she's just sat there. She's not even been to bed for two nights. She's not eating or even drinking. I'm at my wits' end . . .'

'Let me see her.' Fleur pushed past him and almost ran through the front room and into the back part of the house.

Just as Robbie had said, Meg was sitting by the fire, her hands lying limply in her lap She was just staring into space, oblivious to everything around her. Across the hearth, the old man sat huddled in his chair, staring helplessly at his daughter. He didn't speak, merely nodded at Fleur and then wiped away a tear running down his wrinkled cheek.

Fleur knelt in front of Meg and touched her hand. It felt cold, almost lifeless. 'Mrs Rodwell,' she began gently, 'I've come to ask you a big favour.'

There was no response from the woman. She seemed unaware of Fleur's presence.

'See?' Robbie said as he limped into the room. 'I told you. I can't get her to do anything. She won't even speak to me. I can't get through to her.'

Taking both Meg's hands in hers, she said firmly, 'Mrs Rodwell, listen to me. My dad needs you. *Jake* needs you.'

Meg blinked and seemed to be trying to focus her eyes on Fleur. It was the name 'Jake' that had prompted a tiny response. Fleur latched on to it. 'Jake wants to see you. He's asking for you. Please, will you come and see him? Come and see Jake.'

Meg's lips moved stiffly and her voice was husky. 'Jake?'

'Yes – Jake. He's in hospital. He's drifting in and out of consciousness. I can't reach him. I've tried. I've been there all morning and he won't wake up. Not for me. And the only name the nurses have heard him say is "Meg". Oh, please.' She gripped the woman's hand even tighter and her voice was full of tears. 'Oh, please, say you'll come.'

Meg stirred as if she was awaking from a trance. 'Me? He . . . he's asking for me?'

'Yes.'

But Meg was shaking her head. 'I can't.'

'Why ever not?' Fleur cried passionately. 'Don't you want to help him? Surely – whatever happened in the past – you can put it aside to . . . to save his *life*, can't you?'

'You don't understand. It's not *me* who doesn't want to see *him* . . .' Her voice trailed away and tears trembled on her eyelashes.

'But he's asking for you.'

Meg shook her head. 'He doesn't know what he's

saying. He must be delirious. He – he won't want to see me. Besides, it wouldn't be right. With poor Betsy only just – only just . . .'

'It can't hurt my mother now,' Fleur insisted. 'She's gone. If she was still alive, then I wouldn't be asking you, but she isn't. Dad is and he needs you.'

'What will people say . . . ?' Meg asked. 'Folks have long memories.'

'Look,' Fleur cried passionately, 'I don't give a damn about what anyone might say. I don't care about what happened years ago. I don't even care that my mother hated the very sound of your name . . .' She saw Meg flinch and was sorry she had been so blunt, but she pressed on now. 'I don't care about any of that. All I care about is my dad and trying to keep him alive. I – I can't bear to lose him.' The final words ended on a sob and she buried her face in Meg's lap.

She felt the older woman's gentle touch on her hair and heard her say, 'Neither can I, Fleur. Oh, neither can I.'

The ward was quiet and peaceful in the middle of the afternoon. The morning flurry of doctors' visits had passed and the daily routine of work finished.

'It's not really visiting time,' the sister greeted them, 'but you, I take it, are Meg?'

Meg, still looking anxious as if she didn't feel she had the right to be there, nodded.

The sister turned to Fleur. 'There's no change, I'm afraid, since this morning. But maybe now . . .' She did not finish her sentence, but glanced hopefully back at Meg. 'Come this way.'

They followed the sister and, as she led them towards Jake's bed, Fleur heard Meg pull in a sharp breath at the sight of him, but she controlled her feelings and sat down in the chair beside him.

His hands and arms were bandaged and most of his face was covered with dressings. There was nothing she could touch. She couldn't hold his hand, couldn't kiss his face. All she could do was say, 'Jake, it's me. It's Meg. I'm here.'

Fleur and Robbie stood at the end of the bed, their arms around one another. They all saw Jake's eyes flicker open and he tried to turn his head towards the sound of her voice. Meg stood up and leant over him.

His eyes focused slowly and he saw her face as he remembered her. Her red flying hair, her smooth skin, her smile. Oh, her smile! That heartbreaking smile of hers. To him she was still the young girl he had met all those years ago. The girl whose strong spirit had lifted him out of the workhouse. The girl he'd loved and lost and who, despite his contented life with Betsy and his children, he'd never been able to forget.

'Meg, oh, Meggie. You came.' The words were faint and slightly slurred but understandable.

At the end of the bed, Fleur buried her face into Robbie's jacket and wept tears of thankfulness. He was going to be all right. Her dad was going to be all right.

'Yes, Jake,' Meg was saying simply. 'I came. I'm here to stay and I shan't leave you. Not unless you tell me to.'

He tried to lift his hand to touch her face, but winced with the pain. 'I won't do that, Meggie. Not ever.'

'Then just rest, Jake, and get well. I'll be right here. Always . . .'

If the past was not entirely forgotten, at least now it was all forgiven.